SWOONY TYCOONS

Her Greek Billionaire

Cinderella's Jilted Billionaire

The Real Deal

Lucy Monroe

Lucy Monroe LLC

CONTENTS

HER GREEK BILLIONAIRE

LUCY MONROE

LUCY MONROE LLC

DEDICATION

For my daughter-in-law. Thank you, Megan, for being so dear and becoming a daughter of my heart. Your strong spirit, determination and tender heart remind me of Rowan. I hope you enjoy her book.

Chapter One

R owan Johnson pulled her five-year-old, ecofriendly electric compact to a stop in front of a mansion in one of the wealthiest neighborhoods in Athens.

The soaring stone wall that encompassed the huge property in its entirety was broken only by an imposing steel gate. Painted a sandy brown to match the stone in the wall, it was wide enough to let a delivery vehicle through. Right now, it was shut tight.

Taking a deep breath for courage, she got out of her little car. She wasn't going to back out now. This was what she wanted, and if she rightly read the way Lysander Baros, Greek billionaire and most eligible Athens bachelor, not to mention the sexiest one, looked at her, he did too.

Even if he didn't want it as much as she did, the chance to knock his half-brother down a peg might be worth it all on its own.

Rowen walked to the callbox beside the gate, stepping carefully in her three-inch heels. She wasn't dressed to go walking, or even to go out. She would never go to a club in a skirt as tight as the one on the dress she wore. Nor with a neckline as plunging.

She was dressed to seduce and hoped she'd gotten it right.

At thirty, she wasn't a virgin, but neither was she particularly experienced in the art of seduction. Married at the age of twenty and filing for divorce nine years later, there hadn't been a lot of time for her to learn. But she was ready to change that.

She was ready to show her ex, who thought the divorce had been her way of demanding fidelity, not ending their marriage, that she was moving on. And what better way than with the illegitimate half-brother who Cyrus regarded with equal parts jealousy and antipathy?

The fact that Rowan wanted Lysander in a way she'd never craved physical connection with Cyrus only made this little plan both possible and potentially pleasurable.

"Do you have an appointment?"

The voice startled Rowan out of her musings, and nearly toppled her off of her three-inch heels.

She spun around to see that while yes, there was a call box on one side of the gate like on the estate she'd once shared with her husband, there was also a security gate on the other. It was manned by a guard who looked like he knew what he was doing. She supposed that was the difference between security for a billionaire like Lysander Baros and a millionaire like his half-brother and her ex, Cyrus Andino.

"Um, no, but I think Lysander will see me." As she said the words, Rowan realized how foolish they sounded. This guard didn't know her, or that she knew Lysander.

It hadn't been very smart to come over here without calling Lysander first either. What if he was entertaining?

She knew he preferred quiet after returning from extended business trips, but that didn't mean he wouldn't have a discreet companion to welcome him home from his trip to Asia. He'd been gone seven weeks and visited five countries, with stops in multiple cities in each. A grueling schedule, even for a man like her Greek billionaire.

No, not *hers*. He would never be that, but he might be her lover if she handled this right.

The guard was looking at her impassively, and kudos to him for that because he had to have lots of experience turning away women who wanted a little of Lysander's time and were sure that he'd want to see them. Even if he weren't a billionaire, he would be in high demand with his square jawed good looks, wavy dark hair and utterly mesmerizing blue eyes. Not to mention a muscular body most athletes would envy.

Rowan grabbed her bag and dug out her phone. Much easier in the small, elegant bag she'd paired with her slinky designer dress than her usual hold all.

"Let me just call him and let him know I'm here," she said, looking up to give the guard a winning smile, only to find a gun trained on her.

Rowan screamed and dropped her phone.

Not a very practical reaction, she admitted, but she'd never seen a gun in person, much less had one pointed at her. Of course, she knew her security had been armed when she was married to Cyrus, but the guns had always been covered by suitcoats. Or maybe they'd worn ankle holsters?

She didn't know, and neither mattered now as she stared down the barrel of the gun still pointed at her.

Her initial shock wearing off, indignation set in, and she frowned severely at the security guard. "Why are you threatening me with a gun? How could that possibly be necessary?"

"I thought you might be going for a weapon," he said.

She didn't even try to hold back the snort of derision. "Clearly not." She pointed to the phone on the ground a few feet away. "I was trying to get my phone out so I could call Lysander and tell him I'm here."

"What is your name?" the guard asked.

"Rowan Johnson." She'd taken back her maiden name at the divorce.

The guard's expression didn't change. "Your name is not on the list."

"You haven't bothered to look at any list," she said, unimpressed.

"I have it memorized, and your name is not on it."

"Oh, do you have an eidetic memory? Only isn't being a gate guard an odd choice of careers for someone with that kind of skill?" she asked herself more than him.

Rowan always wanted to understand the why of people. It was hardwired into her. At least that's how it felt to her.

"I'm a security specialist, and no I don't have a photographic memory. Mr. Baros's list of approved guests is short."

"Oh. That's not surprising, I guess. I can't help noticing your gun is still pointed at me." And it was making her nervous. Well, strictly speaking, she'd gotten a full dose of scared and worried the second the gun came out.

There was no making about it.

"I haven't yet ascertained if you are a threat."

"Look, how about you call Lysander and tell him Rowan Johnson nee Andino is at the gate?"

"I cannot do that."

"Why not? Did you drop your cell phone too?" she asked sarcastically, but inside she was shaking a little. Her phone was only a few feet away, but she wasn't about to move toward it while he had his gun out.

What kind of security was trained to threaten violence without the least provocation? Rowan wasn't feeling sexy anymore. She was angry and scared, and that only made her angrier.

"Policy is not to bother Mr. Baros with anyone showing up who does not have an appointment."

"Okay, fine. Put your gun away and I will get my cell phone and call him."

"Show me the inside of your purse first," the man instructed.

It was a rude request, and surely unnecessary, but Rowan wanted that gun put away more than she wanted to argue about the invasion of her privacy.

So, she opened her small clutch and turned it so he could see the inside. "There. No weapons of any kind. I don't even carry a nail file with me. Satisfied?"

He nodded and holstered his gun.

Rowan surged forward to grab her phone, forgetting she was wearing heels rather than her usual more sensible foot attire and promptly twisted her ankle, falling forward to land heavily on her knees. She cried out and then gasped as sharp pricks of pain from her skinned knees and a resounding throb in her ankle assailed her.

Shoot. This was the worst plan ever. What had she been thinking?

Seduce Mr. Sexy himself and make sure Cyrus heard about it so he would stop hounding her about reconciling? She wanted to get her dad and brothers off her back as well. They were business partners with her ex and apparently the divorce had made things uncomfortable for them.

Like that was all that mattered. But considering the fact they'd all known Cyrus slept around during her marriage and had never told her, there could be no question where their loyalty lay.

Anyway, this plan was definitely a bust. Climbing to her feet without flashing her panties was the kind of struggle she'd never thought to face and told her why she never dressed in this kind of clothing. She was far too clutzy for femme fatale gear.

Taking a step, she nearly fell again from the pain. No way could she walk another step in these heels, much less back to her car. Leaning against the wall, she removed first one sandal and then the other. Then she limped to her phone, her ire getting worse with every painful step.

When she reached the phone, she was faced with another dilemma. How did she bend down to get it without her skirt riding up indecently? If she tried to squat, she'd be equally exposed but in a different area of her anatomy.

Finally, she managed a combination squat-bend and got the phone.

She unlocked it and called Lysander.

"Hello, Rowan, what an unexpected pleasure," he said in his smooth, deep voice answering after the second ring.

"So, you have my number in your phone, but my name isn't on your list. I can't believe I thought having sex with you was a good idea. You have your guards trained to pull guns on people just for trying to use their phones? What kind of man is that paranoid?"

"What are you saying? You aren't making sense."

"You're right. My idea was completely nonsensical but I don't think I needed to pay for that with skinned knees, a twisted ankle and having a gun drawn on me."

"Slow down, Rowan, who drew a gun on you?"

"Your gate guard, excuse me, *security specialist*," she emphasized. "He scared the bejeebees out of me. I don't like wearing heels."

"I know. You mentioned it once when we were dancing."

He'd asked her to dance at one of the dos for a charity both her ex and Lysander had supported. That the two men agreed on even that was almost a miracle. She'd learned that after the dance though. When Cyrus had berated her for dancing with the other man.

"But he's your brother."

"My half-brother. Why my father chose to acknowledge him, I'll never understand, but we aren't legal family."

Which meant what? She'd always wondered. They weren't legal brothers, but they shared half their DNA and they'd been raised by the same father, though saying Baptiste Andino had had a hand in raising his mistress's child was a bit of a stretch. But he had acknowledged Lysander as his son publicly and paid for his support and schooling, something that Cyrus resented. The connection had never been a secret. Her ex had resented that too.

Rowan had quickly learned that Cyrus took it as a personal affront if Rowan so much as smiled at Lysander, much less talked to him. Cyrus had frozen her out for a week after that innocent dance.

"We have only danced once," she pointed out now. "And trust me the exercise isn't likely to be repeated. I'm totally off men who have their security trained to treat visitors to their estate like the international most wanted."

"Gregor will bring you to the house." Then the call dropped. How rude. He hadn't even said goodbye.

Suddenly the gate started to slide open, and the security specialist headed toward her with rapid steps. His gun was still holstered, but the look on his face showed intent. Rowan just knew that intent had something to do with her.

Just how ridiculous her plan was washed over Rowan and filled her with embarrassment. Why had she thought Mr. Eligible Bachelor himself would want to sleep with her when he could have pretty much any woman, or man if he swung that way, in Athens? Like heck she was sticking around so he could laugh in her face at the very idea.

She took a step toward her car and nearly fell again. Crud, that had hurt.

Her knees were still stinging and any movement made the pain more acute, but it was her ankle that was making walking difficult. She limped as fast as she could, but hadn't yet reached her car when a hand came around her wrist like a manacle.

She gasped and yanked against the hold instinctively. Her wrist remained firmly in the security specialist's grip.

"Mr. Baros would like you to come to the house so he can speak to you." The guard's tone was polite, but that didn't make her any less his prisoner.

"Mr. Baros can call me at his convenience. I want to leave," Rowan said tartly. "Let go of my hand."

Even if she still thought her idea was a good one, and she didn't, she had no desire to meet up with Lysander with skinned knees, a sore ankle and a sweaty brow from stress.

Chapter Two

"Please be reasonable, Miz Johnson. You came here to see Mr. Baros. If you come with me, you can do that."

"I would rather go home."

"Klaus is bringing your car up to the house already."

Sure enough, her little electric car was being driven through the gate by a man as large as the one in possession of her wrist, but with blond hair. He grinned at her and tipped an imaginary hat in her direction through the window of her car.

"Hey, you can't steal my car," she shouted at him. To no effect.

"He's not stealing it. He is merely parking it for you. It is a courtesy," Gregor said, his own expression as impassive as it had been since the beginning of their discussion.

However, there was something around his eyes. Something that told her he was amused by this situation. Rowan was not.

"How am I supposed to get up to the house? I don't know if it escaped your notice, but I twisted my ankle."

"I saw." No apology for his part in her debacle, just an admission he'd seen it happen.

She glared at him. "So?"

"I have a vehicle here." He helped her over to a vehicle that might have been a golf cart in another life. In this one, it was painted a discreet grey with the logo of a security firm emblazoned on the side.

The ride up to the house was a short one. When they arrived at the front door, there was no sign of her compact.

"Where is my car?" she asked.

"Klaus has parked it in an empty garage bay." The answer did not come from Gregor.

Butterflies waged war in Rowan's tummy like peaceful, innocent butterflies were not supposed to do and Rowan turned her head to see the object of her visit. And quite a few of her recent fantasies.

Lysander Baros. He stood there in a pair of slacks and white dress shirt, sleeves rolled up to reveal the tanned skin and defined muscles of his forearms. The top two buttons of his shirt were undone, and she could see a hint of his dark chest hair.

Despite the situation she'd found herself in, her body had a predictable response to this man. The same response she'd had to every image she saw of him, or the rare times she saw him at an event in person since her divorce. She wanted him. She'd never wanted Cyrus this way and the fact was that she didn't want any other man like this either.

It was like her body had tuned to Lysander's station and everything else was static.

Nevertheless, the utmost emotion in Rowan at the moment was anger.

Uncertain if she could stand at the minute, she didn't try to get out of her seat in the security vehicle. Instead, she turned her body so he could receive the full weight of her displeasure. "Well, he can just unpark it and bring it back round. I want to go home."

"But you came to see me, yes? And here I am."

"What? Do you want a gold star for participation, or something? First, you have your goon pull a gun on me. Then you hang up on me without saying goodbye. That is rude and I know your mom taught you better. She's a nice lady."

Lysander's eyes widened at Rowan's tone, but he didn't say anything.

So, she continued. "Then you send another goon to steal my car." She ticked each offense with one finger. She had three fingers up so far. "But that wasn't enough? No, you had to have your—"

"Goon," Gregor supplied helpfully, cutting into her words.

She let him have some of her ire filled gaze before turning her attention back to the man who had infuriated her to the point of raising her voice. "Right, your goon—"

"His name is Gregor," Klaus said, coming up, his expression showing all the humor he found in the current situation.

Rowan crossed her arms over her chest and frowned at him this time. "You'll notice I'm not laughing. Your boss had me kidnapped and that is not only illegal, it's—"

"Let me guess, rude?" Gregor asked, his own tone now showing his amusement as well.

"So is interrupting people."

"You'll have to forgive me, I grew up in an orphanage and the streets of Athens. No mother to teach me polite behavior."

"Goodness help you then, because clearly you aren't going to learn it from your boss."

Both the security specialists laughed out loud at that.

Which made Rowan feel just a tiny bit vindicated. They didn't mind seeing the arrogant self-made billionaire taken down a peg. Funny, but before today she'd had no desire to see that herself. Apparently wealthy men forgot what they learned in manners in their pursuit of money.

Maybe she should write an op-ed about that. She wondered if any of the fringe press would publish it.

"You were saying," Lysander prompted when Rowan had been lost in silent thought for several seconds.

"Oh, uh, right. I want to go home."

"You said you had skinned knees and a twisted ankle?" he asked, sounding solicitous, if she could believe that.

She didn't. "Yes, because you have your goons—"

"I prefer security specialist," Klaus said.

Rowan felt like a tea kettle about to go off. She never screamed shrilly, but these men. They thought they were so cute. "Seriously? Act like a security specialist and that's what I'll call you. Act like a goon and that's your title."

"I didn't do anything goonish," Klaus said, all innocence.

"You stole my car."

"I parked it for you. I often park guest's cars for Mr. Baros."

"So, you're a valet, not a security specialist?" she asked with raised brows.

"Apparently, he's both," Lysander said, finally speaking. "I apologize that my security specialists' methods were distressing for you, but I would appreciate you allowing me to have your wounds seen to."

"They're not wounds." That sounded so serious.

But Lysander wasn't listening. He was in fact, sliding one strong arm under her hips and the other behind her back. Rowan let out a squeak she would deny later having made as she was lifted right against the rock-solid chest that had played a pivotal role in several fantasies of late.

"Now you're kidnapping me?" she asked with more breathlessness than she would ever admit to, and very little of the ire she'd intended.

"You have not been kidnapped. You came to see me. You see me. Klaus did not steal your car. It is waiting for you safely in the estate garage." He said nothing about Gregor drawing his gun on her, but Lysander had already said he was sorry she'd found it distressing.

Like that was the end of it, like a simple apology could make up for her terror at having a weapon pointed at her for no reason at all.

"If you aren't kidnapping me, then put me down and have my car brought back around."

"We have yet to see your wounds doctored," he replied.

"They're hardly wounds. Just..." She wasn't sure what to classify her skinned knees as. Saying owie felt rather juvenile, especially with how her body was responding to his in such a very adult manner. "Do you ever listen?" she demanded, even as she tried to steady her breathing.

"I listen to you. I distinctly heard you say you want to have sex with me." His deep tone held a wealth of satisfaction.

"Of course, you heard that and ignored everything else I said." Typical man.

"I do not ignore you, but surely you did not come all this way simply to turn around without having the discussion you hoped to with me."

"That was not my original plan, no, but it became my plan after Gregor pulled his gun on me."

"So, you do remember his name."

"Seriously, Lysander. Do you really have such a problem with women showing up at your gate that pulling guns on unexpected visitors is your people's go to?"

Lysander shook his head. "We have had some threats."

"What do you mean we?" She tried to read his handsome features. "Do you mean you? Someone is threatening you and in a serious enough way that you've got your security on high alert?"

The thought of someone doing him harm sent a wave of dread over her.

"I cut business ties with and funding for a group with ties to shady, but powerful businessmen who want to see clean energy regulations loosened or done away with altogether."

Lysander's support of the EU's stance on clean energy was well known. It was one of the things she liked about him.

"And they think threatening you will get you to do business with them again?" she asked incredulously. She and Lysander were not close, but he was a force to be reckoned with in the business world, not someone to be intimidated.

"Intimidation might work for someone without my security resources," he said with a shrug as they entered an inviting living area, and no mention of his powerful influence in the global world of business.

Rowan let her gaze scan the room. This was not an entertaining space for business contacts. Family photos made up a collage on one wall Rowan was sure was courtesy of Iona Baros, Lysander's mom. She'd never taken him to be the sentimental type, but the photos were there, regardless of who had them framed and hung.

A large screen television was on and paused on a stock report. There was an oversized chocolate brown sectional sofa with lots of cushions and a square coffee table that held a coffee cup and a tablet.

This had been where Lysander was when she'd called him. He'd probably been reading the news on his tablet while listening to the stock report on the TV. He laid her on the chaise lounge part of the sectional and sat down beside her, their hips touching, and his body oriented to face hers.

"This is a cozy room," Rowan observed.

"My private sanctum."

Before he could add anything else, like why he'd brought Rowan in here rather than a more public room in the mansion, a woman dressed in the no nonsense uniform of a housekeeper with her salt and pepper hair pulled back into a severe bun briskly walked in. She carried a laden tray. She spoke in rapid Greek to Lysander, telling him she had the supplies to tend to his guest.

Clearly expecting her boss to move out of the way, the housekeeper stepped toward Rowan. However, Lysander put his hand out with an imperious gesture. "Give it to me."

"You are going to put bandages on my skinned knees?" Rowan asked with shock. *He* was?

"Not until I have cleaned them," he said, like that should be self-evident. "But first let us get some ice on your ankle. Which one is paining you?"

Rowan pointed to her left ankle, which did not look swollen, so she had hopes it wasn't a full-on sprain.

He laid a cloth neatly over her ankle and then carefully placed an icepack on top of the cloth before instructing a smart speaker to set a twenty-minute timer. "Do you want something for the pain?"

"If you have a couple of ibuprofen, I'll happily take them." At some point she would have to walk out of here on her own steam. She'd like to be able to do that without making an absolute cake of herself.

Lysander sent the housekeeper for the ibuprofen and then took a damp cloth from a pile of neatly rolled ones just like it and dabbed oh so gently at her left knee. It still stung and Rowan winced.

He blew on it. "Better?"

Unable to form even the single word *yes*, Rowan gulped and nodded.

Chapter Three

The housekeeper returned with a tumbler of water and two tablets. Thanking the other woman in Greek, Rowan took the pain relievers with a sip of water.

"Drink at least a cup. It is better for you and will make the pain reliever work faster," Lysander instructed.

Rowan did as directed because she knew he was right, not because she was usually amenable to being bossed around. Even for her own good.

Lysander repeated the gentle dabbing to her knee with the wet cloth, then soft blowing to take the sting away until he was apparently satisfied with the results of his ministrations. He then put some ointment on the abrasion before picking out the perfect sized bandage and applying it. After he had shown her right knee equally careful attention, he moved the tray from the sofa to the coffee table.

However, he made no move to put any physical distance between them.

"How is your ankle feeling?" he asked.

She shrugged. "The ice seems to be helping."

"We'll check it after the timer goes off and determine if you need a doctor to look at it."

"Oh, I'm sure that's not necessary," she assured him. "It didn't look swollen."

He made a noncommittal noise.

"I do not like going to the doctor's," she informed him. Her antipathy was rooted in a childhood spent in too many doctor's offices monitoring a heart condition that had required surgery when she was six.

Since then, her heart was the strongest muscle in her body, she was sure of it. It would have to be to survive the betrayal of both her husband and her family.

"Understood," Lysander said.

"What does that mean? You understand I don't want to go to the doctor's office, but I'm going anyway if you think my ankle needs attention?" she asked with heavy sarcasm.

He gave her a slashing white smile. "It is like you know me, but not exactly. I understand if your ankle needs attention, my concierge doctor will be called to attend you here."

"You have a concierge doctor?" Of course, he did. He was a billionaire after all.

"It is a matter of time, efficiency, and security."

"Does it ever bother you?"

"What?"

"That you cannot live like a normal person. If you run out of milk, going to the grocery store means taking a whole entourage of security and staff?"

"First, I don't care for dairy milk. Second, I would never think to go to the grocery store. Helen would be appalled at my choices, I am sure."

She'd heard him call the housekeeper, Helen. "Your housekeeper, not your cook?"

"Helen rules the house," he said with a shrug. "Even Etienne would not think to oppose her."

"Etienne is your chef?"

"He is. He makes an even better moussaka than Mama, but if you tell her I said so, I will deny it."

Rowan laughed as she knew she was meant to.

"Your divorce has become final?" he asked, apropos of nothing.

Though considering she'd told him she wanted sex with him, maybe not nothing.

"Yes, last week." Since she'd been married in the USA, she'd filed in a US court, but it had still taken over a year to finalize.

Her ex had not been cooperative. Lucky for her, his infidelity had been easy to document and the divorce laws in her home state favored her petition. She also hadn't asked for maintenance, or a financial settlement.

The prenuptial agreement she'd signed had dictated certain financial arrangements she'd been happy to forego for her freedom from the marriage. The judge presiding had not agreed and had ordered a fulfillment of the contract to the letter.

Cyrus and her own family had been livid, but now she had a nest egg. She was still deciding how much of it she intended to keep, and how much she would donate to causes close to her heart.

With her degree in human resources, Rowan was perfectly capable of supporting herself, if not in the lifestyle she'd known growing up or during her marriage, in one she found comfortable.

Lysander smiled at her answer. "Good."

"That's not the usual response I get." Mostly people told her they were sorry. She was sorry too, not to be divorced, but that she'd ever been duped by Cyrus to begin with.

Lysander shrugged. "You were not happy in your marriage even before you found out that Cyrus had broken his marriage vows."

"That's a very old-fashioned way of putting it," she said.

"I am an old-fashioned man in some ways. I believe promises are meant to be kept. It is why I never intend to marry."

She didn't believe for a minute he was engaging in idle chit-chat. He was warning her. Sex might be in the offing, but commitment wasn't.

"Don't worry, Lysander, I'm not looking for another husband." Rowan didn't believe all men were lying cheaters like her ex, but Lysander had been right. She hadn't been happy in her marriage long before she'd learned of Cyrus's ongoing and frequent extra-marital bedroom activities.

"I don't think I'm cut out for marriage," she told Lysander with more honesty than was probably smart to engage in. "I didn't enjoy having my *I* constantly subsumed by the *we*."

"I do not believe all marriages require that, but I am by no means an expert, having never been married and being the product of a relationship that was never going to include that particular element."

"Did that bother you?" she asked, wondering even as she did so if he would deign to answer.

It was a cheekily personal question.

"There were times in my life it bothered me a great deal," he said surprising her with his honesty. "Now is not one of them."

"What changed?"

"I made a place for myself in the world where it does not matter."

"I would have to agree." Lysander wielded influence his brother and even his father could not hope to match.

It infuriated Cyrus, making him jealous and mean about the sibling he refused to acknowledge in any meaningful way.

"It clearly does not matter to you," he said, a wealth of meaning in his words.

Heat climbed into Rowan's cheeks. Why had she said that about wanting to have sex with him?

"You do realize having a gun pointed at me was a real turn off, don't you?" she asked repressively.

His gaze skimmed down her body, noting she was sure the way her beaded nipples pressed against the thin fabric of her barely there bra and slinky dress. "Funnily enough, no, it had not occurred to me."

Before she could make a blistering retort, or at least say something about looks being deceiving, the alarm on the smart speaker went off.

"Time to check your ankle," he said, shifting so he could lift the cloth and icepack to reveal her foot and ankle closest to him.

He trailed his fingertip from the tip of her big toe over her foot and up her ankle. "How does that feel?"

"F..." She coughed. "Fine."

"Try rotating your foot."

She did and felt only the tiniest twinge. Oh, thank goodness, it really was going to be fine and there would be no need for wrapping or crutches.

"Let us see how you do putting weight on it." He suited action to words, standing up and holding his hands out to her.

She grasped them and stood, relief flooding her when the twinge didn't grow into a throb. "I should have no trouble walking on it now. Thank you. Did you want to have my car brought round?"

He shook his head.

She cocked her head to one side, eyeing him warily. "I'm still a kidnap victim then?"

"We still have your original reason for coming to visit to discuss."

"I think I'd rather discuss it sometime when I haven't been accosted by your goons." If ever. The reality of what she'd planned to propose to him was hitting her hard.

Had Rowan really thought suggesting they have sex to stick it to her ex was a good idea?

"I would prefer to discuss it now," he said with certainty. "You came dressed so enticingly and for my benefit, how can I do anything but give you my full attention?"

"I'm sure I'm not the first woman who showed up at your gate dressed to seduce."

"You're the first one I have any interest in though."

"Oh."

"This chemistry between us, it goes both ways." He touched her face with his fingertips.

That small connection sent electric shocks through Rowan's body. If she'd responded this way to her ex, maybe their marriage wouldn't have been such a sham. Instantly shaking off those thoughts, Rowan reminded herself that her former husband's choices had not been her fault. He'd never been faithful, not from the very beginning, as his longtime mistress had been happy to point out.

The other woman hadn't been his only extramarital relationship, so she probably had her own axe to grind. Delphine had insisted that powerful men like Cyrus could not be expected to be faithful.

Maybe Rowan was naïve, but she *had* expected her Greek husband to honor his promise of fidelity.

Delphine had only been too happy to provide evidence against Cyrus in the divorce. Perhaps because he'd lied to her once too often?

Rowan didn't know and neither did she care. Her life with Cyrus was over and this, right here, this was how she intended to show that to the world.

"I don't think you'll like my stipulations," she said now to Lysander.

His expression instantly wary, he asked, "What stipulations?"

"In the morning, or whatever time I leave in the night, I want to be caught by the paparazzi."

"You want to have sex with me to have revenge on your ex?" Lysander asked.

She couldn't tell from his tone how he felt about that. His expression wasn't a happy one, but then Lysander wasn't known for his affable personality. Gorgeous? Check. Uber wealthy. Double check. Personable? Sometimes. But he was more aloof than charming. In fact, she would have called him downright grumpy, though no one else seemed willing to.

"I want to have sex with you because I want you. I want the paparazzi to catch me so my ex-husband will realize the divorce wasn't some kind of feminine plea for fidelity."

"He doesn't accept that your marriage is over?" Lysander asked.

"Not even a little. He sent me roses just yesterday. I gave them to my neighbor."

"You do not like roses?"

"I love them, but I don't like the sender. I want him out of my life completely, only my family and he still have dreams of dynasty building. They're all sure that once I start having babies everything will fall into place."

"You were married ten years."

"Nine. Our marriage ended when I learned of his infidelity."

"But the divorce only finalized last week."

"Yes. Now it isn't just a matter of how I see my life, but that I am legally no longer bound to him in any way."

"My point was that if they are looking for dynasty building, a marriage that did not produce children in nearly a decade is not one likely to in the future either."

"I was on birth control for the first few years."

"And after?"

She sighed. "We didn't have sex that often and it just never happened." Now she was really glad it hadn't. Rowan couldn't imagine being tied to Cyrus Andino indefinitely through a child.

But for a while, her lack of motherhood had been a real source of grief for her.

"So, not dynasty building," Lysander said, almost musingly.

Chapter Four

"What do you mean?" Rowan asked Lysander.

"Cyrus wants you back. It could be as simple as not being willing to let go of what he believes is his, but the fact you didn't have children and he is narcissistic enough to insist on leaving his imprint on the next generation, leads to an important question."

"What would that be?"

"Why won't he let you go? Of course, he may well know the fertility problem lies with him already. He has no children with any of his lovers either. Not even Delphine, and they've been together since before your wedding."

"You knew all this?" she asked, feeling betrayed. Only Lysander hadn't betrayed her.

They hadn't been considered family. Their combustible chemistry aside, they weren't even friends. He hadn't owed her the truth. Not like her own family, all of whom had been aware of Delphine, if not Cyrus's other pillow friends.

"How?" she asked.

"I keep tabs on my family, especially the ones who would prefer I did not exist."

Rowan couldn't deny that interpretation of Cyrus's feelings.

"You're more than a little paranoid, aren't you?" She hadn't forgotten his goon drawing his gun on her, even if Lysander preferred to pretend it hadn't happened.

"I am cautious, that is all. And I have good reason to be. Cyrus is not a good man."

"I wish someone had said as much to me before I married him," Rowan muttered.

"Had I known you, I would have."

She believed him. "But Cyrus and I met in the States and that's where we got married." After a whirlwind courtship, that looking back on, had all sorts of red flags.

But her family had been all in on the idea of her marrying an Andino and Rowan had been completely taken in by Cyrus's charm and good looks. He'd known just what to say and how to act. Of course, at the time she'd had no idea he'd been getting coaching from her own father.

"Tell me about your prenuptial agreement."

"Are you saying you haven't managed to get yourself a copy?"

"I admit I never even tried. It was of little interest to me. You, the most intriguing woman I'd met, were married to my detestable half-brother."

Rowan hadn't been the only one avoiding Lysander since that dance. He'd done a good job of avoiding her as well. The feelings she had around him confused her and only later had she realized they were attracted to each other. By then, she'd been grateful for his discretion. Unlike her ex, Rowan had considered her wedding vows inviolate.

"Why do you want to hear about it now?"

"Because you assume that learning you have had sex with me will end Cyrus's interest in you. Forgive me, but my brother clearly didn't appreciate what he had in you when you were married, why so adamant now to get you back?"

"And you think something in the prenuptial agreement explains it?"

"Yes."

"Okay. You can read it. I'll send over a copy after I get home."

"Why not move back to the States?" he asked. "You went back to get the divorce?"

"I'm thirty years old," she told him. "I built a life for myself here in Athens. I have a job, even if it's one neither my family, nor Cyrus ever considered much of."

"You work as a career counselor for women going back into the workforce after a prolonged absence."

"Yes, and I find it very rewarding. I believe in what my organization does. I like my coworkers. My boss doesn't hover. My apartment isn't big, but it has a great view, and I can walk to work and all the shops from there. I have friends that are closer than my brother and sister are to me. This is where my life is, and Cyrus isn't chasing me out of Athens."

Besides, moving back to the US wasn't going to make it harder for Cyrus to pursue her. He had a private jet and spent at least one week a month in New York on business.

No, she had to get him (and her father) to understand without a doubt that she had moved on and wasn't ever going to be amenable to reconciliation. If she still loved Cyrus, that would make her decision harder, but once he'd stopped playing the part of perfect man for her, she'd discovered they had almost nothing in common and certainly nothing of substance.

"Cyrus wants me back because he doesn't like losing. Full stop."

"Tell me, was there a clause in the prenup that ensured you retained ownership of all gifts given to you over the course of your marriage?"

"There might have been. I only read the document once. I didn't ask for it to be enforced in the divorce."

"But it was?" Lysander asked.

"Yes. The judge decreed that all stipulations and clauses would be adhered to the letter."

"As I thought. It is likely that Cyrus put things in your name as a tax shelter, or even to hide their existence. Now you have ownership and I am guessing it impacts his business in a seriously negative way if he doesn't get control of those assets back. Did you get shares in his company as part of the divorce settlement."

That she *could* answer. "Yes. I got ten percent of his company and he got ten percent of my father's company, but now that the divorce is finalized, us getting remarried isn't going to change that."

"It could."

"If he convinced me to sign them over."

"Both your father and Cyrus have reason to want that outcome."

"Then you think if I sign the shares back over to Cyrus, he'll stop trying to pursue me?" She'd wanted to donate them to her organization as an ongoing source of income, but if it meant getting Cyrus out of her life entirely, she'd give them back in a hot minute.

Or would she? There was a lot of good that could be done with that money and Cyrus was never going to do it.

"It depends."

"Right. You think he may have put other assets in my name."

"It's almost a certainty. He is too short sighted to realize that he would not always have control of you, much less those assets that legally now belong to you."

"That does sound like Cyrus. What if I give it all back? Then he'll leave me alone."

"Is that what you really want?"

"I wanted to do some good with the money I got out of the divorce. I didn't ask for it, but it is mine and I thought I could make a difference."

"You still can."

"Once I give it all away, he won't have any reason to keep after me either," she said, realizing that was the truth. Oh, Cyrus, not to mention her father, would be furious.

She'd no doubts that they had some kind of deal to exchange the shares in each other's company if they succeeded in pressuring her into remarrying him. Not that she expected Cyrus would honor his side of the bargain. Her father was a fool if he did, but that was his lookout.

"So, this isn't necessary," she mused aloud.

"No, I don't think it is." Lysander gave her one of his rare slashing grins. "Not for the sake of ridding you of Cyrus, anyway."

And suddenly, she wasn't thinking about how to get rid of her ex, but what it would feel like to have Lysander's hands on her body, to have license to touch him as much as she liked. Those thoughts made her heart race.

Her mouth opened and a small puff of air expelled from her chest.

She wanted him.

And it didn't have a darn thing to do with revenge.

"I'm not married anymore." That felt like something important to say right then.

"No, you are not. I do not have a lover at present either."

"You don't sleep with more than one woman at the same time?" she asked, not sure she'd believe him if Lysander said no.

He shook his head. "I do not. I have had many lovers, but never more than one at a time."

"You don't do commitment."

"No, but I do temporary fidelity when the sex goes beyond a single night."

"What about Adele Fournier?" The French supermodel had been photographed on Lysander's arm several times over the past couple of years.

"Adele and I have a mutually beneficial arrangement. She likes to attend the functions I have to for business."

"Are you saying you never sleep with her?"

"I am saying that there is no expectation of commitment or fidelity on either side."

"The billionaire's version of friends with benefits." Of course, his *friend* was considered one of the most beautiful women in the world.

"While I find Adele's company less irritating than some, I would not say we are friends."

Why didn't that surprise her? Rowan wondered if the Greek tycoon considered anyone an actual friend.

Regardless, she wasn't looking for long term either. She was in fact, only proposing one night.

However, the knowledge that if they started something that lasted longer, he would not be sleeping with other women as well resonated. It settled inside her with a much stronger positive vibe than she would have expected it to.

It was like that mattered. A lot. And really? It shouldn't matter at all.

Her plan was to get rid of her ex once and for all, but also to prove to herself that she could move on. That the bad choice she'd made at twenty didn't have to define the rest of her life.

"I expect the same," he said almost warningly.

She thought about that. She didn't desire anyone but him and couldn't imagine jumping from his bed to someone else's. "I'm not sure why we're discussing this."

"We are getting the expectations out of the way before anything happens between us."

"You mean sex."

"I mean sex."

She sighed. "This feels very calculated."

"Did the prenup you signed before marriage feel calculated?" he asked.

"No, but that was different. People in our world sign prenuptial agreements all the time."

"And people discuss expectations before going to bed together." His hand slid around to cup the back of her neck, his thumb rubbing up and down softly against her skin. "Stay with me today. We'll watch a movie, have dinner in and relax together. Whatever happens, happens."

That sounded way better than a calculated move to the bedroom. "You watch movies?" she asked, infusing her voice with humor laced skepticism.

"Sometimes."

"Not often, I bet."

"No, not often, but even self-made billionaires have to have down time."

"I thought your version of down time was doing business in your shirt sleeves. I mean, correct me if I'm wrong, but you were in here reading the business news while listening to the stock market reports." She looked toward the television that was still paused on the screen showing a graph for stock prices on a global tech company.

"Caught, but I'm happy to pivot to something entirely nonwork related."

"What kind of movies do you like?" she asked, really curious.

"Documentaries are my favorite, but I indulge in action adventure too."

"I love documentaries. Have you watched the latest on hummingbirds?"

"I haven't had the pleasure."

"Neither have I, but my coworker said it's amazing."

He leaned down and grabbed the remote. "See if you can find it. I'll organize some refreshments."

"I'd love something bright and fizzy, but no alcohol." Being around him was enough of a challenge to her equilibrium without adding wine or hard liquor to the mix.

Chapter Five

"Something bright and fizzy coming right up." He grabbed his phone and sent a text.

She did a search for the documentary she wanted to watch and found it on the first try. She clicked into it and then paused it, so they could get comfortable before starting the show.

"I wish I'd worn more practical clothing," she lamented. "I don't think femme fatale is really in my repertoire."

"You look amazing, but maybe not very comfortable."

"I'm not." She tugged down the hem on her skirt which seemed to want to ride up. "Who knew dressing to seduce could be so irritating?"

She never would have twisted her ankle if she'd been wearing her normal shoes.

"Tell me your sizes and I'll get something delivered."

"What? No. That's a waste of energy and money when I have perfectly good clothing at home."

"But I want you to stay here, and I want you to be comfortable. You like that designer?" he asked, referring to her dress.

"Usually, yes." The dress she was wearing was from a different line than she usually shopped. And now that she was supporting herself, she needed to eschew designer labels all together.

If she did keep the money and assets she'd gotten from her divorce, she wasn't using them to continue supporting a lifestyle that had never made her happy. She liked hanging out with her friends in places that did not get written up in the social pages, or go viral on social media. She liked her little apartment and her neighbors that came from so many different walks of life.

"Give me a moment and I'll take care of it."

"Wouldn't it be easier to simply give my apartment key to one of your goons and send them to pick up some clothes for me?"

He shrugged. "There is nothing difficult about sending a personal shopper out for some outfits for you to choose from."

"You live in a very rarified world." Even more rarified than the one she'd known most of her life.

They settled on the couch after that, he insisting she put her ankle up on a cushion on the chaise. She didn't mind because it gave her some breathing room with the attraction threatening to overwhelm her. Not a lot, because he sat right beside her, but it wasn't instant sexy times.

They started watching the documentary on the hummingbirds. Despite having the most tantalizing man she'd ever known only inches away, Rowan quickly found herself engrossed. The housekeeper came in with drinks for them. Rowan's turned out to be a splash of cranberry and pineapple juice mixed with club soda and served over ice. It was refreshing and the cookies brought with it delicious.

Lysander put his arm around her shoulder and she let herself relax against him. As much as she was enjoying the documentary, this closer proximity soon began to wreak havoc with her senses. The heat of his body so close, the hard muscles of his chest pressing against her arm and shoulder, the scent that was so much more than the masculine aftershave he wore.

She shifted to get closer, inhaling that delicious smell that was all Lysander Baros and felt her skirt sliding up her legs. Darn it.

Vowing never to wear this dress again, she tugged her hem down, squirming as she did so.

"You really are uncomfortable in that dress," he said, sounding surprised.

"I thought I wouldn't be wearing it long," she admitted and then wished she hadn't.

He already knew she wanted him. He didn't need more proof.

"If things had gone according to your plan, you wouldn't have," he said with certainty. "I want to touch you badly."

"But I like that we're not just jumping into bed," she admitted.

"Not all sex happens in the bedroom." The tone of his voice made her look away from the beautiful little birds fighting over territory on the screen and up at him.

He was looking at her, specifically at how much of her curvy breasts were on display with her plunging neckline. She wasn't model thin, or anything close to it. Her tummy wasn't flat, and her butt filled out a pair of jeans very nicely. Her large breasts would easily fill his hands.

At six and a half feet tall, Lysander had big hands. And the thought of them on her body made Rowan's nipples tingle.

"I've never had sex outside of a bedroom," she admitted, just a little breathless at the idea.

Sure, she'd read about it. Books made lots of things seem possible that she'd never experienced in real life. Like a happy marriage. Like parents that put their children's happiness above their own desire for money, power and prestige. Like passion and fun and lots of other stuff besides.

Stuff that felt all to possible when she was with this man.

Lysander Baros.

His eyes had darkened, looking nearly black, his expression intent. "Never?"

Incapable of speech, Rowan shook her head.

Lysander pulled his phone out and sent a text. "We will not be disturbed." Then he got up and pulled thickly paneled pocket doors together, closing off the entrance to his sanctum from the hall. He crossed the room and shut another pocket door, closing off the entry the housekeeper had used earlier. "We are now entirely private."

"What about when my clothes arrive."

"I've instructed they be delivered to my bedroom."

"Oh, that's efficient." But hadn't the idea been for her to change into something less sexy for their television time?

He rejoined her on the sectional, shocking her when he settled them back into the position they'd been before. "Relax, watch the show. If your skirt rides up, no one is here to see it."

"You're here."

"Yes, I am." The meaning behind his words sent heat pulsing through her body. Yes. He was. And that was what she wanted. To be here with him.

They went back to watching the show and Rowan felt herself relaxing again. When she shifted and her skirt inched up her thighs, she didn't worry about it. In fact, it excited her a little, just thinking he could see her body.

The idea of exposing her thighs to her husband had always stressed Rowan out. Cyrus always had something to say, and it was never complimentary. He'd made cutting comments about choosing a different designer for her clothes and not showing skin if it was dimpled with cellulite.

Why didn't she worry that Lysander would be turned off by her less than perfect body?

Maybe because despite him never making a move on her, she knew he wanted her. Just like she now wanted him. And maybe, just maybe, the self-made business mogul wanted her as much as she wanted him.

Because this? This relaxing in front of the TV? It was just for her.

Lysander's thumb brushed up along her neck and he traced her earlobe with the lightest caress of his fingertips. Rowan shivered.

"Cold?" Lysander asked.

She shook her head. "No."

"I would like to kiss you."

Rowan turned so their lips were only a breath apart. "I'd like that too."

His mouth pressed against hers softly. Once. Twice. Three times. Each touch of their lips teased and delighted in turn. She loved it. She wanted more. She wanted to taste him.

She initiated the next kiss, parting her lips just the littlest bit and exploring his mouth with hers. It was so good. The connection between their lips electrifying. Before she realized what was happening, her hands were buried in his dark hair as she tugged his head closer to hers, prolonging the kiss.

The tip of his tongue slid along her lips and she let hers meet it.

Her body felt like it was on fire, heat surging through her in volcanic waves.

Rowan wanted more. Not just more kissing, but touching. She climbed over Lysander so she was straddling his lap. Part of her brain was vaguely aware of him shifting so no pressure was on her hurt ankle. She ignored the tiny sting from the pressure she was putting on her knees.

This was too good to worry about minor discomfort.

His big hands cupped her bottom and kneaded, sending pleasure arcing through her. Their kiss became more intense as they explored each other's mouths and her breathing grew ragged.

His hands slid up her back until he reached the halter clasp on her dress. He stopped, breaking the kiss and panted. Then asked, "All right?"

"Yes," she said and dove back into the kiss.

The clasp came undone and then he was peeling the fabric down so her breasts were exposed. Her nipples were already hard, but now they tingled from being exposed to the air and she wanted oh so badly for him to touch her there.

Like he read her mind, Lysander brushed his palms over the turgid nubs, sending an arc of need directly to her core. It felt so good to be touched by another person, to know that person was as keen to touch her as she was to be touched. She arched her back, pressing her breasts into his hands, seeking more.

He gave it to her, gently squeezing the round globes in his hands and swiping his thumbs more firmly over her nipples.

She didn't know how long they kissed and touched each other, but at some point it just wasn't enough. She needed all of him, right now. Rowan broke the kiss and panted. Lysander's lips moved to her throat then down her chest.

She gasped as he sucked on the top of her breast. "More, Sander, I want more."

Tearing herself away from him, she shimmied out of her tiny dress and reveled in the look of approval and need he gave her. Then she put her fingers into either side of her panties and stopped. "You too. I want naked."

"*Ne.*" He said *yes*, slipping into Greek. She didn't mind. She was fluent and it showed how into the moment he was.

He stood and stripped with rapid movements, tossing his clothes to the floor. Rowan sucked in a breath of air, trying to move oxygen into her suddenly deprived lungs. Her soon to be lover was sculpted and bronze all over.

She licked her lips. "Do you sunbathe nude?"

"I swim laps in the morning."

"Without a suit."

"I like it better that way."

She nodded. She'd like it better that way if she were swimming with him too.

"The way you look at me is such a turn on," he said, his tone guttural.

She swallowed. "Same."

He looked at her like she was the sexiest thing he'd ever seen. Like airbrushed and botoxed wasn't perfection. She was.

They kissed again, their bodies pressing against each other, skin on skin. Every one of Rowan's nerve endings went zing. His body was hard all over, but the urgency of his need pressed into her stomach and she couldn't help wanting to touch him there. She grasped his hardon in her hand and slid up and down the impressive length.

Rowan wanted him inside her. She hoped he had condoms somewhere in this sanctuary of his.

When she'd decided to go through with this scheme, she'd gotten the birth control shot, but Lysander was sexually active, and she had no idea if he'd been tested recently. She wasn't taking any chances.

At least, that's what she told herself.

CHAPTER SIX

L ysander maneuvered them to the sofa, and they spent glorious minutes exploring each other's bodies with hands and mouths.

At some point he grabbed a condom out of the first aid supplies.

Rowan laughed, even as relief washed over her. "You had Helen bring condoms with the bandages?"

"You said you wanted sex. I wanted to be prepared for whatever happened."

"I guess you've had sex outside the bedroom many times." He was too sexually confident to be limited by the standard location for intimacy.

Rowan, on the other hand, had never had sex anywhere but the marital bed. Her defunct marriage had not been a place to explore her sexually adventurous side.

"Yes," he agreed. He looked around them and then back at her. "It's the first time in here though. I don't usually bring lovers to my home and never in this room."

Right, because it was his inner sanctum.

She liked hearing that, but didn't make the mistake of saying so. They'd been very clear that they weren't dating. They were having sex. She had no claim on him, but still...she liked the sense that she was special.

"Let me," she said, taking the condom from him.

She opened the packet and then rolled the protection down his length, taking her time about it. Once she finished, she brushed up and down over the thin latex and reveled in how his body jerked in involuntary response to her touch.

He brushed her hands away. "Enough. You're going to make me come before I'm even inside you."

"Then I'd just have to entice you to hardness again, wouldn't I?" she asked without repentance.

The sound he made was pure sex.

Seconds later, she was under him, her thighs spread wide and his hardness pressing against the entrance to her body. "Ready?" he asked.

"Yes." More than.

He thrust with his hips, pushing himself inside her body. Sensation after sensation coursed through her as they found a rhythm that brought wave upon wave of ecstasy. Pleasure built from her core until she was tossing her head and canting her hips upward to meet every one of his thrusts.

He kissed her, his mouth passionate and desperate against her own before rearing up to change his angle slightly. He used one hand to steady himself, but the other was all over her, touching her breasts, her neck, her thigh, her stomach and finally sliding between them so his thumb could rub against her clitoris.

Rowan's climax took her by surprise, throwing her body into a rictus of ecstasy that did not end. Lysander kept moving, his handsome features set in stark lines of sexual need and then his head fell back and he shouted, his body going rigid above hers.

They moved together in aftershocks of joyous pleasure for long moments before he rolled to one side, pulling her into him as if unable to bear losing the physical connection.

He'd have to deal with the condom shortly, but right now, she let herself wallow in the aftermath of the most amazing sex she'd ever had. Her entire body tingled with lingering pleasure.

"I believe it is time to move to the bedroom."

"Oh, yes?" she asked, not really inclined to move at all.

"I want to bathe with you." His tone made the words an invitation to more pleasure.

"I've never bathed with someone before," she said thoughtfully. "It sounds fun."

"It will be," he promised.

He called for robes and they donned them before she followed him up a private staircase that led directly to his suite of rooms. The bedroom was large and decorated in dark wood, every piece of furniture substantial, including the bed that looked like a family of five could easily sleep in it.

But they hadn't come up for the bed, no matter how decadent, as evidenced by him walking directly into the ensuite. She followed without hesitation, but stopped when she saw the large whirlpool tub that dominated one corner of the bathroom as big as the bedroom in her current apartment.

"Wow." Steaming water was already bubbling away. "Did you have Helen run us a bath?"

She wasn't going to be embarrassed by that. She wasn't. She was a grown woman who had decided to have sex with the one man she wanted. She had nothing to be embarrassed of.

"Her, or one of her minions." He shrugged. "I sent the text to her."

Amused, Rowan smiled. "She has minions?"

"In a house this size? She has a full staff at her beck and call."

"I bet every one of them adores her."

"They do. She's a good employer."

"But aren't you their employer?"

"I pay them, but she has full discretion for hiring and firing."

"You trust her a great deal."

"My mother hired her."

She loved that he trusted his mother that much. "I'm surprised your mom doesn't live here with you."

"I'm well past the age of living with my mother and she is not who I want to think about right now."

Rowan found herself grinning. She played teasingly with the tie on her robe. "I wonder who exactly you would rather be thinking about."

"I think you know," he said with a mock growl and then he was helping her with that pesky tie and leading her to the bubbling tub.

Rowan learned that waterproof lube made lovemaking in the bath much easier and a lot of fun. She also learned that as intense as Lysander could be, he liked to laugh, and intimacy felt even more intimate when that laughter was shared.

~ ~ ~

They ate dinner in their robes on the balcony, though there was a temporary wardrobe rack filled with clothes in Rowan's style, preferred colors and size. When he opted for a robe, rather than dressing, so did she.

Rowan enjoyed the privacy of eating the delicious moussaka and salad on the balcony with Lysander her only companion. They talked about everything from the road works projects in Athens to her desire to go parasailing.

"You've never gone? But why not?" he asked.

Rowan savored a bite of salad before answering. She loved olives and feta in her salad and Lysander's chef mixed a dressing that had just the right balance of tangy vinegar, olive oil and herbs.

"My ex strongly discouraged me from wearing a swimsuit in public," she said after swallowing all that yumminess.

One of the things she missed sometimes about the life she'd left behind was never having to prepare her own food. She was learning to cook though, and it wasn't going too badly. She'd burned a few things, and over salted others, but all-in-all, Rowan thought she was getting the hang of it. She couldn't make anything like this meal though.

Her one and only attempt at moussaka had turned out more like a soup than a casserole.

Lysander's brows drew together, a storm brewing in his dark eyes. "I know Cyrus is a fool, but why not?"

"He wasn't enamored of my body." He'd been embarrassed by her, or at least that was what his words and actions implied.

Rowan had thanked the powers that be more than once that she'd fallen in love with a phantom and not the real man. Yes, Cyrus's attitude had hurt, more in the beginning than the end of their marriage. But once Rowan had realized he'd played a part to woo her into marriage and that the real Cyrus was selfish and lacking in both empathy and compassion, she'd stopped giving his opinions much weight at all.

And that had been before she'd found out he'd been cheating on her since before they even said, "I do."

"So?" Lysander asked with the dismissiveness he always directed toward his half-brother. "Why should that stop you trying something you wanted to?"

"It's not going to now," she said with a shrug. "I'll probably even go on the cruise to Mexico I've always wanted to. I may even combine the two."

"You want to go...on a cruise?" he asked, like the idea was beyond his comprehension.

She stifled a giggle at the look of horror he couldn't quite hide. "Oh, yes. I've always wanted to."

"But Cyrus has a yacht. Surely you spent time sailing on it."

"It's not the same. Whenever we traveled it was with his friends and business associates. Cruise ships are full of strangers, interesting people I can get to know and lots of things to do." She'd found the views the only redeeming element to otherwise nearly unbearably boring trips aboard her ex-husband's yacht.

"You want to meet strangers?" This time the horror was right there for her to see and hear.

She couldn't help laughing. "You sound like you wonder if I'm using all my brain cells."

"I would never imply otherwise," he said quickly, but his expression didn't match his words.

Even as she felt a little bubble of warmth at this indication that though he could be a cranky so-and-so with other people, he was trying to be careful of *her* feelings, Rowan burst out giggling again and shook her head. "There's world class chefs providing the food, nightly entertainment, decks you can hang out on."

"But you have all of that on a yacht."

"Didn't you ever watch *The Love Boat* as a kid?"

"No. What is it?"

"It was a show in the 1970s."

"You weren't even born then."

"Syndication," she replied with a roll of her eyes. "People fell in love on board and there was a cruise director who made sure everyone had fun, and a bartender who was a real chick magnet."

"And this made you want to take a cruise?" he asked doubtfully. "You do realize real life is not like television. Especially television from many decades ago."

She shrugged, not bothered he didn't share her vision. She wasn't asking him to come with her. She would find a friend to share a cabin and go on her cruise. Someday.

"Why Mexico?" he asked. "You do realize where we live?"

The look on his face. The general bewilderment in his tone. She had to stifle a giggle. He really did look perplexed.

Lysander Baros was Greek, through and through. The idea of wanting to soak in the sun on any sea but those surrounding his beloved country was beyond his comprehension.

Oh, he was well traveled and sophisticated in his tastes as only a man who had eaten food from the best chefs in most of the world's largest cities could be. But that travel? Those meals? They had mostly been to further his business interests.

Maybe the idea of taking a vacation, of traveling simply for the sake of enjoyment was as baffling to him as where she wanted to go.

Poor, driven tycoon.

She'd thought about a cruise on the Mediterranean, but as much as she loved the beauty and people of her adopted country, she wanted to experience something entirely different. "I have lived in Greece for the past ten years. I want to go somewhere I have never been."

"Your parents never took you to Mexico?"

"No. When we traveled, we came to Europe." Her parents had considered places like Paris, Rome, and London worthy destinations.

And of course Athens, where her father had worked so hard to build business relations with Lysander's father.

"I love the colorfulness of Mexico, the way the Mexican language is different from Spanish in other countries, especially Spain." She had taken Spanish in high school and been taught by a woman from Mexico. Rowan's teacher had been very clear on the differences. "I want to learn more about the country, its culture and its people."

"I'm not sure a cruise is your best way to do that."

Could he sound any more condescending?

"There are shore excursions. I'll get a little taste of lots of places." And she would do tons of reading before her cruise. She loved learning new things.

"More like a taste of the tourist areas."

"That's as valid an experience as anything else," she insisted.

"But hardly the authentic Mexico."

"First of all, Mexico is a whole country, so no one city is authentic to all of it. Second of all, you're probably right, but I still want to do it."

He just looked at her, his dark eyes asking why?

"I'm sure that the days I spend on shore will give me an idea for where I'd like to come when I return to Mexico for a hopefully longer visit." She smiled, thinking about the prospect.

Maybe she would use just a tiny bit of her divorce settlement for travel.

She could still do a lot of good with what was left over.

"The point of the cruise isn't just the shore excursions or getting to visit another country." Rowan was also excited about what she expected life onboard to be like.

It was the experience on the ship. Getting to know the other passengers. Meeting people from all walks of life. Playing shuffleboard. Did they still play shuffleboard on cruises? She'd find out. Some day.

"You're a very unique woman." He didn't sound judgy now. In fact, he was almost admiring.

"I don't think so. Lots of people go on cruises and even more dream about it." Maybe just not people as wealthy and driven as Lysander.

"But few of them have access to a private yacht and the Mediterranean."

"I *had* access to a yacht during my marriage. I don't anymore." Her family had never had a yacht. Her parents had borrowed Cyrus's a couple of times every year. She wondered if they had last year, while she'd been fighting the legal battle for her divorce?

"Do you want access to a yacht?" he asked.

Was he offering his? "No. I told you; I want to go on a cruise."

He shook his head, like he couldn't quite believe what he was hearing. "To Mexico."

"Exactly."

CHAPTER SEVEN

The next morning, Rowan woke beside Lysander, her body still lethargic from the surfeit of pleasure their night together had brought. She didn't want to leave the warmth of his body, much less his bed, but they'd set the parameters very succinctly. No commitments. Just sex. Not feelings.

Rowan frowned, her heart squeezing a little in her chest. It wasn't a great time to realize she might be one of those people for whom sex was never just a physical act. Even married to a man she'd rapidly fallen out of love with, she'd felt an emotional connection to him because of the sex they shared, no matter how infrequent.

Which was why she'd been so hurt to find out about his infidelity. She hadn't loved him any longer, but that act of sex between them? It had still felt like something important, something he should not have been doing with other people while married to her.

However, what she'd experienced last night with Lysander blew ten years of tepid emotional connection out of the water. Every time she'd taken Lysander into her body, she'd felt like their souls collided and entwined.

And hers felt bruised this morning from all the mental reminders she'd had to give herself not to settle into the feelings.

They weren't real.

It was just sex. Amazing, mind blowing, never before experienced emotionally intense sex. At least for her. But still, it had only been a temporary pleasure. Nothing lasting.

Lysander didn't do commitment and did Rowan really want one? Regardless of how incredible the night before had been, how connected she had felt to her Greek billionaire lover, she didn't want strings that tethered her to a life that wasn't hers to lead as she saw fit.

After losing ten years of her life to a bad marriage, Rowan wanted to experience all the adventures life had to offer. She was never going back into the wife-of-an-important-businessman box again, that jail cell that only allowed for certain behaviors and certain friends.

She'd always bucked against the constraints, but her efforts had been thwarted by both her husband's and her own family's expectations. She'd wanted to take a paid, fulltime position with her organization from the beginning. Cyrus had allowed part-time volunteer work. Looking back, she hated that she'd agreed to keep the peace.

She'd made friends that didn't further her husband's or father's business interests, but the time she'd had to spend with them had been minimal. She'd been used to juggling the life she wanted with the life she led. She'd been doing it since she was a child, being encouraged by her mother to invite certain children home to play.

At some point that juggling had felt more like trying to catch spinning plates in the air. Rowan had been so stifled in those last couple of years, it had been hard to breathe.

So, she needed to get out of this bed, get dressed and get the heck out of Lysander's house. They'd had their fun, now it was time for her to go.

Moving very carefully, so as not to wake him, she slid toward the side of the bed.

"Where are you going?"

Rowan startled and turned quickly to face him. "Um, it's morning."

"I am aware. We didn't close the curtains to the balcony," he said.

Right. The sun shone into the room brightly, though it had risen only a little while before.

"I should get going."

"Why? You do not have to work. Today is Saturday. You have clothing here for any eventuality we may plan."

"That wardrobe hanger is pretty full. Why is that?" Had he planned on her staying the weekend? Was that what he wanted?

Was that what *she* wanted?

"I am thorough."

"We agreed to one night."

"Did we?" he asked.

"You said you don't do commitment."

"Are you saying you got enough?"

She stared at him, pretty sure she could never make that particular claim. "What are you saying?"

"Your intention was to get the message through to Cyrus that your marriage is over. One night *might* do it, but a full-on affair? That would *definitely* get the point across."

"You want to be my lover long term to stick it to your half-brother?"

"I want to be your lover, for whatever term, because last night was not enough for me. Was it for you?" The demand she answer the question this time was in his tone, but his face was neutral.

"No."

"Yet, you were leaving."

Seriously? He was stuck on that. "That was the agreement."

"When you make a deal, you stick to it." No question how he felt about that. He approved. It was in his tone, but also the warmth of his gaze left no doubt.

"I do."

"Make a deal with me now. We are lovers for as long as we both want to be."

"Okay." She could live with that. More than. Though she didn't know how her heart was going to handle the inevitable breakup. That was a problem for the future. Today, she was going to live the life she wanted to and that included being Lysander's lover.

She sat up and tugged the bedding with her to cover her naked breasts. "But if either of us decides we want to see other people, we tell the other *before* a date, or anything else."

She didn't want to feature as the cheated-on girlfriend in the tabloids any more than she'd enjoyed being featured as the betrayed wife in the many salacious articles detailing Cyrus's bedroom behavior. She'd first learned of his infidelity through a friend who'd seen one such article.

When confronted, Cyrus had dismissed the article as journalism at its basest at first, claiming the pictures were photoshopped.

Her mom had been the one to finally confirm Rowan's suspicions. Calling her to give her a *pep talk* about how men and women saw marriage differently and that she couldn't take Cyrus's affairs personally. Coming from a woman who had consistently turned a blind eye to her own husband's indiscretions, the words had carried more weight than the tabloid article.

Cyrus had been unfaithful, and Rowan's mother knew it. Had, as Rowan learned later, known all along.

"Agreed."

"That included your friends with benefits thing with Adele Fournier." He wasn't getting any other *benefits* while he was sharing Rowan's bed.

"I told you. While I am in a liaison with one woman, I do not have sex with others." He tugged at the sheet covering her. "Now, since we are both awake, let us make better use of our time than talking."

And they did.

The next two days were idyllic for Rowan. Lysander was an inventive and eager lover. She learned a lot about her own body's responses she'd never known. His personal shopper had excellent taste and Rowan felt no urge to return to her apartment before she absolutely had to.

That was Sunday night.

Only Lysander wasn't keen on her leaving.

~ ~ ~

"Why can't you go to work from here in the morning?" Lysander asked Rowan. He liked having her in his home and the sex was something outside his experience.

He liked sex. It was both pleasure and stress relief. What was not to like? But with Rowan, it was more. It was fun. And he wanted her all the time. Like now.

She stood there in a pair of jeans and a top that hugged her generous curves, looking like she didn't understand the question and all he wanted to do was strip those clothes off her and start touching.

"Lysander, we've spent the entire weekend together and if I know you, you'll be up and out of bed hours before I am." She sounded reasonable.

He didn't want practical. He wanted her, in his bed every night until they burned out this conflagration of desire between them. "We'll have the night together," he pointed out, not sure why he had to.

Surely, that was obvious.

"More sex?" she asked, sounding surprised. "I've never had so much sex in a week, maybe even a month, much less a weekend."

He liked hearing that. Which was strange. Although he expected monogamy during his temporary liaisons, he was not a possessive lover. However, with Rowan, all his atavistic instincts were kicking in.

"Probably." He grinned at her, feeling...happy. That was not usually a word he used to describe himself.

Driven. Focused. Determined. All those and more, but happy? It was odd. He liked it, though.

She gave him an assessing look. "You're way less grumpy than I remember."

"I am not grumpy," he said, feeling offended. He wasn't antisocial, just not overly friendly. It was necessary to maintain a certain distance from others.

"You hardly ever smile. That first time we danced, I thought you were angry at me."

"I was not angry with you." He'd been furious to learn she was married to his estranged half-brother.

Lysander had been attracted to Rowan from the first moment he saw her luscious curves in no way diminished by her designer gown's attempt at modesty. She was beautiful, and everything he found sexually appealing in a woman, but she'd been married.

That she was tied to his selfish prick of a sibling only made it worse.

"Oh, I figured that out. Cyrus was mad, but I figured out that you pretty much frown at everybody."

"I do not frown at everyone. A lack of a smile is not de facto a frown. My most common expression is neutral boredom." At least when surrounded by people like his father and brother.

Lysander did not enjoy superficial and made no attempt to pretend he did.

"Um, if you say so, but you have to admit that you don't bother with polite conversation either."

He shrugged. "When a man with my wealth and influence smiles at someone, they take it as an invitation to make an approach."

Could he sound more pretentious? But what he said was true.

"And that's a bad thing?" she asked.

"They almost always ask for something. Usually money."

"The price of success, I guess. I'll probably hit you up for a donation for the foundation I work for too sometime."

Why didn't that bother him? Because she was so open about it? Or just because it was her?

"Anyway, I'm sure some people just want a chance to talk to you. You're like a celebrity." Her tone was teasing.

So, he ignored the celebrity remark. "I have no time for small talk."

She laughed softly, like he'd been joking. He wasn't.

"My father and Cyrus excel at discussing golf, stock prices and the next big thing. They smile a lot too," she said, like she was thinking about that and wasn't sure what she thought.

"And that signifies what?" Lysander asked. "Both are men that would approach me for business capital with the least encouragement. Even my half-brother, who refuses to speak to me otherwise, would leverage our tenuous family ties if he thought he had a chance of sharing in a business venture."

Regardless of how they liked to be seen, neither man approached Lysander's wealth or power in the business world. When he'd been younger, he'd had nothing compared to them, but now? He could buy either man several times over. He didn't say that because he didn't think the tender-hearted Rowan would appreciate it.

"You really wouldn't do a business deal with Cyrus?" she asked. "I always thought that was all in his head. You don't go out of your way to be rude to him."

Not like his brother, she meant. Cyrus got his petty thrills from making it obvious that though their father acknowledged Lysander as a son, Cyrus would never acknowledge him as a brother. He was sure the other man regretted taking that stance now, but he was too entrenched in it to backtrack without losing major face.

"No," he said in answer to Rowan's question. "I choose my business partners carefully." And his brother was not a good bet.

For many more reasons than the family drama.

"Not too carefully, or you wouldn't have had to sever ties with a company that has connections to an organization that thinks threatening you will get you to back off on your clean energy stance," Rowan pointed out with sass.

Lysander frowned, not enjoying this reminder of his fallibility, despite how charming he found her teasing. "That was an unfortunate oversight on the part of one of my upper managers."

Rowan's eyes widened. "Does he still have a job?"

"Yes, but he has been demoted and placed under the mentorship of a director I know I can trust." The remaining acquisition managers had been required to do additional training in asset assessment as well.

Lysander wasn't risking the same thing ever happening again.

"You thought you could trust this man."

Lysander shrugged. "I don't pretend to be perfect."

Something shifted in Rowan's gaze, almost like she admired him all the more for having made an error in judgment. She didn't react like other people, and he liked that about her.

"No. You don't pretend anything," she said with satisfaction. "But there are a lot of tycoon level businesspeople who think they can do no wrong. It's nice knowing you can acknowledge your mistakes."

"If we cannot learn from our errors, we cannot grow." No matter how good a person was at something, there would always be those moments when they fumbled. "For the sake of my employees and shareholders, I try to manage the risk so mine are not catastrophic."

Her eyes shone with approval that he was fast growing addicted to. "I love that you included your employees in that statement."

"Of course I do. The people I employ are why I am where I am."

"I don't think many billionaires would say that. I know a few millionaires who definitely wouldn't."

She was talking about her father and Cyrus. "You cannot judge all businessmen by your father and my half-brother."

"I'm not. I've been around men like my father my whole life."

"And still you married Cyrus."

"We're doing this now?" she asked.

Chapter Eight

"It appears we are." He had a hard time understanding how a woman like her had ended up with a waste of space like Cyrus.

"My parents coached him on how to win me over. I didn't know they were feeding him intel on my likes and dislikes. I'm still not sure why everyone was so vested in me marrying Cyrus, but even my older brother got in on it."

His own father would have no qualms about betraying his own child in the same way. Lysander's mother, on the other hand, would sooner kill a user like Cyrus than help him marry her daughter.

Lysander had no siblings, but he knew his mother would have done her best to protect her daughter, just as she had him.

"How did you find out?"

"After we'd been married a while, I pushed Cyrus to explain why he'd changed so much. It was one of our rare fights, not because we agreed on all things but because we didn't have a relationship in which open and honest discussion was encouraged. Anyway, he let it slip that he'd done what he had to make me fall in love with him."

"You stayed."

"I did, but my love died when I realized that the man I thought I loved didn't exist and never had."

"And still you stayed."

"I made promises."

"And then you found out he'd broken his."

"Yes."

"You're very old world in some ways."

"If you're saying that I believe in justice and that him having a plethora of lovers while married to me was justification for divorcing him, you're right."

"Yes, that is what I was saying." But he stood by the way he'd said it. She had a way of looking at the world that reminded him of a medieval knight.

Her honor mattered to her, but so did the integrity of the people she'd sworn her allegiance to. He wanted to be one of those people.

She smiled brightly at him, the warmth in her gaze doing something strange in the area of his heart. "You're kind of amazing, do you know that?"

"Does that mean you are spending the night with this amazing man?" he asked as he pulled her into his arms like he'd been wanting to do since she started making noises about going back to her apartment.

"Hmm..." she said, tilting her head and exaggerating a thoughtful expression. "There's my empty apartment where chores that I usually spend the entire weekend taking care of are waiting to be done before bed."

"Yes?"

"And there's you."

"And there is me." He couldn't help it. He kissed her.

When he lifted his head, her expression was hazy, but she was still smiling. "You win. You definitely win. I mean laundry doesn't feel all that urgent when I still have a week's worth of new outfits I've never worn, courtesy of my very generous lover."

"An investment in clothing has never been so well spent, then."

She reached up and kissed him. "You are so not the grumpy guy everyone thinks."

"I am not a grumpy guy at all."

She just laughed, like that was funny. But he was being serious. He wasn't bad tempered. Was he? What would his mother say? He knew what she'd say when she found out he was dating Rowan. She was going to be over the moon.

She lived with the perpetual hope he would marry one day and give her grandchildren. He never told her how unlikely that event was. He did not want to break her heart.

"I know you planned to call in the paparazzi for your *morning after* walk," he said. "However, I wonder if it might be more pleasant to announce our status as a couple by attending the Vasileiou Gala."

The look on her face made it clear Rowan had completely forgotten about calling the paparazzi to catch her leaving Lysander's house after staying the night. He, on the other hand, rarely forgot anything.

"I think you might be right about him wanting me back for reasons other than sheer bloody-mindedness, so I'm not sure it matters if he knows we're together, but that doesn't stop me wanting to go to the gala with you."

He liked hearing that. Liked it a lot that she made it clear spending time with him was what was important, not her plan to turn Cyrus off her.

Lysander liked that plan though and had his own ideas of how to make it happen. He did need a look at her prenuptial agreement though. He thought it might take some business acumen rather than just showing Cyrus that Rowan had moved on. Lysander had to admit that he didn't mind that bit either.

She'd been right about one thing. Though it was nowhere near the top reason he wanted to take her to the gala, rubbing his half-brother's face in the fact that Rowan was with Lysander now had a great deal of appeal. If for no other reason than to show Cyrus what an idiot he'd been to treat his marriage with so little consideration.

The Vasileiou Gala would work very well as an opportunity to let Athens society know Lysander and Rowan were seeing each other.

Lysander found he liked the thought of that. He and Cyrus had little in common, including the charities they supported. With one exception. This one. In fact, he'd seen Rowan for the first time at that year's Vasileiou Gala. He'd asked her to dance and he'd been charmed by her. He had also been turned on. Then he'd learned she was married to his brother.

Oh, yeah, Lysander could be certain his half-brother would be at the gala. It was such a high-profile event, the Andino family never missed it.

Cyrus would get the memo about Lysander and Rowan all right.

So would their father, which would probably have more effect on cooling Cyrus's enthusiasm for trying to get back together with his ex-wife. Cyrus didn't take being shown up well. Knowing Rowan was with Lysander would irk the other man, but having the rest of the world know it? Would make her radioactive where Cyrus was concerned.

Rowan had been right that if she was seen leaving Lysander's house *the morning after*, it would nix Cyrus's desire for reconciliation. Provided that desire was motivated by possessiveness, or even some type of affection. However, Lysander was not convinced that it was. He needed to get a look at her prenup and maybe do some digging into holdings she might not even realize were in her name.

"Does it bother you seeing your father with his wife?" Rowan asked, interrupting his thoughts.

Lysander frowned. His father had presented the image of solidly married man, with his wife on his arm at every public event for Lysander's entire life. That couldn't be what Rowan meant. "His current wife, you mean?"

Rowan nodded.

"That's a heavy question for me, are you sure you want the answer?" he said, being more candid than he would have been with anyone else, except his mother.

"Yes." Rowan pressed in closer to him. "I want to know everything about you."

Why did hearing that make him want to smile. Their liaison was temporary. He had to admit, if only to himself, he was just as curious about her. "The short answer is no."

"And the long answer?" she prompted.

"It bothered the hell out of me that he did not marry my mother when his first wife died, but it did not surprise me." Lysander was too pragmatic not to have realized a long time ago what a shallow human being Baptiste Andino was.

Citing adherence to his religious beliefs that did not allow for divorce, Lysander's father had kept his mother on a string, living as his mistress, for decades while remaining married to the socialite wife with all the right connections. When the first Mrs. Andino had died three years before, Lysander's father had started dating a bare six months after he buried her. And he'd married another socialite whose family had business connections he wanted a year later.

The fact she was twenty years younger and considered beautiful had no doubt played their role as well, Lysander thought cynically. His father was all about the image.

His loyal, trusting mother had never even been in the running, despite the fact that Baptiste recognized Lysander as his.

"A man of his ilk does not marry his mistress," Lysander said.

It had devastated his mother when she'd realized all the promises and if-only-I-wasn't-married refrains she'd heard from the man were nothing but hot air, but it had been the best thing that could have happened to her too. At least as far as Lysander could see.

It had never been Baptiste's religious conviction that kept him married, no matter what he'd told the woman who had born him his second son. It had been pure self-interest. Just as self-interest had prompted Baptiste's second marriage to *someone suitable*.

Lysander's mother had finally broken things off with his father the night he announced his engagement to his current wife. Lysander had been so proud of her, even as he'd held her while she cried.

He'd vowed in that moment never to cause a woman that kind of heartache. Lysander would never make vows he could not keep.

He would never have more than one lover at a time, but he would not make promises to any of them. He didn't do forever, wasn't sure it was even possible.

CHAPTER NINE

"You don't think much of him, do you?" Rowan asked perceptively.

"No. Do you?" he asked. "You lived in the same house with him for years. You probably know him better than I do, despite me being his son."

Rowan's lovely features twisted with distaste. "No, I never did think much of him. He didn't even try to be discreet about his affairs. I guess that's one reason why finding out Cyrus was a philanderer came as such a shock."

"Because he was better at hiding it."

"Yes. I think modern sensibilities are less forgiving of that sort of thing. When your father was a young man, it was common for powerful men to have what they called their *pillow friends*."

Lysander hated thinking of his mother in those terms, but she'd never been anything else to Baptiste. Even the house Lysander had grown up in had not belonged to her. A mistress didn't own her home, she lived at the behest of her lover and provider.

"Culture swings on a pendulum." At least on the surface.

Lysander wasn't sure there were any fewer men of his standing that took lovers, but they weren't as forthright about it. It all sickened him. His mother's life, his own life, could have been so different if his father had been a man who kept his word.

"What put that look on your face?" Rowan asked.

Lysander shook his head before moving to take her hand and tug her out of the room and toward the stairs.

"Where are we going?" she asked with laughter in her voice.

"Where do you think?" he riposted.

More laughter was his only answer.

When they reached his bedroom and he'd shut the door on the rest of the world, Lysander shocked himself by saying, "My father paid for my schooling. He paid for our lifestyle, but the car she drove belonged to him. The house she raised me in was his. One of the first things I did when I reached my initial financial goal was to buy my mother a house and a car that were in her name."

"You wanted her to be independent."

"I wanted her to leave my father, but that didn't come until later." As had his mother's move into the house he'd bought for her.

"He must have loved her, in his way," Rowan said. "He stayed in a relationship with her for longer than a lot of marriages last."

"While remaining married to another woman."

"Yes, but I saw him after Iona broke up with him. I'm pretty sure it happened the night he announced his engagement to his current wife. He was all smiles at the engagement party, but the next morning he was haggard, like he'd aged ten years in a night."

Lysander had never thought his father would grieve the breakup. "It was probably something else."

"No, I don't think it was. He used to slip and call his new wife Iona. He did the same thing to my mother-in-law when she was alive. I don't know if he still does it as I haven't seen him with her in over a year."

Lysander shrugged. "I wouldn't know." He rarely saw his father and almost never in the company of his wife.

Still, something shifted in Lysander's chest at the knowledge that his mother breaking things off had affected his father so badly. Regardless, the man had been selfish and manipulative in his relationship with Lysander's mother and Lysander would never forget the pain she'd suffered because of it.

"Enough about my father," Lysander said. "It is you I'm focused on right now."

"Oh, yes?" Rowan walked across Lysander's sitting room and opened the doors leading to the balcony. She stopped only when she stood at the chest high wall surrounding the balcony and took in a deep breath. "I love the privacy here. We're outside but no one can see us."

"Only the birds," he agreed. It was one of the reasons the wall was so high, privacy and safety. "There are no good angles for the paparazzi no matter how good their camera's zoom lens."

"Not unless they can fly." She turned to face him, her hands on the hem of her top. "We can do anything we want and no one can see us," she repeated.

Then she pulled her top off over her head, leaving her in hip hugging jeans and a lacy bra that put her luscious curves on display.

All melancholy inevitably brought on by thoughts of his parents' relationship were swept away by the tsunami of lust that slammed through his body. He went painfully erect in a matter of seconds, which no matter what people wanted to believe was not the norm. Not even for a viral man in his prime like Lysander.

But she affected him as no other woman ever had.

Rowan's lips curved in a come-hither smile. "Like what you see?"

"I wouldn't mind seeing more," he said.

"Like this?" She reached behind herself and suddenly her bra was sliding down her arms and her generous breasts were spilling out.

Wanting to cup them in his hands he took an involuntary step forward. His mouth watered with the desire to suck on her nipples. The little noises of passion she made when he did were one of his new favorite things.

But he couldn't move any further than that half step. He was frozen into immobility by his reaction to her. He was so hard, it hurt to have himself confined in his slacks.

Rowan's beauty was Rubenesque, not conventional. Her tummy had a little curve he loved to caress, her thighs and butt were lush and he was addicted to every inch of her.

"It hardly seems fair for me to be the only one undressing," she teased pointedly.

He agreed, but his legs were still locked. Finally, Lysander managed to pull his polo style shirt over his head before tossing it to the floor.

The setting sun turned Rowan's body golden as she unzipped and wiggled out of her jeans, leaving her in only a pair of panties. Since she could have taken them off with the jeans, she'd left them on with a purpose.

To tease him.

And tease him, they did.

He wanted to see the copper curls nestled in the apex between her thighs. His mouth salivated with the desire to taste her there.

"You make me burn with that look in your eyes," she said huskily.

He had to swallow before he could speak. "Fair. You make me burn just being in the same room."

She expelled a soft sigh. "I don't care if you say the same thing to all the women you sleep with, I like hearing it."

"You're the only one."

Cupping her own breasts, like she was offering them to him for his pleasure, she smiled. "Even better."

Making a primal sound he'd never heard from himself before taking this woman to his bed, Lysander stripped out of the rest of his clothes with lightning speed. Then he crossed the few feet that separated them and pulled her against his body.

Her arms came up and landed on his shoulders, her pillowy breasts pressing into his chest. "I thought maybe you were going to stand there and look at me for the rest of the night."

"No chance." Not when touching and tasting were in the offing.

Her laughter went straight to his dick, succeeding in the impossible...making him even harder. This is what she did to him. Every time.

Even before her divorce, she'd turned him on. Lysander had avoided her because she was so completely off limits, but now she was *his* lover. He reveled in the ability to slide his hands down Rowan's silky back and over her curved bottom. His hips thrust forward of their own volition rubbing his erection against her stomach.

She gave a throaty purr and he was lost.

Lysander picked her up so their sexes could kiss and she helped him, spreading her legs and hooking them around his hips. They kissed, eating at each other's mouths, her moans vibrating against his lips and his hardon pressing against the silk barrier of her panties.

She broke from the kiss. "I want you, Sander!"

He didn't bother to respond with words, but lowered her so she was once again standing. Then he dropped to his knees and slid her panties down her legs. The scent of her arousal perfumed the air around them.

Pressing her legs further apart, he shifted forward and tasted her.

She cried out and leaned back against the stone wall of the balcony.

There was something so decadent and primal about making love outside. The balcony gave them complete privacy, but the air brushed their skin like another lover's caress.

He pleasured her with his tongue and fingers, sliding one into her slick, hot entrance. He pressed up and rubbed on that spot that sent her into raptures. She squirmed, her legs buckling, and he held her up while he tasted her sweet nectar.

"Please, Sander..." she moaned out. "I need you inside me."

Swiping at his face with the back of his hand, he stood and gave her exactly what she was asking for, thrusting inside her with unerring accuracy honed over the multiple times they'd made love in the last two days.

Her silky flesh gripped his cock tightly as he pushed deeper into her soaked depths.

Lysander was grateful she'd told him after their first time that she was on birth control. He'd shown her his health results and told her he hadn't had a lover since the tests. She'd had hers on her phone and insisted on doing the same before agreeing to forego the condom.

He'd realized he didn't need to see her test results to believe her though.

He trusted Rowan like he never trusted anyone. Lysander knew deep in his gut that she would never lie to him.

Their bodies locked together, he took her mouth in a breath stealing kiss just in time to stifle her scream. Rowan was a noisy lover.

And that turned him on more than he thought it could.

They moved together for long moments, but as much pleasure as this joining afforded, he couldn't get the angle he wanted. Rowan seemed frustrated as well, breaking from the kiss to shake her head and moan.

"Try a different position?" he asked, his voice just above a growl.

"Yes. *Something*. I'm so close."

He disentangled their bodies and turned hers, so she faced the balcony. "Lean on the wall."

She did, arching her back and thrusting her behind toward him. It was all the invitation he needed, and he entered her from behind, sliding back into silky smooth, welcoming heat. He reached around and cupped her breast with one of his hands, lightly pinching the hard nipple while sliding his other hand down her body until he could press his middle finger against her clitoris.

She moaned, canting her hips forward and then arching back as if she couldn't decide what stimulation she needed more. His dick deep inside her, or the press of his finger against her sensitive bundle of nerves.

Lysander alternated between making circles around her clit and sliding directly over it with his fingertip until she was panting and pleading for more. He continued to touch her in the way she'd shown him she liked, driving her closer and closer to orgasm.

Increasing the pace, he drove into her with hard thrusts until she went rigid under him and cried out her release. Her vaginal walls contracted like a vice around his sex pulling him even deeper into her body and making him come. His shout joined hers and Lysander didn't care if everyone on staff could hear them.

This was so damn good.

Perfect.

They were both sweaty and heaving after, but he sat on the L shaped outdoor sofa and pulled her naked into his lap, running his hands over her body as their breathing slowly returned to normal.

This lazy touching was another of his new favorite things. He found Rowan's luscious curves addicting.

~ ~ ~

Rowan nestled into Lysander's arms, enjoying the soft glide of his big hands over her body. He made no effort to hide how much he relished touching her and she loved that. There was no one upmanship when she was in bed with Lysander.

He didn't make a big deal about who came first, but he always made sure that they both did. He didn't ask her how it was, maybe because it was always so obvious that it had been very, very satisfying.

For both of them.

Best of all, Lysander never critiqued her *performance* and told her what she could do to make it better in the future. Her ex had done that. It had hurt her at first, and then just annoyed her. Sex wasn't a job Rowan performed.

It was an experience between two people, both of them equally responsible for how it went.

It was that way with Lysander. He paid attention to her responses and listened when she said anything. Like earlier, changing their angle. What they'd been doing had felt so hot, but she'd hung on the edge of that precipice of pleasure and wanted to soar right over.

He'd listened and then they'd both gotten what they needed.

"I like this," she said, kissing his neck before she laid her head against his shoulder.

"I do too."

She knew he did. The languid touching afterward usually led to another bout of lovemaking, and she doubted this time would be any different. Sex had never been so consuming for her, and she had thought it was a myth that men could do it more than once in a night.

Apparently, it wasn't, and she was the lucky recipient of repeated proof of that.

Chapter Ten

The next morning, Klaus brought Rowan's car to the front of the villa. Lysander was already in a meeting, though he'd offered to have her driven to work and picked up afterward. This time, she'd stood firm on her plan to return to her apartment. She was a grownup with things that needed tending.

Only later that evening as she let herself into the silent and empty place, she had to try hard to remember what they were and why they were so important. If she'd gone back to Lysander's, they'd be sharing a drink before dinner and she'd be looking forward to another night of amazing lovemaking.

No matter how tantalizing, that wasn't her life. Rowan had spent years living in a loveless marriage because it had been what was expected of her. She'd had every creature comfort seen to, but her soul had starved. Well, her soul wasn't starving anymore. She thrived working full-time for an organization she believed in. The only constraint on her time with the friends of her choosing were the things she had committed to doing, not things committed to on her behalf.

Not that her family hadn't tried. Rowan's mom had expected her to move back into the family home and do what she'd always done, support her father's business interests. Of course, she'd expected Rowan to stay married to Cyrus too. Neither were going to happen.

She'd gone back to the States, but only temporarily, so she could start divorce proceedings. She'd returned for the necessary arbitration and hearing, but her life was in Greece now and that was where it would stay.

Rowan hadn't walked away from Cyrus only to move back into the same constricting existence with her parents. In the last two years, she'd worked hard to make a life for herself, one that she could be proud to live. One that fed her soul.

And that was why she was here, making a sandwich for dinner, instead of dining with Lysander in five-star splendor, she reminded herself. After starting a load of laundry, she started going through the mail that had piled up in her absence. How was it that there was still so much physical mail when almost all of her bills were paid online and no one ever sent her any letters?

Although most of the mail was simply junk destined for the recycling bin, a few things were invitations to events her parents would expect her to attend. For the sake of maintaining some semblance of a relationship with them, she would say yes to at least one.

Although invitations were handled via email and social media among her chosen friends, certain organizations that catered to the wealthy elite still insisted on printed invites with RSVP cards and their embossed return envelopes. It was a matter of fulfilling expectations.

Rowan considered consulting with Lysander before choosing the invitation to say yes to. If he was already planning to go, then if it worked for her schedule, she'd prefer to RSVP a yes to that event. She wasn't kidding herself though. She knew he worked long hours and if she wanted to see him during whatever time they chose to remain lovers, she had to be creative about making that happen.

She might even have to accommodate, but unlike every year until she'd walked out on her ex, Rowan wasn't going to be the only one doing the accommodating. Lysander would have to make time for them in his schedule or they wouldn't last very long. No matter how mind blowing the sex was.

He'd already taken an entire weekend to spend with her and though she knew he liked his decompress time when he returned from a trip, she'd heard him giving instructions to reschedule some calls and a dinner meeting the night before with some consortium out of Belgium.

Rowan grabbed her phone and called him.

Not because she missed him already. No. It was simply a matter of expediency. She needed to know his plans to see if they meshed with hers. Yes, that was it. She didn't miss his infrequent smile, or the way he looked at her with such heat, or his surprisingly teasing manner.

He kept calling his security specialists *goons* just to rile her up.

She refused to back down on that score though. They'd behaved like goons and she'd let them know it. Strangely enough, both Klaus and Gregor seemed to like and respect her. Gregor had even apologized for pulling a gun on her and promised it wouldn't happen again.

She should hope not. And not to anyone else either. When she'd said so, he'd just given her a slightly enigmatic smile and walked away.

~ ~ ~

Lysander picked up after the first ring.

"Hello, *glikia mou*. Have you changed your mind about coming over tonight?" he asked in a tone meant for the bedroom.

Sudden heat washed over Rowan and she fanned herself with a piece of junk mail. He'd taken to calling her *his sweet* and the endearment did things to her all on its own. In that tone? It was deadly.

"I was wondering if you had plans to attend any events that I've been invited to," she said. "I try to go to at least a couple while my parents are in Athens, and I would prefer to make it an opportunity to see you as well."

Her father's business interests in Greece were a big part of his company's revenue, but her parents still spent the majority of their time in their home outside of Atlanta. Her mother enjoyed her social position there as a Queen Bee around whom many buzzed, more than in Athens where she was not married to one of the wealthiest men in any room.

Oh, her father was rich all right, but he didn't make the Forbes list. Lysander was near the top and Cyrus was nearer the bottom, but he was still on it.

"You could have called my personal assistant for that," he said, his tone teasing. "And yet you called me."

"You've given me access to your PA?" Rowan asked with shock she made no attempt to hide.

Neither her father, nor Cyrus, had done so. They expected full access to her schedule, but had never returned the favor. She'd spent so much of her life in a controlled bubble, she thought disconsolately.

"Yes." Lysander's response was tinged with surprise at his own behavior. "I have just sent details to your phone. Did you want to call her instead?"

"No. I want to talk to you," Rowan offered with more honesty than was prudent.

"And I am pleased to speak with you," he said, rewarding her truthfulness with his own, his tone warm and approving.

"Lysander..." She let her voice trail off, not sure what she wanted to say.

"Have you accomplished the chores you set out to do?" he asked.

She nodded, remembered they weren't facetiming and said, "I've started them anyway."

"Ah, you are going through your mail," he guessed. "One benefit to being a billionaire executive is that I have people to do that for me."

"So, if I sent you a card or a letter, your PA would read it before you did?" she asked, her voice going sultry. "I'd better be careful what I write then."

"Just as any correspondence from my mother has special instructions to be brought directly to me, so does yours."

"It does? Already?" They'd only been seeing each other for a minute.

And really, they hadn't even had their first date. They'd spent the weekend together, mostly in bed.

"I am an efficient man."

"I wish I was as efficient. I have another load of laundry to do and my apartment needs a good dusting and vacuuming." She'd meant to do it on the weekend, but those plans had gone by the wayside in the face of the opportunity to spend that time with him.

"If I offered to send a cleaning service so you could return to my home, would you be charmed, or offended?"

"Good question." But her heart had already answered it. She was definitely charmed.

He wanted to spend time with her and that he was pressing for her return to his home when he made a habit of working long hours and into the night, meant he planned to change his own schedule to make that worth it. Didn't he?

She said, "It depends on if you plan to spend time with me out of bed if I return to the villa, or just want a convenient bed partner."

"If I planned to work while you were here, I would not ask you to come," he said with easy assurance.

He hadn't had to think about his answer for even a second. Which meant what? Lysander really did want to spend time with her.

"This thing between us, it's intense, isn't it?"

"Yes."

"That's kind of scary."

"It doesn't need to be. Neither of us has made any promises."

That wasn't as reassuring as she was sure he thought it would be.

"I don't live with women."

Well, that had come out of nowhere. "I wasn't asking to move in. You're the one trying to finagle my presence in your home, if you'll remember."

"I am aware." He paused like he was thinking. "I don't live with my lovers," he said again. "But I want to live with you. You are right, most nights I work after dinner and I leave early for the office, but I want to spend as much time with you as possible."

She should be shocked, but she wasn't. Because Rowan wanted the same thing. Whatever they had between them, it was burning hot and bright right now. She wanted to indulge in every second that blazing hot passion lasted. It was bound to burn itself out, but until then?

Rowan wanted to spend every available moment with Lysander.

"Not just in bed," she said, certain that she could not live with that kind of arrangement. It would just be another box to stuff herself into and she was done being stifled.

"Not just in bed," he affirmed. "I want to eat breakfast with you, even if it's two hours after I've started my workday. I want to see you when I return to my home, to find you watching your favorite show or haranguing my security men about their manners."

"That sounds very domestic."

"I have never said I don't like domesticity."

Only commitment. "All right."

"You will move in with me?" he asked.

"Well, I had been thinking about getting a cat. I guess that will have to wait."

"You want a cat?"

"Yes." Getting a rescue pet had never been an option when she was living at home or in the Andino mansion. "But it can wait. I'm keeping my apartment though. This thing between us could fizzle out in a week."

"Or not."

"Or not. Either way, I'm keeping my place."

"Naturally."

"And I'm not coming over tonight," she said firmly. Both for his sake and her own. "I'm going to finish my laundry and pack some things like a normal person. I'll come to the villa tomorrow after work."

"I will not be home." He sounded chagrined.

He was home now and she was refusing to come over. In way, that was good. He needed to know from the outset that he couldn't have everything his own way.

"Then you'd better give your goons instructions to let me in," she told him saucily.

"They prefer security specialists."

She laughed. Then his rich chuckle came through the phone and she felt like she'd won something.

"Those instructions have already been given regardless," he said.

"You really are efficient."

"Or it is important."

She wasn't touching that. How could she be important to him already? But then, she was upending her own life to be with him, even if it was temporary. He was definitely already important to her.

~ ~ ~

The next evening when she arrived at Lysander's gate, her backseat and trunk full of clothes and other things she needed for an extended stay, Gregor sent it sliding open as soon as he saw her. He smiled and saluted as she drove past.

She smiled back and waived. She noticed a second security guard she hadn't seen before, standing alertly on the other side of the drive, his attention fixed on the area around the gate and not her car. She didn't wave to him, but she did wonder if he was added security, or if she just hadn't noticed him before.

When she stopped her car in front of the villa, Klaus was standing at the top of the steps. Gregor must have called him. Movement flickered in her peripheral vision and she turned her head to see what it was. Another guard walked the perimeter around the house.

Rowan got out of the car and took a moment to really examine her surroundings. She could see two more guards on patrol in the distance.

"The threat to Lysander has increased?" she asked worriedly.

Klaus shrugged. "Not that I am aware. He ordered additional and tighter security last night when he told us you would be moving in."

"I'm not moving in." She shouldered a bag with a long strap and pulled another wheeled suitcase from the car.

"It certainly looks like you're moving in," Klaus drawled.

"I'm staying a while." And that was all he needed to know. "And I'm keeping my own apartment."

Okay, maybe that too. She was no clinger-on, expecting her rich lover to support her financially.

"Does Mr. Baros know that?" Klaus asked skeptically.

Her reply was firm. "Yes."

"If you say so." Klaus stepped forward and opened the back door on the other side of her car and immediately began pulling stuff out.

Since he grabbed her largest case which was unwieldy and had a wonky wheel, she didn't object. When the wheel showed its temperament, the burly security specialist just picked up the bag and carried it.

"Impressive," Rowan quipped. But she meant it. She'd had to strain to get the bag up into her car. "I've got a box of books in the trunk you're free to manhandle as well."

Chapter Eleven

"Are you flirting with my goons?" Lysander asked from the top of the steps.

Rowan spun toward him, knocking over the case she'd been pulling. "Sander! I thought you were going to be gone."

"I took my conference call here. The wi-fi is just as good."

"Wasn't it supposed to last another hour?" He'd told her that, and then asked if she minded waiting to have dinner until later.

Since Rowan had long since adjusted to the European tendency to eat at 8 pm or later, she'd acquiesced easily.

"It is over," he said.

She couldn't help wondering if he'd cut it short to see her. But that was really egotistical, wasn't it? No matter how much he liked her, a man as driven and focused as Lysander wasn't going to cancel an important meeting so he could spend time with her.

He reached her and kissed her. It was no sweet buss of lips to say hello, but a meeting of their mouths that made no attempt to deny the passion between them. By the time she'd been thoroughly greeted the bag she'd been carrying had fallen to the ground as well.

She stared down at it, unable to parse what she was supposed to do now.

"I think you befuddled her, boss."

"Befuddled?" Rowan mouthed to Lysander.

"Klaus is very proud of his vocabulary."

"I like the word befuddled. I've never seen someone it fit so well either."

That had her frowning, though not really upset. "I am not confused."

The look the security specialist gave her put that into question, but all Klaus did was grab the box of books she'd mentioned and ask his boss, "Where do you want these?"

"What are they?" Lysander asked.

"Books."

Lysander looked at Rowan. "You brought books?"

"I like to read." She'd been teased by both her family and her ex for being too bookish. Like that was a bad thing.

"I read business journals."

"No fiction?" she asked, appalled and trying not to show it.

Fiction was amazing.

"Perhaps you will recommend a book."

Well, that was an unexpected response. "Sure."

"Where would you like your books?"

"Anywhere I can find them easily."

"We can put a bookcase in the lounge." That's what he called his inner sanctum. "Or the bedroom."

"I doubt you'll get much reading done in there."

Rowan almost laughed, but then she thought about it. Though she'd done most of her reading in bed in the past, she had to admit that even she could think of something she'd rather do in there than immerse herself in her favorite fictional worlds.

"The lounge it is then."

Klaus left without having to be instructed further.

"You don't have to install a bookcase just for me." She could keep her books in the box. It wasn't a permanent home for them after all.

Lysander didn't reply. He simply picked up the two bags she'd dropped and headed into his villa with them. Somehow seeing the billionaire carrying her luggage made this move in with him all the more real. Also, she couldn't imagine the other men in his world doing such a mundane chore.

Rowan grabbed the last box from her small trunk. Most of the space was taken up by the large battery that powered her electric car.

She passed Klaus on her way inside. "I'll put your car in the nearest garage, bay two. Your keys will be on a hook by the door."

"Is that secure?" she asked before thinking better of it.

She was for all intents and purposes now living in a secured compound. No one was getting inside without an invitation and Lysander's guests weren't likely to steal a car that could be bought for what they paid in golfing fees yearly, if not monthly.

"It takes a fingerprint to open the door into the garage."

"Oh, then how will I open it?"

"Yours will be added to the biometric lock system."

"That's pretty high tech, isn't it?"

"Television may make it look easy to bypass biometric locks, but it's not, and this system in particular is one of the most secure."

"Not *the* most secure?" she teased.

"Those can be unwieldy, and with our other measures would be overkill," Lysander answered, stopping next to her.

He took the box from her arms without comment, and she let it go. She'd never been averse to gentlemanly behavior, so long as it was not accompanied by an attitude of male superiority.

She arched her brows at him. "I didn't know you and your cohorts thought any security measure could be overkill."

"We're cohorts now?" Klaus asked. "Not goons?"

Rowan ignored him and kept her gaze pinned on Lysander.

He smiled that gorgeous smile that always made her heart flutter. "We do not need military grade tech to protect automobiles."

"Are you saying you have it elsewhere in the villa?" she asked.

"The panic room is second to none for security and ability to withstand efforts to gain entrance."

"Oh." She wondered if he was going to show it to her. She knew that the location of the panic room in her old home was secret to anyone outside the family.

Even the staff who had worked for the Andino the longest had not been told where it was. Rowan had always determined that if there was ever an occasion to use it, she would make sure to bring as many of the staff with her as she could.

Luckily, she'd never had to use it for any reason.

"All the staff and security team know it's location and the domestic staff knows to head there if the need arises."

Rowan cast a glance at Klaus's retreating figure. "And the security staff?"

"If the panic room becomes necessary, it would be because they had been neutralized already."

By neutralized he meant killed. Rowan shuddered. "Being a billionaire isn't without its drawbacks."

Her family home had not had a panic room as her father had never considered one necessary. That Lysander did only showed how aware of his own vulnerability to attack he was. She hated knowing his wealth and position of influence made him a target.

"If you do not want the world to know we are together, we can skip the gala," he said, clearly misinterpreting her look.

"It's not me I'm worried about. It's you. I noticed the increased security."

"It became necessary when you agreed to live here."

"But I'm nobody." Maybe not poor, but certainly not rich in comparison to this man.

"You are my girlfriend. That makes you vulnerable to kidnapping for ransom."

"That only happens in movies," she quipped, knowing it wasn't true. "Besides you aren't going to pay a million dollars to get me back."

"I would pay whatever was necessary, but it is a moot point as you will not be taken."

"What are you going to do, send Klaus with me to work?" she asked facetiously, not as convinced as he was that simply by dating him she became a potential target for kidnappers. "Your mother would be way more at risk than me."

"She has her own security team."

"I'm glad." Rowan liked Iona Baros and didn't want her hurt in some misguided attempt to extort money out of her son.

"It is good to hear you say that. I thought you might balk at having one assigned to you."

"What? That's not necessary."

"For as long as you remain living here, it is."

"But you never said anything about that last night."

He shrugged, like it should have been obvious.

"Are you telling me that you assign security to all your lovers?"

"No."

"What makes me special?" she demanded.

He turned and headed toward the stairs. "What's in this box? Does it go in the bedroom?"

"Probably." It had come out of her bedroom, but she'd stored things wherever they fit in her small apartment. "Now, answer my question. What makes me special?"

They reached his bedroom suite and he placed the box on the table by the settee in the sitting area. "Staff will unpack your cases. Would you like to go for a swim?"

"Yes." Rowan loved the water and had really missed access to a pool since moving into her apartment with no amenities. "But my bathing suit is in one of the cases."

She tried to remember which one she'd packed her swimsuits in. Rowan had pared down to two suits, when she used to have seven. The rest of her clothes had gone through a similar winnowing. There simply wasn't room in her apartment to store a wardrobe meant for a socialite, only a social worker.

"There are a couple for you to choose from in the drawer already."

"You got me swimsuits?" she asked. "You know I thought you were only buying an outfit for me so I could be comfortable and would spend the night."

"I do not buy clothes to get women into bed with me." He headed into the bedroom and then to the walk-in closet that had conspicuously empty racks.

For her clothes. He was quite literally making space for her in his life.

Touched, Rowan started pulling open drawers, only to find most of them already had an item or two of clothing, all clearly meant for her. Even socks and underwear.

She pulled a pair of lace panties out and dangled them on her finger. "There's almost nothing to these." They were just a triangle of lace and three strings. "I can't believe you had a shopper buy these for me."

"I ordered them."

At her askance look, he shrugged. "I had time between meetings and did not want to get immersed in a report."

"So, you went online and bought me underwear."

Color burnished his cheekbones, but he nodded resolutely.

"You're kind of amazing, you know that?" She hugged him tightly. "Thank you."

His arms came around her automatically and he held her close. "You are thanking me for buying you sexy lingerie?"

"One should always express appreciation for a gift," she said in a lecturing tone and then smiled. "I like that you were thinking of me. And I like even more that you personally picked these out. Though I can't promise I'll ever wear them. I know some women just love thongs, but I've always found them uncomfortable."

"I promise that if you put them on you won't wear them long enough to be bothered."

She laughed and stepped away from him. "You promised me a swim."

He indicated a drawer she hadn't opened. "You'll find swimsuits in there."

She opened the drawer and found three suits inside. None of them one-pieces. She did find a tankini, but feeling daring, she opted for a black and white polka dot bikini that reminded her of a 1940s pin up girl. The top supported her ample breasts and the bottom was high waisted, flattering her curves, but not hiding them. A one-piece in a similar style had made it into her keep pile when she'd gone through her clothes.

"This is really me," she said, a little surprised he knew her so well.

It wasn't as if they'd ever been swimming together.

"Your favorite designer has a lot of 1940s inspired styles in her collection," Lysander said with a verbal shrug.

"Well, I love it," Rowan said happily.

Lysander's smile was wolfish. "I'm going to love seeing it on you."

Somehow, they both got their suits on without falling into bed naked together. It was touch and go, but Rowan wanted that swim. She also wanted to know they could spend time together outside the bedroom. That was, after all, a condition of her moving in with him.

She wasn't just a convenient booty call.

And neither was he.

Chapter Twelve

Lysander dived gracefully into the pool and immediately started swimming laps.

Rowan opted for entry into the water via the steps, but she dove under as soon as she reached water deep enough to swim in and began her own laps, swimming in the opposite direction to him, so they passed each other on every lap. She didn't know how long they'd been doing laps when she felt that perfect release from tension that swimming gave her.

Soon after, she finished her laps and stopped in the shallow end of the pool. Lysander executed a quick turn at the wall in the deep end and then joined her seconds later, erupting out of the water like Poseidon.

Gorgeous and powerful.

And his gaze was locked on her.

Needing to focus on anything but his nearly naked body, she brought up the security detail again. "You never explained why I have to have bodyguards when the other women you've dated didn't."

"I have never invited a woman to live with me." He brushed his hand over his wet hair, causing rivulets to travel enticingly down his neck and over his shoulders. "I don't even bring my lovers back to my home."

She wanted to follow those drops of water with her fingertips...maybe her tongue.

Forcing her attention back on the discussion, she asked "Where do you take them?" She couldn't imagine a man with his need for control being okay with all the sex happening at his lover's home.

"That is what hotel suites are for."

"Huh." She waived her arms back and forth through the water, loving its silky feeling against her skin. "Not the point right now, but just so you know, I'm not adverse to hotel rooms. They're a little impersonal to be the exclusive venue for such an intimate relationship though."

"Sex is not always intimate." He sounded very definite.

She was just as definite. "It is with us, though."

"Yes."

She smiled. "Still not sure I get why me temporarily moving into your villa makes me a target for extortionists."

"You are clearly important to me, different from my other lovers."

"Are all billionaires as paranoid as you?" she wondered out loud.

"They should be, but some show more concern for the security of their cars than the safety of the people in their inner circle."

Thinking of some of the billionaires that made it into the media, especially back in the States, Rowan had to agree. "I don't think I want a security detail."

"They can accompany you, or follow you. Your choice."

In other words, she was getting security if she wanted it or not. How easy it would be for her guards to protect her would be determined by her actions.

She sighed. "You're not going to budge on this, are you?"

"No."

"Okay, but fair warning, I'm putting them to work when they come with me to the org." There was always stuff that needed doing and never enough staff or volunteers to do it.

"So long as they are in the same room with you, or the room through which anyone would have to go to get to you, that is fine."

Not sure the security specialists would agree with him while stuffing the job placement packs with reading material and the donations from companies wanting the people her org served to feel valued and seen. Regardless, Rowan couldn't help but smile at the thought of another set of helping hands.

"You are pleased to have the help?"

"Yes."

"If not the protection."

"That's nice too, in a way." It made her feel like he cared about her, or at least her safety. But she added with honesty, "It might get a little stifling as well."

"We make sacrifices for the life we choose to live."

"True." She made a faster move with her arm than those before and a wave of water arced up and splashed him. "You have sacrificed your almost dry face."

He laughed and sent water cascading over her. Her hair was already wet, so she just laughed. They splashed and played until they ended up plastered against each other in water too deep for her to stand.

She wrapped her legs around his waist and her arms around his neck. "I like this."

"I do too." His eyes were dark with unmistakable passion.

She'd been playing, but he was thinking about a whole other kind of physical exercise than swimming.

It sparked a response in Rowan that whooshed through her like a tsunami of sensual need. "Do you think they'll hold dinner?"

"Yes," he growled before kissing her breathless.

Water was covering her lower face before Rowan realized what was happening. Lysander wasn't paying attention to where they were, and he had been shifting toward the deeper end.

She broke the kiss, inhaled some water, coughed and started laughing. "I thought making love in the pool was supposed to be sexy."

Lysander was already moving them the opposite direction with quick strides in the water and soon only her feet dangled in it.

"It is," he assured her, before sitting on a tiled cement bench that went down both sides of the shallow end of the pool. He pulled her astride his lap. "It is," he said again, his mouth taking hers before she could reply.

Rowan lost all thought of saying anything as passion once again erupted inside her. Oh sheesh, she hoped his staff were nowhere around because she had the feeling things were about to get very sexy indeed.

"Do not worry," he said as he unhooked her bikini top and caressed her back. "I gave instructions for privacy."

"What about the patrolling guards?" she asked, stopping him removing her top entirely by pressing her arms down to hold the fabric in place.

"No patrols on this side until I give the word."

"That's safe?"

"We have motion sensors on the wall and cameras covering every angle but the pool itself right now. That camera will be turned back on at my instruction."

"You planned for this."

"Rowan, you are irresistible to me. I always plan for the possibility of this." He canted his hips upward, letting her feel the hardness of his erection.

With her legs splayed over him, his hardon pressed against her clitoris and she moaned, pushing downward with her hips to increase the friction. The two swimsuits stopped anything but contact that teased at pleasure.

She climbed off his lap, her gaze locked on his. "No one can see us?"

"No."

"You promise?"

"You have my word."

She pulled her top away from her body and tossed it to the side of the pool, her nipples going instantly hard in the evening air. It felt so good, she moaned a little and then she reached down to remove her bottoms. It was easier than she expected. Unlike a wet swimsuit outside the pool, the fabric glided down her legs, helped by the water.

Throwing it in a pile with her top, she motioned with her other hand toward Lysander. "Now you."

With a choked sound, her lover surged to his feet and shoved his suit off too, not bothering to retrieve it from the water before pulling her against him and kissing her with open mouthed passion.

The water ebbed and flowed around them adding to the sensations bombarding Rowan. Seconds later, he'd maneuvered them back to the bench and she was once again astride his lap, but no fabric separated her sex from his. This time when they arched together, his erection pressed directly against her pleasure spot, rubbing up and down as they shifted together in the water.

She rode him like he was inside her, the water acting as a lubricant that allowed smooth movement. The stimulation to her clitoris felt amazing.

"That feels so damn good, *glikia mou*."

"Yes, it does." Was that throaty purr her?

Lysander brought out a sexual side that Rowan hadn't known existed in her and she reveled in every ecstatic second.

He cupped her breasts, squeezing and brushing his thumbs over her nipples. Rowan increased the speed of her thrusts. So did Lysander so they were rutting together in a beautiful frenzy.

The water added to the pleasure, but it also made it hard for her to get enough sensation to tip over. It all felt too wonderful to stop though.

One of Lysander's hands slid down her back, over her bottom and between her thighs. He pressed a single finger inside her, and Rowan's vaginal walls contracted around it. Now every thrust brought pleasure to her most sensitive flesh both inside and out.

Pleasure coiled tightly in her belly and then exploded, fireworks going off in her body as ecstasy roared over her. Lysander thrust upward sending aftershocks of pleasure through her as his body went rigid and he shouted with release.

Rowan collapsed against him, her head resting on his shoulder. Her lungs were working like bellows, but then so were his.

"Definitely sexy," she managed between gasping breaths.

"Yes, you are."

It was a cheesy line, but the sincerity in his tone and the way he held her close made it something more. Lysander didn't need Rowan to be thinner, or less chatty, or anything different than exactly what she was, to be sexually enthralled with her.

She would take it.

If her heart insisted there should be more, she ignored that little voice in favor of the sense of repletion she felt.

"I'm so glad you arranged for our privacy. This was amazing."

"Even if we had not made love, I would not have wanted the staff watching our every move. Sometimes, it is good simply not to have eyes of other people on you."

"Even security?" she asked.

"When our safety can be assured, yes."

Oh, she noticed that caveat. He wasn't backing down about her having a bodyguard. Rowan let it go.

She'd lived with some level of security most of her life, though it had increased after marriage. She'd only known full autonomy since leaving Cyrus.

And if having a bodyguard was the price she had to pay for being Lysander's lover, she would pay it happily.

Chapter Thirteen

The morning of the Vasileiou Gala dawned bright and sunny, as most did this time of year in Athens.

Rowan watched the sunrise from her spot on the terrace, a cup of coffee in front of her. Lysander had risen at 4:30 for an international video conference. Rowan usually went back to sleep after he left the bed, but not this morning.

She was going to see her parents and her ex-husband, as well as his family. Tension thrummed through her at the prospect.

Her mother had called to confirm that Rowan would be at the gala. Confirming her intention to attend, Rowan hadn't mentioned who her date would be. Nor had Rowan told her mother that she wouldn't be sitting with them.

"What has you up so early?" Lysander's deep voice had Rowan turning from the sunrise to face him.

He was dressed immaculately in one of his bespoke suits, a crisp white shirt and perfectly knotted tie. She was sure her lover had made an impressive sight on the video call, as he always did.

Anyone interacting with Lysander Baros knew the man was put together and powerful. But she, little ole' Rowan Johnson, had seen him disheveled and naked.

It gave Rowan an intrinsic thrill to be one of the few people in the world to know more than just the public persona. She had witnessed the real man: the loving son, the passionate and surprisingly earthy lover, the charming friend.

She had a bookcase in his inner sanctum and closet space in his bedroom suite.

"I couldn't go back to sleep after you left. I thought I would watch the sunrise."

Lysander put his hand on her shoulder, his thumb brushing along her neck. "One of the things I enjoy most about this property is the ability to watch either the sunrise or sunset in comfort from a terrace, or a balcony."

"I do too."

"But the sunrise is not what got you out of bed this morning."

She sighed and shook her head. "No, it isn't."

"Are you stressed about seeing Cyrus tonight?" Lysander asked, his tone carefully neutral.

"Not as tense as I am about seeing my parents," Rowan admitted.

Lysander moved to take the chair on the other side of the small table. His dark gaze bore into hers. "Why?"

"Unlike your mother, mine constantly looks for fault and isn't shy about voicing her criticism."Rowan grimaced. "Unless she helped pick it out, my dress is never right for the occasion. Same with the amount of makeup I choose to wear, and she's appalled I won't get a weekly manicure like she does."

"Does it help to know that I think you look lovely?" he asked, waggling his sexy eyebrows.

She laughed. "How do you know? You haven't seen what I picked out for tonight."

"It won't matter. You are beautiful, with or without makeup. So long as your clothing isn't some monstrosity intended to hide your figure, it will be gorgeous because it will be on you."

Warmth spread through Rowan. "That's a very nice thing to say."

"I am not a nice man."

He did have a reputation for ruthlessness in business, but since that ruthless attitude rarely got directed toward the rank-and-file employees, she didn't hold it against him.

Personally, Rowan thought that the management Lysander was known for winnowing were probably not *all that*. Or her lover would never let them go. He was too savvy for blunders like that.

"Maybe to other people, but you are to me."

"It is not kindness when it is truth," he said in a tone that sounded like a warning.

She merely shook her head in response. He wanted her to think he would be ruthless with her, and they both knew he would not. Not until it came time to say goodbye. For however long this thing between them lasted, Rowan had a unique position in Lysander's life, similar to his mother's.

"I guarantee my mother won't agree and my father will be livid I'm not sitting with him and trying to make things up with Cyrus."

"It is unfortunate that he will be angry, but that was the point of this, wasn't it?" Lysander reached across the table and took her hand.

He was always touching her. A fingertip brushing along her jawline. Sitting close enough to her on the couch so their thighs touched, and he could easily put his arm over her shoulders. But her favorite was how he cupped her nape.

That gave her shivers every time. And it made her feel special. There was not a single photo of Lysander in the tabloids or society pages touching a woman in a similar way. Yes, Rowan had paid attention over the years. She'd been curious.

Her inner voice said now might be the time to admit it had been more than innocent curiosity, but Rowan wasn't admitting anything. Not even to herself.

When she didn't reply, Lysander asked, "You wanted to let both families know that you are unequivocally over Cyrus and have moved on from your failed marriage, did you not?"

"Yes." She sighed. "In theory anyway." In practice, facing the guaranteed censure from her family made acid churn in Rowan's stomach.

He tugged at her hand until she was standing and then pulled her to him and into his lap. "If you want to cancel tonight, we can." He kissed the corner of her lips. "My donation is the same whether I attend, or not."

Rowan sucked in a shocked breath at the offer. She knew attending this gala was important to Lysander, though she did not know why. He never missed.

"No." She turned her head so his dark brown eyes could see the sincerity in hers. "Thank you for offering that. It means a lot, but no. We are going. I will deal with my parents like I have always done."

The best she could and with antacids tucked into her evening bag.

"This time I will be with you."

It was a sweet sentiment, if not as reassuring as she was sure he intended it to be. What could Lysander do to mitigate motherly disapproval, or fatherly disappointment?

~ ~ ~

The answer to that question came later in the evening.

Rowan walked into the gala, her hand tucked in the crook of Lysander's tuxedo clad arm and chatter had started immediately.

She heard things like, "Isn't that Rowan Andino with Lysander Baros?" and "What is she doing here? I thought she'd moved back to the States."

Lysander ignored it all and Rowan did her best to pretend she did too, though the back of her neck was hot with embarrassment. She kept her head up though and her face placid as she and Lysander followed the server leading them to their table.

Her father stepped in front of them, his expression stern, forcing the server to halt.

Lysander had no choice but to stop as well, though he did it so naturally, it seemed like stopping to talk to her father was Lysander's idea.

"Mr. Johnson." Lysander acknowledged her father with a slight dip of his chin.

"Mr. Baros, my daughter's seat is over there." He pointed to the table where her mother sat with the Andinos.

"You are mistaken." Though his face showed not the slightest emotion, Lysander's voice was cold as the arctic. "She is sitting with me."

"But Cyrus bought her ticket."

"My brother may have purchased an extra ticket, but it was not for *my* companion."

Her father turned away from Lysander's steady, unperturbed gaze, turning his look of disapproval on her. "You knew we were expecting you at our table," he hissed in an undertone.

"If you will excuse us," Lysander said to her father as if he hadn't spoken and subtly shifted his body forward.

Now, if he didn't want to create a scene, her father was the one who had no choice but to move.

"Rowan," he barked as she followed Lysander.

"Do not acknowledge him," Lysander instructed, his voice loud enough to carry, his arm dropping around her waist. "If he cannot speak to you in a polite tone, he won't be speaking to you at all."

Rowan couldn't remember the last time someone had taken umbrage on her behalf like that, much less publicly stood up for her.

Lysander did not allow the server to pull out Rowan's chair, insisting on doing it himself. Once she was seated, he introduced her to the others at their table.

"My mother, you know," he said. "This is her companion, Garret Landry."

"That sounds like an English name," Rowan said after the usual *pleasure to meet you*.

"American," Mr. Landry said with a smile that he turned on Iona. "Apparently like mother like son."

Iona's pleased expression showed how much she enjoyed the man saying that about her and Lysander. Rowan liked the comparison too. It implied that she and Lysander were a real couple.

Which they were, even if their time together had an as yet unspecified sell-by date.

Lysander continued his introductions his attitude that of a man both pleased by and proud of his companion.

Rowan learned that the rest of the table was made up of high-level managers in his company. Inviting them to share his table had been a nice thing to do.

Buying the table cost six figures. She knew because the Andinos bought one each year. However, her father-in-law used his tickets to curry favor with other tycoons and their wives. Her own father had to reimburse Baptiste for his and her mother's tickets, if he wanted to sit at the table with them.

Lysander could have used the gala as an opportunity to gain kudos with business associates too, but he opted to give his management team the chance to make connections at the prestigious event.

Which showed just how confident he was that they wouldn't leave his employment.

Time passed much faster than it usually did at events like this for Rowan. She liked Lysander's people and they liked the positive influence she had on him. More than one had remarked on how much more relaxed Lysander was with her there. One even said he'd been in a better mood since she'd moved into his villa.

"You knew I moved in?" she asked the man, and then turned to address Lysander. "You told them?"

"No." He frowned at his manager. "I am the same as I've always been."

"If you say so, boss," said one of the women at the table and then she smiled at Rowan. "The paparazzi have nothing on the office grapevine."

"They must not because news of my move hasn't made it into the papers yet." Rowan was fully expecting a distressed phone call from her mother when it did and a lecture from her father when he found out.

"After tonight, you can bet they'll be watching at the gate with their telephoto lenses and microphones, hoping to get a comment," the same woman said.

Rowan wasn't worried. She'd dealt with her share of the gossip press while married to Cyrus and more than when news of the divorce became public.

To avoid them, she'd spent a few months in the United States after filing for divorce in a state court. However, she had a job to do and a life to build as Rowan Johnson, not Andino, in Greece.

She'd returned to Athens months before the divorce was finalized and for a while the gutter media hounded her every step.

Lysander's security was pretty tight right now because of the threats made against him. The press would find her a lot harder to access than she had been after she moved into her apartment.

"Rowan will have security to run interference for her," Lysander said.

Was that one of the reasons he'd insisted on her having bodyguards?

"Good," the woman said.

"I'm glad," Iona added with a look of approval for her son. "She deserves looking after."

"I can look after myself," Rowan felt compelled to point out, but once again she felt something warm inside her at the knowledge Lysander was watching out for her.

"But you needn't. The paparazzi can be so tiresome," Iona added. "I dealt with them for years because there was no secret who my son's father was."

Rowan hadn't considered that aspect of Baptiste Andino acknowledging his illegitimate son.

"The security detail my son has assigned to me make sure I am not bothered by reporters now. Their photos..." Iona waived her hand in dismissal. "You cannot hide from the cameras, but I do not care if they take my picture. Only if they don't get my good side."

Everyone at the table laughed. Including Rowan. "I know what you mean. They're very good at taking pictures that get you at your worst so they can run stories with all sorts of speculation. One tabloid insinuated that Cyrus and I had divorced because I had a drug problem. The pictures they ran with the article made it look like it could be true."

"Disgusting," Mr. Landry said. "I hope you sued them for libel."

"I didn't need to. They ran a retraction before the other outlets had picked up the story. I guess Cyrus didn't want even his ex-wife besmirching his reputation that way."

"That wasn't Mr. Andino," an affable man who had been introduced as Lysander's media liaison, said. "That was all Lysander. He instructed me to get the story quashed and I did."

CHAPTER FOURTEEN

Rowan was flummoxed. Lysander had forced the retraction? But why?

She turned to him, needing to know. Why was this ruthless billionaire her secret knight in shining armor? "Why would you do that?"

"You were dealing with enough and I don't like the gutter press."

She had no doubt that was true, but it didn't explain why he'd wielded his immense power on her behalf. There were dozens of licentious and libelous stories out there he could have turned his attention to.

But he'd protected *her*.

"He gave me permission to set the big dogs on them." The media liaison named a prestigious and exclusive law firm.

The look Lysander gave him, said the media liaison had been a little too open about his activities on her behalf. The younger man stopped talking and took a hasty sip of his water.

Rowan felt badly for him, but she was glad to know Lysander deserved the White Knight credit and not her ex. Even if she still didn't understand why.

"Wow. Well thank you. It helped. A lot." She'd handled everything else to that point with a pretty even keel, but being accused of drug addiction with those awful pictures as proof had hurt. "If that story had gained traction, my boss would have had no choice but to fire me. The organization can't afford to be associated with that kind of story."

Her director had brought her into his office and told her that very thing. Rowan had been devastated, but then the tabloid had printed the retraction, on the front page no less. Her life had been allowed to go on as normal and she'd kept her job.

She didn't know why Lysander had protected her. They hadn't even been friends then. But she was grateful for it.

He had all the makings of a fairytale knight, but she needed to remember that this story didn't have a happily ever after. No matter what her heart kept insisting it wanted.

She needed to be content with happy for right now. Because she was.

Very happy.

"That is my son, a gentleman and a protector," Iona said complacently. "He is too soft hearted for his own good sometimes, but in this case, I can only applaud his instinct to protect."

The people around the table reacted to that statement with varying degrees of amusement and disbelief.

Lysander shook his head, his own expression well...cranky. "You see me through the eyes of a mother's love. I assure you, I am not soft."

Rowan could attest to that. As soon as she had the thought, she nearly choked on her before-dinner champagne. *Naughty Rowan*, she chastised herself, but the urge to laugh at her own private little joke was still there.

"Are you alright?" Lysander demanded.

"I'm..." She sucked in air for several seconds. "Fine. Just swallowed my champagne wrong."

"Perhaps wine without bubbles?" he asked, looking at the expensive champagne like it was pig swill.

"It wasn't the champagne. It was something I thought...it was funny and I started to laugh, but I was drinking." She shrugged. "Not a great combination."

Lysander's expression turned thoughtful, and she knew he was replaying their recent conversation in his head. She could see the moment he realized what had amused her.

He leaned forward and said sotto voce, "I am never *soft* when I am around you."

Rowan laughed again, the sound low and throaty, garnering several speculative looks from the others at their table.

But no one said anything, and the conversation turned to the Greece National Lacrosse Team and its chances of making a showing in international competition.

Rowan knew the team had been created in 2018 and that was about it. She wasn't big on sports, much preferring a comfy chair and a good book for her downtime. Several guests were clear enthusiasts though and the conversation carried them through the starter and into the main course.

Lysander was knowledgeable, but not keenly interested, though no one else at the table seemed to notice that.

Huh.

"Does your company support a lacrosse team?" Rowan asked him as she cut into what looked like a perfectly cooked sea bream filet. It flaked apart with her fork, no knife required.

"Several of my subsidiary holdings field teams for competition. It has become a near mania." He gave her a look. "Few things can make me that excited."

That look said she was one of them.

Heat washed through her, and Rowan smiled. "I can return the compliment."

"I didn't say anything."

"Didn't you?"

His smile was all the answer she needed.

"I have never seen the boss smile this much in a year," the media liaison said, back to his chatty self. "Not even when we managed to quash all rumors of a takeover so the stock didn't rise before he could make his move."

"He was talking about the many lacrosse teams the subsidiary companies in Baros International field."

"I'm on one. It's a lot of fun," said another man at the table. "But Baros International is a sponsor for the national team."

"I hadn't realized that."

"We have a budget for that sort of thing and one of my management team was passionate about it, so..." Lysander shrugged, like donating millions to supporting a new national sport was no big deal.

"It's not really your thing though, is it?" Rowan asked, wanting to know if she'd read him right.

He shook his head. "No, I am a traditional man and football is my sport of choice."

Rowan remembered learning how popular what they called soccer back home was in Europe. Some businesses even shut down so employees could watch the world cup.

"You may prefer football, but I don't think you're much of a traditionalist."

"You do not?" he asked, his brows raised.

What did that mean? "Considering our current situation, no."

"Oh ho, she has your number my son," Iona said with glee. "My son who sees himself as *traditional*, does he marry? No. Does he give me grandbabies to dote on? He does not!"

Rowan was in danger of choking on her champagne again, so she set the glass down and reached for her water. But Iona cracked her up. The mom who had lived anything but a conventional life, wanted her son to settle down and get married.

And give her grandchildren.

The sincerity of the desire was there in her eyes, though it was not accompanied by the censure her words might have indicated.

So, although Iona did not see her son as perfect, that did not bother her. Not like Rowan's parents.

Speaking of Rowan's parents. What were they doing coming toward Lysander's table when the main course hadn't even been cleared?

It wasn't at all appropriate and could easily cause the kind of scene they both abhorred.

"Rowan, dear, I think there must be some misunderstanding. You were meant to sit at our table." Her mother's opening salvo was only surprising in its timing, not its content.

"I received no invitation," Rowan said calmly. "And as you can see, I am here with Lysander."

Her mother's mouth pursed like she'd just bitten into a lemon, her expression as sour as the fruit too. "I cannot imagine why, but it would be better if you joined us. You sitting here is causing all sorts of speculation."

"Is it?" Rowan asked. "If people are guessing that Lysander and I are a couple, they are right."

"Nonsense. You are married to Cyrus," her father said in a crushing undertone.

Rowan wasn't crushed. In fact, unlike most times when her parents joined forces to castigate her, she didn't feel small at all. She was proud to be here with Lysander and positively wallowed in the joy of being his lover.

"I am not married to Cyrus. Our divorce finalized over a month ago. I have not lived with him in over a year."

"Mr. and Mrs. Johnson, it would be best if you returned to your seats. You are causing far more gossip than your daughter is by being with me."

"Like hell we are. Everyone is talking about it," her father said more loudly than he probably meant to.

"Good," Rowan said firmly. "My marriage to Cyrus is over and the sooner you all come to terms with that, the better."

"Are you *trying* to humiliate the man you said vows to?" her mother asked with freezing censure.

"He negated those vows very early in our marriage if I had but known it. Again, *we are divorced*," Rowan emphasized.

"And furthermore..." she let her own voice rise just enough that the tables around could hear her if they were listening, as she could tell many were.

Her parents really hadn't thought this through.

"There is nothing humiliating to Cyrus in his ex-wife dating his brother. He's lucky to be related to a man as amazing as Lysander and I'm sure he knows it." Even if her ex was too proud to ever admit it out loud. "The key word there is *ex* and who I date has absolutely nothing to do with Cyrus, or you two for that matter. No more than who I choose to live with."

"Live with?" her mother practically shrieked.

Ooops. She hadn't meant to let that particular cat out of the bag at tonight's gala.

That's what came from waiting so long to stand up to her parents. Her primary way of dealing with them since becoming an adult had been to avoid them as much as possible and not do anything to draw their attention and inevitable criticism.

That strategy had been blown out of the water when she filed for divorce, but even then, she'd never come right out and said that they had no say in her life.

"Yes, live with," Lysander said, twining his fingers through Rowan's and then setting their joined hands on the table in full display.

After letting his action sink in for a count of two, he looked off to his left and nodded. Seconds later, servers appeared to usher her parents back to their table. Klaus also stood a couple of feet away, clearly ready to step in if necessary.

Rowan felt badly for the embarrassment both her parents had to be feeling in that moment, but she also acknowledged that they'd brought it on themselves. Trying to spirit her away from Lysander's table in the middle of dinner? Ridiculous.

And not something she would ever have guessed they would do. She'd expected a frontal assault like this, but after dessert when many guests would get up and move around.

"You moved in with my son?" Iona asked, her lovely eyes the same warm brown as Lysander's wide with shock. "I did not realize you two had been dating that long."

"She has a bookcase in my inner sanctum," Lysander said by way of an answer, sidestepping the length of their dating relationship entirely.

If possible, Iona's eyes grew wider. "You installed furniture for her?"

"It's just a bookcase. I think Lysander was offended by the look of my carboard box of books on the floor of his room."

"Certainly, I had no desire to trip over it, but so long as you live there, my house is your home and should accommodate you accordingly."

Iona sucked in a shocked breath of air, but she wasn't the only one. Every person at the table looked gobsmacked at the idea of Lysander making that sort of claim.

A little dumbfounded herself, she was not at all offended.

After dinner, Lysander asked Rowan to dance. Remembering that dance they had shared years ago, she agreed without hesitation.

Their bodies fit together smoothly, and it was as if they had been dancing together for all the years in between.

Lysander held her close, his body heat reaching out to her, his muscular thighs rubbing against her own during certain moments. Forgetting the crowd surrounding them, Rowan gave herself up to the pleasure of being in his arms and moving to the music.

Someone tapped on Lysander's shoulder, and he tensed. Rowan looked up and into her ex-husband's mocking eyes. He thought he had them over a barrel, but only because he didn't understand his half-brother's character.

"Get lost," Lysander said without compunction.

Just as she'd expected him to.

And then he danced her away from Cyrus, who stood fuming and who had finally, truly been humiliated. But only because he'd tried to get Rowan to dance with him, believing that social conventions would force her to comply.

"You do not mind?" Lysander asked as they once again found the rhythm of the music with their bodies.

"No. If you hadn't said it, I would have." The very idea of Cyrus touching her, even for nothing more than a dance, made Rowan's skin crawl.

"He is an idiot."

"When you're right, you're right."

They danced through another song without interruption, heat building between them as it always did when their bodies were so close.

Until another unwelcome voice shattered the intimate bubble around them. This time the voice was feminine.

Chapter Fifteen

"Mon ami, Lysander, what a pleasant surprise," the voice coming from behind Rowan could be no other than Adele Fournier.

Of course, she was at the gala, Rowan thought with a dose of sarcasm she tried to keep off her face.

Lysander stopped dancing, but he kept his arms around Rowan.

Adele laid her hand on Lysander's arm. "Shall we?"

The tall, willowy blond was sophisticated with an ethereal beauty often remarked upon by the press. Tonight, she was dressed to impress in a form fitting copper colored silk gown cut low in the front, making it impossible for her to be wearing one of the designer bras she modeled.

Rowan looked up at Lysander, wondering what he would do.

He was looking back, his expression asking her how *she* planned to respond. He had sent Cyrus on his way. Now, it was her turn.

Rowan gave Adele her best plastic social smile. "I'm afraid Lysander's dance card is full."

The supermodel looked her up and down and then focused on Lysander. "Is she why you aren't answering my texts or calls? Couldn't bypass the opportunity to stick it to your brother by bedding his wife?"

Lysander's big body stiffened and the air around them supercharged. Too busy trying to gauge Rowan's reaction to her barb to notice, Adele remained oblivious. Rowan knew why Lysander was with her and it wasn't to stick it to Cyrus.

They were so hot together, the sheets should be ash after every time they touched.

"Rowan is living in my house because I want her there. Because I want *her*."

Adele's gaze snapped back to Lysander, her expression one of disbelief.

Rowan's billionaire wasn't done though. "If I had wanted to be that petty in regard to my brother, it was taken care of the first time I had sex with you, wasn't it?"

Without waiting for Adele's reaction, Lysander swept Rowan back into movement and away from the frowning supermodel.

"What did you mean? Was Adele one of Cyrus's women?"

"They had an affair a few years ago. She broke it off with him when she learned about Delphine."

So, him being married hadn't bothered the other woman, but that he already had a mistress did? Typical. "And then she came after you?"

"Yes. Once I learned she had been in his bed, I told her she had to stay away from him if she wanted our arrangement to continue."

"It didn't bother you that she'd been with Cyrus first?"

"I didn't care what men she took to her bed, or how many. Ours was a transactional relationship. She got entrée into events like this and I got a companion that didn't expect anything beyond it."

That made Adele sound more like an escort than a girlfriend. Nothing against escorts, but if he had hired someone to attend functions with him, word would have gotten out and the press would have had a field day.

Just like they were bound to do with her moving into his house. His half-brother's ex-wife.

"Wow. I thought my sex-with-you-to-get-rid-of-Cyrus plot was such an outlandish idea and now I find out I'm the second one to think of it."

"Adele wanted revenge. Full stop. You wanted to give your ex a message that could not be misinterpreted."

Whatever their motives, clearly both she and the supermodel had desired Lysander. Still did from what Rowan could see. Adele had been willing to stay away from Cyrus to keep her no-strings access to his half-brother.

Whereas, Rowan had moved into his home against her own better judgment. But Lysander had made a commitment to her, even if it was temporary.

And he hadn't hesitated to reject Adele's overtures now.

Lysander pulled her just a little bit closer to his hard body, like he couldn't help himself. "I looked into your prenup."

That was not what she expected him to say, so it took Rowan a moment to respond. "Oh?"

She'd given him a copy the day after she moved into his house, but he hadn't brought it up again. She'd assumed Lysander hadn't had time to read it. He was a busy man, working long hours to increase his billions, after all.

"Find anything interesting?"

"I put my team onto researching property purchases and tax shelters created in your name during your marriage. Not only did you get ten percent of Cyrus's company in the divorce, but you retained ownership of a plot of land that wasn't worth much when he bought it."

"You mean he intended it to be a loss to write off?" she asked.

"Precisely."

"But?" She knew there was a *but* or Lysander would not have brought it up.

"He has gone into business with a development company. They need ownership of that parcel of land for the development to go ahead."

"Why?" she wondered out loud.

"There are utility accesses they cannot get with the land they purchased that is adjacent to it."

"Wouldn't it be cheaper to bribe officials?" She knew Cyrus had done exactly that in the past.

"It is not merely a matter of permits, but accessibility."

"What do you mean?"

"There is no connection point to the main utilities if they do not have access to your parcel to lay the connecting lines and pipes."

"Okay, then why not buy it from me? He had to realize I'd have no idea of its value and be willing to sell."

"As to that, I think we covered it with my first statement."

Cyrus was so caught up in his own machinations, it hadn't occurred to him to simply try to buy the land from her.

"With the development in the offing, that piece of land is worth millions."

"If it will get him to leave me alone once and for all, I'll give it to him and good riddance." Marveling, she looked up into Lysander's handsome features. "I can't believe you figured this all out so quickly."

She was sure Cyrus had done his best to cover his tracks and his motives. Rowan would never have thought to even look into the assets she'd gained in the divorce, happy to leave that to her lawyer and accountant.

"My people are good."

She loved that Lysander didn't feel the need to take all the credit.

"Well, they have an amazingly astute boss."

His smile flashed and then he kissed her. Right there in the middle of the dance floor. And she loved it.

Uncaring of what others at the charity gala thought, Rowan kissed him back.

"You aren't giving that land to my half-brother."

Looking deliciously befuddled from the kiss that left him hard as a rock, it took Rowan a beat to focus and parse Lysander's words.

He waited.

Her brows drew together in a frown. "Why not? Is there something legally binding in the pre-nup that says I can't?"

"No."

"Then, I *can* give it to him. You just don't want me to."

"Why would *you* want to?" he asked, furious at the thought of Cyrus taking advantage of Rowan like that.

"To get him and my family off of my back?" she asks, like it should be obvious.

"One, you can sell the property to the developer yourself which will quash my brother's interest in reconciliation." If our father's heir was only after the parcel of land. Maybe he had figured out too late what he had in Rowan and now wanted her back. "And two, curtailing Cyrus's interest in you will not stop your parents from blaming you for the breakup."

She sighed, her lips twisting with discontent. "You're right about that. And from a financial viewpoint, your first suggestion makes sense."

"Is there a viewpoint it doesn't make sense from?"

"The one where I don't need Cyrus holding a nasty grudge against me. I escaped my marriage relatively unscathed, but I'm not naïve enough to believe that Cyrus couldn't make my life here untenable if he wanted to."

"I will never allow him to hurt you." He'd been protecting her for ten years. He wasn't about to stop now.

"That's sweet, but eventually, you'll end this thing between us." She grimaced. "Or I will. And when that happens, you won't be standing as a barrier between me and your half-brother. He holds grudges."

"Never does not have an expiration date," he assured her.

He didn't know why it was so important to protect this woman, but it was a course he had committed to years ago.

She was looking at him like she had back at the table. Like he was some kind of hero. He wasn't. He was a ruthless businessman.

Having those pretty blue eyes fixed on him with that expression felt good though. So, he didn't remind her of the darker side of his nature. She'd been unwilling to see it thus far anyway.

"Okay, so we, I mean *I* sell the property to the land developer. I guess I have my lawyer approach them?"

"I will take care of it for you."

"Um, even if we were in a committed relationship, I wouldn't ask you to do that. I have a lawyer. She can take care of it."

"We agreed to exclusivity," he reminded her. "It doesn't get much more committed than that."

Giving him a teasing grin, Rowan said, "Your mom would disagree."

Despite her own life choices, or perhaps because of them, his mother would not be happy until he had bound himself legally to a woman. But that wasn't something Lysander had ever wanted to do.

It didn't make him shudder with distaste when she'd made her comments at dinner. Perhaps he was growing inured to the guilt trips.

"At the risk of sounding arrogant, I will get you a better deal than your lawyer," he said, getting back to the topic at hand.

Rowan's soft laugh affected him like it always did. Straight in his libido. But there was an odd tight feeling in his chest too. Had the food given him heartburn?

"I'm sure you can," she said with a smile. "And yes, you do sound arrogant, but it's part of your charm."

"I'll remind you that you said that the next time you aren't finding it quite so charming."

Her eyes lit with sweet humor. "You do that."

"Why do I get the feeling, you will conveniently forget this conversation?"

"Because you are a very smart man."

"Smart enough to negotiate a deal with the developer."

"Wow, you just are not going to let this go."

"I want what is best for you." In a way that would bother him if he let himself think about it. So, he didn't.

"Okay, if you really want to handle the sale, then by all means, do it."

"Tell me if Cyrus or Baptiste attempt to contact you, or threaten you in any way." He knew how vindictive both men could be, but Cyrus had a wide streak of petty as well.

"You're being bossy again."

"It's part of my charming arrogance."

"I might chalk it up to that if you charm me with another kiss."

He didn't need to be asked twice. Kissing this woman was addictive and he was greedy for another fix. Pulling her flush against his body, he let her feel what dancing with her did to him before pressing his mouth against hers.

Rowan's lips parted on a soft sigh, and he was damn tempted to ravage her mouth with his tongue. However, while he didn't care what they said about him, he did not want to give the tabloids a story to tell about her tomorrow.

Her sweet tongue came out to taste his lips and Lysander's reaction was primal and immediate. He broke the kiss and guided her from the dance floor with a firm hand at the small of her back.

"It is time to go home."

"You'll get no arguments from me," Rowan quipped.

But when they reached the table to collect her purse, Cyrus and Lysander's father were sitting in wait.

Lysander gave his father an impassive look. "Trying to poach my people?" he taunted.

"Trying to have a quiet word with my son."

Lysander usually at least listened to his father, but right then? He wanted to be home and inside his beautiful lover. "Call my assistant and make an appointment."

"Is that any way to treat your father?" Baptiste asked with a frown.

"We are leaving. If you would like to walk us out..." Lysander left the rest unsaid.

If his father wanted to talk to him that badly, he would say what he needed to between the table and the door to the outside.

Unfortunately, as soon as Baptiste stood, so did Cyrus.

CHAPTER SIXTEEN

"You must realize how badly this looks for our family," was his father's opening salvo.

Baptiste waited until they were almost to the exit doors, where few gala attendees were around to overhear the quietly spoken words. Lysander's father was more circumspect than Rowan's, but no less obvious to him.

With that sentence, Lysander knew that the property deal was not Cyrus's alone. Their father had a stake in it as well, or Andino Enterprises did. If Baptiste were genuinely concerned about the effect of his son's behavior on the family's reputation, he would have told Cyrus to keep it in his pants during his marriage to Rowan.

No, his worry was about that parcel of land, and no doubt the shares in Andino Enterprises that Rowan had been given in the divorce too. Baptiste had a vested interest in seeing Rowan and Cyrus reconciled.

Over Lysander's dead, cold and bankrupt body. No way in hell.

Lysander was not an Andino and the success of that company meant nothing to him. He couldn't care less who controlled the family shares, and he definitely had no compunction about gouging the land developer on Rowan's behalf.

Lysander did not slow his and Rowan's progress across the cavernous hotel lobby. "I disagree."

"Taking your brother's leavings as your mistress is beneath you." Baptiste's voice echoed with disgust.

Rowan stiffened beside Lysander, a soft gasp falling from her lovely mouth. Rage rolled through him with gale force.

His body stiff with fury, he stopped in the middle of the lobby, and turned to face his father and Cyrus. His brother's smarmy features looked smug, the look he gave Rowan full of superiority.

Neither Baptiste, nor Cyrus, were targeting Lysander. What they didn't seem to realize was that by aiming their vitriol at Rowan, they might as well have been.

"Do you know why my company has grown exponentially faster than Andino Enterprises in the past decade?" he asked, his tone flat.

Neither his father, nor his brother, liked that reminder and both scowled.

He did not wait to see if they would hazard a guess and answered his own question. "Because I do my research. I make sure I know my opponents before I take them on."

"I know my wife," Cyrus said scornfully. "She'll get over this little rebellion and come back to me."

"Ex-wife," Lysander gritted, the look on his face making his half-brother take a step backward.

It wasn't enough. Lysander wanted him and his father gone. He turned his sulfuric glare on his father. "I am not married. Rowan is not my mistress. She is my lover and she is nobody's leavings."

Rowan squeezed his hand. She had something she wanted to say. He refrained from adding the demand his father apologize so she could say it.

Drawing herself up, she gave the two men she'd once called family a scathing look. "Comments like that are beneath you, Baptiste. I am an independent, *single* woman who can sleep with whomever I want. And right now, I want that to be Lysander."

He didn't like the *right now* even though he had specified that their relationship would not be permanent.

Damn it. What was she doing to him?

"I apologize, Rowan," Lysander's father said stiffly.

She inclined her head regally and looked directly at her ex. "I understand why you think I'm such a pushover, Cyrus. You mistook my naivete and desire to please my parents as an indication of a lack of intelligence and weak will. Neither are attributes I carry."

"He doesn't know you at all, does he?" Lysander looked down at the magnificent woman at his side.

She held herself like a queen and her tone revealed no emotional upheaval. She had this locked down.

"No, he doesn't."

Cyrus sputtered, but slicing his hand through the air, Lysander cut his words off. "Don't bother. It's obvious you never even tried to figure out what makes Rowan tick. If you had, you would not have risked the assets assigned to her in the prenup by cheating. She's not a woman who would tolerate that. Ever."

No, his brother had assumed that because Rowan put up with their unhappy marriage, she would not balk at being cheated on. He'd completely misread her commitment to loyalty. Once he gave her an out, she was going to take it.

And she had.

"Surely that is something for Cyrus and Rowan to work through. They cannot do that if you have her in your bed." Lysander's father hissed his disapproval in a quiet tone, his attention clearly on the proximity of others and the potential for their discussion to be overheard.

"They aren't working anything out," Lysander said with bite, making no effort to modulate his own tone. "Regardless, you and Cyrus mistook my meaning. I wasn't talking about Rowan when I mentioned an opponent. I was talking about myself."

His father reeled back like Lysander had struck him. "You are my son, not my enemy."

"If you come for Rowan, I will be," he assured the older man.

"No. That's ridiculous. You don't have relationships," Cyrus said. "You're the consummate playboy." He gave Rowan a pitying look. "You must realize you are not the only woman in his bed."

"That just cost you the deal you're trying to make with the Japanese conglomerate," Lysander informed his brother. "I do not tolerate slander."

"What? How did you know about... You can't..." Cyrus stuttered.

Baptiste's expression revealed that he had finally figured out how badly he and Cyrus had messed up. "Do not be hasty, son."

If he thought calling Lysander son was going to sway the outcome, Baptiste was a fool.

"Let's make something very clear here," Lysander bit, his tone cold and threatening. "I do not care if Andino Enterprises goes bankrupt, much less loses a few million on a deal. I damn well do care if you harm someone under my protection."

"You're telling us that Rowan is under you protection?" his father asked, clearly shocked. "Since when?"

"You would know the answer to that if you had bothered to pay attention." Lysander had never been impressed with his father and brother's lazy approach to accumulating necessary information.

"She's *my* wife," Cyrus said belligerently.

"*Ex*. I'm your *ex*-wife," Rowan piped up with that reminder, emphasizing the ex. "I haven't lived with you for over a year. The divorce is final. I changed my name back to Johnson. We're as over as over can be."

Cyrus and Baptiste looked at Rowan with twin expressions of consternation. Baptiste's gaze turned considering, but anger tightened Cyrus's face.

"I know you're a petty, vindictive man, Cyrus," Rowan said, showing she knew her ex much better than he'd ever known her. "Refrain from trying to get back at me for having the audacity to divorce your cheating ass, or I will sign my shares in Andino Enterprises over to your biggest competition."

"You're not giving shares in *my* company to that bastard," Cyrus shouted, pointing at Lysander.

Baptiste grabbed his legitimate son's arm in warning.

Rowan laughed, the sound more mockery than humor. "You think you're in competition with Lysander? You're not even in the same stratosphere. He doesn't need shares in Andino Enterprises to crush it."

Her words filled Lysander with unexpected pride. Not only did she know more about his business than his so-called family, but she recognized the financial power he wielded.

His reaction to her approval was disconcerting though. It was too intense.

"Who are you talking about then?" The snide condescension rolled off his half-brother.

Rowan named the company Lysander himself considered most likely to launch a hostile merger attempt on Andino Enterprises if they were able to add a block of the company's shares to their portfolio.

"Lysander, you may not be part of Andino Enterprises, but you are still my son. You owe family loyalty." His father sounded almost desperate.

Was Andino Enterprises in trouble financially? Why else would Baptiste and Cyrus be so fixated on bringing the shares and the land parcel back into their greedy little hands?

Rowan had had a point earlier. Why hadn't they simply offered to buy them from her?

It was something he needed to look into.

"The only family I owe loyalty to is my mother." He was a Baros, not an Andino as Cyrus had so eloquently pointed out when he called Lysander a bastard. "The woman you disrespected by taking to your bed but not the altar when you had the chance."

His father winced, eyes so like Lysander's own, going bleak.

Perhaps Rowan had been right, and the older man *had* grieved for the loss of Iona Baros. However, that loss was entirely his own doing. Lysander had no sympathy for Baptiste or his regrets.

Nor did he feel unswerving loyalty toward him. Yes, Baptiste had acknowledged Lysander as his *illegitimate* son, but in many ways that had only made Lysander's life more difficult in the predominately conservative business world of Athens.

His father had never attempted to bring Lysander into the family business or his own life in any meaningful way. Expecting loyalty to a family name that Lysander did not carry was ludicrous.

If Baptiste did not want to lose his company, he had better keep a tighter rein on Cyrus as Rowan's ex than he had when he was her husband. If Rowan didn't bring them down by selling her shares to their keenest competitor, Lysander would take the company apart piece by piece.

Dismantling the deal with the Japanese conglomerate would show both men how serious Lysander was about keeping and protecting Rowan.

He'd meant his promise to her earlier. Even after their liaison ended, Lysander would keep Cyrus's revenge impulses in check where she was concerned.

"Marriage is a sacred institution," his father said, trying another tack.

Lysander gave the older man a disbelieving look. "You are saying this to me? The result of you not keeping your *sacred* vows to your first wife."

Rowan's hand squeezed his. She was trying to comfort him. He did not need it. He'd long since come to terms with his own origin story. The gesture warmed him though.

She was just so damn sweet.

"You don't want me back," Rowan said to Cyrus, with unwavering conviction. "This is all about what I got in the divorce settlement. Newsflash, you aren't getting any of it back."

She'd gone from wanting to just give him the parcel of land to refusing to give him anything. Rowan had a temper that spurred intransigence, as he had learned the day she'd shown up at his gate with her intriguing proposition.

Rowan rolled her eyes when Cyrus's face went slack with shock, and she shook her head. "Did you really think I would be fooled a second time by your attempt at romance? How gullible do you think I am?"

"I don't know what Lysander has told you, Rowan, but keep in mind that he has an axe to grind with our family."

Lysander was done.

Rowan's feisty side turned him on, and he'd already been aroused by their dancing. His tuxedo jacket was hiding a raging hardon he was ready to bury in his lover's enticing body.

As if she could read his mind, or maybe her body was reacting to his pheromones, Rowan looked up at him with a sultry smile. "Time to go, don't you think, Sander?"

"Yes," he growled.

Chapter Seventeen

T he sexual tension in the car on the way back to Lysander's home was palpable. Rowan pressed her thighs together trying to alleviate the ache between them.

It did not work.

Lysander gripped the steering wheel with white-knuckle intensity. "Why didn't I use a driver tonight?"

"Because you like handling this super expensive, finely tuned machine?" she teased.

"I like handling you more."

"I'm flattered. I think."

"You should be. You're the only woman in that category."

"I guess I'm special then."

His gaze flicked sideways to her before returning to the road. "You are that."

They barely made it through the front door before they were tearing off each other's clothing. Rowan ran her hands over the hard plains of his chest, reveling in her freedom to touch this sexy man however she liked.

His hands gripped tightly around her hips, he lifted her against the wall in the foyer and took her mouth forcefully.

Rowan gave back as good as she got, tangling her tongue with his, spreading her legs so the juncture of her thighs rubbed against the hard ridges of his eight-pack. She was so wet, it soaked right through her panties and made his skin slick.

He dropped her legs and jerked her panties down. She kicked off her shoes and stepped out of her underwear while he yanked her dress over her head. Then she stood naked because she hadn't been wearing a bra.

With a groan, Lysander brought his mouth down to her breast and he laved her peaked nipple. "So sweet," he breathed against her sensitive flesh.

"Please, Sander...I *need*."

He maneuvered her a couple of feet to the right and then she found herself perched on the edge of a console table while his raging erection pressed against her most intimate flesh.

"Yes." She wanted this. So much. "Put it in me."

He surged forward, his huge manhood getting stuck after only a couple of inches despite how ready she was.

Pulling back and thrusting forward in short jabs, he worked more of his hard penis inside her swollen channel. "So damn tight."

She tried to help, but she had no traction with her legs dangling off the side of the console table.

Finally, the root of his sex pressed against her vulva. A mini starburst of pleasure went through her. And then he started to thrust for real, pistoning in and out of her body in an uncontrolled rhythm that quickly brought her to the brink of ecstasy.

His pelvis pressed against her clitoris with every forward thrust and that ecstasy flooded her in a tsunami of feeling.

Her head tilted back, she screamed with an abandon she couldn't hope to leash.

Lysander stopped thrusting, just grinding his pelvis against her to prolong her bliss.

He stared down at her, his face tight with need. "You are so beautiful like this."

Then he started canting his hips again and soon his big, muscled body went rigid with his own climax. His shout was loud and guttural.

But recognizable for all that.

He'd yelled her name as he came.

Something cracked inside of Rowan. Something she had no desire to acknowledge or examine.

~ ~ ~

Blissful days turned into blissful weeks, and Rowan realized she'd been living with Lysander for two months.

With no signs of either of them growing bored with the other's company.

And the sex was hot and plentiful.

It was almost too good to be true and Rowan kept waiting for Lysander to change. To start treating her like a piece of furniture as Cyrus had done. As she had seen so many men in her life do to their society wives.

Maybe it was because she was his lover and not his wife, but Lysander wanted to talk over dinner. He cajoled her into getting up ridiculously early so they could have breakfast together before he left for the office.

They had dinner with his mother and her husband. Rowan met Lysander's business associates because he liked having her with him when they had a dinner meeting.

She got to know his staff and security specialists, but she still called them goons so they wouldn't grow complacent.

She was in danger of growing more than complacent; she was becoming attached. To Lysander. To his life. To the life they shared together.

~ ~ ~

Upon her return to the villa after work, Rowan was surprised to find Lysander home as well. He relaxed on the leather sectional in his inner sanctum, the television showing the stock markets somewhere, his tablet in his hand.

It was so like that first day she'd come here, she smiled. "You're back early."

He swiped and tapped something on his tablet and put it down. Looking up at her, his dark eyes heated. "And you are late."

"Couldn't be helped." Though if she'd known he was already here, she would have tried harder to leave on time.

He stood and put his hand out. "You are here now. Come."

"Are we having sex for dinner again?" she asked, tongue in cheek.

"Have I ever let you skip a meal?"

"No." He was kind of militant about making sure she got dinner, even if it was in bed after making love.

"Helen packed for you, but you'll want to check and make sure she got everything you'll need."

"Are we going somewhere?" It was Friday. So, they had the weekend. Or at least she did. Lysander almost always had to work at least part of the weekend.

It took a lot of effort to stay at the top of the tycoon food chain.

"We are going on a cruise."

Excitement made Rowan's blood bubble in her veins like champagne. "A weekend cruise?"

It wasn't Mexico, but it was a cruise. And he'd booked it for her. If she didn't watch out, she was going to fall head over heels for this man.

"We'll be spending ten days in the Mexican Riviera."

Rowan stopped walking, her heart thudding. She stared up at Lysander, certain she'd misheard him. "What did you say?"

"You want to go on a cruise in Mexico." His tone and expression said he was still confused as to why.

"Yes, so?"

"So, we are going. I've spoken to Ariston Spiridakou. He owns a cruise line and has provided accommodation on one of his luxury ships."

Rowan couldn't even fathom what level of opulence would cause a contemporary of Lysander to refer to the vessel as a *luxury* ship.

"No way are you taking ten days away from work."

Lysander shrugged. "I will work remotely for a couple of hours a day. I can take conference calls as necessary."

That sounded more like her workaholic lover, but still. "I can't just take off for vacation without making sure everything is covered at work."

"Taken care of."

"What do you mean?"

"I contacted your org's director. She okayed your absence."

"But we're in the middle of a fund-raising push."

"A couple of my people will be filling in for you."

"You think of everything."

CHAPTER EIGHTEEN

Rowan realized how true that statement was as she found herself on a private jet flying toward Los Angeles, California. The Greek cruise line embarked from the Port of Los Angeles.

Lysander had arranged for her things to be packed, very efficiently, by Helen. He'd ordered dinner to be served on board the plane. But best of all, he had an entire itinerary with shore excursions for her to pore over.

"Choose the ones you want to go on and I'll have them booked for us."

"You're going on a group shore excursion?" Rowan couldn't help the surprise in her tone. "*You* are?"

"No." His gorgeous smile slashed across his face. "We will have private guides and transportation."

Of course, they would.

After selecting the places and things she wanted to see and do in each cruise port, Rowan stared at Lysander and wondered how long it would take him to feel her eyes on him. It was no hardship.

Her Greek tycoon lover was gorgeous. And that look he got on his face when he was concentrating on work? It made her heart rat-a-tat-tat and her panties damp. He was just so sexy in his king-of-the-business-world mode.

Was it the intelligence shining in his dark eyes as he read through reports? Or maybe how incongruous his perfectly sculpted body was to his tycoon role. Billionaires were just *not* this gorgeous. The proof was in every business journal and tabloid on the planet.

Most of those men were at least a decade older than Lysander and none of them had his rugged good looks. At least in her opinion. Which might be biased.

Is that what love did to you?

Rowan's brain screeched to a silent halt like an incomplete music download. Love? Who said anything about love?

She could not love this man. That emotion was strictly off limits in their temporary relationship.

Lysander looked up from the email he'd been writing to one of his subsidiary CEOs and found Rowan staring at him like she'd seen a paparazzi outside the plane window. Disbelief tinged with disgust dominated her beautiful face.

It was not the expression he expected to see after she'd been going over their itinerary options for Mexico.

"What is the matter? Is there an excursion you find distasteful?"

Shaking herself, Rowan's expression cleared. "No. They're all great. It was hard to choose, if you want the truth."

"I always want the truth from you."

She winced and then shook her head. "Pretty sure you don't."

"I do." He had no doubts on that score.

"Do you have a lot more work to do?" she asked. "Only, I thought we might make use of the bedroom. I've never been on a private jet with one before."

"Are you tired?" he teased.

Rowan's libido easily matched his. No way was she talking about sleeping.

"Not so much, no." Whatever had put the distressed look on her face wasn't at the forefront of her mind now.

Sex was. And just like that, it was the overriding thought in his brain too.

He shut his laptop and set it aside before standing. Putting his hand out to Rowan, he said, "Let's go see how comfortable the bed is."

"You don't know?"

"No."

"Why have a bed on your plane if you don't use it?" she asked with a tilt of her head, her expression curious and little judgy. "I know you aren't keen on sleeping more than a few hours a night, but even you must rest on the longer trips."

She was right on both counts. He didn't require much sleep, but using travel time to get what he did need was only logical. "It is not my plane."

Surprise widened her lovely blue eyes. "It isn't?"

"It belongs to a friend." He had considered how much he wanted to say to her, but Lysander had decided that she would want to know the full truth. "I did not want our travel arrangements easily tracked."

"What? Why not?"

"The threats have escalated and now include you." The anger and tension that had simmered inside him since being made aware of her name being mentioned in the latest threat threatened to boil over.

"You didn't say anything."

"I'm saying something now."

"I guess you are." She chewed on her lip. "You wouldn't be leaving if it wasn't for me being threatened, would you?"

"No." A man in his position received threats too often to let them dictate even a modest change to his schedule.

Having her targeted changed things.

"So, we're flying incognito?"

"We are not listed by name on the flight manifest."

"Is that legal?"

"No."

"Oh."

He didn't want her frightened. "My security company has a plan for smoking out the culprits."

"That's good."

"I wanted you out of Europe while they do it."

"And you came with me to keep me company? You could have just sent me on the cruise alone."

That was not going to happen.

"The look on your face. Are you worried I'd flirt with the other guests on board?"

"No." He was understandably concerned a woman as beautiful and vivacious as she was would get hit on by other men. "As long as we are together, we are exclusive."

"That's what we agreed."

"Then there is nothing to be concerned about."

"And yet, here you are, flying anonymously on a plane to another country in order to go on a cruise with me." She shook her head, disbelief etched on her face. "That whole incognito thing, it seems really cloak and dagger."

"It is a little. Body doubles will be living in the villa, pretending to be us while we are away." The fully trained security agents would be engaging in activity meant to draw the threat out into the open.

"This really is a working vacation for you. Can I expect to see much of you at all on the cruise?" she asked, disappointment clear in her drooped shoulders.

"Yes. I said I would only work a couple of hours a day. You don't think I'm sending you ashore alone, do you?" Like hell.

Not only would he be with her, but they were traveling with a full complement of security.

"I'm glad you aren't." She grinned, her natural enthusiasm coming to the fore. "I'm surprised you didn't just plan for us to visit one of your company headquarters outside Europe."

"You wanted to go on a cruise. To Mexico." And he wanted to see her eyes light up the way they had when he told her about their trip.

"So, you got in touch with one of your Greek tycoon friends who just happens to own a luxury cruise line?"

"Ariston is more a business associate than a friend." Lysander didn't have friends. He had family, some of whom he would happily live without.

His father. His brother.

One he cared deeply about. His mother. Others he considered important because his mother did. Her relatives.

But friends? No.

"Are we traveling under assumed names?" Rowan's voice was laced with excitement.

He chuckled. "Nothing so mysterious. I'm sorry, but I don't have a fake passport for you, or any super spy gadgets."

She gave him a moue of regret. "It is a little disappointing."

"I'll make up for it," he promised.

"You can start back there." She tilted her head toward the bedroom in the back of the plane.

Arousal whooshed through him in a heated wave. "Yes, let's test the firmness of the bed."

"If it's anything like your bed at the villa, I'm sure it's as firm as can be."

"Are you saying my bed at home is too hard for you?"

"Nothing about you is *too* hard," she teased in a low, sultry voice. "Your hardness is just right."

Then she jumped up and rushed to the back of the plane, her laughter trailing behind her.

Cheeky minx.

He would show her just how hard she made him and he could only hope the bed would withstand his efforts.

~ ~ ~

There were three cruise ships docked when Rowan and Lysander reached the harbor. The one owned by Ariston Spiridakou gleamed pristinely white in the sunshine. It wasn't quite as large as the other two ships and she just knew that meant it was because fewer guests were accommodated, not because it lacked any amenity.

Fizzing with excitement, she clutched her hold all on one side of her body and Lysander's hand on the other. "I can't believe you made this happen. Thank you, Sander."

"My pleasure." He laced their fingers and pulled her close as they walked toward the ship.

No passport or check-in lines for men like Lysander Baros. Their security detail surrounded them and handed over all necessary documents to ship personal.

"Where are all of the other passengers?" she asked the purser, who was personally escorting them to their cabin.

"General boarding does not begin for three hours."

Of course.

He ushered them through a door marked *cruise personnel*. It led to a surprisingly well appointed corridor with an elevator in the center.

"This is your personal elevator," the purser explained. "It is accessible via doors in the same position on every deck and requires your keycard and thumbprint to call."

It sounded like excessive security measures to reach their cabin, but this was the world of a billionaire. The purser left them at the elevator after scanning both their thumbprints and giving them each a keycard with their pictures on them.

She'd read that the card with their picture was used as identification to get on and off the ship, but again, Rowan doubted it worked that way for friends of the owner of the cruise line.

When the elevator doors opened, Lysander held Rowan back from exiting. All but one of their security detail did though. "This is their suite."

From the glimpse Rowan got through the open doors, the suite had a large living area with four doors off of it. The security specialists' rooms?

But her curiosity about the sleeping arrangements for their guards disintegrated into nothingness when she saw their suite. "This place is bigger than my apartment back in Athens. I thought cabins on cruise ships were supposed to be small."

She'd expected a suite and more space than the typical cabin. She was traveling with Lysander Baros after all, but this? This was over the top luxury and space.

The security specialist did his thing making sure the rooms off the main living area were empty. "All clear, Mr. Baros," he said.

Lysander nodded. "Make sure at least two men are available at all times to guard Rowan and I if we leave the suite."

The man nodded and left via the elevator.

"Pfft," Rowan said. "This isn't a suite. It's a luxury apartment."

Lysander's brows rose. "Is that a complaint?"

"You know it's not. This is amazing." She twirled and indicated the beautifully appointed space with her hands out.

Lysander grabbed her by the waist and pulled her in. Like he couldn't help but touch her. "It is Ariston and Chloe's personal accommodation."

"They keep a palatial suite like this on all their ships?" Wow. Just, wow.

"Not all."

"More than one though?"

He nodded, his eyes fixed on her lips.

"But..." Talk about excess.

"It is good to be king."

"Says one monarch about another."

Her *king* bent and pressed his mouth to hers in a kiss that quickly turned carnal.

Rowan was breathing hard when he lifted his head and stared down at her with an expression she couldn't begin to read. "You are too damn addicting."

"Pot, meet kettle," she teased.

But he didn't smile. Shaking his head, he stepped away. "Come and see the balcony."

Lysander tugged Rowan toward a huge sliding glass door that led outside. The balcony was huge, covering the entire width of their suite. With lounge furniture and a large hot tub to the left, as well as a family size table for outdoor dining to the right, it was easily as large as one of the terraces off Lysander's villa.

They were on the top deck of the ship with a 280° view around them. The wall surrounding the balcony was clear, which surprised her.

"I would think someone like Ariston Spiridakou would be more intent on his privacy."

Lysander pressed a button on the wall by the door and the walls around the terrace went frosted and opaque.

"Ooh, clever." She stepped into Lysander's personal space. "I can think of something we could do with the privacy."

Lysander took a step back, away from her. "I need to do some work as long as we're in port. Why don't you get settled?"

He disappeared inside the suite.

CHAPTER NINETEEN

Doing her best to ignore the sting of the rejection, Rowan went back inside too.

She wasn't anywhere near done exploring.

Lysander had said he would have to work a couple of hours each day and there hadn't been much time for it this morning. They'd landed at a private airstrip outside of Los Angeles and then been driven to the port.

He'd spent some time on his phone in the car, but she was sure he needed some privacy to make calls and whatever else tycoons did to fill their work hours. Of which there were many.

Opening one door, Rowan found a small but well appointed bathroom with a shower. The next two doors, on either side of the bathroom revealed small bedrooms. Across the living area, there were only two doors.

She could hear the muffled tones of Lysander's voice behind one and assumed that was some kind of office. She doubted Ariston was any great shakes about taking time off from his mega empire either. The next room was a master bedroom complete with an en suite with both a full separate tub and shower.

This place was *bigger* than her apartment in Athens, by a bedroom, an office and at least 50% more living space in the main room. There was no kitchen, but then on a cruise ship, she assumed there was no need for one. There was a small fridge and fully stocked personal bar area.

This place was set up to accommodate a family. Did Ariston and Chloe travel with their family? She didn't know much about the other Greek tycoon. Not even his age. For all she knew, their children were grown, but Rowan still felt a twinge in her chest when she thought about traveling like this with children.

It wasn't the opulence surrounding her that had her feeling wistful. It was the idea of having children. Something she hadn't wanted after the first year in her marriage to Cyrus.

What would Lysander's child be like? Willful and stubborn, for sure. She could see a little boy with his father's intense dark eyes in her mind's eye.

Pushing thoughts better left to old and buried dreams, Rowan strolled over to the dining table.

In the center of it, a platter of fruit and cheese tempted her. Sitting next to it was a bucket with a bottle of champagne chilling in the ice. She read the note beside it:

Lysander & Rowan:
Enjoy your trip. My staff has been instructed to get you whatever you need.
Ariston
Short and to the point, but a nice touch all the same.

Now, if only she had a lover to share the champagne with. Drinking bubbly on her own was not exactly Rowan's norm. Especially this early in the day.

She grabbed a bunch of grapes to nibble on and wandered outside again. The sounds of the cruise port were muted, but still discernable from her place on the top deck. The hot tub made a sound, like it was running a routine filtration cycle.

Hmm...nothing was stopping her from putting on her bikini and availing herself of the warm bubbly water.

She wanted to watch the ship leave port, but that would not be for hours yet. Who knew how many of those hours Lysander would spend holed up in the suite's study?

Putting thought to action, she hurried into the bedroom and opened her suitcase. She could unpack. That was probably what Lysander meant by settling in, but the hot tub beckoned. And unlike her temporary lover, Rowan was not a workaholic.

Unplanned, or not, this was her vacation and she meant to enjoy every minute of it.

A couple of minutes later, after changing into her swimsuit and pulling her hair into a messy bun, Rowan padded out barefoot to the balcony. Not wanting anything to impede her view, she pressed the button turning the glass back to clear.

The water was hot, but not too hot and Rowan let her body sink onto a seat under the bubbles. She had an unimpeded view of the harbor and watched boats coming and going. The suite was on the stern of the ship, so all she saw on the deck two stories below was an empty outdoor eating area.

When the ship was full, she was sure it was busy and was grateful for the option to turn the glass opaque. Maybe she was too spoiled by her lifestyle to truly enjoy a regular cruise with regular people, but the idea of being watched while she relaxed felt like nails on a chalkboard to her brain.

This was perfect though. And she *did* want to eat in the public restaurants. She wanted to play trivia with the other guests in the bar area. And take dance lessons on the pool deck. Rowan had read about all these activities and more when she'd looked into taking a cruise by herself.

She'd never worked up the enthusiasm to travel alone though.

Being here with Lysander was perfect. Well, it would be when he wasn't working. Which she wasn't going to complain about. Not even to herself. She wasn't about to become a vine and cling either. Not her style.

So, if participating in onboard activities meant doing it alone, that's what Rowan would do. She couldn't help hoping she'd convince Lysander to join her at least part of the time, though.

She thought she was in with a chance. Lysander had tried things with her he hadn't done before. Like moving her into his home. She was the only woman he'd ever lived with besides his mother.

That meant something, didn't it?

More importantly, what did she want it to mean?

When this thing between them first started, she had been no more interested in commitment than he was, certain her emotions were locked down tight. Feeling bereft when he chose to work rather than make love? That said otherwise.

Sure, she could pretend to herself it was all about sexual frustration, but she didn't make it a habit to lie to herself like that. And she wasn't going to start now.

Their relationship had a sell by date and while she'd wanted that to start with, now it felt like the Sword of Damocles hanging over her head.

Neither of them knew what that date was, and she was sure Lysander didn't spend a single second worrying about it. However, the inevitable end of their liaison was starting to color their time together in shades of grief she couldn't let herself show.

She didn't even know which one of them would end it. Because it could be her. No matter how much she craved him in her life, she might walk away to protect herself from further pain.

Since that first dance they'd shared, she'd felt a connection to Lysander she'd never known with another man. While married she hadn't acted on that feeling, or even allowed herself to dwell on it. No secret fantasies of a man she wasn't married to.

Unlike Cyrus, Rowan was loyal. And she believed in keeping her word. Even if that meant letting go of a man she wasn't sure she could live happily without when the time came.

It was time to stop pretending she'd approached him with her plan solely in order to get rid of her ex-husband's attention.

Rowan had dressed up like an amateur seductress and gone to Lysander because she wanted him. Full stop. Having had him...over and over again for the past weeks...she only wanted him more.

Far from working him out of her system, he had worked his way into the fortress that had been her heart.

The only man on the planet who could.

And she'd been the fool to come to him, to suggest they have revenge sex that turned into the most intimate and fulfilling sex of her life.

"What are you doing out here?" Lysander barked.

Rowan jerked in surprise, slipping from her perch on the molded seat below her and sputtered as water splashed up into her face.

She'd been so lost in her thoughts, she hadn't heard him approach.

Allowing the momentum from her slide into the water to propel her, she floated to the side of the hot tub. Settling her crossed arms on it, she lifted her head and gave him a wry glance. "I think that's pretty obvious, yeah?"

"It sure as hell is." He jabbed the button turning the glass of the surround frosted once again. "I don't want men leering at you in your bikini."

"So possessive," she teased.

She should probably at least put up a token resistance to such blatant jealousy, but it secretly thrilled her. He wanted her to be his and his alone. Even the right to look at her swimsuit clad body. At least for now.

Not that she was giving up public swimming, but she liked the way his over-the-top reaction made her feel.

"Are you done working?" she asked with an inviting smile. "Only, it's a little lonely in this hot tub."

"How can you be lonely when you're displaying your body for anyone to see?"

Okay. No matter how much this version of her lover turned her on, enough was enough.

"Newsflash, we are on a cruise ship, Sander. There will be other men by the pool when we use it. I can't stop them leering, though I doubt I'll be the only woman down there in a bikini." She put her hand up in a stop gesture when Lysander looked like he wanted to speak. She waived toward the outdoor dining area two decks below. "And there are no people down there right now."

"We won't be using the pool when other guests have access to it," Lysander dismissed.

"Maybe you won't, but I'm not spending the entire day holed up in the suite while you are working."

He looked taken aback by her words, like it had never occurred to him that she would explore what the ship had to offer without him.

"That is not acceptable."

"It's cute how you think you get to dictate to me, but here's another bit of news, Mr. Greek tycoon, you aren't the boss of me."

Chapter Twenty

"I thought it was King?"

"I'm American. We don't do sovereigns."

"You chose to have a life in Greece."

"Greece abolished the monarchy in 1974." Her words said one thing, her mind another. Because Lysander had the presence and bearing of royalty.

He began unbuttoning his shirt, his suit jacket and tie nowhere in evidence.

"What are you doing?" she parroted his question.

He gave her a look that asked what she thought he was doing because it should be obvious. "Undressing so I can join you."

"You're not wearing swim trunks under your slacks. I saw you get dressed."

"Nor do I need them in a private spa."

"Oh." She wasn't sure why a small piece of clothing made a difference, but it did.

The idea of him sliding into the hot tub naked made her core pulse. She pressed her thighs together to alleviate the ache, but all that did was make her more aware of what she wanted.

Him. His hands there. His sex *there*.

The predatory look in his eye was like a brush straight over her clitoris.

Peeling out of his clothes, soon Lysander stood naked and proud, the sun shining on his tanned skin and sculpted muscles.

"Corporate sharks shouldn't look so much like ancient Greek gods," she muttered.

His laughter said he'd heard her. "From a king to a god, what is next?"

She didn't answer, too busy watching him walk toward her, his sex already half mast. His defined muscles bunching with each movement of his legs.

"You look like you're ready to eat me," he said, a sexy smile slashing across his face.

What that tone and look did to her. She had no hope of nonchalance in the face of such masculine beauty and strength.

Sexual hunger washed over her.

Rowan was not complaining. Not even a little. She reveled in the way her body responded to him.

"Getting my mouth on you sounds about right," Rowan said throatily.

Only this man brought out the Siren in her.

Eschewing the handrail and steps, he lifted one long powerful leg over the side and turned, bringing the rest of his lower body into contact with the water. But he didn't sink under.

Instead, he sat on the side, and indicated his now fully erect length with his hand. "Have at it."

He didn't need to ask her twice. Rowan's mouth watered for a taste of him. She turned and propelled herself across the hot tub, only stopping when she was between his knees.

Kneading his hard thighs with her hands, she said, "Don't mind if I do."

Leaning forward, she nuzzled into the skin between his hip and his torso. Taking a deep inhalation of his masculine scent, Rowan exulted in her right to this intimacy no other woman was allowed.

For now.

Ignoring the sting of that reminder, she took in the hint of the sandalwood soap he used in the shower mixed with the distinctly intimate fragrance of his skin here. This amazing god of a man was hers.

However temporarily. Right now? His body was her playground. And she meant to play to her heart's content.

She bit gently on his inner thigh and then laved the spot with her tongue. He groaned and she smiled to herself before turning her head to do the same to his other leg. She was oh so careful not to touch his balls or his hard shaft.

His big hands gripped her on either side of her head. "What you do to me, *yineka mou.*"

His woman. Oh, she liked when he called her that. Way too much.

Until one of them said otherwise, she was his. Just like he was hers.

Mouthing along his skin she traveled down his rock hard thigh toward his knee before making the reverse journey up his other leg. She stopped with her mouth pressed against his groin and kissed him there.

With a sound of sexual frustration and desire, his hips canted upward.

She loved teasing him, pushing him to the limit of his vaunted self-control. Loved even more when she managed to shove him right over into pure animal lust.

Right now, she didn't want him taking over though, so she slid her lips toward his sex. Dipping her head so she could lick delicately at his scrotum, she rubbed her cheek against his erection.

~ ~ ~

Of their own volition, Lysander's fingers tunneled through Rowan's silky hair. He was not at all disappointed when the tie that held it on top of her head in a messy bun was dislodged.

Her hair fell around her face and shoulders in a silky red curtain, brushing over his thighs like a mass of butterfly wings. The soft skin of her cheek brushed against his fully erect cock while she licked at his aching balls.

It all felt so damn good, but he wanted more.

Why had he rejected her sexual overture earlier? There had been nothing in his inbox so damn important it could not wait.

When he realized he was hiding from her and the way she made him feel, he'd told himself to man up and go claim his woman.

Only now, she was claiming him.

Sensually. Perfectly. Irrevocably.

Ignoring the implication of that last thought, he directed her head up so her mouth was right there. Warm air puffed over the head of his dick, her lips only millimeters away.

Heavy lidded, her beautiful blue eyes teased him with sensual promise. "Do you want something?"

"Your mouth on me," he said in a guttural voice.

This woman drove him to the brink of his restraint. She licked up and down his turgid pole, kissing the head with an open mouth, but not taking him inside her wet heat.

"What are you doing to me?" he demanded.

In answer, she grasped him in her wet hand and pulled along his length. It wasn't enough.

"I want your mouth."

"Then take it." She opened her lips wide, but left her mouth poised at the end of his cock, her gaze challenging him.

His grip on her head tightened and he pulled her face forward, lust riding him, but he watched for any sign this wasn't what she wanted. She gave none, flicking her tongue out to lick the pearls of precum gathering on the end of his dick.

Pushing forward, he tugged her onto his cock and she hummed with approval, but she didn't move her head. What did she want?

Her hands came up and gripped his. She tugged, directing him to guide her. A wildfire of lust burned through his control and he pushed to the back of her mouth. When he touched her throat, she didn't gag, but swallowed, pulling him deeper and he was lost.

He thrust in and out of her mouth, the sounds of arousal she made around his thick flesh increasing his need until he was nearly mindless with it.

"I'm going to come," he warned her.

Her hands gripped his harder while she sucked and swallowed. Ecstasy exploded in a cataclysm of pleasure as he shot his ejaculate down her throat. Everything in his brain went white, his body transported by a level of rapturous pleasure he'd never experienced with anyone else.

Only this woman.

She licked him clean as she pulled her head backward and then turned to nuzzle into his hand.

That small act of affection set his libido right back to overdrive. He grabbed her waist and yanked her up until their lips came together in harsh passion. She wrapped her arms around his neck and kissed him back with violent fervor.

Surging up, he brought her body with his and she wrapped her legs around him. Somehow, he got them out of the hot tub and into the bedroom and he laid her on the bed, uncaring about the water from her body soaking the duvet.

"You are beautiful in this, but even more gorgeous out of it." He tugged her bikini bottoms down her legs.

Rowan lifted up on her elbows, giving him easy access to the clasps on her top's straps, but made no move to take it off herself.

It took him only seconds to undo both the neck and back straps so he could pull the wet and clinging fabric away from her generous mounds. His mouth watered as nipples beaded and flushed with arousal were revealed to his eyes.

He dove down and took one of those tempting little gems into his mouth, sucking and nipping while he kneaded the fleshy mound around it. His dick was still hard despite shooting like a geyser down Rowan's throat. Nudging her thighs apart, he rubbed his hard flesh against her wet folds and clitoris.

Moaning, she thrashed beneath him and splayed her legs wider in invitation.

Surging up her body, he took her mouth as he invaded her. Rowan's slick wetness allowed him to seat himself in her tight channel in a single hard thrust.

She cried out and he stilled.

Squirming against him, she broke the kiss. "Don't you dare stop, Sander. It's too good."

The words were all the permission he needed to start pounding into her. He had no intention of stopping until they were both wrung out from pleasure. She climaxed quickly, but he was nowhere near done with her.

He pulled out only to renew his attack on her senses with his mouth and hands. He'd wrung three orgasms out of her before he pushed his now throbbing cock deep inside her and brought them both to a final climax that was a near out of body experience.

~ ~ ~

Rowan didn't know what had come over Lysander, but there was no hope of leaving their suite to explore the cruise ship that first night. He kept them both naked and played her body like the sexual virtuoso he was, building her arousal and need over and over again.

She woke the next morning with a delicious ache between her legs and a not so delicious one in her lower back. She groaned as she went to sit up, the bed beside her empty.

No surprise there. Lysander rarely stayed in bed until she woke.

After going to the bathroom, Rowan slipped a sleeveless t-shirt dress over her nakedness and gingerly made her way into the main room.

Lysander sat at the dining table, his computer in front of him and a cup of coffee off to the side.

His eyes narrowed on her. "What's wrong?"

"Nothing. I'm just a little sore from all our calisthenics yesterday."

Jumping up from the table, he crossed the room in a few long strides. "Sore? Where? Did I hurt you?"

"No, Sander, you did not hurt me." She reached up, offering her lips for a kiss. Which he took. Gently.

She smiled. "You gave me a surfeit of pleasure. My muscles just aren't used to the exercise."

"You haven't been like this before," he said, accusingly.

"We tried a couple of positions we haven't before. Both of which I enjoyed very much by the way." She'd lost count of her orgasms long before they fell into exhausted slumber in each other's arms. "After breakfast, I'll have a soak in the hot tub."

Which sounded way too good. Maybe hot tub first and breakfast after.

Lysander shook his head. "I'll get you some pain reliever and order a massage for you."

"Ooh, I can't wait to see the spa. I bet it's gorgeous on a ship like this."

"You won't be going to the spa." He walked toward the bedroom. "They will come here."

"There's no point in being on a cruise ship if I spend all of my time while at sea in this suite," she called to his retreating back.

Not waiting for him to reply, she picked up the phone and ordered some breakfast.

Lysander returned from the bedroom and held out two gel caps. Rowan took them gratefully and the glass of water he offered with them.

Tossing the pain relievers into the back of her mouth, she took a gulp of water to swallow them down. Then she picked up the phone receiver again and pressed the button to connect to the spa.

A chipper voice said, "Serenity. What can we do for you today, Mrs. Baros."

Rowan flushed hot all over at being called Mrs. Baros, but didn't correct the other woman. She didn't know if it had been a mistake or if the suite was booked under Mr. and Mrs. Lysander Baros.

"I would like to book a massage sometime today if that's possible."

"Of course, but we can send a masseuse to your suite if you'd rather."

Was this a conspiracy, or something? "That won't be necessary. I prefer to come there for the service."

"Of course, Mrs. Baros."

They finalized the details for the massage while Lysander stood glowering beside her. "I don't like you wandering the ship on your own."

"I very much doubt I'll be alone. Unless you aren't planning to have the security specialists shadow me like they do back in Athens?" she asked hopefully.

"No chance."

"Then I'll hardly be *wandering the ship on my own*, will I?" She rolled her eyes. Billionaires. They didn't see the world like regular people.

"I would prefer to be with you when you leave the suite."

"No." She wasn't hanging around in the suite all day while he worked. "Not going to happen."

"You do not want to spend time with me?" he asked. "You were keen enough for my company yesterday."

Rowan blushed at the reminder of how ardent she'd been in their lovemaking.

"But then we were having sex," he continued, his dark brow raised. "Weren't you the one who said this relationship had to be about more than sex if you were going to move in with me?"

"Let me clarify. I'm happy for you to join me whenever you have the time to do so, but I will not limit my expeditions outside of the suite to those times."

"Call Serenity back and book a couples massage."

"You want to get a massage too?" she asked.

"I would prefer doing so in the comfort of our suite."

Rowan sighed. "All right. I'll ask them to come here."

"You want to go to the spa." His tone was the same as when he'd acknowledged she wanted to go on a cruise.

He didn't understand why she wanted it, but he was willing to indulge her. She hoped.

Rowan looked at Lysander appealingly. "Yes."

"Then book our couples massage at Serenity."

"They might not have another masseuse available," she warned. "I read that days at sea are busy for the spa and other onboard services."

"They will accommodate us, Rowan."

"Because we are staying in the private suite of the owner of the cruise line," she guessed, feeling silly for even doubting they would make room in their schedule for her and/or Lysander.

"Perhaps, but the room is booked in my name."

And billionaire tycoon Lysander Baros was kind of a big deal.

"You really want to get a couple's massage with me?" she asked.

"Yes."

Unable to help the grin spreading over her face, Rowan called Serenity again and made the arrangements. Lysander checked his phone while she was talking to the receptionist.

"Klaus will be up momentarily with your breakfast," he said after she put the handset down.

"Not a steward?"

"No one but our security staff and the approved cleaning staff while in their company will be allowed into the suite."

And apparently staff from the spa if they so desired. She'd bet they got vetted before being allowed up though.

"Isn't that overkill?"

Lysander looked at her like he didn't understand what she was asking.

"Is this how you usually travel?" she asked, trying to fathom living like this all of the time. "With a layer of security between you and the rest of the world?"

"Unvetted people are not allowed access to where I am staying, no."

"Doesn't that get exhausting?"

"I don't do the vetting."

"Of course, you don't." She still thought it sounded like it had to be mentally taxing to be so security conscious all the time.

If she really was Mrs. Baros, that would be her life as well. Rowan did her best to ignore the small voice inside her that insisted it would be worth it.

Chapter Twenty-One

Lysander found the couple's massage in the spa surprisingly enjoyable. The ambiance was tranquil in a way the suite could not match regardless of its luxury.

He was glad to see Rowan walking without a single twinge afterward because he had more plans for her in the bedroom later. Or on the balcony...or perhaps they would make use of the sturdy dining table.

However, she looked tired, so he convinced her to return to the suite for a nap. If the sleeping came after he stripped her, spread her legs and tasted the honey between them until she screamed out her climax, he certainly wasn't complaining.

The massage was not the last of Rowan's attempts to draw him into life on-board the cruise ship. Not that she tried to convince him to join her. It was simply that she refused to stay in the suite, and he wasn't about to leave her on her own with a ship full of men looking for a vacation romance, a one-night stand, or both.

Rowan was warm and engaging with everyone they talked to, her beautiful smile on display constantly, her gorgeous body drawing attention wherever they went. Not that his irresistible lover noticed the lascivious stares of other men.

The only thing that kept Lysander from getting homicidal was how totally focused on him she remained.

Right now, they were in the buffet dining room. Not that they were eating here. He drew the line at communal eating from self-serve cafeteria style lines. No matter how high the star rating was for the food here.

It was late in the afternoon on their second day at sea and the large dining area was practically empty.

So, despite having a perfectly adequate study in which to work, Lysander's laptop was on the table in front of him while Rowan read on her tablet in a chair beside the window. She could have read on their balcony, but she wanted to *enjoy the view from this deck*, or so she said.

How much view she was enjoying with her eyes fixed on her eReader was up for interpretation.

An Asian family played Mahjong behind them, the click-clack of tiles interspersed with talking and the occasional sound of victory or groan of defeat.

A few tables away a woman worked on some kind of art project with little gems she painstakingly placed on the picture in front of her. She told every passersby and server who came within six feet of her table about it. Each one heard about how she planned to leave it there for them to finish at the end of the cruise, like she was doing them a favor.

She hadn't tried to talk to him, or Rowan. No doubt because of Klaus and the other three security specialists surrounding them.

Lysander wasn't distracted. He was too focused for that, but he was aware. He noticed everything because that kept him on top and moving forward.

Which was why it really pissed him off that he hadn't realized his father had been wooing a partner investor for his company. He'd discovered that reading a report from his corporate investigator this morning.

Lysander hadn't talked to Rowan about it yet, but he now understood why getting access to her stocks and the piece of real estate was so important to his father and half-brother.

A deal worth hundreds of millions of dollars was at stake.

"Seriously?" Rowan harrumphed.

Lysander looked at her over the top of his computer. Her gaze was on the woman doing the craft project.

"What is it, *glikia mou?*"

"That woman," Rowan hissed and shook her head. "She keeps talking about leaving her gem painting here for the staff to finish, like they have all the time in the world. Like they're on vacation just because she is."

"Why does this bother you?"

"I don't know." She blew out an annoyed breath. "It's just, she's so clueless. No fewer than three servers have tried to politely tell her they don't have time for stuff like that and she keeps overriding them like she knows their workday better than they do."

"And this annoys you?" Lysander asked.

"Yes."

"Why?"

Rowan sighed and looked off into the distance, like she was asking herself that same question.

"It reminds me of traveling with the Andinos," she said after a minute of silent reflection. "They're always so dismissive of anyone paid to serve them in any way."

"She thinks she's doing something nice."

"Right. I know. That makes it worse." Rowan's blue gaze met his, her lovely mouth turned down in a frown.

"Because she wants to be kind?"

"Because she's proud of herself for being *kind* when in fact she's being extremely rude."

Lysander shrugged. "The world is full of oblivious people."

"You're right. And she's not being rude on purpose. Not like my ex and his family, who think they are above anyone not as wealthy as they are."

"They treated you like you were less than because your father's company is not as big."

"I had no voice in that household and I only realized how bad it was after I left, when suddenly I got to make all the choices about my life and how I spent each day." She put her tablet down in her lap and stared out at the ocean again. "My father used me as a bargaining chip to leverage better deals with a company out of his league beforehand."

Was Richard Johnson part of the land development? Rowan was right that her father wasn't a big enough player to be involved in the investment partnership. He would have to have his investigator do some more digging. Knowledge was power.

And Lysander always acted from a position of power.

"Are you ready to return to our suite?" he asked.

Rowan gave him a once over that had his cock hardening. "That depends? Are you done working?"

"I can be."

"Then yes."

~ ~ ~

Their first port of call was Cabo San Lucas.

Rowan had picked an adventure on camelback for their excursion, and she loved it. The guide was voluble and full of anecdotes about the area and its history.

At one point, Lysander made it clear he thought she was paying too much attention to the handsome young man.

Rowan shook her head and laughed at her tycoon. "I'm supposed to hang on his every word. He's telling us about the area."

"And his family. And his own studies at university."

"Which is exactly what makes him so interesting. He's sharing more than what I could read in a guidebook. Thank you so much for finding someone like him to be our guide."

Lysander defrosted enough after that to ask a couple of his own questions.

Afterward, they stopped for lunch at a restaurant in the courtyard of a beautiful building in downtown Cabo San Lucas. Rowan found the outdoor seating charming and spent time people watching while Lysander checked his messages and email on his phone.

Their security detail used a table on either side of them, but there were plenty of other tourists and locals for Rowan to observe. Careful not to get caught staring, she soaked in vignettes of human interaction around her.

But when the fried cheese appetizer arrived, Rowan's attention went to her empty tummy and the delicious food.

"I've never had anything like this," she said.

Lysander hummed an assent, his attention fixed firmly on his phone as he typed away on the screen.

She warned, "If you don't watch out, I'll eat it all."

She'd been expecting something like cheese sticks, but this was cheese flattened and fried, to be eaten like chips with the plethora of salsas in little dishes on the table.

"I'll wait for my lunch," Lysander said without looking up.

At the reminder that more food was coming, Rowan had one last bite of the cheese and then pushed the platter away.

Taking a sip of her fresh coconut water, Rowan noticed a familiar woman walking purposefully between the tables.

Adele Fournier stopped beside their table. "Lysander, darling, if you are that bored with your companion, perhaps you should have answered my latest text."

Lysander's head jerked up. "Adele."

His expression was filled with surprise and in no way welcoming. Rowan was gobsmacked. What was the supermodel doing here? Was she on a shoot? What were the odds?

"You don't mind if I join you?" Adele asked, finally deigning to acknowledge Rowan with a lift of her perfectly shaped eyebrows.

Neither Rowan, nor Lysander had a chance to reply before the model sat down in one of the empty chairs at their table.

Rowan opened her mouth to say she did in fact mind, but didn't get a chance.

Klaus was already there physically lifting Adele from the chair. "This is a private lunch, Miz Fournier. Let me help you find another table."

"What? Klaus, release me at once. Lys, tell this behemoth to take his hands off me."

"I prefer *goon*," Klaus said in an aside to Rowan, inexorably guiding the still complaining supermodel away from the table.

"Why bother inviting me to Mexico if you're going to treat me like this?" she shouted at Lysander over her shoulder as she struggled against Klaus's grip. "I won't stand for it."

Lysander ignored the mini temper tantrum happening behind him and snagged Rowan's gaze with his own. "I did not invite her. I don't know what she's doing here."

"How did she know you were here though?" Rowan asked. "I thought no one was supposed to know where we are."

"That is something Klaus is no doubt attempting to find out."

Klaus, who apparently preferred Rowan's teasing moniker of goon over behemoth, was speaking quietly to Adele as he marched her out of the restaurant.

"Did she let you know she planned to be here too?" This all felt a bit surreal.

How was Adele Fournier, of all people, in Cabo San Lucas the same day they were?

"If she did, I don't know about it. I deleted her contact info from the text app we used to communicate." Nothing about Lysander's demeanor said he had wanted to see the other woman, much less done as she claimed and invited her to join him in Mexico.

"She doesn't have your number?"

"No."

"I do."

"Yes."

Rowan sighed. "One word answers? Really?"

"What would you like me to say?"

"I'm not sure. You were dating her last year."

"You know that is not true. I explained it to you. She was my plus one at a few events. We were not dating."

"You never answered when I asked if you have sex with her." It had been implied, but not spelled out.

Suddenly, Rowan needed things to be crystal clear in her mind.

"Does it matter?"

"Yes." She could do one-word answers too.

Lysander looked amused rather than worried. "Jealous? You were married to Cyrus for most of the time Adele acted as my plus one."

Rowan pretended not to hear the question about her jealousy, not sure if that was what she was feeling, or not. She'd never been jealous before. Not even when she'd discovered her husband had a mistress and a string of extra-marital lovers.

Angry and betrayed? Yes. Jealous? No.

"Did you?" she pressed.

"Once."

"Oh." Although Rowan had no doubt that Adele wanted to be in Lysander's bed, the feeling had not been mutual.

"Before I learned she'd been with Cyrus."

Okay, so maybe not so much he hadn't wanted the supermodel, but Lysander didn't want his brother's ex. Only that didn't make any sense, because he definitely wanted Rowan. He showed her several times a day.

"Oh." Rowan cringed inwardly at how inarticulate she sounded.

"I don't talk about women after I've had sex with them, but the fact it only happened one time and she was my companion on multiple occasions should tell you something."

It wasn't about Adele being one of Cyrus's exes. Lysander was clearly implying that the sex hadn't been great. Simply put, Lysander hadn't been that into the supermodel.

That's what the admission told her. Also, Lysander was a gentleman, if a ruthless one, because he didn't say anything overtly disparaging about Adele. Which he could have done to make his case seem more believable.

But the Greek billionaire didn't think he needed to make a case. He expected Rowan to believe him. Which she did.

Relief washed over Rowan, though really...it should not matter. But it really did.

"She calls you Lys."

"Which I have instructed her multiple times not to do. It is one of the reasons I stopped having my assistant set her up as my plus one."

"Your assistant set it up?"

"Yes."

"Huh."

"I would never have personally invited her to Mexico if I wanted her here to attend a function with me. I would have left it up to my staff to arrange."

Did he think Rowan had doubts? She didn't. "I believe you," she spelled out, in case he needed her to.

He nodded, like he expected no less, but the tension around his eyes lessened. "Before you, I didn't do relationships that mattered. Hell, I didn't do real relationships at all. I had sexual liaisons that lasted months without a single personal discussion between us."

Not like them. Rowan and Lysander talked about everything from their favorite music, food, and entertainment to family and their hopes for the future.

"What we have, it's real." It wasn't a question. Rowan knew it was.

Whether it was temporary, or not, what they shared went deeper than convenience, or even sexual hunger.

"It is."

The rest of their lunch went uninterrupted. When Klaus returned from seeing the supermodel on her way, he did not sit back down, but remained standing on alert until they were ready to leave.

No other uninvited guests would be sitting at their table.

Chapter Twenty-Two

On their fourth day aboard ship, Rowan finally convinced Lysander to have dinner in one of the specialty restaurants.

Their security team filled the tables around them, but Rowan didn't let that bother her. Soaking in the over-the-top luxury décor, including a chandelier the size of her car, she observed the other diners and the waitstaff interact.

"You like to watch people," Lysander remarked.

"I always have. I'm an extroverted-introvert. I'll chat with people, but I'm just as happy to watch them from the background."

"You are hardly in the background here."

No. He'd made sure they had a very nice table with a view of the ocean. Other passengers kept sending them looks. She supposed with their entourage of bodyguards, they looked famous, or something. People probably wondered who they were.

"We are a little conspicuous in how our group takes up five tables." Two security personnel sat at each of four around them. And then of course there was their table.

"Klaus and the others could be eating in the privacy of their suite if we were eating in ours," Lysander pointed out, not so helpfully.

Rowan gave her lover a look. "Maybe they would have eaten here anyway."

"I'm sure they would not."

"Let's ask them." Which is what she did, proving her point.

Every single one of the security personnel said they preferred eating out in such a controlled environment.

Huh.

That wasn't something Rowan had considered, how guarding Lysander aboard ship, even when he was out of the suite, was easier than back in Athens.

"Don't get smug," Lysander told her, but his eyes were smiling, even if his lips weren't.

Dinner was delicious and even he had to admit it. Which she made him do before she would leave the table.

"You are a challenge." He shook his head. "Why do I put up with you?"

"Because you like my body?"

"I like more than your body. And I adore your body, let's be clear on that."

"Hmm, I think I like being in the adored category."

"You are the only one that ever has been."

This man.

When he said things like that, Rowan had a hard time remembering he didn't want long term commitment. Only maybe he'd changed his attitude about that just like she had?

It was such a tantalizing thought that Rowan had to banish it very firmly. If she let herself hope for a future with Lysander and he decided he was done with her a month from now, her heart would break.

She'd never had a broken heart before, but she'd known plenty of emotional pain with her family and her ex. She suspected Lysander had the power to devastate her in a way no one else had.

~ ~ ~

Their next day at anchor was in Puerto Vallarta where she'd chosen a private tequila tasting, followed by a fiesta lunch with traditional dancers and a discussion of their history in the area.

Although Rowan was not a big drinker, she easily discerned the vast difference between aged tequila and what she'd had in margaritas when she'd gone for a drink with coworkers after work.

She listened avidly to the lecture on the process of harvesting the agave and distilling the tequila.

She even got to meet a *jimadore*, one of the skilled workers who harvested the agave. They chatted for nearly half an hour, and he proudly told her about the long line of men in his family who had been *jimadores*.

After lunch, they visited the cathedral, which was awe inspiring and had such an air of peace, she'd put off leaving as long as possible.

That peace was shattered when they stepped outside.

"Lysander, fancy seeing you here." It was Cyrus.

"You have a serious security breach," Rowan said to Lysander. "First your ex and now mine."

"What the hell are you doing here?" Lysander demanded of his half-brother.

"Taking in the sites like you, I would imagine."

"Cut the crap, Cyrus. I don't know how you tracked us down, but your intrusion is not welcome."

"Oh, was this little trip to Mexico supposed to be a secret?" Cyrus asked. "I'm sure I saw some speculation about it with a picture of you two."

Lysander said a very ugly word. Rowan didn't chastise him. She was feeling the same way.

Until the threats to him were dealt with, Lysander was at risk. She hated knowing someone had revealed their whereabouts. Could it have been Ariston Spiridakou? But why would he?

Lysander did not bother replying to Cyrus, but ushered Rowan into one of the shops on a side street near the cathedral. His security team prevented Cyrus from following them or speaking to them.

Unless he wanted to shout and that was below her ex-husband's self-perceived dignity.

Rowan didn't want to let Cyrus showing up spoil the day, but tension made her shoulders tight as she and Lysander perused the shops. He even helped her find tchotchkes to give her coworkers back in Athens. Which she found endearing.

However, she didn't relax again until she and Lysander were strolling along the sea walk, marveling at the view of the harbor and her annoying ex was nowhere in sight.

"There is someplace I would like to go, if you're up for one more stop?" Lysander asked. "I know Cyrus showing up put a pall on the day."

Rowan shook her head vehemently. "No. It has been an amazing day and I've really enjoyed how you've indulged my inner tourist."

"Then you don't mind one last stop?"

"Not at all." Since Rowan hadn't had anything else on her itinerary, she had no idea where Lysander wanted to take her. "What did you want to see?"

"It's a surprise."

The surprise turned out to be a jewelry store with a team of jewelers on hand who either worked on new pieces or made adjustments to jewelry bought on site. They did all of this at their workbenches in full view of the store.

Rowan was fascinated.

"Here, try this on," Lysander said from beside her.

A large pendant with a gorgeous teardrop shaped Mexican fire opal and a cluster of diamonds at the top dangled from a gold chain in his hand.

He'd been over on the other side of the store, and she'd assumed he was checking his phone again. Apparently, he'd been perusing the jewelry cases.

"It's beautiful," Rowan breathed.

"An opal that size is very rare, but especially a fire opal," the jeweler who she'd been watching fashion a one of a kind ring said.

"It reminds me of your hair," Lysander said as he fixed the chain around her neck.

The shimmery red stone with streaks of opalescence settled just above her cleavage.

Brandishing a mirror, the salesclerk said, "Ah, it is almost as lovely as the woman wearing it."

Rowan looked at her image in the mirror and something tugged at her heart. Not because of the necklace, but because of the expression on Lysander's face beside hers.

There was more fire in his eyes than in the opal.

"It suits you, *yineka mou*."

For some reason, Rowan's throat was too tight to make speech so she nodded. She loved it.

"There it is finished." The jeweler held up the ring he'd been working on. "You must try it on."

The ring was a delicate brushed gold band that came together in two hearts entwined around a much smaller fire opal than the one in her pendant.

Rowan was going to refuse when Lysander took the ring. Grabbing her hand, he lifted it so he could slide the golden circle onto her left ring finger.

In Greece that ring finger had no particular significance, as wedding rings were worn on the right hand, but in America, it symbolized promises and engagements.

"Perfect," Lysander said.

Rowan's gaze snapped up to his, but he was looking at the ring on her finger.

"Such a special woman deserves this special ring," the jeweler said.

It was then the haggling began. Lysander might be a billionaire, but he was also Greek. After several minutes of a spirited back and forth, Rowan walked out of the store wearing both the pendant and the ring.

"There you are," a feminine voice filled with satisfaction said when they walked out of the shop.

Klaus and the other guards immediately surrounded Rowan and Lysander, preventing Adele from getting close.

She gave them a moue of displeasure. "Really, this is too much. You all know me. I am no threat to Lys. I am a world renowned model."

She was a world class pain in the backside. However, she'd found them the first time, learning their itinerary once she knew what ship they were sailing on wouldn't have been hard. What Rowan couldn't figure out was why she was here in the Mexico to begin with.

Finding it difficult to believe that such a famous woman would be stalking Lysander, Rowan's mind chewed over the possibilities.

Was she here on her own? Or had someone put her up to it? Rowan knew who she suspected for the latter. Cyrus or Baptiste Andino. Cyrus being at the top of her list because he too had shown up today.

But honestly? What could her ex-husband hope to gain?

"Whoever put you up to this won't be able to protect you if I decide to torpedo your career," Lysander said to Adele, echoing Rowan's suspicion that the supermodel was not in Mexico on her own agenda.

Fear flashed in the model's eyes, but then she smiled and gave Lysander a flirty look. "Don't pretend you don't know why I'm here."

"Leave, Adele, now. And I won't make a call to your agency. Don't leave and you won't be able find work in an online clothing catalogue."

Tears welled into the other woman's eyes and she looked at Lysander reproachfully. "Stop threatening me. I haven't done anything wrong."

"Now." That was all Lysander said.

But Adele spun on her heel and walked away.

"Follow her," Lysander said to Klaus. "I want to know if she meets up with Cyrus."

So, he suspected collusion between their exes as well.

Whatever was driving her, they didn't see Adele Fournier again.

CHAPTER TWENTY-THREE

Rowan woke early to an empty bed. Again.

She forced herself to get up and throw a cotton sundress on. After running her fingers through her hair to try to tame it, she left the bedroom, determined to join Lysander for breakfast.

He had been working longer hours since Puerto Vallarta and she'd barely seen him the last couple of days. He'd been so busy, he didn't even bother to complain, much less offer to join her, when she left their suite to experience all she could of shipboard life.

They ate dinner together, but even then, he spent more time on his phone than talking to her.

She couldn't help wondering if he was growing bored with her, or maybe Cyrus's shenanigans were getting to be too much for Lysander, Mr. No Drama Here Folks, to deal with.

He hadn't come to bed until almost three in the morning last night and they hadn't made love. He'd slept only a few hours before getting up again.

Would this be their new norm when they returned to Athens? And if it was, how was she going to handle it? They'd spent more time together before the cruise than they did now, on their so called vacation.

A vacation necessitated by security, but still.

How long before he asked her to move back into her apartment? Or before she decided to go to save herself the grief of rejection?

Today, she was inserting herself into his day, if only for breakfast. Rowan found him on the balcony, looking at his phone. Of course.

There was a cup of coffee on the table, but no food.

"Good morning. Have you had breakfast?" she asked.

Lysander looked up from the small screen, satisfaction covering his handsome features. "We've got them."

"Who them?" Then she realized. "The people threatening you? They've been arrested?"

"Better." His dark gaze burned with purpose. "I dismantled the business. The men in power are now scrambling to keep their homes and cars as their company implodes. Newsflash: they won't."

"You're going to bankrupt them personally?" she asked. Wouldn't that make the men's hatred for him more personal too?

"It is already happening."

"But won't that make them want to kill you even more?"

"They won't have enough money to buy toys for their children's birthdays much less hire muscle to come after me."

"That's awful. Children should not suffer for their parents' bad judgment."

"You would prefer I left these men with the resources to remain a threat to me? To you?" The way he said *to you* told Rowan that she was one of the main reasons he was being so thorough in dismantling the business empire and the lives of the men who ran it.

Which meant what? He *wasn't* bored with her? She cautioned herself not to read too much into it. Apparently, he'd been protective of her before they'd ever shared a bed.

"No," she denied quickly. The thought of something happening to Lysander made her sick. "But can't you make sure their children don't end up on the streets?"

Even as she asked the question, she realized how foolish she sounded.

Lysander didn't look at her with judgment or pity for her naivete though. His gaze burned, but no longer with the zeal of revenge. Something else entirely smoldered in those brown orbs now. Something she was afraid to name.

"Come here," he said.

With zero instinct to protest, Rowan obeyed and as soon as she reached him, Lysander pulled her into his lap. Cupping her face, he kissed her. She wrapped her arms around his neck and kissed him back.

Things were heating up nicely when he broke the kiss. She made a sound of protest.

But he pulled back until their gazes met. "You are something special."

"I don't think so."

"I know so." He kissed her forehead and then her lips again, but chastely this time. "For you, *glikia mou*, I will arrange something for the wives and children."

It took several seconds for Rowan's scattered senses to understand what he was referring to. Protecting the children.

Worry that doing so would leave him vulnerable instantly filled her heart. "It will have to be resources those men can't leverage. They can't be left with any way to hurt you."

"Do not worry. When I take an enemy down, they stay down."

She shivered, but it wasn't with fear. It was with arousal. His power and confidence were a total turn on for her.

"You like that."

She shrugged. "Maybe. A little. You're like a tycoon superhero."

The kiss he gave her sent all of Rowan's concerns for the future into the ether, right along with her ability to string two thoughts together.

They spent the entire day at sea together, but never once left the suite and rarely left the bedroom, unless it was to spend naked time together in the hot tub.

~ ~ ~

When the ship arrived in Ensenada and they disembarked, Rowan was not surprised a private car waited to take them to the Kumiai Reservation. And she was relieved to see no sign of either Adele or Cyrus.

She was stunned, however, when they were joined by a group of tourists from the ship after they got there. Lysander had not booked a private experience.

It was because she'd said she wished they could be regular tourists, just once. It had been a throw away comment when she was drowsy after lovemaking.

Despite his clear desire to give her what she'd said she wanted, Lysander's security team created a wall between them and the other guests while they listened to a fascinating lecture on the history and traditional ways of the Kumiai people in the museum.

Well, she listened. He took a call outside. He returned only after they had been ushered to a long dining table and everyone else had been given samplings of food that would have been staples of the Kumiai people's diet in the past.

He frowned when he reached the table to find all the seats around Rowan taken. And not by his security. She'd told the men to stand back unless they planned to participate. Nothing was going to happen to her with them looming against the wall less than six feet away.

Rowan sat across from an older couple who acted like they were on their honeymoon, only to tell her they'd been married for decades. They were near the end of the table where a man from the ship who was supposed to rate the tour for their cruise director was seated.

He was friendly, but not as outgoing as the man to her left, who seemed intent on learning everything that there was to know about her. Rowan evaded answering his probing personal questions, wondering if he was some kind of paparazzi on Lysander's scent.

"So, you're single?" he asked, his gaze well south of her eyes.

Not a reporter. A guy on the make.

Rowan wasn't interested and she opened her mouth to say so, but Lysander's hand landed heavily on her shoulder, surprising her into silence.

"No. She is not," he gritted out.

Oh, somebody's phone call hadn't gone well.

"Is this a shipboard thing, or something more?" the man asked.

Wow. That was so bold, and deluded, Rowan had to stifle a laugh.

"None of your business. There's an empty seat further up the table. Take it." Lysander's voice was deep with unspoken menace.

Without another word, the overly friendly man vacated his chair.

Lysander sat down and then took Rowan's hand in his. He didn't try any of the food, but he paid attention when the guides spoke. He even turned his phone to silent.

Afterward, they learned how to make a woven pendant for a necklace. Rowan's reeds broke almost immediately, and the teacher had to weave extra fibers onto it so she could continue. Naturally, Lysander's turned out perfectly. And he finished first.

"Show off," Rowan muttered as she worked on finishing hers off.

He cocked an eyebrow. "Do you want me to help you?"

"No."

But he got up to lean over her anyway and his hands came around hers, guiding her fingers in twisting the wet reeds. Rowan's breath sped up and her body reacted predictably to his touch and nearness.

She was just grateful no one else seemed to notice.

Until the woman who'd sat across from her during the food demonstration said, "What a sweetheart." And her husband gave Lysander a knowing look. "Yep. Sweet. That's the word."

He knew exactly what her Greek billionaire was doing to her, and his expression said he approved. With the way he cuddled his wife during the lecture from the elders, he no doubt did.

There. She got it.

Needing a break from Lysander's nearness before she combusted or begged him to take a walk behind the buildings with her, Rowan joined in the traditional dance. She was out of step as often as not, but she had fun.

It didn't give her the reprieve she'd needed though because her tycoon watched her with burning eyes.

She was more than a little grateful for the private car on their trip back into the city. As soon as he closed the privacy panel between the back and the front, Lysander made good on the promise of those heated looks.

Chapter Twenty-Four

They stopped at the city center on the way back to the ship and did some shopping.

"These are all tourist shops along this road. Are you sure this is where you want to shop?" Lysander asked her for the third time as they entered a store filled with t-shirts.

"Yes." Rowan perused the t-shirts and chatted with the salesperson in Spanish.

Her Spanish was rusty as she had little chance to use it in her life in Athens, but the salesclerk didn't seem to mind. She told Rowan about her family, including her younger sister who was attending college.

Rowan insisted on getting matching t-shirts for herself and Lysander.

"I will never wear it," he warned.

"Didn't anyone ever tell you to never say never?"

"No."

She smiled and shook her head. "We'll see."

She picked out t-shirts for Iona and her husband as well.

"Who are those for?" Lysander asked.

"Your mom and her husband."

"You think my mother will wear a souvenir t-shirt?"

Rowan shrugged. "Probably to paint in."

Lysander's mother was an artist. Her paintings were swaths of color and no discernable shapes, but they made her happy. And Rowan really liked the few that Lysander had hanging on his walls.

They always evoked emotion.

"And where do you think her husband will wear his?"

"He probably won't, but it would be rude to get her one and not him."

Lysander just shook his head, but his lips tilted in an almost smile that turned into a full on grin when he said, "Perhaps we should get one for my father."

Rowan laughed, but Lysander went on the hunt for the tackiest possible t-shirt with the loudest colors to buy for Baptiste. She didn't suggest getting anything for Baptiste's latest wife, not even as a joke.

Rowan was sure the woman would never be anything but a sore spot for Lysander.

They visited handbag shops and Rowan bought a roomy beach tote that would bring back memories of this trip when she used it.

Her feet were sore by the time they returned to the ship and Lysander suggested she soak in the hot tub while he got some work done. "I would like to join you, but dismantling a company takes time. Things that were not critical are now because of the timing."

Oh. That made sense of the days he'd worked pretty much nonstop. They weren't a harbinger for the future, except when he had a big deal going. And Rowan could live with that, so long as it was the exception and not the norm.

Besides, when he was done, he'd taken a full day off to be with her. *In bed,* that little voice of caution in her head reminded her.

While their relationship was more than sex, at her insistence, it existed because of their explosive sexual attraction. Letting herself forget that would set her up for heartache.

Unwilling to dwell on those thoughts, even if she also refused to ignore them, Rowan changed into her bikini.

She came out onto the balcony to find a bowl of frozen grapes and a carafe of chilled water (with ice, which was her preference and an American habit she'd never let go of) on the hot tub ledge.

Lysander.

She gave a swoony sigh she never would have let anyone else hear.

He could be so incredibly thoughtful.

When her body was fully relaxed from soaking in the bubbling water, and she felt refreshed from the frozen grapes and crisp, cool water, Rowan got out. Taking the remainder of the carafe of water with her, she settled on a lounger. The sun felt so good on her body, she just lazed while her thoughts drifted and she watched the people come and go on the deck two stories below.

She should have brought her tablet out to read, but couldn't make herself get up and retrieve it.

"You have forgotten to frost the glass again," Lysander said as he pressed the button.

"I didn't forget." In fact, she'd had to turn it back to clear.

Given his way, Lysander would have left it frosted twenty-four-seven.

"And yet here you lie with your luscious body on display."

"Thank you."

"For what?"

"Calling my body luscious." She smiled up at him. "You make me feel beautiful."

"You are beautiful, and I do not want my goddess of a lover the subject of other men's fantasies."

Rowan laughed. She could not help it. "You are always so complimentary." But she was no goddess. "The only way anyone can see me up here is if they have better than normal vision, or binoculars and who is going to go to that effort?"

The sun loungers were set toward the back of the balcony as well. The angle would make spying on her even more difficult than the distance. If anyone were that keen to do so.

"You refuse to see yourself as the irresistible woman that you are."

"As long as you can't resist me, that's all that I care about."

"I cannot. Why do you think I am out here when I still have a dozen unopened emails marked urgent in my in-box?"

Warmth curled through her all the way down to her toes. "Am I keeping you from your work?" she teased.

He growled and started stripping off his clothes.

~ ~ ~

It was more difficult than Rowan expected to return to normal life in Athens. Well, her new normal, living with her sexually irresistible billionaire lover.

Living with Lysander wasn't the hard part and hadn't been since the day she moved in. Getting used to his demanding work schedule was. He'd always worked longer hours than her, but since they got back from Mexico, he worked less from his office in the villa.

There were days the only time she saw him was when he woke her in the middle of the night to make love.

With one exception, the evenings he made it home for dinner, his attention was entirely on Rowan however. That exception had been when they had dinner with his mother and her husband. The older couple had been charmed by the kitchy t-shirts, though Iona's husband had clearly been more impressed with the aged tequila Lysander gifted him.

Most nights they ate alone at the villa. However, sometimes Lysander took her to A List restaurants, where he always arranged for some sort of private dining for them, so they could eat undisturbed.

Being the center of his intense focus was becoming as addictive as his lovemaking, but on the days she didn't see him at all, Rowan spent way too much time thinking.

Before their trip to Mexico, they texted back and forth throughout the day. Since returning to Athens, he often took an hour, or longer, to reply to her texts. There were times when she hadn't asked a specific question that he did not reply at all. And, unlike before their trip, he rarely initiated a text conversation.

Their first week back, she'd chalked that up to him being busy catching up with work. By the second week, the pang she got when her texts went unanswered felt more like a knife jab to her tender heart.

She'd been so sure she could keep deep emotions out of this thing between them.

Boy, had she been wrong about that.

Rowan's heart was fully engaged while she suspected Lysander's was still firmly locked behind the protective barriers he'd never let down.

The fear that he was growing bored with her that she'd managed to banish aboard ship came rushing back. She'd convinced herself that his distant behavior had been due to how busy he'd been de-toothing the bite of his enemies.

Now, she questioned that belief.

Because there were no more enemies to crush into corporate dust and he was just as distant, if not more so. At least he hadn't told her about any further threats. She only had one bodyguard assigned to her now though. Which supported her belief that it was back to life as usual for her tycoon.

Was he hers though? While he still called her *glikia mou*, his sweet, he hadn't used the more intimate and meaningful term *yineka mou*, his woman, since their return to Athens. Not even during sex.

Deciding she needed a break from her disquieting thoughts, Rowan accepted her coworker's invitation to get drinks after work.

"I believe Mr. Baros plans to be home this evening," Klaus told Rowan when she informed him of her plans.

So, he had time to text his security, but not her? "If he expected me to be there as well, I'm sure he would have let me know."

Ignoring Klaus's frown, Rowan joined her coworkers on the walk to the bar. Drinks turned into dinner, and she didn't get back to the villa until after nine.

She found Lysander in his inner sanctum, a laptop on his lap and the television playing international news in the background.

"You have a real problem relaxing, don't you?" she asked with a shake of her head as she dropped her oversized purse on the floor near one end of the sectional.

Lysander glared at her hold-all like it offended him. "Are you going to leave that there?"

"Until I need it again tomorrow morning, yes. Why? Is there somewhere else you'd rather I put it?"

"Your closet." His tone implied she should realize that was the appropriate place to store her bag.

Her pleasant buzz from her evening was disappearing like the mist. "Okay," she said drawing out both syllables. "If it bothered you, you could have said something before."

"I'm saying something now."

"Noted." She picked up the bag and headed out of the room to stow it upstairs in her closet.

"Where are you going?" he asked, sounding surly.

"To put my purse away, like you so pleasantly told me to."

"Petulance doesn't become you."

"I'm not being petulant. I *was* being sarcastic because you have *not* been pleasant, but I am also adult enough to respect your wish for me not to clutter your home with my things. Now, if you will excuse me."

"It is your home too." Take surly and add it to supremely irritated and throw in a dash of righteous indignation and that was Lysander's tone now.

Her patience about used up, Rowan gritted her teeth and nodded. Because right now? This didn't feel like her home so much as somewhere she was staying on sufferance.

"Put it away later. I haven't seen you all day."

"It's hardly the first time this week." It was in fact, the first time he'd gotten back to the villa before she went to bed since the weekend. "I'm going to take a shower and then go to bed."

"Is that an invitation?" He stood, his masculine presence dominating and intense.

Her lady parts immediately pulsed with heat and wetness flooded her panties.

Refusing to show how easily he got to her, she forced a casual shrug. "You're welcome to join me. You can work on your laptop while I read."

There. He could put that in his pipe and smoke it.

She dropped her hold-all on the floor of her side of the massive walk-in closet before kicking off her shoes and stowing them with her others. Passing Lysander on her way through the bedroom, she did her best to ignore his brooding presence. Which was a total failure as every nerve ending in her body sparked from his nearness.

Rowan stripped and tossed her clothes in the hamper before stepping into the oversized marble shower. Turning on the water, she jumped as cold water showered down before the hot water followed. It was only a second or two, but it woke her up.

"No need to punish yourself with a cold shower," Lysander drawled as he stepped in behind her.

"I'm not," she groused. "I've done nothing that needs punishing."

"You know I work long hours. I expect you to be here when I am."

Heck to the no. "If you want my company, you can *ask* for it."

"I told Klaus I would be home tonight. Are you saying he didn't inform you?"

"No." Rowan put her head back under the cascading water and closed her eyes. "So, why didn't you come home?"

"Because I was invited by my friends to join them for drinks."

"You could have gone for drinks with them any other night."

Lathering her hair, she opened her eyes to glare at her arrogant lover. "And you could have texted me instead of Klaus if you wanted my company."

Even if Lysander had texted *her*, Rowan would like to think that it was not a given she would have blown off her plans with her coworkers. Not in the habit of lying to herself, she acknowledged she probably would have. She missed spending time with her lover.

"Do not be childish. You knew I was going to be here."

That was the second time he'd implied she was behaving immaturely, and man did it prick her temper. "There is nothing puerile about expecting common courtesy."

His dark gaze traveled over her body, leaving heated sensation in its wake. "No, there is nothing childlike about you. I should have said obstinate."

"You think I'm being stubborn?" she asked, her own gaze narrowed even as her vaginal walls contracted with the need to have him inside her.

Ignoring her body's cravings, she rinsed her hair and waited for his answer.

It came in the form of his hands cupping her breasts. "Yes, I think you were foolishly stubborn to spend the evening with your friends when you could have been here, doing this with me."

CHAPTER TWENTY-FIVE

"Sex isn't everything." And they'd agreed it wouldn't be the only thing between them either.

"But it is something good," he said. "Something special."

Rowan wasn't feeling all that special, no matter how intensely her body reacted to his touch. Not with him expecting her to abandon her plans at the last minute because he was going to be unexpectedly available.

Even worse if it wasn't unexpected. If he'd known from the beginning of their day that he would be back at the villa in time for dinner.

Unaware of her tumultuous thoughts, Lysander took the conditioner bottle from her hand. "Let me."

He squirted a fair amount in his hand and then worked it through her hair, massaging her scalp until she relaxed against him. Then, showing he remembered her routine, he began to wash her body with soapy hands.

As she might expect, her lover paid particular attention to her breasts and between her legs, but he also knelt so he could thoroughly clean each of her feet, rubbing his fingers between her toes.

Pleasure zinged straight from her feet to her core. Shocked at how good that felt, she gasped.

"You like that, *yineka mou?*"

The physical sensation mixed with his use of that endearment made Rowan's knees buckle. He caught her. Of course. Rising, he snaked one arm around her waist and used his other hand to help rinse the conditioner from her hair.

When he was done, he turned off the water and moved them from the shower. He dried her off before handing her a fresh towel to wrap her hair in, turban style. He took a lot less time drying his own body than he had hers.

"I have to dry my hair." She hated going to sleep with wet hair. Not only did it look like an awful mess in the morning, but it soaked her pillow.

"Sit down. I'll do it."

"Are you trying to make up for being so grumpy when I got home?" She sat on the stool in front of the built in vanity.

"Maybe I just enjoy spoiling you." He carefully pulled the towel from her head and then used it to wick more moisture away from her hair.

Afterward, he gently brushed her hair and then used her blow dryer to finish drying it.

"You're awfully good at this." Was it something he'd done for all of his lovers? Only it was the first time he'd dried *her* hair.

"I watched you and I am a fast learner."

"Are you saying you don't make it a habit to dry your girlfriend's hair?" she pressed, unsure why it felt so important to know.

"You are the only woman I have done this for." His lips turned down in a frown and his jaw hardened.

"You don't have to do it. I can finish."

His head and shoulders moved like he was shaking off his thoughts. "No."

Okay, then.

He finished and ran his fingers through her long red hair, smoothed by his near professional attention to it. "It is so silky."

"That's what the conditioner is for," she quipped.

Leaning down, he slid his hands over her breasts and cupped them. "I think it is you. Everything about you is soft to my touch. Your hair is silk, your skin smooth like satin."

Heat bloomed in her cheeks. "You're awfully complimentary."

He didn't answer, but his big hands gently kneaded her fleshy curves. Mesmerized, she watched him watch her in the mirror as her nipples beaded and the flush of arousal washed over her chest and up her neck.

His own dark gaze flared with arousal.

"These luscious, pink buds are irresistible." Lysander plucked at her nipples, sending sensation thrumming through Rowan.

More wet heat gathered between her legs, and she squirmed, that feeling of emptiness in her core growing.

"You respond so beautifully to my touch, *yineka mou*." He leaned down and kissed her neck, his tongue tasting her clean skin. "It makes me very happy."

Warmth unfurled inside of her and her annoyance at his grumpiness melted under the heat of their combined arousal. The scent and heat of his body surrounded her as he straightened, once again meeting her gaze in the mirror. The storm raging through her reflected in the depth of his eyes.

Rowan turned her head so she could rub her cheek against the join of his hip and torso, her hair brushing over his erection. The engorged flesh jumped, and he groaned.

His hands tightened on her swollen mounds, his fingertips pinching her rigid nipples to the point of pain before brushing over them in a soothing caress. "I want you."

"You have me." She turned on the stool and licked a pearl of pre-ejaculate off the tip of his hard penis.

She reveled in the salty sweetness of him before he came, swiping over his slit a second time.

His hands came to rest on her head on both sides, his hold firm but not harsh and he pressed against her parted lips with his erection. "Open."

She did as he ordered, and he pushed the head of his shaft into her willing mouth. She sucked and laved him with her tongue.

They both loved this. Him in her mouth, Lysander controlling their pleasure. Rowan didn't touch his sex with her hands, but let him use her mouth as he liked while she steadied herself with a hold on the rock hard muscles of his thighs.

He pushed a couple of inches of his oversized sex into her mouth. "That's good. Take me."

Rowan sucked, welcoming him as he stretched her mouth wide, pushing toward the back of her throat. He didn't gag her, but pistoned in and out of her as she sucked and licked. She tasted his copious precum as his erection swelled and became even more granite-like.

He was close and her mouth watered with anticipation of his climax, but he pulled out of her mouth with a pop. Saliva covered her chin and glistened on his rigid sex.

Confused by his withdrawal, her gaze flew upward. A look of carnal need hardened his features.

Lysander grabbed her under her arms and jerked her up and kissed her almost brutally before spinning her body around. He positioned her so she faced the mirror, her torso leaning forward on the vanity, balanced on her forearms.

His features cast in vicious desire, he shoved into her dripping channel from behind. She was tight and he was big, so even though she was slick with arousal, shock reverberated through her at the intimate intrusion.

Rowan watched in the mirror as his handsome face reflected the savage ecstasy he found in their connection.

He hammered forward, drilling his big erection deep into her body, stretching her vaginal walls as only he ever had. Lysander hit that spot inside her that brought so much pleasure and she moaned.

"Mine," he growled as he bottomed out against her cervix.

Mild pain mixed with pleasure, intensifying it to near unbearable levels. And she shuddered as her own climax loomed. He pulled back before pounding into her again, repeatedly sliding over her G-spot and battering her cervix with his bulbous head.

When she thought she might pass out from the tension inside her, Rowan finally detonated. Bliss exploded from her core outward, forcing a scream from deep inside her.

He shoved forward, going rigid as his penis pressed against the very depth of her as he gave a guttural shout, their orgasms feeding off each other. He filled her with his heat, making her shudder with renewed pleasure, his grip on her hips so tight it would probably leave bruises.

The idea of having his fingerprints on her skin sent another wave of ecstasy crashing through her before she collapsed forward, boneless in the aftermath of the mind numbing bliss.

She was too wiped afterward to protest when he carried her to bed without showering again. But also...she liked the scent of them together on her skin. She'd bathe in the morning. Maybe.

~ ~ ~

Lysander got into his office before dawn, wishing he could have stayed in bed to make love to Rowan again, but there was too much to do.

He had lost out on not one, but two lucrative deals while playing tourist with Rowan in Mexico. Since starting his company, he had never let the ball drop when there was profit to be made.

Not until taking the maddening woman as his lover.

Why had she insisted on going to dinner with her coworkers when she knew he was at the villa waiting for her? He didn't like this feeling of need she engendered in him. Lysander controlled every aspect of his life and his business until Rowan Johnson had offered him her body.

He'd begun to work shorter hours until making the inexplicable choice to take her on the cruise in Mexico she'd always wanted. When logic would dictate he spend the time out of country at one of his other headquarters.

Lysander hadn't minded the money he lost by not being available to orchestrate the deals. And that had bothered him a hell of a lot more than losing the money. He ran a multi-billion dollar company. He had thousands of employees relying on him keeping that company in the black.

How could one small woman disrupt the discipline of a lifetime?

He'd thrown himself into work since returning to Athens, determined to make up for his slacking, only to leave his office early the day before. Because he'd missed her.

And she had opted to spend the evening with others.

It pissed him off. And it...hurt. Though he would never admit that particular vulnerability.

Her schedule was a lot more flexible than his. She should accommodate him. Why did she not realize that?

~ ~ ~

"Excuse me? You think we're going where?"

Rowan couldn't quite wrap her mind around what Lysander had just said.

"Japan."

"Another time, I would love to travel to Japan with you." Or anywhere else. "But I just got back from a vacation. I cannot take another one. Especially right now."

"I will get one of my employees to cover for you," he said dismissively.

"No. That won't work this time." Like in most nonprofit organizations, employees like her wore many hats.

Rowan had been put in charge of their major fundraising gala. The director believed the connections she'd made during her ill fated marriage could be leveraged to bring in bigger donations than ever before.

She agreed, but needed to reach out personally to donors and sponsors for that to work.

"You were okay with it in order to take the cruise you wanted. Now you refuse so we can spend the next two weeks together."

That was so unfair. Did she want to spend two weeks apart? No. But that did not change the fact that Rowan could not leave Athens right now.

"First, you did not actually give me a choice. Second, we left Greece for safety reasons and the choice to go on a cruise was subordinate to that. Third, I am up to my ears in planning the biggest fundraising gala of the year. A temp cannot fill in for me right now."

"What do you expect to raise at the gala? A couple hundred thousand? I'll donate it."

"Money is not always the answer, Sander. I have a life I am building that means something to me."

"And I mean nothing to you?"

"What do you want to mean to me?"

He shook his head. "Is it so much to ask? I have offered two valid solutions and you refuse both," he said, refusing to answer the question that really mattered. Naturally.

"Neither of your solutions work for me. My role is to build connections with donors. Having someone fill in for me won't do that. You making a large donation won't do that either. What happens next year?"

"I am not going to commit to millions of dollars of funding for your org in order to convince you to come on a single trip with me."

"I'm not asking you to. That is my point."

"I cannot send someone else on this trip in my stead. Thousands of employees and investors rely on me to do my job."

"I know."

"So, why are you being so difficult?"

Rowan grabbed onto her patience with both hands. He wasn't being thick on purpose. It was just hard for the billionaire to understand that regular people had important commitments too.

Maybe she wasn't going to impact thousands of people by putting on a successful fundraising gala. That didn't mean it didn't matter though.

"I'm not trying to be difficult. I am your girlfriend, not your mistress. My life does not revolve around your schedule."

Lysander's expression went completely emotionless and a steel door slammed down between them with a clang that echoed in her heart. "I have never once said or implied that you are my mistress."

Oh, crap.

That was the wrong thing to say, but it was accurate, darn it. Lysander wanted her to drop everything, like a mistress who was expected to be on call twenty-four-seven, always willing to accommodate the important man's plans.

"I don't know why you are making such a big deal out of this, anyway. If this trip is anything like your work schedule since we returned to Greece, we'll barely see each other."

"You'll be there for me. Every night. In my bed."

Oh, heck no. "Are you sure mistress isn't the word you're looking for?"

"It is not just sex. Knowing I will be able to hold you through the night gives me comfort."

Something melted inside Rowan. That was no admission of love, but it was something much deeper than body driven lust. Maybe she could make the calls from Japan, although the time difference would make that problematic.

Lysander shook his head again. "Never mind. Clearly your job takes precedence. I will not ask you to compromise it again."

"Lysander."

But he'd turned away and was already making a call on his phone. That he was telling his personal assistant to take Rowan's name off the flight manifest, and cancel the employee fill in for her, made her heart twinge and her brain ignite with irritation in equal measure.

He had been so confident she would drop everything, he'd already made the arrangements for her to travel with him.

It was actually the pain in her heart that prevented her from chasing after him and apologizing. Or, worse, offering to figure out a solution that didn't leave her org hanging.

This arrangement of theirs was supposed to be no strings. More than sex. Less than love. No long term commitment.

Only her heart was already involved, bound to him with indelible bonds he had never asked for. And that scared her to death, considering how determined Lysander was to keep their relationship in the temporary category.

Rowan knew with everything in her that her feelings wouldn't end when their arrangement inevitably did.

Chapter Twenty-Six

Lysander joined Rowan for dinner but refused to be drawn into personal conversation.

Honestly, she didn't try very hard. Rowan was too busy attempting to come to terms with the reality that she was deeply in love with a man destined to let her go.

Seemingly unbothered by her own silence, Lysander reverted to his cold, ruthless business mogul persona. When the last dish had been cleared away, he excused himself to make some calls.

Eventually, Rowan went to bed. Alone.

How had they gone from the idyllic bubble they had ended the cruise in and brought back to Athens to this? Him so cold and aloof? Her so freaking doubtful and confused?

It took her a long time to fall asleep and when she did, it was fitful, not deep. She woke immediately when Lysander climbed into bed beside her.

He didn't reach for her like he usually did. Not to hold her. Not to initiate lovemaking. He didn't shift restlessly either. His breathing was even and deep. Was he already asleep?

Unwilling to let the distance between them remain, Rowan slid across the bed and put her hand on his chest. He said he found comfort by her presence in his bed. Maybe they both needed that comfort tonight.

Rowan softly kissed his shoulder and then sighed as she snuggled into his side. The unresolved conflict between them didn't stop her needing his closeness.

Lysander exploded up and came over her, kissing her with angry passion. Rowan's desire rose to match his and the kiss grew carnal as their hands roamed over each other's bodies.

"You are not my mistress," he growled as he surged into her body. "Even if you allowed me to support you in every way, you would be my girlfriend, not a woman kept in the sidelines of my life."

Oh, man. He expected her to talk now? To think?

Only, he clearly didn't, because when she tried to speak, he kissed her, pushing her words back with his thrusting tongue.

They were up for hours, sating their bodies with sensual pleasure in silence broken only by their erratic breathing and moans.

Every time she tried to talk, he stopped her. And part of her was grateful because Rowan was afraid she'd confess her love if she managed to say anything at all.

~ ~ ~

Lysander was gone when her alarm woke her the next morning. She didn't remember him kissing her goodbye, but that doesn't mean he hadn't.

Rowan had fallen into a deep, exhausted slumber after their last bout of love-making. She moved sluggishly as she got ready for work and would have been late if she had to make her own breakfast.

Thankfully, she didn't.

Helen had made her breakfast. It was waiting on a tray when Rowan came out of the bathroom, drying her hair with a towel. Vacillating between whether to text Lysander and tell him to have a safe trip, or not, she ate as she got dressed, and did her hair and makeup.

Finally, she decided to send the text.

Rowan: *Tell your pilot no risky flying. I'll miss you. Be safe.*

Lysander: *I will miss you too.*

Rowan didn't know what possessed her to send him three heart emojis. She wished she hadn't as soon as she'd pressed send. How obvious was she?

Her phone rang.

It was Lysander.

She answered. "Hello."

"I apologize for undervaluing your commitments."

Air whooshed out of her and it took her a moment to respond. "Thank you."

"You are important to me. Therefore, so are the things that are important to you."

"You're important to me too." Why were her eyes stinging?

"Sometimes we will have to be apart, but I will make a more concentrated effort to spend time together when we are both in Athens."

Rowan was too choked to say anything.

"Losing lucrative deals because of the time I spend with you is not going to sink my company."

Her laughter was watery. "Is that what happened?"

"My focus on business has not been what it was before we got together."

"I'm sorry."

"I am not."

"Oh. Well, then I'm glad." Did that mean he was coming to love her too?

Or was he resigned to being a less efficient corporate shark for the time they were together because he knew it wasn't going to last?

"I have to go."

"Okay."

"Do not forget to eat your breakfast. I reminded Helen to prepare you something."

"She did."

"Good."

"I..."

He waited in silence, but Rowan couldn't say anymore. She wanted to say those three little words that meant so much. Only she knew she couldn't. It wouldn't be fair to Lysander to burden him with her love when she'd agreed to a no strings affair.

That included bindings of the heart.

"I have to go too," she finally said. "Or I'll be late to work."

"Do not work too hard," he replied.

"You either." Though she doubted that admonition would be listened to.

They said goodbye and he disconnected the call, but he texted her later that afternoon to let her know when his plane was taking off.

Longing to be with him filled her. Had she been foolish to refuse to go with him? Their relationship had an end date. Why hadn't she jumped at the chance to spend every minute with him that she could?

Because for however long this thing between them lasted, she wanted it to be real. More than sex. More than his convenience. For however long they had together, they would be in a relationship.

A relationship in which they were equal partners.

It wasn't just about pride. It was about value. Her heart would shatter when they broke up, but she wasn't going to let him stomp all over it while they were still together.

Lysander would never play the role her family or her ex-husband had in her life. He would not dictate her schedule or her behavior.

Yes, she would compromise for him because he was worth it.

No, she wouldn't subsume herself to him, because *she* was worth it.

When her coworkers invited her for a drink after work again, she refused. As much as she did not look forward to going home knowing Lysander would not be there, she was not in the mood to socialize either.

She ate dinner by herself in the den, sitting on the sofa where Lysander usually sat and let the news play in the background as she read a book. Tired from the night before, she went to bed early, but found it impossible to go to sleep.

Until she pulled one of Lysander's dress shirts out of the laundry and put it on. Hugging his pillow and surrounded by his scent, she finally fell asleep.

Her phone woke her.

She fumbled for it and when she saw the unknown number, she considered not answering. What if it was Lysander? He should still be on his jet ten thousand feet in the air though.

Still, something told her to answer. So, she did.

"Hello."

"*Yineka mou*, did I wake you?"

"Sander. It is you. I thought it was, but I didn't recognize the number."

"Satellite phone on the jet."

"Oh."

"I wanted to wish you goodnight."

"Shouldn't you be sleeping? Tokyo is six hours ahead of Athens." She'd looked it up.

"Did you have a good day?" he asked, rather than answer.

Typical Lysander. He probably thought he didn't need sleep like other mere mortals. Arrogant, exasperating...*amazing* man.

"Yes. I found two big sponsors for the gala and talked to a couple interested in opening a branch of the organization in Thessaloniki."

"That is good news. What you do is important."

"Thank you for saying that." She put the phone on speaker so she could get more comfortable. "Tell me about what you're hoping to do in Japan."

"It is not a hope. It is a plan."

"Of course it is. And what is this plan?"

"I told Cyrus and my father that they would lose the deal they had going with the Japanese conglomerate. I worked on it while on the cruise, but I need to go to Tokyo to finalize the details."

"You're inserting your company in their place?" she asked. "Was that what you meant by losing money? Did you have to make concessions to push your father and Cyrus out of the deal?"

No wonder he'd been frustrated with her for refusing to go with him. Lysander was making this trip for her sake, to show his father and half-brother he'd meant business when he warned them off of her.

He was protecting her.

"No. My company brings more to any partnership than Andino Enterprises could. The conglomerate is happy to adhere to my requirement of cutting ties with my father's company in order to make a deal with me."

She didn't doubt it. She still felt guilty though. Because whether he was making money on this deal, or not, he was there for her.

"I wish you'd told me this was the deal you were using to show your father and Cyrus that they can't mess with me."

"I am glad I did not. You would have come with me out of guilt and there is nothing you have to feel guilty for. I take care of my woman."

Why did hearing him call her that in English send tingles through her body.

"You took very good care of me last night."

"As you did me." His voice had gone husky and deep.

She groaned. "I'm never getting back to sleep, am I? I should have just gone with you. I'll be a zombie by the time you get back."

"You will sleep tonight, I will make sure of it."

"How do you plan to do that?"

"Put your phone on speaker."

"It already is."

"Good. Now put both of your hands on those mounds I like to play with so much."

"What? We aren't doing phone sex, Sander."

"Cup them."

Why were her hands moving? As if he was moving them like puppet arms on a string, she undid the buttons on his shirt so it fell away to expose her breasts and the rest of her body.

"Are you doing what I said?" he asked.

"Yes."

"Rub your thumbs over your nipples. They're already hard like lush raspberries, aren't they?"

"Yesss." She drew the word out as pleasure washed over her. "Please tell me no one is there listening to you have sexy times over the sat phone with your girlfriend."

"No one gets to hear your sexy little sounds but me, *yineka mou*."

His voice went directly to her core, making it pulse, making her ache for him.

As if he could read her mind, he said, "Do not touch your vulva. Your hands stay where they are for now."

"Sander..." Was she begging? Or just saying his name?

She didn't know. Any more than she knew why she was doing what he said and why doing it was turning her on so much. She could feel the wetness gush between her legs, soaking her panties.

"Pinch your nipples."

She did and moaned at the sensations coursing through her.

"Harder."

"I can't." But she did and it sent a jolt of electric bliss straight to her center. Her vaginal walls contracted.

She needed him. But he was on a jet, hours and miles away.

"Slide your right hand down your body and into your panties. You wore panties to bed didn't you?"

"Yes."

"You don't when I'm there."

She didn't wear anything to bed when he was there beside her. Neither did he.

Her fingertip grazed over her clit and she gasped.

"Does it feel good, *glikia mou*? Do you know why I call you that?"

"Because I'm sweet?"

"Because you taste like honey."

"My mouth?"

"Mmm...and the nectar that flows out of your delicious little vagina."

She said a word she never ever said and he laughed.

Dipping into the wetness he was talking about, she drew it up to her clitoris, making it slick and easy to slide her fingers over. It felt, so, so good.

"Roll your nipple between your fingers while you touch your clit."

She did as he said, his voice sending sensations along her nerve endings just like her own fingers. Her orgasm took her by surprise, pulling a cry from her throat as her body bowed on the bed.

Even more surprising was the yawn that followed.

"Will you sleep now, *glikia mou*?"

"Yes," she said on a sigh, having an entirely different reaction to him calling her his sweet now.

It felt very personal. Very intimate.

"Good. I need to go take care of the hardon listening to you and imagining you in our bed gave me."

"Send me a picture," she joked and then yawned again.

She fell asleep almost immediately.

The next morning she found a text from him. No words. Just a picture of his still hard penis covered in his ejaculate.

Even as the image shocked her sensibilities, her mouth watered for his taste. She sent him her own text. A close up of her pursed, slightly parted lips with the words, *my mouth is watering*.

He texted back almost immediately. *I miss you.*

Not *I miss your mouth*. Not some kind of sexual inuendo. But *I miss you.*

This time when she sent him three heart emojis she didn't second guess herself.

Chapter Twenty-Seven

Even though Lysander was in Tokyo and Rowan was in Athens, things were more like they'd been right after she moved into his villa.

They texted each other throughout the day. Even the six-hour time difference didn't stop him replying immediately to her messages, so she did her best not to send any after ten at night in Tokyo.

He video-called her every day at lunch to talk and every night at bedtime for other things. Which meant he was waking up at four a.m. to do it. Sometimes, he told her how to touch herself. Sometimes, she told him what she wanted to do to him, what she wanted him to do to her.

She always came and so did he. Rowan fell asleep afterward feeling wanted and cherished.

On Thursday, she went to her director and asked if she could work remotely the following week. Since she was working pretty much fulltime on the fundraiser, she didn't need to be in the office for her usual appointment sessions with the women her organization served.

The time difference wasn't insurmountable for her to make the phone calls she needed to, and any in-person meetings could be scheduled for the following week. She really could not have been gone the past few days, but she'd worked hard to make working remotely possible for the remainder of Lysander's time in Japan.

After some discussion and making sure her bases were covered, Rowan's director agreed. Then, she called Lysander's personal assistant and let the woman know of her plans to fly to Japan on Friday's redeye. Sounding relieved, the woman insisted on upgrading Rowan to first class and promised to arrange her return with Lysander on the company jet.

"I would have booked first-class if there had been any seats available, but there aren't," Rowan told her.

No, she wasn't a billionaire, or even a multi-millionaire like her ex-husband, but the divorce settlement was still sitting in her bank account, and she was prepared to use it to get herself to Lysander.

The PA harrumphed. "We'll see about that."

"Thank you for trying." She wasn't convinced anything could be done, but if anyone could get Rowan a first-class seat to Japan, it would be Lysander's terrifyingly efficient personal assistant.

"I'm very glad you will be joining him, Miz Johnson. He is so much happier when he gets to see you."

"Are you saying Lysander has been cranky this past week?" she asked, a little surprised. He was always warm and charming, not to mention dead sexy, on their phone calls.

"He is very much like his old self," the personal assistant said neutrally.

"Old as in before what?" Rowan pushed.

"Before you moved into the villa."

Rowan shouldn't be surprised her coming into his life had impacted Lysander. Moving in with him had changed her. A lot. She woke looking forward to every day. Even bad days were better because she got to see him.

Still, knowing he was different *did* surprise her. It also gave her hope.

She loved him. Could the change in him mean that he loved her too? Even if he did, would he ever allow himself to admit it?

Vulnerability was not her billionaire boyfriend's strong suit.

Rowan was making notes on a list of potential donors when her mother called and invited her to lunch. Her first instinct was to refuse. She didn't want to miss her video call with Lysander.

But then Vanessa Johnson pulled out the guilt card. "I have barely seen you this trip."

Before Rowan left Cyrus, when her parents had come to Athens, she had lunch with her mother a couple of times a week, at least. And since they had travelled in the same circles, Rowan had seen her parents at all of the social events.

Rowan had only been in Greece at the same time as her parents twice in the last year. The first time, she'd been learning to navigate her new life and thought she'd successfully found a compromise with them by attending a few social functions.

However, she and her mother had only had lunch together once the last visit and none at all this time.

"We're flying home soon. I wanted to see you before we do. Is lunch too much to ask?"

"No, of course not." She didn't particularly miss seeing either of them, but apparently her mother felt differently. "I'll warn you now that if you bring up Cyrus even once, I'm getting up and leaving."

"Really, Rowan, I didn't raise you to be so acrimonious."

"I mean it, Mom."

"Very well, no discussion of your husband. Can we make it an early lunch?"

"Yes." Rowan preferred it. She would text Lysander and ask him to video call her a little later than usual.

"Good." Her mother named a time and restaurant to meet.

"That's not your usual haunt," Rowan said with surprise.

The restaurant had an excellent chef but was small and out of the way. Not a spot to see and be seen.

"It's quiet and we'll get a chance to catch up without having to worry about paparazzi or running into acquaintances."

Particularly having an early lunch like her mother planned. Their social set didn't do lunch at eleven in the morning. That was for brunch and brunch wasn't done midweek at small eateries, no matter how good the chef.

Was it possible that her mother actually just wanted to catch up with Rowan? The idea made her smile. Although her mother's criticism had hurt over the years, she had also been the one parent who showed interest in Rowan's life both before and after her wedding to Cyrus.

~ ~ ~

Rowan was taken to the table where her mother waited as soon as she arrived at the restaurant. The dining room was practically empty.

Most Greek city dwellers ate lunch much later, but the restaurant served breakfast as well, so they probably saw little benefit in closing down when they might pick up some tourist business.

Not that it was anywhere near the typical tourist areas. Okay, she didn't know why they stayed open for what had to be a very quiet couple of hours midmorning. Did it really matter?

Rowan only knew she preferred the lack of people in case lunch didn't go well with her mother.

As soon as Rowan reached the table, Vanessa Johnson stood to hug her. It wasn't effusive and warm like Iona's hugs, but it wasn't entirely social fake either.

Vanessa sat down, carefully spreading her napkin over her lap. "I've already ordered our lunch."

"Okay."

"Do not look at me like that. I am your mother. I know the food you like to eat. I ordered you fish."

Rowan loved seafood and had to smile. "Thank you."

Although since coming to Greece, she'd learned that people typically ate their largest meal for lunch and lighter fare for dinner, Rowan wasn't surprised to see a small grilled fillet served with a leafy salad when their food was brought to the table.

Her mother had never approved of her curvier figure. Rowan was comfortable with her body though and that was all that mattered. Okay, it was pretty nice that Lysander found her sexually irresistible as well.

Without an iota of embarrassment, she requested pita bread to accompany her lunch and pointedly ignored her mother's look of disapproval.

Carbs were not her enemy.

Lunch was surprisingly pleasant without her mother making a single overt criticism. Discussion moved to her parents' upcoming social engagements and her mother asked if Rowan planned to attend any of the functions the following week.

"No." Rowan didn't explain that she would be out of the country.

That would only lead to more questions that would result in an argument if answered.

Any sense of pleasantness went right out the window when Rowan spied a familiar and unwelcome figure approaching their table. Adele Fournier.

Vanessa stood with a smile for the supermodel. Adele kissed the air beside both of Rowan's mother's cheeks in greeting before the women both sat down.

This had been a setup.

Unaccountably disappointed, Rowan tossed her napkin on the table and stood up.

Her mother grabbed her arm with surprising strength, halting her. "No. Do not leave. I invited Ms. Fournier to join us, and she took time out of her busy schedule to do so. The least you can do is listen to what she has to say."

"No." Rowan tried to pull her arm away.

"I really think you are going to want to hear what I have to say," Adele said, the French lilt to her voice no mask for the malice in her eyes. "More to the point, you will want to see what your mother has to show you."

"I doubt it."

"Rowan, please," her mother pleaded, appearing, and sounding genuinely distressed. "I'm only trying to look out for your best interests."

Whatever her mother's reasons for setting up this lunch, Rowan had no doubts that whatever drove Adele Fournier's presence, it was not altruism on the model's part.

The woman had stalked them to Mexico. Now she was going to...what? It was that *what* that had Rowan pausing. Forewarned was forearmed.

As much as she had no desire to spend a single minute in the other woman's company, Rowan cared too much about Lysander not to at least try to figure out what game the supermodel was playing.

While Rowan wouldn't believe Adele if she said the sky was blue, that didn't mean others wouldn't and Rowan wanted to protect her lover from being blindsided by the media if she could.

Her phone buzzed with a text. "Excuse me," she said to her mother and turned away before she swiped to see the message.

Sander: *I miss you.*

Love fluttered in her chest. They were going to video call in less than an hour, but he missed her because it was going to be thirty minutes later than usual. Or maybe he just missed her. Full. Stop. Like she missed him.

Smiling, she typed a reply telling him so before sending a second text to her bodyguard. She tapped on another app and then slid back into her seat before setting her phone on the table, face down.

Rowan looked at Adele with all the skepticism she felt. "You have something you want to say?"

"It's not going to be easy to hear." Rowan's mother patted her arm. She frowned. "Or to see."

Rowan wanted information, so she tamped down her immediate inclination to tell her mother she would never believe a word spoken against Lysander. Especially if it was said by Adele, a bunny boiler, if there ever was one.

"Adele is here as a favor to..." Her mother's voice trailed off. "To our family," she finally said. "But before she says anything, I need you to look at some photos."

Vanessa pulled out her phone. "These were taken this last week in Tokyo."

Tension stiffened Rowan's spine. This was going to be some kind of claim about Adele and Lysander in Tokyo. Someone had done their homework or had access to privileged information they shouldn't.

Yes, sometimes Lysander's trips were made public, but there had been nothing in the media, much less his company's social media alluding to his current visit to Japan.

Lysander wasn't just going to be annoyed; he was going to be raging.

"I admit I was surprised Lys asked me to join him on such short notice, but I had a break in my schedule." Adele's gallic shrug was perfectly executed to imply a lack of tension.

Maybe the woman should try acting as well as modeling.

Too bad she was playing to a wholly unreceptive audience. Even if Rowan and Lysander had still been arguing, she wouldn't have believed the narrative the supermodel was trying to create.

He had said no other women as long as they were together, and she had believed him.

She still did.

The calculating gleam in the model's eyes was subtle, but she was watching Rowan with unmistakable interest to see how she reacted to the story. Rowan *did not* roll her eyes, but it was hard.

"Let me see the pictures." She put her hand out for her mother's phone.

With a sad, almost pitying expression her mother handed over her smartphone. "Swipe right for additional photos."

The first one was a picture taken from a distance of Adele and Lysander looking very chummy while the model took a selfie with her phone.

"That's the café on the ground floor of the hotel we stayed in. The next picture is the hotel."

Rowan swiped right. Sure enough the next photo was a picture of the two of them in front of the hotel, again taken from a distance. There was a picture of them at dinner and one of the model coming out of a hotel suite Rowan assumed was the one Lysander was staying in.

There were even a couple of photos of them kissing, one through the sheers on his hotel suite windows taken with a telephoto lens. It was rather grainy and only someone who knew his build well would suspect the man in the picture was Lysander.

The other was in the back of a car, the driver standing beside the open door making the shot possible.

Each had a time and date stamp that coincided with the previous week. Rowan quickly sent all the photos to her own phone before handing her mother's back.

Chapter Twenty-Eight

"Where did those pictures come from?" Rowan asked, finding it difficult to keep her fury in check.

"Cyrus hired a private investigator to follow Lysander," her mother confided. "He didn't trust his brother not to be using you to get back at him."

Rowan almost laughed. If anything, it was the opposite way around.

Only, it wasn't. Not really. And never really had been. Whatever excuses Rowan had given herself for approaching Lysander, she was adult enough to acknowledge the real reason she'd shown up at his gate that day.

She'd wanted him and once her divorce was final, she could have him.

Rowan shook her head, hoping the older woman had been as taken in by the lies as Cyrus had hoped Rowan would be. Regardless of their strained relationship, she hated to think her mother was playing not only a willing but witting role in this farce.

Lysander didn't just get angry. He got even. And Rowan didn't like the chances of any of the players purposefully creating the false narrative coming out of this unscathed.

Rowan looked at Adele. "You want me to believe that you and Sander went from you being his platonic escort to necessary social events to having sex behind my back?"

She made no effort to disguise the skepticism in her tone now that she knew the details of the scam.

"Is that what he told you?" Adele trilled a mocking laugh. "That we only slept together once?"

"Adele, you said you wanted to help my daughter, not hurt her," Vanessa Johnson admonished.

The words surprised Rowan. It almost sounded like her mother cared.

"The truth sometimes hurts," Adele replied.

Rowan rolled her eyes. Cliché much?

"Surely by now, you realize what a powerful libido Lys has. Is it even remotely believable that he and I would have spent so many evenings together without having sex?" Her tone said: *Look at me, who wouldn't want to worship this?*

What Rowan realized was that Adele was a very proficient liar. Just like Cyrus.

Unfortunately for Adele and this little scheme she and Cyrus had come up with, Rowan was no longer the woman who had let herself be manipulated into a loveless marriage to a narcissist.

She'd grown in ways people like them would never understand. She knew her own value and *because* of her years with Cyrus and before that, growing up with her father, she knew the difference between a manipulative liar and an honorable man.

Lysander was the latter.

He'd told her that his relationship with Adele had been platonic after the one time of having sex. And him? She believed. 100%.

"I do know how deliciously strong Sander's sex drive is," she said now. "We've spent the last week having fantastic and very satisfying phone sex over video chat. You have not been in his bed."

Rowan's mother gasped. "Do not be vulgar. We are not here to discuss your...what you and Lysander do behind closed doors."

As amused as she was by her mother's clear embarrassment, Rowan was much angrier about the lies Adele was spouting and her mother's willingness to give them credence.

"But discussing his supposed sexual exploits with Adele is all right?" Rowan shook her head. "I don't think so."

Adele's face was pinched. The conversation was clearly not going the way she had expected.

"It is naïve to believe a man like Lysander Baros would be satisfied with that kind of thing. When he had a *companion* at hand." Her mother waived her hand, her discomfort with the topic clear.

Had she meant to make Adele sound like a sex worker? Considering the narrow-eyed look her mother cast the supermodel, Rowan thought the wording might have been deliberate.

The offended glare Adele shot Rowan's mother said she'd gotten the implication as well.

"Vulgar, or naïve, which is it mother? I'm pretty sure I can't be both."

"Do not let your heart rule your head," her mother said. "You cannot simply ignore the truth of Adele's claim and the proof of those pictures because you want to. You are smarter than that."

"I think you might actually be worried about me and not merely Dad's business relationship with the Andinos," Rowan said with surprise. "Regardless, you are right."

Her mother and Adele both perked up at that.

"I am intelligent. Intelligent to be aware of what a blatant liar Adele Fournier is. Smart enough to know that Cyrus has his own reasons for wanting to drive a wedge between me and Sander, but not one of them is for my benefit."

She stood up, done with this farce. "After living for most of my life with liars, I am savvy enough to recognize an honorable man. Sander promised me fidelity for as long as we are together and when he makes a promise, he keeps it."

Adele's tinkling laugh was mocking. "He's not a saint."

No. Lysander was no saint. He could be cranky and demanding. His pathological need to keep things tidy would be really annoying if he didn't have household staff. He was a workaholic and terrifically competitive. Possessive. Even jealous.

And she loved him with every fiber of her being.

"No, but he is a man who keeps his word."

"You're so sure?" Adele asked with more mockery.

There was nothing but certainty in Rowan's answer. "Yes."

Adele looked pityingly at Rowan. "You're a fool."

"Please, Rowan, I don't want to see you hurt," her mother pleaded.

Where was that concern when Rowan's father was feeding Cyrus information to make her fall for a man who had never existed? Where were those pleas when Cyrus cheated, and her parents were so adamantly opposed to Rowan filing for divorce?

Rowan shook her head. "I'm not the dangerously reckless one here, that would be you three."

Despite the immovability of her Botox treated face, her mother managed to look hurt. "For trying to protect you?"

"Let's leave the fact you're actually trying to make Sander's lover leave him and just address the reality that you two and Cyrus have conspired to slander a very wealthy, very powerful man who holds grudges."

"It's not slander! He is my lover," Adele claimed passionately.

"When was the last time you had sex with him?" Rowan asked. This was almost fun.

"Three nights ago, before I returned from Tokyo." Adele was cockily sure of herself.

"Let me be absolutely sure I have this right. Ms. Fournier. You are saying that you had sex with my lover, Lysander Baros, three nights ago in Tokyo?"

"Yes!"

Well, that was unequivocal. And Rowan was done. She picked up her phone, sent another text with attachments copied to Lysander and Klaus. Then she texted her bodyguard again, happy to see him materialize near the table within seconds of her sending it.

Her first text had been to tell him to come inside the restaurant and be close by in case she needed him.

Rowan stood and frowned down at her mother. "I don't know if you believe this charade, or if Cyrus has duped you into playing the part of concerned parent, but I hope for your sake it's the latter. It might save you from Sander's wrath."

"Those pictures! Rowan. You can't ignore them."

"Oh, I haven't. And neither will Sander." She glared at Adele. "I don't know if AI or CGI, or just plain photo manipulation was used, but Sander has the best tech experts on the planet working for him and they will find out."

Adele was trying to appear unaffected, but fear flickered in her gaze.

"I imagine you'll be hearing from his lawyers very soon, but I doubt that will be the extent of his wrath," Rowan drove the point home. "He once told me that when he knocks an enemy down, they stay that way."

"I'm not his enemy. I'm his lover!" the supermodel shrieked.

Unimpressed, Rowan continued, "You have stitched yourself up nicely and I think you know that Sander isn't a forgive and forget kind of guy."

After tapping her screen, the women's voices played from the phone's speakers, replaying the conversation they'd just had.

Adele leaped for the phone, screaming, claiming it was all a joke, but the bodyguard was there, and he didn't let the furious supermodel within a foot of Rowan.

"Rowan!" Her mother's distraught tone halted her. "You recorded us?"

"I did. I sent the recording and the photos to Sander already. Don't bother trying to convince me to keep this little drama between ourselves."

"I wasn't going to. But Adele and he...the pictures. After Cyrus...your own father. You know men cheat."

Hadn't she been listening? It was because of them that Rowan knew the difference. "Petty, insecure men with no honor cheat, Mom. Not men like Sander."

"You really believe in him."

"Yes." More than that, Rowan loved him.

However, the first person who was going to hear those words was going to be Lysander.

"I thought the pictures were real, that Ms. Fournier was doing us a favor by talking to you."

"Did you really? Or did you think that Cyrus had found a way to drive a wedge between me and Sander? I don't know why you think I would ever go back to that waste of space, but it will never happen. I don't care what that costs you and Father socially, or even financially. I'm done being a family pawn."

"Women do what they have to for their family, Rowan."

That sounded more like her mother.

Rowan just shook her head and walked away. She and Vanessa Johnson were never going to agree on what that meant.

One day, she hoped she'd have her own children and she would never, ever allow them to be used as bargaining chips.

She would never counsel her daughter, or her son for that matter, to stay with an unfaithful spouse.

CHAPTER TWENTY-NINE

L ysander's phone buzzed with a text. Maybe Rowan had finished lunch with her mother early.

He grabbed his phone and opened their text thread.

Rowan: *Cyrus had (maybe still has) a private investigator following you in Tokyo.*

Several photos came through and each one increased the dread inside him until he was clammy with fear. An experience he'd never before encountered.

By the time an attached recording came through, he was throwing his clothes into the garment bag and barking orders over the phone to the top company executive he'd brought with him for this trip.

"You'll have to handle the rest of the negotiations. I won't be there."

"But Lysander, it's you they want to talk to. Mr. Takamasa made that clear. It's a respect thing. If you leave now, he could very well back out of the deal."

"I am aware."

"Good," the other man sounded relieved.

"Handle it. I'm flying back to Athens as soon as there's a takeoff slot for the jet."

The executive was still squawking when Lysander hung up and sent a barrage of texts to his people. He wanted the jet ready for takeoff within the hour and a takeoff slot arranged.

He told Klaus to get their techs on the photos to figure out what had been done to create them. He was sure his head of security was already looking into the PI working for Cyrus angle.

Then he dialed his brother's number.

"Lysander, to what do I owe the pleasure?" Cyrus asked, sounding so damn smug.

"I would have been happy to leave it at slapping your wrists with the land developer deal and cutting you out of the negotiations with Takamasa and his conglomerate, but now I will not rest until Andino Enterprises is in bankruptcy."

"What the hell? You can't threaten me, Lysander."

"It wasn't a threat." Lysander hung up and blocked Cyrus's number mid-ring.

His father's call came minutes later. Lysander blocked him too. If he lost Rowan over this, he was going to make sure that not only was Andino Enterprises destroyed, but he would burn his father and brother's entire lives down to ash.

Once he was on the way to the airport, he called Rowan.

~ ~ ~

Rowan's phone rang and she saw it was a video call from Lysander. Unfortunately, she was on another call, and she had to reject the video chat request. She'd been trying to connect to the woman well known for her philanthropic ventures the past two weeks.

She texted her lover to apologize. *Sorry I couldn't take your call. Talking to a potential donor. I'll let you know when I'm done.*

Twenty minutes later, she hung up from a successful call with the donor. The woman would be hosting a table at the gala as well as committing to a generous monthly contribution.

Wanting to share her good news and yes, curious to find out what Lysander thought of Cyrus and Adele's machinations, she tried to return his video call. It didn't connect and there was no text forthcoming.

He must be in a meeting.

A little deflated but reminding herself that she'd see him in person soon enough, Rowan went back to work.

Her phone rang again a half an hour later. It was the sat phone from the plane.

Rowan quickly swiped to accept the call. "Hello?"

"Rowan."

Sander. "Why are you calling me from the plane?"

"I'm flying home."

"Did you finish your negotiations then?"

"No."

"Then why are you flying back to Athens?" Seeing the time, she quickly closed down her computer and texted her bodyguard to bring the car.

"You ask me that after sending me those photos?" There was an odd quality to Lysander's voice.

He almost sounded a little unhinged.

"I know they're problematic, but do you really think they're that big of a deal? I'm pretty sure Klaus has it covered." That's why she'd copied him on the texts, so he could start working on the problem immediately. "Are you worried the Japanese conglomerate will back out because of them?"

"No," Lysander said, his voice strangled.

He was really upset.

"It's not like we're married or something," she soothed him. "Even if Adele or Cyrus sends them to the tabloids, the story doesn't have enough legs to make it onto the front pages, much less through a whole media cycle."

"I know we are not married, but I made you a promise."

"Just like I made a promise to you, but I don't think the media is going to care about that. Do you think Cyrus and Adele have been working together since Mexico? That's weird, right? Do you think they're together again?"

He cursed viciously. "I do not care."

"Are you okay? I know this sucks, but you sound more upset than I would have expected you to be." And he was flying home.

Like the drama his brother and ex-escort were trying to create was a lot bigger than Rowan thought it was.

"What is going on?" she asked as she stepped outside to find her bodyguard behind the wheel of the hybrid SUV Lysander had purchased for her use.

It was more comfortable for her bodyguard than her compact electric car, which was why she hadn't argued about using it. And it was a hybrid. So, there was that.

"Rowan..." he ground out. "Just be there when I arrive. Promise me."

Since he would arrive sometime in the early hours of the morning if he was leaving now, where else would she be? The trip from Tokyo was nearly fourteen hours and that was just the flight.

"I'm not waiting up for you," she warned him in a teasing tone as she buckled her seatbelt. "Though, I might as well admit I was going to fly out to Tokyo tonight."

If she didn't, he'd learn soon enough from his PA.

"You were coming here?"

"Yep. It took most of the week, but I got things settled so I can work remotely next week."

"You did not want to come with me."

"I never said that. I said I *couldn't* go with you. At least not this week." She sighed. "I know that concept is hard for your tycoon brain to take in, but some of us cannot make the world bend to our will on a daily basis. Honestly, Sander, I don't want to. Life might not always be convenient but fulfilling my obligations and making a way to join you was satisfying for me. Can you understand that?"

"Yes."

"You sound weird."

Looking out the window, Rowan was happy to note that her bodyguard had gotten the memo and they were headed to the villa and not the airport.

"Do I?"

"I guess we can talk more about our different approaches to life when you get back. Are you sure it's a good time to leave Japan? The deal won't sour, will it?"

"I don't give a..." He said a four-letter word that he almost never said around her. "I'm coming home. Those pictures are faked."

"I know."

"You know?" Lysander's voice was heavy with disbelief. "But you sent them to me."

"So you could be aware of the latest Cyrus gambit." Wait. "Did you listen to the recording?"

He didn't answer. Had the call dropped?

"Are you still there?"

"I'm here."

"Why haven't you listened to the recording?"

"When I got the pictures, I thought you were breaking up with me." The bleakness in his tone hurt her heart. "I thought the recording was a voice message telling me we are over."

"What the heck? Why would you think that?"

"You sent me pictures of myself with another woman. You said your ex-husband had me followed."

"Well, yes, I assumed you'd look into who the PI was. He had to be in your hotel to get the backgrounds he used for the pictures. I mean, I'm not excited about paying skeezballs, but you've got deeper pockets than Cyrus. The easiest way to prove the fakery of the photos and stop the story in its tracks is to get the PI to admit his part in it."

"Klaus is looking for the *skeezball* now. Is that another one of your American-isms?"

"Most people say sleazeball but I like skeezball better. It implies sleazy and skeevy at the same time." She laughed, but it was forced.

He'd thought she was dumping him. And his response had been to fly back to Athens post haste. She hugged that knowledge to her heart. Maybe her three-word confession would not go unanswered.

Hope buoyed her heart. "You need to listen to the recording."

When he did, he'd have his own buoy because only a woman deeply in love would be so certain of her man's honor in the face of the evidence Rowan had been presented with at lunch.

"I will."

The silence between them was laden with words unsaid, emotions not given expression.

"Now," she prompted.

"Yes."

They hung up without saying goodbye. For Rowan there were only three words she wanted to say and she wasn't saying them until he was there, in the same room with her.

CHAPTER THIRTY

R owan woke to soft kisses and whispered words as the sun was just beginning to rise.

Turning, she slid her arms around Lysander's neck and pressed into his hard, naked body. "Welcome home."

"Those words." He stilled, his eyes closed, his face a mask of emotion. "Say it again."

"Welcome home."

"This is our home. Yours and mine."

"Yes."

He opened his eyes, his dark gaze intently fixed on hers. "I listened to the recording."

"And?"

"You were never going to break up with me."

"No."

He swallowed, like he was trying to control strong emotion. "You *aren't* ever going to leave me."

"No. If you try to send me off, I warn you, it won't be easy. I've got squatters rights now to the den. Just ask my purse."

He frowned. "Did you leave it by the couch again?"

"Yep."

"You're a troublemaker."

"Not a slob?" she quizzed, arching against Lysander's body, inhaling his scent.

"I might be a little uptight about where things go."

"A little?" she teased.

"I admit that the purse wasn't the problem."

"Oh no?"

He kissed her softly and then shook his head. "No."

"Care to share?"

"You know."

"You didn't want to go to Japan without me."

"I didn't want to go to Japan without you," he agreed.

"Next time, lets focus on the real issue."

"I thought you didn't want to come, that you were getting tired of me."

"Funny, that's what I thought when you stopped working from home at all and I saw more of your staff than you."

He cupped her cheek. "I will never get tired of you."

"Promise?"

"Promise."

"That sounds suspiciously like a long-term commitment." She tried to tease, but her voice got all choked and Rowan had to blink back tears.

His answer was a prolonged, tender kiss, but when it started to turn hot and heavy, he pulled back and sat up against the headboard. "As much as I want you, we need to talk."

Rowan climbed into his lap, her knees on either side of his hips. "Maybe you shouldn't have come to bed naked then."

"I don't want any barriers between us."

That he was talking about things more important than clothing did not escape her.

"What do you want to talk about?" she asked.

There were more words she wanted to say, but for some reason they weren't popping out of her mouth like she'd expected them to.

"The recording."

"Adele overplayed her hand for sure," Rowan opined. "She was so sure I would believe her."

"I don't care about Adele."

"You don't?" Rowan asked. "What do you care about?"

"Ask me *who*."

"Who..." She had to clear her throat and take a deep breath before she got the words out. "Who do you care about?"

"You. *Agape mou*."

He'd never called her that before. It could be as innocuous as sweetheart, but in the right context, it meant, *my love*. Was this the right context?

"I care about you too." It wasn't all she wanted to say, but it was true.

"I know. You offer a loyalty that goes to the depths of your soul. You did not doubt me for even a second. You turned your recording app on immediately. You never once wavered."

"Of course not. You might be a workaholic and seriously grumpy about where I choose to leave my handbag for the next morning, but you would never lie to me."

Lysander sat up against the headboard, pulling her with him. "About the workaholic thing."

"Are you going to try to deny it?"

"No."

"I don't like the way things have been since we got back from Mexico." She wasn't dumping him because he worked long hours, but she wasn't pretending to be okay with it either.

"I didn't either."

She just looked at him.

"Yes, I know. It was my fault. I was trying to prove something to myself."

"What?"

"When you first moved in, it was easy to curtail my work schedule. I assumed our relationship would burn out quickly, especially if we lived together."

She'd half suspected as much, so she should not be surprised. Or hurt. She was both.

"I guess it worked." Rowan went to slide off his lap.

Lysander held her in place with firm hands on her thighs. "No, *agape mou.* Stay."

There was that endearment again. That little buoy in her heart bobbed, reminding her that he'd left an important business deal in Japan to come home when he thought he'd lost her.

"It did not work. In fact, the opposite happened. Having you here only made me crave you more. Not just in bed, though I will never get my fill of your sexy body."

The erection pressing up between them gave credence to this claim.

"Every minute we spend together is precious to me and only makes me want more minutes, hours, days, weeks..." He shook his head. "Just more. Since we returned from Mexico, I have tried to prove to myself nothing had changed for me."

Did that mean things *had* changed for him? She loved this man and if she wasn't deluding herself, he loved her too.

"Nothing about our relationship fit what I believed about myself. I have never been a jealous lover, but the idea of another man so much as looking at you makes me livid."

"You demanded monogamy though."

"Yes, and had no twinge of feeling if my sex partner decided to move on before I did."

"You wouldn't have let me go so easily." He *hadn't* let her go. He'd fought for the one night to become something more and for that more to become them living together.

"When the threats escalated and you were mentioned, I should have sent you away while I dealt with the problem—"

"Like that would have worked. I'm not going anywhere."

He grimaced. "I am aware of how stubborn you can be."

"Good. I wouldn't want you to be misled by my usually sweet nature."

He kissed her again, tasting her mouth for long minutes before pulling his head back. "You are sweet, *yineka mou.* Everywhere."

Her face heated with a blush, which felt silly because how many times had they made love? How many times had they explored each other's bodies thoroughly? She was sitting naked with him in bed and memories of why he called her *glikia mou* had her squirming.

His knowing expression said he was aware of exactly what she was thinking about.

But then he shook his head. "Later."

She sighed, but nodded.

"Instead of sending you away, or going to my New York office, I decided to use the need to get out of Athens to give you something you wanted."

"The cruise was amazing." Even with his hot-cold treatment and the stalker supermodel showing up as well as her ex-husband.

"I am glad you found it so. We can take another one in the future, if that is what you want." The words were so obviously forced, Rowan had to stifle an urge to smile.

"Once was enough. Thank you."

Relief washed over his handsome features. "If you are sure."

"I am."

"You need to understand that I've never put anything or anyone ahead of my business. Not even my mother. When I didn't even consider sending you away, much less going to my New York office, alarm bells went off. I ignored them. Just like I ignored my business to resolve the issue with those bastards as quickly as possible, so you were no longer at risk. The more I felt for you, the more I fought those feelings."

He'd been fighting himself, not her, which had led to his hot-cold treatment.

"That explains a lot. Is that why you threw yourself so intensely into work when we got back to Athens?"

"Yes."

"It hurt, but I understand."

"I never wanted to hurt you."

She believed him, but that didn't change the outcome. "I think when you love someone, they have the power to hurt you in ways you would never expect."

"Don't say it."

"What?" But she knew. Or thought she did.

"Let me say it first. I love you, Rowan. Your soul is entwined with mine and I will never let you go. I can't. To lose you would be to lose the other half of myself."

"That sounds like a lifetime commitment." Marriage.

"I'm not looking for a lifetime together."

"You're not?" she asked, her heart squeezing painfully.

"I want eternity."

Wow. Okay. Trust Mr. Billionaire Greek Tycoon to be an over achiever when it came to love too.

He reached for something on his bedside table and then put his hand out, offering it.

A ring with a huge yellow diamond surrounded by a cluster of marquis-cut smaller stones sat in the center of his big palm. "Will you marry me, Rowan?"

She couldn't get any words out; she was trying too hard not to cry. He hadn't bought that ring on the way home from the airport. This wasn't a spur of the moment thing.

"How long have you had that?" she asked, emotion clogging her voice.

"Since the day after you moved in."

She pushed herself up to look at him in shock. "You knew you wanted forever then?"

"I was still fighting it. I told myself it was a gift, not an engagement ring."

"But you never gave it to me." And that ring couldn't be mistaken for anything but the kind of bling a man gave a woman to claim her.

"Because no matter how I lied to myself, I knew giving it to you came with a question I wasn't ready to ask."

"I want children if we can have them." Images of a baby girl with his dark eyes, and a little boy with Lysander's chiseled chin filled her mind.

Rowan's ovaries clenched with anticipation.

"Is that a yes?"

"It's a negotiation."

He laughed, his eyes warm with the emotion she had no trouble naming now. Love. "I'm eager to hear your terms."

"My purse has a spot beside the sofa in the den."

"Done."

"I know you aren't going to work forty hours a week, but I need you to be present or there's no point in getting married." She wasn't having children to raise as a single parent either.

"I'm already working on a more manageable schedule. Losing a few million in deals is nothing in comparison to losing you."

From her tycoon? That was heart-meltingly sweet.

"I want vacations. A minimum of four a year."

"Done."

She gasped. She'd expected major pushback on that and had thought she'd have to settle for two at the most.

She narrowed her eyes. "A vacation is defined as seven or more days without working more than two hours a day."

He kissed her. "It will go in the prenup."

"Speaking of, there will be no monetary incentives, or otherwise for longevity or children in this prenup." That was becoming a common thing and she didn't like the cynicism of it. "Our staying together won't be because I'm looking for a bigger payout."

He didn't say *done* this time. He kissed her with voracious need. They made love and somewhere along the way, the ring ended up on her finger.

Afterward, while their hearts were still racing and her breathing was still ragged, she said the words, "Yes. I will marry you, Sander. I love you more than anyone or anything. I didn't know this kind of love was even possible. I've never felt it. Never seen it. But I feel it now. You are my everything."

"We are everything together."

"Yes."

"If you hadn't shown up at my gate, I would have gone looking for you."

That was a big admission for him, revealing a need and vulnerability that filled her with joy.

She owed him the same level of honesty. "I didn't come to you because I wanted revenge on my ex. That was my excuse, for myself and for you. I came because I wanted you."

She had always wanted him, even when she hadn't allowed her conscious brain to acknowledge it because she was married to another man. Lysander was it for her.

"I'm sure you realize by now that my suggestion we have an affair had nothing to do with Cyrus either." Lysander kissed her, his hand rubbing up and down the naked skin of her back. "I never realized what real desire was until I met you and you were married to my damned brother."

"Half-brother. You're not an Andino. You are a Baros and I love you, Lysander Baros."

Chapter Thirty-One

Rowan's mother called to apologize. Apparently, she had believed the photos were real and had been trying to protect her daughter for once.

If she could be believed.

"It was clear that you felt something much deeper for Lysander than you ever did for Cyrus. I wanted to save you the pain of years being married to a philanderer."

"You didn't feel that way about Cyrus."

"By the time you left Cyrus, he held no piece of your heart. He could not hurt you."

"Oh, it hurt all right." It had been the hurt of betrayal and not heartbreak, but it had been painful all the same.

"But you were not devastated. Not like..."

"Like what, Mom?"

"Like I was the first time I realized your father had a mistress. Our marriage was arranged by our parents, but he was so charming. So handsome. When he walked into a room, his presence filled it."

This was a side of her mother Rowan had never seen. "You fell in love."

"Yes, but he didn't."

"Why did you stay with him?"

"Because that is what women in our station did. Falling in love with Richard was my weakness to bear. My father had other women, but he and my mother were not unhappy. Later in life, they became devoted to each other."

"You thought that would happen with Dad?" Rowan had a hard time imagining her father devoted to anything but his own search for more wealth and power.

"Yes." Her mother sighed. "Your father wasn't like mine. He didn't mark our anniversaries or get me beautiful jewelry for my birthday."

Rowan remembered her father giving her mother money and telling her to buy something with it to show off at the country club more than once. She'd thought that was normal, so when Cyrus had done it for her first birthday as a married woman, Rowan hadn't been bothered.

Now, she was, but not on her own behalf. On behalf of her mother. Her mother was no saint, but Rowan's father was a real piece of work.

"The only time we socialized together was when he needed me by his side for his image's sake."

"I thought that was the way you wanted it." Her mother had never acted like it bothered her that she and her husband led such separate lives.

"After you were born, we stopped sharing a bedroom. I resented you for that, though it had nothing to do with you. You came six years after Michael. Neither of us was expecting me to get pregnant again. Your father was not pleased and refused to risk it happening again, so he moved me to another bedroom."

"That had to have hurt." Rowan couldn't imagine what it would feel like if Lysander tried to relegate her to a different bedroom.

She did know that she would make him regret it. In so many ways. Murder would not be out of the running for one of them.

Reining in her thoughts, Rowan asked, "Why not just use birth control?"

"I was on the pill when I became pregnant with you. I offered to get a tubal ligation, but he said not to bother."

Ouch.

Rowan saw so much about her mother she'd never seen before. The pain and discontent she'd been forced to live with day in and day out had manifested in the way she treated others. The resentment she felt toward Rowan for being the catalyst to losing what was left of intimacy in her marriage had made sure that Rowan got the brunt of that negativity.

It wasn't fair. And it wasn't okay. But she understood it now.

"We'll never be close, Rowan. I've made too many mistakes with you and we're very different people, but I never wanted to see you unhappy."

"I sure wasn't happy married to Cyrus."

"You seemed content."

"You really don't know me very well."

"No, I don't suppose I do, but that doesn't stop me being very glad you are happy now."

"Thank you." Rowan didn't know what else to say.

"Your father is very regretful that he backed the wrong horse in this race." Her mother's tone was almost gleeful.

"What do you mean?"

"He supported Cyrus's attempt to get you back, and even when he knew you were with Lysander, he assumed a man like him wasn't going to marry you."

"Now that we're engaged, he tried to leverage my relationship with Sander into a business opportunity, didn't he?" Lysander hadn't said anything, but Rowan could easily imagine how that meeting had gone.

"Yes. Your fiancée made it clear that he'd happily see your father begging on a street corner rather than ever go into a deal with him. Your father was livid."

"Sander is very protective of me."

"I am glad. You deserve that."

"This is weird," Rowan couldn't help saying.

Her mom's laugh was different than usual. It actually sounded like she was amused. "Yes. I imagine it is. It's taken me thirty years and being made a pawn by yet another scheming businessman to realize you were never the problem in my marriage."

"Uh...I'm glad."

"So am I."

Even after that phone call, Rowan was shocked when Lysander pointed out an article from a newspaper back home about her mother and father separating. Vanessa Johnson had moved out of the family mansion and filed for divorce.

She hadn't heard from either of her brothers in a couple of years, but the oldest sent a text demanding Rowan talk some sense into their mother. Her second brother sent her an email telling her that it was Rowan's fault their mother was doing something so bad for the family business.

If Rowan hadn't divorced Cyrus, apparently none of this would have happened.

Considering that both men had shown not a single iota of concern for their mother, Rowan ignored both the text and the email.

She kind of liked thinking her actions had spurred Vanessa's behavior. Rowan certainly wasn't ashamed of it. Maybe her mom would finally find some genuine happiness in her own life now.

~ ~ ~

Feeling bone deep contentment, Lysander cuddled his soon to be wife on the den sofa. Instead of a stock report, the television played a nature documentary about monkeys.

Rowan loved any kind of animal documentary and Lysander loved Rowan. Ergo, his unlooked for education about monkeys.

She shifted against him, unbuttoning his shirt so her hand could slide over his stomach. Usually, by halfway into whatever show they were watching, she had his shirt open and at least one hand on his bare skin.

It was a game he played with himself to see how long he could last before either pulling her to straddle him or throwing her over his shoulder and taking her to bed. Her complaint that she never got to see the end of her shows wasn't much of a complaint when accompanied by the heated look in her beautiful blue eyes.

"Have you figured out how Adele Fournier stalked us to Mexico?" Rowan asked, surprising him.

She hadn't seemed inclined to discuss the doctored images after the night they got engaged.

Lysander ran his fingertip over her ring. Soon it would be joined by a wedding band. That couldn't happen fast enough as far as he was concerned.

"She had a sexual relationship with one of my personal security detail and managed to put a tracker in his tactical watch."

Rowan sat up and climbed astride Lysander's thighs, her face filled with shock. "How did you find out?"

"Klaus discovered it after scanning every item the security team brought with them to Mexico. There is no way of knowing how long it had been in there, but they'd been having sex for months."

Rowan's brow furrowed and she shook her head. "Wow. That's some next level thirsty-stalking. The guy probably feels so used."

"What he feels is unemployed." And unemployable.

Klaus hadn't taken it well to find out one of his men had put Lysander at risk.

"You fired him? But Adele tricked him."

"Do not worry. She is getting her comeuppance as well." Fury surged through him when he thought of what the supermodel's machinations could have cost him. "She and Cyrus will regret trying to take you from me."

"You can be a little scary."

"Not to you."

"Never to me." Rowan's happy smile caused a much different feeling than anger to fill him.

"I'm thinking about selling my stock in Andino Enterprises to a competitor. I don't suppose you could help me with that?"

"It would be my pleasure."

"I can think of something a lot more pleasurable than facilitating a stock sale." She rocked her hips, rubbing herself over his rapidly growing erection.

They didn't make it to the bedroom.

Chapter Thirty-Two

Rowan was in her office at the org when she heard an unwelcome, but unfortunately too familiar voice in the hall.

Looking up, she found Cyrus standing in the doorway to the small room.

It was a Cyrus unlike she had ever seen before. He had several days stubble on his face. His hair was unkempt, his suit worse for wear.

"You have got to get him to stop, Rowan. He's going to bankrupt us."

Uh oh.

Lysander hadn't said anything about what he planned to do in response to Cyrus and Adele's scheme to convince Rowan he'd cheated. She'd only asked once, and he'd told her not to worry about it.

So, she hadn't.

But she'd never doubted for a minute that Lysander would accept the faked photos and spurious claims by the supermodel lying down.

"You knew your brother holds grudges, why would you risk his wrath trying to make me believe that garbage about him and Adele?"

"I didn't know he wanted to marry you!" Cyrus looked unhinged. "How would I? Lysander doesn't do commitment."

"Sucks to be you, I guess."

"Is that all you can say? We were married ten years!"

"But were we? Really? I mean if you negated our vows within hours of speaking them, how married were we?"

Cyrus shook his head like she made no sense. "Look, I don't care about the land developer deal."

He didn't care about losing out on the 3.5 million dollars Lysander had negotiated making the sale on her behalf?

"That's a lot of money, but then again, it's not." It had never made sense to her that Cyrus would go to so much trouble to try to get back together for a few million.

Her dad? He wasn't swimming in a pond as big as the one the Andinos were in. Richard Johnson would have fought harder for less, but not Cyrus.

"What do you care about?" Rowan asked.

What had driven Cyrus into showing up at her work?

"The stock shares. We need them, damn you, and Lysander is negotiating a deal for them with a rival."

"I know. I asked him to."

"You didn't even want them," Cyrus snarled. "You were going to waive all benefits from the prenup to get out of our marriage."

"I am aware." The judge had refused to allow it.

"So, sign them over to me now."

"No."

"What the hell do you mean? No?"

"I mean, you tried to take the man I love from me with a lie, just like all the lies you told while we were married."

If Cyrus had told the truth, Rowan would have divorced him long ago and would already be married to Lysander. They'd been connected from that first meeting and only her useless marriage had kept them apart.

"I need those stocks."

"Why?" she asked, only mildly curious.

"None of your business."

"Really? That's the way you want to play it when you're asking me for something?"

"We're trying to merge with another European company. I need those shares to meet the percentage vested requirement." Cyrus tried to look at her appealingly. "The merger is worth hundreds of millions to Andino Enterprises."

Like she cared. She'd been bartered for the good of that company and her father's, even though she thought she'd been getting married for the sake of love.

Rowan knew what love felt like now and was sad for her younger self that she'd been so easily fooled.

"That makes a lot more sense than you wanting to get back together when you never cared about our marriage to begin with."

"I need those shares, Rowan."

"It *really* sucks to be you."

"Get the hell out of my fiancée's office." Lysander was practically breathing fire.

Cyrus spun to face Lysander. "You're going to bankrupt us!" he accused. "Your own father's company."

"Did you think I would let you get away with trying to take Rowan away? You did not succeed and that is the only reason you're still breathing." Lysander's chilling tone probably terrified Cyrus.

It turned Rowan on to have all the fury focused on the idea of losing her though.

"Are you threatening to kill me?" Cyrus asked with disbelief.

"No. I am telling you what would have happened if the woman I love left me because of your lies."

"I just wanted the shares," Cyrus whined.

"Then you should have offered to buy them."

"I'll buy them now. I'll pay you twice what they are worth," he said to Rowan.

"Lysander has already found me a buyer."

"You heartless bitch!"

Lysander grabbed Cyrus, jerked him backward and then punched him so hard he made a dent in the wall when he hit it. "Apologize."

Cyrus told Lysander where to get off. It lost a lot of its impact because his tone was so nasally from his now broken nose.

Lysander yanked his half-brother up by his shirt and this time sent his fist straight into his solar plexus.

He dropped the now groaning and gasping man to the floor and put his hand out to Rowan. "We have an appointment with the lawyer to sign the prenup."

The prenuptial agreement wasn't anything like the one Rowan had signed with Cyrus.

There were no monetary incentives for longevity as she'd asked, but it spelled out quite clearly that what was Lysander's would now be hers. That if she filed for divorce, for any reason, she would get half of Lysander Baros's assets.

"I can't sign this."

"Why not, *agape mou*?"

"You're not giving me half of your wealth."

"No, I am not."

She breathed a sigh of relief, but then she frowned. "Was this some kind of test?"

"Not at all. Sign the document, Rowan."

"No. You just said—"

"You will never be divorcing me, nor will I ever end our marriage. The point is moot."

She wanted to believe that, but life had a way of taking unexpected turns. "It's not moot if it's in the contract."

"We can skip the prenup all together if you like."

"Not on your life." She wanted the promise of no more than 50-hour work-weeks they'd agreed on, and four vacations per year, in writing. Signed by him.

"Then you agree to take half of my fortune if you ever leave me."

"I know what you are doing."

"What is that?"

"You know I'll never allow you to hand over half of your wealth and posses-sions."

"There is no handing over. What is mine is yours already. Nothing I have built would matter if you stopped loving me and walked away."

Tears burned her eyes. "Iona told me that under all that scary tycoon armor, beat a romantic's heart. I didn't believe her."

"It is not a matter of romance, but of truth."

"If you say so." She grabbed the contract and signed it. "You're stuck now, Sander. You're never getting rid of me."

The satisfaction that settled over his gorgeous features made her breathless. And wet.

His grin said he knew it too. "Are you ready to go home?"

"Yes."

~ ~ ~

They ripped off each other's clothes in the foyer and made love against the wall. She trusted him to have alerted the staff to give them privacy. He was efficient like that.

And it was a good thing, because once they started kissing and touching, Rowan's higher thinking skills went right out the window.

Afterward, he carried her to their bedroom. "I love you with everything in my ruthless tycoon heart, Rowan."

"Not nearly as much as I love you."

"Impossible." He made love to her again. This time in their bed with whisper soft touches, long slow thrusts and so many words.

Words about her beauty. About how much he needed her. About what he meant to her. About how perfect their children and life were going to be.

"Happy children aren't perfect," Rowan said.

"Then they will be imperfect, because with you as their mother, they can only be happy."

There were tears in her eyes when she told him she loved him again.

"Always and forever, Rowan."

"Always and forever."

Finis.

If you enjoyed Her Greek Billionaire, please consider leaving a review. Thank you!

Want to read bonus content, including a bonus scene for Her Greek Billionaire, and to be kept up to date on her books? Sign up for Lucy Monroe's .

Read more passionate contemporary romance by Lucy Monroe:

Read Lucy's new mafia romance series, .

CINDERELLA'S JILTED BILLIONAIRE

Lucy Monroe

Lucy Monroe LLC

For Jadesola James, a new friend, a fabulous author, and someone who appreciates a good Cinderella story, but most importantly, loves a truly emotional romance. This story is for you and other authors and readers like you! Hugs!

Chapter One

Annette Hudson rushed around her tiny studio apartment, grabbing last-minute items. She was late leaving for the airport, but she'd had a last-minute emergency at work.

Nothing new in that. Understaffed and underfunded, her nonprofit organization expected her to wear multiple hats on a daily basis. Getting the week off for her little sister's wedding had been nearly impossible, but for once Annette had refused to back down about taking the time.

Joyce was getting married and Annette wasn't going to miss it. Not only was Joyce the only family who still had anything to do with her, but Annette was one of Joyce's bridesmaids. She had the dress to prove it.

That she would see the man she'd jilted at the altar five years before had nothing to do with the discordant concerto playing along her nerve endings. No, of course it didn't. He was just at the center of the biggest mistake of her life, costing her the family she'd dreamed of and the family she'd grown up with, not to mention the man she'd loved beyond reason.

Although the society pages showed him escorting a bevy of beautiful women to his mother's charity galas, Carlo Messina was still single. He would play best man for the groom. In a cruel twist of fate, Annette's baby sister had fallen for, and was marrying, Carlo's younger brother, Fantino Messina.

The similarities between the two couples were uncanny. Joyce was the same young twenty-two Annette had been when she'd left Carlo standing at the altar. Fantino was eerily the same age Carlo had been then as well, twenty-nine.

But there was no chance Joyce would take flight as Annette had done. Not only was she a far more self-assured twenty-two, confident in the love of her Sicilian tycoon, Joyce was also seven months pregnant. The plans had already been in place for the *wedding of the century* when Annette's younger sister told their families the happy news.

Their mother had been livid, but everyone else, even Carlo's conservative Sicilian relatives, had been delighted.

Annette was thrilled for her sister, if a little envious.

Joyce was building the very life that Annette had always dreamed of, and it was no one's fault but her own that she hadn't realized it first. Determined to show nothing but happiness for her sister, Annette rushed for the MAX line that would take her to the airport.

Several hours and a plane ride later, Annette dragged her suitcase out of the back of the taxi in front of an exclusive building in Manhattan. She might be willing to travel public transport in Portland, Oregon, but wasn't as confident of doing so alone in New York City.

You could take the girl away from wealth and privilege, but you couldn't stop the tapes playing in her head of all she'd been taught by parents who had a distinct *us and them* mentality when it came to the money *haves* and *have nots*. She didn't want to be afraid to ride the subway alone, but she was.

Would she ever be wholly her own person, leaving her parents' narrow view of the world behind completely?

She walked into the lobby of the apartment building and gave the doorman her name. Fantino had an apartment here and Annette was staying there for the week before the wedding. She could have stayed with her parents, but that would have been awkward when they hadn't had a real conversation in five years.

Not since her father had all but forced her to leave New York, by offering a substantial gift to her organization, if they transferred her to their office across country. She'd spent the last five years in exile, very pointedly not invited to family gatherings. Returning for a visit had been out of the question. Labeled an ungrateful daughter who had humiliated her family by standing her billionaire groom up at the altar, Annette had been shunned by everyone except Joyce since that fateful day.

Okay, so there could be a lot of reasons for the butterflies tap dancing in spiked cleats in her stomach right now, and Carlo Messina was only one of them.

The doorman requested her identification and then sent her up in the elevator to Fantino's penthouse floor. The man himself was there to greet her when she knocked on his door.

Looking so much like his older brother, it hurt her to see him, his teeth flashed white in a warm smile. "Annette! Welcome! Joyce will be so glad you have made it."

It was all Annette could do to summon a smile of acknowledgement to Fantino's words. She should have it together. She'd been wholly on her own since leaving New York. Annette had stood up to drug dealers who were messing with the kids in her program. She'd stared down cops doing the same thing.

The prospect of seeing Carlo Messina again shouldn't be so darn scary, much less her own parents.

Only it was.

She was shaking inside but hiding it, and that was the best she could hope for.

"Who is it?" Think of the devil and he will appear. Six feet, four inches of Sicilian male perfection, Carlo stood there looking amazing in a bespoke suit, his dark hair styled perfectly.

No pallor beneath his sun kissed skin to reveal nerves to rival hers. But then, he'd never actually loved her, and she'd never gotten over loving him. He hadn't had neatly trimmed facial hair six years ago. It gave him a sexy edge he didn't need. The man was already sex on a stick with a side of dark chocolate sauce.

The look in his grey eyes when they landed on her was indifferent. So much worse than anger. It indicated that while she hadn't been able to move on, he had.

"Oh, I see," he said dismissively. "Joyce is in the living room," Carlo turned to walk away.

Say something, she instructed herself, but Annette couldn't get a single word past the obstruction in her throat.

"Don't mind him. He's had enough girlfriends since you broke up, he can't claim he's been pining for you," Fantino said airily, leading her into the swank, modern living room of the penthouse.

If that was supposed to make her feel better, it had failed spectacularly.

"Annette!" Her sister's shout reached her ears only a second before the lithe brunette pulled her into a breath stealing hug.

Joyce was the only member of their family who called her by her full name, Annette. The rest of the family and extended family called her Netta, as if trying to erase the existence of her deceased birth mother, Anne.

"Isn't that sweet?" a smooth, feminine voice asked. Annette couldn't see the woman speaking through the crowd of well-wishers attending the prewedding party. "Only I thought Cinderella's family had disowned her."

Joyce let go of Annette and spun around. "The past is the past. My sister is one of my dearest friends and nothing will change that." It was like she was warning everyone in the room.

Annette knew Joyce had fought family pressure to maintain their relationship. Though the younger woman had said nothing, it must have been a battle royal when she insisted on inviting Annette to the wedding. Making her a bridesmaid would have been even worse in their parents' opinion.

Warmth and gratitude surged through Annette.

"Naturally not," Valentina Messina said smoothly as she arrived beside them, looking just as put together and lovely as Annette remembered the woman who had been meant to be *her* mother-in-law. "Family is family."

"Hello, Signora Messina," Annette said in a huskier tone than usual, but it was taking all she had to form words.

This was so much harder than she thought it would be.

The gorgeous woman now clinging to Carlo's arm like a limpet only made things worse.

Annette had never been a liar, so she'd never lied to herself and claimed to be over the man. She doubted she ever would be.

"It is Valentina, as I am sure you remember," the elegant older woman instructed. "So, you did not marry my eldest son." She waved negligently with her elegant hand. "Life has its little turns. However, your sister *will* be marrying my younger son and that is all that matters now."

Annette just nodded, all the time her focus inexorably drawn to the beautiful brooding man she had so foolishly walked away from five years ago.

"Thank you for the card and flowers when Alceu was in the hospital. The food baskets and coffee deliveries from my favorite barista were lovely," Valentina went on. "It was a kindness."

"I...it was the least I could do."

"What a kind thing to say, but under the circumstances untrue." She meant because Annette had no longer been a de facto member of the family. "His accident was such a worrisome time for us all and your thoughtfulness was very much appreciated." Valentina gave her husband a significant look. "I warned him for years to stop driving like he wanted to enter *Le Mans*. But would he listen?"

The weeks after her failed wedding were some of the hardest of Annette's life, made infinitely worse when Alceu, a man she'd come to love like a father, was in the car accident and was taken to the hospital. She could do nothing but watch from the sidelines, hoping he would recover.

The look on Carlo's face and her own parents' expressions said Valentina might be the only person who thought the way she did.

Though she'd had nothing to do with the accident, hadn't even been in the same country it happened in, they definitely blamed Annette. For all of it.

When Annette hadn't shown up at the church, the media had a heyday with their awful headlines and salacious innuendo laden articles and it only got worse after Alceu's accident. There had been speculation that, humiliated by his son being stood up at the altar and the subsequent media frenzy, Alceu had done it on purpose.

Cinderella Jilts Billionaire had morphed to *Even Billions of Dollars Can't Get Cinderella to the Altar*.

The whole Cinderella angle was her older sister's fault, not that anyone in her family would admit it. Lynette's friends used to make fun of Annette because more often than not, her mother would find fault with something about her appearance or behavior at a social function they were hosting and send Annette to the kitchen to help the cook or the serving staff.

She'd say if Annette couldn't handle her responsibilities as a daughter of the host, she might as well make some use of herself. Lynette's friends had dubbed her Cinderella and that's how that whole group referred to her on social media. Lynette had been the one to give an interview after the failed wedding to a gossip rag journalist about Annette, sharing the nickname and what a supposed failure Annette had been as a socialite.

Lynnette hadn't mentioned Annette's adopted status either, but then that would have sparked ire from their parents and Lynette was too smart for that. Only she hadn't been smart enough to realize that her words could be twisted, and they had been. Her family and Carlo had been raked over the coals by the press. They'd said that despite his billions, he was no Prince Charming.

Which was not true. He'd been her prince, she'd just been too insecure to realize it, much less fight for what they could have had.

Regardless of her lack of foresight, Lynnette had come out of the debacle smelling like a rose. As per usual. Completely ignoring her role in it, everyone had acted like it was Annette's fault the family had drawn censure for *making her into a modern-day Cinderella*.

It had taken two years of therapy for Annette to realize she had not been at fault. Yes, she'd jilted Carlo at the altar, and she could have handled that differently, but the media frenzy that ensued had not been on her. No matter what her family thought.

"Enough talking of the past, it is time to toast the happy couple," Alceu Messina announced with authority that would never leave him, no matter that he was officially retired now.

He'd worked hard coming back from his accident, and if she didn't know he'd spent six months in a hospital bed recovering from terrible damage to his body, she would never suspect it.

One toast followed another and soon the room was filled with laughing, chatting partygoers. If some gave Annette the side-eye, she ignored it. She was here for Joyce and that was what mattered.

Just as he had for the past six years, Carlo did a great job of ignoring Annette's existence. With his date always there, touching him and flirting with the Sicilian tycoon, Annette was happy to return the favor and kept her focus on Joyce, Fantino, and their friends that didn't seem interested in rehashing six years ago.

The rest of the week was more of the same. Annette spent the rehearsal doing her best to avoid looking at either Carlo, or her parents. It helped she was just a bridesmaid and not maid of honor. That position had been filled by their oldest sister, Lynette.

Annette didn't mind in the least. While she wasn't exactly an introvert, she really didn't like being the center of attention among this crowd, and Lynette's role meant she was the one giving the formal toast to the happy couple at the reception.

Annette didn't mind a bit when the youth she served focused on her. She was comfortable leading workshops for them, but that was different.

Carlo brought yet another beautiful companion to the rehearsal dinner, much to Lynette's obvious chagrin. Apparently, her older sister expected Carlo, as best man, to be her escort and complained to both sets of parents loudly enough to be overheard.

Annette would have found it all laugh worthy if she wasn't fighting her own jealousy over the date's presence. After five years, she should be more inured to such feelings, regardless of her feelings for the man.

After all, she had been strong enough to walk away when she realized it wasn't working. Which wasn't the show of strength she wanted to believe it was, because she doubted that decision almost every day, wishing she'd tried to at least talk to him again, wishing above everything she'd handled the cancelled wedding better.

Texting her parents and asking them to alert everyone else had been a colossal mistake.

Because of course they hadn't. They'd let everyone think she'd skipped town without a word to them. Why Carlo had shown up at the church when she'd told him to his face it was over, she didn't understand to this day.

The wedding was beautiful. Joyce's Regency inspired gown had not been designed to hide her pregnancy and she glowed with joy from the moment she entered the church.

Annette could see not a single sign of wedding jitters.

The reception was held in one of the old grand hotel ballrooms, so exactly the way that Joyce had always said she wanted things to be, Annette couldn't help smiling. Though she was operating on her last reserves after a week of being her family's pariah and the recipient of censure from Carlo's extended family and friends.

His parents were wonderful, and of course so was his younger brother.

Carlo simply ignored her and that hurt most of all.

Done with it all, Annette had tucked herself into a corner of the ballroom away from everyone, just waiting for the bride and groom to leave so she could too.

"I cannot believe you were selfish enough to come to Joyce's wedding, Netta." Lynette's spiteful voice invaded Annette's solitude.

Sighing, Annette looked up. Lynette was glaring down at her. Nothing new there.

"Don't you have things you need to be doing as the matron of honor?" she asked.

"Can you believe our sister wanted to make you *maid* of honor?" Lynette asked derisively, as if the distinction between maid and matron was a negative one.

Annette didn't see it. Yes, Lynette had married since Annette left New York, but she had also divorced. That made them both single, if not technically *maids*.

Unlike Annette, Lynette had a busy social calendar though. She'd never landed the catch she really wanted to, however. Carlo Messina showed no more interest in Annette's older sister than he ever had. Despite being best man and Lynette being the matron of honor, Carlo had managed to finagle a change in the dance partner line up and Annette's sister had been stuck dancing with a cousin while Carlo had escorted his grandmother around the floor.

It had been the highlight of an otherwise miserable few hours for Annette, seeing her grasping older sister thwarted.

"I believe you owe me this dance," Carlo's voice startled both women.

Lynette turned, her expression going from sour to sweet in a heartbeat. "Do I?" she asked throatily.

But Carlo was looking at Annette, his hand extended to *her*.

Without really thinking of what she was doing, she reached out and took it.

He pulled her from her chair, the cornflower blue chiffon of her bridesmaid dress floating around her legs. The three-inch heels of her delicate silver strappy sandals bringing her petite height to average.

Lynette said, "Netta? But why would you want to dance with her?"

Carlo ignored the remark and pulled Annette toward the dance floor.

"What did Lynette ever do to you?" Annette asked as Carlo pulled her into his arms for a slow dance.

He looked at her like she had to be kidding. "She leaked that you broke things off. She's the one that got the whole media storm going in the first place, doing that tabloid interview."

"No one else blamed her."

"In her jealousy, she made an already difficult situation worse."

"My parents believe she was just trying to get ahead of the story, to protect the family, but it backfired."

"Your parents wear blinders where that one is concerned."

Annette agreed, but didn't realize anyone else saw the truth.

"So, you're mad she did the interview? But I'm the one that didn't show up at the church." Why had she said that? Why bring up her own culpability?

Because therapy had only increased Annette's need to live honestly. She'd hated the subterfuge and subtle untruths that permeated her childhood hiding her adopted status like it was something to be ashamed of.

"I am aware." With that, Carlo pulled her in close, making talking difficult.

Unless she wanted to speak into his shirtfront. Annette didn't complain. Her body was responding as it always did to his nearness and it was all she could to not to melt into him. She inhaled his delicious masculine scent, knowing this was probably the last time she would ever do so. She had no idea why he'd asked her to dance after avoiding her all week, especially if, as it seemed, he didn't want to talk.

He still wore the cologne she'd picked out for him while they were dating. She wondered why. Did he like it that much? He had to overlook his antipathy toward the first person to have bought it for him every time he put it on. Or had he simply forgotten it was her?

What a demoralizing thought.

Soon any thought of cologne or gifts floated right out of her head as controlling her libido became her overriding concern. Desire bloomed deep in her belly and spread throughout her body so that everywhere they touched zinged with the electric current of need.

One song bled into another and rather than let her go, Carlo simply pulled her that much closer. Close enough that she could tell the dancing was having the same effect on him as it did on her.

"You want me," she whispered in shock.

He chuckled darkly, like he was laughing at himself. "We often want what is not good for us."

"We should..." she made a feeble attempt to step back.

He held her firmly. "Continue dancing, I agree."

He separated their bodies only when the music had shifted to something with a faster beat. Annette looked around them and realized he'd maneuvered them away from the crowded dance floor, toward the back of cavernous ballroom.

"We must have looked ridiculous dancing back here by ourselves." Not that Annette really cared about things like that.

"I doubt anyone even noticed."

Catching the glare of both her sister Lynette, and their mother, Annette had to disagree. Even Joyce was looking at them, but she was giving Annette the thumbs up and grinning.

Going on the principle that if she couldn't see them, her mom and oldest sister couldn't ruin the moment, Annette smiled back at Joyce and then turned so the only person she could see was Carlo.

"Why did you dance with me?" she asked baldly.

"Because I want you."

She stared. How was she supposed to respond to that? With honesty. She wasn't a naïve virgin, neither was he. "I want you too."

He passed her a black and gold keycard. "I have a suite here. Meet me there after Fantino and Joyce have had their sendoff."

Annette took the keycard automatically, but then immediately regretted doing so and tried to shove it back at him. "No. I can't. What about your girlfriend?"

"I do not have a girlfriend. I had a date."

"Had?"

"I sent her home in a car."

"Won't she be angry?"

He shrugged. "Perhaps, perhaps not. She got entrée to the event and the chance to make the connections she wanted."

"You're saying she only dated you for the access you could provide her? I don't believe that."

"The sex was a bonus," he said cynically.

Annette winced. It hurt to hear that cynicism in his voice, but it hurt even more to think about him having sex with another woman.

"You don't like the idea of me in bed with her."

"No." Again, honesty was her only fallback. Not a naïve virgin, but a possessive ex. She'd like to sink through the floor as she acknowledged that maybe honesty was not *always* the best policy.

"Then, you be that woman tonight."

"You're not some playboy who has a different bed partner every night."

"You sound very sure about that."

"It's not who you are."

"It has been five years. You don't know who I am."

"You could be right." She would have turned to leave, but something in his expression arrested her. "You want to make love with me, tonight."

"I want sex with you, *sì*."

Annette really didn't care what terminology they used. If they joined their bodies, emotion would be involved. Whether he acknowledged that emotion, or not, didn't mean it wouldn't be there.

The question was, could she live with all the emotion being on her side?

She'd spent five years unable to get over him. Maybe having sex with him without any commitments or even the tenuous tie of dating would give her what she needed to move on.

Closure.

They said that if what you were doing wasn't working, then you should change it. Being deprived of his company for five years hadn't given her the ability to let him go, but maybe this would.

Besides, Annette's body was already at nuclear meltdown levels, just from dancing with him. She'd been celibate so long, she hadn't bothered to have her IUD replaced when the time had come to remove it. Her body craved what her heart told her only he could give her.

By tomorrow morning, maybe both of those things would have shifted.

Determined to see through the sensual promise in his expression, she nodded to herself. "All right."

His gorgeous eyes flared infinitesimally, like she'd surprised him.

Annette tucked the keycard away in a hidden pocket in her dress and headed back into the ballroom.

Carlo watched Annette walk away from him, her honey blonde hair coming down from its formal updo, her beautiful curvy body moving enticingly in her blue dress, and wondered if he'd just made the biggest mistake of his life.

He'd known since sending Cynthia home that he was going to do it.

Annette had made it easy, but even if she hadn't, Carlo knew he would have pursued her with everything in his arsenal. Because he wanted what his brother had. A wife who wanted children with him. A wife who wanted to raise those children herself and not leave it up to others.

Someone unlike his own mother. As much as Carlo loved her, he wanted a mother for his children who would make time in *her* life for them.

And he wasn't going to find that until he'd worked Annette Hudson out of his system. Five years. It had been five years since she had jilted him, made him the butt of every kind of joke.

And in those years, Carlo had had sex with exactly two other women, one time each. On both occasions he'd been left feeling hollow and unsatisfied, regardless of the physical climax they'd both achieved. He could not forget the way it felt to make love to Annette.

He still dreamt about the woman who had as good as thrown his ring back in his face.

After the debacle, she'd sent the custom-made diamond and sapphire engagement ring back via her father. Carlo still had it stored in his wall safe. Maybe he could get rid of it after he finally got her out of his system.

Because he wasn't just being pedantic, he intended to have sex with her tonight, not make love. And in so doing, exorcise the demons that would not let him go.

The rest of the reception was a blur for Annette. She couldn't stop thinking about what was going to happen after. She'd meant to return to her spot out of the way, but Joyce had called Annette over, insisting she take Lynette's empty matron of honor seat.

"Lynette isn't going to be happy if she comes back and finds me here."

"I don't understand why she resents you so much," Joyce said with a familiar younger sister eyeroll. "You always did everything she didn't want to, making her life easier."

And been made into a meme because of it.

"Mom was lucky you were so accommodating. Lynette never would have been," Joyce said warmly.

She called Annette *Cinderella* with affection, finding it a great joke. She would never understand how much all the publicity that had circulated around Annette getting that moniker had hurt. Joyce had been a sunny dispositioned teen when it had happened and Annette wasn't about to go into old hurts now.

"I saw you with Carlo."

"I know." Annette shook her head. "Don't go getting romantic ideas. That man despises me."

"It sure didn't look like he hated you when you were dancing."

It hadn't felt like it either, but Annette knew something Joyce didn't seem to want to realize. When the sex happened, it wasn't going to be because Carlo wanted to start again with Annette.

They'd always been sexually compatible. Combustible more like.

The sex had been amazing, and Annette thought Carlo just wanted some more of it. Five years ago, she'd mistaken amazing sex for love, but she wouldn't make that mistake again.

She was looking for closure.

Nothing more.

If her heart accused her of lying to herself, Annette ignored that too savvy inner voice.

She had a keycard to his room, and she intended to use it.

CHAPTER THREE

Annette stood outside the hotel room door, her palms sweaty, and her heart beating a mile a minute.

Was she really going to go through with this? Was she going to have sex with Carlo Messina, when they hadn't spoken before this week in five years?

He'd refused all her attempts at communication, blocking her email address, her phone number, and on social media. He'd wanted nothing to do with her and she was sure that would have continued if their siblings hadn't fallen in love and decided to marry.

So, what was she doing here?

Getting her own closure and maybe giving him some too, not that he acted like he needed it. But if he did? She owed it to him. Not via sex, that was her choice, but if she could give him closure too, she wanted to.

Sure, and you aren't trying to rekindle anything. That heart voice was back, and it was laced with sarcasm.

Ignoring it, Annette lifted the keycard toward the door, but still she hesitated.

A sound down the corridor decided her. The one thing she was certain of was that she did not want to be caught standing outside his door.

She passed the keycard over the electronic reader and the door clicked. Taking a deep breath and letting it out, she opened it.

Annette stopped stock still at the sight that greeted her, the door swishing shut behind her.

Carlo was already inside, reclining naked on the bed, his dark hair wet from the shower. He had a drink in his hand. It looked like the Scotch malt whiskey he favored in a rock glass.

"You look like you've seen a ghost."

She shook her head, mute with overwhelming desire.

He put his hand out to her. "Come here."

"I'm still dressed." She'd found her voice. Just barely.

"Then allow me the privilege of undressing you."

So similar to things he'd used to say all the time to her, the words triggered a visceral reaction in Annette, her eyes stinging with emotion.

Carlo stood, his body rippling with even more muscles than she remembered. He'd always been well formed, but now he was really fit, his skin glowing with health.

"Do you work out a lot more?" she asked inanely.

He did not seem to mind, giving her a slashing smile. "Maybe. Are you saying I'm in better shape than I was five years ago?"

She licked suddenly dry lips. "Your muscles are more defined."

"And you like that?"

She nodded, incapable of speech.

He started by pulling the pins from her updo, allowing her long hair to completely release from its confinement. He took some of her long honey-colored curls between his fingers, seemingly mesmerized by the sight. "Your hair used to be darker."

"Lowlights." Annette had been getting brown streaks added to her honey blonde hair since she was an adolescent. Her mom had suggested them, and Annette had been desperate to fit in with her adopted family, so she'd gone along.

No amount of hair dye was going to make her part of the Floyd Hudson family, but she hadn't understood that until she was in Portland, letting her own blond roots grow out.

Carlo touched her natural blonde hair like he was rubbing silk between his fingers. "I like this better."

"I do too." And that was all that mattered anymore. Annette had given up all vestiges of trying to fit into her adopted family when she was exiled from New York.

"You are so different from the rest of your family," he mused, like he was just now making that observation.

Annette just shrugged. They'd never talked about the fact she was adopted. Her parents treated that fact like it was a state secret, and therefore so had Annette.

If tonight led to anything more, she would tell Carlo the truth of her past. It might help him understand her actions six years ago.

Though she wasn't counting on it. It had taken two years of therapy for Annette to understand herself.

And why was she thinking like that? This was closure, no matter what her inner voice said.

"Stop," he instructed as he unzipped the back of her dress.

She shivered in anticipation of what was to come. "What?"

"Thinking."

"No thinking?" she asked, perplexed. When had thinking become a bad thing?

"Only feeling. Only pleasure. Only me."

Ah, so he wanted her focus on him. That she could do. "Only you."

He tugged her dress off, letting it pool in a cloud of blue chiffon around her feet. She wore only a pale blue bra and panties set she'd bought just to wear under the bridesmaid dress.

"I like these." He touched the tiny pink rosettes where her bra cups met with a fingertip. "But I like these best of all." He cupped her lush breasts, brushing his thumbs over her nipples poking against the delicate silk.

Pleasure zinged a direct path from her tightened peaks to her core.

He leaned down and put his mouth over the blue silk, gently nipping and then sucking her nipple through the thin fabric.

Bombarded by sensations she hadn't felt in years, Annette shuddered. She'd tried sex with other men, but had balked at the final hurdle. Their kisses never felt right. Their touch felt too alien on her skin. Ultimately, she simply couldn't share her body with them.

She'd talked to her therapist about that too.

The revelation that she still loved Carlo had not been surprising. Her therapist's suggestion that she give her heart and body all the time she needed to move on had shocked her as it was so antithetical to how her family expected her to handle emotion. Learning that being told to simply forget one father while embracing her uncle as her dad was not in fact okay, had been freeing. Being told by someone that she could take all the time she needed to move on from Carlo had been too.

Annette had stopped trying to be what her family said she should and had simply accepted being herself.

Being herself had gotten her here and that wasn't so bad at all.

Heat suffused her body as he continued stimulating her breasts through the silk of her bra. Suddenly he cupped her bottom with both hands, lifted her, and carried her to the bed.

She landed on her back looking up at Carlo in all his primal masculine glory.

His pupils were blown, his expression dark with sexual need, his big body glowing in the lamplight of the room.

He reached out and touched the rosette right above her feminine mound. "So pretty."

"I like pretty underwear."

"I know." He gave her a slashing grin filled with sexual heat. "I like how they hint at your feminine beauty."

She always used to demur when he said stuff like that, telling him she knew she wasn't beautiful. Now, she soaked it in.

He smiled again. "No denial? I like that too."

"I've matured."

He didn't reply but slid his hands up her thighs and took hold of her underwear waistband. "All right?"

She nodded, wanting to be naked with him more than she'd ever wanted anything in her life, including her parents' affection and approval.

He tugged the blue silk down her thighs slowly, using the time to amp up the sexual tension between them. Annette reached behind herself to unclasp her bra, wanting it off as well.

"Impatient?" Carlo teased as he *finally* tugged her panties over her feet and tossed them on the floor behind him.

"Aren't you?" she taunted back.

"Maybe, but I'm going to savor you, Annette. We have all night."

She flung her bra aside. "I don't want to wait all night to have you inside me."

He didn't make her wait that long, but at times it felt like it. Carlo was on a mission to taste and touch every inch of her body, to drive Annette to a gibbering, pleading mess.

Finally, done with the teasing and the slow seduction, she pushed him onto his back. "Condom?" she asked in a tone that she hoped let him know she was done playing.

He grabbed one from under the pillow and Annette put it on him, her hands shaking. But she got it. And then, she took him into her body.

Her climax came almost immediately, causing her body to bow backward and a raw scream to erupt from her throat.

Carlo wasn't done though. He flipped their bodies, setting a slow pace of deep thrusts that aroused her all over again. By the time she climaxed the second time, he was pistoning into her body and shouting his own release.

Afterward, he got rid of the condom, but it was obvious he wasn't done.

"More?" she asked, a little awed.

He'd been a keen lover six years ago, but this was like pent up need finally finding an explosive outlet. She knew he hadn't been celibate. He'd been featured in too many gossip rags with sexy, beautiful women over the past years.

However, something was driving him, and she was happy to go along for the ride, finally falling into an exhausted sleep somewhere near dawn.

Annette woke feeling more comfortable in her skin than she had in years. Maybe ever.

Even five years ago, she had held parts of herself back from Carlo, afraid that if he knew the real her, he would lose interest. She'd still been dying her hair, dressing like her social set and socializing with the *right* people.

It was a lot more than her hair that had changed in the intervening time.

Annette's friends were more social activists now than socialites. She spent her spare time marching and organizing for her causes. She'd rather read than play tennis, and hike rather than play golf. She ate at food trucks and family-owned restaurants, instead of the latest hot spot with a Michelin Star.

She couldn't help wondering how the *new* Annette was going to fit in with Carlo's life. He came from wealth and privilege that far exceeded her own.

Refusing to let worry cloud her sense of wellbeing, she opened her eyes.

Annette was not surprised to be in the bed alone. Carlo had never needed as many hours of sleep as she did. The only times she'd ever woken with him beside her, he'd been up and working, only to return to bed to make love.

So, the empty bed and bedroom was no surprise. Annette got up and took a shower, a little surprised when the sound of hot running water hadn't brought her highly sexual lover into the bathroom. He must be on a business call.

She took her time drying her hair before donning one of the suite's complimentary robes to go in search of Carlo.

Annette cautiously looked through the cracked door as she opened, not wanting to be caught in the camera lens of a video call in a hotel bathrobe.

The living room was empty though. There was a cold breakfast of pastries and juice on the coffee table, obviously left there for her as the clear plastic dome was still over the plate of mouth-watering pastries. No note, but breakfast itself was a message.

Carlo was taking care of her.

No doubt still very much a workaholic, he must have gotten called away on business.

Annette sat down and uncovered the pastry plate, suddenly ravenous. She inhaled a perfectly flaky croissant filled with berries and cream before pouring herself a cup of coffee from the thermos style carafe. The dark liquid smelled divine and still steamed before she added milk and sugar.

Annette found her dress and the secret pocket that still had her cell phone in it. She used it to call his number.

He picked up on the third ring. "Hello?"

"It's Annette." She couldn't expect him to still have her number in his phone. They hadn't called each other in more than half a decade.

"Yes?"

"If you were expecting me to save you some pastry, you might be out of luck," she joked. "They're delicious."

"I have already eaten."

"Of course you have. What time did you get up anyway?"

"Does it matter? Did you need something, Annette?"

The coolness of his tone finally registered. This wasn't about talking in front of business associates. This was about how he was responding *to her*.

"You were gone when I woke up," she pointed out, but at what point last night had she decided he would be there?

When had she shifted from seeking closure to looking for something more?

"Naturally."

His neutral tone was getting to her. "You didn't leave a note."

"Why would I have?"

"Um, because that would have been polite?"

"I wasn't aware that there was an etiquette for one-night stands."

All the air whooshed out of Annette's lungs like she'd been sucker punched. "What do you mean?" she forced out.

Okay, he'd said it was just sex before it even started, but did that mean he couldn't treat her with common decency? Is this how men and women who had one-night stands treated each other?

If it was, she was glad she'd been celibate. Annette didn't like it. At all.

She'd had enough of being treated like an afterthought that didn't matter by her family.

"We weren't starting something last night, Annette. If anything, we were finally finishing it."

"Last night was closure for you?" she asked through suddenly dry lips, envious if it was true.

She'd wanted to give him closure if she could, but she'd also wanted it for herself and the way she'd woken up this morning thinking about a future with him was proof she, at least, hadn't gotten it.

"*Sì.*" Which was an admission that he'd needed closure.

That was something, what she wasn't sure, but something.

"A one-night stand," she reiterated.

"*Sì.*"

"I've never had one," she mused mostly to herself.

He made an odd sound. "Now you have."

"Carlo..." Her voice trailed off. She didn't know what she wanted to say to him.

"If that is all?" But he didn't sound as unmoved as he had earlier.

It was almost like he needed to get off to the phone.

"You left me breakfast." Why had he done that?

"It seemed the polite thing to do."

Ah, manners. Carlo had impeccable ones. And apparently, he knew what was called for these situations. Unlike her. "So, there is an etiquette for one-night-stands, only I didn't know."

"We had great sex last night, Annette. I wouldn't mind repeating the experience, but that is all it was."

"You wouldn't mind repeating the..." Oh, the arrogant so-and-so!

She'd blast him, but the truth was, Annette couldn't be entirely sure that if he asked, she'd say no. She'd walked into this hotel room with both eyes open.

But then they'd started kissing and touching and nothing about that had been emotionless. "It wasn't just physical pleasure, for either of us." He could acknowledge it, or not.

The truth was the truth.

"Perhaps not. We do share a past."

"Last night we shared a lot more than a past." They'd shared their bodies in every imaginable way. "You couldn't get enough of me."

And if she knew him at all, he'd left that morning, so he didn't give into the temptation of having her again. Because he might not trust her, but he still wanted her, and closure wasn't sex until you literally could not stop collapsing from exhaustion.

That was wanting more.

Only he had no intention of admitting it, did he?

"Thank you for breakfast," she said as he began to say something. "I'll see you around."

But she fervently hoped not before she'd developed some defensive walls where he was concerned.

Annette was not built for one-night stands.

She hung up before he could reply. When her phone rang a few minutes later, she ignored it.

However, she read the text that came in a few seconds after the call went to voicemail.

It isn't polite to hang up on people.

She texted back. *I thought one-night stands didn't need to be polite.*

I left you breakfast.

Yes, he had, but he'd also left her with the painful realization that Annette was no closer to being over Carlo than she had been before their wild night of lovemaking.

Chapter Four

Annette refused to pick up when Carlo called, but she replied to his texts.

Sometimes he sent ones laden with sexual innuendo, other times he sent her memes that made her laugh out loud. Some were just comments about his day.

They didn't text every day, but a full week did not go by before he would reach out again.

He always initiated the communication. It was her rule.

It felt right after spending five years being blocked by him, which she noticed was no longer an issue. She'd never unfriended Carlo on social media platforms and suddenly his posts started showing up in her newsfeeds.

He also reacted to her posts, which led to one spectacular donation for the summer youth camp she organized.

Were they *friends* now? She wasn't sure, but it seemed like it.

Apparently closure for Carlo meant they could be friends. But those sexy texts? They implied he wanted more.

Annette just wasn't sure what she wanted.

Annette flew to New York as soon as she could get a flight when her sister went into labor and made it in time to be in the room when Jocinda Valentina Messina was born. Her name filled Annette with warmth since her sister had told Annette that she and Fantino had agreed to name their daughter after both Joyce and Annette, using a derivative of the nickname Joyce still called Annette in their private calls and texts. Cinderella.

For once the moniker brought nothing but pleasure to Annette.

Joyce was euphoric after the birth of her daughter and Annette hated having to leave that much happiness to return to Portland, but she'd been recently promoted to regional director for her organization, and it could not be helped.

A month later, she flew to Sicily for the christening, and was shocked at her sister's wan appearance and Fantino's unhappy demeanor.

Annette waited until they were alone together on the terrace overlooking the pool and a fabulous view of the Mediterranean at the Messina family mansion to approach Joyce about it. "Is everything okay, honey?"

Everyone had congregated for a celebratory lunch and the grandmothers were currently taking turns holding the little sleeping Jocinda, cooing over the baby and saying what a sweetheart she was.

"What do you mean?" Joyce asked defensively, her wan face pinched. "Of course, it is."

"You and Fantino look a little worn, is all," Annette said soothingly. "Can I help?"

"With you living across country? What are you going to do, rock my daughter to sleep via video call?" Joyce's derisive tone took Annette aback.

"I could come stay if you want me to."

"I'm fine. My baby is fine. I can handle it," Joyce said with more anger than confidence, turning and storming to the other side of the terrace.

She pressed her hands on the rail, her grip so tight Annette could see the whites of her knuckles from where she stood in worried bewilderment.

"Trust you to upset your sister on such a special day." Her mother's voice had Annette spinning around.

Annette took a deep breath and let it out before speaking. "I wasn't trying to upset her."

"Not to be too indelicate, but you need to butt out, Netta. Your sister is fine."

The woman who had just snapped at her and looked like she hadn't slept in a week was not fine. "I guess we don't see the same thing when we look at her."

"No, we don't. I am not jealous of what she has."

The accusation hit too close to the bone for Annette to respond immediately. She wasn't jealous of her sister, but she'd had moments of envy she'd had to work through. Her therapist said that was normal, but Annette still felt guilty about it.

Without another word, Annette's mother walked away.

Typical. Why try to have a conversation with the daughter you barely acknowledged? If it wasn't for Joyce, Annette was pretty sure her family would simply have stopped acknowledging her all together.

"That didn't sound good." Carlo's concerned tone coming from behind her had Annette spinning around.

She'd seen him from a distance at the Christening, but had managed to avoid talking to him until now.

She frowned at him. "I wasn't being nosy. I'm concerned."

"Did I say anything?" he asked, his hands up in that gesture that meant he wasn't guilty.

Realizing she was reacting to her mother's words and not his, Annette felt heat steal up her neck. "I am sorry, I should not have snapped at you."

"What was that all about?" he asked, waving away the apology.

"Have you noticed that your brother barely smiles and that my sister looks like she hasn't slept in a week?" she asked, unable to believe she was the only one who saw how beleaguered both new parents had become.

However, Carlo flicked his hand dismissively. "New parenthood is hard. It is to be expected."

"You say that like you know something about it, but you don't have any children." And his mother had always had help, so Annette doubted sincerely this attitude was coming from Valentina or Alceu Messina.

"No, I don't. The woman who promised me marriage and a family left me standing at the altar." He said it sardonically, with little emotion, but the anger banked in his gaze said all she needed to know about how much he'd forgiven her.

Which was not at all.

Despite their night of uninhibited passion after their siblings' wedding and the texting and online *friendship* they'd built since then. It would be smart of her to remember that.

"Okay, so neither of us is parents. Noted. That doesn't change the fact that they need our help." How could he not see that?

"I could offer to hire a nanny for them, but my brother is perfectly capable of doing so. I am unclear on what kind of help you hope to offer?" he asked, reflecting her sister's attitude almost verbatim.

"I could go and stay with them if they need me," she said, repeating what she'd told Joyce.

The look Carlo gave her was odd. "You realize that would require you taking time off of work. I thought you were busy with the new regional directorship."

"I did not say it would be easy, but I could do it."

"If you were needed." There was something in Carlo's tone. It wasn't quite derogatory, but it was something. He shrugged. "Look, If Joyce needs help, your mother is there in New York for her to call on."

"My mother isn't going to offer to babysit." But honestly, Annette wasn't sure that was true. "Okay, maybe she will. She loves Joyce after all."

Unlike the adopted daughter she'd taken on sufferance.

"So, you have nothing to worry about."

Only that everyone else seemed to think how wan her sister looked was normal and okay.

Maybe Annette was being paranoid and feeling guilty because she wasn't in town and able to offer real help with the baby. Her sister was right. Annette couldn't rock her baby niece to sleep, or help by changing a diaper, or in any other tangible way from across the country.

Unlike the rest of her family, she wasn't wealthy and couldn't pay for once a week help for her sister to get a break, or anything like *that* either.

Perhaps the time had come to move back to New York. If her father balked, Annette would tell him to deal with it. She'd lived in exile long enough. She had stayed away for over five years. Surely that was enough time for the embarrassment her actions had brought her family to have subsided and her notoriety with it.

She couldn't afford to live in the city, even if she left the nonprofit sector, which she didn't want to do. But she could move close enough to make it possible to see her sister weekly, instead of only for the major events in Joyce's life.

"You don't look like you are getting much sleep yourself," Carlo remarked.

He didn't sound concerned exactly, but he didn't sound like he was reveling in her misfortune either.

"Jetlag," she dismissed, though she knew that was only part of it.

She hadn't been sleeping well for weeks. Her promotion had been eye opening in some very negative ways.

Now that Annette had access to what all the employees in her region were being paid, the realization that there were gross inequities in pay for marginalized staff had hurt. Finding out that she was not allowed to address those inequities because of national policy for the organization had been soul destroying.

She was currently fighting for pay raises for three of the employees and the amount of red tape being thrown her way opened her eyes to realities she found beyond unacceptable.

"How long will you be in Sicily?" he asked, speculation in his grey eyes.

"Just three days."

"That is a rather short stay for such a long flight."

He was right. Flying commercial from Oregon made for an extremely long day flying, especially when she'd had a four-hour layover in Rome because her flight to Sicily had been delayed. The flight home would be worse. "I couldn't take any more time off from my job."

Disappointment flashed in his grey gaze. "Ah, yes, your career comes first."

He didn't point out the fact that if she wanted to help her sister in any meaningful way, Annette's job could not take the precedence it always had. They both knew it and clearly, he believed she wouldn't make the necessary changes.

Why should he think any differently? Annette had refused to change jobs to move to Sicily with him after their wedding. Looking back, especially knowing what she did now about her organization, regret sat heavily on her heart.

"It's all I have right now," she admitted baldly. Particularly if Joyce didn't *want* Annette's help or presence.

Annette had no social life to speak of. All of her friends were from work and their socialization happened around work. Her new position was making her take stock of how the management expected that kind of commitment from employees that were not paid enough to make rent and utilities without a partner.

Like her. She'd had to sell stuff and work a seasonal second job to make ends meet.

"Being named our niece's godparent meant nothing to you then?" he asked, this time the disappointment in her was easy to see.

"That's not what I said. I just..." Being named Jocinda's godparent wasn't going to change Annette's life appreciably.

Not as long as she kept living in Portland.

Joyce was the only member of Annette's family who wanted anything to do with her, but she lived across country. They video chatted weekly, and Annette had been able to return to New York for important events, like Joyce's wedding and Jocinda's birth, but it wasn't enough.

Annette could only see one way to fix that.

Carlo stepped closer to her, leaned down and spoke in that low tone that sent shivers through her. "You just what?"

"Oh no you don't." She hurriedly stepped back, her progress blocked by the railing. She put her hand up in the *stop* gesture. "You stay over there."

"What is the matter, Annette?" Carlo had remained in her personal space, his body giving off pheromones that hers reacted to regardless of what her mind insisted she do.

Do not give in. Leave him alone. Steer clear of his brand of Sicilian seduction.

"You've got that look in your eye," she accused.

"What look is that?" he asked, stepping forward again so her hand pressed against his chest.

How had he gone from being disappointed in her, to wanting sex with her? What did that say about him wanting her at all? That he was only interested in her body and not the mind of the woman he didn't understand.

"You know what I'm talking about, and we aren't going there."

He tugged her hand up to his mouth and tickled her palm with the tip of his tongue, sending shivers down her arm and to places more intimate. "I think we should." He kissed her palm.

Desire burst into flame inside her so potent her knees wanted to buckle. Annette gripped the rail behind her and stood firm. This was not happening.

"I'm not one-night stand material," she told him tightly.

He gave her a devilish smile. "How about friends with benefits?"

"We aren't friends."

"Aren't we?" he asked with amusement. "You know me better than anyone, surely that makes us friends."

"*Friendship* makes friends, and we don't have that." Only, they sort of did. Now.

"I text you more often than I do anyone else. We follow each other on social media."

Now they did. "For five years, you wouldn't take a single call or text or email."

"I was angry. My Sicilian emotions run deep."

"Are you saying you've forgiven me?"

"I am saying I want to spend the time you have here in Sicily together."

"In bed."

"And out of it."

Annette went still. *That* was different.

"And when I go back to Portland?"

"I've never tried sexting, but I'm game."

"No," she said quickly, before her own temptation to indulge in both suggestions that sounded wildly interesting showed on her face. "I'm not wired for casual sex."

Which she knew was true, but she also knew that sex with Carlo would never be casual for her, at least.

"Isn't that old fashioned?" He brushed her nape, sending frissons of enticement traveling along her nerve endings. "What about the sexual revolution women have fought so hard for?"

That was rich coming from one of the original throwbacks. "It's about having the freedom to have sex, or not, as we see fit, Carlo. Not a mandate to have sex."

"You do want me," he said with conceited assurance.

That was unfortunately entirely justified.

"But I don't want no-strings sex."

He stepped back, a cloak of cold withdrawal going around him. "I'm not offering strings to you."

"I didn't think you were." Which was why, this time, Annette was thinking with her head and not her sexual desire, or her heart. "You made that abundantly clear the last time."

"So, you refuse to give into what we both want because I know better than to trust you with anything other than sex?" His tone said he couldn't quite believe his ears.

She wanted to shout, *Welcome to the club, buddy!*, but asked instead, "You don't think you can trust me?" She made no attempt to hide her own shock.

"How can you be surprised by that?" He stared down at her, that disbelief now written clearly on his handsome features. "You left me standing at the altar."

"I told you I wouldn't be there." She still didn't understand why he'd shown up.

"I thought it was prewedding jitters. I made the mistake of trusting you to keep your promise and all that got me was public and private humiliation and vilification," he said with grim judgement.

Carlo had really believed she would show up at the church. That just boggled her mind.

Was it because he'd believed in their relationship that strongly, or simply could not imagine her refusing to fall in with his plans?

"You wouldn't listen to me, not about the honeymoon, not about moving. It took too long for me to realize that there were compromises we could have made, that we needed to talk more." How many times had Annette wished over the last seven and a half years she'd gone through with the wedding and then offered up those options, or at least insisted on discussing them beforehand?

"Compromises?" he asked with scorn, the usual urbane charmer no longer in evidence. "Your actions showed you weren't interested in compromising in any way."

She could see why he thought that. She'd told her parents the wedding was off after trying to give Carlo back her ring. Then she'd run away. She'd turned off her phone and found a no name motel to hole up in. She hadn't even realized the media frenzy was happening until it was too late to do anything meaningful to mitigate it.

By then Alceu had his accident and Floyd Hudson had already spoken to the head office of her organization, making an offer they had no intention of refusing. Her transfer had happened in a matter of days. "I am truly sorry. There are reasons—"

"There is no excuse for you running away like you did," he said adamantly.

"I didn't say excuses, I said reasons. And honestly, even understanding myself better now, after the highhanded way you planned our future and the length of our honeymoon without consulting me, I'm not sure I could have done anything differently." That had been a hard thing to acknowledge.

Almost as hard as realizing she had reacted more to the fear of being rejected than what he'd said and done.

It was a conundrum she'd never quite found a solution to. She knew her reaction had been knee-jerk and over the top, but even knowing that she should have pressed for another talk with him, she could not be confident that the end result would have been any different.

As much as she'd wished over and over that she'd gone through with the wedding, she'd also thought an equal number of times she'd been right to call it off. Not how she'd done it maybe and not because she was afraid of him eventually dumping her because she wasn't the perfect woman for him, but because their relationship had been too unequal.

She'd been too used to unequal relationships to see it. Then anyway.

Now, she saw the past through a very different lens than the one she'd used to look at life through when she was twenty-two. Which did not mean they couldn't have found more even footing to stand on.

Was that why she found it so hard to let him go? The unknown of whether they could have worked things out, or not?

"Good to know your apology just now was as sincere as your promise back then." Carlo turned and walked away, but unlike Joyce, he headed back inside the traditional Mediterranean style mansion.

Annette didn't call him back.

She was too busy reliving the conversation that had prompted her to call off the wedding.

Chapter Five

"So, we'll take two months, using a house on the Dalmatian Coast as our base, and my new yacht, exploring every bit of ancient culture in Croatia, Italy, Greece and Turkey that we can." Wealthy Sicilian tycoon, Carlo finished speaking and looked at Annette with expectation in his grey gaze, like he'd just offered her the world, not tried to take hers apart.

"I can't take two months off for a honeymoon," she told him, quite reasonably she thought, when really? She wanted to scream.

At 22, she'd only graduated university the year before and she'd landed her dream job as a program coordinator for an organization that serviced youth in the Foster Care system.

His handsome face settled into a frown. "But you love travel and history. It is the perfect honeymoon for you, *bèdda mia.*"

For once, Annette didn't react to him calling her *his beauty* in Sicilian. She could not let herself get sidetracked by the way he made her feel. She loved him more than anything else and still, something inside her was screaming a warning because of his words.

This was too important. "And if you were talking about the two weeks we had planned, not two months, right when we are supposed to be launching a new STEM program for our youth, I would be leaping on you with gratitude."

"I expected you to leap regardless." His sexy grin did predictable things to her insides.

"You know two months is too long for me to take away from my job," she told him, needing her Sicilian tycoon lover to understand.

"I run a worldwide consortium and *I* am taking two months," he pointed out.

If that were true, she would feel very differently. Maybe.

"But you aren't taking two months off, are you? You have a state-of-the-art office on board that new yacht and you'll spend a few hours every day making sure that your family's multiple companies continue to run like clockwork."

His expression said he didn't get her point. "You require more sleep than I do, my few hours a day keeping my hand in will not impinge on our time together."

"I believe you'll do your best to make sure they don't, but I also know if an emergency arises, you'll deal with if it. Even if that means you calling in a helicopter to take you to be onsite."

"That happened once."

"During a date," she pointed out because the memory still rankled. He'd left her without a backward glance when they'd been very close to making love. "But in a space of two months, how many emergencies do you deal with?"

"We cannot foresee that."

"No, but we do *know* that my organization will have to hire a program coordinator to take my place, and there can be no guarantee they'll have a place for me when we return. Not to mention the fact that I will not have time to train my replacement how to get into the building, much less how to do the job, between now and our wedding." Which was only two days away. "And we also *know* that there will be lots of emergencies over the next two months getting that program up and running, but *I* won't be accessible to deal with them."

"You cannot compare your job to my role in Messina Shipping & Exports."

The company had started off as a humble exporter of olive oil and other agricultural goods from Sicily four generations in the past. Now it was one of the world's largest import-export brokers and had an entire fleet of cargo ships.

And even that hadn't been enough for her power broker fiancé. The tall, dark-haired Adonis had his own Venture Capitalist firm which had made him one of the richest men in Europe in his own right by the age of twenty-nine.

Not that any of that mattered to Annette. She'd fallen in love with Carlo the man, not Carlo the billionaire.

"No, and I've never tried to," she said now. "But I do ask that you respect that my job is very important *to me* even if it doesn't make me rich."

"You do not need to work once we are married," he said with arrogant assurance.

Pain filled her as she realized where this two-month long honeymoon was really coming from, and it wasn't her fiancé's desire to spend two months working parttime and remotely. He wanted her to quit her job. Had done since almost the moment she'd first taken it.

Only she thought they'd worked out that was not going to happen. "So, you've said."

She didn't understand his attitude. While his mother might not earn a salary for her volunteer work, the Sicilian socialite easily worked fulltime hours on her various charities and projects.

"Your job should not be more important than me." This time Carlo's frown was more of a scowl and she could see that something more than natural male arrogance was there, under the surface.

Only her own feelings of panic were taking precedence. This felt way too much like conversations she'd had with her father. Why must Annette choose to work in a career with no prestige? Didn't she see how her desire to work with at risk youth made their family look?

She thought it made them look like maybe they'd raised someone who cared about the world beyond her own front door. Her parents did not agree.

Social activism had its role, but not the one Annette wanted to take.

"No, of course not," she said responding to Carlo's words and not her father's playing over and over in her head. She wasn't putting the job ahead of him, but ahead of the luxury of a two-month-long honeymoon. "But how I feel about what I do *should* be important to you."

"You will find other worthy causes to support after we are married, *bèdda mia*."

"Like your mother?" she asked. Was the problem Annette earning an income?

"Perhaps not with the same level of time commitment."

Things started to become clearer in Annette's mind. She might be five years younger than him, but she was not ignorant. "You mean projects I can throw your money at, but not my time?" she asked with more anger than she'd realized she was holding.

His gorgeous grey eyes widened, like the anger in her tone surprised him too. "I am not being unreasonable."

"Telling me two days before the wedding that you want me to take practically the entire summer off from my position at a critical time for the program is more than unreasonable, it's selfish and manipulative. You don't want me to work and you're hoping that this will be the catalyst to force me into giving up my job."

She wanted him to deny the words so badly, her body ached with the tension it was holding.

"What if I am?" he demanded, slashing through the bubble of her dreams so they deflated too fast for even a pop of sound inside her heart. "I am a wealthy man, from an old family. Your job is an embarrassment to me."

She couldn't breathe for the pain in her chest.

His words were so like her father's they'd already been sharpened to such a fine point, they lacerated her heart with ease.

When she said nothing, he added. "We will be living in Sicily after the honeymoon, so you couldn't keep that job anyway."

And just like that, he dismissed her job as of no importance, telling Annette that the things closest to her heart didn't even register with the man she'd fallen in love with.

As a program coordinator for a social service organization, she could not be his perfect wife. But if she did not help others as she had always dreamed of doing, Annette could not, would not be herself.

So, that meant what? That he wanted to marry a different version of her, one that did not in fact exist. Annette had learned early and young that being something other than what was wanted, or expected, led to rejection and abandonment.

"When were you going to tell me that?" she asked painfully.

"I just did."

"But your office is in New York."

"My younger brother will be taking over the New York office. My father wants to retire and that means me taking over Messina Shipping & Exports."

"Your father wants to retire?" she asked, dumbfounded. Alceu Messina was an even bigger workaholic than his son.

"His doctor has told him he needs to minimize the stress in his life."

"Your father isn't well? Why didn't you tell me?" The feeling of being shielded from the truth did not wrap around her like a protective blanket, but upbraided her every exposed nerve ending.

She'd been left out of the loop with her own family too often to ever take it in stride from the man she intended to marry.

"He is not unwell, but he is ready to make a change in his life. He is sixty-seven after all, he has earned it."

"Yes, of course." Alceu and Valentina had their children later in life.

Annette didn't know if that had been on purpose or because there had been complications. It wasn't something she and Carlo had ever talked about. Like too many things, it looked like.

"I still don't understand why you didn't tell me he wanted to retire."

"Papa doesn't want it getting out before I take over."

"But I'm not the media."

Carlo shrugged.

And so many things were becoming awfully, painfully clear she couldn't deal with the emotional fallout. "How long have you known?"

"Does it matter?"

"I think it does."

"He asked me to take over three months ago and we've been moving toward that transition since."

That explained why Carlo made so many extra trips to Sicily in the past months. "You didn't think I deserved to know *then* that you were going to move us to Europe?"

"I am telling you now."

"Why?"

"Don't be dense."

"I'm not being dense. I want to know why you didn't even talk to me before making that kind of monumental decision for both our lives."

"Why would I?"

And that, in a nutshell, said it all. Her opinions were unimportant. Her dreams were unimportant. Her desires were unimportant. They only mattered when they coincided with his.

Ultimately, *she* was unimportant.

She existed to him only as he wanted her to be, only he saw her as some construct he'd created in his own mind, not the woman she was. Could never be. Playing arm candy to a wealthy husband and socialite in training with his family was a role Annette was destined to fail at.

Just like she'd failed at being the kind of daughter her parents had wanted her to be.

She stared up at him, drinking in his gorgeous face, his muscular body, knowing she was likely seeing him for the last time. "You're so arrogant."

"You've said that before," he said with a slashing smile.

"But I'm not finding it charming right now. Your arrogance and selfishness are hurting me, and you don't even care." Could she get through to him?

Could she make him see that she was herself, not some version he'd concocted in his brain and Annette simply could not be anything other than *herself*?

"You will get over leaving your job," he said with absolute assurance.

"And leaving my sister? And the rest of my family," she tacked on, though Joyce was the only one Annette would actually miss.

Or who would miss her.

Their older sister had always resented the younger sibling who had been adopted when she was an only child. Their parents didn't even pretend anymore that they saw Annette the same way they did their two biological children.

But then, their reasons for adopting her had not been emotional, or even altruistic.

Carlo frowned. "You knew that one day we would have to move back to Sicily."

"One day in the future, not right now!"

"Now or then? What's the difference?"

She could see why he felt that way. For him, there was no difference. He'd never given any credence to her desire to do certain things with her organization before she left, how committed she was to starting a STEM program and building it into something she could be proud of. Something that would make a difference to children too often overlooked by the very agency created to serve them.

"It's always going to be like this with you, isn't it?" she asked as her heart cracked inside her chest.

"What do you mean?" He was starting to look just a tiny bit worried.

If business moguls ever actually worried about personal stuff, and she was not convinced they did.

"My feelings will always be secondary. The things I want, or need, out of life will always come down the priority list for you, if they make it on there at all."

"You want me. You need me. That is what is important."

"Not if it means losing *me*." She tugged the engagement ring off her finger.

The symbol she'd thought of love he could not express with words. It had been designed for her. Yellow gold with a beautiful floral design accented by diamonds and sapphires. Platinum was *de rigueur* in their set, but he'd had her ring made from her preferred precious metal. The floral design reflected her love of flowers and natural beauty.

He'd taken her desires into consideration when he'd had it made, why did they matter so little now?

"What are you doing?" he demanded.

She extended her hand with the ring in it toward him. "The wedding is off."

"Do not be melodramatic, *bèdda mia*. The wedding is not off. If it is that important to you, find a charity organization to support with your time once we return to Sicily after the wedding," he said, like making a hugely magnanimous gesture. "Parttime of course."

"Your mother easily works fulltime."

"I know."

And once again in a matter of minutes, lightbulbs went on in her brain, illuminating truths Annette had overlooked during their time together.

What she had always seen as a point of concurrence for them, was in fact a wedge that would drive them apart. "How did I never realize you resented your mother's time on her work?"

"I never said I did." But his expression? That closed off, emotionless mask said it all.

Something about Valentina's commitment to her various causes had hurt Carlo, leaving him with the certainty that *his* wife should put their family first.

And Annette had never even realized that was an issue. How unseeing had she been? So wrapped up in her own glowing version of their relationship she'd ignored every indicator that their views of the world did not mesh.

"This," Annette indicated him and her with a gesture of her hand. "It says it loud and clear."

"I want our children to have your attention."

"We aren't having children right away," she said with exasperation. They'd discussed it and agreed to wait at least a couple of years. She was leaning more toward five or six.

She was marrying young because she'd fallen in love, that didn't mean she wanted everything else happening at a pace.

"My father wants to meet his grandchildren before he dies."

"His health is that serious?" she asked, her heart squeezing in her chest. She *liked* Alceu, though he was every bit as much of a workaholic as his sons had been raised to be.

"No. As I said, he is not ill, but he is nearing seventy."

And would probably live to see ninety at least.

"Yet another decision you planned to make without me?" she asked, her tone harsh.

She'd spent years working so hard to earn her family's love, being placid when inside she was roiling with anger sometimes, pursuing activities she didn't enjoy in the least to please adopted parents that never seemed to think she measured up.

Annette had promised herself she wouldn't marry a man who expected the same from her. She'd thought she'd found him.

She'd been spectacularly wrong.

"I could hardly do that, could I?" he asked, this time annoyance and impatience loud and clear in his tone.

He referred, of course, to the fact that she had opted to use an IUD for birth control, once they had become physically intimate. It was only coming out on her say so. She was talking about something far more important than the mechanics of birth control. Annette was referring to sharing decisions as equals, to respecting one another's goals and dreams.

She didn't have to run a multinational corporation for the time she spent at work to have value. No, she didn't employ thousands of people, but she made a difference in the lives of the youth she served.

Apparently, he did not see things the same way.

At all.

"I cannot marry you," she said again, each word a slashing wound to her heart. Annette tried to hand him the ring again. "I'm not the right woman for you."

"I will be the judge of that, *caro*." Carlo looked at her with indulgence rather than anger, and totally ignored her outstretched hand. "Of course, you can marry me. Things may be happening more quickly than either of us expected in certain regards, but it is nothing to fear."

She wasn't afraid of being a mother, but neither was she ready for that role just yet. "You expect me to jettison my job and move to Sicily."

"You knew we would have to move there at some point, that you could not stay with your organization long term."

"Yes, but I had plans, goals for what I could do while I was there."

"So, make new plans. Set new goals." His tone implied this was not rocket science.

"If I married you, it would always be like this, wouldn't it? Me changing to fit your plans, you making decisions without my input."

He sighed. "Perhaps, I should have spoken to you about the move, but *cara*, you must understand, the last weeks have been intense. It took a great deal to clear my schedule for the honeymoon. My father's decision to retire came unexpectedly, even for me."

A two-month-long honeymoon she had not asked for and did not want. Not to mention emotionally painful and stressful, not that Carlo would admit to anything that might resemble weakness.

"He works too many hours and dines on stress," Annette said, realizing she might as well be describing Carlo. She still found it hard to believe Alceu wanted to retire.

His health *must* be more precarious than Carlo was acknowledging. But was that because Carlo refused to see it, or he simply didn't want to share it with her?

Her Sicilian lover shrugged. "He will have to learn to eat food instead," he joked.

"Yes, but it's not your father that's worrying me." She sighed, realizing how callous that sounded. "I don't mean I don't care about him. I do care. Very much, but he's not the problem."

"No, your job is the problem."

She shook her head. "It's not my job. It's me. You want me to be something I'm not, someone I'm not even sure I could ever be, even if I was willing to try."

"You are talking nonsense. Listen, this is just prewedding jitters. You will feel better after we are wed."

"I am not going to marry you." She held the ring out again, pain so heavy she wasn't sure she could hold it inside. "Take it. I mean it, Carlo."

But he remained with his hands stubbornly down. "I will not. I will be standing at the front of the church waiting for you in two days' time. I expect you to be there. Whatever problems you think we have, we can work them out later. We have a lifetime."

He turned and strode away without another word.

Annette tried to shout after him, but she could not make the words come.

No matter what he thought, that was not how it worked. Whatever problems they had would follow them into marriage. And this problem was insurmountable.

She was not the right woman for him.

And as much as it hurt to admit, *he was not the right man for her.*

One thing she knew with absolute certainty, being alone was better than living with someone who needed her to be something other than her authentic self to accept her. She'd lived that way since she was five years old, until she'd gone away to university.

She could not live that way again.

Not ever.

CHAPTER SIX

Annette came out of her fugue of memories to note her sister had left the terrace and she was entirely alone. It was not a new feeling.

She'd basically been alone since becoming the unwanted baggage from her birth father's first marriage, dumped with his brother to appease his new wife. Named Annette after her mother, Anne, her adoptive family had instantly started calling her Netta in deference to the woman now married to William Hudson. Apparently, Annette looked too much like her birth mother as well, serving as a continual reminder of a past both her birth father and his second wife would prefer to forget.

She was blonde and blue eyed, like her deceased mother. Everyone else in the Hudson clan were brunettes. Kimber, the woman who her birth father had married, was even a brunette, though she had salon perfected red highlights. At five-feet-three inches, Annette was shorter than all the other women in her family too. Where they were tall and svelte, she was short and curvy.

Unlike her sisters, she could never wear a garment straight off the runway.

Carlo hadn't seemed to mind though. He'd called her his pocket Venus and complimented her blue eyes, often saying they glowed like sapphires. When they'd had sex after her sister's wedding, he'd said he liked her natural blonde hair better than the lowlights too.

If only his appreciation for her body translated to him caring about and approving of the person she was. It didn't though.

And now she understood better where five years of silence had come from.

He had truly believed she would show up at the church. He'd trusted her to keep her promise to marry him and because she'd left telling people the wedding was off to her parents, no one had disabused him of that notion.

She'd literally left him standing at the altar and all her reasons for her behavior five years ago didn't change that. Not for the first time, she realized she owed him an apology. One without qualifiers or explanations.

She thought he should be sorry too, for the high-handed way he'd tried to dictate her life five years ago. However, if therapy had taught her anything, it was that Annette could not dictate the actions of others. She only had agency over her own, but she did have that agency and had to always remember that.

Needing to make sure things were okay between her and Joyce, or simply looking for a way to put off the upcoming discussion with Carlo, Annette went back inside the villa.

She found her sister sitting between their mother and their oldest sister, Lynette.

The look she gave Annette indicated that had not been happenstance on her part. Joyce didn't want another private tete-e-tete with Annette and she'd chosen the perfect avoidance.

Hurt, but unwilling to approach her younger sister when she'd placed herself between allies so hostile to Annette, she looked around the large drawing room for sign of either the baby, or Carlo.

She found them together with Fantino. Carlo was holding Jocinda oh so carefully, his expression one of wonder and unabashed affection as he looked down at the tiny infant.

Fantino was talking about some business deal and for once it was clear he only had half his brother's attention on the company matter. The way the young father kept reaching out to run a finger down his daughter's soft cheek, or touch her little foot showed that maybe his attention wasn't fully focused on what he was saying either.

The younger Messina looked up as Annette approached. "Ah, Annette. Joyce was hoping the two of you could spend some time together alone."

Not anymore, she wasn't. But Annette didn't say that. She simply gave Fantino what she thought of as her *family* smile, the one that hid all real emotion. "That would be nice. I wouldn't mind some time with this beautiful little girl, either."

Carlo's head snapped up, like he'd just now realized Annette was there. For one second his grey gaze flashed with welcome and the heat that was always there, under the surface, between them. Then his face shuttered, and he looked to his brother. "Set up the meeting. I'll have my team put together the numbers and proposal you and I have discussed."

So much for him only listening with partial attention. She should have known better. Nothing got between Carlo and business. Not even their adorable new baby niece.

"*Bonu,*" Fantino said. "I appreciate—"

Carlo interrupted his brother's thanks, saying something like no problem, that's what brothers are for in Sicilian. Close enough to Italian, which she spoke fluently, for her to understand, Annette still wouldn't have tried to speak the native dialect of Sicily.

"May I hold her?" Annette asked Fantino, indicating Jocinda.

"If you can prise her away from my brother." Fantino laughed at his own joke, though Annette still thought he looked exhausted.

"Jocinda isn't sleeping through the night?" she asked.

She'd thought the baby was because of something Joyce had said on one of their video calls, but neither parent was rested enough for that to be true.

Something skittered across the younger brother's features, but he shrugged. "Jet lag."

Funny, she didn't believe him when he said it any more than she'd believed herself using the excuse earlier. "If I can help in any way..." She let her voice trail off, worried Fantino would throw her offer back in her face as Joyce had done.

He didn't, but his shrug said it all. How could she help?

"Tonight. I can stay with her and get up with her so you and Joyce can sleep the night through."

"Oh, would you?" The abject relief on Fantino's face was hard to bear.

"Why haven't you hired a nanny, or something?" she asked.

Fantino and Carlo shared a significant look. "Joyce and I are raising our daughter, not a nanny," Fantino said, sounding defensive.

Annette had no desire to push it and perhaps have him back out on letting her stay with the baby that night. If she could give her sister and brother-in-law a night of uninterrupted rest, she was going to.

"It sounds like you'll have plenty of time holding little Jocinda tonight," Carlo said smugly. "She is content with me right now."

"Until your phone rings," Annette teased.

Carlo shook his head. "You are feeling very brave when I have a baby in my arms."

"I don't remember Annette ever hesitating to tease you before," Fantino offered with a tired smile.

"Why Jocinda?" Carlo asked, ignoring his brother's comment. "Mama and Papa were wondering as well. It is not a family name on either side."

"Isn't it?" Fantino asked, his tone implying he thought Carlo should know the answer to his own question.

"I have never heard it used."

"Do you have to use family names for your children?" Annette asked lightly. "Surely, that would get confusing."

"No, of course not. We Messinas are not that hidebound," Carlo said.

"Well, then..." Annette didn't know why, but she was loathe to be there when someone explained to Carlo that his baby niece had been named for her, and not just her, but the nickname that had played so heavily in the scandal that followed their breakup.

Cinderella.

All discussion was abandoned when Valentina arrived on the scene, insistent on holding her first grandchild. "Your father and I are keeping the baby tonight, so you and dear Joyce can sleep through."

"I already offered," Annette said when Fantino just stared at his mother, like he was trying to parse her words.

"Nonsense," Valentina said with finality. "You are young. Go out, enjoy yourself tonight. I am sure my son can be prevailed upon to accompany you."

"Fantino?" Annette asked senselessly.

But Valentina couldn't possibly mean Carlo, could she? And she didn't have any other sons.

Valentina's laugh startled the baby, who was quickly settled, but not before Joyce arrived looking harried. "Is she alright?"

"She is fine, *cara*. Do not worry. Her grandmother has her."

Both Messina men stared at their mother like the sight of her with a babe in her arms was entirely unexpected.

Annette rolled her eyes. "She had you both, if you will remember."

But the two brothers just shrugged. Like that didn't signify.

Valentina cooed down at the baby, ignoring her sons. Or so Annette thought.

"The boys think because I left certain care to their nannies and grandmother that I do not know how to care for a baby, I suppose. My causes kept me from them too often, but just as Alceu has had to slow down, so have I. I have every intention of spending lots of quality time with my first grandchild."

The look on Carlo's face was a cross between shock and pain.

And another thing about this man slotted into place. Valentina had been an absentee mother and Annette already knew their father had been a workaholic. So, that left their grandmother and the nannies.

Annette finally understood why his mother's volunteerism was not a source of pride so much as pain for Carlo, and clearly Fantino as well.

What she did not understand was why they didn't seem to blame their father for being equally, if not more absent from their formative years?

Annette would never question the power of Valentina's will again. Not when she sat in the passenger seat of Carlo's sleek black sports car.

"You'll be 35 this year, don't you think it's time for a more sedate form of transportation?" she joked as the scent of the leather upholstery teased her senses.

"Don't you know that 35 is when most men buy their first sportscar?" he bantered back.

"Not the men I know." But then the men she knew were her father, who had a luxury sedan and the requisite driver to go with it, and the men associated with her nonprofit organization.

The latter drove electric cars, sometimes hybrids, and none of them still had the new car smell clinging to them.

"Let me guess, your dates drive sedate fuel-efficient compacts."

"If we're going to save the planet, somebody has to." She didn't launch into her usual speech about the *reduce* part of the reduce, reuse and recycle motto.

For one thing, Carlo had heard it all before.

For another, she was enjoying the ride in the luxury sports car too much to say anything without feeling like a hypocrite. She also didn't mention that she didn't date. That was a little tidbit Annette thought she'd rather keep to herself.

They were sharing a lovely meal at a tiny restaurant that catered to the wealthy locals. No tourists here. Very few guests at all and a menu fixed by the chef that changed nightly based on local produce.

Annette was enchanted and said so.

"It is one of my favorite places to eat. Other places, it can be difficult for security to keep people who want to meet a Messina away from the table."

She knew he spoke the truth. While Carlo and his family would move countries before being in a reality television show, they were as well known in Sicily as the Kardashians were in America.

Security was such a natural part of the billionaire's lifestyle, Annette hadn't really paid attention when a car kept pace with theirs on the drive to the restaurant.

Or when one of the men from it had taken up an inobtrusive position on the periphery of the establishment. He wasn't the only security man watching over a client here, but the restaurant had been designed to give the illusion of privacy, if not the reality.

"I owe you an apology," she said after the wine had been tested and poured.

Carlo jerked his head in the negative. "I did not want to talk about it five years ago, and I do not wish to discuss it now."

"But I am sorry. Please believe me, Carlo. If I had it to do over again, I would have done things differently."

"If *differently* doesn't include showing up at the church, prepared to speak your vows, I'm not interested."

"You have a very binary view of the world, did you know that?"

"In some things, like keeping one's promises? Yes, I suppose I do."

She stifled a sigh. "I never meant to hurt you."

"I never said you hurt me, but you did humiliate me. The media vultures were just a small part of it."

"I know. I'm sor—"

"Do not say it again. We start afresh. Now. You are the sister of my sister-in-law. The aunt and godmother to my very precious niece. Our history is no longer what is important, but our family's future."

"I agree, but—"

"No buts. This is the way it has to be, Annette."

Hearing him call her by name hurt in a way all its own, she realized. He'd always used to call her his beauty, or darling. He'd only used her name when they were making love and it had felt special then.

Now it felt like another barrier between them.

Despite the barriers, Annette had a wonderful time with Carlo. So long as she kept the conversation well away from their shared past, he was an interested and interesting companion.

He took her dancing and somehow, they found themselves on the dance floor for all the slower songs. Carlo held her close, sometimes singing along to the song lyrics in a surprisingly fine baritone.

As the night wore on, Annette's defenses against his sensual pull crumbled bit by bit.

Because he treated her like a date, not a woman he despised and could not trust.

When he took her to a hotel after dancing, she did not demur. Once again, Annette was making her own choices and she chose to spend the night in Carlo's arms.

This time she was fully aware she would not wake up with him beside her.

Their lovemaking was every bit as frenzied as after her sister's wedding. Only this time, it felt like a beginning, not an ending.

Which is what she'd told herself the last time, so she could hardly trust it.

However, Carlo was there the next morning when she woke. Working, yes, but still in the hotel suite. He'd ordered her breakfast again, but this time it was her favorite crepes and cups of the freshly brewed Sicilian coffee she adored.

Annette took her time over breakfast, noticing quickly that again, Carlo was very intent on steering the conversation in decidedly non-personal channels. He even told her about his latest deal, for goodness's sake.

She listened raptly though, interested despite herself.

He asked about her work and Annette found herself telling him about what she'd learned about hiring and salary practices at her organization.

Instead of dismissing her concerns to naivete, Carlo listened and offered his attorneys to help her set things right if she needed. "Even if you don't want to pull that trigger, you can text me any time for advice."

Overcome, Annette swallowed back emotion she knew he didn't want to deal with. "Thank you."

They made love again but took post coital showers separately by silent agreement. She wanted to get back to the villa and see her sister. He had work to do. The fact he'd stayed so late with her on a Monday sent warm fuzzies fizzing through her like just uncorked champagne.

However, when they got back to the villa later, it was to find Valentina in a state. Joyce had insisted on returning home early. She, Fantino and Jocinda had left for the airport right after breakfast. Since they were flying in the company jet, they only had to wait for a takeoff slot, not a scheduled flight.

And the Sicilian airport wasn't nearly as busy as the one in Rome.

Chapter Seven

As worried as she was for her sister, Annette couldn't help enjoying her time with Carlo. She spent her last day and a half with his parents during business hours and with Carlo after. He worked his schedule so he got off much earlier than usual both days and they visited sites in Sicily she'd yet to see.

As wonderful as their time together was, Annette was very aware how Carlo never wanted to discuss the past or any prospect of a future.

When it came time for her to go to the airport, his father drove her because Carlo had a business call he had to take.

"I could have caught a taxi," Annette said, pretty sure it was true. "Or simply ridden with one of your security people. You didn't have to go out of your way."

As she said the words, she realized how much she wished that Carlo had gone out of his though. But the last three days had been a sexual tryst, nothing else, and if she let herself forget that, she was in for a world of hurt.

"Nonsense, you are family."

Unable to deny that assertion, Annette simply said, "Well, thank you."

When her brother-in-law called two weeks later and asked her to come, Annette was worried, but not surprised. She'd only had one video chat with Joyce since returning from Europe and her sister had swung between snappish and apathetic with erratic frequency.

Annette had already arranged to step down from her new job, and to take a sabbatical from the company. She'd begun packing to move back to New York, so it was simply a matter of getting a storage container and asking her coworkers to come by and help her fill it. Her things would be shipped to New York and stored at a facility until she'd found a place to live.

Although she and Carlo had been texting even more regularly than before, Annette didn't tell him of her plans to move. He was still in Sicily, so Portland or New York made little difference to him, she was sure.

They'd tried sexting, but both had found it far more hilarious than sexy, and they'd advanced to video chats for their *booty calls*. There could be no question that their relationship was mainly about sex, so Annette didn't tell Carlo about Fantino's call either, or her plans for the present to stay with her sister's family and help however she could.

When Joyce called Annette after the Messina jet landed in the small Upstate New York airport, the younger woman was sobbing and begging her sister to come. Annette had never been so grateful for timing in her life, because she was already in the car Fantino had had waiting for her and on her way to their home.

When she arrived, Joyce was in no better state than she'd been on the phone and Fantino looked wrung out, though he was admitting no weakness.

Typical Messina man.

The first week flew by as Annette did her best to take care of Jo-Jo without help. Fantino spent the weekdays in the city and while he did his best to care for his daughter on the weekends, he also had an emotionally fragile wife to contend with.

Annette never knew if she was going to be dealing with weepy Joyce, angry Joyce, or lost and confused Joyce from one minute to the next. She did her best to shield the baby from the tension that laid a pall over the adults in the beautiful Upstate New York mansion, while struggling with unexpected exhaustion.

Taking care of an infant who did not sleep through the night by any stretch was far more taxing than she'd expected. Annette could not nap while Jo-Jo did during the day, because then she was busy with her sister. Joyce had confided to Annette only yesterday that she'd had thoughts of harming herself and the baby.

Annette was trying to convince both Joyce and Fantino that the new mom needed professional help. Until then, she was doing her best, with the help of the mansion's staff, to make sure that neither the baby, nor Joyce, were left alone. The stress was taking its toll and Annette felt constantly nauseated and tired.

She still hadn't talked to Carlo about the move, but she planned to change that tonight. They had a video chat scheduled, but instead of having cybersex, they were going to talk.

Joyce had Fantino's promise that he would stay with his wife and not disappear into his study for work, after dinner. Annette had a baby monitor set up in Jo-Jo's room, so she could hear if the baby cried. With her preparations in place, she shut the door to her room and got comfy in an armchair by the window, tucking her feet under her.

Her guestroom was on the west side, and if it had been earlier, she would have had a gorgeous view of the sunset as she sipped a cup of herbal tea and waited for Carlo's call. As it was, she stared out into the inky blackness of a winter night too cloudy for stars.

When her phone buzzed, she swiped to answer, the video taking a moment longer to connect than a voice call.

From the angle, it was obvious Carlo had his phone in a stand that would allow him hands free movement, but she held hers close so her face took up most of the screen. "Hi, Carlo."

"*Bèdda mia*, it is good to see you."

"It's good to see you too." She realized how true the words were as she said them.

Just seeing Carlo's capable and handsome face on her phone screen gave her a sense of calm that had been missing for the past week. She wasn't alone. He would have an idea of what to do, how to convince both Joyce and Fantino to get Joyce help.

Both were equally intransigent about therapy and the need for it.

That was for other people. Joyce could sort her own problems. Or so they assured Annette. The fact Annette had spent three years in therapy after moving to Portland was seen as unfortunate, not the shining example of rational behavior she'd hoped they might acknowledge it.

Joyce simply said she thought her sister should be able to help her then.

Neither wanted to admit that Joyce was suffering any sort of depression. And Annette was no professional. Despite all the training she'd taken to work with at risk youth, Annette wasn't about to diagnose her sister with postpartum depression, but she desperately wanted Joyce to see someone who could determine if that was the cause of her sister's doldrums and frightening thoughts.

"You look contemplative," Carlo said.

"I am." She sighed. "We need to talk about Joyce and Fantino."

He frowned, his body tensing. "No."

"What do you mean, no? I need your advice." Maybe even his help. He could talk to Fantino, couldn't he?

Tell his younger brother that there was nothing wrong with seeking psychological support for Joyce.

"My advice is to stay out of your sister's marriage."

"Carlo, you don't know—"

"No. Listen to yourself, Annette. You did not want to marry and have a family. That does not mean it was a bad choice for Joyce."

"It hasn't turned out to be all sunshine and roses for her either," Annette insisted.

"Who said it would? Or even should be? Life is not always easy, but she and Fantino must work through their own problems."

"Have you been talking to Fantino?" she asked suspiciously. Was *Carlo* the reason the younger Messina brother was so anti-therapy?

"I talk to my brother frequently."

So, he knew about what was happening and he thought she should butt out? Like her mom and dad did.

"Look, sometimes people need professional help dealing with their problems."

"Fantino and Joyce do not have those sorts of problems."

"You are not serious."

"Listen to me, Annette. You need to let Joyce find her happiness."

"That's what I'm talking about."

"By driving a wedge between her and Fantino? By filling her head with ideas of starting a career when she's still settling into new motherhood?"

"What are you talking about? Though if getting a job would help her, I'm all for it. It's her choice, Carlo."

"Exactly. Not mine. Not *yours*."

"You act like I have some kind of agenda here."

"Don't you?"

"Only to help my sister get better."

"Regularly sleeping through the night will help more than any sisterly advice, I am sure."

Exhausted and on edge herself, Annette was in no mood to deal with Carlo's opinions on that score. She was the one losing sleep so her sister could get some. After a week, Joyce didn't show any improvement from it.

"When your father asked me to talk to you and suggest you let your sister find her feet in her new marriage and motherhood, I told him I didn't think it was necessary, but I can see I was wrong."

"You've been speaking to my father?"

"We talk regularly. We share common business interests, you remember."

"I am not a business interest!" She was losing her cool and that was not okay, but Carlo and her father?

Annette could just imagine what had been said about her and none of it good.

"No, but as his daughter, you are a concern."

"You know what? Never mind. If you and my father have the same view of the situation, you're not going to help me." Once again, the weight of being on her own pressed down her.

"Gladly. I did not call you to talk about our siblings." He gave her that slashing smile that usually sent her nerve endings zinging.

Tonight, all it did was make her want to cry.

Because that smile in that moment might as well have been a meteorite hitting her world. It told her that their relationship wasn't just mostly about sex, but it was all about sex. She was an easy booty call. He didn't even have to leave his apartment, because here she was on the other end of a video call.

And if Annette was wired for easy, casual sex, that would be fine.

She wasn't. No matter what she tried to tell herself. And this pseudo friendship that wasn't really a friendship at all wasn't enough of a relationship to make the sex okay with her brain, much less her heart.

"I need to go."

"You look tired. Get some sleep. We'll set something up for later in the week."

Yeah, no. She just shook her head and signed off the video call.

Joyce's voice risen to the point of screaming had her running from her room in search of her sister. She found her in the living room, sobbing on the floor in front of a large ornate mirror, now broken like someone had thrown something at it.

The culprit, a small statue that used to sit on the mantle lay on the carpet below.

Fantino was trying to comfort his wife. Between the two of them, he and Annette finally got Joyce up to their bedroom and into a soothing bath.

"You are right. She needs help that you and I cannot give her." Fantino sounded so sad, but also determined.

It took another month, with more incidents just like that one, before he and Joyce took the Messina jet to California to check her into a private clinic. Joyce had insisted on Southern California because she'd wanted away from New York's cold winter.

Annette was just glad her sister was willing to get help. She deserved to be happy.

Annette sat in numb silence, waiting for the lawyer to speak. She didn't understand why she had to be here for this. Surely Carlo could handle the business stuff.

She didn't understand why everyone else was there as well, a living will wasn't like a regular will, was it?

But everyone was there. Her parents, Lynette, Carlo and his parents.

No Joyce or Fantino though. They were the reason everyone had been called to the lawyer's office. Annette's baby sister was in a coma along with her husband. A semi-truck driven by a man who'd had too little sleep on roads slick with ice had crossed three lanes to run into their car as they returned from the airport. Annette shook her head, unable to believe what was happening.

Joyce had worked hard at regaining her equilibrium at the clinic. Their last video chat before she and Fantino returned to New York had shown the sister Annette remembered, a vibrant woman who couldn't wait to see her baby in person.

Now, she hovered in a no man's land between life and death, her injuries so severe, she could die before she ever woke up.

With both her parents in comas none of the doctors could be sure they would ever come out of, Jo-Jo was as much an orphan as Annette had ever been. She was determined her niece would never feel the pain of not being wanted as she had. Annette would take care of Jo-Jo, making sure the baby knew she was absolutely loved and wanted.

Annette's numbness turned to horror as she heard the terms of her sister's and then her brother-in-law's respective living wills. In the unlikely event that both were incapacitated for any length of time, they had placed Jo-Jo under the sole guardianship of Carlo.

"But that can't be right!"

The lawyer stopped speaking and gave her a censorious glance. "If I could continue?"

What else was there to say? What else mattered? "But he barely knows Jo-Jo."

He'd met the baby when she was born and then seen her again at the christening. It was the only time he'd held the baby that she knew of. Yes, Carlo had been good with her, but he hadn't been to New York to see his niece in the intervening months. And now they were saying Carlo was to be the baby's guardian?

"For the past three months I'm the one who has fed Jo-Jo, woken in the middle of the night to comfort her, played with her, bathed her, changed all her diapers." Joyce has spent six weeks at the clinic. Fantino had been there for the first two and then on the weekends thereafter.

One thing neither one had moved on though was their unwillingness to hire a nanny, so Annette had been on her own taking care of Jo-Jo. Not that she'd ever really considered herself on her own with a house full of staff.

"Perhaps pushing your way in where you don't belong is why your sister had such a hard time coming to grips with motherhood," Elise Hudson said with angry judgment.

Old pain from her adopted mother's many rejections pricked at Annette's soul.

"You know that's not true," Annette said softly, her voice cracked with emotion. "I only stepped in when Fantino asked me to help, when it was obvious Joyce wasn't coping."

"So you claim. However, both your sister and her husband have made it crystal clear who they wished to take guardianship of the child," Annette's father said coldly. "And it wasn't you. I'm sure we all have no difficulty understanding why."

"I don't understand why." Despair and desperation became a tight vice around Annette's heart. She owed her sister. She owed Jo-Jo.

Annette had to take care of the baby until her own parents were capable of doing so. She refused to believe they wouldn't come out of their comas.

Carlo just sat there in silence, his expression unreadable.

"If you need help securing a flight back to Portland, my administrative assistant will see to it." That was Carlo, finally putting his oar in.

This was him getting back at her for ignoring his texts and other attempts to get in touch over the past couple of months. Annette simply hadn't had the wherewithal to deal with her complicated feelings where Carlo was concerned. She'd accepted he only wanted sex and she had admitted to herself that she needed more.

So, she'd ghosted him. Fair? Maybe not, but Annette had spent a good part of those months exhausted herself, finally adjusting to her new sleep schedule just this past week.

She'd thought it was a sign. Everything was getting better. That incessant stress nausea had finally settled down too.

"I don't care what those papers say, I'm not going anywhere until Joyce and Fantino are well enough to care for their child." Annette tried to sound firm, but her voice broke at the last.

Joyce and Fantino had to get better. They just had to.

Chapter Eight

Carlo frowned. "Pamina will be with Jocinda. You do not need to worry about her safety and well-being."

"Pamina? You're trusting her care to a woman who has known Jo-Jo less than a week?"

"Pamina is her nanny, naturally I trust her to care for our niece." He looked pained, like explaining himself was far from what he wanted to be doing. "She came with the highest of recommendations from a reputable agency."

Who cared? Pamina was not Annette. "Jo-Jo needs *family*." The baby needed *her*.

Annette was the only consistent in the baby's life right now. None of the rest of the family, on either side, had enough of a bond with Jo-Jo to take over for Annette. As much as it hurt Annette to acknowledge, Jo-Jo did not cry for her parents when she was distressed now. She wanted Annette.

Annette had offered to come with them to California and bring Jo-Jo, but Joyce had been adamantly opposed to the idea. They'd learned that was part of what turned out to be a pretty severe case of postpartum depression. Joyce had not bonded with her daughter because she'd been emotionally unavailable. She'd wanted to change that as soon as they got back to New York. It was Annette's job to make sure Jo-Jo felt loved and secure until that could happen.

Once her sister and Fantino were well. They *would* get well.

And nanny, or no nanny, Annette wasn't going anywhere until Joyce and Fantino had come home. Ridiculously duped, she'd believed Pamina was Carlo's clumsy attempt at giving *her* support after the accident. Valentina and Alceu had gone straight to the hospital, dropping in twice to see how she was doing and murmuring their approval upon finding a nanny in residence to help her.

Carlo had not been to the house in the week since the tragedy, not that Annette blamed him. His brother had been in ICU that entire time. What time he wasn't spending overseeing the company and covering for his brother, he'd been at the hospital.

While Annette had longed to be there as well, at her sister's bedside, she'd only been able to visit once because she had to do what was best for Jo-Jo.

The nanny had taken direction easily from Annette and had never once alluded to the fact that Carlo was her employer, not Annette. She'd seen the bond Annette had with Jo-Jo and remarked upon it with approval, expressing relief the baby had someone consistent in her life.

Annette had liked Pamina and considered her a godsend.

"How can a workaholic like you take care of a baby?" she demanded. "You've been her effective parent for a week and you knew that, but you haven't made the time to even check in on her once!"

"I speak to Pamina daily."

"She never told me that." And it did not help Annette's feelings. Because how involved could those discussions have been if the fact Annette was there had never come up? "Anyway, it's not the same as being there. What if Jo-Jo didn't like her?"

"My parents assured me that Jocinda and Pamina were a good fit."

But clearly they hadn't mentioned that Annette had been there, taking care of the baby already. Did no one in her life think she was worthy of being family, much less even mentioned?

Jo-Jo needed her. Couldn't they all see that? She looked wildly around the office filled with people Annette couldn't help feeling despised her, regardless of anything said in the past.

Valentina was looking at her with pity. Alceu wasn't looking at her at all. He seemed entirely checked out of the proceedings, grey with stress that only seemed to grow the longer his son stayed in a coma.

Annette's parents were looking at her all right and their expressions were not warm.

"If you'd left well enough alone, Joyce would have stepped up and been the mother she needed to be," her mother accused. "They would never have been in California in the first place."

Those words hit Annette like a body blow and she stumbled. "No," she whispered. "Don't say that."

"Jocinda is better off without you in her life, just as your sister would have been," her mother went on remorselessly.

"That is enough." Carlo's words came out like bullets. "Annette did not cause the crash."

"We are all upset," Valentina added. "However, blaming one another will do nothing to bring either of our children out of coma any faster."

Elise pressed her lips together tightly, saying nothing more, but the look she gave Annette was filled with condemnation.

Guilt beat at Annette because she knew her mother was right about one thing. Jo-Jo's parents would not be in hospital if they had not gone to the clinic in California for treatment.

"She needed help," Annette said to no one in particular. "Joyce was suffering from a hormone and chemical imbalance." Her sister had continued to have thoughts of self-harm and hurting Jo-Jo, even when Annette was there taking care of them both. "It wasn't going to get better on its own."

"Back in my day, a woman knew she had to do whatever it took to be a mother. My daughter would have gotten over her *hormones* if you hadn't interfered," Elise said staunchly.

"I'm your daughter too," Annette couldn't help saying. She might be adopted, but she was still *theirs*. Hadn't they all said it often enough?

Her dad wasn't her daddy anymore. Now that was Floyd Hudson, not his brother William. She'd been punished every time she'd forgotten that important fact and called the wrong man dad.

"No daughter of ours would make the kinds of choices you've made with your life." Her father's expression was every bit as repudiating as his tone.

One might think he had never forgiven her for calling off the wedding, but really her father had never actually forgiven Annette for catching Carlo's eye in the first place. He'd wanted the billionaire businessman for Lynette.

Annette cracked right down the center of her soul. These were her parents and they wouldn't help her.

No one was going to help her and she wasn't going to be allowed to help Jo-Jo.

The room pressed in on Annette, pain and fear making her heart ache in her chest, her breath come in unsatisfying pants. Lightheaded, she stumbled back to her chair, only vaguely aware of a strong, guiding hand.

"Sit. Let the lawyer finish and then we will speak." That was Carlo's voice, sounding kind.

Annette nodded, but did not speak.

The lawyer continued, his voice an indistinct drone going on about financial details she paid no attention to. All Annette could think was how to convince Carlo to let Annette remain in Jo-Jo's life until Joyce woke up from her coma.

Her whirling thoughts were not coming up with anything though, and her desperation and sadness grew.

"Here, drink this." A cup of coffee hovered in front of Annette's gaze, its scent bringing her out of the morass in her head.

The strong olive toned hand holding it was steady. Annette's gaze flicked up to Carlo. His face was set in stoic lines, his body language giving away nothing of how he was feeling.

"Carlo, please. Don't take Jo-Jo away from me," she begged.

"Drink your coffee."

The smell of coffee mixed with brandy wafted toward her and she shook her head. "No. No brandy. I have to be able to think."

"To do what? You aren't going back to the mansion tonight."

She had planned to do that, but now she thought the next day would be better spent consulting an attorney. "I'm going to fight the guardianship assignment." Though she had no idea how.

He shook his head.

But she was determined. "I have to protect Jo-Jo."

"You don't have to protect our niece from me."

"Not from you, but from the pain of neglect, of being unwanted? Yes, I do!" But that had been her, not Jo-Jo. Annette had been neglected and unwanted.

Even if he was a workaholic, Carlo loved their niece.

"You are being irrational. Have you even slept since getting the news?" He put the coffee down on the low table beside her chair. Had it been there before? She couldn't remember.

Annette looked around the lawyer's office, meeting room, whatever...and re-alized it was empty. Her family were gone and so was his. So was the lawyer and his paralegal.

"Where is everyone?" she asked.

"All the necessary legal matters have been seen to. They left."

"Jo-Jo is the only thing that matters as far as I'm concerned."

"I think you would find it difficult to take care of her without a place to live," he said prosaically. "You cannot think to take our niece back to Portland with you."

"I can stay in Joyce and Fantino's home. They'll return to it." She felt compelled to add, "Eventually."

Because even if her sister and/or brother-in-law woke up today, they both had healing to do before leaving the hospital. Their injuries had been severe, though Joyce's most serious injury was the head trauma that had put her in a coma. She had numerous lacerations that had required stitches. With a broken leg and shoulder, Fantino would need physical therapy as well.

"And pay the staff with what? Buy groceries and pay the not insignificant utilities with what exactly?"

"I have some money set by." She moved restlessly. "What does any of that matter? Jo-Jo needs me."

"You keep saying that."

"Because it is true!"

He nodded. "I am willing to concede the point, though I have always been told that babies are resilient. One way, or another, Jocinda will be fine."

"Stop calling her that! Fantino and Joyce called her Jo-Jo. She deserves to be called by the name her parents gave her."

"They named her Jocinda."

"After me and Joyce. Doesn't that tell you anything?"

"Your name is not Cindy."

"Joyce thought it was funny to call me Cinderella. She didn't find the stories in the media the tragedy everyone else did, but laughed at them." And her baby sister had said the name fit too well, the way Annette had always served her family.

Carlo didn't look like he believed her.

"When have I ever lied to you?"

"When you promised to marry me."

"Get over it!" For once the guilt of jilting him was not paramount. "Rela-tionships end. You can't let your personal feelings toward me hurt Jo-Jo. You're responsible for her now." At least until Joyce and Fantino could take back the responsibility.

"I am aware." Carlo's tone and expression said he realized how serious that commitment was and maybe it wasn't one he'd been looking for.

"You need to listen to me, Carlo."

"I have listened to you, but I also listened to what my brother and my sis-ter-in-law did not say in their living will. They did not name you as co-guardian to Joc..."

She glared at him, demanding he acknowledge the six-month-old as her own person, not just a name on a piece of paper.

"Jo-Jo. They made no provision for you to take care of the baby."

"But I *have* been taking care of her!" She looked at him imploringly. "Please, Carlo, Jo-Jo needs me."

He frowned, like her easy agreement angered him instead of pleasing him. "Meet me for dinner tomorrow night and we will discuss options."

"But I was going to go back to Upstate New York tonight, for Jo-Jo."

"She has Pamina. The baby will be fine."

Annette hoped that was true. Jo-Jo might be used to her father being gone during the week and seeing her own mother occasionally despite living in the same house, but for the last three months, Annette had been there all day, every day.

Nevertheless, she nodded. "Where do you want to meet?"

"I will send a car for you. Where are you staying?"

"I'm not. Like I said, I was planning to return on the train tonight."

"I will have a room booked for you at my hotel."

"Okay."

"No arguments about paying your own way or choosing your own lodgings?"

She stared at him. "None of that matters right now."

Annette wasn't even sure she *could* book her own hotel right now. She was beyond exhausted and doubted she'd sleep any better tonight than she had been since news had reached her of Joyce and Fantino's accident.

Chapter Nine

Carlo called his father after his nightly phone call with the nanny. Pamina had said Jo-Jo wasn't settling and had been fractious since lunchtime.

He'd asked if he needed to dispatch a doctor to check on the infant. The nanny had said no that she thought it was simply a matter of Jo-Jo missing Annette. "She's used to her aunt being there all of the time from what I've seen. She doesn't want to accept substitutes," Pamina had said.

Carlo had mentioned that opinion to his father and been shocked at the older man's response. "Of course, the baby misses her. Annette is practically the only mother she's known these past three months."

"What do you mean?" Carlo demanded. How much had Fantino neglected to tell him?

Was it because for the past five years, Carlo had made it clear he expected his family not to mention Annette to him?

He'd tolerated the occasional and inevitable times he would see her in person once Fantino and Joyce became serious about each other, but Carlo wanted no reminders of the most humiliating and *sì*, painful, episode in his life.

Not that he would ever admit to the emotional pain. He'd locked it away and chalked the relationship up as a learning experience.

But the cost of that learning experience had been steep. Not only had he nearly lost his father, but then a distant cousin had tried to take over the company because of Carlo's notoriety and the rumors circulating about him after he was jilted at the altar.

"Joyce was too ill to be a parent. You know this."

Only Carlo hadn't. Fantino had never said anything of the sort when they spoke or texted. The first he'd heard of the clinic had been today.

"She rejected Jo-Jo completely," his father went on, his voice heavy with sadness. "Fantino said she had postpartum depression. That's why he took her to California. He checked her into a clinic there that specializes in treatment of severe cases."

"And Joyce's case was that serious?" Fantino had never once mentioned his wife's illness to Carlo, and Carlo did not understand why.

"*Sì*. So severe she had thoughts of hurting both herself and her daughter. Without Annette's help, Fantino would have drowned under the pressure and Jo-Jo would not have thrived. Annette tried to help Joyce without professional intervention, but things were getting worse, not better. Fantino told me when they left for California that Joyce had not so much as held Jo-Jo in several days and she struggled to get out of bed each day."

Well, that explained why Fantino hadn't opened up about what was going on after the birth of his daughter. Carlo may have gotten a little over the top when Annette's name had been mentioned for the past five years.

None of his family knew about the sexual relationship that had started at the wedding. He hadn't wanted anyone assuming he was getting back together with her, but he could see now he should have at least told Fantino he and Annette were *friends* again.

Not that she had been acting very friendly the past couple of months. Ever since that less than successful video chat, she'd been ignoring his texts and phone calls.

"You know Annette took a leave of absence from work to take care of the baby and help her sister?" his father asked. "I think she had plans to move back to New York."

Stunned, Carlo did not answer. He had *not* known.

That was not the story Annette's father had been spinning to Carlo the past months. Moreover, his on-again-off-again lover had never mentioned plans to move across country, much less take time away from her job to care for their niece.

"I hadn't known that, actually. I thought she only came to watch Jocinda when they left for California."

"Oh, not at all. I know you have your reasons for thinking less of Annette, but she's been a good sister to Joyce and a loving aunt to my granddaughter."

"I wish Fantino had told me." His younger brother could have told him about Joyce's illness at the very least. They could have gotten in home therapy, or something.

"He didn't want you thinking less of him."

"Why would I?"

"Because he thought less of himself. He left Joyce on her own during the week, staying near the office in the city. He only went to her and the baby on the weekends and he thought her depression was his fault."

Apparently, his brother and father had discussed the difficulties going on extensively, but Fantino had not once brought them up to Carlo. According to Annette, Fantino had initially been the one to call and ask her to come help with the baby.

And he had not said word one to Carlo.

"He could have taken time off." Carlo hated knowing his younger brother had not been willing to share his difficulties with him. "I would have covered for him."

"He didn't want to take time off." His father's tone held resignation, not censure for her younger son's choices. "He spent the first two weeks in California with Joyce, but after that he flew back to visit her on the weekends."

The company had been both men's lives since they reached adulthood, and for the first time Carlo had to ask himself if that was best. He rang off with his father, his mind busy reframing the past three months with what he knew now. That video call and its outcome made a lot more sense.

Annette had been furious because he had misconstrued her motives and her actions. All based on her father's say so. A man whom Carlo had never considered unbiased when it came to his children. He and his wife played favorites, making it clear they did not feel the same way about their middle child as the other two.

Had she been an oops baby, or something? He'd always wondered, but never asked, not wanting to hurt Annette's feelings pointing out her parents' lack of affection.

Carlo had a great deal of work to do in his brother's office before he could sleep that night, but he found himself thinking about the only woman he had ever asked to marry him. His current lover, though he thought she was doing her best to avoid that role lately.

Because she'd been overwhelmed taking care of Jo-Jo, or because she was tired of him?

She'd turned off him easily enough five years ago. He wished his own craving for her was so easy to turn away.

He'd been shocked when she stood him up at the altar and he'd almost welcomed the media storm that followed because it had got his pride up and he hadn't gone chasing after her as had been his first inclination. By the time he'd dealt with the fallout of his botched attempt at marriage, he'd had no such inclination.

But just as he'd known might happen, the minute he'd seen her, he'd started wanting her again. This time, he'd been careful not to set up expectations. No strings sex.

And still, it had *hurt* when she stopped answering his texts and phone calls, when she cut him out of her life as he had once cut her out of his.

An idea began to form, a way for Carlo to finally get a little of his own back against the woman who had very nearly cost him his beloved father and the company that had been in their family for generations. A woman who had rejected him not once, but twice.

First as a husband, and then more recently as a lover.

Not because she didn't want him, he was sure of it. She responded too strongly to his touch for that to be the case, but because she'd discovered she wanted the strings of relationship she'd so cavalierly cut five years ago. She'd said as much in Sicily at the Christening.

A woman who had humiliated and betrayed him, making him an object of pity and anecdote to his Sicilian family and the media.

How the mighty are fallen. That's what several cousins had said, one in particular before trying the takeover bid. That man was selling cars in Rome now, and off every guest list Carlo was on, family, or no family.

Even being a billionaire is no protection from heartache, others had said, meaning well perhaps, but flaying Carlo's pride nonetheless.

Heartache? Five years ago, he had been far from some lovestruck teen, but he'd been painted as a tragic figure by his family and the media. Turned into an object of pity.

Carlo had hated it.

Now, here she sat, in a prime position for him to get what he wanted for himself, and for his baby niece. All of it on *his* terms.

A small niggle of worry said he was tired and stressed and should think before following through on his fantasies, but he ignored it.

The idea of getting anything on his terms seemed like a colossal joke the next day when he got Annette's text saying she was taking the train back to Upstate New York. He could come there and talk about her role in their niece's life while Jo-Jo's parents were still in hospital.

Feeling very much like he was chasing the wind, Carlo had his executive team shift things in his schedule and took the helicopter to Fantino's home, arriving shortly before Annette.

Annette searched out Jo-Jo, the minute she arrived back at the mansion, finding the baby playing with the rattles and things hanging above her plushy blanket on the floor in her nursery while Pamina read a book in the rocking chair.

With no thought to the business suit she'd worn to go into the City, Annette laid down on the carpet beside her niece and started talking to her. "What do you think of that giraffe? He looks like he would be fun to play with. Can you make him rattle?"

Jo-Jo's head turned at the sound of Annette's voice and then joyous baby babble filled the air between them. Dressed in cute, flowered stretchy pants and a long sleeved top with a big flower in the middle, Jo-Jo looked up at her aunt with joy in her sweet gaze. Her little feet covered in fuzzy booties kicked a mile a minute.

"Oh, she's happy to see you. I told *Signore* Messina our little Jo-Jo was missing you." Pamina's voice reminded Annette that someone else was in the room.

Annette looked up and smiled. "It's very good to be back." And she wasn't leaving.

If possession was nine tenths of the law, Annette was going to bolster it with squatter's rights. She wasn't going anywhere until Joyce came home to take care of her baby.

"I should have known you would come straight to the nursery." Carlo's voice came from the doorway.

She sat up, trying to keep her straight skirt from hiking up her legs. "You're here!"

"As you see."

"But I thought you were spending the day in New York."

"And I thought we had dinner plans. Apparently, we were both wrong."

Annette felt heat creep into her face, but she refused to be embarrassed. "I wanted to see Jo-Jo. I can't wait for Joyce and Fantino to be moved out of the ICU so we can take Jo-Jo to see them. I know hearing the baby talk will help."

"She doesn't talk yet, surely," Carlo said with disbelief.

"Well, not talk...but she babbles. It lifts my heart when I hear it. I know it will affect her parents the same, even in their comas."

Carlo's expression flashed pain and grief, but it was soon gone. Mr. Stoic.

He nodded. "I am sure you are right."

"Perhaps you could finish your visit with our niece and then meet me in the study later?"

"She'll be ready for her nap soon," Pamina said.

Annette frowned but nodded. She didn't want to upset Jo-Jo's schedule. The baby had had enough discontinuity in her six months of life already.

An hour later, after changing into clothes that fit her style way better than the business suit, Annette went down to the study to meet with Carlo.

He was on the phone when she entered, so she turned to go out again, but he shook his head and waved her into a chair. He said something in Japanese and then tapped his phone screen.

"I'll be finished here in just a couple of minutes. Mrs. Banning has already laid lunch out on the table in the dining room. I thought we could have our discussion over a meal."

"Still looking for your dinner date?" she quipped.

"It's lunch and not a date." His tone was a lot more serious than hers. But then he went back to his call, and she took that as permission to leave.

Annette took a few minutes to chat with Mrs. Banning about the coming week before entering the formal dining room, where the table had been laid at one end.

Memories of stilted meals with her sister in here while Joyce did her best to pretend she didn't even have a baby bothered Annette. She knew her sister hadn't meant it, that hormones had dictated how she responded to life and her infant, but the memories still hurt. Especially with Joyce unable to come home and start bonding with Jo-Jo as planned.

"You look like you've seen a ghost. What is wrong?" Carlo asked upon entry into the room.

"It's not my favorite room, that's all."

"It's a dining room."

"Yes, I know." One with memories she'd rather forget.

"Would you prefer to eat our lunch somewhere else?"

It was too cold outside, and the breakfast nook was no doubt being used by the staff to eat their own lunch. Besides, the food was already laid out. "No of course not. I wouldn't put anyone to the bother."

"But something about this room bothers you."

"Joyce insisted on eating in here and when we were at the table, she didn't want Jo-Jo mentioned."

"But she was so happy to become a mom."

"Yes, but her hormones betrayed her." Annette shivered. "It's hard to accept how a chemical in your body can make a person think things that are so different than their true feelings, or do and say things they would otherwise never do."

Carlo looked at her speculatively. "Were you having hormone imbalances five years ago?"

"No. At least I don't think so." She settled into one of the chairs at the table and started dishing up her plate from the gorgeous Greek salad with smoked salmon Mrs. Banning had left for them.

Annette had been craving fish lately. She could eat it every day and be happy. Mrs. Banning had teased her about it, but the wonderful housekeeper had still prepared this mouthwatering salad with salmon instead of chicken as she usually did.

"Does it matter? Now?" Annette asked him, forcing herself to wait for him to sit down and serve himself before taking a bite of the salmon.

"No. It is water under the bridge as you Americans are so fond of saying."

Was that an American saying? Annette thought she'd look up its etymology later, but she doubted he would care the origination of the saying when he'd gotten it from his American business associates and friends.

"How was the train ride up?" he asked her.

As a subject change it was not inspired, but it was obvious. Once again, he had no interest in discussing their past in any meaningful way.

Annette tucked into her lunch. "These garlic bread knots taste as delicious as they smell."

Again, an uninspired topic for conversation, but a safe one.

Carlo waited until they'd eaten most of their lunch before broaching the topic he meant to.

Annette had shown a willingness to keep their conversation on totally inane topics, which revealed how nervous she was about their conversation to come, even if she didn't realize it. She'd expressed her near manic need to care for their niece the day before. Her emotions had been all but out of control, shocking him.

Funny how five years ago he would have told anyone who cared to listen that Annette was both sensible and practical, in everything but her choice of attire. She loved her whimsical clothing pieces, usually purchased at market stalls, not in high end department stores.

Now, he wondered if the way she always made sure everything was running smoothly, and never reacted with anger to her family's foibles, was more a result of family dynamic than personality and her way of dressing was Annette showing her true nature.

Dismissing the speculation, he observed, "You seem calmer today."

"Yesterday was a shock. I thought I was attending a meeting with the lawyer to go over things like finances for Jo-Jo's care and long-term plans for our siblings, and honestly, I resented having to take time away from the baby for something I thought you could handle. *That's* why I thought the rest of you were there. It never occurred to me that anyone *but me* would be named the baby's guardian."

"Nevertheless, I was named her legal guardian while her parents are unable to see to her care."

"I know." She frowned at him like she did not appreciate the reminder.

"I have a proposition for you."

Annette swallowed and nodded. "I understand."

"I doubt it, but you will."

Chapter Ten

"What do you mean? You can't expect to take Jo-Jo back to Sicily," Annette asked with clear disapproval.

"None of us will be leaving New York until..." He let his voice trail off, unwilling to voice the options.

Until one, or both of, their siblings woke up and began to recover...or died.

"That's what I thought, but then you said you had a proposition..." her voice trailed off, her expression quizzical.

"I want you in my bed." There, he'd said it.

Though a voice inside him, which sounded suspiciously like his brother, called him a fool and demanded he retract the demand that she pay for the chance to care for their niece with her body. He didn't mean it. He knew he didn't mean it, but did she?

"What?" Shock held Annette's lovely face immobile.

"I think the strings of shared guardianship should satisfy your need for something more than casual sex."

"You want me to pay for the privilege of taking care of Jo-Jo with my body?" She laughed in disbelief, when he expected an air clearing explosion.

Why was she laughing instead of angry? Did she think he was joking?

"Those are my terms." But were they? Even as he said the words, his conscience squirmed.

Annette shook her head. "You have to know you don't have to blackmail me into your bed."

"You've ignored my every text and phone call for the last three months," he pointed out.

"Didn't like that much, huh?"

"No."

"I didn't like it when you did the same to me."

"Was it payback?"

"No. I was furious with you for ignoring the serious issues here and listening to my father about me."

"What is the deal with your parents?" He was sure she already realized that Carlo had had the wrong end of the stick during that conversation, so he didn't belabor the point.

"Maybe someday I'll tell you."

In other words, she didn't trust him enough to do it now. Could he blame her? He'd just tried to blackmail her into his bed. And she'd said it wasn't necessary.

"So, you intended to call me again?"

"I did, but I meant to offer you my own bargain."

"Oh?" Intrigued and growing increasingly uncomfortable with *his* bargain as stated, he was more than willing to entertain hers.

"Strings. I want strings."

"Shared guardianship," Carlo reminded her.

"What does that mean, exactly?"

"We will live here, together, with Jo-Jo, for the present."

"Only we share a bedroom."

Said like that, it sounded way less messy and even less ugly than the thoughts that had entertained him the night before. "Exactly. I am not promising a lifetime. In fact, it is my plan to get you out of my system. I want what my brother had, even if it ended badly. A wife who adores me, children. A family."

As he said the words, that same small voice he'd done such a good job ignoring so far asked why she couldn't be that woman? He'd changed in five years, maybe she had too. Maybe she regretted jilting him.

"And you have to get me out of your system for that to happen?" she asked, her tone odd and her expression unreadable.

"Apparently." But he was seriously beginning to doubt if he would *ever* get this woman entirely out of his system.

"Only you do expect our liaison to end sooner than later?"

"I do not know how long it will last," he replied truthfully. More honest than he'd been to this point.

But then if she knew him as well as he'd believed she had at one time, Annette was perfectly aware that he would never refuse her help with Jo-Jo. Their niece's welfare came first.

She sighed and put down her fork, finished with her lunch. "All right," she said, almost to herself, her focus on the table. Then she looked up and met his eyes. "Yes."

"Yes, what?" Was she agreeing to his ludicrous proposal?

"Yes, I'll be your lover for the foreseeable future."

"But..."

"Do we have to discuss terms right now?"

He shook his head, reeling from her easy acquiescence.

Something inside Carlo went cold at the knowledge she had just agreed to become his lover in exchange for a role in their niece's life. The old adage to be careful what he wished for filled his brain with biting clarity.

"What is the catch?" he asked, hoping there was one.

Because that at least would prove she understood his character even a little.

That damn shrug again. "Is there one?"

"No."

"You seem angry."

"Do I?" He shoved his plate away.

"Yes, but you are getting what you want." She smiled, almost teasing, if he could believe it. "Me."

"Or the use of your body," he pointed out.

Her smile did not dim. "And I am getting the use of yours."

"I have a contract I want you to sign."

"A contract?" *That* seemed to throw her.

"Knowing me as well as you do, I am surprised you did not expect one."

"I suppose that is true. It just feels odd having contract terms for something so personal."

"Come with me to the living room. I have the contract in there." There was an edge to Carlo's tone that Annette did not understand.

She asked, "Not the study?"

He just shook his head.

There was a neat stack of papers on the coffee table nearest the fireplace.

Oddly, Carlo took a moment to light the gas fire before joining her on the sofa in front of it. Like he was setting a cozy mood, only too much anger made his body rigid and his expression grim for any kind of warm atmosphere to prevail.

Annette took the proffered seat beside him and began to read the contract. As she read the over the multiple page document, her amusement just grew and grew. "I cannot believe you put this stuff down on paper."

It was obvious the contract had been written by him, not a legal team. There had been an attempt to make the document feel like a legal contract with binding this and first party that, but some of the clauses came straight out of Carlo's fantasies.

He'd gotten very specific about what he wanted in bed and out of it. There was something endearing about that. Even more so because from Carlo's expression, he expected her to be horrified.

And it occurred to Annette that everything to this point about the *deal* had been offered to get a reaction from her and she hadn't given the one he expected.

Unsure why that was the case, she simply pointed out, "You do realize none of this had to be put in writing, don't you? You have to know how much I want you, and we were never boring lovers before."

Annette wasn't ashamed of her desire and saw no reason to pretend otherwise.

"Will you sign it?"

She grinned up at him. "If you say so, but I'm pretty sure no judge in the country would hold me to these terms. I'm not even sure it's legal to put them down like this."

"You will honor your word."

"Will I? Only I thought you didn't trust me like that anymore." She couldn't help the taunt, not when it was becoming obvious to her that his intent here had been to get some of his own back in the humiliation department.

She didn't feel humiliated, but that was beside the point.

Carlo did not respond to her words.

Annette went back to reading, her amusement taking a sudden nosedive when she reached the terms outlining her responsibilities and rights with Jo-Jo. As she read the final clause, her heart stopped in her chest and then started pounding again. So fast, she thought she might faint from the blood rush.

In the event of the death of both of Jocinda's parents, the second party (Annette) agreed not to sue for custody of the child.

Everything inside Annette froze. "You put it in writing." She was so upset, her words came out in a hoarse whisper from the strain of pushing them past a tight throat. "That they could *die*."

She surged to her feet and glared down at him, tears already burning in her eyes. "You put it in writing! How could you do that?" Nowhere near whispering now, she swiped at the tears already running down her cheeks. "How could you say that? They aren't going to die!"

Joyce couldn't die. It wouldn't be fair. Life wasn't fair. But this was Joyce. The one person in Annette's life who truly loved her. A woman who was finally ready to be a mom and bond with her baby when fate had sent her to the hospital in a coma instead.

Suddenly, Annette could not breathe. The walls of the huge room were closing in on her, the fire so hot sweat prickled along her spine.

Spinning away, she ran from the room.

Carlo followed, calling her name.

Annette ran faster, rushing up the stairs, her eyes blinded by moisture. She tripped, falling backward, terror gripping her as she swung her arms wildly, trying to catch hold of something.

But it was Carlo who caught hold of her, stopping her fall. She wrested herself from his arms.

He put his hands out again. "Be careful, *bèdda mia*!"

She ignored him, turning and continuing her headlong rush toward her room.

"You were supposed to get mad about the other, yell at me. You never do what I expect..." Carlo's voice trailed after Annette, but she was no longer listening.

Her need to find the solitude and privacy of her room had morphed to an acute physical emergency. If she didn't get to the en suite, she would throw up all over her sister's plush carpet.

Annette made it to the toilet just in time, losing her lunch and then a dry heaving that resulted in nothing but pain and difficulty catching her breath. Carlo was there the whole time, offering her a glass of water, trying to calm her with words that didn't matter.

The only words that mattered were the ones he'd put in that darned contract.

A cold cloth settled on the back of her neck, a hand rubbed circles between her shoulder blades. The heaving finally stopped and Annette could drink the water, but first she rinsed her mouth and took in several deep lungfuls of air.

Carlo squatted beside her, finally silent.

She turned to glare balefully at him. "They aren't going to die."

"We have to be prepared for—"

"No," she cut him off without mercy. "We don't. We believe for them. We have to."

He nodded, looking like he was observing a particularly volatile creature, he wasn't sure how to deal with.

"I thought the stress nausea was gone. No thanks to you for bringing it back."

"Stress nausea?" he asked carefully.

"When I first got here. Things were rough. I was nauseated all the time, but it got better when Joyce got better."

"That was a little over three months after the Christening?" he asked, his tone curiously flat and his expression blank.

"Yes, I guess so. Does it matter?"

"Probably not." He shook his head, like he was clearing it. "I've been imagining all sorts lately."

"No, what are you trying to get at?" Had there been a bout of flu or something that went around after she left Sicily? Why would it have affected her so long?

"I'd say you were showing signs of pregnancy if you didn't have an IUD. Mrs. Banning said you were exhausted the first few weeks you were here, that you'd only started looking like you were getting your sleep recently. You still have dark circles under your eyes."

"Don't we all?" From what she'd seen of the two families at the lawyer's office, Annette didn't think anyone was getting enough sleep since news came of the accident.

"Yes, of course, you are right. I have not been myself lately, either."

Was that his oblique way of saying that the Carlo she knew would never have written that contract?

"I'm not signing your ridiculous sex contract."

"I never expected you to." He sighed, suddenly looking even more weary than before. "I wrote it when I was tired and maybe I'd had one too many glasses of whiskey from my brother's stash in his office. Writing that contract was a stupid thing to do."

"And you showed it to me why?"

His chiseled features reddened, but he just shook his head.

"You wanted to humiliate me," she guessed.

Sex hadn't given him closure. Maybe this had.

"You were not humiliated." He sounded disgruntled, but also kind of in awe of her.

Her lips tilted in a half smile. "No. You missed out on your bit of revenge for being stood at the altar. Poor you."

"That is not the way I see it."

"If you don't rip it up, I'm going to ask Mrs. Banning to burn your breakfast every day until you go back to Sicily."

Annette wasn't leaving those words about Joyce and Fantino's possible deaths in writing. She did not care if it was rational. Annette did not feel rational. She felt terrified. Terrified of losing Joyce permanently. Frightened for Jo-Jo and what the baby's future held.

"Your plans for revenge are so much more prosaic than mine." Carlo sounded admiring.

On that, they could agree. "But effective. You don't do well without a proper breakfast."

"You know me well, or I thought you did."

"And now you've decided that I don't?" Annette heaved herself up from the floor and washed her face with cold water before drinking some more water.

Her stomach felt settled, but for how long? The source of her stress was standing right in front of her.

"You were going to sign the contract."

"Until I read that clause. How could you put that in there?"

"I was being thorough."

"And the list of sexual fantasies wasn't thorough enough?"

He grimaced, high cheekbones burnishing an even deeper red. "That was..." He waved his hand. "It was late at night when I wrote that. I had been working nonstop for days and I had not slept properly since leaving Sicily. I thought you would be offended by the sex stuff, yell at me..."

He'd said something like that when she'd been running for her room.

Annette sidestepped Carlo and went into the bedroom, but then she stopped, just looking around, unsure what she wanted to do now. Jo-Jo would not be up from her nap for another hour. She still slept longer in the afternoon than during morning nap time.

"Why would you want me to yell at you?" she asked him.

Because of course Carlo had followed her, like he'd been doing since she dashed out of the dining room.

"I wanted some of my own back. I will not deny it," he said stoically, like admitting a huge secret but doing it *manfully*. "But I also thought you would yell and I would yell and we would clear the air on five years ago."

"That's..." She didn't know what that was. Ludicrous? Only not. "But I've offered to talk about what happened back then several times and you've insisted we already drew a line under it."

He shrugged. "I am Sicilian. I am proud."

"And you needed to be angry to talk about something that hurt you deeply."

"I never said I was hurt."

No, but he'd never been willing to talk about it at all.

"I don't want to have to have an argument to talk. My body's taken to handling stress through my stomach."

Again with the look. "An IUD is more than 99% effective, but there are out-liers."

"True. I don't have an IUD anymore though."

"You don't?" he asked, his tone laced with shock. "But I thought..." He shook his head, like thinking better of what he'd been about to say.

"When the last one expired, I didn't have another put in. I wasn't in a relation-ship, or sexually active. How is this any of your business?" she demanded, realizing she was rambling personal details she wasn't sure she wanted to share with Mr. Get-Her-Out-Of-His-System.

"It is not, except that we had in person, penetrative sex when you were in Sicily. Quite a bit of it and I was unaware we were relying entirely on condoms for birth control."

"You didn't ask."

"No, I didn't. I'm not assigning blame, merely explaining."

"What exactly?"
"Why I think you should take a pregnancy test."

Chapter Eleven

arlo would have smiled at the stupefied expression on Annette's face, but in her current state of emotional volatility, he wasn't taking any chances in her misinterpreting his smile.

"But we always used a condom."

"All birth control has a failure rate, even when used perfectly, and I admit I wasn't as careful, believing you had an IUD." He realized he was mansplaining to a woman who worked with at risk youth.

Annette's knowledge of birth control no doubt outstripped his by miles. However, she was acting like the idea of pregnancy had never occurred to her.

"I can't be pregnant," she said, shaking her head as if her will alone could repudiate the possibility. "Joyce and Fantino are in comas. Jo-Jo needs me right now. I...It's..."

"Your choice, naturally."

She stared at him. "Yes, I...wait, I don't want. Nothing I'm saying is making sense, is it?"

"You are upset."

"Yes, but I'm also a grown up. You're right. I need a pregnancy test. Then we can talk about what's what."

He knew what *he* wanted, but Carlo didn't fool himself into believing it was the same as what she did. She'd jilted him five years before, and unless something had drastically changed for her, happy families was not in their future.

"And just to clarify something. I do know you. I never doubted you would let me stay with Jo-Jo because that's what's best for her and you would never do anything less. I agreed to become your lover because I wanted to. Full. Stop."

Flummoxed, Carlo watched Annette walk out of the room, not a single word in answer coming to his lips.

She'd been prepared to sign that ridiculous contract because she wanted to be his lover and for no other reason.

Carlo went to the pharmacy and bought the pregnancy test, leaving it in Annette's room before going in search of her. He found her returning with a bundled-up Jo-Jo from their walk.

Pamina stepped forward and offered to remove Jo-Jo's outer clothes for Annette.

Her cheeks rosy from the cold and her hair windswept, Annette nodded. "If you don't mind, bring her down to the kitchen and I'll feed her before her bath."

Despite everything, Carlo's body reacted like it always did to Annette's presence. Desire coursed through him as she undid her own outer layers in a thoroughly unsexy striptease that nevertheless resulted in him having to adjust his stance, so his arousal wasn't too noticeable.

Annette noticed anyway. Her eyes widened. "What's that about?" She nodded toward his erection. "Developed a fetish for the outdoorsy vibe?"

"I want you in all your vibes. I thought we'd established that."

"Are you saying you haven't been with anyone else?"

He was not sure how she drew that conclusion from his words, but it was true. "Not in a long time, no."

"What? You've got gorgeous women on your arm at every social function."

"Not every date ends in bed."

"Ours always did."

"That should tell you something."

"That we're sexually compatible." She waved with her hand. "That's chemistry. It doesn't mean much."

"It meant a lot to me five years ago."

"But not now. You're the one who said he wanted to get over me so you could go looking for the perfect paragon to marry."

"I never used that term and naturally, if you are pregnant, my plans will change."

"You think so?" she asked enigmatically.

"I do think so." Carlo spoke with all the arrogant confidence at his disposal.

It had always been his policy to begin as he meant to go on. And if she was pregnant, he meant to marry her.

Annette was getting ready for bed when a firm knock sounded on her door. She hurried into her sleep pants and grabbed a cardigan to put on over her sleep tank before opening the door.

Carlo stood on the other side, his gorgeous face cast in expectation. "Well?"

"What?" Then she realized and grabbed his arm, tugging him into her room. She wasn't having this conversation out in the hall.

Annette shut the door and locked it for good measure. "I'm not taking the test until tomorrow morning. They're most accurate when used first thing in the morning."

She didn't mention that was mostly true for testing early in a pregnancy and if she'd gotten pregnant in Sicily, Annette would now be almost four months along. She'd had a short period that first month and none since, but her periods had been sporadic since taking out the IUD. Her body was still adjusting, or so her doctor assured her.

Annette certainly didn't mind the months she got to skip her monthly.

"Oh. I had not realized."

"Why would you? Unless you'd thought you'd gotten other women pregnant." She looked at him expectantly.

"No. Never." Carlo looked at her attire and smiled. "Interesting pajamas."

Her cardigan was dark orange, her sleep pants were lime green and her sleep tank was grey with a black and white picture of iconic cartoon characters kissing on the front. Under were the words, *closet romantic.*

"I wasn't expecting company."

"Weren't you?"

"No. I thought you might wait until we knew for sure on the pregnancy thing before launching the seduction offensive."

"There is nothing offensive about my seduction techniques," he assured her.

No, there really wasn't.

"You haven't been with anyone else while we were having our *friends with benefits* thing?" she asked, wondering what it meant if he said no.

"Not since before the wedding," he offered.

"What about the no strings, it was just a one-night stand, yadda yadda yadda?"

"I have never said yadda in my life and I have no answer for you. I did not believe myself committed to you and yet I had no desire to have sex with other women."

Why did he say bone melting things right along with the cold hard truth? "You said you wanted to get closure. To be able to move on. Are you saying that having sex with other women hasn't worked for you since our breakup?"

Because that would put them in the same boat, and she wasn't sure how she felt about that. She'd been the one to walk away (or more accurately run away) five years before. If she hadn't, what would their life be like now?

"Have there been other men?" he asked, rather than give a straight answer.

Typical Carlo.

"None successfully."

Something flared in his eyes. Was it satisfaction or relief? Or both?

"Why should it matter?" she asked. But she knew.

For the same reason she liked knowing his sex life hadn't been great since they broke up.

A very primal part of Annette still saw Carlo as hers. She wanted to be the only woman who spurred him to all night long intimacy.

"You know," he said, moving into her personal space. "You feel it too."

Annette's breath caught, her body suffusing with heat that had nothing to do with embarrassment. She wanted him.

She always wanted him. And he always wanted her.

Wasn't that something worth pursuing? She'd downplayed the power and importance of the chemistry between them earlier, but after five years of unsuccessful and mostly nonexistent (because of the unsuccessful part) dating, she now knew just how rare that kind of sexual compatibility was.

Annette tipped her head back, so their gazes met. His simmered with desire.

She knew he could see a matching need in her own.

"I do feel it."

He smiled, white teeth flashing in that sexy way that got her every time. "This." He cupped her waist beneath her cardigan, his big hand warm through the thin cotton of her sleep tank. "But you feel the other too. You like being the woman I can't get out of my head."

"More like your pants, but yes."

"I'm going to kiss you."

"I'm going to let you."

She didn't see the smile that time because she'd closed her eyes as his lips met hers. She felt it though at the beginning of the kiss.

Kissing back with all the passion she had unwittingly banked for the past three and a half months, Annette shrugged out of her cardy before grabbing his hair and holding him in place for the kiss to go on and on and on.

He growled against her lips as he cupped her bottom with both hands, pulling her up his body so his sex aligned with the apex of her thighs. Annette wrapped her legs around him, rubbing herself against his hardness.

Oh, how she'd missed this. And no way was it all about sex.

Not when neither of them could manage satisfying sex with anyone else.

But that was a thought for another time. Annette's body felt on fire with need to be touched, every nerve ending sparking the conflagration of need inside her.

She felt their bodies moving and then her back hit the familiar support of her bed. Only everything else about this was unfamiliar. Having a masculine body above her, rutting between her thighs even though they were both still fully clothed.

It took bare moments for that to change as they both threw their clothes off with abandon, needing to get to skin on skin.

He knelt above her, his hard honed body leashed with power, sexual need emanating off him in electric waves that connected to her body, creating a sexual current between them that only seemed to get more intense second by second. His sex jutted from his body, already glistening at the tip.

"You are so beautiful," he said, his gaze traveling all over her like the sexiest caress.

But she shook her head. "No, that's you."

His laugh was strained. "Always arguing with me."

"You wouldn't want things too easy." Though she was about to make things very easy for him. Or maybe very good. Easy wasn't all it was cracked up to be.

"No, if I wanted easy, I never would have fixed my sights on you, Annette."

She begged to differ. Five years ago. She'd been very accommodating. Until she wasn't.

Maybe not so easy after all.

"Right now, I want you to fix something."

"What is that?" he asked, cupping her breasts, kneading them and playing with her nipples in the way he knew drive her wild with need.

She told him, in intimate detail. One thing their video sex chats had done for Annette was obliterate her shyness about speaking her sexual needs aloud. It had made cybersex more intense and she realized from his ferocious reaction, it was going to do the same for in person intimacy.

When he stopped to don a condom saying, "If you are not pregnant, now is not the time to make decisions like this," she was filled with another feeling all together. Love.

He was taking care of her, and she had to admit that he always had. If sometimes in a very high-handed way they *would* have to talk about if she were pregnant and he thought that meant fulfilling the plans that she'd leveled five years ago.

He entered her and she surged upward to meet him, needing this connection to the very core of her being.

They made love, their passion building along with a certainty inside of Annette.

She was always going to want this man. If she was pregnant, they were going to have to find a way to make it work between them because she *was* too easy for this man.

Annette's climax hit her without warning and she screamed her pleasure even as Carlo found his own release, his shout ringing in her ears.

Later, cuddled into his body, the covers over them rather than under them, Annette said, "Well, even if no one saw you come into my room, everyone who lives here knows you've been in my bed now."

"Pamina and Mrs. Banning are the only staff that lives in." Carlo said it like it made all the difference that only two people and not twenty knew they'd just had sex.

"Mrs. Banning is the only one that matters. She'll tell Joyce for sure."

"I do not think so. She's an imminently respectable housekeeper. She wouldn't gossip about the household."

"First, respectability has nothing to do with it. Second, what era do you think we live in?" Though she wasn't convinced that staff had gossiped any less in past eras than they did now. "She and Joyce are friends. She'll tell her for sure."

He shifted so he was on his side looking at her in the shadowed moonlight. "Does that bother you?"

"Did you tell Fantino about us?" she asked him, playing his own trick back at him.

Question for question. No answers in evidence.

"I did not, and I regret that. Maybe he would have confided in me if I had."

"Why do you think neither of them named me as guardian, or even co-guardian, of Jo-Jo in the event they were both incapacitated?" She didn't say dead, because she was *not* saying that out loud.

Not with both of them still on some form of life support.

Carlo waited to answer, so she knew he was doing her the courtesy of really thinking about it. "I do not know. They made us both godparents. Why not name us both guardians?"

"Because they assumed I wouldn't drop everything to be here for them." She didn't wonder why they hadn't changed the wills they'd had drawn up when they'd gotten married.

There'd been no reason to believe two young, healthy people needed to update their will, even after she'd come to stay and care for Jo-Jo. They'd all believed everything would work out for Joyce.

It had. And then it hadn't.

It hurt more than she could express that Joyce, the one person she'd believed was her *true* family, the only one in her family who loved Annette, had not seen her as a good bet as her daughter's guardian.

"Perhaps your father influenced her. He seems to see through a cracked lens when looking at you."

"Not cracked, just not the same color as the one he has for his biological children."

Carlo went still, his expression unreadable in the dark. "What do you mean?"

CHAPTER TWELVE

U nwilling to have this conversation without being able to see his reaction to her words, Annette reached out and turned on the lamp by the bed.

Then she sat up, pulling the bedding up to cover her naked breasts. Not because she was embarrassed by her nudity with him. How could she be? However, she didn't want this discussion derailed by sex. It was something she should have talked about with him five years ago.

"I'm adopted."

Carlo stared at her, his jaw going slack for the first time in their acquaintance. "Say again."

"I'm adopted," she repeated.

Sitting up, he made a visible effort to regain his usual composure. "And you have found this out recently?"

"I've always known." Then she explained about her father giving her to his brother when he wanted to remarry after her mother's death. "He paid my Father and Mother a monthly stipend for my care until I turned 18."

"That explains you having to work your way through university." There was something strange in Carlo's tone.

He was right though. She'd always known her parents wouldn't pay for it and Annette had worked hard to get a scholarship to make college even possible for her. She'd done it too. "They let me live in their home until I graduated."

"Generous of them." Sarcasm dripped from every word.

Annette shrugged. "I thought it was at the time. I knew I wasn't wanted, not by my biological father, not by them. Anything they were willing to give me felt like a gift."

"So, you tried to make a place for yourself by being useful."

The Cinderella complex the media had made such a meal of. He was right. "Not exactly. My mom didn't like the way I dressed, or how gauche I was with important people, so she'd send me back into the kitchen to make myself useful. None of us really had chores growing up, other than cleaning our rooms really. Only somehow, I always ended up doing stuff that Lynette didn't want to and Joyce was too young to do well. A last-minute cleanup of the guest bathroom before important visitors, and the like."

"But your parents had staff to do that sort of thing."

"Yes. But she kept the staff busy and my mom resented me. It didn't matter to her that the money she and Dad got for taking care of me was more than a nominal stipend, or that it made it possible for Dad to build his business."

"You never told me any of this."

"No."

"Why?"

"My parents did not allow us to talk about it. Lynette knew of course. She was six and I was five when my biological dad dumped me with his brother."

"What about Joyce?"

"She figured it out when she was a teenager, not long before we met."

"She never treated you any different."

"No, she didn't." Which was why her sister making Carlo her child's guardian with no mention of Annette hurt so much. "She always acted like I was her sister and that was that."

"She didn't make Lynette Jo-Jo's guardian either," Carlo pointed out, like he knew what she was thinking.

"Can you imagine? Lynette doesn't have a nurturing bone in her body. She's never made any bones about the fact she does not crave motherhood."

"That is not what she implied to me."

"She wanted to hook you."

"It did not work."

"No." And Annette felt a great deal of satisfaction at that truth.

"You kept an important truth about yourself from me. No wonder everything fell apart five years ago."

"I didn't back out of the wedding because I am adopted."

"Didn't you? Are you saying the insecurity you felt with your family did not contribute to you walking away from me?"

Annette opened her mouth, but no words came out. She couldn't deny that because she now knew that feeling unworthy of her family's love *had* been part of why she'd run away so far and so fast. She'd been certain he needed perfection and she'd never lived up to that with her family. How could she with him?

But had he needed her to be his perfect wife? Or had she played a part five years ago that somewhere deep inside she knew she couldn't keep playing for a lifetime?

Cinderella.

A woman who had been her family's perpetual servant and was destined to be an extension of her future husband rather than his partner.

"It was a secret," she reminded him now, rather than acknowledge the truth of his words out loud. "I wasn't supposed to tell anyone. Ever."

"You were going to marry me," he pointed out, like that mattered.

"I was ashamed." She hadn't realized that until therapy, but it helped Annette understand why she found it so easy to think everything was her fault.

"Of being adopted?"

She didn't answer for several seconds, looking for the words that hadn't come easily even in the therapist's office. "Of being unwanted. Unworthy of my father's love, of not being enough to inspire love in my adoptive parents."

"But your father's lack and frankly the lack of your parents now is not your fault."

"After three years of therapy, I mostly know that, but the feeling of shame is a hard one to shake. I work on it every day, reminding myself that my birth father didn't give me up because there was something wrong with me, but because he lacked something inside himself that allowed him to give up his five-year-old daughter without a backward glance."

"He was an ass."

She laughed, but privately agreed. Looking back at how her adoptive parents had treated her, she wasn't too impressed with their nurturing instincts either. Whatever their reasons for always finding the fault, the actual fault hadn't been in who she was, but who they wanted her to be.

The next morning, Annette peed on the stick and then stared at it in shock for several minutes before a knock sounded on the bathroom door.

For once, she'd been up well before Carlo, needing to do the test and show him she *wasn't* pregnant. Only, she was. Nearly four months along. Why wasn't she bigger? Her tummy looked the same, or maybe a little poochy, but Annette had always been curvy. Though goodness knew she'd tried for willow thin when she was younger, trying to look more like her tall, svelte adopted sisters and mom.

The knock sounded again. "Annette." Just that one word. Her name. No demand to be let inside though she knew he had to be itching to ask her if she'd taken the test yet.

"I took the test," she said through the door, strangely reluctant to open it.

"Let's talk about it."

Like they hadn't talked five years before. She got that. Annette wasn't a young and uncertain 22-year-old any longer. She knew how she fit in the world and accepted the things that could not be changed.

At least she thought she did.

She was pregnant.

That could be changed, but Annette really had no desire to take steps in that direction. She wanted this baby. Her baby. Carlo's baby. Family.

She opened the door, the stick still in her hand.

"What do the double blue lines mean?" he asked.

"Well on some tests, they would mean I'm not pregnant." She always taught her youth to read the instructions on the package because those lines and their colors meant different things to some of them.

"And on this one?" he pressed, standing there naked and every bit as confident as if he'd donned one of his bespoke suits.

"It means I'm going to have a baby."

"*Sì?*" he asked, excitement glinting in his grey gaze. "Am I allowed to celebrate?"

Was he? Was she? Annette's hand went to her stomach, and she smiled. "Yes, I think we are."

"You are going to have my baby." His eyes filled with moisture that shocked her. "I am undone."

And then he undid her with lovemaking that was so tender, it was her eyes that burned with emotion as she climaxed.

They were eating a late breakfast when Carlo's phone rang. He looked at the screen and went pale.

"What? What is it?" Annette asked.

He shook his head. "I do not know, but it is the hospital."

"Well, answer it! Maybe one of them has woken up." They had plans to visit the hospital later while Pamina watched Jo-Jo.

Somehow, Carlo had finagled an appointment with an obstetrician for her in the hospital complex as well.

"*Sì.* I mean, yes, it is Carlo Messina." His voice reverberated with stress.

He was not expecting good news, but Annette would not let herself consider anything else.

"He has? Yes. Yes. *Sì.* We will be there directly." He hung the phone up and looked at Annette, his expression filled with shock.

"What is it? Is Fantino...he's all right, isn't he? Did they have to take him back into surgery?"

"He woke up. He is awake." Carlo surged to his feet and came around to pull her up and into his arms. "He is awake. He is stable. They are moving him to a private room." He hugged Annette so hard she squeaked.

Releasing her immediately, he stared at her in abject horror. "*Scusami*! I am sorry. Did I hurt the baby?"

"No, you didn't hurt the baby. Or me." She wrapped her arms around him and hugged him back, hard. "I'm so happy. He's going to be okay."

"You always said, but I feared..." His voice choked off and she let him have his moment. Finally, he went on, his voice still clogged with emotion. "I feared the worse, but you did not. You had faith enough for us all."

She held onto Carlo tight, wishing her sister was awake as well but rejoicing no less in her heart for Fantino's start to recovery. "Can we take Jo-Jo to see him?"

"I do not know." Carlo stepped back, his usual urbane manner completely eclipsed by his relief at the news about Fantino. "I should have asked. Why did I not ask?" He rambled on in Sicilian.

"Do you want me to call your parents?" she asked.

If the hospital had called him, Carlo was the contact on file.

"*Sì. Sì.* We must call them."

"Okay, here's what's going to happen. You contact your executive team and deal with how this is going to impact your schedule. I'll call your mother. She'll tell your father."

"I have already cancelled my calls for today. We have our own appointment to attend."

"You are coming to the OB with me?" She'd just assumed she'd be going alone while he did business in the back of the limo like he'd done on some occasions when they were dating.

"Of course, I am going with you, unless you do not want me there? It is your choice, after all."

He kept saying that. It was her choice. And it was true. She appreciated that he recognized that. "Then if it is my choice, I would like you there."

She'd spent four months pregnant and not even realized. She wasn't feeling great about that and why his presence made her feel better she didn't choose to dwell on.

"*Bene.* You call my mother. She will cry all over you. I will call my father."

"As if he is not going to cry all over you," Annette teased.

Neither of them said anything about Carlo's own tears of relief and joy.

Annette's phone call with Valentina had gone much as Carlo thought it would. Valentina had interspersed her joy at her son's waking with tears and promises to Annette that Joyce would wake eventually too.

"These Sicilian tycoons, they are too cynical to believe like us, but we will hold faith for your sister."

Annette was so touched, she could barely get out a heartfelt, "Thank you."

"*Famigghia esti famigghia,*" she said prosaically. "We are family, *sì?*"

Yes, they were family. And soon that tie would be made even stronger by a child. Carlo and Annette's child.

She and Carlo hung up with their calls about the same time.

"Your mother is overcome with joy," she said to him.

"My father also." He looked entirely too smug, so she should have guessed what was coming next. "He is also delighted to have another grandchild on the way."

"You told them?" she asked, her voice risen in shock. "Surely now is not the time for that news."

"It is the best time. It gives my father a reminder that life wins." He reached out and laid his hand over her belly. "Our baby is *my* reminder that life wins. Sometimes, life wins."

Not always. Not even Annette believed that, but yes sometimes life did win.

It certainly felt like it when they entered Fantino's hospital room later to find him already talking to his parents, who were staying at a hotel only minutes from the medical complex.

His smile when he saw his brother was beautiful to see, but then that same smile was turned to her. "Annette, our savior."

"How can you say that?" She shook her head, tears clogging her throat and washing into her eyes. She spun on her heel and rushed from the room.

She collapsed against the wall outside, unable to control the tears.

A hand landed on her shoulder, but it was not Carlo's as she'd expected. It was Valentina's. "There, child, let it out. You were not to blame for this accident. Whatever your parents said in their grief, they do not believe it either."

"They do." It wasn't just grief. It was lack of love.

"Then they are fools." Valentina's bald statement without trying to convince Annette otherwise came as a surprise that almost stopped her tears.

"Yes, you pushed for your sister to get help. And I am grateful for it. We are all grateful. She deserves to be happy in her motherhood, but that is not such an easy thing always."

"No," Annette choked out.

"Fantino knows Joyce is still in a coma. He needs us to remind him she will come out of it."

"Cynical tycoon." Annette was still crying, but not as hard. A golden tanned hand reached out with a box of tissues. Carlo.

Of course, the man who did not love her nevertheless always knew what she needed. Except when he didn't, she reminded herself.

Jilting him hadn't happened in a vacuum.

Annette took the tissue and mopped herself up. "Thank you."

"Are you alright?" Carlo's gaze searched her face. "Fantino wants to see you."

Annette nodded. "Yes, I just..."

"Carry too much inside. I will remember that even when you don't look like you are going off the rails like the rest of us, you are inside. I should have realized after that appointment with the lawyers, but then you were your usual feisty self. Now, I know."

What he thought he knew she wasn't entirely sure, but one thing stuck. Carlo had acknowledged going off the rails. That was big. He put his hand out and she took it, concentrating on the warmth of his clasp and not the hospital sounds and smells around them.

They re-entered the hospital room that looked more like a high-end hotel room, but for all the machines and the IV hanging to the right of the bed. Alceu made a place for her beside the bed and Annette forced herself to approach and then stand there, looking down at the man whom she loved like a brother.

And whom her advice had nearly killed.

Chapter Thirteen

"Annette, sister." Fantino's voice was not his usual strong tenor, but it was unmistakably his. "You saved my family."

"I..."

Fantino grasped her free hand. "Did not cross three lanes of traffic because you were too tired to be driving."

Annette stared first at Fantino and then at Alceu Messina, who looked back stoically. "You told him all of it, is that wise?"

"I remembered most of it," Fantino said.

"You wouldn't have been in California if not for me," she said. "I'm sorry. Carlo mentioned in home therapy, and it never even occurred to me."

"The decision to go to California was Joyce's and I agreed with it, even though it meant leaving our baby in your provenly capable hands. I want to see Jo-Jo." Fantino looked to his brother like he expected Carlo to make that happen.

"As soon as the doctor approves the visit, we will bring her." Carlo's voice rang like a promise in the room.

Fantino nodded, clearly satisfied. "Joyce will wake soon and she'll be annoyed I got to see Jo-Jo first."

"She's really looking forward to finally bonding with her baby," Annette said, doing her best to keep emotion from her voice and pretty sure she'd failed miserably.

"She is," Fantino agreed. "The treatment made such a difference for her. I got my wife back, thanks to you."

"You won't lose her," Annette said in as much a plea as a promise.

She could not stand losing her sister.

"No, I won't. She's more stubborn than me. She'll wake up soon."

Annette nodded, too overcome with emotion to get any words past her tight throat. Carlo seemed to know and pulled her into his body, his arm coming protectively around her.

Fantino looked at them with speculation. "Is there something you want to share with the class?"

"We are having a baby," Carlo said, his own tone suffused with joy at impending fatherhood.

He might not think she was great shakes as potential wife material, but he was ecstatic she was having his baby. And Annette knew now that it had been confirmed, whatever his previous plans, Carlo was now set on wooing her into a wedding.

Again.

Only this time, she wasn't living in the fantasy that he loved her. The fantasy that had popped like a soap bubble when he'd laid out his plans for their future without her input, or even taking her feelings into consideration.

"When's the wedding?" Fantino asked. "Only I don't recommend waiting like we did. The wedding was a lot of stress on Joyce in her last trimester."

"Now is not the time for a big wedding, regardless," Carlo said, his tone brooking no argument.

He wasn't going to get one from her. "I agree."

"But there will be a wedding?" Alceu asked, *his* tone equally intransigent.

Before Annette could stutter some kind of answer that basically said she wasn't sure, or Carlo could say whatever he'd just taken a breath to get out, his mother said, "Leave them alone, *caro*. Today is for celebrating Fantino's recovery. Tomorrow is time enough to begin badgering your eldest about his love life."

Fantino started to droop soon after that, so Annette and Carlo took their leave. Valentina refused to be moved and declared she would read while he slept.

Considering that the furniture in the hospital room was as comfortable as any Annette had had in her living room, she wasn't worried the older woman would make herself exhausted with a bedside vigil. Valentina deserved having whatever moments of wakefulness her son gave her throughout the day after the worry he would not wake at all.

Annette and Carlo looked in on Joyce and found Lynette there, reading to their younger sister from a fashion magazine. "You'll adore this new line from..." She let her voice trail off when she saw them. "What are you doing here?" she asked pointedly of Annette.

"She's my sister too," Annette said, wishing her older sister's words no longer had the power to hurt her.

She'd come a long way to believing it wasn't her fault her family didn't love her, but that didn't mean she didn't love them, or that they couldn't hurt her.

"I guess," Lynette said grudgingly, surprising Annette.

But then she chanced a side glance at Carlo and the glower he was giving her sister was pretty ferocious. Lynette was doing her best to avoid his gaze at this point.

Annette probably shouldn't feel like smiling, but she did. Lynette was so used to everyone being okay with the way she treated Annette; she didn't know what to do with herself when someone disapproved.

Lynette stood up abruptly. "If you're going to be here for a while, I'll take a walk."

"Have you been here all day?" Annette asked, surprised.

"Yes, not that you'd know. You barely bother to visit, despite living less than an hour away."

"I visit as much as I can, but Jo-Jo needs me right now."

"So you've said." Lynette flipped her highlighted brown hair. "She has a nanny. We all heard Carlo say so."

"And yet a nanny cannot substitute for family. The better question might be why neither your parents, nor yourself have taken the time to check on Jo-Jo's welfare during all this."

"She's fine. You said so yourself."

"But none of you stepped in to offer help in her care."

Lynette frowned. "Why would we? Joyce needs us. The baby has carers."

Her sister's blatant dismissal of their niece's needs didn't surprise Annette, but it did hurt. "Jo-Jo deserves to be surrounded by people who love her while her parents can't be there."

"If they ever wake up," Lynette said, genuine regret in her voice as she looked down at Joyce. "It has been more than two weeks."

"Fantino woke up earlier. It's just a matter of time before Joyce does," Annette said, believing it.

She had to believe it.

"What? Fantino's awake?" Lynette asked in shock and then she looked at Annette accusingly. "Why weren't we told?"

"By we you mean?" Carlo asked in a tone that wasn't exactly friendly.

Lynette didn't seem to notice. "Me and my parents. Joyce's family. Fantino is my brother-in-law."

"Annette is also Joyce's family, but as long as you refuse to acknowledge that you cannot expect to be in either my parents or my favor." It was a warning, clear as day.

Annette heard it. Lynette did too because the look she shot Annette was positively venomous.

"There are things you don't know," she said to Carlo. "Besides, she is the woman who jilted you at the altar five years ago and humiliated you in the process. Or had you forgotten?"

"I have forgotten nothing, least of which the role you played in the social and tabloid media storm that followed.

Lynette sucked in a breath, her mouth opening and closing like a fish. She was so obviously trying to think of what to say to spin the past in a different light, Annette almost felt sorry for her. Almost.

But while Lynette was undoubtedly a good sister to Joyce, she was not a nice person.

"As to apprising you of my brother's improved condition, my father called yours earlier today."

"Oh!" Lynette grabbed her phone out of her bag and said a word they would have been punished for uttering as teens. "I had my phone on silent. Dad texted me."

Annette knew she had gotten no similar text, but chose to believe that was because Alceu had told her father that she already knew.

Lynette turned to go, but before she could leave the room, Carlo said, "I know Annette is adopted and I know why. That does not reflect badly on her, but your family's behavior reflects very poorly on all of you."

The brunette spun and stared. "You told him?" she demanded of Annette, accusation in every syllable. "That's a family matter."

"That I am adopted is a *personal* matter and who I choose to tell is none of your business." Annette was done pretending her past was something to be ashamed of or hidden.

"But nobody wanted you. Why would you want people to know that?" Lynette asked, incomprehensibly.

"Our parents wanted me, or at least the money I could bring them. It was their choice not to love me, but that is not my fault." And finally, Annette believed that, to the very core of her.

Whatever was lacking in her family's feelings toward her, it came from a dearth in their own hearts, not in her.

"I didn't want a sister," Lynette said baldly. "Joyce was different, she was a cute baby and full of smiles for me, but you? That first year, you were either crying, or quiet and sullen. You ignored me."

"And you couldn't stand that." Annette shook her head. "It never occurred to you that I'd lost both my parents within a year of each other and the grief was overwhelming."

"I was six. Of course, I didn't think about that."

"But you are no longer six," Carlo pointed out.

"No." Lynette shook her head. "I got in the habit of resenting you and it never went away."

"We don't ever have to be friends, but maybe you could work on not being such a complete mess of a human?" Annette suggested.

"I'm not a mess. I just don't like you."

About to quip that the feeling was entirely mutual, Annette cast a quick glance toward the bed, guilt immediately wracking her for having this discussion at her sister's bedside. What she saw nearly sent her to her knees.

Joyce's eyes were open. And they were clear. Her hand not tethered to an I.V. was moving toward her face like she wanted to grab the apparatus there.

Annette leaped toward the bed, but her hand was gentle when she put on her sister's wrist. "Don't. They'll take it out for you. You are okay. It is all going to be okay."

Joyce looked at her with trust and a lot more alertly than Annette expected.

The doctors had said that Fantino took a couple of hours to become fully coherent, but Joyce's eyes were clear.

Lynette rushed to the bed. "You're awake."

Joyce shifted her head slightly toward Lynette's voice and winced.

"Shh...shh...don't move just yet. Let the doctor and nurses check you over," Annette said.

"I've got to tell Mom and Dad." Lynette left the room to make the call.

Joyce's eyes followed her.

"She's been with you almost every day," Annette said. "Give her a minute to get herself together. You know she doesn't like for anyone to see her cry."

Joyce blinked, but her eyes asked questions.

"There was an accident. Do you remember?"

Joyce's expression filled with horror, making it obvious she did.

"Fantino is fine. He's awake in another room. Maybe now you're awake, you can be moved from ICU to join him."

"That's for the doctor to decide." A nurse came in and approached the bed. "It's good to see you awake, Mrs. Messina." She said to Annette. "We'll need you to leave for the present, but you can come back after she's been assessed by the doctor."

Annette brushed her sister's cheek. "We'll be back. I have some amazing news for you."

Joyce's eyes shifted to something at Annette's left and she realized Carlo was standing there. He must have gone for the nurse when Annette realized Joyce was awake. But he was here now and Joyce was asking silently if he was part of the amazing news.

"Yes, he's part of it," Annette said aloud. "But I'm not telling you more until I come back."

The laughter in Joyce's eyes said she understood Annette was giving her something to look forward to, and also teasing a little, as big sisters did sometimes.

"Fantino is going to be ecstatic that you have woken," Carlo said. "We will go tell him."

Joyce's relaxed expression said that was all she needed to hear right now.

Carlo and Annette left the room, but ran into Lynette as she was coming back.

Carlo put his arm out. "The doctors want a chance to assess your sister and hopefully remove the tubes that are preventing her speech."

Lynnette nodded and then just fell on Annette. "She's all right. I didn't think she would be."

Annette let their oldest sister cry, even as she stood in stunned silence that Lynette would choose her as a point of comfort. It ended as abruptly as it began as soon as their parents voices could be heard in the corridor.

Lynette broke from Annette and ran for them.

They stood together, a tableau of three, no room for her.

Carlo once again slid his arm around her, pulling her into his body. "Come, we have an appointment to keep and then we will return and share our good news with your sister."

Annette was nervous going into her appointment, still bothered by the fact it had never even occurred to her she might be pregnant. The youth in her program would be laughing their heads off at her if they knew. However, the doctor was kind with an approachable manner.

"We could do another urine test to confirm your pregnancy, but as we would then perform an ultrasound, we might as well start there, with the added benefit of not emptying your bladder."

So, there was a reason the office had instructed her to drink at least four cups of water an hour before her ultrasound. And it wasn't just to leave her with an urgent need for the restroom.

Laying on the exam table a few minutes later, naked from the waist down and her stomach covered in cold gel, Annette wasn't prepared for what she saw on the monitor. "I can see their little mouth and eyes."

"It is our baby," Carlo said, his own voice heavy with suppressed emotion.

"Yes, and our measurements match your calculations. You are four months pregnant."

"She's not showing though. Should we be worried?" Carlo asked.

The doctor gave him a look that said *new fathers, what can you do?* "There's nothing to worry about at all. The baby's size is commensurate with being eighteen weeks along. Some women show early, some quite late."

They were given a thumb drive with the ultrasound pictures on it and instructions for foods to avoid during pregnancy. Thankfully none of which she'd been indulging in since returning from Sicily.

"You haven't been drinking coffee?" Carlo asked with surprise as they walked out to the car waiting for them at the curb.

"It made me nauseated. I thought I was getting a stress ulcer, to tell you the truth."

"Because of your worry about Joyce?" he asked, his dark brow furrowed.

"That was only part of it. I told you what was going on in the organization and all that I had uncovered since becoming a regional director. Knowing how I'd supported and worked for an organization that didn't practice the core values it claimed to uphold was soul destroying."

"Were my legal staff not able to help?"

"Oh, they're helping the employees I got them in touch with, but that didn't change my own sense of personal responsibility."

"You take too much on yourself."

"You think so?"

"You blamed yourself for the accident."

"My parents did too."

He frowned. "If anything, they should be grateful, as we are, that you were willing to step in and help your sister and Fantino when the rest of us ignored what was happening, telling ourselves it was just part of being new parents."

"You really feel that way?" she asked.

"*Sì.* So do my parents. We are all very grateful to you, just as Fantino is."

Warmth unfurled inside Annette. He and his family appreciated her and it felt good.

As nice as that was, by the time they had visited with Joyce and Fantino again, sharing their good news with her sister, Annette was exhausted and ready for dinner and an early night.

Chapter Fourteen

The next morning, Annette woke with a complete sense of wellbeing.

She remembered the last time that had happened and what had come after. The prick of that memory threatened to burst the sense of contentment surrounding her.

Warm breath exhaled over her temple and Annette smiled. Not the same.

Carlo was beside her in the bed, his body wrapped around hers, his hand settled over her lower abdomen even in his sleep. Carlo really wanted this baby, and Annette really wanted a family. With him. That bit was something she had to come to terms with for her own sense of equanimity.

Both Joyce and Fantino were awake now, and soon enough Jo-Jo was going to have her own family back. The six-month-old would not need her aunt like she did now, but the baby growing inside Annette would always need her. She could love that child without telling herself not to get too attached, to remember she was not the mom.

But this baby had a father too, one very keen to shower his child with love and affection, protection, and care.

Annette didn't know if her biological father had felt that way at one time about her, but whatever feelings he had for her died with her mother, she was sure of that. Could Carlo get turned off his own child that easily?

She didn't think so, but how could she know?

Carlo stirred, his hand rubbing a slow circle over her belly before leaning down to kiss her neck and then shifting so they were face to face. "You look thoughtful," he said.

"So, no big wedding?" she asked, rather than ask a question sure to offend him.

"Are you saying there is going to be a wedding at all?"

"You haven't actually asked me."

"I did that five years ago." And his tone said, *look where that got us.*

She had to acknowledge he had a point. "So, *if* there is a wedding, no church?" she rephrased her question.

"No." That was definite.

But then he probably had very bad memories of standing in the front of a full church only to have a no-show bride.

She nodded. "Good."

"You did not want a church wedding before?" he asked, clearly surprised.

"I didn't want a spectacle." She'd hated the thought of saying their vows in front of hundreds of people that were strangers to her.

"You did not say."

"My mother took over planning the wedding practically from the moment I told my parents that we were getting married."

"Surely she wanted your opinion on things."

"Trust me, she didn't."

"A celebrant and only the necessary witnesses," Carlo said. "Perhaps in our sibling's shared hospital room."

If all went well, the doctors thought Joyce would be able to be moved into Fantino's room before the end of the week. Alceu was already looking into what it would take to bring them both home soonest so they could see their baby and Fantino could get his physical therapy in familiar surroundings.

"You want to get married this week?" she asked with an embarrassingly shocked squeak in her voice.

"You heard Fantino, you do not need the stress of a wedding late in your pregnancy."

And maybe he thought that if they didn't put it off too long, she was more likely to follow through.

"If we get married, we already agreed there will be no big production. Therefore, no stress."

Frowning, Carlo nevertheless nodded. He withdrew from her, though, and got out of bed.

"Carlo?"

"I have some work to attend to this morning. I cannot keep putting off my responsibilities."

"Visiting your brother is part of those responsibilities, isn't it?"

"*Sì*. Even so..." He shrugged, grabbed his slacks and slid them on before heading to the door, the rest of his clothes in hand.

Something had happened there and Annette wasn't sure what it was. "Carlo. Stop. What is going on?"

"I have work. I said."

"Yes, you did. I just..."

"What?" He turned to face her. "You think my pride likes the constant reminders that I'm good enough for sex, but not good enough for marriage as far you are concerned?"

"I never said that!"

"You have said it in too many ways to count, but jilting me at the altar was the biggest one."

"I didn't jilt you at the altar. I jilted you to your face, but you were too arrogant to believe I meant what I said."

"Arrogant? Trusting you to mean what you said was arrogant?"

"I meant it when I said the wedding was off."

He ran his hands through his hair. "Why? Why was it off?"

"Do you remember saying my job was an embarrassment to you?"

"*Sì*. That was unacceptable, but you do run away from your own wedding because your groom says one foolish thing?"

"Even if you meant it?"

"I was arrogant about that, I admit it. I had ideas, this picture in my head of what a perfect family would be like."

"And in that family, I didn't have a job." She scooted up in the bed, making no attempt to hide her nudity.

His grey eyes flared with interest, but then he met her gaze, his expression almost contrite. "That was wrong of me."

Not almost. He was sorry. Good. Maybe there was hope for them yet.

She nodded. "It was, but it wasn't just that."

"What else?"

"I had this feeling, like I could never measure up to the perfect wife you wanted me to be, and I'd spend my whole life trying to be perfect and never being able to earn my family's love."

"So, you thought I would eventually treat you like they do?" he asked, clearly appalled at the idea, and also offended. "I would not have done that. You were, and are again, precious to me."

She about melted on the spot, but precious wasn't the same as loving. "I wanted you to love me. I thought maybe you did, only then you made all those plans without even talking to me and I knew you couldn't, could you?"

"Love?" He shook his head, letting out a sigh. "I'm not a romantic. Not like my father and brother."

Right. That's what she'd finally realized. "But you wanted to marry me. Why?"

"We fit. In bed and out of it, or so I thought."

"I did too. Until I didn't."

"Until you did not." He sighed again. "I guess you need to take some time and decide if you think we can fit again."

"I thought you were going to try to persuade me."

"I make no promises not to do that, but for now, I think we both deserve time to think."

She nodded. He was right. Of course, he was right.

So, why did him leaving her room like this feel so wrong?

Annette found the next week odd and if she were honest with herself, trying.

She and Carlo were living in the same house, but he'd started sleeping in his own guest room. They ate breakfast together every morning, though he had to interrupt his already busy workday to do so. He also joined her and Jo-Jo on their daily walk.

Both of which showed his commitment to spending time with her and their niece, but the intimacy they had shared even while at odds was gone.

They talked about Joyce and Fantino, the business, and even Annette's job and what she might want to do going forward. They did not talk about their relationship and the topic of marriage was not brought up again between them. Annette was afraid Carlo had changed his mind and was interested in shared custody rather than a shared life.

She had no idea what her Sicilian lover was really thinking, though.

They'd finally cleared the air about their failed attempt to marry the first time and yet Annette felt like they were further apart than ever in some ways.

Carlo was unfailingly polite, but he did not touch her. At all.

She missed his touches and wasn't ashamed to say so. To herself. Alone. In her room when she was missing them most and trying to sleep, but often failing miserably.

The night before Fantino was supposed to return home, Annette fell asleep when her head hit the pillow from pure exhaustion, only to waken in a cold sweat sometime later, the echo of nightmares she could not remember reverberating through her consciousness. She didn't remember the dreams, but she remembered the sense of loss.

Knowing she would not get back to sleep right away, she got up. Maybe a cup of chamomile tea would help. She shivered and grabbed her robe. She pulled it on over her pajamas. She'd taken to wearing a long-sleeved t-shirt and flannel sleep pants the last couple of nights because she'd been cold in her bed. She missed Carlo's body radiating heat.

There was a light under the door into the kitchen when she reached it.

Pushing open the door, she was unsurprised to find Carlo sitting at the table, drinking a mug of something. The kitchen was dimly lit from the light over the stove, the overhead lights not on.

"I hope that's not coffee. You'll never get any sleep if it is."

His head jerked up like he hadn't heard her come in. "Oh, uh...no." He grimaced. "I'm embarrassed to say it is warm milk with vanilla and sugar like my mother used to make when I couldn't sleep as a boy."

"Sounds yummy, though I don't know how the sugar was supposed to help you sleep."

He shrugged. "It always worked back then."

"Maybe I should try it then."

He stood. "Sit down, I will make you some."

"You don't have to do that. I'm sure I can figure it out."

"Sit, Annette. You look as drawn out as when I first arrived. And we had good news today."

"Yes, Fantino is coming home and if this last infection stays gone, Joyce gets to come home in a few days."

"She will need help."

"Yes." And while Jo-Jo transitioned to bonding with her mother, that help needed to be Annette, but not for too long. She needed to leave so the family could find its footing together again.

Without her.

Carlo moved around the kitchen with surprising efficiency, preparing her a cup of warmed milk in a saucepan, not the microwave as she would have done. He handed her the steaming mug and then returned to his own seat and proceeded to stare at his own cup like it held the secrets of the universe.

"Is something the matter?" she asked after several seconds of silence.

He looked up, again like he was almost startled to find her there. "Drink your milk while it's warm or it won't do you any good."

"Really?" She took a sip and the flavor of vanilla slid across her tongue. "Mmm...yum. I wonder why it matters if it is warm."

"Warmth and comfort, I guess. I do not know. It is something my mother used to say to me."

"Valentina was a good mom."

"*Sì*. She was, but for many years I did not think so. I thought she neglected me and my brother, because she was not the one to come to our football matches, or volunteer at school like the other mothers."

"She didn't neglect you though, did she?" Valentina had always had her causes, but she loved her family.

"Not really, no." He frowned. "When I was young, I resented the time she spent on her causes, her many trips away to service them. We always had nannies, and our grandparents were active in our lives, but Fantino and I both felt badly that our mother was rarely around for the things that mattered to us."

"I am sorry. If she knew she hurt you, she would be sorry for it."

"She was a wonderful mother," he said, like he'd come to the conclusion long before. "Her life was about more than my brother and I and she has done so much good."

"But when you were a child, you wanted her to be like the other moms."

"*Sì*. Now, I appreciate the woman she is."

"But that's why my job was such a problem for you. You saw my dedication to at risk youth as a competition for dedication to our own family."

"We didn't even have children yet, and yes I know I tried to guilt you into having them earlier than we planned. I've done a lot of thinking this past week and I ask myself if I set out to break us up because my actions couldn't have ended with any other scenario."

"Do you think you wanted out of the marriage, but didn't want to break your word?" she asked, pain at the idea a solid lump in her chest.

He shook his head decisively and then met her gaze, his own intent. "No. I think I was what you accused me of being. Arrogant. I believed that because you were so malleable with your family, you would be malleable with me when it mattered. Or when I thought it mattered. My entire life, I have found it easier to ask pardon than to ask permission. And so, I did what I always had done, made my plans and then told you about them after the fact, assuming that even if you were angry, you would get over it."

"And you would get your way." She took another sip of her warmed milk, finding it comforting but his willingness to talk even more so.

He nodded, looking chagrined. "In no scenario did I actually expect you to dump me."

"You were very sure of me."

"You told me you loved me."

"You said you aren't a romantic."

"I am not. I am pragmatic and I thought if you loved me, then so much the better."

"How did that work out for you?" she asked with only a little sarcasm.

"As you know, it did not work at all."

"And now?"

He came around the table, dropping to his knees beside her chair and taking both her hands in his. "Now? Now, I must tell you how very sorry I am for taking you for granted, for treating you like you were not the most precious person in my life as you were. I should never have planned that honeymoon, hoping to get you to quit your job. That was inexcusable, and I paid dearly for my arrogance."

He considered losing her a dear price to pay?

He kissed her knuckles, and then looked into her eyes, his shining with sincerity and something she'd never seen before in them. Humility. "I am so sorry I made the decision to move back to Sicily without talking to you first. When I told my father, he was livid with me. Said he'd raised me better."

"It shocked me."

"No matter what happens between us going forward, you have my word I will never attempt to manipulate you like that again."

She went to draw her hands away, but he held tight. "I'm not done."

Chapter Fifteen

"There's more?" she asked.

"I have not yet said how much I regret not listening to you that day. You would not be you if you did not want to help others. Your heart is too big to keep it caged in a Sicilian mansion."

"You're positively poetic."

"I am not trying to be."

She smiled. "I believe you. Neither of us is the same person we were five years ago."

"No, we are not." He gave her a slashing grin, some of his usual confidence shining through. "I think now, you would make me listen."

"Yes." She so would.

"But I would not make the same choices either."

"No, I don't think you would." He'd grown, just as she had. That very heartfelt apology showed it. "Just like you didn't with Jo-Jo. You listened to me about her."

"I'm glad you realize that and don't hold the contract against me. That was such a—"

She interrupted before he could start self-flagellating. She was glad he was sorry, but she didn't want him being so down on himself. "You burned it." She'd seen the ashes in the study fireplace. "You never had any intention of forcing me to sign it."

"No. I promise you; I never did."

Since she'd never thought he was serious and it was his version of going off the rails, like he'd said at the hospital, she believed him.

He let go of her hands and stood up. "Now, I do not know what you want." It was a big admission for such a confident, take-charge man.

"I want a family," Annette assured him. "But I want to work and make a difference for at risk youth too."

"*Sì*. Absolutely. You would not be the precious woman that you are otherwise. I finally understand that."

"It's only taken five years." Which really? Wasn't all that long in the scheme of things.

He smiled. "You always take the positive view."

"I didn't five years ago," she admitted.

"You were wrong about one thing."

"What's that?"

He reached down and grabbed his mug, drinking what appeared to be the last of his warmed milk and then put the mug down. "I didn't need a perfect wife. I wanted you. I still want you."

"Even though I'm a bad bet?" she teased.

"You are not. Neither am I, because I will never again make choices for you without consulting you, this I promise you."

"There are other deal breakers, but that's a big one."

"Oh, yes, what are they?" He got up and put both now empty mugs in the sink.

She stood, yawning, suddenly very tired. "I'll put them in the prenup."

He went very still. "You are saying you will marry me?"

"Yes, Carlo, I will marry you. This time we both have a better understanding of what we expect going in."

"We do, but there will be no prenup."

"What?" Even the shock of that statement couldn't rouse much energy in her. "Did you put sleeping pills in my milk?"

"No, you are just worn out worrying about everyone. It cannot be good for you, or the baby."

"No, I don't suppose it is." She covered her mouth before yawning again.

He guided her from the kitchen, his arm at her back all the way up the stairs and down the hall to her room.

She stopped in front of her door, but didn't go in. "Sleep with me. I'm cold without you."

Carlo didn't reply but he followed her into her room.

The next morning Annette met Carlo for breakfast like usual. What was not usual was the ring box sitting beside her plate.

It was the same jeweler that had done her engagement ring before. "Is that?"

"Your engagement ring? *Sì*. It has been sitting in my safe since your father returned it to me." He shook his head. "I thought that told me how little regard you had for it. You didn't want me or the ring I'd had custom made for you, but the expression on your lovely features says the opposite."

"I love that ring." But she'd felt wrong keeping it after calling off the wedding.

Carlo opened the box and took out the ring. Annette offered her hand and he slid the ring on her finger. It was déjà vu and not. They'd done this once before, but this time, Annette knew they were getting married to build a family.

She wasn't building castles in the sky around love and happily ever after.

They would be good together if they were good to each other.

She loved him and had every intention of being the best human in his life she could be. Annette trusted that Carlo was just as determined. He'd grown in the past five years, just as she had.

Smiling she sat down to the table, thrilled to see her favorite smoked salmon and gouda omelet on her plate. There was fruit and toast as well, but she ignored both to take and then savor a bite of the omelet, making *mmm* noises.

"You know some doctors claim cravings are your body's way of getting the nourishment it needs," Carlo said with a smile. "Have you had your iron levels checked recently?"

"I'm sure it was included in the panel the obstetrician had run." They'd taken two vials of blood after all. "The nurse said everything came back normal when she called."

"I'd feel better if you checked your health chart app."

"Fine. After breakfast. Right now, I'm going to eat this yummy omelet before it goes cold."

"A very prosaic way to celebrate our engagement, but not a bad one."

She grinned at him. "I can't drink champagne, but I can eat fish."

"Not too much fish. Some studies—"

"Shh...after breakfast."

He dutifully went silent, making a sign of zipping his lips. However, Annette had no doubts he'd be having a talk with Mrs. Banning about how much fish should be served at meals in future.

"I am still the President of Messina Shipping and Exports," Carlo said as they finished their meal.

"Yes, I know."

"It is possible we could move my offices to New York."

Touched at the proof that he was not taking anything for granted this time around, Annette shook her head. "Not necessary. I'm not staying with my organization so now is as good a time as any to make the move to Sicily. I speak Italian and can look for a job over there, but honestly after the past few months, I'd like to take some time to regroup. Maybe a sabbatical at least until after our baby is born and we see how mundane things like breast feeding and sleeping through the night go for us."

"If that is what you truly want?" He wasn't being diffident. There was too much quiet confidence in his demeanor, but he was taking nothing for granted this time around. She approved.

"I do."

"That will make my next request an easier one to make then."

"Yes?" she inquired.

"I hoped you would be willing to wait to look for another position until after our honeymoon."

"We're going on a honeymoon?" For a marriage of convenience because they liked having sex and didn't seem inclined to stop doing it together and she'd gotten pregnant as a result?

"It is customary."

"All right, but I want to give Joyce, Fantino and Jo-Jo a few days to settle in after Joyce comes home, before I leave."

"Naturally. It will be hard on both you and Jo-Jo when you leave, but if she is going to bond with her mother..." He let his voice trail off and shrugged.

"She has to see Joyce as mommy and not Aunt Annette. I know." Emotion washed over her. Worry and doubt and fear a maelstrom that always seemed ready to take over.

And it made no sense because Joyce and Fantino were improving every day.

"I just wish I knew how to make it easier on all of them," she told Carlo.

"You take too much on yourself, but I have been making plans."

"You have?"

He just looked at her.

She almost laughed, but was afraid she'd start crying if she did. Darn hormones. "Of course, you have. What are they?"

"I've spoken to the clinic she went to, and they are sending a psychologist who specializes in adoption transitions to facilitate those first weeks with Joyce home."

Relief washed through Annette. It wasn't on her to fix it this time. Someone who knew what they were doing was going to guide Joyce and Fantino. "Jo-Jo isn't adopted though," she couldn't help pointing out, nevertheless.

"No, but many things about the situation have a similar emotional makeup, or so the director for the clinic claimed."

That made sense, Annette supposed. Joyce and Jo-Jo's bond was tenuous at best. While Jo-Jo seemed happy for Fantino to hold her and play with her, she still reached for Annette when she needed comfort. That had to change for the baby's sake and her parents' sakes.

"My parents will remain in New York for the next few months. My father will cover Fantino's office until my brother is able to return to work fulltime."

"Aren't you worried for his health?" The senior Messina had recovered from his accident, but he was in his seventies now and she worried the stress of working the long work hours he and his sons were known for could be detrimental.

"No," Carlo said with assurance. "Mama will be policing his time and she can be a dragon if she needs to."

Annette agreed. She thought Valentina Messina was a formidable woman even when she didn't need to be, but she was also very occupied with her own projects. "Will she be able to keep track of Alceu's hours when she herself is so busy?"

"Mama has slowed down her involvements since Papa retired. They spend more time together. They travel a great deal."

"Oh, that's good then."

"I have also used my time here in New York to identify additional members of management staff who will make solid adds to Fantino's executive team. He approved my choices this morning and I have had human resources contact each with their promotion offers. This will free up more experienced executive team members to take some of the daily burden from my father."

"You're a good son."

Carlo looked pleased with her assessment, and it occurred to Annette that he'd always liked praise from her when he seemed indifferent to it from everyone else. Except his family.

Further proof that in his mind she was on equal footing with his family, which was not a bad place to be in the life of the Sicilian tycoon.

Fantino came home that evening and Joyce five days later. The psychologist from California arrived at the same time. He fit right in with the household, insisting on being called Ray and began facilitating the adjustment of the little family toward what would be *their* normal almost immediately.

Annette and Carlo were out walking together with Jo-Jo, since neither parent could manage the task just yet, when Carlo said, "Ray is a good man and competent doctor, I am sure, but I am glad I am not Fantino right now."

"Because you'd have to talk about your *feelings* at least daily?" she teased.

But Carlo nodded quickly, his look of utter horror at the prospect making her laugh.

"Feelings don't make you weak, Carlo."

"Nor does talking about them make them any more real," he countered.

But Annette wasn't sure she agreed. "Maybe it does."

"No. All this talking, it brings up more bad than good."

"At first, maybe, but not talking about it doesn't mean the bad wasn't there, under the surface."

"You think they have a bad marriage?" he asked, sounding shocked.

"I didn't say that. You're the one that used the term bad. I would say difficult. Joyce and Fantino stopped communicating during her depression and now they have to find their way back to each other and being able to freely share their hearts and ideas once again."

"We are open with each other." Carlo took over the stroller as they started up a muddy, steep track. Annette had slid backwards on this before and he wouldn't risk her falling.

She walked beside him. "Yes, we are, but we weren't always."

"That is true," he admitted, his tone grudging. "We didn't need a psychologist to get us to open up this time though."

"Speak for yourself. I was in therapy for three years after I moved to Portland."

He didn't reply. She cast him a sidelong glance and found him looking back, his expression questioning. "It helped?"

"It helped."

"I am glad."

She was too, but that wasn't what she wanted to talk about. They'd set a wedding date, one week from today, after which, they planned to go on the long-delayed honeymoon. They'd agreed on who should be invited to the wedding.

Annette had thought long and hard and finally decided against inviting anyone in her family except Joyce. It was her wedding day and while she wasn't marrying her Knight in Shining Armor who loved her to pieces like she'd always dreamed, it was still special.

Annette loved Carlo. Deeply and forever.

She wanted nothing but goodwill on her wedding day and she was certain that if she invited her older sister and her parents, that would not be her experience.

One thing she'd definitely gotten out of therapy was that she was not responsible for the actions of others. If her parents were toxic to her, even if they were good to their other children, Annette did not have to give them room in *her* life's special moments.

Whether she would give them space in her child's life was something she would decide based on their behavior.

She'd told Carlo as much and he had agreed, but hadn't been happy. He wanted to cut off all ties with her parents for their past treatment of her, but Annette wasn't willing to go that far. For one thing, she knew it would strain her relationship with Joyce and that bond was too important to Annette to harm unless she had no other choice.

None of that was what was on her mind uppermost today though. "Carlo, we haven't signed the prenuptial agreement yet. You know I have a clause or two I want to put in."

"I told you, there will be no prenuptial agreement."

"But why not? I signed one last time."

"And you walked away. This time we are doing things differently."

"But you're a billionaire. You can't just marry me without a prenup." She'd been raised by Floyd Hudson, if not with affection, with all the same strictures her sisters had been taught.

And one of those was to always have a prenuptial agreement to protect their assets. Annette had no assets to speak of, but Carlo had a business empire.

When Carlo remained silent, she asked, "What does your father think about it?"

"He has asked me to sign over my shares in the company to him to protect Messina Shipping and Exports."

"What? No. You've nearly doubled the size of the company since you took it over." The workaholic that he was. "That's not fair."

"I would still draw a more than adequate salary. And I have my own firm."

The venture capital firm he'd created as a young man in business school was now one of the world's leading ones.

"No, I won't let you do it. You tell your father we're signing a contract."

"Fine, if you want one, you work with the lawyers and my father and draw it up, but I warn you that if you try to shortchange yourself somehow, I won't be signing it."

"Why? What is this really about?"

He stopped the stroller at the top of the hill and turned to face her while Jo-Jo babbled at her favorite view. There were cows in the distance and sometimes people walking. The baby seemed to love this vantage point.

Carlo brushed Annette's cheek, the soft leather of his glove making her shiver a little. "This is about making a lifetime commitment to build a family. You are agreeing to it because you are pregnant with my child. That makes it no less real and lasting."

"How does a prenup change that?"

"It gives us a prescription for the way out if things get hard."

"And you don't want that?"

"No. Like anything else worth having, I want to work for our marriage, in the good times, but also the difficult ones."

"You say you are not a romantic." Annette's voice was clogged with emotion. Darn hormones again.

"I am not, but even I recognize that marriage is not a business contract."

"Last time..."

"I did everything expected."

"I still don't see why that is bad."

"It wasn't." Left unsaid was a truth between them: but it hadn't worked.

And in Carlo's mind, it wasn't enough to change how he handled decisions about their lives together, he had to change everything leading up to the wedding.

"You can be a little irrational," she pointed out.

"I am perfectly rational," he said, affronted.

Said the man who had written up that ludicrous sex contract.

"Okay. I will draft the prenup, but don't come whining to me if you don't like some of the clauses."

"I assure you, I will not."

Chapter Sixteen

He was singing a different tune two days later.

Annette, Alceu and Valentina had pounded out a prenup that satisfied Alceu for the safety of the Messina empire, Valentina about her son's future fatherhood in the event the marriage did not last and Annette about how that marriage and their family life would be conducted.

"You have put limits on the number of hours I may work and how often I can leave the family for business trips."

"There are also limits on the number of trips you can expect us to take each year with you for the sake of business," Annette agreed serenely. "You'll notice there is also a limit on the number of hours I spend working, or volunteering."

She'd put a forty-hour cap on hers because honestly, Annette had always wanted to work only part time when her children were in school, but she didn't want to work extra hours later either. She wanted balance in life.

Carlo's sixty-hour max was generous on her part, but she didn't think the tycoon would countenance any less. However, there were other family centric provisos. Like both of them attending their children's events at least half of the time. Annette had every intention of being there for everything she could, but she expected Carlo to make an effort too.

"It is not reasonable to expect me to make a football match in the middle of my workday, or go to every dance recital."

"It's only half, not every, and why not? You know what I never heard you say when you were talking about the resentments you held toward your mother for not being there when you wanted her?"

"What?" Carlo asked, warily.

"Any resentment toward your father for missing *all* of them."

Arrested, Carlo stared at her. "I...he was running the company."

"A global concern, I know, but he could have delegated more."

"Not without risk."

"Life is made up of risks. You choose which ones you want to take."

"You want me to risk my company for the sake of time with our child?"

"Hopefully children, but yes." He'd been willing to risk the whole shebang by marrying her without a prenup. It shouldn't be a big stretch.

"You want more than one child?"

"You know I do." Five years ago, they'd agreed on at least two children, but she had always wanted four. So, there was no middle child to be lost on her own.

"I did not know if your desires in that regard had changed."

"A good conversation to have *before* marriage."

He shrugged. "Perhaps, but ultimately, whether we agreed on how many children to have did not matter. You *are* pregnant with our child. We are getting married. If you choose never to get pregnant again, that will not change those basic facts."

"I still think being on the same page about expectation in that regard is nice."

"Certainly, but life does not afford us the luxury of always being on the same page as the people most important to us."

"Is this about your father?" She knew it had hurt Carlo when Alceu had asked him to sign over the shares to the company.

The prenup had allowed Alceu to withdraw the request, but she knew it still rankled with Carlo that the older man had made it.

Carlo shrugged. "It does not matter. My point is that *nice* is not always our luxury."

Since she could not argue with that, Annette didn't try. "He still thinks the world of you, you know?"

Carlo looked at her, the contract pages spread out between them over the library table. Although library was a misnomer. There were books in the room and lots of bookshelves, but they held more objects d'art than reading material.

Joyce was not the reader that Annette was. Apparently, neither was Fantino.

Still, it made a nice room to have this meeting in, having a door that shut snugly with a lock. With his parents staying and both Joyce and Fantino back in residence, along with the psychologist, privacy in the mansion was in short supply.

"I know my father respects me. Do not worry about my tender feelings, Annette. I am fine. It was business and that is one thing I understand very well."

"If you say so." She still wasn't convinced. Something was bothering Carlo and she was certain it was his father's apparent lack of faith in him.

This contract negated all the older Messina man's worries though, so Annette felt good about that. She didn't want father and son at odds. The family had been through enough.

Carlo finished reading the last page and then signed the prenuptial agreement with a flourish. "So, it is done."

"Just like that?" she asked, a little shocked. "I expected some push back and to have to negotiate the number of weeks of vacation time each year at the very least." She'd stipulated six. Two weeks at the winter holidays and four more weeks throughout the year.

She would prefer they were taken in at least weeklong clumps, but she would settle for lots of long weekends so long as he made real time in his schedule to spend with her and their children regularly.

He seemed perfectly willing to do just that.

"I give my top executives six weeks of vacation and an additional two of personal leave. I cannot justify giving myself any less to spend with my own family." Carlo stood, his smile filled with something he usually reserved for the nighttime when they were alone. "I think that sofa looks quite comfortable. Would you like to join me on it?"

He was talking about a large brown leather sofa situated in front of another gas fireplace. It was blocked from the windows by standing bookcases behind it.

She darted a glance to the door.

"I locked it on the way in."

"You were planning this then?" she asked with laughter as she got up and did as he asked, joining him on the sofa.

"I was planning privacy. Now, I want to celebrate."

"Celebrate?"

"Oh, yes. That contract has us both stitched up tight."

"You liked that clause then?"

"Can you doubt it?" he was stripping methodically all the while watching her do the same.

She'd put a clause in that was her solemn promise to show up for the ceremony. She thought a businessman like him would appreciate her putting it in writing. He really did, it looked like.

An hour later, his suitcoat (which they'd used to protect the couch) would never be the same and Annette was left in no doubt just how enthusiastically her tycoon fiancé felt about the prenuptial contract he had just signed.

Annette woke on her wedding day feeling more anticipation than she thought she should. She *should* be worried, but she wasn't. She was excited.

Today, she started building the family she had always craved.

Five years ago, she'd run from Carlo, out of fear of not being enough, and of quite honestly losing herself. She wasn't worried about that now. Carlo had promised he would never try to manipulate her into a big life change again, nor would he make choices that affected her without her input and buy-in. She trusted him to keep his word.

Equally important, Annette was no wilting flower. She could and would hold her own with the billionaire businessman.

Carlo might not be her Prince Charming, and head over heels in love with her, but she'd stopped believing in fairytales, so that was okay.

He was honorable and he believed entirely in the importance of family. He was willing to give what his own father had not. Carlo had promised his time to Annette and their unborn child, and to any other children they might have.

Maybe there was just a tiny bit of Prince Charming in him after all. At the very least that Knight in Shining Armor.

Annette's hand slid down to rest over belly. Their baby. Her family.

All of Carlo's actions to this point indicated a man intent on making a real go of their marriage. Annette couldn't ask for any more than that. Suddenly she felt a movement inside. The baby. She'd felt the baby move! She shifted, hoping it would happen again.

It did.

She was laying there, happiness just bubbling through her when a knock sounded on the door and Annette sat up. "Who is it?"

That hadn't been Carlo's usual knock and besides his mother had threatened him with dire consequences if he tried to see Annette before the wedding. Which meant she had slept alone the night before, but it had been surprisingly soundly.

"It is me, Valentina," her soon to be mother-in-law said through the door.

Annette jumped out of bed and grabbed her robe, calling, "Come in."

Valentina pushed open the door, a sweet smile on her face. "Happy wedding day, Annette."

"What is that?" Annette pointed to a pile of ivory silk shimmering with crystal beading, foaming over Valentina's arms.

Valentina walked forward and laid out the most exquisite antique gown. It had copious crystal beading in an art deco design. "This was my great grandmother's wedding gown."

Annette reached out and touched the embroidered silk. "It looks like it's from the 1920s."

"It is. My great grandparents married in 1927."

"Oh. It's beautiful."

"I've always thought so."

"If it fits," Annette couldn't help offering the caveat because she was a curvy five-foot-three. "I will be honored to wear it."

Not drop waisted but designed like a 1920s evening gown Clara Bow might have worn, the dress fit like it had been made for Annette, hugging her breasts and hips and the beading design accentuating her waist. Valentina had bought shoes in Annette's size to match it, 1920's inspired heels with a t-strap. She had also managed to find a veil with an art deco styled jeweled circlet that could have been made in tandem with the dress.

Joyce joined them with Mrs. Banning in tow, a laden breakfast tray in her hands. All four women found somewhere to sit in Annette's room and ate.

Joyce rested on the bed, her expression as happy as on her own wedding day. "Oh, Annette, I'm so glad you and Carlo found your way back to each other. You two are soulmates and I think the universe would be really mad if you hadn't."

Annette laughed and shook her head but left her younger sister to her romantic fantasies. Soulmates or not, she was marrying the love of her life and that had to be enough.

Annette looked in the mirror ninety minutes later and felt tears tighten her throat.

"Don't you dare cry and mess up your makeup," Joyce warned her. "You'll ruin all of Valentina's efforts and start your marriage on the wrong side of our mother-in-law."

All three women laughed as did Mrs. Banning and the stylist Valentina had brought in to do all their hair and the other women's makeup.

Valentina had insisted on doing Annette's makeup herself though. She'd done the same with Joyce, despite their mother's protest. Valentina really was a formidable woman when she wanted to be. And continuing family tradition brought it out in her.

"I'm just...it's..." Annette shook her head.

"It is your wedding day. You are overcome with emotion," Valentina said complacently. "It is as it should be."

"Exactly as it should be," Joyce agreed.

Alceu met the women at the top of the stairs and surprised Annette by putting his arm out to escort her, and not his wife.

He walked her down the stairs and to the formal living room in the Upstate New York mansion. Decorated in a more formal style than the rest of the house, it would have made a pretty setting for the ceremony to come without all the gorgeous winter floral arrangements giving the space a festive air.

Annette did not know who was responsible for the flowers, but she was grateful. She hadn't wanted a spectacle, but it *was* her wedding, and they gave the ambiance that took from convenience for the sake of an accidental pregnancy to something more.

Looking gorgeous in a dark bespoke tuxedo with short waist and tails, Carlo stood with a judge who had been chosen to officiate near the large, ornate fireplace.

Fantino sat in a wheelchair beside Carlo, his broken leg raised as it was supposed to be. Alceu leaned in to kiss Annette's cheek before stepping back and leading his wife to a white Queen Anne style sofa, where they sat down together. Pamina sat in a matching armchair, with Jo-Jo, who had been provided a frothy lace dress for the occasion in her lap.

Joyce took her spot beside Annette, as it was supposed to be.

Only one other person was in the room: a professional photographer. It was a private ceremony for a private event, but there would be pictures to put out with the press release.

Annette met Carlo's gaze as she crossed the floor toward him. His grey eyes were almost black, his face inscrutable, like he was intent on not letting any emotion show through. However, the heat in his gaze could be felt across the expanse of the large room.

That warmth gave her feet the impetus to move. She could do this.

When she reached him, he handed her a beautiful bouquet of crimson roses mixed with white star lilies and baby's breath. It was the bouquet she'd wanted five years ago and been vetoed by her mother, who had wanted pastels.

Annette's gaze flew to his. She was touched and she let him see that in her expression. Carlo smiled, the pleasure at her approval seeping through the emotionless façade.

"Thank you," she said, her voice low.

Carlo nodded. "It is my pleasure."

She saw the flowers around the room with new eyes. They were all in the same festive, red and white theme. Suddenly she knew Carlo had ordered them and no one else.

Yes, maybe there *was* a bit of Prince Charming in the man she was marrying.

The ceremony was brief, but they both spoke vows they technically did not have to. The judge could have signed off on the marriage without any verbal promises being made.

She and Carlo had agreed that they *wanted* to make verbal promises. And so they did.

Vows of fidelity, honesty, respect, and to live together for as long as they were both alive. The weight of those promises hit Annette much harder than she expected.

The kiss took Annette by surprise. They hadn't talked about including *that*. However, she responded immediately, allowing her lips to part and soften under his.

He didn't turn the kiss intimate, but the passion surged between them like an electric current all the same. It probably only lasted a matter of seconds, but Annette felt dizzy, like she'd been holding her breath for a long time.

She swayed a little and Carlo put his arm around her waist to hold her up as everyone in the room took turns congratulated them on their marriage.

Chapter Seventeen

C arlo watched Annette, though he pretended interest in the lively discussion around the table as they shared a family lunch to celebrate the wedding.

He was married.

To the woman he had once thought he *would* marry and later believed to be the one woman he would *never* marry. But when they'd discovered she carried his child, all his determination to get over his sexual obsession with her went by the wayside.

Not that said determination had been bearing much fruit.

He could feel nothing but satisfaction that she had spoken her vows with him today. He understood better now how much those promises meant to her and that her walking away five years ago had not been about breaking her promise to him. She'd been trying to avoid what she was convinced would be a disaster.

Oh, she'd put it differently, but it amounted to the same thing.

Annette had refused to fit into the mold he'd set for her. Not because she did not care about him as he'd made himself believe, but because she simply could not do it. He understood that. How hollow had he felt when his father had asked Carlo to sign those shares over to him?

And it had not meant that Carlo would no longer be President of the company, but he'd still felt like part of him was to be stripped away.

Annette didn't run a multinational corporation, but the work she did with at-risk youth was just as important to her. He would never forget that again.

Nor would he forget all those family time clauses in their prenuptial agreement. Because as important as her work was to her, it was clear that her family would be as well. And she expected their family to be important to him too.

She always made him stop and think in new ways and he hoped she would always care enough to do that.

His father stood up to make a toast. "To my dear son, Carlo, may your marriage be filled with joy and blessed with many children."

Annette smiled, winked and mouthed *four and that's it* to him.

Everyone else read her lips as he did and burst into laughter.

Fantino tapped his glass and made his own toast, followed by Joyce and then his mother.

Carlo was unaccountably touched by the very personal well wishes and realized that he was glad they had not had a big wedding like they'd planned five years ago.

This felt so much more real, like a day of promises, not a production put on for the guests.

Carlo lifted his own glass to toast his bride. "It might have taken five years, but we got here in the end."

"When my brother knows what he wants, he doesn't stop going after it," Fantino said with a lift of his own glass.

He sat beside his wife, their daughter in Joyce's lap, the picture of family contentment. They had been through the wars, but they got their happy endings as modern fairytales promised, and Carlo couldn't be happier for them.

Everyone around the table laughed, but Carlo was struck by his brother's words as sure as if they had been a blow. Because he'd wanted Annette five years ago and he'd given up pretty damn easily. What did that say about his supposed stubborn resolve?

Or had he been lying to himself five years ago when he said he'd let her go? How quickly he'd fallen into bed with her after seeing her again gave credence to that theory.

Whatever his past mistakes, he was married to the woman now and his satisfaction was greater than he'd ever before experienced in his life.

He wondered what she would think if she knew? Call him a throwback no doubt, but he couldn't deny it. He was done lying to himself.

Carlo had only ever wanted to marry Annette and now their lives were joined.

A few hours later, they were ensconced in side-by-side seats on his jet, sipping bubbly, though Annette's was of the nonalcoholic variety.

"Where are we going?" she asked him.

Finally.

When he'd asked if she wanted to make the plans for their honeymoon together, she'd told him no. She wanted to be surprised. Like she was intent on erasing the past with new memories.

He was happy to oblige, though she might think he'd taken it too far. "The Dalmatian Coast."

A near identical trip to their aborted honeymoon. However, rather than two months, they had two weeks.

He would have preferred longer, but after everything he had to get back to the office. He would make a concentrated effort in the year to come to build up his own executive team so he could work shorter hours and take more time off.

"In Croatia?" she asked, her tone laced with surprise.

"*Sì.*" She had always wanted to go to Croatia, and particularly the Dalmatian Coast because of the heavy influence from the ancient cultures of Italy and Greece that could be found there. Did she think he had forgotten that?

"I was half afraid you'd never want to vacation in Croatia, or Greece because of the honeymoon that didn't happen."

"That was not going to happen." He'd bought a house there, hadn't he?

Not that he'd stayed in it in the past five years, but he hadn't taken a real vacation in that time either. Which brought up something he wanted to say to her. "You are right. I never considered my father's hours at work, or weeks away from home a problem, and yet I begrudged my mother her work in a very childlike fashion, even into my adulthood."

It shamed him to realize the double standard he had entertained for his parents. He was not a product of the last century, but a man of today.

"That's an amazing breakthrough in self-realization," she said with some awe.

Which both irked and pleased him. He liked when she looked at him like that, when her voice took that tone. But she should not be so surprised he could make such strides. "I'm no throwback."

"Are you sure about that?" The obviously teasing glint in her eyes took any sting the words might have had.

"If I am a throwback, you are too." He was thinking of the near primal possessiveness they felt toward each other.

"You might be right. In some ways, anyway." She yawned and then blushed. "Sorry. I don't know why I'm tired. I slept well last night."

"While I barely slept."

"Why?"

"I'll tell you all about it when we reach the Dalmatian Coast house."

"If this jet is anything like the one you had five years ago, it has a bedroom." She gave a near comical waggle of her brows, but then yawned again.

He laughed. "It does and I expect you to use it, but we will not have our first night making love as a married couple in bed on an airplane."

"Why not?"

"Because you, my dear, *pregnant* bride, need your sleep."

He could see she was gearing up to argue, but the third yawn in as many minutes made even his stubborn bride realize she needed rest.

Carlo spent most of the hours of the flight working while his wife slumbered alone in the plane's bedroom.

Carlo roused Annette to prepare for landing and she followed him blearily back into the main cabin, taking her seat and buckling in as the plane began its descent.

They'd arrived in Croatia in the middle of the night, and everything was cast in shadows of darkness as they disembarked the private jet and transferred to a luxury SUV. One bodyguard rode up front with the driver and the rest of the team followed in a second SUV.

Annette had slept on the plane, but she was still tired. She didn't even try to see the countryside out the window in the darkness, but as exhausted as she felt, Annette was also too wired to fall asleep.

Carlo put his phone away after checking something and then tugged, so Annette rested against his chest. Suddenly, that nervous energy keeping her awake just disappeared and she slumped into him, her body going boneless for sleep.

It took only about twenty minutes to reach the house from the private airstrip, but Annette was already dozing against his chest when the SUV pulled to a stop.

Carlo caressed her beautiful, silky blonde hair tenderly. She was exhausted and needed her sleep.

His body was taut with need. It was their wedding night, but he would have to be a monster to try to seduce her into making love in her condition. No matter how much he knew she thought she wanted the same thing.

Stifling his baser urges, he reached down and released the catch on her seatbelt.

Her scent wafted to him, triggering an atavistic response he had no control over. However, while he might not be able to stop himself getting a hardon, he had absolute control over whether he acted on it.

Ignoring his body's need, he cupped her shoulder and shook gently. "Wake up, *bèdda mia*. We are here."

Her eyes fluttered open, their emerald depths warming in recognition. "Carlo."

That was all she said, like his name was a sentence all on its own. It went through him like a lightning bolt, this unfiltered reaction from her.

Giving into one urge, he leant down and swept her up against his chest.

"You're going to carry me over the threshold," she said with sleepy approval.

He was doing just that, so did not think she needed verbal agreement. In fact, he carried her up the stairs to the bedroom he had designated as theirs. It was decorated in the colors she preferred with warm, traditional wood furniture.

He helped her undress and get into the king-sized bed, but Annette did not lay down. She looked ready to fall asleep sitting up.

"Why don't you lie down?" he asked her as he kicked off his shoes.

"I'm waiting."

He shrugged out of his suitcoat and hung it on the wooden rack that had been installed for that purpose. "For what?"

"You," she said like that should have been obvious.

Carlo finished stripping out of his clothes with efficient movements, adding to the pile of hers on the floor. Domestic staff would see to the clothing the next day. Though he did hang the trousers from his bespoke suit over the rail below his jacket.

He climbed into the bed and Annette immediately scooted toward the center. Pulling her into his arms, he settled them against the pillows.

"We aren't going to make love?" she asked in a voice laced with exhaustion.

The obstetrician had warned Annette might need more than her usual amount of sleep. It appeared that possibility had finally caught up with them.

"In the morning."

"Promise?" she asked, snuggling into him like she liked to do.

"*Sì.*"

"Good." She patted his chest and relaxed fully, her breathing going even in sleep only minutes later.

With the feel of his wife's delectable body wrapped snugly against his own, it took Carlo considerably longer to find slumber.

Annette woke feeling fully refreshed and alert. She was feeling something else, too. Desire.

Carlo's arms were tight around her, his big body pressed against hers. She felt protected and cared for, whatever their reason for getting married.

He'd brought her to bed, but he hadn't pushed making love. Annette had been almost completely out of it the night before, she'd been so tired, but she had felt the hardness of his erection against her.

He'd been turned on, but he hadn't tried to seduce her into staying awake to make love.

Nevertheless, she did not think it would bother him if she woke *him* for that purpose.

Annette carefully extracted herself from Carlo's arms and went to use the bathroom. When she returned, she found her husband's steel grey eyes open.

Oh, she did like the sound of that. *Her husband*. She could revel as much as she liked in the privacy of her own heart and mind, too. Though she thought Carlo might be the one person who understood and would not judge her somewhat primitive urges where he was concerned.

Smiling, she rejoined him on the bed. "Good morning." She gave him a heated once over. "I have plans."

"For me?" he asked, desire thick in his voice, and his grey gaze filled with sensual need.

She returned the look with interest. "For us both."

His smile stole her breath, but not her ability to move. She pressed her naked body right up against that of her husband. The man she had always craved and would always love.

He slashed a smile at her. "You look like the cat that got the cream."

"Do I?"

"*Sì,*" he growled and then he kissed her, all possessive demand.

She kissed him back the same way, laying claim to the only man she'd ever really wanted to. The kiss went on for minute after minute, while they ate at each other's lips, the slide of his tongue against hers tantalizing and sensual. Their bodies pressed tightly together, his strong arms circling around her, holding her close.

Annette buried her hands in his hair, needing his head to stay just where it was, craving this kiss as she'd never craved another.

Even with him.

They were married. She hadn't thought that would make any difference to this, to sex.

Only, somehow, it did. She felt a confidence that often eluded her, a sense of belonging, a certainty of connection. They hadn't married for love, but her sense of connection with him went to the very core of her soul.

Finally, she could wait no longer to touch him in all the ways she yearned for, and she broke the kiss.

He resisted at first when she wanted to pull away, but then he let her go.

She slid back just a little and smiled at him with a sense of feminine power. "Trust me."

His eyes narrowed, but he nodded his proud Sicilian head nearly imperceptibly.

She smiled again, but then she leaned down and began to kiss along his neck, using her teeth gently to increase the sensation for him.

"*Bèdda mia,*" he groaned.

She liked when he called her beautiful. She liked it even more when he added the possessive *mia* to it.

Taking her time, Annette mapped her new husband's body with her mouth and hands, touching him in ways she knew excited him, and taking note of spots heretofore unknown that elicited masculine groans of excitement.

Her body had brushed against his rigid sex over and over, but she had not touched it directly yet. She didn't want to simply touch.

Annette wanted to taste. This wasn't something she'd done much of, not out of distaste, but she'd been insecure in her technique.

This morning, she decided technique did not matter. She wanted to taste, so she would.

Carlo nearly came off the bed when Annette lapped at the tip of his penis with delicate little licks. Her hands were wrapped around his erection, making subtle movements up and down. Not enough to send him over the precipice, and he was grateful for that. Enough to turn a hardon into steel though.

Her mouth popped over his sex, taking him into her moist heat and Carlo shouted. The loud sound didn't shock her into stopping, but increased her efforts at exciting him. She'd taken him in her mouth before, but never with this abandon. Something had changed, but he was too excited to try to figure out what. Perhaps it was as simple as being husband and wife.

Ecstasy flowed through him, and he knew he was close. No matter how much she might be enjoying herself, he wasn't going to climax in her mouth.

His sweet wife was not ready for that. Many women never enjoyed the taste of a man's ejaculate.

Carlo pressed against Annette's shoulders. "Stop, *cara mia*."

Chapter Eighteen

Annette ignored his demand, sucking at his sex with delightful enthusiasm.

"Please, *bèdda*. Stop."

She came off his sex with a pop and swiped at her beautiful mouth, swollen from their kissing and what she'd just been doing. "Why?"

"I want to be inside your beautiful body when I come."

She thought about it, which turned him on even more. She was thinking what she wanted more and that idea that she'd been enjoying pleasuring him that much was as exciting as a touch.

"Okay." She scooted up his body until she straddled his thighs nearly kissing his erection with her feminine heat. "Hold yourself steady."

Carlo did, turned on by her sexual confidence.

She lowered herself onto his erection, her slick heat enveloping him as she pressed downward. He reached up and cupped her luscious rosy tipped breasts. She threw her head back, her gorgeous curvaceous body flushing with desire. Shifting back and forth, she rocked herself until he was fully seated inside her.

They both groaned.

Unable to stand the passivity any longer, Carlo began to thrust upward, one hand moving to her waist to hold her in place.

But Annette leaned forward and began her own pace. Their bodies came together with more force than he expected, but it felt good. Almost too good.

Annette's moan of pleasure and demand he do that again said she felt the same.

His climax was riding him hard, and Carlo knew he wasn't going to last many more thrusts, much less minutes. He shifted one hand so his thumb could press against her clitoris.

Her cry of delight was followed by a shimmy that about sent him over.

He rubbed her swollen nub, and she shifted her body for maximum pleasure, taking the pleasure he wanted to give and guiding it toward her own moment of ecstasy.

She looked down at him, her face flushed with pleasure. "I'm so close."

"Bèdda mia." He could get no other words out, her beauty so intense in that moment, it dazzled him.

Her eyes sparking like sapphires under a spotlight, Annette's body went tight above him and she cried out as her vaginal walls tightened around his sex. Carlo thrusted upward, coming so hard he shouted with the pleasure of it.

They moved together after, drawing aftershocks of ecstasy from each other's bodies before she collapsed on top of him. "How does it get better and better?"

"I do not know." No more than he understood why it was not all that great with other women anymore.

Though he was starting to get a glimmer.

After a leisurely breakfast and shower with more sexy times, Carlo asked Annette if she wanted to go into Dubrovnik. Eager to see the mixed architecture and explore the ancient streets of Old Town, Annette agreed.

"It's like Sicily, but not," she said as they walked in the Stradun with buildings on either side that had been built centuries ago.

"Both have similar cultural influences from Italy and Greece."

She nodded, delighted by the red tiled roofs and stone walled buildings, some with ornate columns and others more elegantly simple. "The weather is amazing too."

Sunny, but not too hot, it was the perfect day for walking down the limestone streets. They spent two hours in the Rector's Palace, which now housed the Cultural History Museum. Carlo held Annette's hand and they brought each other's attention to displays that caught their eyes.

It was so much like the past, when they had found each other's company easy and pleasurable, that Annette felt a sort of time displacement.

When they came back out into the sun, she squinted at the bright light and Carlo handed her a pair of designer sunglasses to put on. They were clearly women's glasses and meant for her.

"Thank you." She hadn't brought a pair with her, but he'd been prepared. "It's been wonderful, but everyone is closing for *pižolot*." She had been surprised by the afternoon nap similar to the Spanish *siesta* observed here. "There are so many more things I want to see. I think I could spend a year in this town alone, just soaking in the architecture, atmosphere and history."

"We can come back tomorrow. We have two weeks here, this time."

"This time?" she asked as they made their way to the SUV waiting for them.

"I bought the villa."

"You did?" It did have some things in it that didn't feel like they would be in a rental property, even one in use by billionaires. "The bedroom. It's done in the colors I told you I loved for a bedroom." The same colors she'd used when decorating her space when she'd gotten to Portland.

"I bought the house five years ago."

"Oh, Carlo." And the man still denied being a romantic. "I love it."

"I am glad. It is yours."

"What? No, it's not."

"I assure you, it is. You signed the deeds with the prenuptial agreement five years ago."

Which didn't say much for how closely she'd read that document back then. She blushed, knowing her father would be appalled if he knew.

She turned and threw her arms around him, kissing him soundly. "Thank you."

"You can thank me like that any time," he promised.

The following days fell into a pattern. After waking to make love, Annette and Carlo did touristy things, then in the evenings they took out the boat that was moored at the house's slip. She was not at all surprised to find out Carlo owned the mini yacht, but was stunned when she read the name *Sapphire* painted on the side.

He'd named it for her. Annette remembered how he used to say her eyes glowed like the blue precious stones, and her gut told her his intention had been to play on that connection. Or was that her heart?

Sometimes, Carlo worked while Annette lounged by the pool or read on the terrace. He was always solicitous and kind. Like with the sunglasses, he seemed to just know what Annette needed and make sure she got it.

He treated her like he valued her. He consulted her on how they should spend their days, and he'd even asked her if she wanted to live in the family home in Sicily, or get their own place.

Several generations of his family had lived in the mansion sized villa outside Palermo, but he was willing to buy another home for them, so she would feel comfortable. Annette had told him she had no trouble living with his parents.

Annette *liked* Valentina and Alceu. Equally importantly, she knew they liked her. She wouldn't hurt them for the world, and she thought having their oldest son break with tradition and move out would have done so.

Besides, the villa was big enough for Carlo, Annette and their children to have their own wing. Which she said to Carlo.

"*Sì*. We will have our own space." His expression was odd though.

"What?" she asked.

He looked at her like he didn't understand the question.

"You've got a strange look on your face," she explained.

"I was thinking about having more children with you."

"Good thoughts?" she quipped.

He indicated evidence of his arousal in his trousers with a flick of his masculine hand. "Very good thoughts."

Annette smiled contentedly, pleased that the idea of having more children with her turned him on like that. Which was probably another *throwback* reaction on her part, but then so was his visceral response to the idea.

Despite being okay with living in the Sicilian villa with his parents, Annette was glad they were still in New York when she and Carlo returned from the Dalmatian Coast.

She had a chance to settle into her new life without anyone else looking on.

If she didn't count the myriad staff, but like security, live in staff were an inevitable part of the life of wife to a billionaire businessman.

"What does that look mean?" Carlo asked, his hand reaching for her nape.

He was always touching her, and Annette loved it. She'd spent most of her life bereft of touch from loved ones and he seemed intent on making up for those barren years all at once.

Annette leaned into him, sliding her own arm around his trim waist. "I was just thinking that it's nice to settle into the villa without worrying what your parents think."

"And that amused you?" he asked as they headed out onto the terrace.

Carlo liked being outside as much as she did, and they had spent a lot of time relaxing together on a luxurious double lounger with a shade covering on their honeymoon. Well, Annette had relaxed, sometimes reading, sometimes napping.

Carlo had been on his phone, no doubt working, but he'd been there with her, and he was the one who would take her book from her hands and kiss her, or wake her from her dozing with the same.

"I was amused at my own lack of logic," she told him as they sat down on an outdoor sofa. It was a large corner shaped seating area, but they sat close together at the end with a chaise. She kicked off her sandals and put her feet up. "We're hardly without prying eyes, not with a whole villa full of staff."

"Does that bother you?" He put his arm around her shoulder, his fingers brushing back and forth over shoulders bared by her floral sundress.

Annette shivered, her nipples reacting to the light touch as if they were in the bedroom and not out on the terrace.

"No," she answered him, her tone husky.

"Papa and Mama will be returning early next month," Carlo said, like he was warning her.

Annette grinned. "I'm so glad things are going so well for Joyce and Fantino that they are able to do that. Besides, I can't wait to see them."

His parents treated her like a beloved, longed for daughter, just like they did Joyce, and Annette reveled in that kind of parental affection after a lifetime without it.

"*Bene*. I am glad."

"When do you return to the office?" she asked, dreading the answer and yet aware that their idyll could not last forever.

"Tomorrow."

"Oh." So soon.

"You are disappointed. Will you miss me?"

She nodded, seeing no reason to pretend otherwise. Her phone buzzed before she could give a verbal response. Annette looked down. Another text from her father. He wanted to know when they were going to have a formal reception to celebrate the wedding.

"That look is definitely not amusement," Carlo said.

Rather than explain, she showed him the phone.

Carlo swore succinctly. "How long has he been bothering you with this?" Rather than wait for her answer, he scrolled up in the text thread to check for himself and swore again, this time more inventively.

"I've been ignoring their calls and texts. I should have blocked their numbers." But they were her parents and she had felt wrong about doing that.

Again. Five years ago, she'd only blocked them for a few days, but they had been furious. Even though they didn't want her in the family, they expected her to be available to them when they needed something.

Boundaries. She still struggled with them, even after three years of therapy and five years in exile.

"I will speak to your father."

"No, it's my responsibility."

Carlo's jaw tautened, but he nodded.

He really was making every effort to prove that he had no desire to control her life.

Just this minute, she could wish he wasn't trying so hard. It would be so easy to let him field the call. Her father would never say the things to Carlo she knew he would say to her. But Annette wasn't weak. She could handle one uncomfortable phone call with her parents. After all, she'd survived their treatment most of her life.

"I'll go call him back," she said, getting up with reluctance.

Carlo's big body was tense with the need to act. "Are you sure you don't want me to make the call?"

Annette shook her head, unable to force out another verbal denial.

Annette had walked halfway around the house, on the wrap around terrace, looking for a private spot to make the call when it occurred to her that she was only putting off the unpleasant. She stopped and sat down on a bench that overlooked the olive grove to the side of the house.

This was as private as it was going to get.

Checking the time, and confirming it was neither too early nor too late, she dialed her father's number.

"It's about time you called," her father said by way of a greeting, his tone filled with annoyance and censure.

"I was on my honeymoon."

"Not that we were invited to your wedding," he replied with cold disapproval.

She wasn't going to feel guilty for that. "You made it clear you no longer consider me part of your family."

"Asking you to move so the scandal you caused could die down was not an excommunication from our family."

How easily he rewrote history to suit himself. Just like when he and her mom had rewritten history to say she was their daughter and not her biological father's. Had they followed that rewrite up with love and acceptance, Annette's life and perception of herself would be very different.

"First, I didn't cause that scandal. Lynette did," Annette said firmly. "Second, you didn't just ask me to move, you bribed an organization to transfer me to a job in another state. And you and mom refused to have me *home* for any holidays. That definitely qualifies as being kicked out of the family."

"You were at your sister's wedding and the baby's christening," he scoffed.

"Because Joyce never stopped seeing me as her sister."

"You cannot blame your poor choices on Lynette." Typical. Deflection when he had no answer for the truth.

"No, but I can blame her for feeding the media frenzy."

Her father started to say something, but Annette cut him off. Suddenly she was done, just done with parents who didn't care about her and a sister who actively disliked her. "Listen, there isn't going to be any reception."

Although maybe the Messinas wanted one? Annette would have to ask them. "I don't think. Carlo and I haven't talked about it."

"Of course, there will be a reception. Events like that are necessary for business."

"My marriage is not a business deal."

"What else could it be? Carlo married you to solidify his company's connection to mine. Even you should have enough intelligence to see that."

Annette knew why Carlo had married her and it had nothing to do with business. It had to do with the baby growing inside her, another tidbit she had yet to share with her parents. Maybe Joyce would let it slip and Annette could avoid another phone call like this one. Or not. She would fight one battle at a time.

"Even me?" she demanded, tired of the put downs. "Which of your children was it who won an academic scholarship for college? Oh, right, that would be me. I'm plenty intelligent, dad, but I'm not a pushover. Not anymore."

"Is that how you justify not inviting your parents to your wedding?" he asked scathingly, "Telling yourself you're not a pushover. You owe us. We raised you."

"If you had ever bothered to even try to love me, that might mean something, but you were paid for the services you rendered. That precious business of yours wouldn't exist but for your agreement to *take me in*."

Her father was silent for long seconds, clearly unsure how to take this new less than tolerant attitude from her. She'd never fought them on anything important.

"I'm sure the Messinas were there," her father finally said.

"Yes, they were." As Joyce had been, but saying so would have been petty and Annette was not that. Firm? Yes. Determined to stop being the Cinderella figure in her family's life? Yes. But she had no desire to hurt anyone unnecessarily.

"So, we should have been invited as well."

"No." She wasn't going to bother going into the why again. If he didn't understand now, he never would.

"Carlo isn't going to be your golden goose business partner," she warned her father, finding his claim that her husband had married her for the business connection ludicrous.

It was clear who benefited most from their business connections, and it wasn't her husband.

Chapter Nineteen

"Have you been poisoning him against me?" Annette's father demanded with rancor.

"He was appalled by both your and mom's behavior at the lawyer's office. When I told him about me being adopted and how you only did it to get money from your wealthier, older brother, he wasn't all that impressed either."

"That's ridiculous. We were on his side. You can't tell me he took that against us." Typical of her father to completely ignore any reference to her adoption, or the reason for it.

Yes, they'd been on what they considered Carlo's side, just like they had been five years ago. She was their daughter, but she didn't matter. Her feelings didn't matter.

She wanted to hang up, but she had one last thing she had to say. "I'm pregnant. I will take your congratulations as spoken," she said sarcastically before her father could speak. "Whether you are allowed into my family's life will be determined by your choices. How you choose to treat me. Whether you attempt to play the same favorites with your grandchildren that you have your own children."

Whatever their reasons, they'd adopted her, darn it. And they had forced her to recognize them as her parents. Now, they could either recognize her as their daughter with all rights and privileges, or they could stay well out of her life.

"You think you've landed yourself in clover, don't you? Carlo Messina only married you because you're pregnant with my grandchild."

Man, it had taken mere minutes for her father to change his tack on that one. First his business, now *his* grandchild. Not *her* baby. What a narcissist.

"You've insinuated yourself in his life, but he'll see you for what you are." What her dad thought that was, he left unsaid.

But she'd had a lifetime to figure it out and it wasn't something good.

"What I am is a loving person who will be a great mom, because there was a time many years ago that I had one." She would hold onto that memory always and they could not take it away from her, even if they'd managed to erase the connection between her and her biological father. "And if nothing else, you and mom have taught me important lessons about raising all my children with the same love and affection."

A hand was suddenly in front of her, open like ready to take the phone, but not reaching for it.

She stared at that hand and then looked up into her husband's face. His handsome features were cast in fury.

How much of their conversation had he heard? Had he been there the whole time? Annette's phone was a cheap model that bled a lot of noise. No such thing as a truly private phone call if anyone else was around.

"May I speak now?" he asked politely.

She almost laughed but stifled the sound and handed him the phone. She'd said what she needed to.

"Floyd, this is Carlo," her husband said in a chilled tone, so different than the one he used with her.

The sound of her father's voice, which had been raised in a litany of the usual complaints against her, cut off abruptly.

"Listen carefully. If you ever speak in this cutting way to my wife again, not only will we cut you from our lives, but I will cut all business ties with you as well."

Annette stood up from the bench and stepped away to the edge of the terrace, not wanting to hear her father's response.

Though she couldn't miss Carlo's next words. "No, there will be no further business dealings, but I will not cancel current contracts. That is as far as my generosity takes me."

Carlo and her father spoke for only a few moments more before Carlo informed the other man that all communication from the Hudsons needed to come to him, not be directed toward Annette. When he looked at her, like asking if that was okay, she nodded.

She was done. Annette would not waste any more energy trying to earn love or respect from her adopted family and she frankly never wanted to see her biological father again. Not that he'd shown any desire to build a relationship over the years.

She just knew *she* no longer wanted to, either.

She had a new family, and she was going to concentrate all her love and energy on them.

That night, when they made love, Annette said the words out loud.

"I love you, Carlo." She needed him to know.

He was on top this time, setting the rhythm. His grey eyes dark with passion, he shushed her. "Shh. Just feel. No talking."

Annette told herself it didn't matter, that he deserved to know she loved him. Carlo had given her a family who loved and accepted her, a family she adored as well. He was such a good man. Yes, a little controlling and used to getting his way, but he listened and stepped back when he needed to.

She said it again when ecstasy took them and ignored the echo of silence that came after.

Carlo lay in the darkness, awake and thinking, his precious wife lost to slumber beside him. They had made love more than once tonight, exhausting, but also eliciting word of love.

Did she mean them? Did she love him again? Still?

He hadn't said the words back, but for the first time he accepted he felt them. Why had he fought the admission so hard?

Because five years ago, he'd believed himself in love and loved in return only to be humiliated and rejected on his wedding day. His pride had not allowed him to acknowledge the deep wound, not even to his brother.

Now that he had better perspective on the past, Carlo knew Annette had meant the words when she said them five years ago. So, why did he doubt them now?

Because of the baby. She'd married him for the baby's sake.

Wasn't that what she thought about him? That he'd only wanted to marry her because she was pregnant?

Who was the genius that told her he only wanted sex to work her out of his system?

That would be him.

But he loved her. And he had to tell her. Would she be upset if he woke her up to do so?

He could wait for the morning, surely.

Carlo lay, rigid, fighting the need to wake his wife with tender kisses and whisper sweet words of adoration in her ear.

Annette shifted and then groaned. "I have to pee," she said, as if talking to herself.

Never had a bodily function been so welcome by Carlo. "I would like to tell you something when you're done."

She jerked as if startled. "Carlo? You're awake?" she asked, sounding more alert herself.

"I am."

"And you want to tell me something? In the middle of the night?"

"It can wait for your bladder."

"Baby more like. It's like she rolls right onto my bladder every other hour."

They'd found out the baby was a girl at the OB's visit just before their wedding. Joyce and Annette had been ecstatic, promising each other their daughters would be the best of friends. Just like sisters.

Carlo replayed that sweet memory in his head as he waited for his wife to return to their bed.

When Annette came back into the bedroom, Carlo had turned on a lamp and was sitting up, his expression filled with an emotion she was afraid to name.

"You didn't say it earlier, when I did," she blurted. "Or five years ago. You never said it."

"Five years ago, I planned to say it on our wedding night."

"You did?" she asked faintly.

"Si."

"And tonight?"

"I was still fighting admitting it to myself."

"Why?"

"Because if I loved you, then I'd been lying to myself for five years and telling real whoppers since Joyce and Fantino's wedding."

Annette climbed back into the bed, letting Carlo pull her right onto his knees so they were practically eye level. He tucked the blankets around her with solicitous care.

"You're always so attentive, doing stuff like that. I just thought you were *that* guy, you know?"

"That guy?" he asked, leaning in a little to inhale her scent.

He did that sometimes. She did the same thing. No other man she'd ever met smelled quite like Carlo and it wasn't just his cologne.

"You know, the good guy. The honorable guy. The man who will marry the mother of his baby even if he doesn't trust her to keep her promises."

"But I do trust you *bèdda mia*."

"Yes, I believe you, only when we got married, I was sure it was all about the baby."

"Our baby is a gift, but our marriage was all about you. It has always been all about you."

"Not for anyone else. Never for anyone else."

"Your family do not deserve you."

"But *Famigghia esti famigghia*," she said, quoting the Sicilian saying. Family was family. "If they can be decent, even if they aren't ever loving, I'll allow them space in my life and that of our child."

"And if they are not, I will destroy your father and see them bankrupt."

"I think you're kidding. You *are* joking, aren't you?"

Carlo just shrugged. "I did not wake you to talk about your family."

"You didn't wake me at all. Our baby did that." Then the baby kicked and she gasped. "Here..." She grabbed Carlo's hand and placed it against her hard abdomen, though it was still a pretty small baby bump. "Feel."

"I can feel her," Carlo said with awe.

"Isn't it amazing?"

He just nodded, his eyes shiny.

This man. He did her in with emotion. "You said you had something to say to me, when I woke up to pee," she reminded him.

"Ah, yes. I wanted to wake you so badly, I think I willed our daughter to move onto your bladder."

Annette laughed and shook her head. "Whatever you say."

"I say that I love with all that is within me for all of this life and beyond."

For a moment, she was so overcome, she could not speak. "That's a lot of love," she said finally.

"There is no man who loves another more than I love you," he assured her in all seriousness.

And Annette just soaked it in. All that love, all that assurance. "I love you. I always have. I am so sorry I ran five years ago."

"I am so sorry I was such an ass that you felt the need to run."

"Next time you're an ass, I'll stand and fight."

"You're so sure there will be a next time?"

"There has to be. Otherwise, you would be perfect, and I cannot live up to, or with, perfection."

"We shall see."

She smiled and then kissed him, not bothered at all when that led to more. Later, they lay entwined and whispered words of love until they fell asleep together.

Her dreams were sweet and she woke beside the man she loved and the man she now knew loved her.

She looked at the clock and then started. "Aren't you supposed to be at the office?"

"I am playing hooky. We are celebrating."

"What are we celebrating?"

"Being in love."

They spent the day doing just that, but it didn't stop with a day. Carlo thought that their love should be celebrated often and well.

Annette agreed. It was an amazing gift.

EPILOGUE

The evening of their first anniversary, Annette met Carlo on the terrace outside their bedroom with a sheaf of papers.

"What is this?" he asked.

"I've got a contract for you to sign."

"Do you?" He took the papers and began reading, his laughter ringing soon thereafter.

Annette settled onto his lap, enjoying how much easier it was to do so now than it had been six months before. She'd barely shown for the first five months and then ballooned to a basketball sized tummy at supersonic speed.

Carlo had spent the last months of her pregnancy kissing her stretch marks and telling her how beautiful they were, a mark of her motherhood. Now, their adorable little Joy was six months old and wonder of wonders, sleeping through the night.

"What's so funny?" she asked him, as if she did not know.

"This reads more like a teenaged girl's sex fantasies than a contract," he told her, echoing her words from a fateful day that had brought them here. He went serious. "But it's this final set of articles I can't live without."

Annette had poured her love onto those pages, promising the many ways she would show it to him throughout their life.

"I will only sign this if I can add some clauses of my own."

"Of course. It's a love contract after all and love is both give and take."

"In this case, I want to give it to you. Every day for all of our lives."

And that is what he did.

THE END

THE REAL DEAL

Lucy Monroe

Lucy Monroe LLC

DEDICATION

To Lori Foster for her generosity and friendship, which are an indescribable blessing to me and to her Book Junkies, authors and readers that have enriched my life letting me hang out with them online. Thanks, guys! Major hugs.

PROLOGUE

T hunk.

Pain jarred through her shoulder as the baseball bat connected with the treadmill, but the darn thing didn't even shift. The black metal monster taunted her just as it had for the past two years. Her nemesis.

The symbol of her husband's dissatisfaction with her body.

Of her failure as a woman.

Swinging the bat in a high arc above her head, she then brought it down with the force of all the anger and despair warring inside her.

Thunk.

This time the pain was so great her fingers flexed open in an involuntary spasm and she dropped the bat.

"No. You aren't going to win!"

Briefly, for one horrifying second, she saw herself as someone else might see her - a mad woman in a Jackie-O dress and heels attacking a piece of exercise equipment with a baseball bat and screaming at it as if it were animate.

She didn't care. She hated that pile of molded metal as much as she hated what she'd allowed herself to become. She bent over, her shoulder and arm throbbing and grabbed the bat again. Melodious chimes, discordant with her mood, halted her mid-swing before she could bring the bat into connection with the treadmill again.

She spun on her heel and stomped through the perfect Southern California showplace that had never felt like a home. Sun glinted off the polished tile floor of the foyer, causing a white glare that hurt eyes gritty from crying.

She didn't want to deal with a visitor. Didn't even know if she could. It was probably someone for Lance. Today was Saturday, golf day. Her husband usually spent it with his tanned and toned business associates on one of the many prestigious private courses found along the Southern California coast. Only today, Lance was otherwise occupied.

Which was something she had every intention of telling whoever was on the other side of that door, right before telling them to go away.

It would serve the lying swine right if she told his visitor just what was occupying her faithless wretch of a husband.

Red hair stuck up in a wild tangle showed through the glass semicircle insert in the door. Jillian. Thank you, God. Amanda could deal with Jillian. She would understand. Heck, she'd probably ask for her own bat.

She yanked the door open. More sunlight glared and little black spots wavered before her eyes, obscuring the flamboyantly dressed woman in front of her. "Hey, Jill."

"Amanda! What happened?" Jillian swept inside with her usual dramatic flair, her day-glow orange dress competing with the sunlight for brightness. "I came by to talk you into some serious mall walking, but you look like you're competing with Tammy Fay what's-her-name for the Miss Raccoon title."

Amanda scrubbed at the hot wetness on her face with one hand. "I'm thinking more along the lines of Lorena Bobbit."

"What did that SOB do this time?"

Amanda almost laughed. Almost, but she couldn't quite make it. Jillian was the only person in her life who considered Lance less than an ideal husband.

"You're implying that he makes a habit of screwing me over." Which couldn't be further from the truth.

Jillian's brightly painted lips twisted in a grimace. "He's a condescending jerk who wouldn't know a truly sexy woman if she fell on her knees in front of him and offered him a blow-job."

Remembered humiliation mixed with her anger as Amanda recalled doing almost exactly that. And getting turned down. A sob tore from her already raw throat and she felt her knees buckle. Wiry but strong arms wrapped around her, stopping her descent to the floor. A string of curses that would do any movie director in Hollywood proud stung Amanda's eardrums.

"Come on, honey." The familiar fragrance of Jillian's perfume wrapped around her, as soothing as her friend's voice. "Let's go in the kitchen and get you something to drink. You look a little shocky."

Shock didn't begin to describe how Amanda was feeling. "He was in his office. He was naked, Jill. It's been so long since I saw him that way, I almost didn't recognize him." Her pathetic joke fell flat as another keening wail snaked up from her battered soul. She gulped and breathed before trying to talk again. "He wasn't alone."

"I kinda figured that, you being so upset and all. I didn't think him jacking off to a copy of Playboy would have left you white-faced and shaking."

That did make her laugh, just one small, choked giggle, but it was better than the crying that had been making her throat raw for the past two hours.

"So, who was it? The new paralegal?"

Three little words. Who was it? And it all came rushing back. Walking into the anteroom of his plush law office. The sounds coming from the other side of his door in an otherwise silent building. The mesmeric pull of those sounds. The long walk across deeply piled carpet, making no sound herself except for shallow breathing that seemed to grow thinner with each step. The feel of the cold doorknob under her hand. The excruciating slowness as she turned it. The door swinging inward on silent hinges and the tableau that burned like acid against her mind's eye.

"No. Not his assistant." Amanda stopped abruptly, pulling Jillian to a stand-still beside her. She leaned back against the white wall, needing the support, the connection with something solid and real. "He was with..."

She took a deep breath and Jillian waited for Amanda to continue, for once totally silent.

She closed her eyes, trying to block the picture swimming before them, but the image only grew more prominent against the inside of her eyelids. "He was standing there. Naked." She'd already said that. "He wasn't alone."

Jillian didn't remind her she'd already said that too and Amanda was grateful.

"He had his arms around a woman. She was up against the wall. H-he was inside her. Standing up. I don't know who she is." Amanda didn't know if she could finish it. "A m-man was standing behind him, only he wasn't just standing. Lance was... He was..." She couldn't say it. Couldn't repeat the exact nature of the threesome's lewd activity, couldn't tell her best friend who the man copulating with her husband had been.

She didn't even want to think it. The double betrayal was ripping her guts out.

"Both of them? He was screwing both of them?"

Amanda's eyes flew open at Jillian's shriek and she stared into green eyes dilated by the same shock that had her trapped.

"Yes. Well, Lance was doing it to the woman and the other man was doing it to him." Even saying it made her sick and she felt bile rise in her throat.

Jillian followed her mad dash to the bathroom, handed her a glass of water afterward and kept up a steady stream of cursing the whole time. "What did you do?" This time her friend's voice came out in a whisper.

"They were really into what they were doing. They didn't notice me. So, I snuck out."

"He doesn't know you saw him?"

Amanda shook her head, her formerly neat French twist rubbing against the wall. She could feel hanks of her long hair coming loose and settling against her shoulders.

"What's the bat for?"

Her mouth twisted. "I was trying to beat up the treadmill, but it didn't work. The damn thing is indestructible."

Jillian made one of the expressive sounds she was so good at. "Honey, you said the d-word. Next thing I know, you really will be sharpening the knives."

Amanda grimaced. "I'd rather destroy the treadmill. I can't go to prison for that one."

Jillian nodded, her red hair waving like some mad monkey on top of her head. "You've got a point."

The next thing Amanda knew Jillian had grabbed her wrist and she was being dragged toward the garage. "Come on, I bet even Lance has a cordless screw driver. All men have them. Even men who don't know the difference between a flathead and a Phillips. They're status symbols or something."

"And do you know what to do with one?"

"Sure. I've been living on my own since I was seventeen. I even know how to use a snake on a backed up toilet."

Amanda chose not to comment on that dubious accomplishment.

Ten minutes later, she and Jillian were both armed with cordless screwdrivers. Her husband, who Jillian had guessed rightly wouldn't know how to use one, had not merely one, but three screwdrivers. All different models.

It didn't take long for Amanda to get the hang of using the tool under the competent instruction of her friend. Soon, the whirring of the battery powered motors mixed with metal scraping against metal. Before long, the treadmill lay around them in pieces. They moved onto the stairmaster and even managed to dismantle the pneumatic weight bench.

Amanda squeezed the trigger on her screwdriver, making it whir noisily. "This is really therapeutic. I wish my aerobics tapes could be dealt with the same way."

Jill grinned. "Hey, the baseball bat oughtta work on those."

It did, but Amanda still felt dissatisfied. She needed more. She'd spent two years married to the food and exercise Gestapo and she wanted revenge. She let the bat fall to her side and wiped the sweat from her forehead. "It's not enough."

Jillian's eyes twinkled with a look that had been scaring those who knew her since before she could talk. "Come on."

Amanda followed her into the entertainment room and her gaze fell on the giant screen TV that filled up half of an entire wall, Lance's newest and most prized toy. She swiveled her head and met Jillian's eyes. Their green depths reflected the same sense of purpose beating a rhythm in Amanda's breast. It took a lot longer than the treadmill and they both had to jump out of the way when the heavy screen crashed to the floor, splintering into pieces, but when they were done, she felt better than she had in months.

They both stood, staring at the remains of the exorbitantly expensive piece of equipment and then Jillian looked up. "Anything else?"

Amanda thought about it. She could think of several things it would bother her husband to lose, but her blind desire for destruction seemed to be satisfied.

"No. I just want to pack my stuff and get out of here."

A curious sense of relief was beginning to pervade her being as she realized she never again had to suffer the critical comments and sexual rejection that typified her marriage to Lance. She was tired of feeling like a failure.

Maybe her womanly attributes were overblown in comparison to the boyishly thin chick her husband had been bonking. Maybe she was too pale for Southern California beauty, too short, too chesty, too hippy, too pretty much everything, but who said a woman was defined by her sex appeal?

She was on the inside fast track at Extant Corporation. Investing her time, energy and emotion in her career made more sense than giving those precious resources to her jerk of a husband, or any other man for that matter.

One thing was certain – she was never going to make the mistake of giving a man the power to hurt her again.

CHAPTER ONE

With an accuracy born of years of practice, Simon brought the katana down in a precise arc that left the silk scarf hanging in two even sections from the hooks in the ceiling. Moving into the next position, he swung the Korean sword in a horizontal path that sent two scraps of red silk fluttering to the floor.

Pushing his muscles to burning point, he worked through his form three times and completed an entire set of stretching exercises before taking care of his katana and hanging it back on the wall of his private gym. He wiped the wet sheen of sweat from his chest and arms with a small towel.

He crossed the room and turned out the lights, leaving the only illumination the light filtering in through the wall of windows that made up one side of his gym. He moved to the center of that wall and then sank to a cross-legged position on the floor mat. Facing the glass, he took in the view of the dark waters of the Puget Sound, their cold depths calling to the chill in his soul as they always did.

He'd built his home on an island, less than an hour's ferry journey from the mainland and only two hours from Seattle. It was the perfect location for a man who liked his privacy, but whose research often required access to technology resources available in a major city.

The sun had set some time ago and moonlight from a full moon glinted on the water, hinting at mysteries yet unexplored.

But he had his own mysteries to unravel.

The entire computer industry was racing to see who could develop a usable prototype of a fiber optic processor and he was determined to be the first. It was that need that had sent him in here looking for clarity of mind and an ease of the physical tension that always accompanied his deep immersion in a project.

He hadn't found it. His mind, usually so clear after a workout, spun from one thought to another.

For some reason, instead of focusing on the results of his most recent experiments, old memories demanded his attention tonight. Memories he would have been happy to bury into oblivion, five-year-old memories that had no place in his life today.

He could see Elaine's face, the beautiful features taut with stress, the exotic eyes glistening with tears as she said good-bye. "You've got to understand, Simon. You live in the shadows. I want to live in the light. Eric likes being around people.

You're always looking for excuses to avoid them. You want to spend all your time in that stupid lab of yours. A woman can't live like that."

He remembered each word verbatim.

A woman can't live like that.

At the time, he had wanted to believe she was wrong, that she'd been making excuses for her own choices. But five years on, he had to concede she was probably right.

After Elaine, he hadn't had a relationship last long enough for him to even start considering marriage. His infrequent girlfriends invariably bailed after the novelty of the sex wore off. He was too intense. Insensitive to their needs. Too wrapped up in his designs and experiments. Too cold. Too uncommunicative.

Some had even decided after having sex that he was just too big. He wasn't a monster, but damn it, he couldn't help the fact he was not average.

He wanted marriage. A family. A life like the one he had known so long ago before his mother's death, one that had warmth and companionship. Hell if he knew how to go about procuring one though. He didn't know how to turn down the intensity. He could no more give up his computer experiments than he could will his sex to stay at half-mast during intercourse.

His current project fascinated and challenged him in a way that nothing, particularly no woman, had since he was six years old and programmed his first robot. So, why was he letting old memories taunt him?

But he knew. Eric's ecstatic voice over the phone. Elaine was pregnant with their second child. He was hoping for a girl this time. Simon wasn't jealous of his cousin's relationship with Elaine. He had accepted a long time ago that they made a more natural couple than he and Elaine had ever done.

The fact that their relationship had not progressed to the bedroom should have clued him in long before Elaine's big good-bye scene. But part of his problem, he freely admitted, was a certain amount of cluelessness where women were concerned.

Simon counted her family and friend now, just the same as Eric. He made himself a frequent visitor to their home so he could spend time with them and their little boy. The kid called him Uncle Simon and he liked it. It made him feel like he belonged to someone.

But none of that changed the velocity of the lonely winds that howled through his soul as he contemplated a bleak future.

He picked up one of the pieces of red silk that had landed near where he sat. It was soft against his skin, but so light it weighed almost nothing. If he closed his eyes, it would be like it wasn't even there.

Just like him.

Sometimes he thought if he closed his eyes long enough, he would cease to exist, fading into the cold mists that often surrounded his home.

Amanda mentally went over the game plan for her upcoming meeting with the president of Brant Computers as the elevator made its ascent.

She could barely believe her luck. When she had put the proposal for a friendly merger before the Executive Management Team at Extant Corporation, she hadn't been sure they'd go for it. She'd been almost positive if they did pursue her plan, they would choose someone higher in the management hierarchy to negotiate terms.

That hadn't happened. She'd been chosen over several colleagues to make the initial approach to Eric Brant. He had been receptive and the Executive Management Team had appointed her point man for negotiations.

Her boss had wanted her to take a team with her, but she had convinced him that Eric and she had already developed a rapport that could be undermined if other negotiators were introduced this early on. He had acceded to her arguments, allowing her to make the trip to Port Mulqueen, Washington to talk to the president of Brant Computers alone.

Her relief had been enormous since a representative from the company's law firm had been one of the suggested team members. It was inevitable that she have business dealing with her ex-husband given that his firm handled all of Extant's legal issues, but the last thing she wanted was for her first really big break with her company to depend on Lance Roger's cooperation.

So far, negotiations had gone very well indeed.

She watched the buttons light up as the elevator went past one floor after another without stopping to pick up further passengers. She willed each little circle to lighten and darken without the elevator stopping. She didn't want any delays in her meeting with Eric Brant today, not even small ones.

She wasn't nervous, not exactly. Just impatient. It was a honey of a deal. She couldn't imagine Brant's board of directors not going for it. Not once she'd gotten buy-in from the company president and that's what she was here for. After his encouraging reaction to her first proposal, she wasn't expecting a lot of resistance.

When the deal closed, she'd be one step closer to that position on the Executive Management Team she coveted. At twenty-seven, she was the youngest female junior executive in the firm. Her goal was to be the youngest executive, male or female, and she was two years into a five-year plan to make that happen. Her plan would get a major boost when she successfully negotiated the merger with Brant Computers.

A smile of professional satisfaction hovered on her lips as the elevator doors slid open. She adjusted the strap of her purse over the shoulder of her ultra-professional, favorite red blazer and tightened her grip on her briefcase before stepping out of the elevator. Taking a cleansing breath, she walked toward the semicircular desk in the center of the large reception area. Her two-inch heels made whisper soft noises on the carpet that seemed to fit with the soft music playing in the background and the almost silent clicking of the receptionist's keyboard as she worked at her computer.

Amanda stopped in front of the desk and a blond of indeterminate age turned to greet her. "Ms. Zachary?"

"Yes." Amanda smiled.

"I'll just call Mr. Brant's executive assistant and let her know you're here."

The receptionist picked up the phone, dialed a number and spoke into mouthpiece attached to her headphones. As she listened to what was being said, her gaze flitted to Amanda and then back to her computer screen. "All right. I'll tell her."

She hung up the phone. "Mr. Brant's earlier meeting has run over. If you would like to take a seat, his executive assistant will come for you when he's finished."

Amanda acquiesced with carefully concealed impatience, seating herself in an armchair on the opposite wall from the elevator. She ignored the magazines laid out in an attractively arranged pile in order to spend her time waiting in thought.

What was going on?

It could be that a meeting had legitimately gone over. The man was president of a major company after all. He could also be exercising psychological strategy in making her wait. But to what purpose? Her previous meetings with Eric had led her to believe he was as excited about the possible merger as she was.

Several minutes had passed before an older woman in a dove gray suit cut in classic lines approached Amanda. "Ms. Zachary?"

Amanda stood. "You must be Fran." She had spoken to the executive assistant several times on the phone, but this was their first opportunity to meet.

The older woman's mouth tilted slightly in a smile. "Yes, won't you come this way?"

Amanda got up and followed the other woman. They stopped in front of double doors, one of which was cracked open a few inches.

"What the hell is the matter with you, Eric?" The deeply masculine voice came out in even tones, but was laced with unmistakable anger. "This is a family held company. Merging with Extant would destroy everything our Grandfather and fathers built here."

"Nonsense." Eric's voice sounded conciliatory, but louder than the other man's. "Look, Simon, you promised to give her a fair hearing and I'm holding you to your word."

"I would have promised anything to get Elaine to turn off the waterworks, including listening to some snake-oil salesman's pitch."

"Our arguing upset my wife and Amanda Zachary is no snake-oil salesman."

Before the other man could respond, the executive assistant had knocked on the already opened door.

The voices ceased abruptly.

Fran pushed the door open. "Eric, Ms. Zachary is here."

There were two men in the room. One stood in front of the windows so his face and expression were cast in shadow, but she could tell he was big, easily six-foot-two.

The other man wasn't quite so massive. His sandy brown hair and engaging smile gave him a look of boyish charm, but his blue eyes glinted with unmistakable intelligence. "Thank you, Fran. We'll take it from here."

The other woman turned and left. For one completely insane moment, Amanda wanted to call her back. The brooding presence of the man by the window unnerved her.

Then Eric caught her attention by coming forward to take her hand. "It's a pleasure to finally meet you, Amanda."

She shook his hand, being sure to grasp it firmly. "The pleasure is mine. I'm looking forward to our discussion."

Or rather, she had been before this other man had entered the equation.

Eric released her hand and turned slightly. "Amanda, this is my cousin Simon Brant. He's in charge of research and development for Brant Computers. Simon, this is Amanda Zachary, the representative from Extant Corporation."

Simon stepped away from the window and she got her first clear view of the man. She knew her negotiators smile had slipped a little, but she couldn't help it. Simon Brant was a force of nature. Dark exotic looks mixed with a smoldering presence in a Molotov cocktail that set something on fire inside her she was absolutely sure no longer even existed.

Desire. Hot. Molten. Unstoppable. And it washed through her body as if her receptors had forgotten, or never even known, she wasn't a very sexual person. She felt betrayed by her body. Now was not the time for it to rediscover long dormant feminine hormones.

Everything important to her was on the line with this deal.

"M-Mr. Brant." Great. She'd stuttered. She never tripped over her words, not since going through an endless series of speech therapy sessions as a child. However, she'd never met a man who looked like a cross between a Scottish warlord and Apache chief before either.

She put out her hand and wished to Heaven she'd ignored the urge for politeness when his big, warm fingers enclosed hers.

For the space of seconds, she didn't speak. Couldn't speak. Something elemental and downright terrifying passed from his hand to hers as he completed the shake.

"Ms. Zachary."

"Call me Amanda." The words slipped out, unbidden. She wouldn't have taken them back if she could. It would be awkward to have his cousin calling her by her first name while Simon stuck with the more formal address.

He dropped her hand, his gray eyes roaming over her with tactile intensity. "Simon."

That was it. Just his name, but she knew what he meant.

"Now that the introductions are over, why don't we all sit down?" Eric's voice sounded far away and Amanda had to force herself to decipher the words before nodding her agreement.

Despite the fact it was Eric's office, Simon led the way. He waited for her to sit in an armchair across the room from Eric's large executive desk. Eric and Simon sat at either end of the matching black leather sofa, with Simon taking the end furthest from her. She should have felt relief that his choice had given her a reprieve from his proximity, but the angle at which they sat gave him a clear view of her and vice versa.

It was an effort to turn her attention to Eric. "I didn't realize your cousin would be joining us for the meeting."

"It's a family held company, Amanda." Simon gave special inflection to her name. "I'm family and I happen to own a sizable chunk of the business."

"I see." She smiled tentatively. "But I had the impression from Eric that none of the other family played a principal role in management of the company."

"That's true." Eric gave Simon a hard look. "I'm the president of the company and my cousin rarely shows interest in my day to day decision making."

"I don't call proposing a merger with one of our chief competitors your average day to day decision. Wouldn't you agree, Amanda?"

He'd put her on the spot and in all honesty, she couldn't gainsay him. "It is a big decision, but certainly not one Eric has entertained lightly. We've been discussing the possibilities and ramifications of a merger for several weeks now."

"It's a pity I wasn't brought in before this then, because you've wasted your time talking to my cousin. I'll never approve what you propose."

"You don't own controlling interest in the company, damn it." Eric glared at Simon.

"Neither do you," Simon pointed out with a silky menace that sent shivers down the back of Amanda's legs.

"What do you plan to do, make this a family war?"

Simon's shoulders tensed infinitesimally and Amanda had the distinct impression that war was the last thing he wanted.

"Perhaps if you would allow me to present Extant's proposal, there won't be any need for bloodshed." It was a weak joke, but Eric smiled.

"Great idea."

Simon settled against the sofa cushions and kicked his denim clad, long legs out in front of him. He crossed them at the ankles, one booted foot resting on top the other. His arm stretched along the back of the couch pulling the knit of his dark crew-neck shirt taut over the well-defined muscles of his torso. He was the epitome of relaxed.

So, why did she get the feeling he was a tiger waiting to pounce on her unwary person?

One black brow rose. "I'm ready for you to begin, Amanda."

She'd put up with all the patronizing from men she was going to tolerate in her lifetime during her marriage. She didn't care how sexy this guy was, no one knew their job as well as she knew hers. It was after all her life. And she was no snake-oil salesman as he would soon see. She gave him a smile meant to convey her confidence in what she had to say and then launched into the initial proposal she'd given to Eric.

The smile would have knocked him on his ass if he hadn't already been sitting down.

Man, this woman was hot. Beautiful. Built to stop a strong man's heart, even if she did hide it behind a boxy jacket and long skirt that only hinted at the legs underneath. And she was the damn enemy.

Simon's jaw set and he listened while a husky voice that could have played a starring role in his favorite wet dream told him why he should let his cousin go through with his plans to destroy their family held company.

All right, so she didn't see it as destruction. Why should she? It wasn't her grandfather's dreams at stake here.

She was going on about the increased market share the two companies would enjoy once they were merged.

"Where did you come up with those figures?" he asked, interrupting her mid-flow.

He had to give it to her. She didn't so much as frown at his rudeness, nor did she hesitate before explaining the marketing statistics she'd used to develop her proposal.

"What about the employees? I'm still unclear as to effect this will have on overlapping human resources."

He wasn't unclear at all. It meant letting people go. Loyal employees that had a right to expect some loyalty back from the company they worked for. But he wanted to hear her say it. He wanted to see his cousin's face when she said it. Didn't Eric care?

She sat forward on the edge of her chair, her expression earnest. "Not unexpectedly, there will be a certain amount of employee attrition, but nothing on the scale of a major layoff."

"What do you consider a major layoff, Ms. Zachary?"

"Less than five percent of the total workforce for both Brant and Extant will be affected." She said it like she was expecting accolades for keeping the numbers down.

Eric sat there looking as if he thought laying off five percent of their workforce was no big deal.

Simon uncrossed his legs and leaned forward. "Do you realize how many jobs we're talking about here? I'd be willing to bet that for the guy who loses his job, just one person let go seems pretty major."

It interested him that she scooted back in her chair even though he was several feet away from her. "The computer industry is dynamic. Employees who have chosen their career in it understand that."

"How would you feel, if it was your job on the line, Amanda? Would you still be in favor of the merger?"

She blanched, actually flinching at the question. The woman's job meant a lot to her.

He waited to see how honestly she would answer the question, but Eric intervened. "That's not a fair question, Simon. This is about what is best for the company, not individual employees."

Simon stood up, his patience disintegrating with his mood. "Maybe I think the company's welfare is tied up with that of the employees."

Eric ran his fingers through his hair, disturbing the usually immaculate style. "Calm down, Simon."

"I'm not upset."

Eric's expression said he wasn't fooled. Simon wasn't shouting, but his cousin knew he was pissed. Big time.

"Mr. Brant... Simon... You agreed to hear me out, I thought. I'm barely through the first point in my presentation."

She had guts and eyes the color of Hershey's dark chocolate syrup that a man could happily drown in.

Nothing about this merger appealed to him, but the woman did. He'd listen, if for no other reason than to spend more time in her company, learn more about what made her tick. He sat back down.

"I'm here." He turned to Eric. "But don't you ever use your wife to manipulate me again."

Eric's relieved smile froze on his face. "It wasn't like that."

Suddenly Simon knew it had been exactly like that. He'd been spouting off, but Eric had known Simon couldn't withstand Elaine's tears. He'd also known his pregnant wife was bound to be upset by their argument. "You son of a bitch, you brought it up in front of her on purpose."

Eric had the grace to blush. "We'll talk about this later."

"Why? Don't you want Amanda privy to family business? You seem pretty free with the idea of handing over the family company to her."

Eric's eyes narrowed and the muscles of his jaw tightened. "I'm not handing the company over to her. I'm not handing it over to Extant for that matter. We're talking about a merger, a friendly merger."

"Eric is right. Brant Computers isn't going to cease to exist, it's going to be bigger than it has ever been." She was leaning forward again and her blazer parted to reveal the thin white silk of her blouse.

Did she know he could see the shadow of the top swell of her breasts when she did that?

Somehow he doubted it. She seemed completely focused on business. It wouldn't hurt him to do the same thing. He hadn't had as much trouble with his libido since he was a fifteen-year-old wiz kid attending college with fully developed, sexually active women who had turned teasing into a national league sport.

"There may be a company left. Hell, you might even agree to keep the Brant name, but the company my grandfather founded and my father spent his life building will cease to exist and all the softsoap in the world isn't going to make that any less of a reality."

"I don't think you're looking at the big picture."

"Maybe that's because the picture of Brant employees standing in the unemployment line keeps getting in the way."

She frowned at that. "Over the long term the employees will be better off because stability will be increased for both the companies." She grabbed her briefcase and started pulling papers out. "If you just look at these long term sales forecasts, you'll see that the initial five percent of employee attrition will not only be made up, but there will be steady growth in the number of positions available within the merged companies."

Simon looked at the papers, but all he saw were two exquisitely feminine hands with neatly manicured nails. He'd give his most recently acquired antique katana to have those delicate fingers on his body. He'd give the whole collection to have met this woman in other circumstances.

"Eric, trade places with Amanda. Presumably, you've already seen these numbers."

Her head came up and he read startled uncertainty in those gorgeous brown eyes before she masked her reaction.

Eric was already standing and the poor little darling had no choice but to do what Simon had suggested. Her initial reaction told him that the idea of being in close proximity to him made her nervous. Was that because he was on the opposite side of this issue from her and she saw him as the enemy?

Or was it because she felt this gut wrenching physical attraction too?

"Here, let me see that." He let his hand brush against hers as he pulled the paper from off the top of the pile.

Her fingers trembled.

An immediate and unexpected reaction took place just south of his belt buckle. He started a mental recitation of the laws and formulas related to thermal dynamics.

"As you can see, future employment projections are quite good."

He didn't comment. The recitation of the formulas sparked an idea related to his latest fiber optic experiment. He needed a notebook. Dropping the paper in his hand, he stood up and crossed the room to Eric's desk. It took rifling through three drawers, but he found a legal pad. He started taking notes as rapidly as possible.

He had to test this.

The pad in one hand, he started from the room.

"Simon!"

He stopped at the door and turned his head to the sound of his cousin's demanding voice. He didn't see Eric though, his mind's eye was too focused on his project.

"What about Amanda's presentation?"

"If I've said something to offend you..." The soft, husky voice trailed off and succeeded in claiming a corner of his attention.

Amanda.

He wanted to see her again.

"Bring your proposal to my house."

Her eyes widened and he heard Eric groan.

"My cousin can give you directions." Then he turned and left, his thoughts consumed with his upcoming experiment.

Chapter Two

Amanda watched the maddening man walk out of the office, feeling like Dorothy before she'd found the yellow brick road. What had just happened?

"He wants me to go to his house?"

Eric's expression was one of rueful resignation. He nodded. "Don't take this personally. Simon's brilliant and his mind doesn't work like everyone else's. When he gets an idea, it holds his complete attention."

"But..." One second he'd been reading her figures and the next he'd gotten up and was rummaging through Eric's desk.

"One Christmas, when he was about nine I think, he got up in the middle of opening his presents and disappeared into his lab until New Years Day."

"When he was nine?" Eric had to be exaggerating.

"Simon was a child prodigy. He graduated from high school when he was eleven. He had a double bachelor's degree in physics and computer design engineering by the time he was fifteen. Four years later he had a PhD in physics."

She knew what Eric was telling her. Simon was a genius. A cold, sinking sensation settled somewhere around her stomach because that genius didn't want his company merged with Extant. She could see all her carefully laid plans crashing and burning.

"Why does he want me to go to his house?"

A wrinkle appeared between Eric's brows. "I'm not sure. I think he wants you to finish your presentation."

"But why at his house?" A straightforward business deal had taken a distinctly unbusinesslike turn.

Eric's expression turned thoughtful. "I really don't know. He's a total privacy nut. Him inviting you to his house is out of character, but then his showing such a strong interest in the business side of Brant Computers is too."

"I'd feel better about finishing the presentation here in your office." She'd feel more comfortable not having to be in the disturbing man's presence at all, but going to his house seemed way too intimate.

Eric shook his head. "If he's on a new project, it could be days, weeks even, before he comes back to the mainland."

"Comes back to the mainland?" Her voice came out faint as she considered how disastrous that would be for the timetable on the merger.

"He lives on one of the islands. The Puget Sound is full of them. At least he opted for a home on one that has regular ferry service. You should be able to go and come back in one day."

Was that supposed to make her feel better? "But couldn't you call him and ask him to meet me here?"

Eric shook his head again, his mouth twisted grimly. "No. Simon is stubborn and like I said, his mind doesn't work like the rest of us. If we want him to hear your presentation, you'll have to go to him."

"Won't you be participating in the meeting?"

"Like Simon said, I've seen all the numbers." Eric stood up. "I can't really take the time from my schedule for a duplication of effort. You convinced me. I'm sure you can convince Simon and until you do, further meetings on the subject between the two of us would be ineffective."

She wasn't sure of any such thing, but she had no choice other than to try. She couldn't let Simon Brant jeopardize her goals. If that meant visiting him at his island home, that's what she would do.

Which was how she found herself breathing in the smell of burning diesel fuel on a ferry bound for a small island in the Puget Sound the next day.

She'd tried calling Simon to ask him to meet her again in Seattle. According to the crotchety old man that identified himself as Simon's housekeeper, Simon wasn't available for phone calls. When she identified herself, she'd been told Simon was expecting her.

Since he hadn't so much as given her a time or day for their meeting, she didn't see how that could be, but apparently Eric was right. Simon didn't think like other people.

His housekeeper had told her she was expected for lunch today.

William Tell's Overture started chirping away in her purse and she grabbed for her cell phone. Flipping it open, she put it to her ear. "Hello?"

"Hey, chicky-poo, how's it hangin'?"

"Jillian. Why aren't you on the set?"

"We finished taping early. They wanted to do this sunrise scene. I've been up since two-thirty this morning."

"Uh...Jill, we live on the West Coast. Sunsets over the ocean are beautiful, sunrises hidden behind LA's smog and skyline aren't exactly awe-inspiring."

"We did a desert taping, smarty-pants."

"Oh."

"Anyway, I called to say you've gotta watch today's episode. I've got amazing dialogue and I emoted with all the energy of Bette Midler."

Shoot. "Honey, I've got an afternoon appointment and the VCR in my hotel room doesn't have a timed taping function." She thought fast. "But my Ti-Vo is saving it for me at my condo. I'll watch it the minute I get home, I promise."

"Amanda..." Jillian drew her name out for at least six syllables. "I really wanted you to watch this. It's just the first half of the show. Can't you sneak away to the bathroom or something and find a television?"

What would Simon think of taking a thirty-minute break in the middle of their meeting to watch Jillian's soap opera?

"Jill—"

"Please, Amanda. I haven't been this excited about my work since I got the job."

That was saying a lot. Jillian had had her bit part on the soap for the past six years, longer than Amanda's marriage had lasted. She was a regular, if not a star.

"Okay, I'll try." She couldn't believe she was saying this. "But I can't promise anything."

"Thanks, hon! You're the best friend a girl could have. Have I told you that lately?"

"Not in the last week, no," Amanda said, laughing. Jillian had always been there for her. Through a disastrous two-year marriage, a divorce that took a year to finalize and a year of learning to be her own person completely again, Jill had been a rock in Amanda's life. "But listen, if I can't watch it, can you Fed-Ex me the tape?"

"The way I feel today, I'd fly the tape up to you to watch myself if I didn't have to work tomorrow and Friday."

Jillian was right. Amanda hadn't heard this much enthusiasm in her friend's voice concerning her work in years. "Hey, maybe you can fly up for the weekend anyway."

Silence met that. "Are you okay, Amanda?"

Darn. Why were best friends so discerning? "I just asked if you wanted to come up for the weekend. We could do the Seattle thing. Why does something have to be wrong?"

"Because when it comes to work, you are worse than anal retentive. You're so focused, you could give a Zen Buddhist monk lessons."

She sure didn't feel like a monk or a nun rather, not when every time she thought about Simon Brant her hormones started hopping around like rabbits hyped up on sugar. "There's a glitch in the deal I'm trying to work out," she admitted.

"What kind of a glitch?"

"A big one." About six feet, two inches of glitch.

"Bummer, hon. I'm sorry."

"Me too, but I'm not about to give up."

"Of course not. The only thing you've ever given up on is men. Everything else gets your try-til-you-die mentality."

Driving down the same road for the third time in twenty minutes, she was having a difficult time applying the try-til-you-die approach. Where the heck was the turn off? She'd missed it twice and was now driving slower than she could be walking in attempt not to miss it a third time. Wait. Was that an opening in the trees? It was. Carefully camouflaged, the opening to Simon's drive could have easily been taken for a natural break in the flora and fauna alongside the road.

Eric had said Simon was a privacy nut, but this was ridiculous. One of them could have mentioned that the entrance to his property was as well hidden as your average state secret. Not that Simon had mentioned anything. He'd told Eric to give her directions and then dismissed the whole situation by leaving.

It was a good thing he was just a business associate and not her boyfriend. That kind of behavior would be really hard to take in a lover.

Thankfully she reached the gate before her wayward thoughts had a chance to go any farther afield.

She stopped the rental Taurus and pressed the automatic window button. It whirred softly as the glass disappeared between her and the small black box she was supposed to talk into. She reached through the window, inhaling a big breath of fresh, forest-scented air and pressed the red button below the box.

"Yeah?" There was no mistaking that crotchety voice. She'd only heard it once, but Simon's housekeeper was unforgettable.

"It's Amanda Zachary."

"Expected you here a good twenty minutes ago, missy. It don't pay to be late if you expect to catch the boss out of his lab."

She glared at the box and reminded herself that this was business. For business, she could put up with a cranky old man.

"I'm sorry. I missed the turn."

"Guess you missed it more than once if it took you an extra twenty minutes."

What was this guy, the timeliness cop? "Perhaps, since I am already late, you would be kind enough to buzz the gates open so that I won't keep your employer waiting any longer."

"He ain't come out of the lab yet."

She ignored that bit of additional provocation and simply said, "The gate?"

"Can't."

"You can't open the gate?" She stared stupidly at the black box, at a complete loss.

"Right."

"Is it broken?"

"Nope."

Anger overcame confusion and good sense. "Then what exactly is stopping you from opening he darn thing?"

"You got to get out of the car. I need to make a visual I.D. before I can open the gate."

"Since you've never seen me before, what exactly are you trying to identify?"

"No need to get snippy. I done my job. I got a picture of you. No use you asking how. I don't share my trade secrets with just anybody."

For Heaven's sake. She got out of the car and stood so her head and shoulders were clearly visible above the car door.

"You'll have to step around the door, if you don't mind."

Now he decided to be polite, while asking her to do something totally ludicrous.

"What difference does it make?" She glared with unconcealed belligerence at the camera at the top of the gate.

"You got something to hide, missy?"

"Not if you discount a body that wasn't femme fatale material," she muttered to herself as she stepped around the silver car's door.

Thoroughly out of sorts, she threw her arms wide. "Look, no automatic weapons, no hidden cameras, no nerve gas. Are you satisfied?"

"I think I could be."

No! No. No. Darn it. No. That had not been the housekeeper's voice. It was another unforgettable voice though, that of Simon Brant. In a reflex move, she crossed her arms over her chest as she felt heat crawl from the back of her ankles right up her body and into her cheeks. She was going to kill that housekeeper when she got her hands on him.

She was going to pick him up by his toes and hang him above a tar pit. And then she was going to let go.

"Hello, Mr. Brant. I've been informed that I'm late."

He didn't answer, but the gate swung inward.

If Simon tried to talk, he was going to laugh and that would just encourage Jacob in his irascible ways. So, he pressed the button for the gate release without answering Amanda. He watched as she climbed back into her car, her dark hair all twisted on the back of her head in a tidy knot. The severity of her hairstyle and suit she was wearing could not erase the image he had of her with her arms flung wide, her generous breasts pressing against the fabric of her blouse and her eyes glittering with pure temper.

"She's a tad feisty, sir."

Simon didn't know why the old man called him sir. He'd never been in doubt who was in charge between the two of them and it wasn't Simon Brant. "I have no doubt she has cause."

Jacob just shrugged his thin shoulders. "Might have upset her a bit, I suppose. I got poor company manners, sir."

Considering the fact the man had at one time been on the Presidential detail of the secret service, Simon took that comment with the credence it deserved. "What you have is an unfulfilled wish to go undercover and it comes out in the parts you like to play here."

Jacob's gray head cocked to one side. "Could be. Or could be I'm just a crabby old geezer who's lucky to have an eccentric billionaire for a boss."

Simon didn't have a chance to answer as the first few bars of Beethoven's Fifth played over the house-wide sound system. He did not like doorbells.

"I'll get it. I think Amanda could do without another dose of your company manners." And he wanted to be alone when he greeted her. He didn't want any distractions when he discovered if his reaction to her in Eric's office had been an anomaly.

Amanda's hand clenched and unclenched on the handle of her briefcase while she waited for the door to open.

Okay, the guy was a genius and so sexy he made her heart imitate a Morse code operator, but that did not mean he would succeed in scotching the deal. If he was so smart then he would definitely see the benefits of merging with Extant.

She had a briefcase full of reports and graphs that he'd have to be a fool to ignore.

So, stop worrying, already.

He was just a man with some preconceived notions she needed to help him reprogram.

The door swung open.

Simon Brant stood with his strong, masculine hand curved around the edge of the door. "Amanda. Welcome to my home."

How did he do that? Five words, none of them remotely sexual, and her insides were turning into warm honey.

Just a man.

Uh huh.

Right.

Her professional, let's-talk-the-deal smile fought with her rebellious lips' urge to pucker up and beg for the gorgeous man's kisses. Oh, man, she was losing it.

"Mr. Brant."

Firm lips curved in a smile, revealing perfectly even, white teeth. "I thought it was Simon."

"Simon," she conceded. "Thank you for inviting me."

He inclined his head and stepped back, indicating she should come inside.

She stepped over the threshold of the door and for one disconcerting second felt as if she'd made an irrevocable decision that would change the rest of her life. Shaking the feeling off as highly fanciful, she extended her hand toward him. "I look forward to showing you the many benefits of the proposed merger between Brant Computers and Extant Corporation."

Simon took her hand, but he didn't shake it. He squeezed her fingers and bent forward. For one incredulous moment, she thought he was going to kiss her hand, but he didn't. He simply dropped his head forward in a cross between an Oriental bow and an Old World gesture.

He straightened and dropped her hand. "Jacob's prepared lunch. It's waiting for us in the great room."

Was that a veiled hint about her slight tardiness?

He turned and led the way down a hallway, his feet making no sound on the hardwood floor while her shoes tapped out a firm tattoo with each step.

The hall took a sharp right and she stopped in awe at the sight of room exposed to her gaze. The room itself gave great room new meaning. It was huge, at least twenty by forty feet, but it wasn't the size that had her so captivated. The entire thirty-foot wall opposite the entrance was glass with a view of the Sound and Mt. Rainier off in the distance.

Simon stopped and turned to her. "Like it?"

"It's fantastic." No wonder the guy preferred to work out of his home with a home like this.

"Other than necessary structural bracing, this entire side of the house is made up of reinforced glass and windows."

"How many stories are there?"

"Three. The pool and gym are on the floor below us. Jacob's living quarters, the kitchen, guest room and this room are on this level and my living quarters and lab are upstairs."

Her gaze slid around the room they were in. It's simplistic design and fur-nishings had Oriental overtones, but nothing glossy and lacquered. It was all fruitwood, simple lines and natural hues for the upholstery. "This really is mag-nificent. You must enjoy living here quite a bit."

The house was much bigger than the home she had shared with Lance and in many ways more grand, yet it still felt like a home. It reflected it's owner's complex, but deceptively simple appearing approach to life.

"Thank you." He took her arm and led her to the dining table in front of one of the twin massive stone fireplaces at either end of the room. "Let's have lunch and you can tell me a little about yourself."

She allowed him to seat her, feeling strange about a business associate observing the courtesy. In LA, she was used to being treated the same way as her male counterparts in the corporate world.

Flicking her cloth napkin open and then laying it across her lap, she said, "I'm not all that interesting, but I don't think you'll find the same true of Extant's proposal."

His smile flashed along with a determined glint in his gray eyes that gave her pause. "I prefer to know a person before I discuss business with them. It probably comes from working for a family held company."

"I see."

"Good."

She looked down at the pasta in pesto sauce attractively presented in a flat china bowl. "This looks wonderful."

"Jacob's rather proud of his culinary talents."

"He's a unique individual." She meant to be diplomatic.

He laughed, the sound affecting her already off-balance equilibrium. "That's one way to describe him. Cantankerous is another."

She didn't bother asking why Simon kept such a rude man working for him as she took her first bite of the delicious pasta. She thought it was probably just as hard for a recluse genius to find household help as for a cranky old man who cooked like an angel to find a job.

"So, tell me about yourself, Amanda." It was a line tossed out as easily as a common greeting and yet his intent stare and deep, controlled voice made her feel like he was asking for more than a run down on the highlights of her résumé.

She fought against giving into the compulsion to share on a personal level with him. "I've been working for Extant Corporation since graduating from college with a degree in business. This is my second year in the corporate planning division."

"Are you married?"

Her fork paused midway to her mouth. "I don't see how that relates to the merger."

One black brow rose. "I thought I explained I like to know the people I do business with."

"I believed you meant my business background."

He poured wine into her glass and then his own. "Did you?"

No she hadn't. Not really, but it was so ludicrous to think he wanted to know about her. She wasn't the type of woman to inspire personal interest from a man like Simon, from any man for that matter. Or so her ex-husband had taken pains to point out. "I assure you the most interesting aspects of my life relate to my career."

"I'm interested in your marital status."

"Why?"

He shrugged. "It seems relevant to who you are. I'm single and I've never been married. I rarely date and I spend long hours in my lab ignoring the rest of the world."

"Oh..." What was she supposed to say to that? She couldn't begin to understand why he was telling her this stuff. He must be very serious about wanting to personally know the people he did business with. She supposed that made sense considering most of his current business associates were family or employees for his family's company.

"I'm not married." She didn't add that she was divorced. "I don't have time to date." Something flickered in his eyes at that. She supposed he was noticing, as she was, that they had quite a bit in common. "And I'm focused almost exclusively on my work." In fact, her only friend outside work was Jillian.

Which reminded her. "Do you have a television?" She couldn't believe she was asking him this. It was totally unprofessional, but then the man insisted on having a business meeting in his home and grilling her about her marital status. He couldn't be that concerned about professional behavior.

His black brows rose. "No."

She couldn't quite stifle a sound of regret. Jillian was going to be so disappointed.

"I believe Jacob has one, however."

"Jacob?" Asking Simon to allow a thirty-minute break in their meeting so she could keep her promise to Jillian was not nearly as intimidating a prospect as asking Jacob for the loan of his television.

"Yes. He likes British comedies."

That would mean he had cable. He'd definitely get Jillian's soap opera. "My best friend is a regular in a daytime drama. She wants me to watch her show today. She's really proud of her scenes."

It was worth asking to see the bemusement on Simon's features. He'd been knocking her off-balance since they met and she found herself relishing this small opportunity to get her own back again.

"You want to watch a soap opera?"

"Yes. She promised it was only the first thirty minutes I needed to see. I hate to ask for a break like that and realize it isn't quite professional, but I promised." Waiting for Simon's answer, she realized she would never have made the same request of his cousin, Eric Brant.

"What time is the show on?"

"One."

Simon twisted his wrist so he could see the face of his ultra sleek hi-tech watch. "That's in less than an hour."

"I suppose you want to conclude the meeting as soon as possible so you can get back to your project." She'd just have to have Jillian Fed-Ex the tape of the program.

Simon shook his head. "It's important to keep promises to friends. I don't mind taking a little break. I've never seen a soap opera, excuse me, daytime drama before."

That didn't surprise her, his intended desire to watch Jillian's show with her did. "You don't have to watch it with me," she assured him.

"I wouldn't miss it."

"Thank you." It seemed to be the thing to say. "Would you like me to start going over some of the figures for the merger?"

"I prefer not to discuss business while I'm eating. Tell me more about you. Your best friend is an actress?"

"Actor." She smiled. "Actress is considered a sexist term and she'd tear a strip off you if she heard you using it."

"It's fortunate she isn't here to have heard my faux pas then, isn't it?" Silver flecks of humor twinkled in his gunmetal gray eyes.

"She's a little militant," Amanda admitted.

"What about your family?"

"What about them?"

"I presume they aren't all actors."

Actually they all had a fair amount of acting ability. "My parents own a real estate agency in Carlsbad. My brother is a lawyer." And the most accomplished actor of them all.

"No sisters?"

"No. What about you?"

"No."

"No sisters?"

"No brothers either."

She knew his father had died in a plane crash with Eric's father several years ago. "What about your mom?"

Simon's face went blank. "She died of ovarian cancer when I was ten."

She had the sense the loss still affected him deeply and that impressed her. "I'm sorry."

"Thank you."

"Eric told me you got your PhD when you were nineteen. That's very impressive."

He shrugged. "Intelligence is something you are born with. My mother and father encouraged me not to squander mine."

"But to have accomplished so much by such a young age."

Instead of answering, he reached toward her and she watched in mesmerized fascination as his darkly masculine hand came closer and closer to her chest. She couldn't seem to open her mouth to protest, nor could she move.

He stopped, his fingers a centimeter from her body. "You've got a noodle here." Then he pulled the offending piece of pasta off the lapel of her jacket without so much as brushing her chest with the backs of his fingers.

Chapter Three

I t hadn't been a fluke.

Simon's reaction to Amanda was as devastating today as it had been in his cousin's office.

And Amanda was just as affected.

She'd thought he was going to touch her. He could see it in the dilation of the black centers in her eyes, in the way her breath had caught and held, pushing her beautiful curves into prominence. Yet she hadn't protested, hadn't moved.

She wanted him.

Perhaps as much as he wanted her.

But he couldn't let it happen. Not yet, probably not ever.

In the current situation with his family's company, she was the enemy. He wouldn't risk the possibility she might try to use sex to manipulate him into agreeing to the merger. He was almost positive she wouldn't stoop to such tactics. His instincts told him that though she tried to be all business, she wasn't barracuda material.

In fact, she seemed like a really sweet, beautiful woman almost absurdly un-aware of her feminine appeal. He wanted time to see if that was true. He wanted to observer her and get to know her. She intrigued him. He wanted to understand what made her tick, what put shadows in her eyes when she said she wasn't married. He wanted to know why her voice had changed tenor when she mentioned her family.

For the first time in five years, Simon was interested in a woman's friendship. His body craved hers with feral intensity, but he wasn't going to risk her deciding he was too big, or too intense and putting up her guard against him.

His gaze flicked over her heart shaped face. "So, do you usually watch your friend's show?"

"Every day, faithfully."

"You keep a television in your office?"

She looked appalled at the idea. "That would hardly be professional. I record it on my Ti-Vo and watch it when I go to bed to relax me."

"You like to watch television in bed?" He went to bed to sleep, or to make love, period.

She fiddled with her fork, her gaze not quite meeting his. "Yes." For some reason his question had made her blush.

Maybe it had been his mentioning the word bed. He knew simply thinking the word in her proximity brought all sorts of interesting, but impossible, scenarios to his own mind.

"What part does your friend play in the show?" he asked in order to get his focus off those scenarios.

"She started off playing the long lost teenage daughter of one of the love interests on the show. They kept her on. It's a small role, but she gets to do what she has always wanted to do, act."

"And are you doing something you love?"

"My career is very important to me."

"But do you love it?"

"Of course. I'm well on my way to meeting all my goals."

No doubt the intended merger with Brant Computers was a big part of that. It was unfortunate, but she would have to find some other way to pursue her ambitions. Brant Computers was going to stay a family held company as long as Simon had anything to say about it. Considering the fact he had no intention of ever selling his share of the company, that would be for his lifetime.

He searched his mind for a way to steer the direction away from her work. "A friend of mine from my university days is an actor in New York."

With careful attention to directing the conversation on his part, they spent the remainder of lunch discussing her girlfriend's soap opera and the difference between stage acting and television.

Following Simon into Jacob's quarters, Amanda couldn't believe she had gotten so sidetracked.

She'd spent forty-five minutes talking to Simon and after her initial sally, she had not once brought up her proposal. The only other person in her life that kept her so enthralled in conversation was Jillian. Because she was so outrageous. Simon was eccentric, not outrageous, but he was interested in everything and his mind was like a mainframe computer stored to capacity with data.

"You got an addiction to soap opera's have you?" Jacob asked as she took a seat on the sofa opposite a big screen television.

The old man's sneering got her back up. "My best friend is one of the actors in a highly acclaimed daytime drama."

"Ho, is she now? What's her name then?"

"Jillian Sinclair."

Jacob sat in the recliner, leaving the only seat for Simon on the couch with her. "Point her out when she comes on screen." His tone implied he questioned her story.

She consciously refused to grit her teeth. "I will."

Simon sat beside her rather than taking a position by the other arm of the sofa. "This should be interesting."

She turned her head to look at him and couldn't help smiling. His expression was dubious. For a man who didn't even own a television, daytime drama probably had very doubtful appeal. She wasn't sure why he'd decided to watch it with her. Perhaps that genius brain of his so interested in everything wanted to taste a new experience, even a questionable one.

The show's theme music started and she forced her attention back to the television. Opening credits rolled. Jillian wasn't in the first scene, so Amanda allowed herself another peek at Simon, but he wasn't watching the television.

His gunmetal gaze was settled on her. "You don't like the woman on the screen."

He was right. Amanda didn't particularly like the grand dame of the show, but how could he tell? "It's not my favorite storyline."

"If you two are going to talk, sir, there's no sense you staying in here to watch the show, is there?" Jacob's irascible voice interrupted them.

Simon chuckled. "We'll be quiet. It is, after all, your television."

Silence between them did not diminish her awareness of Simon Brant. On the contrary, it heightened it. She had to be imagining that she could feel the heat of his body from six inches away, but the impression would not leave her. The side of her closest to him flushed with warmth.

It got worse when Jillian's initial scene came on screen. "That's Jillian, the redhead," she said, pointing her friend out for Simon and Jacob.

She could have said the half-naked woman draped like a blanket over the blond hunk. Jillian had a love interest. No wonder she was excited. That increased her cache with the show big time. It was, however, not a scene Amanda would have preferred to watch sitting next to the first man in years to spark sexual feelings in her.

She licked her lips as Jillian and the blond hunk kissed. It wasn't a get to know you kiss, but one of supposed overwhelming passion and both actors portrayed the emotion in an amazingly realistic way.

Amanda's breathing hitched and she tried to mask her reaction with a cough, which earned her a glare from Jacob.

Simon caught her eye and winked.

She felt heat crawl up her face. He couldn't possibly know she was thinking about his lips on hers while Jillian and her lover kissed. Could he?

At the next commercial break, Simon turned to her. "Your friend is quite talented. You'd never guess watching her with that guy that they aren't really madly in lust with each other. Or are they?"

She shook her head and laughed a little. "No way. He's married with four kids and the sweetest wife. He dotes on her and she adores him, not at all your average Hollywood marriage." Or any marriage as far as she could tell.

Simon's expression turned thoughtful. "Is Jillian married?"

Why was he asking? She knew her friend was gorgeous. Did Simon want an introduction? "No, but she's got a boyfriend."

More like six of them. Where Amanda lived like a nun, Jillian was out to enjoy male companionship to its fullest.

Gray eyes narrowed, Simon studied her, making Amanda feel like he was looking into her soul. "I don't know. I think I'd go ballistic if my girlfriend kissed a guy like that."

He couldn't be thinking of her when he said that, no matter what his expression indicated. She didn't engender those sorts of thoughts in men, especially gorgeous, sexy men like Simon. "It's not real."

"How can a kiss not be real?"

Amanda wasn't very clear on that herself. Jillian had tried to explain it to her, but for Amanda it always came down to lips against lips, bodies touching bodies. Intimacy.

She shrugged. "She says acting is putting yourself in that person's perspective, so it's not really you doing the kissing."

"And when his penis gets hard and presses against her belly, is that just the character reacting or the man?" He sounded as if he was asking a wholly clinical question.

She didn't feel in the least scientific, or qualified to answer the question in any case. Erect male flesh wasn't something she had a lot of experience with. "He probably doesn't get th-that way."

She'd stuttered. Again. With the exception of the other day, when she'd first met Simon, she hadn't stuttered since spelling militant in her sixth grade spelling bee. She'd dropped out because she'd said too many m's.

"Come on." Incredulity laced his voice. "He's got a beautiful body pressed against his, their tongues are doing the mating dance and did you see where she had her hand?"

Something twinged in her heart when he called Jillian beautiful. She and Amanda were complete opposites physically. "Jill says that with the lights, the people all around and the pressure to get it right for the first take, she doesn't have any inclination to get excited."

Simon looked at her with an expression she couldn't begin to decipher, but which left her feeling ridiculously vulnerable and short of breath. "It wouldn't matter."

Did he mean it wouldn't matter if he had Jillian pressed up against him?

Thankfully, the show came back on and she was saved from having to pursue the conversation further.

They had to sit through another scene without Jillian and a second commercial break, during which Jacob grilled her about Jillian's start in show business.

Then Jillian's subsequent scene came on.

It was in the bedroom and all Amanda could think was how it would feel to be in a similar situation with Simon. Which was highly unprofessional as well as dangerous to her personal well being. She'd never before had a physical reaction to watching a love scene on Jillian's show and goodness knew she'd seen enough of them. But this time, her body was reacting as if she was the one in the bed.

She could feel arrows of sensation shooting down her thighs from their apex and her nipples were pressing against her bra like when she was freezing cold. Only she wasn't cold. She was hot. So hot, she wished she could take off her blazer, but she couldn't. Not with the nipple problem.

She'd die if Simon saw the evidence of her desire, not to mention Jacob. He'd probably say something nasty about it and Jillian's show. As if the show had anything to do with it.

Her wretched imagination was to blame. And the man beside her. Eccentric geniuses had no business being sexy and ultra masculine. He should wear wire-rimmed glasses and dress in polyester pants with checked, cotton button-up shirts, not form fitting shirts and jeans that accentuated his incredible body.

Simon's nostrils flared in primal recognition of the subtle scent coming off Amanda.

Her friend might not be affected by doing the love scene on-screen, but Amanda was affected by watching it. Her breath was coming in shallow little pants and he'd bet his newest computer that if she took off her jacket, her blouse would be inadequate for the task of hiding twin mounds topped by turgid peaks. Imagining the way they would feel against his palm was driving him crazy.

Were they pink or brown? Did she have big aureoles? Were her nipples big or little? Damn. He wanted to touch her. He wanted to see her. Neither was a wise or even possible course of action, so he sat there stewing in his desire.

And getting hard, which could be a problem if Amanda noticed, not to mention uncomfortable.

Stretching his legs out in front of him to relax the constriction around his crotch, he laid his arm along the back of the sofa. He didn't touch her, but she went as stiff as his sex was getting.

He turned his head slightly to see her face better and wanted to explode at the way she was biting her lip.

The sound of the phone ringing came as welcome relief. He jumped up before Jacob could. "I'll get it."

Jacob eyed him speculatively while Amanda kept her gaze set on the television.

"Amanda, go ahead and finish watching the program."

Her head came up then, her features schooled into a blank mask. "All right. Thanks. Jill said she had one last scene in the second half-hour, but it wasn't as big. I'd like to see it."

He nodded already headed toward the nearest telephone.

Amanda went back to the great room after Jillian's soap opera ended, expecting to find Simon waiting for her because he'd never come back to Jacob's quarters.

The room was empty.

Should she go looking for him?

Maybe he was still on the phone. She didn't want to interrupt and surely he knew the show was over by now.

Her gaze moved to the huge wall of windows. The water of the sound was different than the ocean in Southern California. Even in the bright sunlight of late June it looked like smoked glass rather than the shimmering blue she was used to. Simon had a dock that extended over fifty feet out into the water and a sailing yacht moored at the end.

It didn't look like a modern vessel, which surprised her. She was familiar with the sleek lines of the latest boating designs since her condo was located on the bay above an exclusive marina. Simon's yacht looked like something from a nineteen-forties movie. Even from the distance, it's dark wood exterior shone with the gloss of a meticulous finish.

As her gaze skimmed the glass wall, she noticed deck furniture to her right. A pitcher of what looked like ice tea and two glasses sat on the cedar table. Presumably, they were going to continue their meeting out on the deck that extended the length of the house. She picked her briefcase up from where she'd left it earlier and looked for a way outside.

Just like everything about Simon Brant, the exit was cleverly concealed. It took her several minutes before she found the small lever that once pressed, sent a door size piece of glass sliding to the right. She carried her briefcase to the table and set it on one of the empty chairs. Since Simon was not yet there, she didn't sit down but went to lean against the rail, breathing in the warm, salty air.

A small breeze blew across her face, and she closed her eyes, reveling in both the warmth of the sun on her skin and the smell of air free of Southern California smog. She couldn't remember the last time she'd allowed herself the luxury of stopping and just being.

Her conscience reminded her that she could be at the table setting up her facts and figures to present to Simon, but for once, she ignored the inner prompting.

This felt too good.

The quiet was broken only by the distant chatter of Seagulls.

A strange inertia settled over her body as if the overwhelming pace she'd been keeping for the past two years had caught up to her all at once. She'd lived for her job since walking out on Lance. Why that sparked a sense of discontent at that particular moment, she could not understand.

Taking a deep breath, she opened her eyes and forced herself to turn back toward the table. She flicked a look at her watch and was shocked to see she'd stood at the deck rail for half an hour.

Where was Simon?

She scanned the great room, but it was empty.

No doubt Jacob knew where to find his boss. She'd have to locate the cranky housekeeper and ask him what was going on.

Luckily she found him in the kitchen. She hadn't really wanted to wander around the huge house trying to find one of the two men who lived there.

"Jacob, do you know where Simon is? I've been waiting on the deck for him since Jillian's show ended."

Jacob turned from where he was doing something at the sink. "The boss went back to his lab."

"But there's a pitcher of ice tea with two glasses on the deck." They were supposed to talk about the merger.

Jacob nodded. "Told me to put it there."

"But he didn't come out."

"Never does. Not once he gets that look in his eyes and goes off to his lab. Be lucky to see him again today. Probably won't."

"Do you mean he won't be coming out of the lab again this afternoon?" It was the experience at Eric's office all over again. He'd just walked away.

She had an urge to pound on the door to his lab and insist on him coming out and listening to her, but if she got militant, how receptive would he be to what she had to say?

"Not likely."

"You don't think he'll come out again today?" she asked, just to clarify.

"That's what I said, ain't it?"

"Couldn't you knock and remind him I'm here?"

"Wouldn't do no good. He don't hear when he's thinking."

She had some ideas on how to get Simon's attention, but since it had never been her goal in life to get arrested, she dismissed them.

"When do you expect him to come out of his lab? Surely he has to eat sometime."

"Has a kitchen up there, but he comes out to exercise."

Remembering Simon's well-developed muscle tone, she had no problem believing that even if he didn't put his work aside to eat regular meals, he did in order to work out. No one got muscles like those by default. "When does he exercise?"

"Depends."

"On what?"

"On when he wants to."

"I see." What she saw was that Jacob wasn't going to cooperate with her and her patience was a second away from disappearing all together. "Will you please give your employer a message for me?"

"That's my job."

"Oh really? Somehow I thought your job was to drive Simon's visitors crazy enough so that they wouldn't come back. Then he can live as a total recluse." The sarcastic words just tripped off her tongue and she wasn't even slightly apologetic.

Jacob had the gall to look offended. "My company manners may not be what they once were, but I don't try to chase off Simon's friends."

"Merely irritating business associates he has no desire to talk to in the first place. Does he pay you a bonus for your efforts, or do you consider it one of the perks of the job?"

"The boss didn't tell me to try to run you off."

She wasn't buying it. And she wasn't sticking around for more of Jacob's annoying half-answers. Eric Brant wanted this merger too. He could convince his cousin to meet her. She spun on her heel and marched out of the kitchen.

After retrieving her briefcase from the deck, she had her hand on the front door handle when Jacob came into the entry hall. "There's no need for you to leave all in a huff, Ms. Zachary."

"I'm not in a huff. I'm cutting my losses."

"You wanted to leave the boss a message."

"There really isn't any point, is there? He'll just ignore it as effectively as he's managed to ignore me."

Only he hadn't ignored her over lunch, or during Jillian's show. He'd focused his considerable concentration on her and their discussion, which made his subsequent snub feel personal. She was used to male rejection. It wasn't something she would probably ever take in stride, but she had learned not to set herself up for more of the same.

She turned the doorknob. "Good-bye, Jacob."

"Wait."

The command shocked her into stopping. Not only in the fact that the irascible man was actually encouraging her to stay, but also by the authoritative tone of his voice. "What?"

"He doesn't mean anything by it. He's a genius."

"So I'd heard." She found it very difficult to believe Jacob was defending Simon's actions to her, as if her opinion mattered.

"He's not ignoring you so much as so focused on the complexities going through his mind, he's not even peripherally aware of what is happening around him."

"What happened to your bad grammar?"

Jacob's skin took on an interesting burnt hue. "I talk the way I want to."

She let that go. Jacob, she was discovering, was an entity unto himself. "You don't think it was on purpose?" she asked, referring to Simon's second abandonment.

"No, Ms. Zachary. The boss doesn't mean to do it. It's just the way he is."

"No wonder he doesn't have a lot of friends." She was making an assumption based on Simon's lifestyle, but Jacob sighed.

"He's spent his whole life out of step with his peer group one way or another. The boy is more comfortable experimenting in his lab than making friends. I think he finds his computers easier companions than people."

The boss had become the boy and she realized the relationship between Simon and Jacob was more multifaceted than it appeared on the surface.

"If I leave him a message to call, do you think he will?" The prospect of talking to Simon on the phone and seeing him again, even after his habit of disappearing without a word, was much too appealing.

"Yes."

She gave Jacob her cell phone number as well as the name of her hotel and room number. He wrote them down and she left.

The ferry ride back to the mainland passed quickly as she tried to strategize a full-proof plan for presenting the proposal to Simon. Unfortunately, by the time she reached her hotel over an hour later, she was no closer to a solution.

Both Jacob and Eric had made a point of telling her how wrapped up in a new project Simon became. He was evidently in full new-project-mode now and she couldn't help thinking any hope of presenting the merger to him in its entirety was doomed from the outset.

When she got back to her hotel room, there was a message from her manager requesting she call him. She wasn't surprised. She'd had to tell him about the glitch with Simon Brant when her last meeting with Brant Computer's president did not end in a concrete step toward the merger.

"How did Simon Brant respond to the proposal?"

"He didn't."

"What do you mean he didn't? Is he a deep player, keeping his thoughts close to his chest?"

"He's deep all right, but he didn't express any reaction because I didn't get a chance to present the benefits to the merger to him."

"I thought you were meeting with him this afternoon."

"So did I. He didn't want to discuss business over lunch and afterward he disappeared into his lab."

"Don't tell me you couldn't steer the direction around to the merger over lunch. It was a business meeting."

"Simon doesn't see business in the same light most people do. He wanted to get to know me over lunch. He's not comfortable doing business with someone he doesn't know."

Her boss snorted. "And you went along with that? This is no time to decide to let your ice queen persona melt and start pursuing a personal agenda on company time."

"I am pursuing Extant Corporation's agenda to the best of my ability." The ice queen crack hurt, particularly because it wasn't true. She wasn't an ice sculpture, just a flawed one. "I'm not sure trying to convince Simon to support the merger is a practical direction to take right now."

"I talked to Eric Brant and according to him, we need his cousin's cooperation, or the deal is dead in the water. Or at least close enough to justify calling in the coroner." The fact that her boss and Eric had been talking took her aback. She'd been under the impression she was on her own during the preliminary negotiations. Her stomach knotted at the idea that she might be judged and found wanting as a negotiator.

She explained about Simon's preoccupation with his current project. "Even his housekeeper warned me that trying to pin Simon down in one place long enough to hear the presentation is going to be difficult."

"I don't care if you have to camp out on his doorstep until you get him to listen to you. We need that man's cooperation for this deal to go through. If you don't think you can get it, maybe I'll have to come up there and take over the negotiations."

The knots in her stomach drew tighter until she felt in desperate need for an antacid tablet. "I can handle it, Daniel."

"Prove it."

The words echoed through her mind long after he cut the connection.

In one way or another, she'd been trying to prove herself her entire life and somehow she'd always ended up falling short of the mark.

She was determined that this time would be different.

Chapter Four

S he bolted upright in bed, her heart beating erratically. She'd had the dream again, the one where she got fired and driving home to her condo she started shrinking until she wasn't even tall enough to touch the gas pedal. She usually didn't wake up until the car started veering wildly toward the edge of the coastal highway, coming awake just as the car started going over the cliff.

Ring.

She turned toward the sound, still disoriented by her dream and brutal return to reality.

Ring.

It was the phone.

It had woken her, stopping the nightmare right after she started getting smaller. She fumbled for the receiver in the darkness of her room.

"Hello?"

"Good morning, Amanda."

"Simon?" Was it morning? She blearily tried to focus on the clock beside her bed. Twelve minutes after five a.m.. "Do you have any idea what time it is?"

"It's still dark, so not yet six."

"I was asleep."

"I'm sorry I woke you." He paused. "Would you like me to call back later?"

Remembering how easily he lost track of his surroundings and her, she jumped in with a very hasty, "No."

"Jacob said you wanted me to call."

"That's right. You didn't listen to my presentation. You said you would," she reminded him. "I believe it was something you promised your sister-in-law?"

"I promised Eric because Elaine was getting teary eyed. Pregnant women are emotional."

"I wouldn't know."

Lance hadn't wanted children right away and neither had she. She didn't regret that, not since it would have meant putting any child they'd had through divorce. Still, sometimes when she saw mothers with little babies, she felt like she was missing something pretty important in her life.

"Jacob also said I upset you when I disappeared into my lab." He sounded almost apologetic.

"You forgot about me."

"I didn't mean to."

"Don't worry about it. I'm used to it." Why had she said that? She was still too rummy from sleep to control her tongue.

The tendency that first her family and then her ex-husband had had to dismiss her as of little importance was not something she wanted to share with Simon.

"You're used to being forgotten?"

"Never mind." She scooted into a sitting position, dragging the covers with her to maintain their cocoon of warmth. "I'm not quite awake. I don't know what I'm saying. Are you calling to reschedule our meeting?"

Another pause, longer this time. "Yes."

"Can we meet today?" The sooner she got this situation handled the faster she could put Simon Brant and her strange reaction to him out of her mind and life.

"Yes."

That was promising. "When?"

"I'll be between timed experiments late this afternoon."

She took a second to go back over what she remembered of the ferry schedule. "I can be on the three o'clock ferry."

"I'll see you about four then."

"Right."

"Okay, then."

"Simon..." What did she want to say? She had an inexplicable urge to keep him on the phone with meaningless chatter. "Thank you for calling."

"I woke you up."

"I don't mind, really."

"I'm going to bed. If you call me in about fifteen minutes you can repay me in kind."

"You haven't been to bed yet?" He must be exhausted.

"No."

"I'm not into revenge."

"I'm glad. I can use some sleep."

"Sweet dreams."

"I believe they will be. Until later."

She was foolish to think the words had special meaning, particularly directed at her. She was dynamite in the boardroom, but more like a wet sparkler in the bedroom. No fizzle at all. She stifled a sigh. "Bye." She listened for the click on his end before she hung up.

She wished her dreams were sweet, but too often she had the Amanda-shrinks-to-nothing nightmare or one where she relived walking into Lance's office while he had sex with two people. Only in her dream, they realized she was there and they all laughed at her.

She snuggled down into the covers and thought about Simon. She liked his voice. It was deep and masculine, but smooth too, like well aged scotch. He had very sexy lips. She recalled how they moved when he talked and wondered how they would feel moving on her own.

She was still chastising herself for her totally inappropriate, not to mention incredibly unlikely, thoughts when she slipped back into sleep.

This time when she arrived at Simon's, she didn't give Jacob a chance to harass her. She stopped her car, got out and pushed the button to call him. She barely refrained from a few choice expletives when he informed her that now they had met, a visual I.D. through the car window was sufficient.

Jacob answered the door when she rang the bell and she was immediately concerned that Simon hadn't come out of his lab after all.

"Has he surfaced, Jacob?"

"The boss is not a submarine, Ms. Zachary."

That was a matter of opinion. He certainly disappeared as easily as if he were one, and a stealth one at that. "Is he available?"

"Not strictly speaking, no."

"I knew it!" She dropped her briefcase and glared in disgust at Jacob. "He woke me up before dawn this morning and then he didn't even bother to come out of his lab when he promised he would." She dug through her purse looking for headache medicine. She came across an antacid tablet and popped it for good measure. "No wonder the man isn't married. If he had a wife, she would have killed him by now."

"I did not say that my employer was still in his laboratory."

She stopped trying to get the stupid cap off the small white bottle of pain reliever she'd found and looked up at Jacob. He was looking down his nose at her in the best tradition of a snobbish English butler.

"You play more parts than Jillian!"

Jacob in his superior butler mode didn't deign to answer.

"If Simon's not tied up with his experiments, where is he?" She managed to get the cap off and tossed back two small caplets without water.

"Mr. Brant is on the level below."

Hadn't Simon said something about having his gym down there? "Is he exercising?"

"As I cannot see him at this moment in time, I cannot answer that question with any degree of accuracy."

"Jacob, I bet there's a spear somewhere in Africa with your name on it."

The left corner of his mouth tilted up before he schooled his expression into somber regard. The old faker. "I will escort you below stairs if you would like."

She waved her hand in front of her. "By all means."

All humorous irritation with Jacob faded when Amanda found herself standing inside the open doorway to Simon's gym. Everything faded except the sight of him as his foot repeatedly connecting with the kicking bag hanging from a ceiling beam.

He was fast, faster even than her Tae Bo instructor. His ponytail flipped from side to side like a short black whip.

And graceful. He moved with the lithe agility of a human panther.

He was also almost naked.

Wearing a pair of black Karate pants and nothing else, sweat glistened on the smooth, tan skin of his body. His chest had a neat triangle shaped patch of black hair centered between his male nipples. The dark copper circles drew her eyes as did the rippling muscles below them.

He had a six-pack of abs that most weight lifters would die for. The shoulders of his six-foot-four-inch frame were broad and well-developed, as were the bulging biceps of his arms.

He was devastating.

And she was standing there, ogling him like a star-struck teenager on her first visit to Universal Studios.

"It appears he is exercising, Ms. Zachary."

"As shocking as you may find this to believe, I'd figured that out for myself." She couldn't make herself stop looking at Simon while she spoke to Jacob, which she had no doubt the old man noticed and found highly amusing.

She might find her behavior amusing too, in someone else, but in herself, she found it both unexplainable and embarrassing. Nevertheless, she could not look away.

Without warning, Simon whirled on his bare feet to face her. "Amanda. You came."

Had he doubted she would? "Hello, Simon. I can wait for you upstairs while you finish your workout." Even as she said the words, she regretted them. What if he disappeared while she was waiting for him again?

"There's no need. You can talk while I exercise."

"You must have better concentration than me. I can't even tell someone my name in my Tae Bo class, or I lose count of where I'm at."

"You practice Tae Bo?"

She laughed self-consciously. "Not exactly. I'm taking a class in it, strictly for the exercise. My form is terrible."

"I can help you with that." He eyed her as if already determining how best to work with her.

Just the thought of being in her Lycra leggings and sports bra in the same room with Simon in his loose fitting Karate pants was enough to send her temperature spiking. "Well, uh, thanks for the offer, but I doubt I'll have the opportunity to take you up on it."

One black brow rose. "What's wrong with right now?"

She gave him an incredulous look. "I'm not dressed for it." Her smart ice-yellow suit had not been designed with strenuous exercise in mind.

"Take off your shoes."

What? "No."

"Come on. You can be my dummy. Watch my form and later you can work on emulating it."

"I don't need to watch your form." Watching him stand there doing nothing was bad enough on her equilibrium. "I've got an instructor back home."

"He can't be very good if your form is still choppy. You're too supple not to excel at it."

He was a she, as was the entire class, but Simon didn't need to know that.

"You're mistaken." She'd fought the blasted treadmill for supremacy, how in the world could Simon believe she was supple?

"She moves with innate limberness, doesn't she, Jacob?"

She'd forgotten the eccentric housekeeper.

"Yes, sir. She does."

"Oh, please. This is ridiculous. You're not going to talk me into being your Tae Kwon Do dummy by complimenting me on the way I move."

"You said you wanted to talk to me. I'm offering you the opportunity to do so while I exercise." His gaze shifted to the left of her shoulder. "I'll take care of Ms. Zachary, Jacob."

The other man must have left because Simon's gray gaze returned to her. "Take off your shoes," he repeated.

She stared down at her sensible pumps. She couldn't exactly wear them on Simon's exercise mats, even if she didn't act as his dummy.

She slipped the shoes from her feet and lined them up neatly beside the doorway.

"I think you'd better lose the jacket too."

Simon had several panels of glass open in the wall of windows and there was a nice early summer breeze. "I'm sure it won't be necessary. I'm not going to work up a sweat talking to you."

"That's true, but you'll have more mobility without it." Then he stepped forward and started to help her out of her short-waisted blazer.

It was halfway down her arms before she got enough wits to voice a protest. "I don't need mobility to talk."

"But it will make playing my dummy easier."

She was about to tell him what he could do with the idea of her playing his dummy when the conversation she'd had with her manager the day before came back to her. This was for her job. She could and would do a lot to clinch this deal.

Playing dummy for Simon's Tae Kwon Do workout was neither immoral, nor demeaning. No matter how stressful she found it personally, she couldn't justify saying no simply because she was attracted to him.

She had to drop her briefcase before she could let him pull the jacket the rest of the way off.

Goosebumps broke out on her bare arms. From the breeze, she told herself, not because his fingers had brushed against her skin while pulling off the ice-yellow blazer.

He folded her jacket and laid it on top of her shoes, placing her briefcase neatly beside the pile.

Then he looked at her feet. "Those nylons will make you slide on the mats. You could fall."

"They're not nylons," she said before thinking.

"You wear stockings?" For some reason his voice sounded quite strange when he asked that.

Her gaze flew to his face, but his expression gave nothing away.

"I wear thigh-highs. They're more comfortable than either nylons or a garter and stockings." Shut up. Stop blabbering on. He doesn't want to know about the comfort level of your stay-up stockings.

"Thigh-highs?" There went that quizzical brow again.

"They stay up with a lacy elastic band around your thigh."

"Not my thigh." His deep rich chuckle and flashing white teeth made her insides curl.

"You know what I meant."

He smiled. "Yes."

"Why are we talking about my thigh-highs anyway?"

"You need to take them off."

If he'd looked even the least intrigued by the idea, she would have refused, but he spoke completely dispassionately. It was as if the thought of her taking off her semi-intimate apparel was no more interesting to him than the latest stock figures. In fact, those might have excited him. She'd seen that the market was up just a bit today.

She'd look a fool playing the outraged Victorian maiden when he so clearly saw her as the perfect sparring dummy, but not as a woman.

There was nothing new about that.

The knowledge should not have the power to hurt her anymore, but it did.

While not surprising, it was still lowering to admit that the first man she'd been attracted to in years saw her as nothing more than a nuisance he had to spend time with in order to keep his promise to his cousin.

She turned away from him and reaching up under her skirt, she removed first one stocking and then the other. Air brushed her naked legs like a touch and she shivered again.

Schooling her expression into impassivity, she turned back to Simon.

He wasn't even looking at her. He was drinking out of a water bottle she hadn't noticed earlier.

"I'm ready."

He took another pull off the bottle and then put it down. "Okay. Come stand over here."

He maneuvered her into position with his hands on her shoulders. He was so close, she could smell his body's unique fragrance enhanced by sweat from his workout. Would he smell like that after making love?

She would never know and with that acknowledgement, she slammed the lid on that particular line of thought.

"You stand like this." He grabbed the wrist and elbow of her right hand and put it in a blocking position. "Switch arms when I switch sides of attack. Can you do that?"

"Sure." *Just stop touching me before I do something we'll both regret.*

He looked at her strangely. "Are you okay? I'm not going to hit you. I just want a target to aim for. The sparring routine will be completely non-contact."

She nodded. "You can start."

He did and true to his word, though he came within a breath of touching her with each blow, he never made contact. They'd been working out for about five minutes when he reminded her she was supposed to be talking.

"Right. First, I think you need to consider the merger in terms of future growth rather than the minimal cost to the current pool of employees."

Simon didn't respond, he just let her talk. Not by the flicker of an eyelash did he indicate if he was even listening.

Every once in a while, he would change her position to facilitate his workout. He did it silently, but regardless, each time she lost her train of thought and had to search her mind for the point she'd been making.

"You need to change your blocking arm faster."

She stopped in mid-spate while telling him about the projected increase in market share the combined companies would have. "What?"

"I need you to be faster changing which arm you're blocking me with."

So, she increased her speed and found herself moving into basic Tae Bo blocking positions. Pretty soon she was panting between words and sweat was trickling down her back, making the silk of her white tank top stick to her.

"Okay, now let's work on your form."

Without knowing how it happened, she was surrounded completely by Simon with her back brushing against his chest. He took hold of each of her arms and put her into position. "Relax, Amanda. Let your body move with mine."

She was really glad her back was to him and they were facing the windows with a view of the water, not the mirrored wall that would have reflected their tableau with entirely too much realism. Because the thought of her body moving with his had her nipples puckering painfully. Both layers of her silk top and bra were not adequate to hide the evidence and she prayed he would stay behind her.

She tried to concentrate on doing as he'd said and following his movements with the same fluidity his limbs enjoyed.

"This isn't necessary, you know."

He didn't answer, but one big hand landed on her thigh, the fingers exerting pressure for her leg to move into position.

She'd wanted fluidity of movement, but she was in danger of losing control over her muscles as her bones literally turned to water. Her body wanted to melt into a puddle of sexual need on the floor mat below her feet. Only sheer force of will kept her knees from buckling as his fingers moved against her thigh.

Oh, mother! She'd never been this excited, not even in the act of copulation with Lance. And Simon wasn't even trying to turn her on. He was teaching her form, for Heaven's sake.

She stumbled on her stance and Simon's hand slid toward her inner thigh. Only the fact she was wearing a straight skirt that had been stretched taut by her current position stopped his fingers from going between her legs. Nevertheless, his fingertips brushed the very top of her mound and three layers of fabric did not dull the impact on her senses.

She yelped and twisted out of his arms, almost running in her desire to put some distance between them.

"What's the matter? Do you have a cramp?"

Crossing her arms over the telling evidence prominent on her over-generous breasts, she shook her head. He didn't even know what was bothering her. That knowledge, more than any other had her crossing the room and yanking her jacket on. "You're done with your workout, right?"

He nodded. "But we still need to work on your form."

She slid into her shoes without putting on her stockings. "I'd rather finish giving you my presentation on the merger."

"All right, but I had planned to take a short swim. Would you like to join me?"

Not in this lifetime. How did he expect her to swim? Naked? As her body exhibited further evidence of increasing arousal, she chastised herself. Bad thought, Amanda, bad, bad, thought. "No, but I wouldn't mind taking a shower." She wished she had some clean clothes with her. She could feel her perspiration not yet dry on her body.

Simon walked to a small speaking unit on the wall and pressed a button. "Jacob?"

"Yes, sir," came the disembodied voice of Simon's housekeeper.

"Amanda got a little sweaty playing my dummy and she wants to take a shower. I think you two might be similar in size. Could you dig up some clean clothes for her to put on when she's done?"

If Simon had asked, she would have refused the offer of clothing, but he hadn't asked. Knowing he considered her five-foot-four-inch curvy frame on par in size with his housekeeper's masculine, but wiry five-foot-nine, did nothing for her sense of self-confidence.

She could almost feel the sting of one of Lance's love pats on her thigh and hear the words that invariably accompanied it. "Did you get your exercise in this morning, hon?" He'd always managed to make it seem like he doubted the possibility.

When she'd called him on it, he'd told her she was reading things into his words and gone into psychobabble about how damaging that was to the communication of free ideas in a marriage. He'd had the gall to tell her that her reactions made him feel intimidated about being open with her.

She allowed herself a small smirk, remembering she'd told him the same thing about his reaction after she destroyed the big screen television.

"Amanda?"

She looked up and realized that Simon had been saying something to her that she hadn't caught. "I'm sorry. I missed that."

He looked at her quizzically, but she blanked her expression.

"Jacob will show you to the guest room shower and bring you some clothes to wear. I'll see you upstairs in the great room after I've had my swim and shower."

"You won't disappear into your lab again, will you?"

Color burnished his taut cheekbones, but he didn't make any promises. "I don't think so."

She glared at him. "Simon, you're a grown man. Are you, or are you not going to meet me in the great room after your swim? If you aren't, I'd rather go home and shower."

"I have every intention of joining you for dinner after taking my swim."

She picked up her briefcase and shoved her thigh-highs into it. "Okay."

Jacob had materialized at the door and she turned to follow him. "I'll see you shortly, Simon."

He didn't answer and she refused to let that worry her.

His interpersonal communication skills weren't that great, but she'd gotten through at least a third of her presentation already. She could easily outline the last two-thirds over dinner.

If he made it to dinner.

Chapter Five

She wasn't going to wear a pair of bulky men's sweatpants.

This might not be Southern California, but it was early summer and the weather was warm. She had no intention of sweating it out in the thick fabric. If a niggling sense of feminine pride refused to be seen dressed like someone's dotty old uncle that was all right, too.

Tossing the pants aside, she picked up the charcoal gray cotton T-shirt Jacob had leant her and pulled it on. The dark color prevented her lack of a bra from being indecent. She didn't like putting on the same pair of underwear after a shower, but she consoled herself with the knowledge that it had been the top half of her body perspiring during the workout.

She tugged her skirt up over her hips and zipped it, before turning to look in the full-length mirror.

The T-shirt didn't look too bad with the skirt, but tucked in, it outlined her breasts a little too smartly. She pulled it out and the hem fell loosely around her hips. She bit her lip. That was better, but her hair was a bedraggled mess. She'd used a shower cap to keep it somewhat dry. However, that had only aided in ruining the style.

Its customary sleek French twist was coming apart and several hanks of hair hung down her neck. She pulled out the pins she used to secure the bun and then gave it a vigorous brushing with the brush Jacob had left for her.

She didn't have any hairspray to smooth the style back into place, so she used a hair tie from her purse to secure it into a high ponytail on the back of her head. The ends of her hair brushed between her shoulder blades, but the clip kept if off her neck.

Foregoing her shoes, she left them in a neat pile with the rest of her things in the bathroom. She could get them later.

She could not imaging attending a business meeting with anyone but Simon Brant barefoot and in borrowed clothes. She could not imagine playing sparring dummy for a Tae Kwon Do session for anyone else either. Life around him was as full of eccentricities as he was.

She liked it.

She made her way to the great room, her feet drawing her to the wall of windows of their own accord. It was an irresistible view, the ocean looking both infinite and ever changing.

She pressed her hand against the glass, not worried about leaving prints because of her recent shower. It was warm from the sun, its hard, smooth surface a tactile pleasure for her. How long would Simon's swim take?

Movement to her right caught her attention and she watched as Jacob set the table outside for dinner. He crossed the deck and disappeared into the house to her left.

She was still standing at the window when Simon came in.

"You should see the view when there's a storm."

Muscles tensed and her lungs seemed to contract. All this because the man had walked into the room? She needed to get out more. Thinking back over the dearth of dates since her divorce, she amended that to she needed to get out, period.

She forced herself to respond to what he'd said instead of her reaction to him. "I would probably be nervous. Having the only thing between me and the elements a thin wall of glass."

"It's not thin."

That's right. He'd told her it was reinforced. "It's still glass."

"I suppose you'd be more comfortable if there were drapes to draw across the windows so you could block out what is beyond them." He didn't sound condescending, just thoughtful.

And he'd been right. She shrugged. "It's not my house, so it hardly matters." She turned to face him.

His black hair was still wet and though it was slicked back from his face, he hadn't confined the shoulder length strands into a ponytail. He was wearing a pair of jeans and nothing else. Didn't the man ever wear a shirt? With his dark skin tone, he looked like a tribal warrior.

"Did you enjoy your swim?"

It was his turn to shrug and the naked skin on his chest rippled with his muscle's movement. "I don't swim for pleasure. Doing the laps is the most efficient way to end my workout."

"You're not going to convince me you don't enjoy your Martial Arts sessions. You're way too proficient just to do them for exercise. What color belt are you anyway?"

She'd be surprised if he wasn't a black belt.

"Does it matter?" He was looking at her like a bug on a pin, all scientific curiosity and something else that could have been mistaken for male interest if she didn't know better.

"Not really. I'm just making conversation." For some reason, she found the fact that his social skills were not on par with his other abilities rather endearing. "It would be polite for you to answer the question, unless you have some reason for not wanting to do so."

Two thin streaks of red burnished his high cheekbones, indicating he was aware he'd blundered in the politeness arena and was actually bothered by the fact. "I am a Grand Master Black Belt."

"That's pretty impressive."

"Is it?" He seemed genuinely interested in her answer, the storm cloud gray of his eyes reflecting curiosity.

"Yes. I'm impressed anyway. It takes a lot of self-discipline and work to make it that far."

He appeared to contemplate that. "There wasn't anything else to do."

"What do you mean?"

"I started studying Tae Kwon Do with my mother's uncle when I was four years old. I was already in school by then with children that were older and bigger than me. I didn't have playmates, so studying with my great-uncle gave me something to do."

It was hard to imagine a time when he'd been smaller than his peers. He was such a big man now. "Eric said you were a child prodigy."

"Yes."

"Was it hard always being younger than everyone around you?"

An expression that hinted at deep loneliness and pain crossed his masculine features before he nodded briefly.

"Jacob has put dinner on the table."

The abrupt change in topic jolted her.

He stepped around her and pushed the button that slid the glass panel open. "After you." He brought his right hand out with an Old World flourish.

She smiled and walked by him, shocked when she felt a tug on her ponytail.

"I like this. It's not so stuffy." He let go immediately, so she didn't take umbrage.

She looked down at her attire and lack of shoes. "I'd say we're both as far from stuffy as it's possible to get right now." But something twinged inside her at his description of her usual mode of dress. He made it sound like she dressed like an old lady, but though her clothes were conservative in style, she'd always tried to maintain a certain level of chic.

Admittedly, she did not wear anything even remotely sexy or excessively feminine.

"That gray looks good on you. You've got such pale skin for your hair color. It's a fascinating contrast."

She let him seat her before answering. "I take after my great grandmother and fascinating isn't how most Southern Californians view my pasty white skin tone."

"You make it sound as if you look ill and you don't."

"I don't tan. I burn. To most Southern Californians, that is an illness." She laughed lightly, making a joke of it, but she could still remember the sessions in the tanning beds trying to cultivate the right look in her teens.

"People who sunbathe frequently are at higher risk for skin cancer. Their skin ages prematurely as well."

She gave a speaking look to his naked torso. "I appreciate that now, as an adult. As a teenager, I didn't really care. I wanted to look like everyone else." Even if she'd tanned, she still would have had more curves than most of the other girls.

He looked down at himself and then back at her. "I like the feel of the sun on my skin after spending so much time inside my lab, but I don't lay around in the sun for hours on end cultivating a tan."

She looked at his olive skin tone. "You don't need to."

"Neither do you."

That was nice of him to say and maybe he did find pasty white a fascinating skin tone. "It doesn't matter. I gave up trying to tan years ago."

"Good."

She smiled.

"I know what it feels like not to fit in, but trying to be like everyone around you doesn't work."

"Your looks weren't your problem." He was too gorgeous.

He didn't preen under the compliment like so many of the plastic men from her Southern California world would have. "It was my age," he said, repeating what he'd said earlier.

"Did it ever get any easier?"

"I thought it did, for a while when I was a teenager."

"What happened?" Would he slap her down for prying into things that were none of her business, that were further, totally unrelated to why she was there? She couldn't help the interest that burned inside her to know him better.

"I tried doing what the adults around me did."

"That's pretty typical for a teenager."

"Yeah, well most teens try to act like adults with each other. I was surrounded by people several years older than me and light years ahead of me in life experience."

"You got hurt."

"You could say that. I learned some important truths in the process though."

She didn't push for more, but maybe one day he would tell her. Then she chided herself. What was she thinking? Once this merger went through, she'd never see him again.

"Is that why you live on an island now and work at home, so you don't have to worry about fitting in?"

"Maybe. I've never thought about it, but what I do could not be done in a nine to five environment."

"No, I don't suppose it could. Did you always want to be an inventor?"

Jacob materialized, putting a bowl of chilled mango soup in front of each of them. Then he left.

Simon tasted the soup, smiled and took another bite before answering. "I've always hungered to discover new things, new ways to accomplish the same tasks, and more efficient use of the resources at hand."

"That sounds a lot broader than new computer design."

"Computers have always played a central role. It's only natural considering who my father was, but I experiment in other areas as well."

"What are you working on right now?" She tasted the soup. It was ambrosia. Creamy and smooth, it had a hint of coconut flavor as well as peach mixed with the mango.

"One of my current projects is wind powered fuel cells as an alternate form of energy."

Of course he wouldn't work on one thing at a time.

"Any success?"

"Mild."

"What's a fuel cell?" She knew what a windmill was. There were hundreds of them in the California desert. However, she'd never heard of a fuel cell.

"It's like a super-efficient battery run on hydrogen and air. When you need the energy, you run the gases through the layers of the cell with one of the byproducts being electricity."

"What are the other byproducts?" She remembered that Nuclear power had been touted as a clean source of energy and look at the problems the waste by-products had made for the power-plants.

"If hydrogen and air are used for the fuel, the secondary byproduct is pure drinking water. Hydrogen is the most abundant chemical in the universe and preliminary tests have shown the fuel cell to be at least twice as efficient as other energy sources. And there are no moving parts to wear out."

He was so enthusiastic, he was positively chatty.

"It sounds too good to be true."

"There are still a lot of variables that need to be dealt with before it will be a viable alternative for mass energy use."

"And you're working on those variables right now in your lab?"

"Me and probably a hundred other alternative energy source enthusiasts."

She laid down her spoon and stretched her bare toes toward the warm sun. Simon had led her to a seat on the side of the table shaded by an umbrella. "When do you find time to develop prototypes for Brant Computers?"

"I'm not responsible for all prototype development."

"But I thought you were the top design engineer at Brant." She was sure that was how Eric had explained Simon's role in the company.

"I think my title is something like Design Engineer Fellow."

She smiled. "You don't know?"

Gray eyes bore into hers. "It doesn't matter. I do what I do because it is what I like to do."

"But you do design for Brant Computers?"

"I bring new technology to proof of concept phase. Sometimes that means creating a working prototype, sometimes not. Once I turn it over to the design team, I'm pretty much out of it unless they get stuck."

"I hear your design team is one of the top in the industry."

"We like to think so."

"Extant Corporation has some of the most innovative design engineers in the country as well. Can you imagine what the two could do if their resources were pooled?" Surely that was one of the benefits to the merger that would appeal to him.

He frowned. "Forcing the two teams to work together could just as easily destroy the effectiveness of both."

"Why should it do that?"

"New product design is a creative process."

He'd finished his soup before she realized he wasn't going to add anything else. She waited until Jacob had taken away the bowls and laid down plates with their main course before speaking again. "So why does it being a creative process mean it would be bad to bring the two teams together?"

"I don't know that it would be bad. It's a possibility."

"But why is it a possibility? I would think the more brain power the better."

"Haven't you ever heard the old saying, too many cooks spoil the broth?"

"Simon, we're not talking about cooking here."

"But we are talking about the possibility of adding too much of a good thing to the mix."

"What exactly are you saying?"

"One of the reasons I work here is that I have complete creative freedom. That makes it possible for me to try things I wouldn't or couldn't in a corporate environment. Other people don't always spark creativity, sometimes they stifle it. Maybe they've tried something similar before and it didn't work."

"But that could happen in the groups now."

"That's true."

He did it again. Went silent.

"Is that all you're going to say?"

"For now."

Jacob came out bearing a tray with two crystal dishes filled with fresh strawberries topped by heavy cream and a mint garnish.

She gave the old man a dazzling smile just to confound him. "Dinner was fantastic, Jacob. Thank you. And dessert looks sinfully delicious."

"Nothing sinful in fresh berries, missy." He refilled their wine glasses before leaving, the dishes from dinner now on the tray in his hands.

The strawberries were so juicy, they slipped across her tongue with a burst of sweet sensation. "Mmmm," she hummed with pleasure as she took another bite.

She looked up to find Simon watching her, a curious expression on his face. "They're locally grown."

"They're yummy." She scooped another berry out with her spoon, making sure it was coated with the heavy cream. As she went to put it in her mouth, she realized Simon was watching her with disconcerting intensity.

Were his eyes really trained on her lips, or was that her imagination running away with her good sense? She was so attracted to him, she wanted to believe the attraction was reciprocal, but he'd done nothing so far to indicate it was.

More likely he was wondering why a woman with her figure hadn't foregone dessert. If she'd been with her parents, or her ex-husband she would have.

"Aren't you going to eat?" she asked, waving her now empty spoon toward his crystal bowl of fruit.

"I'll eat it later." He looked at the hi-tech watch on his wrist and grimaced. "I need to check on my timed experiment."

"But we're not done discussing..." She didn't finish the sentence, seeing as how she was already talking to his back.

"Simon Brant, someone needs to teach you some manners."

He stopped at the door and turned. His expression registered a vague sort of chagrin. "I'm sorry, but three days of experiments will be wasted if I don't go to my lab right now."

At least he'd stopped to explain. She nodded, but didn't bother to ask if he'd be back down. He wouldn't.

She allowed herself the luxury of finishing her dessert in peaceful silence, the summer evening air cooling around her and bringing out goosebumps on her skin.

"The last ferry sails in thirty minutes." Jacob's voice came from behind her.

She turned to face him. "I guess I'd better be on it."

"Unless you want to spend the night."

"I can't see myself borrowing your pajamas."

The older man shrugged. "Suit yourself, but if you're wanting to talk to the boss, you'd do better to move in here than try to catch him like you've been doing."

She laughed. Right. Move into Simon's house, just so she could be there to talk to him when he surfaced from his lab.

Three days later, she wasn't laughing. She'd called Jacob each day, leaving a message for Simon to call. According the housekeeper, Simon hadn't been out of his lab in all that time.

He certainly hadn't called her.

When the phone rang, she couldn't help hoping it was him.

"Hello."

"How's it going, doll?"

"Jillian! Your new story line is to die for."

Jillian's husky laughter echoed across the phone lines. "Yeah, ain't it just? Even the Grand Dame complimented me on yesterday's takes." The words fairly gurgled with happiness.

"I'm so glad, sweetie. I wish my job was going so well."

"The resident geek still giving you trouble?"

"Simon's not a geek." He was way too sexy to fit that label. "He's a genius. He's also a Grand Master black belt in Tae Kwon Do."

"You're kidding me. The computer nerd is a Chuck Norris wannabe?"

"Simon isn't a wannabe anything. He's completely his own man."

Silence crackled for several seconds.

"You sound really impressed by this guy."

"I am. I'm also totally frustrated."

"Are we talking work frustration here, or something more exciting and totally alien to your lifestyle?"

If she said both, Jillian would be on the next flight out of LAX for Seattle. "I still haven't given him the complete presentation, much less convinced him of the advisability of merging with Extant and I've met with the man three times."

"That does not sound like your usually super-efficient self. Are you sure there's nothing else going on here I should know about?"

"Positive." She didn't want Jillian deciding Simon was the answer to Amanda's lack of a social life. "It's just that he's so wrapped up in his work, it's hard to get more than five minutes of his time. I had to play his Tae Kwon Do sparring dummy to get him to listen to the marketing estimates."

"You played a sparring dummy?" Shock laced Jillian's voice. "I don't believe it."

"In my skirt and blouse no less."

"No way!"

"Yes. You know how important this is to me, Jill. I'd do anything to get this merger tied up."

"And what kind of anything does Simon want you to do?" The suggestive tone of Jillian's voice made Amanda laugh.

"With an eccentric inventor, your guess is as good as mine. I was totally disbelieving when he wanted me to play the dummy. He even insisted on working on my Tae Bo form."

"He did, huh? I gotta tell ya, Amanda, things are sounding pretty interesting around there."

"That's one word for it."

"Have you considered camping on his doorstep until you get his attention?"

Amanda didn't laugh like she knew Jill expected her to. "I'm thinking about moving into his house for the duration."

Jillian sucked in a shocked breath. "Tell me your kidding."

"It was his housekeeper's idea and I think it has merit. How else am I going to get this deal closed?"

"You mean Simon won't mind you just moving in?"

"I don't know, but at this point, I'm willing to risk it. Daniel has been calling non-stop wanting a report on my progress. He's threatened to come up here. If I don't do something, I'm going to get taken off the negotiations."

Telling Jillian she was moving in with Simon and doing it were very different animals, Amanda discovered the next day as she nerved herself to press the red button on Simon's gate callbox.

"Hello, Ms. Zachary."

"Hello, Jacob. Could you release the gate, please?"

"You got an appointment?" He was back to playing belligerent-butler again.

"No."

"Mr. Brant invite you?"

"No."

"You got a reason for coming?"

"Yes, Jacob. Now, are you going to open the gate?"

"Maybe."

She was on to his tricks and she wasn't going to lose her cool this time. "Open the gate, Jacob."

Then before he could reply, she pressed the up button for her window and just waited. He kept her waiting for a full minute before the black iron gate slid open.

She rang the doorbell a minute later, her laptop, briefcase, suitcase and toiletries bag stacked beside her on the porch.

The door opened to reveal not Jacob, but Simon and he looked terrible. His eyes were bloodshot, he had several days of stubble on his face and his skin had the pallor of a sick man.

"Amanda." He shook his head. "Was I expecting you?"

She stepped inside and laid her hand on his arm before thinking. "Simon, are you all right? You look ill."

"I'm not sick. Just tired."

"Hasn't slept more than a few minutes at a time since you was here last." Jacob's irascible voice reached her from further down the hall.

"That's terrible. Simon, you need to be in bed."

He wasn't listening. His focus was on something behind her. "You brought a suitcase."

She sucked in air and courage with the same breath. "Jacob invited me to stay awhile. I'm taking him up on it."

Simon craned his neck around to look at Jacob. "You invited Amanda to stay?" He sounded so confused, she felt sorry for him. He was too tired to understand what was going on, but he wasn't too tired to toss her out on her ear if Jacob gave lie to her bold claim.

"I may have said something to that effect."

She let out the small breath she'd been holding.

Simon stepped back. "Come in then. Jacob, will you see that Ms. Zachary's things are put in the guest room?"

Jacob's wizened gaze caught hers as she passed him and he winked.

It surprised her so much that she stumbled and crashed into Simon. Even tired, he had the reflexes of a trained warrior. He caught her and set her back on her feet without taking so much as an extra breath. "You okay?"

"Yes. Thanks. I'm clumsy today."

Simon covered his mouth and yawned.

"You need to go to bed, Simon."

"I'm hungry. I think Jacob's going to make me something to eat. I don't remember." He was so rummy, his words were slurring.

"I made some beef stew. It's simmering on the stove. Ms. Zachary, you could see the boss gets some while I'm busy with your things."

"No problem. Come on, Simon." She led him to the kitchen where she could smell the savory aroma of simmering stew and recently baked bread.

Simon sat down at the small kitchen table and she served him in a bowl Jacob had left sitting on the counter. She also sliced and buttered some of the bread.

Simon ate in silence while she watched over him like a broody hen. He really did look awful. There was no way they were going to have any sort of intelligent conversation before the man had gotten a good night's rest.

He finished and laid down the spoon. "Can I get you anything, a glass of wine maybe?" he asked her politely, just as if he wasn't practically dead on his feet.

"No, thank you. Go to bed, Simon."

He nodded and stood, swaying slightly on his feet.

She rushed forward and put one arm around his waist. He draped his arm over her shoulder, but didn't put his whole weight against her. For which she was grateful. He let her lead him out of the kitchen.

"Which way is your bedroom?"

He waved his arm to the left. It didn't take her long to find the stairway. They managed to get up it without mishap, but when they reached Simon's bedroom he seemed to lose steam all at once. He went tumbling toward the oversize king bed and took her with him. They landed in a tangle of arms and legs with Simon's body half over hers.

He didn't move.

"Simon."

Nothing.

She fought her head clear of his heavy arm and looked up at his face. His eyes were closed. He was asleep.

No problem. She only had to slide out from under him and he'd never even know she'd been there.

She levered her arm out from where he had it pinned beneath his chest and pushed against him, trying to scoot backwards at the same time. His eyes opened and she fought between relief and embarrassment.

"Uh, Simon..."

He smiled, the beatific smile of a very happy child, said her name and then closed his eyes again.

Without moving.

She pressed firmly against his chest. He said something indecipherable and moved, dragging her into his body like the lover she wasn't. When he was still again, she was wrapped firmly in his arms, his face buried in the curve of her neck and his heavy thigh trapping both her legs.

Chapter Six

She should absolutely get up.

Right this minute.

But she didn't want to move. Simon's breath warmed her throat while the feel of his muscular body wrapped around her gave a sense of warmth and belonging she'd longed for all of her life. It was that sense that had her trying to peel out of Simon's arms. It was way too dangerous.

She wasn't any good at the man-woman thing and if she let herself fall for Simon, she was going to end up hurt.

Badly.

When it came to relationships, she always lost.

She was here for the sake of her career, not to put her damaged heart at risk again.

Unfortunately, even in sleep, Simon was strong. Too strong for her to get away from.

She tried shaking his shoulder to wake him. "Simon. Wake up. You've got to let go."

His face nuzzled more firmly into her neck and his hand shifted until it was cupping her right breast.

Her brain short-circuited while her body started pulsing with unfamiliar desire.

"Simon!"

His hand squeezed and her nipple went rock-hard. She gasped.

He squeezed again and darned if it wasn't with just the right amount of pressure.

Okay. She wasn't going to try to wake him up again. At the rate they were going, he'd be inside of her before she ever got him out of his comatose state. And she'd be loving it.

Which made her wicked and pathetic. For surely only a wicked woman would consider taking advantage of a man's actions while he was sleeping and only a pathetic one would need to.

Maybe if she laid there until he went into a really deep sleep, his muscles would relax enough for her to extricate herself from his arms.

The hand on her breast was heavy and she was tempted to pretend for a little bit. To pretend he meant it to be there. To pretend a gorgeous, sexy man like Simon found her desirable. It should be too much of a stretch for even her imagination. It wasn't. Not with his arms around her and his hard, masculine body pressed all along her side.

Fantasizing was risky.

She might start believing her own delusions.

She had to get her mind off the way it felt to be in Simon's unconscious arms.

She stared up at the ceiling. Not a lot of inspiration there. Simon had a ceiling fan. She wondered if he liked to lay naked on his bed and let the gentle air brush over him like she did. She preferred the fan to running the air conditioner, except on the hottest days.

As things started happening in her body, things like swelling and moistening, she realized wondering about Simon's naked sleeping habits was a bad idea.

She let her gaze roam around the room, at least as much as she was able without turning more than her head. The stark simplicity of Oriental design was in here too, but so was Simon's love of hi-tech. The bed and matching bedroom suite had been designed in molded metal with a flat finish. It didn't look like office furniture gone bad, but rather sleek and almost soothingly simple.

The headboard and footboard on the bed were slatted with horizontal bars. She'd never seen a bed like it.

An image of her lying on the bed, naked but for a silk nothing of a nightgown with her hands tied to the headboard popped into her mind. Simon leaned above her, his hands teasing her body while he whispered shocking things in her ear.

She groaned. Simon's leg insinuated itself between hers, his thigh pressing against the apex of her thigh and the image in her head exploded in favor of tormenting reality.

She had to get out of this bed. She made her body go completely motionless and concentrated on breathing as quietly as possible. Anything not to jar Simon into further movement.

She snuggled into the delicious warmth of her bed, fighting consciousness and trying to cling to the sweetness of her dream. It had been so real, she could still smell the masculine scent of her lover, still feel the strength of his arms around her, the erotic pleasure of his legs twined with hers in the aftermath of loving.

She shifted one leg and fancied she could feel denim rub against the smooth sheerness of her stockings.

Stockings?

She wasn't wearing stockings in her dream. She was nake—Oh, my gosh! Her eyes flew open to a patch of dark blue.

It was a shirt and the shirt covered a male chest.

Simon.

Her head snapped back.

He was still asleep.

That was the only good news she could discern as she came fully alert with a mental bump of huge magnitude. Her legs were indeed twisted together with his, right up to their thighs. This was possible because her skirt was twisted up to her hips, exposing the tops of her stay-ups.

Somehow several buttons had come undone on her once crisp white blouse and Simon's hand was inside, resting against her silk-clad breast. Her hand was underneath his untucked T-shirt, pressing against his well-defined abs.

If he woke up right now, she would have a heart attack and die of humiliation.

With all the caution of a thief leaving the scene of a crime, she gently withdrew her hand from under his shirt. His body shuddered in sleep as her fingertips brushed along his skin and she was terrified he'd waken. He didn't.

He was sleeping too deeply.

Thank you, God.

She'd been right that his muscles would relax in sleep. Moving slow centimeter by centimeter, she withdrew from his embrace until her body was no longer touching him at any point. Heaving a sigh of relief, she rolled onto her back and only registered her nearness to the edge of the bed a second before landing on the floor with a solid thump.

"Not a real graceful way to get out of bed, if you don't mind my saying so, Ms. Zachary."

Jacob? Jacob was here? How much had he seen?

She scooted to her feet in a flurry of movement, yanking her crumpled skirt down over her exposed legs.

"Thought you were going to use the guest room."

She could feel heat scorching into her cheeks. "I am. This was a mistake. He... I..." How did she explain the events that had led up to her sleeping in Simon's arms?

"I don't pry into the boss's private affairs."

"For goodness sake, we are not having an affair. I was trying to help him to bed. He fell asleep with me under him. I mean. He fell. We fell. I couldn't get away. I guess I fell asleep waiting for him to relax."

A lot of falling had gone on.

"Whatever you say, Ms. Zachary. I came to see if you wanted dinner."

"Um, that would be great." She surreptitiously did up several buttons on her blouse, keeping her body angled away from Jacob's too knowing gaze. "I'll just go change my clothes."

She was a wrinkled mess and maybe a return to her usual put together appearance would harbinger a return to sanity as well.

One could only hope.

Eric Brant called after dinner. As soon as Amanda heard his voice, her stomach cramped with worry over his reaction to her coming to stay with his cousin.

"He let you move in? Just like that?" Eric sounded stunned.

"It was Jacob's idea," she defended herself.

"But Simon hardly ever has company and now he's letting a complete stranger live in his house. I have to tell you, Amanda, this is the strangest business deal I've ever been involved in."

"Simon doesn't do things like normal people," she said, throwing his own words from before back at Eric.

"But he doesn't do stuff like this either."

"It was the only way I could think to catch him often enough to convince him of the merits of the merger."

Eric's laughter jangled against her already stretched nerves. "Well, I've got to hand it you, Amanda. You've got real dedication to getting the job done. I only wish my junior executives were half so ambitious and creative."

She warmed under the praise. "Thank you." She hoped her boss, Daniel, agreed with Eric.

Amanda popped the green stem out of the strawberry and tossed it in the waste bin to the left of her on the deck. She dropped the berry in the ceramic bowl and picked up another one. She'd eaten breakfast an hour ago, but the juicy berries were still tempting. The only thing that stopped her popping one in her mouth was the certainty that Jacob would walk out on the deck at that exact moment and catch her.

She wouldn't put it past him to be watching her from the kitchen just so he could do that very thing.

She hadn't seen Simon since practically running from his room the previous afternoon. She didn't even know if he'd woken up from his restorative sleep yet and she didn't have the nerve to ask Jacob. Not after what he had witnessed in Simon's bedroom.

"That doesn't look like the normal occupation for a junior executive from Silicon Valley."

She looked up at the sound of Simon's deep voice and smiled, albeit a bit nervously. She didn't know how much he would remember from her sojourn in his bed. Not that it hadn't been pretty tame as sojourns go, but since she hadn't been in any man's bed in over two years and hadn't done anything worth mentioning in a bed in more than three, she was still uncomfortable about facing Simon.

"Hi. Get enough sleep?"

"I did."

He certainly looked it. His eyes were clear and he'd taken the time to shave. He was shirtless again, this time wearing a pair of cut-off denim shorts. Her gaze slid to his muscualar legs with their light covering of black hair and stayed there for way longer than was politic. She forced herself to meet his eyes again.

They glinted with something she couldn't interpret and a funny half-smile had formed on his lips. "I need some exercise. I came out to see if you wanted to work out with me again."

"You mean play your sparring dummy?"

"I thought we could go through a couple TKD routines."

It actually sounded like a great idea. Her body was craving a workout and she hadn't quite nerved herself to ask Jacob if he thought Simon would mind if she used the pool.

"I'm almost done with these and then I'd love to."

"How did Jacob talk you into doing that?"

"It wasn't hard. I wanted an excuse to sit outside and he gave me one."

"Is he making jam?"

"That's what he said. I've never seen anyone make homemade jam before. He told me I could watch later."

"Your mom didn't do any canning?"

"Are you kidding? My mother's idea of domesticity is having the local maid's service number memorized."

He laughed. "My mom wasn't much better. She was too involved with her painting to want to do much around the house, but she still managed to make it feel like a home."

Then she'd been a world ahead of Amanda's mother who had always managed to make her daughter feel like an intruder the perfectly decorated and maintained California mansion she'd grown up in.

"What was she like?" she asked him.

"Warm. Alive. Fun. She smiled a lot. She could make me and Dad laugh until our sides ached."

"It must have hurt so much to lose her."

"It did. Everything changed."

"Your dad probably took it really hard."

"He found comfort in his work."

"What about you?"

Shrugging those incredible shoulders, he frowned. "I followed my dad's example I guess."

"You were only ten years old, you said." She couldn't fathom a child getting lost in his work.

"And close to graduating high school. Between my experiments and my studies, I got by."

And learned how to shut out the rest of the world in the process.

She finished hulling the last berry and wiped her hands on the wet tea towel Jacob had left with her. "I'll just go throw on something I can do kicks in."

Simon slipped out of his shorts and pulled on a pair of dobok pants. The loose fitting bottoms designed for Martial Arts would be better at concealing his reaction to Amanda when they worked out. He was still reeling from the vivid dreams he'd had of her while sleeping off his three-day-long work binge. They'd been so damned real, he could have sworn her scent clung to his pillow when he woke up.

A cold shower had helped calm his raging hormones, but seeing Amanda dressed in a tank top and jeans had sent his libido into orbit all over again. No wonder the woman hid herself in those boxy looking suits. If she dressed in anything form fitting at work, none of her male colleagues would get any work done.

Not with those curves.

Funny, but he could swear he knew the weight of her breasts in his hands. Wishful thinking, no doubt.

He ran into Jacob as he headed down to the gym.

"Dinner at six."

"Okay, but we haven't even had lunch yet."

"Warning you in advance."

"You mean it's not stew tonight." Jacob occasionally warned Simon when he planned to make a meal that would spoil waiting for Simon to come out of his lab.

"Right. Thought I'd make something special for our guest."

Simon was still having a difficult time believing Jacob had invited her. "Did you really ask her to stay?"

"Told her staying would be the only way to catch you long enough to talk."

Simon didn't want to discuss the merger, but he didn't mind spending more time with the intriguing woman. She was such a mixture of confidence and reticence. She was completely confident in her guise of career woman, but he got the sense that when it came to simply being a woman, she was not nearly so sanguine.

"I assume you entertained her while I slept the afternoon and night away."

"You did a fair job of that yourself, from what I saw."

Simon stopped walking and turned to Jacob. "What do you mean?"

"Came upstairs to check on you. Make sure you made it to the bed all right."

Simon had been known to collapse on the floor in sleep after a work fest like the one he'd just finished. "And?"

"And you were wrapped around a living, breathing Teddy Bear."

"What?"

"She said you fell on her when you got up to your room."

Simon didn't remember anything past the vague recollection of Amanda helping him up the stairs. "I fell on her?"

"Yeah. You were snug as bugs and both sleeping when I came to check the first time."

He couldn't believe it. He'd slept with her, collapsed on top of her in fact. No wonder she'd seemed a little nervous out on the deck. He wondered why she hadn't said anything.

"I assume you checked again."

Jacob's smile was smug. "I thought she might have wanted some dinner."

"I'm sure she appreciated your concern. Was she still asleep?" He wasn't sure he understood how she'd fallen asleep in the first place. It seemed very out of character for a woman with her professional demeanor.

Evidently he'd drug her down to the bed when he fell asleep practically standing up, but why hadn't she gotten up immediately?

"She was trying to get out of bed without waking you up."

"Obviously, she succeeded." He hadn't even known she'd been in his bed.

"Some might say you succeeded too."

The cryptic comments were getting irritating. "In what way?"

"Had your hand inside her blouse. Her unbuttoned blouse. I don't think she minded though. She had her hand up under your shirt."

The scene Jacob was describing had Simon almost bent over double with desire. He'd had his hand on her breast and had been too unconscious to appreciate it.

"Could have been worse, sir."

"How is that Jacob?"

"You've been known to strip completely naked when you fall asleep in your clothes like that."

Simon positioned Amanda in the correct position for the poomse's third step. "Snap your arm like this." He moved her through the correct motion.

"Okay. I think I've got it."

They went through the entire form together and he cursed the clever mind that had come up with this idea. Watching her body move through the poomse's steps after what Jacob had told him, was driving Simon right to the edge of his control.

His hand had been on her breast.

One of the two fleshy mounds that moved so enticingly under the oversized T-shirt she'd put on to exercise in. She probably thought the thigh-length shirt masked her body's attributes adequately. She was wrong.

The Lycra shorts came down about two inches below the hem, leaving the rest of her perfectly formed legs bare. She had such beautiful curves, totally unlike the emaciated look popular among so many women.

He wanted to ask her why she'd stayed in bed with him, but had a sneaking suspicion it could have been his fault. If he'd fallen on her, he could have held her pinned to the bed with his unconscious body. It was just as likely the tableau Jacob had described finding them in had been Simon's fault as well. His dreams had been vivid.

They finished the form.

Amanda swiped the moisture from her temple with the back of her hand. "That was fun."

"I'll show you some one-step sparring."

Her brown eyes lit up. "Like what you were doing the other day when I played your dummy?"

"A little less advanced."

"Let's do it."

His phallus reacted immediately to her words, disregarding the fact she was talking about Martial Arts form, not bodies melting into bodies in wild abandon.

He willed his libido to take a vacation.

Sex was completely out of the question right now, maybe ever. He wasn't going to make another mistake with a woman. And sex muddled a man's ability to reason. Amanda wanted a merger between their two companies, something he was determined to prevent. He couldn't afford to let his hormones put doing what he knew to be right at risk.

His body might disagree with his decision, but he'd learned to control his sexual urges after his disastrous years in college and the lessons they'd taught him about women and making love.

She caught on to the one-step sparring very quickly. "You're good at this, Amanda."

"Thanks. You're a lot more patient than my Tae Bo instructor. She thinks I'm a dead loss."

"Your Tae Bo instructor is a woman?"

"Sure." She worked through the series of one-step sparring techniques he'd shown her without a single mistake. "Simon?"

"Yes?"

"Can we try some sparring? I'm tired of doing everything in order."

"You don't know any kicks yet."

"Sure I do. I haven't been going to Tae Bo classes for a solid year for nothing."

"All right." He was careful to temper his abilities to hers, but what she lacked in skill, she made up for in enthusiasm.

Soon they were both sweating.

She made a reckless move with her leg that was probably supposed to be an axe kick. He pivoted, avoiding contact completely. She lost her balance and pitched forward.

He caught her, instinctively pulling her into his body.

Her palms landed against the sweat-slicked skin of his chest with a loud smack. "Ungh!" she grunted.

"You okay?"

She nodded, her gaze locked with his. "Thanks for catching me."

"No problem." He had to let her go, but his fingers weren't listening to the message his brain was sending. They were too busy enjoying the feel of her silky smooth skin, hot from exercise.

Her lips looked hot too, all red and swollen. The small pink tip of her tongue darted out and wet the fullness of her bottom lip.

Physical sensation coursed through him with an ache that could only be assuaged one way.

He started to lower his head.

Her lips parted on a soft puff of air. He could smell her sweat. It was different from his. Female. Sweet. His body twitched in primordial response to the olfactory message his receptors were getting.

She came up on her tiptoes, her head tilted, her mouth reaching for his. "Simon."

His name on her lips was like an aphrodisiac. He could already taste the ambrosia of her lips, could imagine how good it would feel to rub their two sweat-slicked bodies together. He could picture them writhing on the floor mats in exercise totally unrelated to Martial Arts.

Sexual energy vibrated between them until his body was tight with it.

Her eyelids slid shut, making her look both vulnerable and ready for his kisses. His mouth was centimeters from hers when the last thread holding him to sanity asked him what he thought he was doing?

He said a silent four-letter word that perfectly described what he wanted to do to her and stepped back.

"I think you could stand some work on your axe kicks."

Her eyes flew open and she landed back on her heels from her tiptoes with a double-thud. "Axe kicks?"

"Yes. You don't want to fall flat on your face when you miss your opponent. You need to work on your center of gravity." He dropped one of her arms and used his hold on the other to pull her over to the kicking bag. He let her go and demonstrated an axe kick. It wasn't his best, but he was still hampered by aching stiffness below his waist. "Try a few of those."

It took Amanda several seconds to accept what had just happened. She'd been prepared for the kiss to end all kisses and he'd been thinking about her center of gravity.

Humiliation crawled along her skin, burning and prickling like overexposure to the sun while rejection pulsed through her with the impact of an invading army. She'd wanted him to kiss her and he'd wanted to improve her kicking form.

It hurt. She felt like his foot had connected with her breastbone instead of the sandbag.

Her chest muscles tightened until pulling in air was an Olympic event. How could she have been so stupid? Hadn't she had her undesirability indelibly stamped on her consciousness by her ex-husband? Did she really need a refresher course in that particular lesson?

The questions spun through her mind along with a far more humiliating one. Did Simon realize she had wanted him to kiss her? Was he aware she had wanted it so much she'd gone up on her tiptoes to meet him halfway? She'd learned to avoid the degradation of rejection by not initiating sex somewhere toward the end of the first year of her marriage. So the fact that she had been so close to initiating the kiss both shocked and horrified her.

She forced herself to search his face for pity.

He wasn't looking at her. He was looking at the kicking bag. He executed another perfect axe kick. Thwap. The sound could have been her heart slapping against her chest in mortification. The bag moved.

"Are you going to try it?" He turned toward her, but his gaze was fixed somewhere over her shoulder.

Oh, he knew all right. And was embarrassed by it.

The only alternative left to her pride was to brazen it out. She kicked the bag. "Like that?"

It had been a pathetic attempt.

He didn't criticize her, however. "Try it again," was all he said.

She did. She forced herself to perform several more kicks. She even asked him to demonstrate a snap kick and copied him before telling him she thought she'd had enough and was ready for a shower.

She managed to hold it together until she got under the spray of hot water. Then she let the tears fall.

CHAPTER SEVEN

S imon forced himself not to watch Amanda leave the gym, but focused his energy on a series of dragon kicks. They did nothing to relieve the physical frustration of his body. He wanted her, damn it. But she was off limits for too many reasons to count.

So, he'd backed off from kissing her and she'd followed his lead, pretending like nothing had happened.

She was probably relieved.

The more he got to know of her, the more convinced he was that she wouldn't intentionally use sex to try to convince him of the merger. She simply didn't seem like the type of woman to make it a practice sleeping with her business associates.

She wouldn't have thanked him for taking their relationship to an intimate level. It would probably make her feel like she'd let herself down professionally. He knew the type. Brant Computers had its own share of serious career women.

The computer industry was changing, but there was still a certain amount of prejudice against women making a career in the hi-tech field. Female employees often fought harder for respect in their industry and were less apt to risk their professional standing by engaging in a meaningless sexual fling.

Are you sure it would be meaningless?

He ignored the taunting words in his head. Amanda had her life mapped out and it didn't include making room for a man who spent more time in his lab than he did talking to other people. She'd never give up her job to come live on his island and he couldn't see himself living the fast-paced lifestyle of Southern California.

He was still interested in her friendship though. She fascinated him even more now, but he had no clue how to make room in his life for a long term relationship with a woman, had nothing of value to offer a wife.

Hadn't Elaine made that clear five years ago?

Amanda came out of her room after her shower to discover that Simon had disappeared into his lab again. No matter how much she needed to talk to him about the merger, she couldn't help feeling thankful for the respite from his presence.

The only thing that could make her situation worse would be for Jacob to tell Simon about finding her in bed with him. He would probably think it had been the act of a woman desperate to seduce him.

"He'll be out for dinner, though."

"How can you be so sure?" she asked Jacob after that pronouncement. "From what I can tell, food is no bigger of a draw when he's working than people are."

"The boss invited Mr. Eric Brant and his wife to dinner."

"Eric's coming?" Relief swept through her. Maybe Simon's cousin could help her convince the stubborn man about the merger. Then she could get herself back to California before she made an absolute fool of herself doing something stupid like climbing naked into Simon's bed and completing her humiliation.

At least she had something positive to report to Daniel when she returned the call he'd made while she'd been busy in the gym with Simon.

"You spent the morning working out with him instead of going over the proposal?" Daniel's scathing tones lacerated already taut nerves.

"I told you. He wasn't about to discuss anything until he got his exercise in. He's almost as dedicated to his Martial Arts as he is to his work."

"I thought you were dedicated to Extant Corporation."

This was not going well. "I am."

"Yet he went back to his lab without you discussing word one on the merger with him."

Guilty as charged. "Yes."

"What's he working on?"

"A fuel-cell alternate energy source."

"What? That's got nothing to do with the next generation of computers."

"Simon is an inventor. He works on more than one project at a time. Evidently only some of them are for Brant Computers."

"So, what's he working on for Brant right now?"

"I have no idea." Did Daniel really think Simon was going to share that kind of information with the competition? And until the merger went through, Brant Computers and Extant Corporation were direct competitors.

"You don't seem to know a whole lot about anything of value right now." Daniel's sarcasm hurt.

She was good at her job. It wasn't her fault that Simon was being so recalcitrant about discussing the merger. And the idea she should know what he was working on for Brant was ludicrous. "I didn't get sent up here to be a corporate spy, Daniel. Frankly if Simon did drop proprietary information, I wouldn't pass it on. It wouldn't be ethical."

"I suppose not." But he didn't sound convinced and that worried her. "You said Eric Brant is coming to dinner tonight."

"Yes. He and his wife."

"Well, let's hope he can accomplish what you haven't and get Simon to listen to the merger proposal."

She fumbled in her purse for an antacid, but couldn't find one. She started digging through her briefcase, her cell phone pressed to her ear. "I'm trying my best."

She found a tablet and popped it in her mouth.

"Your best isn't cutting it."

The words sliced through her like a well-sharpened blade. She'd spent so much of her life being judged and found wanting that her reputation as a professional was incredibly important to her. The only place she had ever excelled had been first as a student and then as a career woman.

She couldn't screw that up.

It was the only thing she had left that stopped her from shrinking away to nothing like she did in the nightmare that plagued her.

"Have I ever let you down before, Daniel?"

"No." It was begrudging.

"Then trust me now."

"Don't make me sorry I did."

She was shaking as she hung up the phone. Two weeks ago she'd been on the fast track to success at Extant Corporation and now she felt like her job was hanging by a thread.

Eric and Elaine arrived for dinner before Simon came out of his lab.

"Are you having any success discussing the merger with him?" Eric asked her over drinks in the great room.

Jacob had served them and then said something about fetching Simon.

"I've gotten to tell him the marketing estimates for the merged companies and we discussed the combination of design engineering power." She didn't elaborate on that as the discussion hadn't been a rousing success.

"Simon can be very stubborn." The blond Elaine relaxed elegantly against the sofa's cushions.

She had delicate features and was boyishly slender, even with her obvious pregnancy. Amanda felt oversized beside her and Elaine's chic mint green silk sheath that showed elegant tanned legs made Amanda feel dowdy in her conservative navy skirt that reached almost to her ankles and the matching short sleeved sweater that couldn't even boast and interesting neckline.

Elaine sighed expressively. "When he's not being stubborn, he's usually ignoring the rest of the world in favor of his experiments."

She smiled at Amanda. "I don't envy you the task of trying to hold his attention long enough to convince him about the merger."

"I have to admit his antipathy toward the merger surprised me." Eric took a sip of his scotch. "Half the time I think he doesn't even realize Brant Computers exists."

"His biggest concern seems to stem from the jobs that will be lost."

"I can see that being the case. He's so anti-social, you sometimes forget the level of concern he feels toward others. He spends as much time experimenting with ways to make the world a better place to live as he does on computer development," Eric said musingly.

"You should see him with our little boy," Elaine added, "he's a total pushover for Joey."

Amanda could picture Simon teaching a little boy basic Tae Kwon Do moves and she smiled. He'd be an interesting father, but a good one. "He should have children of his own."

She had no idea why she said it. She didn't know the Brants well enough to make comments like that.

Elaine's eyes widened. "I can't see him noticing a woman long enough to marry her, much less manage to father a child."

"I can't complain about Simon's absentminded approach to relationships. If he'd been more attentive, you might have married him instead of me." Eric's warm regard for his wife left Amanda in no doubt how he felt about the slim woman.

"You silly thing. I loved you almost from the moment I met you. Even if Simon and I had been engaged, I would have ended up with you." She smiled wryly. "That makes me sound awful, but love has its own rules."

"You and Simon dated?" Amanda asked.

"Yes, but dating a genius inventor isn't all it's cracked up to be, let me tell you."

Amanda could not imagine dumping Simon for Eric Brant. It wasn't that Eric wasn't an attractive and powerful man, but Simon was ultra attractive and ultra powerful in his masculinity. He was simply ultra everything.

"So you rightly decided to cut your losses and let my cousin convince you to take a chance on him." Simon's voice sent Amanda's heart skittering.

She schooled her features and turned to him. "Hi, Simon."

He nodded at her.

Elaine got up and went to Simon for a hug. "Hello, stranger. You need to come and see Joey. He's wondering where his Uncle Simon has gone to."

Simon wrapped his arms around her and kissed her cheek. "Tell him I'll be by to see him next week sometime."

Seeing Simon in an embrace with his former girlfriend caused a jealous reaction in Amanda that she had no reason and even less right to feel.

Elaine stepped back. "All right, but a three year old's concept of time isn't that precise. He's going to badger me until you come." There was humor in her voice when she said it, so Amanda assumed Elaine didn't really mind.

Simon and Eric shook hands. "How are the experiments coming along?"

Simon shrugged. "I'll let you know when I have something concrete."

"So, what do you think of Amanda's proposal?"

Simon had been waiting for the question since coming downstairs to discover Elaine telling Amanda why he was a bad relationship risk.

"She hasn't finished presenting it."

Eric laughed. "Well, my money is on Amanda. Any woman who would brave moving in with an old curmudgeon like Jacob and a total eccentric like you has got the moxy necessary to get the job done."

The warm pleasure reflected in Amanda's eyes at Eric's compliment irritated Simon. "I said I'd listen to what she had to say, not that I would agree with her."

"But, Simon, it makes sense." Elaine smiled appealingly. "Extant and Brant together can compete with the bigger companies for market share in a way Brant could never do on its own."

"Market share isn't the only consideration worth looking at." There was so much more to the company than how big a chunk of the market they command-ed.

"But it is a big consideration." This was from Amanda.

Simon turned his attention to her. The way the thin fabric of her sweater stretched across her breasts had been distracting him all evening. "That depends on how you look at it."

"Why don't you tell us how you're looking at it," Eric said, throwing the ball firmly back into Simon's court.

"Extant Corporation is our competitor, not to mention a publicly held company. The only way we could merge would be to go public ourselves. That's not a consideration I dismiss lightly."

"I haven't dismissed it either, but times change, Simon. If we want to stay competitive, Brant Computers has to change with them."

Simon shook his head. "You're not talking about gaining a competitive edge. You're talking about changing the face and direction of our company. No offense, Amanda, but it's a lousy idea."

She looked at him and her expression revealed almost anguished disappointment, but she didn't say anything.

Eric wasn't so reticent. "It's a natural progression for Brant Computers. Your job won't change. You can still do your research and development at home, in your preferred isolation."

"You're assuming I will continue to work for Brant."

He watched as the shock from his words changed his cousin's expression from exasperation to chagrin.

Elaine gasped. "Of course you'll still work for Brant. You're family. You couldn't even consider selling your designs to another company."

He turned to the woman he'd once considered marrying. "Why not?"

"Because it would be betraying your family!"

He leaned back in his chair and crossed his arms over his chest, taking in the others at the table with his gaze. "Not if Brant Computers is no longer a family held company."

Eric said something succinct. He ran his fingers through his sandy hair, leaving it disheveled. "I didn't expect you to look at it that way."

"Obviously."

"Look, why don't you let Amanda finish giving you her presentation and then we can talk more later?"

"Listening to more statistics on sales and growth estimates isn't going to change my mind." He and his older cousin rarely argued, mostly because they usually agreed, but also because they were both stubborn. Eric being four years older had never mattered to Simon.

"What will it hurt? I think you owe it to me to at least hear her out."

"How do you figure that?"

"I've been managing the company with very little input from you for five years. If you ask me, you've chosen a darned inconvenient time to start showing an interest in the way Brant Computers is run."

"You were just as happy with the division of labor between us after the crash as I was."

Eric ran his hand over his face and then dropped it to the table. "I was. I am. I don't think you and I could have worked together the way dad and Uncle John did before they died. They made a great team because they saw things from the same angle. I'm not sure there's a person on the face of the earth that looks at life quite like you do, Simon."

Simon didn't take offense. He knew Eric didn't mean anything derogatory by the remark, but it landed with dead center accuracy in that empty, cold place inside him. The place swirling with the chilling fog of loneliness that had opened when his mom died and never gone away.

"I'm not going to kick Amanda out and send her back to Seattle with a flea in her ear."

"And you will listen to what she has to say?"

"I'll listen."

Eric nodded, looking satisfied.

"Thank you." Amanda's voice pulled his attention back to her. The dark brown eyes were filled with a determination he could not help admiring, no matter how misplaced it was.

Eric and Elaine left for the ferry and Amanda once again found herself alone with Simon.

He poured two glasses of brandy and handed her one before sitting on the opposite end of the sofa from her. "Okay, fire away."

"You dated Elaine before she married Eric?" That was not what she'd meant to say.

Simon looked as startled by her left-field question as she felt. What had prompted her to ask it? She knew he meant to talk about the merger with her. Maybe it had been the three glasses of wine she'd consumed over the course of the evening. They'd loosened her tongue to the point of revealing a personal interest that was better left completely under wraps. If so, she was never going to drink again.

She set the balloon glass of brandy down on the coffee table with an audible thud.

"I wanted to marry her."

If her question had surprised him, his answer shocked her speechless. She stared at him. He'd wanted to marry Elaine?

Simon grimaced in acknowledgement of Amanda's reaction. "Yeah. It was completely impractical. She's much happier with Eric than she could have been with me."

"Did you love her?"

He shrugged. "I wanted her warmth. When she was around the shadows receded."

That sounded like an eccentric inventor's definition of love to her. "How did she meet Eric?"

"I introduced them. He's my closest friend, my family. It seemed like the thing to do."

"And they fell for each other."

"Yes."

"You all seem like friends now."

"We are. I didn't hold her choosing him over me against either of them if that's what you're thinking."

"It was," she admitted.

"What would be the use? Neither of them hurt me on purpose."

But he had been hurt. She could see it in the depths of his somber gray eyes.

"I'm not that understanding, I guess." Lance's betrayal still rankled and she would never trust the man she'd found him with again.

"You know that for a fact?" he asked probingly.

"I do." Maybe she would have understood better if she hadn't been married to Lance though, if her discovery had come before they'd gotten engaged.

"What happened?"

"My husband had an affair."

"You told me you aren't married."

"I divorced him." And her parents still hadn't forgiven her. Neither had her older brother. According to them, she was the one that hadn't lived up to her wedding vows.

"And you haven't forgiven him."

She thought about all the pain still roiling around inside her from marriage to a man who had rejected her femininity so completely. "It's not that simple. If you mean I'm not in a place where I can be his friend like you are with Eric and Elaine, you're right. But I don't wish him ill. So, in that sense I've forgiven him."

"Does he want your friendship?"

"Of course. It's all about appearances in his and my family's circle of acquaintances. He wants everything to look amicable even though it wasn't."

"Did he marry the woman he had an affair with?"

It was her turn to grimace. "No." To this day, she didn't know who the woman had been with Lance and the other man.

"Did he want the divorce?"

"No."

"But you weren't willing to forgive him his lapse and stay married."

She had grown steadily tenser as the conversation progressed. She felt like a pane of fragile glass on the verge of shattering. "No, I wasn't." Then she looked Simon straight in the eye. "Would you have?"

"No."

Some of the tension drained out of her. At least he understood. That was more than her family had been able to do. "We've gotten very profound in our conversation."

His smile dispelled another layer of tension. "Yes."

Maybe asking about Elaine hadn't been such a huge faux pas after all. She picked up her brandy and took a small sip.

"Jacob told me he found us asleep together in my bed."

The strong spirits went down the wrong pipe and she coughed until tears streamed from her eyes. Simon had jumped up when she started coughing and now he handed her a glass of water. She took it gratefully, taking a big gulp immediately.

He extended a box of tissues to her. She pulled one out and used it to wipe the wetness from her face.

"Better?" Simon asked.

She nodded.

"Jacob said you told him I fell on you."

Had he also told Simon about the compromising position she'd woken up in? She could only hope not.

"You fell asleep standing up and on the way to the bed, you somehow took me with you."

"You fell asleep too?"

This was less easy to explain. She averted her head, not wanting to look at him when she tried to make him understand.

"You wouldn't let go. I couldn't wake you up and I couldn't move you. I decided the only thing to do was to wait until you'd gone into a deep enough sleep to relax your muscles." That sounded much better than she had thought it would. "I fell asleep waiting. I'm sorry that I did so. I realize it was a completely unprofessional thing to do."

She peeked at Simon out of the corner of her eye to see how he was taking her explanation.

His expression was unreadable. "I think we can agree it was an irregular situation."

She nodded. That had been easier than she could have imagined. She barely stifled a sigh of relief.

"Why didn't you call for help from Jacob?"

No way was she going to tell him it was because she hadn't wanted to be caught with Simon's hand on her breast. Her reticence had been for nothing as that was exactly what had happened, but at the time she'd been trying to protect her professional reputation. "I didn't know if he would hear me, or not. He spends most of his time at the other end of the house and on a different floor."

Even though the explanation made sense, Simon could tell she was holding something back. He wanted to know what. Had she done it on purpose?

He would have sworn not, but the way she was avoiding looking at him was suspect. On the other hand, she could simply be embarrassed.

If what she said was true, she had no reason to be.

"Eric seems very impressed by your business acumen."

That brought her attention around. "I'm glad."

She looked it, her eyes glittering with satisfaction.

For no reason he could think of, that annoyed the hell out of him. "Maybe he'll offer you a job if your superiors are too disappointed when the merger doesn't go through."

She blanched, her head snapping back and her skin going pale. "You said you'd listen to the proposal before making up your mind."

"I did not. I said I would listen to the presentation, period."

He watched with interest as her brown eyes went almost black with irritation. "But if you've already made up your mind and nothing I can say will change it, why listen at all?"

"Because I promised Eric that I would."

"But you will listen, right?"

"Yes, I'll listen," he said for the second time that night.

That impressive determination burned in her expression again. "And I'll do my best to convince you that your mind should not be made up."

He stood up. "But not tonight. I've got several experiments to catalog before going to bed."

Surprisingly, she didn't complain. She simply nodded and actually smiled. "I'll look forward to seeing you tomorrow then."

By five o'clock the following afternoon, Simon hadn't made an appearance and Amanda's spirits were pretty much in the toilet.

He had as good as said his mind was already made up. His affirmation that he would listen to her arguments had less ability to buoy her up today than it had the night before when she had been mellowed by his company and three glasses of wine. However, even if she thought it would be a complete waste of time, she had to present her ideas to him.

What other choice did she have?

The deal was as dead as her lovelife without his cooperation.

His threat to start selling his ideas to the highest bidder instead of using them for the good of the company was an impressive one. She'd spent the morning clarifying some things with Eric. One of them had been Simon's agreement with the company for his computer designs. He didn't have one.

There was no way Brant Computers could force Simon to give them even first right of refusal on his future technical discoveries. She could not see Eric Brant dismissing such an eventuality as of no consequence. Even if he did, she was sure the rest of the family who held stock in Brant Computers wouldn't.

Though Simon and Eric each owned the biggest blocks of stock, with thirty-five percent each, there were five other cousins who did not work with or for Brant computers that held the remaining thirty percent of stock between them. In other circumstances, she would have considered going to the other stockholders to solicit support of the proposed merger.

But Simon's threat put paid to that idea.

It wasn't one she'd relished anyway. The company was family held and such a move by her would cause untold damage in the relationships among them. No. If this merger were going to go through, she needed the cooperation of one eccentric genius.

And each progressive hour without him coming out of his lab saw her grow further and further depressed.

She was going over her email from work with desultory interest when her mobile phone rang.

She flipped open the palm size unit and said, "Amanda Zachary."

"Amanda, Daniel here."

Already dragging spirits plummeted.

"Hello, Daniel. I'm just putting together that report on the Garvey deal you asked for in this morning's email." Okay, she'd been thinking about it rather than doing it, but she'd send it off soon regardless.

"Great, but I wasn't calling about that. I wanted to know how dinner with Eric and Simon Brant went last night."

Of course he did.

"And don't tell me you didn't discuss business again." Daniel's voice was laced with a fair amount of sarcasm and warning at the same time.

At least she could refute that. "We discussed the merger."

"Good."

Her next words were a lot harder to say. "Simon is still very much against it."

"What the hell..." Daniel's growl left no doubt as to his reaction to Simon's continued reserve regarding the merger.

"He's worried about the employees." Among other things.

"How commendable of him." The tone of Daniel's voice made it clear that employees were the last consideration he would have when looking at a lucrative deal like the one Amanda had proposed. "But that's not as serious as we first anticipated, is it? I read over your latest report and with the cooperation of the other stockholders, Simon Brant's vote can be overruled at the board meeting."

Chapter Eight

S he could feel the beginnings of a tension headache throbbing behind her eyes. She rubbed her forehead. "Neither Eric, nor Simon, want a family war over this."

"But Eric Brant wants the merger," Daniel's voice came out as smooth as a viper striking.

"They're friends and cousins. It's a tight relationship." She pointed out what should be obvious, even to a Southern California businessman. "I don't think Eric wants the merger at the expense of Simon's goodwill."

"Then, I guess it's your job to make him want it, isn't it?"

Bile rose in her throat and she swallowed it down. Daniel could not possibly comprehend what he was suggesting. "You're not talking about a disagreement between faceless stockholders here, Daniel. You're talking about me instigating a war between two men who are not only friends, but are also family."

She hoped reiterating the facts would make them sink in to Daniel's mind.

Pain pounded in her temples. "I think the original plan of trying to gain Simon Brant's cooperation is still the best one."

Eric had two sisters living in Arizona and a mother who split her time between the states her children resided in. He also had a wife and a child, with another one on the way.

Simon had no one but Eric.

She could not come between the two men.

"Then I suggest you use the opportunity of staying in his house to better advantage."

"I'm talking to him every chance I get."

"Perhaps you should consider more than verbal persuasion." Simon had once called her a snake-oil salesman. Daniel sounded like one now.

She stood in stunned silence for several seconds. "What exactly are you proposing?"

"Men are more vulnerable to certain types of persuasion than others. If the lure of getting rich through the merger isn't enough to sway Simon Brant, you might want to consider taking your negotiation tactics to a more personal level."

She would have laughed at the ridiculousness of the suggestion if it wasn't such an offensive one. "Are you implying I should try to convince Simon with sex, Daniel?" She really couldn't believe that was what her boss was saying.

"Don't be so crude, Amanda. You're obviously personally involved on some level or you wouldn't be living in the guy's house."

He believed she and Simon were already having an affair.

"I'm staying here so I can talk to Simon, not because we're sleeping together!"

"Right. Look, all I'm saying is that you should use every weapon at your disposal to ensure the success of this deal. You've got a lot riding on it. Some might even say your whole career path is at stake here. This is a big deal Amanda and I showed a lot of faith in your professionalism when I sent you up there to handle the preliminary negotiations alone."

Anger and fear warred inside her leaving a metallic taste in her mouth and pushing her tension headache into the realm of a migraine. "We must be thinking about two different kinds of professionalism here, because the one you're talking about is illegal in this state."

"Don't be so damn naïve."

Lance had said the same thing when she had insisted on getting a divorce after seeing him engaged in that lewd ménage e trois. She hadn't told him what she'd seen, simply that she knew he'd been having affairs.

He hadn't even denied it. He'd told her not to be so naïve, that all men had affairs. He'd then laid the blame squarely back on her for not being a sexually satisfying partner. She was willing to accede that she'd failed in the sex stakes, but it wasn't all her fault. How could one woman possibly fulfill the sexual function of a man's male and female lovers?

"Amanda? Are you there?"

"Yes, I'm here."

"Good. I thought the call had been dropped."

"No. Port Mulqueen has excellent cell phone coverage being so close to Seattle's transfer towers." Why was she going on about cell phone service when her boss had just suggested she engage in a sophisticated and modern version of the oldest profession in the world?

"Whatever. I've got a meeting in another five minutes, so I've got to go. If you don't think you can get Simon's cooperation, cut your losses and start working on Eric Brant. One way or another, this deal is going to go through."

"Simon threatened to start selling his computer designs to the highest bidder if Brant Computers goes public with its stock in order to accomplish the merger." That ought to spike Daniel's guns. "I don't think you'll get anyone in his family to agree to the merger if it means losing his brilliance to one of the bigger companies."

Even merged, Extant and Brant would find it difficult to compete with the biggest companies in the industry if Simon submitted his designs to an industry wide bidding war.

Daniel swore. "He'd be cutting his own throat."

"That's not how he sees it."

"He'll still own his share of the merged company, damn it!"

"Yes, and he can still draw income from it, but he'll personally make more money selling his designs to the highest bidder."

"Not if it means Brant and Extant going under."

"Why should it? Simon's just one man, Daniel. He may be brilliant, but the design teams for both companies are some of the brightest in the industry." She wasn't arguing because she wanted to dismiss Simon's threat, but because Daniel seemed oblivious to reality.

"Simon Brant is Brant Computers."

"Eric wouldn't agree with that sentiment, I'm sure."

"Eric is management. Simon's working on things that could change the face of the entire industry. We want him part of the merger. He has to be part of the merger."

We who? Extant's executive team? They hadn't even mentioned Simon Brant to her when she'd made her proposal for the merger.

"I can't believe Eric hasn't had him sign an intellectual property rights agreement." Daniel sounded aggrieved.

"Simon owns a big chunk of the company. I doubt Eric ever thought there would be a need.   Besides, there's no saying Simon would ever have agreed to such a thing." The man was pretty independent and he definitely saw his work as his own.

"All the more reason for you to use your influence to get Simon Brant to agree to the merger."

Anger overcame her fear for her career. She was not a prostitute, glorified or otherwise. "You know, I don't think you could possibly mean what I think you mean, because if you did, you'd be making Extant and yourself vulnerable to a huge sexual harassment lawsuit."

When she hung up, Daniel was still spluttering.

Amanda slammed her taped fist into the sandbag. It made a satisfying thud. She did it again. And again. And again.

She was sweaty. Her knuckles hurt. Her muscles ached. And still, the anger burned inside of her. How could Daniel have suggested something so repugnant? She'd worked for Extant for five years and she'd never been asked to do anything remotely unethical.

Now this.

She'd never been so high up on a project before either. Is this the way Extant did business at the executive level? She couldn't believe it was, but Daniel had hinted that she should use her sexual prowess to convince Simon of the merger. There was no getting around it, under it or over it.

Her boss expected her to use her body as a bargaining chip.

She laughed out loud as she stepped back and connected with the sandbag with several roundhouse kicks, one right after the other. Daniel knew she was no sex kitten. She could no more convince Simon of her point of view using her nonexistent sensuality than she could teach Chinese as a second language.

But Daniel was convinced she was already sleeping with Simon and that was why he though she could use her body for the cause. Which didn't alter her disgusted reaction to his suggestion. If she were involved personally with Simon, she would never use emotional or sexual blackmail to try to get his agreement on a business proposition.

With that thought, she switched legs and continued the roundhouse kicks with her other leg.

A disquieting thought nagged at her as she sought physically to alleviate the rage bubbling through her like hot lava. Was she most angry because her boss had suggested something so completely unethical or because she knew there was no chance she could ever follow through on it?

She shook her head at the unpalatable idea and went through the entire repertoire of one-step sparring techniques Simon had taught her, using the bag as a dummy.

Her emotions began to separate themselves as the roiling mass of sensations inside her ebbed slightly. Okay, the anger was definitely at being told to do something so underhanded, but the pain that had nothing to do with tender knuckles or aching muscles was the result of knowing she was as attractive to Simon as a carp to a salmon fisherman.

She didn't want to use her body to seduce Simon, but knowing she couldn't was really bad for her feminine ego. Almost as bad as the night after night of no sex during her marriage. And why Simon, who was nothing more than a business associate when all was said and done, should have that kind of power over her feelings was a mystery she didn't want to solve.

"He wanted you to do what?" Jill's shriek was every bit as indignant as Amanda could have wished.

If there was one thing she could count on in her life, it was Jillian Sinclair's loyalty.

"He suggested I use sex as some kind of weapon in convincing Simon to go along with the merger. He thinks Simon and I are already sleeping together."

"The son of a bitch. I can't believe it. That kind of stuff is only supposed to happen on daytime drama."

Amanda found herself laughing when she was sure she couldn't. "Right. It's the sort of scenario one of your script writers could have come up with."

"Not our script writers. They've got better taste than that."

"Right. I mean that storyline where the show's major male lead's current love interest turned out to be his long lost sister from an affair his father had with his gardener's daughter was more tasteful than Daniel's smarmy suggestion. And more believable too," she admitted ruefully. "I'm not Mata Hari material."

"Mata Hari was a spy, not a corporate negotiator. Of course you would be a poor casting for that role, but if you're trying to imply you couldn't seduce Simon Brant, you're way off." Jillian made an indignant huffing noise. "The male of our species are not all like Lance Rogers."

Remembering the almost kiss that had been all on her side, Amanda laughed with black humor. "I couldn't heat Simon up with a blow-torch, much less use my imaginary sex appeal to manipulate him."

"Just because you don't have an emaciated body like half the women in Southern California, doesn't mean you have no sex appeal." This from someone who made Twiggy look like an overeater. "If you'd let me fix you up with somebody decent, you'd find that out in a hurry."

"Jill, we've been down this conversational by-way."

"And we'll keep going down it until you give in. Though from the sound of things, you don't need fixing up so much as loosening up with the man you're living with."

"I am not living with Simon Brant." Why did everyone seem so confused on that point? "I'm living in his house. It's not the same thing at all." She did her own huff of indignation. "Besides, if you had seen the woman he once considered marrying, you would realize he could never possibly find me attractive. I'd make two of her and she's pregnant, for Heaven's sake."

"Well, he didn't marry her, so that means he couldn't have been that taken with her."

Amanda wished she could convince herself of Jillian's perspective, but she couldn't. "She married his cousin instead."

"That definitely puts her out of the picture," Jillian said with unhidden satisfaction. "There's nothing to stop you from pursuing something fun, if not meaningful, with this guy."

"Simon Brant does not want to have sex with me!" she yelled, totally exasperated and over the edge of her control.

"Are you sure about that?" The words were spoken in a deep, masculine voice from behind her.

Her heart plummeting to her toes, she spun around with the cell phone stuck to the side of her head like a hi-tech earmuff. Simon lounged in the guestroom doorway, the formerly closed door swung carelessly against the wall.

She opened her mouth, but the only thing that came out was air. Jill was saying something, but Amanda couldn't make any sense of it. She was too busy hyperventilating from embarrassment.

"Simon," she choked out.

"Yes, Simon. You're obviously interested in the man." Jill's impatient voice in her ear had a dreamlike quality to it.

Reality was six feet, four inches of masculine perfection and a sardonic gleam in gunmetal gray eyes.

"Jill," she said, breaking into her friend's familiar tirade on Amanda's lack of a love life.

"What?"

"Simon's here. I think he wants to talk to me."

Jillian's gasp was audible. "Simon's there?"

"Yes."

"How much did he hear?" Her friend's whisper was too little, way too late.

"Enough."

Simon's black brow rose in question.

Jill said "Oh."

"Exactly. Look, Jillian, I've got to go."

"Sure. Call me later."

"Maybe tomorrow." If she hadn't died of mortification by then. Could one die from that sort of thing?

She snapped the cell phone shut. "I didn't hear you knock."

"I think your concentration was elsewhere."

It had been. Oh yes, it had been. "Your right."

"You, however, are wrong."

She was wrong about her concentration? Her usually efficient brain was not functioning at anything near normal capacity at the moment. "About what?"

"I do want to have sex with you."

Her knees gave way. Luckily the bed was right behind her and she landed precariously on the edge. "W-what?"

"I think you heard me."

She shook her head, but the buzzing his words produced did not abate. He hadn't moved a centimeter. His entire posture where he leaned in the doorway, filling it, was one of relaxation. He couldn't possibly be discussing sex with her and maintaining such insouciance. It wasn't possible.

"Then I'll say it again. I do want to have sex with you."

She lost her hold on the bed. The carpet muffled the thump as she landed on her bottom on the floor with her back against the mattress and boxsprings. "You didn't just say that."

He moved. Finally. It was to come across the room and offer his hand to her. She took it and he pulled her to her feet. Her bum was sore.

"I did, but that's not what I came in here to talk about."

"It's not?" A modicum of sanity reasserted itself in her beleaguered brain. "Of course it's not."

"I'm truly sorry, but I'm in the middle of an experiment I can't leave right now."

"But you're here." Okay, so her thinking processes weren't completely restored.

"For just a minute. I came down to tell you and Jacob I wouldn't be joining you for dinner. I don't know when I'll be able to break away from the experiment again tonight."

Why was he telling her this?

"We'll have to put off the rest of your presentation until later."

Two things struck her at once. The first was that Simon was capable of divorcing himself from whatever small desire he felt for her pretty darn easily. The second was that he was explaining himself in a way he hadn't so far in their brief acquaintance. She liked it.

"Thank you for telling me."

He nodded. "You're welcome."

His hands dropped from her shoulders. "I've got to go."

"Right."

"We'll talk later."

"Later," she parroted.

Then he left, taking his sinfully sexy body with him. She collapsed back on the bed and wondered if the Peace Corps had any use for a slightly damaged corporate negotiator in a country like Zimbabwe or something.

Simon picked up the calibrator, made note of what it read and wrote a number down on the pad beside his right hand. It was just about what he had expected, but the slight discrepancy bothered him. He would have to find the reason for it before he could go forward with the fuel cell energy project. He started mentally ticking through the list of possible reasons, writing down ideas on isolating root cause as he went.

He stalled at the second likely test while his thoughts went winging back to his brief discussion with Amanda earlier. He could still see the look of shock on her face when she realized he had overheard her telling her friend, vehemently no less, that he did not want to have sex with her.

Was she blind?

Just because he wasn't acting on his desires didn't mean they had suddenly disappeared. She'd been there in the gym when he'd almost kissed her and she'd known what he'd been about to do. He might be clueless about women sometimes, but he knew when one was gearing up for a liplock with him.

He'd been so irritated with her feigned ignorance that he'd told her she was wrong. Not the brightest thing he'd done since first discovering sex. He shouldn't have admitted it out loud. It was a weapon she could use against him.

He wasn't about to give her the chance. He would listen to her proposal and then she could go back to her hotel in Port Mulqueen. With the temptation of her body gone, maybe he would get some actual work done.

He'd never experienced this kind of distraction before. His concentration was usually absolute, but since meeting Amanda he had found himself thinking about her when he should be analyzing a problem. Even the multiple projects he had going right now were not enough to keep his mind off the tantalizing woman. One of the reasons for his three day work-fest had been a test he was forced to restart when he'd messed it up daydreaming about Amanda instead of keeping track of the energy levels.

He could not afford to be distracted right now. Not if he wanted to be the first designer to get proof of concept on a fiber-optic computer processor. His fuel cell project was an interesting diversion, something to keep his mind from getting locked into a single mode of thinking. He'd learned long ago that working on more than one project at a time, projects that were vastly different, kept his thought processes fresh.

Amanda was interfering with that. No doubt about it. Images of her in his bed plagued him far too often. He'd never been so obsessed with the idea of having a woman, so consumed with the desire to know what she looked like out of her clothes, how she felt, how she tasted. Not even his precocious adolescence had elicited this kind of absorption in him.

It was an absorption he could not afford if he wanted to prevent his cousin from merging Brant Computers with Extant Corporation. Amanda's ideas were good, but she and Eric were considering too many of the wrong things in their enthusiasm for the merger. Simon refused to let them forget the company's beginnings, the commitment Brant Computers had always had toward its employees.

The temptation of Amanda's body could very well undermine his efforts in that direction. She had to go.

Out of his house and preferably back to California with a "No," from Eric ringing in her ears.

Warm, salty wind caressed Amanda's face as she sat on the bobbing dock, her feet dangling in the chilly water of the Puget Sound. There were a lot of things she didn't miss about home. She didn't miss the smog, or the stalled traffic on the freeway. She didn't pine for the fast pace or the crowded malls, but she did miss a warm ocean.

Her feet were going numb from the cold. Was that a bad thing? You couldn't get frostbite from water, could you? It probably wasn't worth the risk. Sighing, she pulled her feet from the water and drew her knees to her chest. She watched with much more attention than it deserved as a puddle of water formed around her feet on the sun washed gray wood.

Simon had said he wanted to have sex with her and her mind had gone as numb as her feet were now. Her thought process was still sluggish as she attempted to deal with ramifications of his statement.

He wanted her.

So, why had he pulled away from kissing her in the gym? Or had he? She still couldn't be entirely certain he had meant to kiss her at all. When it came to men's passion and their desire to act on it, she was a total novice, having been married notwithstanding.

She'd been tempted to call Jillian back and tell her everything, but in the end, Amanda had decided against making the call. Because she already knew what her friend would say.

Jill would say, "Go for it."

No hesitation. No other considerations. She would expect Amanda to ignore her own less than successful attempt at sexual intimacy in the past, to ignore the fact that Daniel wanted her to use sex as a weapon against Simon and to forget her sense of propriety when it came to business relationships.

The truly terrifying reality was that Amanda was considering doing just that. Without Jillian's cajoling.

Because Amanda wanted Simon.

More than she had ever wanted another man. More than she had believed possible. She had long ago come to the conclusion that all the hype about making love was just that, hype. Or at least an aspect of reality she was not destined to experience.

She'd read somewhere that there was no such thing as a frigid woman, just an inept lover. She didn't believe it. Or hadn't...until Simon.

Her desire for him put paid to her certainty that she was not a very sexual being. She certainly felt sexual around him. In fact, it was hard to focus on any other aspect of her humanity when he was around. She wanted to touch him. To be touched by him.

Just thinking about it had all sorts of interesting things happening to her body. Her nipples were tightening, puckering, getting hard. The rigid buds pressed against her legs that were drawn close to her chest. Her nipples had never before manifested any sort of sexual excitement until manipulated physically.

She could never remember feeling this throbbing ache between her thighs either, or the fluttery sensation in her stomach. Her breathing didn't usually go ragged and uneven, not even in the act of intercourse.

But all of those things were happening right now and they were all for Simon. And not even Simon in the flesh, but the simple thought of him.

Her body wanted his possession. Okay, it wasn't PC and she'd never say it out loud, but that was what she wanted. She wanted to feel him inside her, surrounding her, owning her for that brief time when their bodies meshed and sought the ultimate pleasure. An experience she'd never actually had.

She was too repressed to pursue it on her own. The mere thought of using mechanical devices made her blush. She'd definitely never known such a thing with Lance. She thought maybe she'd come close once or twice, but now she realized that what she'd mistaken for passion had been at best lukewarm physical pleasure.

"Some people have better things to do than to track down wayward guests and give them messages."

Her head snapped up as a shadow fell over her and Jacob's irascible voice jarred her from her thoughts. "Hello, Jacob. Am I the wayward guest?"

"Don't see nobody else staying in Simon's house, missy."

She was getting used to his bouts of surliness. "I don't either, so that must mean the message is for me," she said with a sunny smile.

Was that approval she could see in his eyes? Maybe the old man was starting to like her.

"The boss said to tell you he would come down about nine o'clock."

"Tomorrow morning?" She had to stifle her disappointment at having missed Simon when he'd surfaced from his lab.

"Tonight. Said to tell you he'd come to your room." Jacob managed to lace the words with disapproval and a fair dose of innuendo all at once.

"At nine o'clock?" Her voice squeaked on the word nine. "In my room?"

"That's what he said. I retire before that unless the boss instructs me otherwise."

So, she and Simon would effectively be alone. In her room. She felt like sticking her head in the frigid water of the sound. Anything to clear the morass of thoughts chasing themselves through her mind.

Was he planning to pursue his desire to have sex with her? She couldn't believe he would have sent the message through Jacob, but then Simon didn't do things the normal way. And she hadn't been around when he'd come out of his lab, presumably to tell her himself.

"Simon wants to meet me at nine o'clock in my room?" she asked to verify the improbable message.

Jacob's snort of impatience barely impinged on her consciousness. "That's what I said. Do you need it in writing?"

She shook her head, as much to clear it as to negate his statement. "No. I've got it."

Simon wanted to meet her in her room at nine o'clock that night. After Jacob had retired to his own quarters. Not exactly at bedtime, but too late to be considered strictly appropriate for a casual visit.

Oh, she had it all right.

The only problem was - what was she going to do with it?

Chapter Nine

Simon laid down the calibrator and stretched. Flicking a glance at the digital atomic clock above his main workbench he winced. Nine-thirty. He'd told Jacob to tell Amanda he would be down at nine.

He hoped she wasn't too irritated.

The thought surprised him. He'd pretty much dismissed the frustration others had with his work habits since he was ten years old. Why were the worries coming to surface now, with a woman who was nothing more than a business contact and an unwelcome one at that?

Even if she was mad, he knew she'd still be up. She wanted a chance to convince him of that damn merger.

She was too dedicated to her job to go to bed in a huff of offended feminine pride at being forgotten. And he hadn't forgotten her. If it had been anyone else, he would probably still be at his workbench. Not doing a quick finger combing of his hair as he rapidly descended the stairs to the second floor.

The sweet fragrance of the peaches and cream candle she'd lit an hour ago filled Amanda's room, but instead of soothing her, it mocked her attempt to create a mood of romance. He wasn't coming. It was after nine-thirty. He'd definitely decided against acting on the mutual attraction between them.

She should be feeling relieved.

After all, she'd only decided at eight-thirty to take the advice she knew Jillian would have offered and go for it. Until then, she'd vacillated between the sane thoughts of her business conscious brain and the insane urges of her heretofore unknown feminine desires.

She should be glad that his decision to stay away had saved her from herself. Maybe if it didn't feel so much like a rejection, she would be. Certainly it made sense that he would have realized the inappropriateness of pursuing any kind of intimate relationship in their current situation. But why in Hades hadn't he figured that out before sending that stupid message through Jacob?

And why hadn't he had at least the courtesy to come down and tell her himself?

The thought that he'd gotten caught up in his lab experiments and forgotten her was no consolation.

That smacked of unpleasantly familiar rejection as well.

A sharp tattoo sounded on her door and all the air in her body seemed to expel. He was here. Heavens. What should she do now?

The knock sounded again. "Amanda?"

Open the door. That's what she had to do. She walked across the room on bare feet, the shimmering burgundy of her painted toenails flashing in the periphery of her vision with every step.

The color went nicely with the Bordeaux satin tap pants and camisole she was wearing. She'd spent a full fifteen minutes applying the nail polish, letting it dry while she brushed her long hair into a dark brown curtain that gleamed like silk in the flickering light of the candle.

She reached for the door handle with a trembling hand and then pulled it open.

Simon's fist was raised to knock again. He let it drop while shock registered on his face. "I know I'm a little late, but I didn't think you'd be going to bed so early."

Why was he looking so surprised?

"It's only nine-thirty," he added.

She looked over her right shoulder at the red glow of her digital alarm clock. "Nine-forty-two actually."

"Look I know it probably irritated you that I forgot the time, but I didn't forget you completely." Far from looking like a man bent on seduction, Simon looked tired and cranky. "I'm here aren't I?"

"Yes." Was she acting annoyed? She didn't think she was.

"I can't believe you're going to dismiss the chance to talk about the merger just because I'm a half an hour later than I said I'd be." Outrage laced his voice. "Hell, you moved into my house so you could catch me between experiments. Going to bed right now is hardly the behavior of a professional career woman intent on pursuing her objective."

On that he had her complete agreement, but the rest of his words weren't making any sense.

"You think I'm angry with you?" she asked, while trying to understand what was going on here. The sensual fog she'd been in since deciding to "go for it" was clouding her ability to reason.

He tipped his head and rubbed the bridge of his nose with his thumb and forefinger. Looking back up, gunmetal eyes reflecting weariness pinned her with unconcealed annoyance. "Don't play this I'm not mad, just tired routine. It's such a female thing to do and not at all what I would expect of a woman dedicated to getting the job done."

As the desire that had overridden her usual caution began to wane under Simon's anger, inconsistencies in the situation infiltrated her consciousness. Inconsistencies she would have noticed immediately if she hadn't been so overwhelmed by the prospect of going to bed with him.

He was not acting like an amorous lover. In fact, nothing he'd said so far indicated any sort of desire on his part whatsoever. As her now nimble brain went back over what he'd said so far, the sick feeling of embarrassment started to crawl along her nerve endings.

He hadn't meant making love at all.

Simon had wanted to meet her to discuss the merger.

How stupid could one woman possibly be? "Why did you insist on meeting in my bedroom?" Her voice was too high, but there was nothing she could do about that.

He frowned. "I didn't insist. I told Jacob I'd look for you in your room so I wouldn't spend a half an hour searching the house for you when I came downstairs. What does where I asked to meet you have to do with your childish display of temper?"

He thought she was being childish? Everything finally made sense. Simon had wanted to discuss the merger. He believed that because he was late, she'd gotten ready for bed in some kind of juvenile act of rebellion. While not exactly flattering, it beat the truly mortifying truth that she'd thought he'd wanted her.

She stepped back into the room, flipping on the overhead light as she went. "I'll just get on some jeans and a sweater, all right? It gets cold in the evenings here. Really chilly, to tell you the truth." She blew out the candle on her way by it. "I'm not used to these kinds of temperatures."

She was babbling, but she didn't care. Maybe if she kept talking it would prevent him from clueing into what she'd really thought. Shame so familiar it was almost a friend surrounded her like the hot oppressive air of the Mojave Desert.

"It won't take a sec," she continued her babbling litany as she yanked on a pair of jeans right over her tap pants. "I'm sorry if you thought I was being childish. I thought you'd forgotten completely. That's all," she lied.

She grabbed a sweatshirt from the top drawer of the dresser she'd been using. She tugged it on over her head, pulling her hair in the process. She ignored the pain as she ripped it loose of the constricting crewneck.

"Let me just clip back my hair." She hadn't looked at him once since realizing her mistake and she didn't do so now either. She spoke to the wall in front of her as she headed for the en-suite.

"Don't pull it back on my account. It looks beautiful down like that."

She wanted to spin around and start screaming invective at him. Beautiful? She wasn't beautiful. She knew it and he knew it. He didn't want her. Not really. She didn't know what he'd meant by telling her he wanted sex with her earlier. It had probably been some kind of joke. An amusing bit of sarcasm she should have recognized as such.

How could a woman with an I.Q. in the top two percent of the populace continue to be so dim about some things?

She didn't bother responding to him as she walked into the bathroom, shutting the door behind her. She needed a minute to collect herself. She needed a lifetime, but she could take a minute.

She searched for the light she hadn't bothered to turn on before coming into the small room. She found it and flipped the switch up.

The sudden brightness illuminated a picture in the mirror she could have gone forever without seeing again. Brown eyes dark with humiliated hurt and wide to prevent the moisture gathering in the corners from slipping to her cheeks. Her face was crimson with embarrassment, her mouth a tight line of pain.

It was a familiar sight. How many nights in the first year of her marriage had she tried to interest Lance in making love only to have him reject her for one reason or another? How many times had she stood in front of the mirror just as she was doing now and tried to see what was wrong with her?

The sad-eyed woman in the mirror was someone she knew intimately, someone she had vowed never to see again.

She'd promised herself, damn it. She was never going to let another man close enough to hurt her this way again. But she had and she was paying the price. The mire of humiliation was closing over her head, suffocating her with its terrifying inevitability.

She hated feeling like this. Hated it!

Suddenly the slide of satin against her skin was as painful as a hair shirt and just as effective a reminder of things she would rather forget. She ripped off her outer clothes, then tore the camisole and tap pants from her body and threw them with all her might into the garbage can beside the sink vanity.

She'd only started wearing pretty feminine undergarments in the last year, having cut every negligee she owned into shreds and disposed of them the second year of her marriage after a particularly brutal rejection from her husband. He'd told her that fat women shouldn't expose so much of themselves to view.

Fat!

She had been five pounds under her ideal weight, but that hadn't been good enough for her husband.

Why had she stayed married to the man so long?

She didn't have an answer now and more than she'd had one the hundred and ten other times she'd asked herself that question.

The closest she could come was to acknowledge that she'd grown up with the feeling that she had no right to be happy. She'd been unlovable to her family. It was only natural her husband had decided he didn't love her too.

Pounding on the door brought her gaze away from the mirror.

"Amanda, are you all right?"

She must have been longer than she thought. "I'm fine. I'll be right out," she called in a credibly even voice.

The only way she could think of to mitigate the pain of Simon's unwitting rejection was to prevent him from knowing how much he had hurt her. At least her humiliation wasn't public, not like it had been with Lance.

She threw her clothes back on, not worrying about a lack of underthings. Simon wouldn't know. It took her longer than usual to clip back her hair because her hands were shaking so badly. She had to get herself under control before she went out there. Closing her eyes, she inhaled deeply, concentrating on breathing in peace and breathing out her stress.

It was a psychological trick one of her friends from high school had taught her. Most of the time, it worked.

Amanda finished zipping up the leopard print suitcase. She'd been up since five that morning after sleeping very little the night before.

Simon had listened to the initial proposal in its entirety, had not interrupted when she outlined her thoughts on the best strategy for joining the two business-es. He had even allowed her to present the rest of her arguments in favor of the merger, all of it with very little comment from him. He hadn't argued a single point, thus not giving her the opportunity to press her own ideas forward.

And she hadn't cared.

She'd been relieved that he didn't want to get into a major discussion because all she had wanted to do was finish the presentation and get away from him. She'd been back in her bedroom by eleven and had started packing five minutes after that.

She should stick around and try to bolster the arguments she'd offered the night before, but she couldn't. While her job was the most important thing in her life, she could not stand the crawling sense of humiliation her mistake the night before had left her with. Not even for a major bump up in her five-year career plan.

She'd done all she could do.

If Simon wasn't convinced, maybe Daniel should consider sending another negotiator to Port Mulqueen. Her stomach cramped at the thought, but she was leaving. Today. This morning. She had every intention of being on the first ferry off Simon's island.

Fifteen minutes later, she went looking for Jacob to tell him she would be going. She found him in the kitchen.

He looked up when she entered, his wizened gaze taking in her perfectly pressed suit. "I'll have blue corn cakes ready in a few minutes. Did you want bacon or sausage with them?"

"Neither, thank you."

"It's not a good idea to start the day without putting a bit of protein in you."

"I'll stop for breakfast when I get back to Port Mulqueen." It was lie. She knew she wouldn't be eating any time soon, but the small deception didn't hurt anyone and it would keep Jacob from haranguing her.

"You going to the mainland today?"

"Yes."

"Will you be back in time for dinner?"

"I won't be back at all. I came in to say thank you for your hospitality and let you know I was leaving."

"Wasn't my hospitality, missy. The bed you slept in belongs to the boss. He bought the food you ate."

"Then please pass my gratitude on to him."

"Why don't you do it yourself? He'll probably be down for breakfast before too long."

Just the prospect of seeing Simon again made her sensitive stomach twist with nausea. "I don't want to miss the ferry." Good. Her voice was steady, professionally void of emotion. She even forced what she hoped was a credible smile to her lips. "Let's be honest, Jacob, there's no guarantee Simon will come down for breakfast at all."

"Thought you were supposed to convince him about that merger Mr. Eric Brant wants."

"Simon listened to the proposal last night." And if Eric wanted the merger so darn bad, he could convince his cousin of its merits. Brant Computers stood to gain by the merger just as much as Extant Corporation did.

"And he agreed to it?" The incredulity in Jacob's voice left her in no doubt how unlikely he found such a scenario.

"No."

"Then shouldn't you be staying to try to talk him into it?"

She didn't know why Jacob cared about her business, but she wished he didn't. "I've done what I could. I can't force Simon to my point of view."

"Seems like a pretty sloppy way to do business to me."

Her tolerance and patience dried up at the same time. "This may come as a debilitating shock to you, but what you think of the way I conduct my business is of no concern to me whatsoever."

Jacob's eyes narrowed. "No need to get snippy with me, missy."

She closed her eyes and counted to ten. It worked in all the books she read. Real life was less disciplined. "You're right, Jacob. I'm leaving now," she said through gritted teeth and then turned on her heel and did just that.

Simon walked into the kitchen, irritated by the anticipation he felt at the prospect of seeing Amanda.

"Good morning, Jacob."

"Morning, sir."

There was a pile of shiny fabric on the counter beside where Jacob stood putting blue corn cakes and bacon on a plate for Simon. The material was the same color as Amanda's pajamas. The pajamas responsible for a night filled with restless sleep interspersed with highly erotic dreams.

"Is Amanda up yet?"

"Up and gone."

"Gone?" Was she walking along the water again? She seemed to really enjoy doing that.

Jacob laid Simon's plate of breakfast on the table. "Took the first ferry to the mainland."

She'd probably gone to have a war council with Eric now that Simon had listened to her arguments. He wondered what her next step in her campaign to convince him would be. He should tell her now that he had listened to her proposal, there was no reason for her to stay on the island.

But what he should do and what he wanted to do were poles apart, especially after seeing her in that wet-dream producing nightwear.

"What time do we expect her back?"

"We don't."

Simon, paused with a loaded fork halfway to his mouth. "What?"

"She's not coming back, sir. Said to tell you she appreciated the hospitality."

"The hell you say."

Jacob just shrugged. "Thought she'd stay to do a little more convincing on that merger business. Told her so, but she pretty much told me to mind my own business."

Amanda had left? Without saying good-bye? There was something about this situation that didn't feel right. Like Jacob said, it made no sense for her to leave without making at least one more effort to convince him about the merger.

"Was there some reason she had to go back to the mainland so early this morning?"

"Don't know, sir. She didn't say anything. Just that she didn't want to miss the ferry."

Simon's gaze slid to the clock on the kitchen wall. The ferry had left the dock twenty minutes ago.

Amanda was gone. Telling himself that was exactly what he wanted did nothing to alleviate the hollow sensation inside him.

Why the hell hadn't she even bothered to say goodbye?

Jacob held up the pile of rich burgundy satin. "She left this behind."

So it was her pajamas. "We'll have to get it back to her." His spirits lifted at the thought of having an excuse to see her again.

"Don't know if she wants it. Found it in the garbage in the bathroom, sir."

"You found Amanda's pajamas in the garbage?" That didn't make any sense. "Were they damaged in some way?" Maybe her woman's thing had started last night and she'd been surprised by it, ruining the silk bottoms to the nightwear.

"Not a thing wrong with them, sir."

"Then they must have fallen into the garbage on accident."

"Could be. Don't see how, but it could have happened."

"Well, what do you think happened?"

"Think she threw them away, sir. She was meticulous in cleaning her other things from the room. Don't see how she could have overlooked these."

Simon measured Jacob with his eyes. The older man had a studiously blank expression on his face. Why had he brought the pajamas to his attention, if he believed Amanda had tossed them on purpose? More worryingly, why had she thrown them away?

The ferry announcement had ended several minutes ago, but the words were still echoing in Amanda's head. Ferry service had been suspended until further notice. There had been an accident on one of the major routes and the single ferry that serviced Simon's sparsely populated island had been re-routed to the busier one. Ferries didn't have accidents, did they?

They were big. They traveled the same stretch of water over and over again. So, how had this happened?

More importantly, what was she going to do? The only public facility she knew of on the island was a small general store and deli - deli being a euphemism for a two-foot long glass case with lunchmeats and potato salad on display. There was a single table with two chairs for customers to sit on. It was not somewhere she would be comfortable staying for several hours while waiting for ferry service to resume.

She could just stay where she was.

She grimaced. She'd been sitting in this poky little waiting room for two hours already. There wasn't even a vending machine where she could buy a bottle of water. According to the ferry officials, it could be hours before service resumed. Considering how much she wanted to get off the blasted island, it would be just her luck that the ferry wouldn't be available until the next morning.

Surely not. She tried to console herself with the thought that they had to have at least one trip to the mainland that day. She wasn't the only one who wanted off the island. Okay, maybe she'd been one of three cars that had been in line for the morning ferry and the other two had left after the first announcement of delay. Looking around the now empty waiting room, she had to accede it was possible she was the only passenger desperate to leave the small island.

"You might as well go back to wherever you've been visiting, ma'am. It's going to be a while before we get a ferry off the dock."

She turned her head at the sound of a man's voice. He was wearing the bright orange vest that indicated ferry personnel.

"How did you know I was visiting?" she asked, apropos of nothing.

"It's a small island. Working the ferry, you get to know all the residents after a while, even the weekenders."

"Oh." What an intelligent response, Amanda. But she felt fresh out of intelligence at the moment.

"Who are you visiting?"

She thought about refusing to answer, but it wasn't a state secret after all. "Simon Brant."

The sandy haired man's blue eyes widened. "He doesn't have a lot visitors, especially overnight ones."

She made a noncommittal sound, not liking the implication his emphasis placed on overnight visitors made about her relationship with Simon.

"The security at his place is pretty tight," the ferry official remarked, obviously fishing for more information on the elusive islander.

Remembering Jacob's insistence on making a visual identification the first time she visited, she had to agree. "I suppose he sees the need for it, being both an inventor and computer designer."

It struck her that Simon had shown a lot of trust allowing her to stay in his home like he had. What if she had been a corporate spy for Extant, more interested in his designs than the merger? The thought brought forth a niggling memory. Daniel had commented on Simon's current project like he knew what it was. How could that be true?

Jacob was as loyal to Simon as any person could be. She would stake her life on that. So, how had Daniel found out anything about Simon's work? Or had he? Perhaps she had misunderstood what her boss had said. She'd been pretty hot about his suggestion she use her body for the cause.

"They say he's a genius."

She nodded.

"And eccentric."

Her lips tilted in a wry smile. "You could certainly describe him that way. You said, they say. Don't you know? Haven't you met him?"

The young man shook his head. "He keeps to himself. Him and that old man who lives there with him."

"Jacob is the housekeeper."

"A security expert too, according to gossip."

She looked more closely at the sandy-haired man. He looked young, but his eyes were filled with the avid curiosity of an inveterate gossip. "For not knowing him, you certainly know a lot about Simon."

"Not as much as you do, I bet." His smile once again implied an intimacy between her and Simon.

She wouldn't let this one slide. "It's strictly a business relationship." Still smarting from her humiliating mistake in the other direction the night before, she was sharper than she intended to be.

The ferry official's smile didn't dim. If anything, he contrived to look smug. "He doesn't bring business acquaintances to the island."

"I suppose gossip said that too," she said in scathing tones that once again went right over his head.

He shrugged. "Yep."

"Well he brought me and I can assure there is nothing except business between Simon Brant and myself."

"You'd say that wouldn't you? Not wanting gossip and all." His knowing look indicated that gossip about Simon's houseguest would be rife on the island, regardless of what she might want.

She stood up, a sense of righteous indignation coursing through her. "Your implication is out of line, not to mention archaic in its perception of the relationship between men and women." Taking a step toward the ferry official, she grimly enjoyed watching him back up. "This is the twenty-first century. Women are a fact of reality in the business arena. I suppose you think we should all stay home and pop out babies until menopause takes us over."

He was starting to look seriously worried. "I don't think that at all, ma'am. Lots of women work for the ferry service."

"But you don't think we have the education or the intelligence to compete in the technology industry. You just assume that a woman could not possibly have business dealings with Simon Brant because he's a genius in a male dominated field. I resent that implication very much."

"I didn't mean that ma'am."

She ignored his lukewarm self-defense, now in the full stride of her ire. "I will have you know that I have a very successful career at Extant Corporation, a company on the forefront of design in the hi-tech industry. Furthermore, there are several women at the executive level with my company. It's attitudes like yours that kept women in strictly supportive roles for so many years."

"He's not old enough to have fought the vote, missy."

She swung around, her finger still pointed accusingly in front of her. "Jacob! What are you doing here?"

Chapter Ten

"Ferry's not running."

His laconic answer did nothing to clarify the situation. "I know that, but how did you?"

"News travels fast on an island."

That sent her spinning back toward the hapless ferry employee. She glared at him. "I suppose gossip accounts for this sort of thing too."

The young man appealed to Jacob over her shoulder. "I didn't mean to offend her. Really. We were just talking."

"Have I suddenly disappeared now that another man is in the room?" she demanded with bite.

"Leave the poor boy alone." Jacob came to stand beside her. "You've got him scared to death."

"Scared of a woman?" she asked derisively, somewhere at the back of her mind realizing she was overreacting, but unable to stop the words from flowing out of her mouth. "Imagine that."

"I'm not a chauvinist," the ferry official asserted, his courage apparently bolstered by Jacob's championship.

"Then how do you explain your inappropriate comments earlier? The result of a bad breakfast?" Her stomach growled reminding her she hadn't eaten anything yet that day, bad or otherwise.

"He made inappropriate comments to you?" Suddenly Jacob's voice had gone arctic, his homey accent dropped for precise diction.

"He implied that rather than business associates, Simon and I shared some kind of personal and intimate relationship."

"My employer does not appreciate speculation regarding his private life." The ferry official blanched.

Amanda didn't blame him. The deadly tone even sent a shiver up her spine.

"I didn't mean anything by it. Honest."

"The implication that a man and woman must have more than a business relationship is never a welcome one," she said before Jacob could reply.

"It was just the shock of you staying overnight. That's all. Mr. Brant hasn't had an overnight visitor since his cousin missed the last evening ferry a couple of months back."

"The secret service has nothing on Washington State ferry personnel, does it?" She was amazed the man knew so much about Simon's life. She didn't even know that much about the neighbors she'd been living next door to since leaving Lance two years ago.

Apparently realizing that everything he said made the situation worse, the orange clad official started backing away toward the office. "I've uh... got a lot of paperwork to catch up on. I'm sorry about the inconvenience the cancelled ferry has caused you ma'am."

"You intimidated him."

She stared at Jacob, disbelief warring with offense inside her. "I intimidated him? You were the one that turned into The Enforcer. You were so cold, I'm surprised the guy didn't get chill blains standing next to you."

Undeniable satisfaction reflected in Jacob's expression. "It's a role I play rather well."

"I'd say you play all your parts with the professionalism of a trained thespian."

"For that sort of flattery, I'll make you a Napoleon for dinner."

Just thinking of the flaky crust and sweet custard filling of the decadent dessert had her mouth watering, but she had no intention of going back to Simon's. "I'll just wait here until the ferry resumes service."

"Not a good idea. Could be tomorrow morning before you can get back to the mainland."

"I find that difficult to believe. They can't just leave passengers stranded without a means to get off the island."

"The island's population is so low it has the least priority of all the ferry routes. Besides, most residents have their own boats to use if they're in desperate need of getting to the mainland."

She remembered the yacht moored on Simon's private dock. "But I have a car. I can't just hire someone to take me across." Though the thought was a tempting one.

"Couldn't hire someone anyway. Jim Fletcher's the only resident that takes paying passengers and he's off island right now."

"So, I'll wait here."

Jacob looked around the sparsely furnished, miniscule room. "Be more comfortable at the boss's house."

That's what he thought. She'd be more comfortable in a thicket of blackberry bushes than she would be at Simon's. "I'll be fine here. If I get tired, I can take a nap in the car."

"What about food?"

She didn't feel like eating, even with her stomach growling, but she was thirsty. "I'll go to the general store for supplies."

"You're being stubborn."

"Think what you like, Jacob. I just don't want to inconvenience Simon anymore. I'll stay here, if it's all the same to you."

"The boss ain't going to like it."

"He won't even notice. By the time you get back he'll have forgotten why he sent you out to begin with."

"The boss ain't senile."

"No, but he is preoccupied with his work. Thank you for your concern, but I'm fine where I'm at."

Jacob left, muttering about intransigent women who might be better off if they never had got the vote.

She couldn't help smiling. Jacob was an irascible old codger, but he'd gotten defensive on her behalf before she mentioned the nature of the ferry official's inappropriate comments. The old faker liked her, even if he would never admit it.

Amanda grabbed the six-pack of bottled water and headed toward the antique looking cash register. The clerk, a middle aged woman in an oversized T-shirt bearing a picture of cats on the front, was talking animatedly with an elderly woman in white slacks and a sweatshirt.

Neither one of them noticed Amanda waiting to be rung up.

She didn't say anything. Why interrupt their discussion when she only planned to take the water and go back to the ferry terminal? She had thought about taking a drive around the island, but what if the ferry came while she was gone? She was fairly certain there would only be one sailing today. She was determined to be on it.

The bell above the entrance jingled. Both she and the chatting women turned to look at the newcomer.

It was Simon.

"Morning, Mr. Brant," the clerk called.

He nodded politely to the two women and then turned to walk toward Amanda. He stopped less than a foot away. "Jacob said you didn't want to come back to the house."

The accusation in his voice was unexpected.

"I didn't want to put you out any more than I had already," she said, giving him the same excuse she'd made up for Jacob.

He flicked a glance to the water in her hand, his expression enigmatic. "I don't mind."

"Thank you, but I wouldn't feel right imposing." He looked like he was about to argue, so she went on. "You allowed me the opportunity to present the merger proposal to you. Our business is concluded and there's no reason for you to feel responsible for my comfort. It's not as if I was a guest in your home."

His mouth quirked. "So you told the man at the ferry. Jacob said you were pretty adamant about it."

She bristled with remembered indignation. "It's the truth. That man had no right to imply otherwise."

"Living on a small island is like living in a very small town." Simon's gaze went temporarily to the two women who pretended to be talking, but were clearly more interested in her conversation with Simon than their own. "Everyone knows everyone else's business, or thinks they do."

"Well, it's not right. That sort of gossip is intolerable." She didn't realize her voice had risen until the woman talking to the store clerk gave all pretense of not listening and stared at her with blatant curiosity. Great. More gossip.

She smiled and nodded, hoping they would go back to their previously absorb-ing conversation, then turned back to Simon. "There's really no reason for you to wait around here. I've got refreshments." She lifted the six-pack of water. "I'll be fine until the ferry gets here."

"But you'll be better at my house. Jacob's set on spoiling you." Simon's voice had taken on a seductive quality that her body did not identify with food. "He's working on the pasty crust for a Napolean even as we speak."

Her face felt tight. The last thing she needed after Simon's unknowing rejec-tion was the high calorie dessert. "I'm sure you will enjoy it then."

"He's making it for you." Simon slid his hands into his jeans pockets, outlining a certain male part of his anatomy she was better off not noticing.

She forced her gaze to his face and kept it there. "I'm sorry I won't be there to eat it," she said, adding another lie to the ones she'd already told that morning.

"Why won't you be there?" He frowned at her, his sensual lips firming into a thin line. "There's no reason for you to wait around in the dinky room when you can relax in comfort at the house. We could even get some sparring in."

He said it like that should be some sort of incentive, but she flinched at the thought.

No way was she going through another tortuous session of touchy-feely Mar-tial Arts training with Simon. "I don't mind. Really. I'm sure you've got experiments or something." She waved vaguely toward the door. "I won't keep you."

She started to turn away, hoping he'd finally get a clue and leave. She wasn't going back to his house. Period. If he thought she was being neurotically polite, so be it. Better that than the chance he would discover the desire that seemed to grow with each lungful of air she took in his radius.

The in-drawn hiss of his breath was all the warning she got. He grabbed the water from her hands, dropped it right there in the aisle and then swept her up into his arms like she was some damsel in distress. Only the real distress started the moment he touched her because her senses went haywire.

"Well, I'm damn well going to keep you. You're being too stubborn for your own good."

"Simon! Put me down. You're causing a scene. It's going to be all over the island by the time we reach my car." And judging from the twin expressions of avid interest on the clerk and her friend's face, Amanda didn't think she was exaggerating.

Simon ignored her and carried her outside. He stopped behind her car. "Push the unlock button."

She didn't even think of arguing with him. If she didn't get out of his arms soon, she was going to do something drastic. Like kiss him. Or bury her fingers in the black, silky hair he'd left loose to hang around his shoulders today.

The snick of unlocking doors sounded and Simon went around to open the passenger door. He bent down and put her inside.

"What are you doing?" She was shrieking. She never shrieked, but then she'd never been kidnapped by an eccentric genius before either. "This is my car."

"I'm driving." And his tone suggested she not argue about it.

She'd never been all that great at taking suggestions. "But the rental agreement doesn't have you on it."

He just looked at her.

"Well it doesn't." She turned to face the front, her mouth in a mutinous line.

He shut the door. Firmly. Seconds later he was sliding into the driver's seat. "Keys?" He put his hand out.

She glared at him in mute defiance. No way was she giving him her keys.

With the incredibly swift reflexes he had exhibited during their Tae Kwon Do sessions, he snatched the keys from her.

She yelped.

He didn't respond to the sound of outrage, but put the key in the ignition and started the car. "Fasten your seatbelt."

She glared at him. "Make me." Where had that come from?

He didn't hesitate. While the car idled, he reached across her, his chest pressing against her breasts and he grabbed the belt. Every rational thought in her head went on vacation and it was all she could do to limit her reaction to breathing in little pants and a heart rate that could be measured on the Richter scale.

He pulled the seatbelt across her and clicked it into the lock. "You're hyperventilating. Calm down. I'm not going to hurt you."

He thought she was frightened? She was, scared silly, but not of him. Of herself.

He put the car into reverse and pulled out of the small store's two-car parking lot. "I need a ride back to the house. I had Jacob drop me off when we spotted your car."

"If you needed a lift. All you had to do was ask." At least her voice worked and she hadn't warbled on a single word. "There was no reason for the he-man kidnapping or for you to appropriate my keys and my car."

His smile was devastating. "Wasn't there?"

She crossed her arms over her still heaving chest. "No."

"You weren't going to come back to my place without an order from the senate."

"That's ridiculous."

"No, your stubborn insistence on waiting out the ferry at the terminal was that. What would you have done if ferry service didn't resume? Slept in your car?"

Since that was exactly what she had planned, she didn't feel the need to answer him.

"This may be a small island, but that doesn't mean it's safe for a beautiful woman to sleep alone in her car all night."

Beautiful woman? Right. She made a rather rude noise in response to his blatant attempt to win her acquiescence with a falsehood.

"And I'd like to know what you were going to eat. All I saw was bottled water. Jacob said you didn't have breakfast. Did you plan to starve yourself?"

She went cold at the question. She didn't starve herself. Not anymore. She wasn't anorexic. It was just that rejection had a negative impact on her ability to eat. "I wasn't hungry."

It was his turn to make a rude noise of disbelief.

"What I eat, or don't eat, has nothing to do with you, Mr. Brant."

"Why not? I thought we were friends."

"We're business associates."

"We can't be friends too?"

Not when she wanted him more than she wanted to breathe, more than she wanted to guard herself against rejection. She'd allowed that want to dictate her actions last night and look what had resulted. She'd been humiliated, even if he didn't know it.

"I doubt I'll even see you again after today."

"You will if you continue to pursue the merger."

They'd reached his gate, which Jacob had left open for Simon. No cat and mouse games from the old codger for the boss.

Simon stopped the car in front of the house and got out. She opened her door and was climbing out when she realized he had popped open the trunk and was pulling out her suitcase.

"What are you doing?"

"Getting your things."

"There's no need." She tried to grab her suitcase and put it back in the trunk, but he placed it on the other side of his body. An impossible barrier in her current state. "I'll be on the ferry in a couple of hours."

He shook his head while reaching in to pull out her laptop. "I don't think so. More likely the first ferry out will be tomorrow morning, but even if it is, you won't be on it."

"What do you mean I won't be on it?" she asked with a fair amount of panic.

"We aren't done discussing this merger business, which I would have told you if you'd bothered to stick around long enough this morning to say goodbye." He sounded really miffed by the fact she hadn't.

But why would he care is she said goodbye, or not?

She ignored the part of her brain that insisted he was right that they weren't done discussing the merger and said, "I've told you all the facts."

"What if I have a question?" He pulled her briefcase from the trunk and turned to look at her with nothing less than accusation. "Or want to discuss some aspect of the proposal?"

"You don't want the darned thing!" This was stupid. Simon wanted that merger about as much as she wanted a cozy friendship with her ex-husband. "Why would you ask me any questions?" she demanded. "You didn't bother to last night."

He picked up her laptop and swung the cases strap over his shoulder, then picked up her suitcase. "I was busy listening."

More like ignoring her. "Right."

His eyes narrowed. "I can prove it." Then he started spouting facts at her like bullets out of an automatic pistol. Every one of them accurate, every one of them something she had told him the night before. When he was done, he looked smug. "Maybe I don't want the merger, but I thought you were going to try to change my mind."

This was too much. He could quote here words back to her verbatim, but that didn't mean he believed a single one of them. "You can't turn a stone into water."

"Are you saying I'm dense like a rock?" Amusement twitched at the corners of his mouth and her temper exploded.

"No, stubborn as mountain of rock!"

He threw back his head and laughed.

Heat surged into her face as her temper continued to escalate. She wasn't embarrassed; she was angry. "It's not funny. This is my career we're talking about. You won't even consider the merger regardless of whether or not it's the best thing for both of the companies."

Suddenly the laughter stopped and his gray eyes fixed on her with serious intent. "And your job is all that matters to you isn't it?"

"A career doesn't let you down like people do."

"And if this merger doesn't go through are you saying you'll get what you want out of your career anyway?"

Remembering the silken threat in Daniel's voice, she grit her teeth against an honest answer. "What difference does it make to you?"

"Maybe I care." He slammed the trunk shut with an excess of force and grimly finished picking up her things. "Maybe I don't want to see you hurt by this, but I don't have any choice about it because what you want isn't best for Brant Computers. You just think it is."

She didn't know what to say. He made it sound like what happened to her really mattered to him and she knew that wasn't possible. She was nothing to him, but an irritant. A blip on the radar of his life and just as temporary.

Without another word, he turned and headed for the house, leaving her to follow or not. She followed.

He went directly to her former bedroom and deposited her things on the end of her bed then turned to face her. "I can't promise to change my mind, but I can promise that if you leave I won't have a chance to."

There was no compromise in his expression. If she stayed, there was a slight chance of success. If she left, the merger was dead. It was blackmail. Plain and simple. Effective too. He'd chosen to hold the lure of the one thing she valued in her life besides her friendship with Jillian. Her career.

She didn't have a clue why Simon wanted her to stay. She couldn't believe it was because he really wanted to consider her arguments in favor Extant's proposal. But what if she was wrong? Even if she wasn't, the longer she held Daniel off from going after the other cousins' support, the better. She refused to be responsible for igniting a family war.

The arguments chased themselves in her head until she was dizzy with it. She felt torn between the familiar hell of staying with Simon and wanting him when he didn't want her and the unfamiliar hell of knowing she had let herself and her company down professionally.

What real choice did she have? She'd survived marriage to Lance. She could withstand a few more days in Simon's home.

"I'll stay."

Simon watched Amanda meander along the shoreline from the lab room window. She'd changed from her starchy suit to a cotton shorty top and matching Capri pants. She'd even pulled her magnificent hair back into a ponytail, letting it loose from that neat bun she constantly wore. She looked incredible, not at all like the buttoned-up woman he'd come to know so well in such a short time.

A timer went off, reminding him he was supposed to be working, but then so was she. She'd told him she had a couple of hours of on-line work to do before lunch after once again refusing any sort of breakfast. That bothered him, but he'd won a major concession and had sensed he wouldn't win another one.

He'd come up to his lab to try to gain some perspective. He had several puzzles that needed solving in his two major projects and that should have been enough to take his mind into a realm populated by circuit wires and computer code instead of people. It hadn't been.

For the first time in his memory, he could not dredge up enough interest in his projects to focus on them. He was too busy thinking about Amanda. Forcing her to stay had to be one of the least logical things he'd ever done. There were several very good reasons for letting her leave and never seeing her again. Reasons he had been convinced were paramount until that morning when he walked into the kitchen and she hadn't been there.

None of those sound arguments stacked up against the reality of her being gone. He'd expected to see her eating at the table and when he hadn't, the light had gone out of his morning. When Jacob told him that Amanda had left without saying goodbye, cold winds had blown across Simon's soul - winds that had been silent since her arrival at his home.

He hated that cold and the shadows that accompanied it. She filled the empty places and pushed the shadows away.

That's why he had kidnapped her from the island's one small grocery store, why he had blackmailed her into staying. It didn't have anything to do with the merger, no matter what he had told her to get her to stay. He wasn't being fair to her. He knew it. He had no intention of changing his mind about the merger. It was the wrong move for a family run company and given enough time, Eric was bound to see that as well, but Simon had still used the carrot of his possible change of heart to lure Amanda into staying.

Because as of this morning when he'd faced a day without Amanda in it, and the prospect of endless more to follow, he had become as determined to keep her as he was to reject the merger.

"I thought you needed to take care of some email."

Simon watched with fascination as Amanda jumped and whirled at the sound of his voice. She acted like a jackrabbit startled by a fox.

She stepped backward, away from him. "I didn't hear you come up."

"You must have been thinking pretty hard."

The twist of her lips could be called a smile, but there was something not quite right about it. She said, "Or you walk as quiet as a panther."

He shrugged at that. "I walk the way I walk."

She chewed on her bottom lip, which looked like it had already had a fair amount of that treatment. It was red and slightly swollen, all of the lipstick eaten off of it. Finally, she sighed. "You're so sure of who you are."

"Are you trying to tell me you're not?" She was easily as focused on her career as he was on his projects.

She looked off toward the water, her expression pensive. "I suppose I am when it comes to my job."

"But not when it comes to being a woman," he guessed, remembering his initial impression of her.

Her laugh was almost brittle. "No, not when it comes to being a woman, but then I'm much better at being a junior executive than I am at being female." The last words came out in such a low voice he had to strain to hear them.

"You don't think you're any good at being female?" he asked for confirmation because he found the idea so laughable. If she were any better at it, he'd need a straight jacket to keep his hands off her.

She whirled to face him, her dark brown eyes shooting sparks like a metal cup in the microwave. "Stop it. I know what I am. And while we're at it, you can quit making those stupid comments about my supposed beauty. I know what I look like, all right? I don't need you patronizing me with false flattery or your sarcastic little jokes about wanting to have sex with me." She sucked in air, drawing his attention to the charms she was so certain she did not have.

"We've got a business relationship. That's all. I don't need you to pretend like you notice me as a woman when you don't. Heavens knows I'm used to it."

"Used to what?" The conversation was not falling into any sort of logical pattern he could recognize.

"Used to being seen as my job rather than myself." She closed her eyes and seemed to battle for control before opening them again. "It's not important. I don't need you to see me as a woman. I'm here to do a job, nothing else."

He had never said otherwise. He might have thought it, but he hadn't said it. "Are you trying to convince me, or yourself?"

Unexpectedly, her eyes filled with tears, their brown depths awash with pain as well as wetness and he felt like a total bastard for having hurt her. He hadn't meant to. All he wanted was to understand what was going on inside her mind right now. He wanted to know why she had left without a word to him, why she had been so adamant about not coming back.

"I need to go." She turned back toward the house.

He could no more let her dismiss him right now than he had been able to leave her in the grocery store and his hand shot out to grab her shoulder. "Wait. I don't understand, baby. I didn't mean to hurt you with that question."

"Don't call me baby," she said in choked voice without turning to face him.

He hadn't realized he had. It fit her though. So tiny. So vulnerable in ways others probably wouldn't notice. "It suits you."

She shook her head, her long hair swinging against her petite back.

Taking her other shoulder in his free hand, he started pulling her back toward him. He didn't know what he planned. To comfort her, maybe, but as soon as her body was flush with his the idea of comfort took on a very intimate connotation.

He wrapped his arms around her front, locking them right under her breasts and nuzzled her shell-pink ear. He couldn't seem to help himself. Touching her seemed both natural and right.

She was in pain and he wanted to make it better. "I don't want you to hurt, Amanda. Tell me what I can do to make it go away."

She'd gone completely still in his arms. He wasn't sure she was even breathing. "Baby?"

"You don't want me any more than he did." The words were filled with so much pain, he winced.

He ignored her ludicrous assertion that he didn't want her. If she couldn't feel the erection growing against her back, he wasn't going to point it out to her and scare her half to death.

But the other part of what she said intrigued him. "Who didn't want you?"

"Lance."

"Your ex-husband?" he guessed.

She nodded causing her ear to brush against his lips, making them tingle. She gave a convulsive shudder.

"Are you crying?" He didn't know what to do with a crying woman, but somehow he couldn't just leave Amanda to her misery, whatever the cause.

"No." The broken syllable gave lie to her word, but he didn't tax her with it.

"Tell me about Lance," he said instead.

"I told you." She sounded belligerent. "He didn't want me."

CHAPTER ELEVEN

"**B**ut he was your husband."

"Yes."

For some reason hearing her affirm it made his gut tighten uncomfortably. He hated the thought of any other man having claim to this woman.

She exhaled on a broken sigh. "And he did everything in his power to mold me into someone he could desire. It didn't work."

What kind of eunuch idiot would want to change her? She was sexy, beautiful and perfect just as she was. "What? Was he gay?"

Her laugh was so far from humorous, it hurt to hear it. "No. He just couldn't force himself to make love with such an inadequate woman."

"You believed that bullshit? That you were inadequate as a woman?" He knew he sounded angry.

He was. Furious in fact. If Lance were with kicking distance, he'd be bruised and bloody right now. While the image gave him some satisfaction, he knew it wouldn't do anything to help the misery he sensed in Amanda right now. He didn't know what would.

She tore out of his arms and whirled on him, her expression feral. "Yes, I believed him! Why shouldn't I? You don't want me either! You made that obvious."

"When have I made that obvious?" He'd told her wanted to have sex with her. Did she think he made a habit of lying?

"Oh, please! Like you don't know."

Her sarcastic words were the last straw and he stormed forward. She backed up, but he caught her with no real effort. They'd have to work on her fighting technique when an adversary had her cornered.

He grabbed her wrist, careful not to bruise her pale flesh, but with a grip she wouldn't be able to get out of easily, and pulled her forward. In a crude act that shocked him even while he was doing it, he placed her small hand against the much larger, irrefutable proof that she was wrong.

"Feel that? I don't walk around with a lead pipe in my jeans, so what do you think that tells you about how much I want you?" He let go of her wrist prepared to take a slap in the face for what he'd done. Or worse.

She didn't slap him, or kick him, or even scream at him. She didn't jerk her hand away either. Instead she pressed her open palm against his erection and stroked its length. His knees almost buckled.

Her tear drenched gaze lifted to his, her expression filled with wonder. "You meant it."

He couldn't make his voice work, not with her hand still pressed against his sex. So, he nodded, but still could not comprehend why she acted so shocked by his arousal.

Her fingers convulsed, squeezing him and his eyes slid shut at the pleasure of it. "If you don't stop, I'm going to take you right here, in front of God, Jacob and the seagulls."

It wasn't the mention of God or the seagulls that did it, but when he said Jacob's name, Amanda forced her hand away from the physical evidence of Simon's arousal.

She felt exultant, like she'd just landed the deal of her career. Simon wanted her and he meant it. There could be no mistaking it this time. A man could not fake an erection, or get one on command. Lance had made sure she knew that. To get hard, a man had to be aroused and Simon was. Very aroused.

She wanted to shout hosannas.

He pulled her against him, letting her feel the hard length of his erection against her stomach. It was an incredible heady sensation and one she had never had before, this standing fully clothed against a man in a state of obvious sexual excitement.

His arms wrapped tightly around her. "You're so sexy, baby. It's all I've been able to do not to lay you down in my bed and keep you there for three days straight."

Bliss shivered through her at the thought. "So, why haven't you?" she asked into his chest with no thought of being coy or playing hard to get entering her mind.

He rubbed himself against her, his hands pressing into the small of her back to increase the friction between them. "I didn't want to cloud our relationship."

"You mean because of the merger?" Remembering Daniels crude advice for how to get Simon to agree to the proposal, she had to admit Simon had a point if that had been his concern.

"That and that fact your life is in Southern California and mine is here."

This evidence that casual sex did not interest him warmed her, but depressed her too. Because nothing could change the fact that their lives were lived in entirely different spheres.

"There's still the merger," she said aloud. "We're business associates, not lovers." Melancholy settled over her as she said the words. Simon might want her, but not enough to overcome the issues holding them apart.

His chin dropped against the top of her head and rested there. "Yes."

Her heart lost its tenuous hold on a possible positive outcome and plummeted. "I guess that means making love would be a bad thing?" she couldn't help asking, even though she knew his answer before he gave it.

His heart sped up at her words, thumping loudly against his chest. With her face pressed against his sternum, she could feel it as well as hear it.

"Depends on how you define bad." One big hand slid down to cup her bottom. "My definition of the word is changing with the speed of a sonic jet."

He had such a sexy voice. She bet he could talk her to an orgasm if he put his mind to it. Just the thought had her growing damp and hot between her legs. "It is?" she asked in an embarrassing croak.

The hand on her bottom squeezed. "Oh, yeah."

She heard his words, but her attention had been caught by his scent. She found herself nuzzling the denim work shirt stretched across his impressive chest muscles. Lance had never smelled like this. No other man in the world had Simon's scent. It was unique and it was intoxicating.

Her fingers lifted of their own volition and started undoing buttons. She wanted skin.

His arms tightened around her. "Keep that up and bad idea is going to lose all meaning for me."

She undid two more buttons for good measure and then kissed the bronzed chest she had just exposed. "Really?" She wanted to taste him. Almost insanely and with a complete lack of her normal sexual reticence, she flicked her tongue out and licked delicately. Salty. Warm. She licked again. Sort of spicy.

His big body shuddered.

For the second time that day she found herself swept up into his arms.

"Simon, what are you doing?"

Had she pushed him too far? Would he make good on his threat to make love to her outside? The thought intrigued her far more than it worried her. To have the ability to push her lover beyond his normal bounds of control was something she had never experienced.

She'd read about it though, and it sounded like a lot of fun if incredibly far-fetched.

His laughter sent sensual shivers arcing through her. "I'm carrying you off to my lair to have my wicked way with you." Suiting action to words, he started making ground-eating strides across the lawn toward the house. "To the victor go the spoils, or some such thing and I did capture you this morning."

"You kidnapped me!"

He shrugged and she clung to his neck, not wanting to fall.

"Same thing," he said.

"Are you saying you see yourself as some kind of conquering warrior?"

He smiled down at her, his eyes full of sensual heat. "You make an incredibly sexy and beautiful captive."

A warrior? She had no problem seeing Simon in the role. He'd struck her as innately dangerous since the moment they'd met. It was only now she was coming to appreciate the true nature of the danger involved. He had the power to stir her emotions in a way no other man ever had, not her few boyfriends and not even her ex-husband.

But her sexy and beautiful? Now that was a lot harder for her to get her imagination wrapped around.

Not so captive. Ooh...she liked that word. After the sexual debacle of her marriage, she was ready to indulge in a decadent fantasy. It might be the only chance she'd ever have. If she disappointed Simon in bed like she had Lance, he wasn't going to play conquering warrior for her again.

She shoved the depressing thought away. No matter what happened in the aftermath, for right now, Simon wanted her. So much he was carrying her off to bed.

"I'm too heavy to cart all the way to the house and up two flights of stairs." It was a half-hearted protest because she found the experience so delightful, but she felt it had to be made.

"Be quiet, captive." His voice came out in a disconcerting predatory growl. "None of your arguments will gain you freedom." His hold on her tightened. "You're mine now."

It was just a game, but it seemed like there was an element of real warning in Simon's voice. She dismissed the thought as fanciful. She was really getting into her role of captive.

"Fighting would be a waste of effort," she agreed, burying her face against him. She inhaled more of his scent, absorbing his essence skin to skin.

If she was dreaming, she'd kill the sleep police if they woke her up before Simon made love to her.

Simon's heart was trying to pound out of his chest as he laid Amanda down on his oversized bed. She looked so incredibly small laying there, her beautiful skin flushed with arousal, her eyes dark pools of sensual promise.

He started reefing off his clothes, stopping when all he had on was a pair of unbuttoned jeans. He didn't take them off. Not yet. He wanted her a lot more excited before he bared himself to her. He would expire from unsatisfied desire if she bolted after seeing his full erection. And it was fully erect, so hard it ached and pulsed with a need only this tiny woman could satisfy.

She hadn't taken anything off.

"If you don't undress, I'll rip your clothes off your body," he said in his conquering warrior persona, but only half-joking. He wanted her so much that if he tried undressing her, that cute little cotton top would probably end up without any buttons left.

Those startled doe eyes looked at him, doubt lurking in their depths. "You want me to take off my clothes?" She sounded just like a nervous virgin.

Another shot of desire surged through him. He didn't know how much longer he could keep up the game. He'd started it on a whim, sensing a need to put their lovemaking on a less intense level for Amanda, but far from lessening the tension, the role-playing was increasing it. At least for him.

He mock glared at her and started toward the bed. "Yes."

Something shifted in her expression and she scrambled to her knees, her hands on the buttons of her blouse. Her eyes questioned him.

"Take it off." Was that guttural voice his? He sounded like primal male intent on subduing his mate. "Wait a second."

Her hands stilled before the reached the blouse.

"Take down your hair." He wanted to see it in all its glorious splendor, like it had been the night before.

She obeyed him, the irises in her eyes growing darker as she did so and the dark brown mass fell down her back. It was as beautiful as the rest of her.

"Now, take off your top," he ordered, his voice every bit as guttural as the first time he'd told her to do it.

Her eyes widened and she moved her hands to the front of her blouse. Fingers trembling, she undid the top button.

Was she scared? He didn't want that. He had to get control of his desire before she decided he was some kind of uncivilized Neanderthal and went running from the room.

He went closer, and reached out to cover her hands with his. "The game doesn't matter, sweetheart. I just want you."

She swallowed. "I um..."

He slipped his fingers under hers and undid the next button, exposing the top of her generous cleavage. He couldn't help himself. "What?"

She cleared her throat. "Simon?"

"I'm right here, baby." He liked calling her that, he decided.

"Could we, um..."

He put his knee down on the bed and loomed over her, slipping the third button out of its hole and giving himself a view of creamy white mounds. She wasn't wearing a bra and for some reason that knowledge upped his excitement ten more notches. He had every intention of seeing her fully naked before long, but there was something about knowing that thin cotton was all that stood between him and her magnificent breasts.

She took a deep breath, pressing soft flesh against the back of his fingers. "Oh!" She blinked her big, brown eyes at him.

He smiled and lowered his head until their lips were a centimeter away from meeting. "Could we what, sweetheart?"

"I want to play."

"I want to play too." And he wanted to play for a very long time. He buried his fingers in her rich dark hair and kissed her, nibbling at that delicious bottom lip that had tantalized him with its fullness earlier.

She tasted so good, better than he'd fantasized. Her mouth was sweet and warm and he explored all of it, starting with her lips and then moving with gentle forays into the interior. Her tongue was shy, but when she let it slide along his, fireworks exploded in his head.

They stayed like that for endless minutes, her shirt half undone, his hands buried in her hair and their mouths molded together like two halves of a work of art by one of the great masters.

Finally, he pulled back. He wanted to finish the job of undressing the treasure in his arms. "Is that the way you wanted to play?" he teased as he undid the final three buttons in quick succession.

Her hands grabbed his wrists before he could peel the fabric back and expose her flesh to his hungry gaze. "I mean I want to play conquering warrior and captive." She said it all in a rush and then blushed crimson.

He'd never seen a woman do that before, but Amanda's cheeks were as red as a ripe apple.

He let the pads of his thumbs caress the inner curves of her breasts. "You want to keep pretending to be my captive?"

Did she have any idea what the scenario was doing to him?

Amanda nodded, terrified of how he'd respond to her request. What if he didn't want to keep up the pretense? She might annoy him with her silliness, but she'd thought that if she could get him to play the game, he would be in charge. He wouldn't expect her to do anything. After all, a captive wasn't required to seduce her captor.

Simon might even mistake her sexual ineptness as an attempt to play inexperienced virgin. It would be his job to seduce her and then maybe she wouldn't mess everything up.

His hands slid inside the opened edges of her top and cupped both her breasts, sending her heart into her throat. "You make a very alluring captive, Amanda."

"I do?" she choked out.

"Oh, yes." His hands squeezed and she felt her pebble hard nipples brush against the hard skin of his palms.

She moaned.

"You may be a virgin, but you cannot pretend you do not want me." Heavens, he really sounded like the conquering warrior now.

Her hands were still on his wrists, but she wasn't trying to stop him from caressing her intimate flesh. She wanted it so much. "Yes, I want you," she said, giving him the words.

Then he kissed her, not gently and tentatively like he'd done before, but with all the passion she'd dreamed of sparking in her lover. His mouth claimed hers with a marauder's skill and she went under without a count.

Her sensory universe shrank to include only this man. His taste. His smell. The way it felt to have his mouth sucking at hers, his tongue invading her mouth. She let her hands slide along his arms and up to his chest, touching him like she had craved doing that first Tae Kwon Do sparring session when he had teased her with his naked torso.

His skin was smooth over rock-hard muscles and she brushed the fan of silken black hair on his chest with her fingertips. She was glad he wasn't hairy all over. She much preferred the velvety expanse of his skin, so warm, so vibrant.

Suddenly the hold on her breasts changed. He took each swollen bud between a thumb and forefinger and began to roll them. She screamed into his mouth, the feeling so electric her fingers dug into his pecs.

His mouth broke away from hers. "I've got to taste you, baby." Then he was tearing her top off and his hot mouth closed around one nipple.

He sucked.

She screamed again, the sound unmuffled and shocking to her.

He sucked harder and it became a pleasure this side of pain, but she would die if he stopped. She knew she would die. He started to play with her other breast again, using his fingers to torment the peak to a level of sensitivity she had never known.

She couldn't talk. She couldn't even beg. All she could do was make incoherent noises with her mouth while the pleasurable tension inside her coiled tighter and tighter. She felt like a spring, ready to snap, but there was no let-up of the pressure. She couldn't stand it. It was too much!

She tried to pull away, but only succeeded in falling backward on the bed, Simon still in possession of her sensitized flesh. He used his knee to push her legs apart and then settled between them, his big body pressed against the heart of her.

She could no more help arching her pelvis toward him than she could stop the feelings shooting straight from her nipples to the core of her femininity.

She reached her hands above her head, needing something to hold onto as the maelstrom of sensations threatened to overwhelm her. Her fingers encountered the bars of the bed. She grabbed them, her whole body tensing as Simon ground the hard muscles of his stomach against the throbbing flesh between her legs.

He released her nipple with a pop and air rushed against the wet, engorged tip. His head came up and his gunmetal gaze raked over her, his eyes narrowing when he saw where her hands were.

He seemed mesmerized by the sight of her fingers clinging to his headboard. "Good idea."

"What do you mean?" Her voice came out in a husky whisper, which was all she could manage at that point.

"A captive should be restrained, don't you think? So she can't run away."

Simon almost laughed at the look that crossed Amanda's face at his suggestion, but he wasn't capable of laughter right then. He was barely capable of speech. He wanted to bury himself between her legs, to feel the liquid heat of her swollen lips and blood engorged tissues surrounding him.

"You want to tie me to the bed?" she asked, her voice squeaking like Minnie Mouse.

He cupped her tip-tilted, luxuriant breasts and squeezed them together, then buried his mouth against the nipples he'd pressed so near one another. "Yes."

She was silent for so long, he thought she was going to say no. He laved the sweet reddened berries with his tongue, totally willing to let the game go if that was what she wanted. He needed her, her body, her generous and giving passion. Her. Nothing more. Nothing less.

"All right."

His head shot up and he looked into doe-brown eyes glazed with desire.

"You can tie my hands to the bed."

He felt a spurt of pre-ejaculate come. Not at the thought of tying his lover up, but at the knowledge she trusted him enough with her body to let him do it.

He came up on his knees and straddled her right over the apex of her thighs. Her breath heaved in and out, making her flushed and excited flesh quiver.

If he didn't need to be inside her so bad, he could watch her just breathe all night. He traced the smooth skin of her abdomen with one fingertip. "Baby, you are stunning."

"I'm not."

Anger equal to his passion coursed through him. "You are and you can damn well stop accusing me of lying. You're the prettiest, sexiest, most incredible woman I have ever known and if you try to deny it again, I'll gag you."

She laughed, the sound almost as beautiful as she was. "You can't gag me because then we couldn't kiss."

She had a point. "Then I'll just have to kiss you silent."

Her mouth curved in a Mona Lisa smile. "Is that supposed to encourage me to be good...or bad?"

He groaned. "Minx."

Leaning over her, he reached for the nightstand drawer and slid it open. The box of condoms Jacob had presented Simon with the day after catching Amanda sleeping in his arms winked up at him, but it was the anti-static straps he had stashed there at some point that interested him at the moment. Their soft composition and Velcro fastening made them ideal for what he had in mind.

Pulling two out, he sat back up, grunting as the movement caused his iron hard flesh to brush against her mound in a way guaranteed to drive him crazy. He wanted to get her pants off and see that place reserved just for him.

She stared at the EST straps in his hands, then looked up at him and smiled such a sweet smile he had to lean down and kiss her.

Amanda reveled under the onslaught of Simon's kiss. She was so close to orgasm that one more movement down there and she was going to go off like a model rocket on a short fuse. He had no idea how tantalizing she found the prospect of having her hands bound. If she couldn't touch him, she couldn't mess up touching him. It was a win-win scenario for her.

And he was so good at this touching thing. He ground himself against her and she felt herself right on the verge of ecstasy, but she needed more, just a little more.

She pressed against him with herself, spreading her legs wider to increase the friction between their bodies. Rotating her hips in a circle, she fought frantically for that final touch that would make the explosion nuclear.

But, cruelly, he pulled away, moving his body so that no matter how she arched and twisted, she couldn't get the contact she needed.

She tore her lips from his. "Simon! Please, I need you to make me come. I'm so close," she whimpered.

His hands cupped her face. "Baby, I want to taste you. I want to touch you. I want some part of my body and I don't care if it's my tongue, my finger or my sex, inside you when you come for me for the first time. Please."

She stared up at him, frustration warring with the undeniable need thickening his voice. His need and hers...to be desired that strongly...won. "All right."

He smiled and kissed her with obvious approval. Then she felt his fingers at work at each wrist and she found herself bound loosely to the bed. If she yanked or worked the bindings, she could get loose, but she didn't want to.

Then he climbed down her body until he could reach the button and zipper on her cotton Capri pants. He undid them and began to pull them off, taking her panties with them as they went. When he reached her feet, her tennies and socks came off too, leaving her completely naked and open to his gaze by the time he stood erect at the end of the bed.

She looked so vulnerable lying there, like she expected him to find her lacking. Her expression of nervous worry was impossible to misinterpret.

He shook his head. "You are gorgeous." Dark brown curls hid the secrets of her femininity and he climbed back onto the bed so he could brush his fingers through the silky fluff.

Her eyes slid shut and she moaned as he pressed one fingertip between the plump lips. He sought out her clitoris and touched it. Just lightly. He didn't want her going off yet. She'd come so close earlier and he hadn't been lying when he said he intended to be inside her when it happened.

He wanted to taste her, to get her so mindless with pleasure that when he went to join their flesh, she wouldn't have enough wherewithal to get nervous about his size. He would never hurt her, but she wouldn't know that until after they'd made love, would she?

He told himself to stop worrying. She'd trusted him enough to play sexy games with him. She wasn't going to freak out when she saw his straining erection.

She arched off the bed, her body flushed with passion. "If you don't do something soon, I'm going to scream."

"You're going to scream all right, but it will be because I'm doing something."

She gave a choked laugh that cut off when he pressed her silky thighs apart and buried his mouth against her wet and swollen flesh. She was slick and sweet and hot, so damn hot. He'd done this for other women, but he could never remember being as turned on by it as he was right now.

Every ripple of pleasure in her flesh echoed in his own.

Every sexy little moan brought a responsive groan from deep inside him.

And she tasted like every erotic fantasy he had ever had.

Her body writhed against him. "Simon, oh... That feels so good. I've never... Oh..."

He slipped his tongue inside and used his thumb to draw circles around her hardened clitoris. She went ballistic, screaming his name while pressing herself against his mouth with so much force he was afraid she'd hurt herself on his teeth.

"More!" she shouted.

And he gave her more. And more. And more. Until she was sobbing with pleasure. Until she was begging him to stop, her body convulsing and jerking with every slide of his tongue, every glide of his finger. And more. Until with a groan of utter abandonment, she went limp beneath him.

He kissed her labia softly, then the sweet spot he'd pleasured so unmercifully and then finally paid homage to it all with a gentle kiss on the very top of her mound.

She expelled a shuddering sigh.

He stood up and shucked out of his jeans and black knit boxers, the relief of letting his sex free an overwhelming pleasure in itself. He walked around the bed and dug a condom out of the drawer in the nightstand. It took two tries to rip open the foil packet because his hands were shaking. He finally got it on and turned to look at Amanda, ready to gauge her reaction to his size, but her eyes weren't even open. Her face wore the most blissful and sweet expression he'd ever seen, but tears ran unchecked down her temples.

Chapter Twelve

Oh, man. Was she okay?

Amanda felt a tentative fingertip trace the path of her tears and smiled. "I didn't hurt you, did I?" He sounded so worried.

She didn't want him to worry, not when she was as close to Heaven as a woman could get and still be living. "No. It just feels so good." She forced heavy eyelids up and turned her head toward the sound of his voice.

He was beside her and leaning above her, propped up on one arm. "You're crying because it feels good?" His tone was one of disbelief.

"Yes." She looked deeply into his storm gray eyes. "Thank you. That's the most beautiful experience I've ever had."

The worry cleared from his expression to be replaced by masculine arrogance. "There's more."

"Not possible."

That made him laugh. Low and husky, sending a skirl of pleasure through her when she thought all pleasure had been wrung from her body.

"Do you want me to release your arms?"

She thought about it. Everything had gone so well so far. He didn't seem disappointed and she'd experienced the most amazing sensations of her life. There was an old saying, "If it isn't broken, don't fix it." It definitely wasn't broken.

"No." Then she peeked at him to see if her answer had disappointed him, but he was already moving over her, pressing her legs apart with his muscular thighs.

He hooked her knees with his forearms, pulling them up, exposing her to him in a way she could not have stood with anyone else. "You wanted more, Amanda, and I'm going to give it to you."

She remembered screaming that sometime during him making love to her with his mouth. Unbelievably, renewed desire sparked to life inside her. She thought she'd been beyond arousal, so satiated her senses could not take in any more pleasure.

She'd been wrong.

At the first tender probe of the blunt tip of his erection, her thighs quivered and the engorged tissues of her feminine core sat up and took notice. He pressed himself inside her opening, stretching her and she felt her eyes widen. "Simon?"

The tentative way she said his name made something protective expand inside him. "What, sweetheart?"

"Are you awfully big?"

"I won't hurt you."

Her smile warmed him. "I know."

"Trust me." He pressed forward a little more and she sucked in air. "I'll be careful. We're going to fit just fine. We just need to take this part slow."

"I do trust you, Simon, but I don't know how slow I can stand for you to take it."

She still wanted him.

Relief had only a second to make itself felt as sexual excitement vied for his attention and won. "I want to bury myself so deeply inside you that our pelvic bones touch."

Her inner flesh contracted at his words. "Oh, yes."

He rocked forward, gaining another full inch and making her moan. "You feel so good, so perfect for me."

She arched toward him, her fingers gripped around the bars of the headboard with white-knuckle intensity. "Stop playing, Simon. You said you wanted to go deep. I want all of you!"

He would have laughed at her demanding tone if he'd had enough breath. He moved again, gaining more, but she was so tight, he couldn't go farther. "Relax for me, baby. Please."

"How?" She sounded both bewildered and as on edge sexually as he felt.

How? He didn't know how. It was her body.

Some of his frustration must have shown on his face because her brows puckered and her lips trembled. "I'm sorry. I—"

He cut off her apology with his mouth. He didn't like hearing her apologizing when she was giving him so much pleasure. When she was once again straining beneath him, he lifted his head. "Can you tighten your inner muscles?"

"I think so." The flesh around him squeezed and he groaned. Okay, she could definitely tighten them.

"Now, try reversing that."

Her face took on the most endearing expression of concentration. He didn't think another woman had ever been so concerned about getting it right for him. And she did get it right, all at once the pressure around him relaxed and she spread her thighs wider. He'd been afraid to press her legs that far apart, but she was incredibly limber.

Hell, she was plain incredible. He rocked into her, finishing the penetration easily now. And then he was where he had most wanted to be, sheathed by her wet, swollen tissues, his sex throbbing from the pleasure her body gave him.

Her entire body went stiff and her gorgeous brown eyes flew wide with shock. "Simon?!"

Had he gone in too far? He'd promised not to hurt her.

Her inner muscles contracted around him again and she shuddered. "So good," she panted and he relaxed.

Oh yeah, it felt good all right. It felt better than anything he'd ever known and he stayed perfectly still savoring the completeness of their joining. He'd been right. She fit him like her body had been made to accommodate his.

As he strained the limits of his self-control by remaining immobile, he could feel sweat soaking his back and muscle burn like he'd been doing a major work out.

"Move, Simon!" She squirmed under him, but she couldn't do much with her knees hooked over his forearms and her hands tied. She glared up at him. "Don't tease me."

"I'm not teasing you, baby. I'm enjoying you."

"Please move. Please, oh please, oh please..."

The begging did it.

He moved. Pulling out until only the head of his sex remained in her warmth, he then surged deep with one thrust... two... three... and suddenly her hot, wet flesh was pulsating around him in release. She screamed, she cried, she writhed and then she demanded more again. He let go of her legs to reach between their bodies and massage her sweet spot with his thumb.

She convulsed again, her body going so taut, she lifted them both up off the bed. He went over the brink, his raw shout joining with her uncontrolled whimpers of surrender and ecstasy. They strained together for endless moments of shared rapture before she collapsed back on the bed.

He went with her, his body feeling boneless. With the last bit of strength he had, he reached above them and undid the restraints on her wrists.

"I don't think I can move them."

His head came up at her ruefully uttered words. She didn't look upset, so he didn't think she meant he'd hurt her.

Her eyes slid shut. "I want to hold you," she whispered on a yawn, "but I can't seem to make my arms work."

He discovered that with the right incentive, he had reserves of energy he had not known possessed. Reaching up, he grasped her wrists and pulled her arms gently down. When he placed them on his shoulders, she linked her hands behind his neck and hugged him to her.

It felt good.

He wrapped the soft luxury of her hair around his fist, careful not to pull. He just wanted another way to anchor her to him.

She kissed his collarbone. "I like this."

He sighed with pleasure. "Me too."

He was still erect inside her, his orgasm having exhausted him, but going nowhere toward slaking the desire she engendered in his flesh.

"Thank you, Simon."

He pulled back so he could see the sweet contours of her heart-shaped face. "Thank you, baby. I've never had it so good," he admitted truthfully.

Hershey brown eyes widened, glistening with suspicious moisture. "Really?"

He kissed her. "Really."

"Me either."

For some reason that admission made him feel ten feet tall. "You liked making love with a conquering warrior, huh?"

"I adored making love with you." Her fingers speared through his hair and she nuzzled his chest. "I've never climaxed before."

The words were muffled and whispered sort of low, so at first he doubted he'd heard her correctly. "Did you just say you'd never come before?"

"Yes." She wouldn't look at him.

He tilted her chin up with his free hand. "Say that again."

She shook her head. "You heard me."

"But you're so responsive!"

She attempted a shrug, but it didn't work very well with his bulk on top of her. "I never have been before."

He liked hearing that. He didn't care if it was a totally archaic attitude to have, but he felt like a true conqueror at her halting admission. Definitely non-PC. "You mean you've never had an orgasm with a man," he said for clarification.

"Did I say that?" she asked, turning her face from his scrutiny, pulling the hair wrapped around his other hand taut.

"No." But the alternative was unthinkable. She was twenty-six years old, or so Jacob had informed him after the initial security check. She was divorced. She couldn't be that innocent. He felt like he'd just made love to a virgin.

He used his hold on her hair to angle her face back toward him so he could see her eyes. "But, baby, there are things…"

She glared up at him. "I didn't feel comfortable trying things, all right? If it bothers you, I'm sorry. I just thought you might like to know."

Hell. He had offended her. "Shh." He kissed her until all the tension that had been seeping into her limbs eased away. "It doesn't bother me. It surprised me. That's all. You are the most sensual woman I have ever been with, but I'd have to be a fool not to like knowing you had your first climax with me."

Her smile was a little watery. "I guess that means you won't mind trying it again sometime."

They were still intimately connected, he could feel her soft wetness clinging to him and she was talking about sometime like what they were sharing right now was over. He stared down at her. Did she think this had been some casual sexual encounter, like sharing a really decadent dessert that they both might want to taste again, but nothing serious?

The hell with that.

But all he said was, "Sure." If his tone was a little surly, she'd have to forgive him. Sometime could mean anything from the next time she was in Washington to the next five minutes. He knew exactly which sometime he intended to make happen and it wasn't some nebulous date in the future.

But first there was something he had to do.

He unwound the silk bonds from his hand, carefully withdrew from her body and rolled away from her. He stood up and turned away from her in pretty much the same motion, still a little leery about her seeing him in all his aroused glory. It was getting more glorious by the second as he contemplated how best to seduce the pocket Venus on his bed all over again.

Amanda watched Simon walk into the bathroom in a state of confusion. He'd sounded angry. Had her question made him mad? Maybe she was clinging. For all she knew, this was a one-off deal for Simon. They hadn't said anything about the future. He might want to go back to business as usual.

Maybe once had been enough for him.

He'd said she was the most sensual woman he'd ever been with, but she knew that wasn't true. Couldn't be true. She was about as sensual as a Raggedy Ann doll, but she had satisfied him. She knew she had. His release had been every bit as loud and wild as her own.

So, why had he vacated the bed so quickly?

Maybe she had disappointed him in some way.

Was she supposed to get dressed and leave while he was in the bathroom? She didn't know the protocol for this sort of thing. She felt lethargic from the surfeit of pleasure he'd given her, but she didn't think he'd appreciate coming back to find she had crawled beneath the sheets and gone to sleep in his bed. She wasn't even sure he'd want to come out and find her in the room at all.

Cold seeped into her where the heat of passion had burned so brightly just minutes ago.

She heard the sound of water running, but it wasn't followed by the distinctive patter of a shower.

What was he doing?

She sat up and scanned the room, looking for her clothes. She could see one tennis shoe over by the door, a sock on the chair by the bed and what looked like her pants in a heap of cotton on the bottom corner of the huge mattress. She got up on her knees and crawled across the bed to retrieve her pants.

When she reached them, she spied her top on the floor about a foot from the bed. She leaned over and reached for it.

"Nice view."

Realizing exactly what he was seeing, her naked backside up in the air, she screeched and scrambled back onto the bed. She turned on her knees to face him. He looked amused, darn him.

Just once she'd like the naked view of her body to inspire uncontrollable desire. Not contempt. Not humor. Passion. Right. That was going to happen in this lifetime, not.

Her top was still on the floor, so she grabbed up her pants and held them in front of her in an attempt at modesty. They'd made love on top of the covers, leaving her nothing to hide behind. The thought of Simon looking at her naked body and noticing her deficiencies made her cringe.

"I thought you were going to take a shower."

But he hadn't. He'd come back wearing nothing but a towel slung low on his hips.

"You look very good sitting on my bed, Amanda." He walked over to the bed. "But you will look even better in my bath."

He reached out and tugged on her pants. "You don't need these right now."

"I..."

He managed to prise the meager cotton barrier to her nudity from her tight grip. He tossed the capris on the floor where they landed almost on top of her shirt.

"They're going to get wrinkled all wadded up like that."

"Jacob can iron them for you." With that, he scooped her up in his strong arms.

"This is becoming a habit with you," she said breathlessly as naked skin met hot, naked skin.

His answering smile was that of a buccaneer who had appropriated a cargo hold full of bounty. "You're such a tiny thing, all my primitive instincts come out. Do you mind?"

"No." Actually, she kind of liked it.

But tiny? She supposed compared to him, her five-foot-four seemed small, but still...tiny?

"I wear a thirty-four D cup bra," she said, stating the obvious, "and I bet I wear the same size all the time that your cousin's wife," the woman he'd cared enough about to want to marry, "wears pregnant."

"Yeah. You're perfect, but so small it scares me a little. I'm really lucky your passion makes up for your size."

Were they talking about the same body? Had he heard a word she had said? Her mother had been after her to go for a breast reduction since she'd finished developing. Lance had joined her mother's urgings, but she had refused. She'd never had surgery and frankly the idea of having such an operation had scared her.

"You really think I'm perfect?" she couldn't help asking.

He stared at her like she'd lost her mind. "You have a luscious body, sweetheart. But I'm not telling you anything you don't already know. Other men must have told you the same thing, ad nauseum."

If she admitted they hadn't, would that lessen her in Simon's eyes? She shrugged noncommittally, not saying anything else until they arrived at Simon's bathtub. It looked more like a small Jacuzzi to her. There was definitely room for two and it occurred to her that Simon meant to take advantage of that fact.

"We're taking a bath together?"

His answer was to step with her into the swirling water.

Simon had come into the bathroom to take care of the condom when the sight of his oversized, jetted tub had given him an idea for his captive's next seduction. He'd never bathed with a woman. He'd taken showers with lovers, but never a bath.

She'd had her first orgasm with him. He decided he would take his first co-ed bath with her.

She made no move to slide off his lap once their bodies were immersed in the hot, scented water. He'd tossed in some aromatherapy bath salts one of his cousins in Arizona had sent him for Christmas. It smelled pretty nice. He hoped Amanda thought so too. Besides it had an oil base, turning the water into an all over body lubricant.

He cupped one of her D cup breasts, smiling at how she had admitted to her bra size like it was a crime. Was she really that ignorant of a man's desires that she didn't realize his reaction to her generous curves would be anything but revulsion?

She circled one of his masculine nipples with a forefinger, making his sex bob in the water beside her hip.

"This is kind of fun, isn't it?" she asked.

Cupping his hand, he scooped up some water and let it trickle over swollen peaks the color of ripe raspberries. "Fun is a pretty tame word for what I feel right now, Amanda."

She laughed, the sound exultant. "Oh, Simon."

He palmed her cheek, angling her head for his kiss. Her lips were pliant and warm. As he played with the ripened flesh of her breasts, she opened her mouth with a purring sound and he took instant advantage of the chance to taste her again. So sweet. He could never get enough of her mouth.

She sucked on his tongue while kneading the muscles of his chest like a cat and he felt like exploding right then. He put up with the torment of her mouth for as long as he could before he knew that one more second and he would come without even having her touch his arousal.

Tearing his mouth from hers, he broke the kiss to suckle the rapid pulse at the base of her throat.

"That feels so good," she groaned, letting her head fall back. "Simon, everything you do to me feels good." She sounded really surprised by that fact.

Maybe she was. She'd been married, but never had a climax. Her husband had to have been a lousy lover because she was amazingly responsive.

She wiggled her bottom against him, but didn't make a move to bring her body into contact with his hardened flesh. He couldn't stand that kind of teasing. Not this time. Maybe never. This woman affected him in ways he would have denied were possible.

He reached down and grabbed her hips, turning her toward him and letting her float in the water just long enough to separate her legs. When he pulled her back onto his lap he made sure she was straddling him.

Her head came up and she stared at him, her eyes glazed with passion. "Simon?"

"I want to feel your sweetness against me, baby."

"Oh, yes." But she didn't move.

Too impatient to wait, he pressed against her tailbone and her bath oil slickened thighs slid along his until their bodies met. He shuddered. So did she.

He adjusted her until her swollen outer labia were lined up with his erection, then he reached around and gently separated the lips. He arched up so his sex pressed against her most sensitive flesh. "Pleasure us, sweetheart."

She made a broken sound. "How?"

Grabbing her bottom with both hands, he slid her up the length of his erection, pressing in when her hardened clitoris was aligned with the mass of nerve endings near the tip. Then he slid her down again until her labia met his sacs.

Her mouth formed a surprised little O that he just had to kiss. "Ride me, baby."

"But you aren't inside me."

Never having taken a bath with a woman before, he didn't know how well a condom worked in that environment. He also didn't have the patience to find out. "This will be good, trust me."

She must have because she started moving against him, doing a little circular motion every time her sweet spot met the ridge at broad tip of his arousal.

"This is so amazing. I can feel bubbles in my..."

"Do you like it?" he asked as he moved his hand around so his fingers could play where the bubbles had found their way.

"Oh... Oh... Yesss... I like it."

Her movements were voluptuous and he was glad they'd already made love. He wanted this to last. And it did.

She rode him for a long time while wave after wave of pleasure washed over him with the oil slick water. Eventually, her movements grew more frantic until she stiffened against him, crying out his name as her body convulsed in what felt like a never ending orgasm.

He came then, too. Shooting into the water. The sensual feel of the bubbling wetness all around him increased the intensity and his orgasm lasted longer than any he had ever had. When it was over, his head fell back against the rest and he closed his eyes. Amanda sank against his chest like a wilted flower and he hugged her to him.

She kissed his chest and he felt that tender salute to the bottom of his soul.

Amanda woke up to the disorienting sensation of being surrounded by living heat. Then she remembered. She was in Simon's bed, in his arms. His quite naked arms. It was almost identical to the time she'd fallen asleep waiting for him to relax his hold on her. His hand was on her breast, hers was against his chest and their legs were entwined.

Only this time, she knew she belonged.

He'd pulled her into his bed after their bath without giving her the option of returning to her own room.

She hadn't minded.

Given her druthers, she'd never leave Simon's bed again.

She allowed herself a small smile at that bit of fantasy. She could just see Jacob bringing them necessary provisions while they pursued a life of debauchery, never leaving the haven of Simon's bedroom.

It didn't feel like debauchery when their bodies were joined though. It felt spiritual. Did Simon experience the same thing? She had no way of knowing. She'd been a virgin with little heavy petting experience when she'd married Lance and she'd never had sex with another man. Until now.

It felt funny, knowing they weren't married.

She supposed in that way too, she was anachronistic. Even feeling odd about it though, she wasn't going to walk away from her first experience with real passion. Because something had hit her about halfway through their decadent bath. It wasn't just a matter of passion, but of love.

She was in love with Simon Brant. Really in love. It was only as the overwhelming emotions coursed through her that she accepted that the lukewarm feelings she had had for Lance had been as much to do with seeking her family's approval as they had to do with any sort of attraction she'd had for the smooth manipulator.

What she felt for Simon was so elemental, it was scary. The thought of him with another woman made her sick and she could not imaging ever letting another man touch her the way Simon had touched her. She wasn't naïve enough to think Simon was considering a long-term commitment to her, but that didn't alter the way she felt.

He'd told her one of his objections to getting involved was the fact their lives did not mesh. Which said to her that he wasn't looking for ways to make them mesh.

Because of her past, she wasn't sure that even if he did want a permanent future with her, she could pursue it. The thought of being married again terrified her. Men changed after marriage. Lance had been complimentary and charming, right up until the honeymoon.

The little digs had started on their wedding night.

Rationally, she knew Simon wasn't another Lance. However, emotions weren't always rational and hers were scarred.

Was she selfish and wicked for wanting to take all she could of Simon, to replace the memories of a devastating failure of a marriage with the amazing beauty of Simon's lovemaking?

Simon stirred, his eyes flicked open and for several seconds they just stared at each other.

"What time is it?"

She went up on one elbow to look over his shoulder at the digital alarm clock. "A little after seven."

"We missed dinner."

Her stomach growled at the words, reminding her she'd missed her other meals today too. They'd made love right through lunch. "We could always go down and raid the kitchen."

"It's not that late. Jacob probably has something waiting for us."

The thought of facing the irascible old man after spending hours in Simon's bedroom daunted her. "Probably."

His hand cupped her chin. "What's the matter?"

"Nothing."

"Come on, baby. You've gone tense."

"Jacob probably thinks I'm a floozy."

"Floozy? Do they still use words like that in Southern California?" he asked with laughter in his voice.

"No, well not that I've heard, but I bet Jacob does."

"You're not a floozy, Amanda."

"I know that. Women and men make love all the time without a major commitment."

His thumb brushed her lips. "But not you."

She felt way too vulnerable, but she couldn't lie. "Not me."

He kissed her so softly, so tenderly that she felt tears prick her eyes. "This isn't casual sex, Amanda. Not for me."

Her breath came out on a broken sigh. "Not for me either."

He didn't say anything else, which left her wondering what the afternoon had been if it not casual sex. No way did he love her, but he didn't sound like the past few hours had been an indulgence of physical pleasure and nothing else either.

That would have to be enough. She put her hand over his on her face. "Shall we go get some dinner?"

He didn't say anything for a second, his gunmetal eyes probing her own, making her wish she could close them and hide whatever he might find.

Finally, his hand dropped from her. "Sure." He slid out of the other side of the bed. "Stay here while I run down and grab your suitcase."

"Okay."

She watched in hungry fascination as he covered his nakedness with a pair of do bok pants. He was only semi-erect, but he was still bigger than Lance had been with a full arousal.

Did the guy ever go totally soft?

He was funny about her seeing him completely excited though. She hadn't noticed at first, but he'd kept his body averted from her when they got out of the bath, wearing a towel until they'd gotten in the bed. And the last time they'd made love, he'd kept the sheet over the lower half of his body until just before joining their bodies.

He also hadn't asked her to put the condom on him. She'd been too shy to ask, but she wanted to touch him there.

Maybe she'd work up the courage later.

She was contemplating the prospect when Simon came back carrying not only her suitcase, but the rest of her things as well.

"Wouldn't it have been easier to just grab my suitcase?" She didn't need her laptop to get dressed.

He dropped the luggage at the end of the bed. "We'd just have to bring it up later. I thought I'd save myself a trip."

That sounded like she was moving into his bedroom. "Uh...Simon?"

He'd turned away to pull clothes out of the dresser. "What?"

"Am I sleeping here now?"

He spun around to face her. "Don't you want to?" He sounded defensive and his expression was wary.

"It's not that I don't want to, it's just that... Are you sure I won't be in the way? What about when you want to work?"

"You're not sleeping in my lab."

"But Jacob said you don't even like him to come up and clean when you're in a work mode."

He grabbed a pair of jeans and dark gray T-shirt from the drawer. "If you want your own space just say so."

She thought about sleeping in Simon's arms, waking up with him and making love to him. "I'd rather sleep here."

Chapter Thirteen

The next morning as she stared blindly at her computer screen having just read an email from Daniel, Amanda questioned the prudence of her decision to move into Simon's bedroom.

Who was she kidding? Prudence had nothing to do with it. For the first time she could remember, she had made a decision based wholly on emotion. She'd ignored the ramifications it might have for her career, the temporary nature of the liaison and even how such a choice would impact how others like Jacob, Eric Brant and her own coworkers saw her.

Why? Because she was in love, and she was discovering that emotion was more powerful than intellect, and more driving than reason. It had to be, or how could she have allowed herself to fall for Simon Brant?

Until the merger went through, if it went through, he wasn't just a business associate. He was a key player for Extant Corp's competition, a rival. With his intransigence toward the merger, he also stood between her and success at her job. Their relationship, such as it was, was temporary. They were from totally different worlds and one day soon, she would have to go back to hers. He'd made that point and he was right.

Love should have no place in any equation that included him as a variable. Not when every indicator on both a business and personal level marked doom for anything lasting between them.

He wasn't looking for permanence with a woman. The only driving compulsions in his life were his inventions and computer designs.

The one woman he had ever considered marrying was the total opposite of Amanda. Elaine Brant was slim, gorgeous and a social butterfly. She'd drawn Simon out of his quiet self-containment at dinner the other evening far more easily than Amanda ever could have done.

How could she have let herself love someone so programmed not to love her back?

If that incredible folly wasn't enough to convince her she'd lost her mind, she'd gone to bed with him. Okay. That part had been wonderful. More than wonderful. It had been life altering. She would never see herself the same way again now that she knew the sensual creature Simon's touch could evoke. Only what was going to happen to her when he decided he didn't want her in his bed any more? Lance's rejection had hurt her, she feared rejection from Simon could come close to destroying her.

If she had two brain cells to rub together she would get off his island and never see him again. Because the longer she let herself be with him, the more it was going to hurt when it was over.

Had she so much as considered that yesterday when he'd come traipsing up the stairs with her things? No. She'd moved in with him instead.

It was incomprehensible to her. She was not an impetuous person. She took her time making major changes in her life. Look how long she had put up with Lance. Yet, yesterday, she had been staying in Simon's house and today, she was living with him. She felt like she'd stepped onto one of the scare rides at Disneyland with no hope of getting off.

The issues that had seemed unimportant yesterday, loomed as shadowy giants in front of her today.

What would happen if Daniel found out she was having an affair with Simon? Bile rose in her throat at the thought he would think she was following his smarmy advice.

When Daniel had given it, he had assumed she was already sleeping with Simon. She had known she wasn't. So, as ugly as the advice had been, it had had no power to really touch her. Now she was Simon's lover and even though she'd done nothing wrong in regard to her business with him, she felt like her professional integrity had been compromised.

She knew she wouldn't try to sway Simon's opinion with sex, but knowing that was what Daniel expected made her feel unclean anyway.

She hated feeling like that, but the only way to change it was to stop being with Simon. Her heart twisted painfully and she acknowledged that she was already past the point of leaving Simon without emotional damage.

She responded to an email from one of her coworkers as the problem gnawed at her conscious.

What if she told Simon about Daniel's recommendation and that she didn't want him to make any decisions based on their intimacy? He might scuttle the merger on the strength of his revulsion toward Daniel alone. Simon had a lot more integrity than her boss. His reaction to the knowledge of what Daniel wanted her to do was bound to be at least as bad as her own. No, she definitely should not tell Simon about that part, but she could still tell him that she didn't want to influence him with their personal relationship.

If he changed his mind about the merger, she wanted it to be because he was swayed by the facts she'd presented to him, not because of sex.

All she had to do was tell him.

Jumping up from the table Simon had installed in his bedroom for her use as a makeshift desk, she crossed the room to knock on the door to his laboratory. He didn't answer. She waited a few seconds and knocked again. Still nothing. She knew he was in there. She knocked one last time. She tried the handle. It turned.

Of course it did.

He didn't have to lock Jacob out. The housekeeper wouldn't dream of interrupting Simon during his work. Well, she couldn't wait for Simon to surface again to settle this issue.

She pushed the door open and peeked inside. She couldn't work with it preying on her conscience like a hungry cayote.

What an amazing room. Looking more like the lab for a several man design team than one man's private sanctuary, it stretched at least ten feet beyond the size of the great room on the floor below.

Workbenches lined the three walls not covered in glass and two long tables bisected the center of the huge space. Several computer systems in various states of build filled one entire workbench and impressive looking equipment with lots of buttons and displays resided on the worktable closest to her. The whir of several super computers struck her ears and an ozone like smell permeated the room.

Her gaze flicked to a nearby corner filled with equipment that looked like it had come straight off of the Star Ship Enterprise. She wasn't very technical, but one of the big black devices looked like a laser to her, its red glow enhancing the room's space age feel.

When she could tear her gaze away from the impressive array of equipment, she found Simon. He was at the other end of the room, sitting behind a U-shaped desk made of the same flat brush metal material as his bedroom set. The rapid clicking of computer keys attested to his concentration on the lap top in front of him.

She walked toward him, stopping a couple of feet from the desk. "Simon."

He kept typing.

"Simon!"

His head jerked up, his eyes widening in shock at the sight of her.

It was a good thing she wasn't a corporate spy. She could have taken pictures of everything in the room before he noticed her. "I did knock."

He flicked a rather vague glance to the door. "I heard."

"So, why didn't you answer?" she asked with some exasperation. She'd stood out there knocking for something like five minutes.

He frowned, his gray gaze sliding back to the computer screen. "I'm right in the middle of something."

And she was an interruption he did not want. He didn't have to say it. Who else would have knocking at his door? Knowing it had to be her, he'd opted not to answer.

Well, that was definitely telling her.

Why had she thought she needed to clarify this whole sex-business thing with him anyway? It was obvious Simon wasn't going to be swayed from his course of action by a few hours in bed with her. He couldn't even be bothered to answer the door when he was busy.

"I'm sorry I interrupted." She backed toward the door. "I'll leave. No more knocking, I promise."

She had her own work to do and would be better off concentrating on it than obsessing over something so unlikely as her in the role of corporate Mata

Hari with Simon as her victim. It was all Daniel's fault for making the revolting suggestion in the first place. Her boss had a lot to answer for.

She spun around and hurried from the room, closing the door softly behind her.

She slid into her chair and logged in to her remote access for work again. She needed to apprise Daniel of the situation with Simon, to tell her boss that Simon had listened to the entire proposal, but still hadn't changed his mind. She wanted to put it off because Daniel would respond in one of two ways. Neither of them did she look forward to.

One, he would give her another talk about doing whatever it took to gain Simon's cooperation and she just might scream at him this time. Two, he could as easily decide it was time to cut their losses and order her to return to Southern California.

She didn't want to leave. With the merger pretty much scuttled, she could take some vacation time and spend time with Simon without business to cloud things between them. That was supposing he would want her to stay, which was not a given.

If he didn't, she might just need the vacation time to pull herself together.

Now that she'd thought about it, she almost hoped Daniel did say to forget the merger negotiations for now. With an irrational sense of anticipation, she flipped open her mobile phone and dialed her office. The phone on the other end had rung twice when she felt a hand on her shoulder.

She didn't have to look up to know it was Simon. Her body had developed a sixth sense for his presence.

She clicked the phone off before the receptionist had a chance to answer and forced herself to turn around and meet Simon's gaze. He didn't look angry.

She swallowed and smiled tentatively. "I'm sorry I barged in like that."

"What did you need?"

Now that she'd thought about it, the idea of telling Simon she wasn't trying to use sex as a manipulative tool seemed really silly. "Nothing important."

"You came into my lab."

She nodded. "I know. I'm sorry," she said again.

"I didn't mind you coming in."

She warmed slightly at that blunt declaration.

"But you were in the middle of something," she said, repeating his own words almost verbatim.

He grimaced. "I should have answered the door."

"Why?" She shrugged. "You don't answer the door for Jacob, do you?"

"You're not Jacob."

"No, I'm not." Not an old man, for sure. Not a housekeeper. Not exactly a lover...not exactly a business associate. What was she to Simon?

"I'm really glad about that." His grin was so sensual, it was a good thing she was already sitting down or her legs would have collapsed under her.

"Are you coming out for dinner tonight?" she asked, hoping he'd think that was what she'd gone haring in there to ask him.

"Actually, I was hoping we could have lunch together down on the dock and then maybe have a Tae Kwon Do session afterward."

Warmth filled her. "I'd like that a lot."

His thumb brushed her collarbone above the scooped neckline of her top. "I want to kiss you, but I'm afraid if I do that I'll carry you back to bed."

Delight that he found her desirable to that extent thrilled through her. "You've really got to watch these caveman tendencies you're developing."

He laughed, the sound deep, rich and very, very sexy. "I feel pretty primitive around you, sweetheart."

She loved it when he called her that. "It's mutual."

"So, why did you come into the lab?"

She hadn't fooled him. She didn't know why she'd thought she could. He was a genius inventor, trained to look minutely at all data. "I thought better of it. It wasn't anything important."

"Which one is it? You thought better of it, or it really wasn't all that important?"

"Both."

His thumb moved to the sensitive spot behind her ear and her concentration on the topic at hand was severely compromised.

"You've got me curious. It'll gnaw at me and I won't get anything done for the rest of the day."

She didn't believe that for a second. The man had more focus than the Hubble telescope. "Try to make me feel guilty, why don't you?" she teased, breathless from his small caresses.

"Is it working?"

She rolled her eyes. "No."

"I really want to know."

She sighed, facing the inevitable. Those amazing powers of concentration of his were focused on getting the information from her and he wasn't about to give up. The man could be so stubborn. Just look at how he'd kidnapped her yesterday. "You'll think it's stupid."

His fingertips trailed up her face. It felt good and it was all she could do not to reach up to trap his hand against her cheek and just hold it there.

He brushed her chin and then let his hand fall. "Nothing about you is stupid. Nothing."

"This is, believe me. But I'll tell you anyway." She owed it to him after pulling him away from his work. She inhaled, hoping she wouldn't sound as idiotic as she felt. "It's just that I got worried you might think, now that we're sleeping together, that I would try to convince you about the merger with a more personal form of persuasion."

"You're worried that I believe you're trying to manipulate me with mind-blowing sex?" He sounded only mildly curious.

She liked the mind-blowing part. "Yes." She smiled wryly to let him know how ridiculous she realized that supposition was.

"Are you?"

"What?"

"Are you trying to use your body to convince me about the merger?" He didn't look like he was teasing her, but again he didn't sound overly concerned by the prospect.

So much for Amanda Zachary as the newest corporate Mata Hari.

"How could you ask me something like that?" It hadn't occurred to her that he might actually have considered such a scenario. "I would never do something so despicable." Not to mention obviously impossible.

Unable to remain sitting with the confusion of emotions roiling through, she shot up from her chair, knocking his hand away from her neck. "If that's what you think of me, maybe I should leave right now."

Stupid! That wasn't what she wanted. Oh God, let him realize how wrong he is and ask me to stay.

Daniel suggesting such a thing had made her angry. Simon believing she was capable of it hurt. But then, Daniel was just her boss. Simon was her lover. He should know her better.

The only thing he knows well is your body. You love him, but his feelings are a lot more basic. Why should he automatically trust in your integrity?

"Amanda, you're the one that brought it up."

"I didn't think you'd believe something so vile about me," she said helplessly, pain radiating outward from the region of her heart.

"Then why did you come into my lab?"

The very reasonableness of the question fanned the flames of her anger. She was feeling vulnerable and she didn't like it. "Because I wanted to tell you I wasn't doing any such thing!"

"If it wasn't a possibility, why bring it up at all?"

"Because I'm not used to sleeping with business associates and I wanted to make sure you understood one had nothing to do with the other."

"I'm glad."

She glared. Bully for him. "Let's be real. It's not like it would ever have worked anyway."

He pulled her into his arms, seemingly oblivious to her stiffened body. "Are you sure about that, baby?"

"Of course I'm sure. You have too much integrity to make a business decision based on sex."

"Thank you." He bent down and kissed the side of her neck.

She shivered. "But it makes me really angry you think I'm some kind of slut who would use my body as a bartering tool."

His hold on her tightened. "No I don't."

"But you said—"

His finger pressed against her lips. "I asked you an academic question. I did not mean to imply I believed the answer would be yes."

"Then why ask it?"

"Why come into my lab to tell it wasn't a possibility?"

"Because!" She took a deep breath, trying for a calm she was far from feeling. "Because I didn't want there to be any misunderstandings between us."

"Exactly."

Oh. Maybe she'd overreacted a little. "Are you sure you're not secretly wondering if I'm just going to bed with you to manipulate your attitude toward the merger?"

"Very sure."

She chewed on her bottom lip.

"Baby, in order for you to be the kind of woman who bargains with her body, you would have had to ask for something in exchange for what you gave me yesterday. You didn't."

"Maybe I was trying to soften you up."

"I don't get soft around you."

When his meaning sank in, she grinned despite a lingering ache inside. "I noticed that yesterday."

"I won't try to manipulate you with sex either."

"I never thought you would."

He squeezed her at the unsubtle dig. "Behave."

She nuzzled his chest. "It still feels funny."

A featherlight kiss landed on top of her head. "What does?"

"Making love with someone I'm doing business with. I'm afraid I'm going to lose my objectivity." She had the terrible feeling she already had.

"Are you going to give up the idea of the merger because I want you to?"

"No." Yet, if he told her she had to choose between the merger and him, she wasn't sure what she would do. Thankfully, it was a moot point because Simon would never stoop to such measures. He was too confident of his ability to get his own way with straightforward means to resort to emotional blackmail as a weapon.

"Then there's nothing for you to worry about is there?"

She shook her head. Nothing she was going to admit to.

"Do you have something urgent you were working on?" he asked in a voice that made her melt inside.

"No."

Then his mouth rocked over hers and she forgot all about the merger, Extant and the phone call she would have to make later to her boss.

Simon had never found watching a woman eat a turn-on before, but everything Amanda did excited him, especially now that his body knew what it felt like to make love to her. He cursed his own stupidity in waiting so long to touch her. All his worries seemed inconsequential now.

The thought that she might have left the island and his life without his ever having touched her passionate nature made him break out in a cold sweat.

He'd never had sex so good, but then he'd never had Amanda. She was the perfect lover. So responsive. So passionate. So giving. So temporary.

Once she realized he wasn't going to change his mind about the merger, he would lose her. Not because she was trying to use sex to convince him, but because her job was the most important thing in her life. She wouldn't thank him for messing things up for her.

He wondered if she would grow bored with his lifestyle before that even happened. Other women had, women he hadn't wanted as much as he wanted her. They'd made it clear being with a man who became obsessed with his work to the point of forgetting they were there grew old real fast.

He'd done that this afternoon to Amanda. She hadn't said anything yet, but he was sure his failure to come out of his lab until dinner had upset her.

She wasn't acting like it, but women were good at hiding things like that. They didn't forget though and then, one day, they walked away, saying he didn't respond to their needs. "I'm sorry I didn't come out for lunch like we planned."

Maybe he would get points for apologizing before it became a major issue.

She laid her fork on the edge of her plate and smiled so sweetly he wanted to wrap her up in his arms and never let go. Right, Simon, women don't do forever with you.

"You had to make up for lost time. So did I."

"But I missed our sparring session too."

"We can have one tonight if you like, but personally, I enjoyed the form of exercise we employed this morning too much to complain." She winked at him.

He was immediately ready for another bout of the kind of exercise she was talking about. "You're not mad at me?"

"No. Why should I be?" She looked genuinely puzzled. "We both chose to spend time we should have been working doing something far more personal and less productive. So, we had to forego the pleasure of a picnic lunch."

"But I forgot about you." Why had he said that? She didn't need to know. She'd come up with a plausible excuse and here he was rejecting the salvation it offered. Dumb, very dumb.

"I forgot about you too, to tell the truth. I had a lot of work to catch up on after taking all of yesterday off."

"You forgot me?" He found that disconcerting. He'd been yelled at, dumped, even slapped for his insensitivity by women, but he didn't think he'd ever been forgotten.

"Mmmm." She popped a bite of the blackened catfish Jacob had made for dinner into her mouth and chewed making a humming sound of pleasure. "This is delicious."

"What if I had come out and wanted to go on our picnic?" he asked, unable to let the subject go.

She shrugged. "Then I would have remembered you."

"Would you have gone on the picnic with me?"

Her mouth twisted as she considered his question. "I'm not sure. Probably, but we would have had to keep it short."

"If you'd knocked on my lab door, I would have answered."

Her smile was radiant. "I'll remember that."

Jacob served chocolate dipped strawberries and champagne after dinner. Simon enjoyed watching Amanda's sexy mouth bite into each succulent strawberry too much to eat his own dessert.

She stopped eating and looked at him. "Aren't you going to have dessert?"

"Later." Only she was going to be the dessert. He wondered if Jacob had any of the chocolate sauce left.

"Oh." She pushed her dessert plate away from her. "Did you want to ask me anything about the merger?"

He shook his head. "Finish your strawberries." The merger could wait. Forever, as far as he was concerned.

"I'm full."

He didn't believe her. "No you aren't."

"Yes, I am."

Something about this scenario bothered him. "You were enjoying your dessert until I told you I wasn't eating mine."

She started to get up. "I'll just go get my briefcase. I thought of something this afternoon that you might be interested in regarding the two companies coming together."

He grabbed her wrist. "If I eat my dessert now, will you finish yours?" He was trying to understand what was going on, but he felt like he was missing an important element.

He hated feeling that way.

She sat back down, but she frowned at him. "Simon this is ridiculous. You're making something out of nothing. I said I was full, can't we just leave it at that?"

"Jacob will be offended if you don't finish." Remembering the old man's reaction to having to serve them Napoleans that had been sitting in the fridge the night before, Simon said, "He'll get cranky."

"Isn't he always?"

"Don't let him hear you say that." He reached across the table and pushed her dessert plate back in front of her.

"Look, it's not as if I need it. My hips won't thank me for the high fat chocolate."

"You think you need to diet?" The idea shocked him. She was perfect.

"I could lose ten pounds, yes."

Like hell she could. "Taking your body below optimum weight can cause problems for your immune system."

"I'm not exactly anorexic."

He was beginning to wonder. "That's fortunate. Anorexia nervosa is a debilitating disease."

She rolled her eyes. "I was being sarcastic. I would think it was obvious that I don't have a problem with eating."

"How is it obvious?" he probed, feeling like he was getting closer to the missing element. Then, as often happened in his lab, several pieces of information clicked together in his head. "He told you that you were fat, didn't he?"

"He who?"

"Don't play dumb."

She looked away, with an air of fragility that had not been there seconds before. "I already told you Lance did not find me the epitome of perfect female form."

"Tell me about it, baby. Please."

She shook her head. "It's over."

"No it's not."

She looked at him and the pain he saw in her face ripped at his gut.

He stood up and pulled her to her feet. "Come here."

Tugging her along, he made straight for his large, overstuffed sofa.

Chapter Fourteen

Amanda let him pull her down onto the couch so they were facing each other. He wanted her to tell him about her marriage to Lance, but what woman wanted to admit to such a colossal failure? She let her gaze travel up his strong, broad chest to his face.

His expression was filled with a compassion she had never expected to receive. "Tell me what that bastard did to you."

"How can you be so sure he did anything?"

Simon's laugh was harsh. "I would have to be a blind idiot not to know that something had happened to you. You are the most beautiful woman I've ever known and you act like your body is grotesque."

"It's not that bad!"

"Maybe, but you sure as heck don't have a clue how lovely and sensual you are."

Maybe that was because she'd never been sensual with anyone but him. Part of her wanted to tell Simon about her past, but for him to understand her marriage, she had to tell him about her family. "My brother introduced me to Lance my junior year in college. I didn't date. I was too shy. Too serious. Too sure I was as awkward and unattractive as my mother claimed. Besides, I didn't fit in with my Southern California peers. I wanted to go to school on the East coast, but my parents refused to pay for anything but a California state college."

He reached out and took both her hands, letting his thumbs rub soothingly over the backs of them, but remained silent.

She took a deep breath and let it out slowly. "Lance got along really well with my family. He was a lawyer with an impressive client list. My parents were both surprised he was interested in me. My brother told me how lucky I was."

"Did you love him?"

"I thought I did. I wanted so much for our relationship to work. I wanted to feel like I belonged to someone."

"But your family..."

Memories of her childhood still had the power to hurt. So, she usually suppressed them, but she wanted Simon to understand. "I was an oops baby. My brother, Brice, is ten years older than me and the only child my parents wanted to have. My mother planned to have an abortion, but unfortunately for her Grandfather's housekeeper had caught on to the fact she was pregnant. He threatened to cut her out of his will if she got rid of me."

Simon had gone rigid beside her. She could imagine. He'd lost his mother when he was a child, but from what he'd said, she had loved him. No one had loved Amanda in her entire life except for Jillian.

"I was three years old when Grandfather died. Alive, but not wanted. The only time my parents ever gave me even the least bit of approval was when I caught Lance's interest. I married him believing I would finally be accepted into my own family with the added bonus of having one of my own. I was on a euphoric cloud for the entire ten months of our engagement. Lance didn't even protest waiting until we were married to make love for the first time."

"You never slept with him?"

She shook her head. "I read a lot as a child. My sense of morality came from my books, not my family because they ignored me or criticized me. Little Women, Anne of Green Gables, The Five Little Peppers, and other classics – books that weren't exactly peopled by your typical Southern Californian."

She turned to stare out over the water, loving the peacefulness of Simon's view all over again. "My wedding night was a disaster. Lance wanted me to do things I'd never heard of. I was scared and embarrassed. Sex hurt. But that wasn't the worst of it. The most painful part of my wedding night was having Lance turn out the light so he could fantasize I had a different body."

"He told you that?"

She didn't look at Simon. "Yes. Over the two years of our marriage, he pestered me to have breast reductions surgery, watched every calorie I consumed and nagged at me if I didn't work out at least an hour every day."

"Why did you stay with him?"

"Because I was used to not being loved I guess. I'm not really sure. It hurt being married to him, but no more than it had hurt living at home. I kept trying to make my marriage work, but nothing I did could fix the problem."

"Your ex-husband is a bastard. That's not a problem you could fix."

She laughed hollowly. "He didn't want me and I was convinced that was my problem. I tried everything to seduce him, but it didn't work. Looking back, I don't know why I bothered. It wasn't as if I enjoyed being intimate with him. He was an extremely selfish, perverse lover." She shivered at her memories. "The last year we were married, we didn't have sex at all and other than feeling like a total failure as a woman, I didn't care."

"You thought I didn't want you either."

Remembering the pain of Simon's rejection, she nodded.

"Why?"

"That day we had the sparring session. I thought you were going to kiss me. I leaned into it and you backed away. I was humiliated. It felt like Lance all over again. Only this time I really wanted you, not just to prove that I could attract you as a woman, but because I wanted you."

"I wanted you too, but our relationship is complicated."

She turned her head and met the silvered gray of his gaze. "It's still complicated."

He didn't deny it. "But I can't keep my hands off you regardless."

She smiled a little. "Making love with you is so different."

"From the sounds of things, sex with your husband was less about intimacy than it was about control. He used his supposed lack of desire for you to make you do the things he wanted."

"I don't know what you mean."

"He controlled what you ate, how much you exercised. I'm damn glad he didn't talk you into that surgery. I find your breasts so sexy, just looking at them makes me want to come."

She threw herself in his arms and kissed him all over his face. "You make me feel good, Simon. Thank you."

He hugged her to him, settling her into his lap where she could feel the rigid proof of his words against her hip.

"Jacob found your pajamas in the guest room's bathroom garbage yesterday." She tensed. "Did he?"

"I thought they must have landed there by accident, but Jacob didn't agree." Jacob was too astute for his own good, she thought wrathfully.

Simon's hand rubbed against her back in a soothing motion. "Tell me why you threw away your pajamas."

She nestled against his chest. "I'd rather not. It was just a misunderstanding and it's over now."

"Does it have something to do with you thinking I didn't want you?" He sounded really disturbed by the prospect and she wished she could lie to him and say no, but she didn't want to lie to Simon. Ever.

"When Jacob told me you wanted to meet me in my room, I thought that was your unique way of setting up an assignation. You've got to admit your mind doesn't work like other people's," she said by way of an explanation for her folly.

"And when I came downstairs expecting you to tell me about the proposal, you were embarrassed."

"Humiliated. I'd got it wrong again."

"You didn't have it wrong. I had erotic dreams all night long about you in those sexy things. When I came down to breakfast and found out you were gone I was ready to howl at the moon in frustration."

"The moon isn't out in the morning."

"Details."

"When I went into the bathroom, I stripped off the lingerie and tossed it away in a fit of angry despair. Lance had once told me how ridiculous I looked in sexy nightwear and I couldn't stand the thought you believed the same thing."

Suddenly she was being held away from him. The compassionate, understanding Simon had been replaced by a furious man. He shook her shoulders. "How could you think that? I told you I wanted you! It was all I could do to keep myself from ripping those silky things off your even silkier body."

"How was I supposed to know that with you rabbiting on about the proposal?"

"You moved in to my house for the express purpose of presenting that information to me, damn it." He sounded even angrier by that fact. "And the only reason you agreed to stay was so you could keep trying to convince me."

An incredible thought struck her all at once. It hurt Simon that she had stayed for business. "But you never let me know there could be anything between us but the merger."

"I told you I wanted you."

It was the second time he'd reminded her of that and this time she laughed. "Lance told me he loved me, but he showed me he didn't."

"Are you saying I showed you I didn't want you?" Simon's voice was dangerously controlled.

But she wasn't going to deny the truth. "Yes."

"Because I didn't put my desires for you above the business that is so all important to you?" Each biting word came out with the power of a bullet.

And she knew, absolutely knew, in a blinding flash of clarity, that what he said was exactly right. She wanted Simon's feelings for her to come before everything else in his life and that was not going to happen. Not ever.

If she kept pushing, she could very well lose what they did have.

She did something she had vowed she'd never do again. She tried a bit of seduction. Rubbing the breasts he said he liked so much against him, she said, "I know you want me now."

It worked.

With a growl, she found herself lying full length on the sofa under Simon with his mouth devouring hers.

"You're sleeping with him?" Jillian's incredulous shriek blasted Amanda from the mobile phone's ear piece.

"You told me I should," she reminded her friend, who was taking the news of Amanda's affair with Simon in a completely unexpected way.

"I told you to go out with my friend, Dave, too, but you didn't do that!"

"I didn't want to go out with Dave." Or any of the other numerous men Jillian had tried to fix Amanda up with since the divorce.

"But you wanted to go to bed with Simon? I don't believe it. According to you, sex is God's joke on unsuspecting women."

"I was wrong about that." Remembered pleasure had Amanda's eyes flicking toward the closed lab door.

He'd said he would answer the door if she knocked. It was tempting, but she couldn't interrupt his work just because at the age of twenty-six she had finally discovered her female libido. Besides, she wasn't ready to risk the possibility of his rejection. She'd initiated that kiss on the sofa the other night, but Simon had already been aroused. She wasn't sure she'd ever have the confidence to approach him cold with seduction on her mind.

"Amanda?"

"Huh?" Indistinguishable words echoed in her mind telling her that Jillian had been talking the entire time she had been caught up in her thoughts of Simon.

"Do you really think this is a good idea?"

"That is a really surprising question coming from you." Jillian had been pushing her to start dating since before the divorce was final.

"I know." She could almost hear her friend doing that thing she did with her hair while she was thinking. "It's just that you're not into casual amore."

No she wasn't. Casual love, sex, whatever you wanted to call it wasn't something in her makeup. "It's not casual," she bit the bullet and admitted, "but it is love."

She'd called Jillian because she had to talk to someone about the overwhelming feelings Simon engendered in her, but saying the words out loud had been harder than she expected. It had also left her feeling stripped naked emotionally. She didn't even want to think how much worse it would be if she told Simon the truth about her feelings for him.

"You're in love with him?" Jillian was back to shrieking.

"Yes." No use prevaricating or trying to take the words back. They were true and Jillian would not be fooled by an attempt at retreat. "Do you really think I could have risked making love with him otherwise?"

"No. That's what has me worried." Her friend's voice dropped an octave with concern. "Sweetie, you pretend to be so tough, but you're not. You're one of the most fragile people I know and I'm scared to death this guy is going to hurt you."

"I'm a little nervous about it myself, but I don't seem to have a choice." She started doodling on a piece of paper. She needed Jill to see how potentially devastating, but equally inescapable this relationship with Simon had become for her. However, she didn't know if she had the words to make her friend understand.

"I never knew how powerful love could be. It's pretty much unstoppable." She could hear the lingering disbelief in her own voice. "Even though I know I'm going to end up hurting, I can't hold back from whatever Simon is willing to give me."

"His body."

"It's a great body, Jillian."

Her friend snorted laughter. "Amanda!"

"He cares about me, too. Maybe it's not love, but it's more than I ever got from Lance. Simon wants me to be happy while I'm with him." He did all sorts of little things to show her, like setting up this office area for her and gaining Jacob's agreement to let her watch Jillian's show every day on his television. "And he never criticizes me. He's sort of blind and tells me all the time how beautiful I am."

"Aw, honey."

"Jill, it's so amazing, but when I'm with him, I feel like I'm not just Amanda Zachary, junior executive and failure in the marriage stakes."

"You're not the failure," Jillian said fiercely.

"That's what Simon says too. He can't understand how Lance didn't want me. He said my ex must have been the most inept lover alive not to be able to please a responsive woman like me. Can you imagine?"

"I tried to tell you that not all men were like that jerk you married."

"Maybe not, but I don't think I would respond to other men the way I do to Simon. I want him, Jill and I've never wanted another man, not like that."

Jillian, who had had an active love life since she was sixteen would probably have a hard time understanding that. She wouldn't make fun of Amanda, though. She never had, no matter how far apart their perception of something was.

"So, tell me more about this guy. I've got that he's hell on wheels in bed, but I want more info on what he's like out of it."

Jillian grilled Amanda about Simon for another twenty minutes, before letting her change the subject. Not that Amanda minded talking about the man she'd fallen in love with. She didn't, but the more she talked about him the more unlikely it seemed that a man like that would fall in love with her. However, when she flipped her cell phone closed forty minutes later, she was smiling.

Jill's initial reaction had surprised her, but the other woman had ended the call by saying, "Go for it."

The next morning, Amanda woke up to the feel of Simon's hand gently caressing her stomach. Her eyes fluttered open to his steel gray gaze.

She smiled. "Hi."

He kissed her, tenderly, sweetly and oh so slowly. "Hi."

"You know what today is?" she asked.

His brows drew together then his expression cleared. "The five day anniversary since the first time we made love. What do you want to do to celebrate?"

She felt her heart constrict. He could be so romantic, even if he did tend to forget everyone else in the room when his mind started chewing on one of his projects.

"That too, but I was thinking that it's Saturday. I don't have to work today. How about you?"

She didn't think he kept regular hours, but maybe he could take a break today.

His forefinger drew a circle around her right nipple, causing the flesh to swell and stiffen immediately. "The only thing I want to work on today is us."

The breath stilled in her chest for a full five seconds and then it came whooshing out on a rush of air. Had he really said that? That he wanted to work on them...that there was a real them to work on, not just two people who were extremely compatible in bed?

Her thoughts short-circuited as he went about once again proving that compatibility.

Simon carried Amanda into the shower. She was right. When he was around her he had some major caveman tendencies, but she liked it. She might haughtily protest his habit of picking her up and carrying her around, but she always curled into him with a trusting sensuality that he found addictive.

Hell, everything about Amanda was addictive. From the way her breath hitched when he first probed the entrance to her body to the way she teased Jacob about having a crush on one of the female leads in Jillian's show. The warm sunshine that seemed such a natural part of her personality dispelled every lingering shadow in his soul but one. He could not dispel the knowledge that one day soon she would be gone.

It made him determined to enjoy her to the fullest while he had her. His libido complied with an enthusiasm he hadn't known since his teens. Their recent lovemaking had been quick and fierce, the perfect beginning to a day spent entirely in her company.

He let her slide down his body, before reaching in to turn on the taps. She liked her shower hotter than he did, so he set the temperature on the two showerheads on the left higher than the overhead nozzle or the two on the right.

He felt a featherlight touch on his back and turned around to face her. She had an odd expression on her face.

"What is it baby?"

"I was just touching you to see if you're real." Her eyes reflected an inexplicable wonder.

His knees about buckled and his recently satisfied male member surged with renewed arousal. "I'm real." Not only did he act like a caveman, he sounded like one, practically growling his response to her.

"Yes." Satisfaction laced her voice. Then she smiled and reached past him to test the water. "It's hot."

He nodded, still a little stunned by the awe he'd seen on her face for that brief moment.

They stepped into the oversized shower stall.

He'd had it built this way because he liked space around him. The five showerheads had been a luxury he'd decided to indulge in that had turned out to be doubly decadent when he and Amanda washed beneath them. He had discovered some very interested uses for the directed jets of water when making love with her, uses that made her blush and come apart with pleasure at the same time.

But today he wanted more than to make love with this beautiful woman full of stimulating contradictions. He wanted her to make love to him. It had taken him a while, but he'd finally realized that she almost never initiated their touching and that she was reticent about touching his body. He'd caught on right away that it wasn't because she didn't want to. She looked at him with a hunger that stirred his baser instincts, but she never acted on that hunger.

At first, he'd been glad. He'd been careful not overwhelm her with his size, but she didn't show the slightest indication that she found his overt masculinity overwhelming. In fact, she went crazy when he touched her so deeply inside with his aroused flesh that he couldn't go any farther. She was tiny compared to him, but her passion made them the perfect fit.

Except she didn't touch him and he was going hungry for the feel of her sweet little hands on his sex.

He handed the soap to her. "Wash me?"

Her head jerked up and she stared at him with those drown-in-me brown eyes. "All over?" she asked as if she needed his permission.

Oh, yeah. "Please."

Her eyes lit with anticipation. "I've been wanting to, but I wasn't sure..." her voice trailed off and she caressed him tentatively with the soap across his chest. "You'll tell me if I do it wrong, won't you?"

Damn that bastard she'd been married to.

Simon reached out and framed her face with his hands, making her look at him. "Any way you touch me is the right way. I'm dying for the feel of your hands on my skin. Amanda, don't you know you're the best lover I've ever had? Please, baby, don't let that bastard stop you from giving me what he was too stupid to want."

Her smile was misty, but brilliant. "Okay." She put the soap aside. "I want to feel you with my hands, both of them, all right?"

He supposed it would take time those little hesitations to be completely dispelled. "It's more than all right, baby. It's perfect."

He couldn't talk after that because her hands were doing things to him he'd dreamed of since the moment he met her. She started with his head, massaging his scalp, playing with the shoulder length strands of his hair before moving on to touch his face with butterfly caresses. His eyelids slid shut as she brushed his cheekbones.

She outlined his lips with a fingertip. "I love your mouth, Simon."

He nipped at her finger. "My mouth loves your body, baby."

She laughed softly, sensually.

Then her hands were on his neck lightly tracing his pulse. "You're heartbeat is a little fast, darling. Maybe you should have your blood pressure checked."

"It wouldn't do any good. It's always high when you're around."

A feathery kiss pressed against his pulse point. Her fingers trailed down his chest, zeroing in on the small brown disks of his male nipples. "They're just like mine. They like being touched too."

He couldn't make his mouth form a response. All he could do was groan with the teasing pleasure she was subjecting him to.

"Do they like other things, I wonder?"

She knew damn well they did. She'd sucked on him last night until he'd taken her in such frenzy that he'd been terrified he had hurt her until she screamed her release in his ear.

She suckled him, first one and then the other. She didn't linger and he didn't ask her to because he didn't want anything to delay her reaching the ultimate goal. A delicate bite on each nipple ended her torment of those erogenous zones.

Her mouth and hands moved downward, caressing a stomach that had gone rock hard with excitement. She outlined each one of his defined abdominal muscles. "You've got an amazing body." Her voice was husky and so sexy it was like a caress on his sensitized skin.

Then she went lower.

He stopped breathing, in a wealth of torment waiting for her to touch his most intimate male flesh, but in a move calculated to drive him insane, she bypassed his sex and went to the tensed muscles of his thighs. She caressed them with all ten fingertips, making him shudder and wonder if he was going to be able to stay standing.

His legs came close to collapsing when she caressed the back of his knees. "You're sensitive here."

"Yes," he managed to get out in a guttural voice.

"And here? Are you sensitive here too?" She brushed the inside of his thighs, letting the backs of her fingers make brief contact with his sacs.

He muttered a short, Anglo-Saxon term that he was usually careful not to use in a woman's presence.

She laughed. "Not yet, darling, but soon."

He liked it when she called him darling. It was intimate, as intimate as her touch.

"Amanda." His hips strained toward her, his erect flesh brushing against her face. "Please, baby, touch me there."

His hands were flattened against the warmed and wet tile of the shower stall and every muscle in his body was tense with anticipation.

When she didn't say or do anything for several long seconds, he opened his eyes and looked down at her. She was staring at his sex with a sort of rapture. He felt a small amount of pre-ejaculate come out in testimony of how much that look turned him on.

She saw it and licked her lips making him groan. She reached out with one delicate little fingertip and touched the bead of moisture at the tip of his penis. Then she brought it to her lips and tasted it.

He groaned. She was going to kill him with her innocently sensual curiosity.

She looked up at him, her eyes darkened almost to black with desire. "I like it."

"Oh, baby..." How could he want to pound into her with every inch of his throbbing arousal while at the same time wanting to hold her and kiss her with a tenderness he'd never felt for another woman?

Her fingers wrapped around him and he choked on his own breath. The tips did not quite touch.

"You're big, aren't you? I mean bigger than average." Her tone was that of a scientist gathering information and it made him smile despite the acuity of his need.

"I don't measure myself against other men," he said truthfully, if evasively.

"Well, you're a lot bigger than Lance was."

Something about the wording of that statement pricked at him until he had an insight that he could not quite believe. "Are you saying you don't have any other standard of comparison?"

She didn't look up at him, her attention was wholly engaged with his hardened rod. "I've never been intimate with any other man except you and Lance."

He wouldn't define what she'd had with her ex-husband as intimacy. "You're practically a virgin!"

Chapter Fifteen

S he did look up then, her expression wry. "I don't think you can be practically a virgin, that's sort of like being almost pregnant. You are or you aren't."

He didn't agree. There were definitely levels to how pregnant a woman was. Just ask any man who had lived through a pregnancy with one. He knew from experience that Elaine three months pregnant was a whole different proposition than she was in her final trimester. And there were levels to a woman's move from innocence to sexual experience as well.

"You're very innocent."

"But I'm learning all the time." Her smile should have warned him, but it didn't.

So when her hot, silky wet mouth closed around the head of his arousal, he went up in flames. He bucked toward her and she caressed his length with both her hands while swirling her tongue around his head.

"I'm going to come, baby. You've got to stop."

She didn't let go. She didn't move her mouth. Instead, she sucked another inch inside the heated interior and moved on him with inexperienced, but highly erotic motions.

He felt like the top of his head was coming off, but he wanted to be inside her when he climaxed. It was the sweetest sensation and one that had become an integral part of his complete satisfaction. He forced her head back and quickly lifting her under her armpits he lined their bodies up for his penetration. Her fingers dug into his shoulders as she spread her legs. Locking them around him, she settled onto his aching flesh in one slow downward thrust.

She was making love to him.

It felt better than he'd fantasized and he went over the brink almost immediately. She came with him, her body convulsing around his pulsing sex while her teeth locked onto his shoulder in pleasure-pain.

Panting from the cataclysmic explosion, he hugged her to him with arms like manacles. It was only as sanity returned in slow increments that the different quality in their lovemaking alerted him to a devastating reality. He had taken her without protection. Or rather, she'd taken him. Not that it mattered. His baby making sperm were swimming inside her right now and that was the only reality he could grasp.

If she got pregnant there was a chance he could convince her to stay with him. As quickly as the thought formed, he felt the shame of it. She deserved something better than to be trapped into a long term relationship.

Guilt followed the shame as close as one Siamese twin is to another. It was all his fault. She'd never had a lover outside of marriage, was as close to being a virgin as a woman could get having been married. He'd been the one to seduce her in the shower, to beg her to touch him...to lose control and enter her without putting on a condom first.

"Baby?"

"Mmm?"

"I didn't use anything."

She mumbled something against his chest.

"What?"

Suddenly, her head flipped back and she looked at him in shock. "Did you just say you didn't use anything?" Then she shook her head, her eyes wide and slightly wild. "Of course you didn't. We were in the shower." She looked down at their still joined bodies. "Oh, Simon, I'm so sorry."

Even now, he didn't want to let her go and one hand settled under her behind. "You're not the one who forgot birth control."

She winced at his tone and he felt worse, but she made no attempt to distance herself from him physically.

"Actually, we both forgot. I didn't give it a thought, but it's all my fault that you did. I seduced you into such a frenzy, you weren't likely to remember anything mundane like that." She didn't sound as upset as she should.

If he didn't think it was beyond the realm of possibility, he would have said she sounded proud of herself even.

"Protection isn't exactly mundane."

"Well, it's not on par with making love either."

"Obviously," he said wryly. "Is pregnancy very likely?" He had to ask.

She blushed and if he hadn't been feeling so guilty, he would have laughed. She'd taken him into her mouth without a qualm, but blushed when asked about her menstrual cycle.

She bit her lip in a gesture that always made him feel both protective and horny. "Do you want the truth or a peace providing lie?"

"The truth."

"If I remember high school health class correctly, we're on the outer edge of the zone."

He couldn't begin to explain the hope that took root inside him and just would not let go, nor could he explain the sudden surge of lust that had him hardening all over again.

Her eyes widened. "Simon?"

He felt heat in his own cheeks. How did you tell a modern woman who was involved in a uncommitted sexual relationship with you that the thought of getting her pregnant was a major turn on? "I guess I'd better let you go."

Her dark brown eyes went liquid with desire. "Um...we've pretty much done the damage, haven't we?"

Was she saying she didn't want him to let her go? His arousal grew in response to the thought. "According to statistical averages, the added increase from a second unprotected encounter to the risk of pregnancy would be minimal."

She laughed, her breath hitching when he moved inside of her. "You sound just like a university lecturer."

"I feel like a man who is on the verge of something earth shaking."

"You say the sweetest things."

Amanda was the first woman who had ever seen him as even approaching romantic. "You say too much sometimes," he growled against her lips before taking them.

Two hours later, replete from a decadent brunch provided by Jacob, Amanda's hand rested in the warm clasp of Simon's as they walked along the shoreline. She'd been trying to work up enough sangfroid to mention that he didn't need to worry about contracting any nasty disease from her, but they'd both been avoiding the topic of their unprotected sex earlier and she didn't know how to open the subject up again.

She inhaled the clean salt air, enjoying the way it woke her senses. "You know, I can understand you wanting to live on an island. Everything is so fresh here, so clean and so quiet."

His hand squeezed hers. "I like it."

"I do too." Which was surprising considering where she was accustomed to living. "The water is cold though."

They were walking in their bare feet and her toes had gone numb from the frigid surf.

"If it weren't, the beaches would be a lot more crowded right along with this island."

"I guess you're right." But it would still be nice to be able to feel her toes.

"My swimming pool is heated." His voice had dropped to that sexy tone that sent messages of delight to the secret places of her body.

"Is it?"

"You haven't been in it since you came."

"I didn't bring a suit." She'd packed for a business trip, one she'd expected to be much shorter than this one had become. And swimming in her shorts and a T-shirt like she had planned to do for exercise didn't cut it when she was with Simon.

He smiled down at her, his usually cool gray eyes warm with the desire that was so much a part of their relationship now. "Swimming without is one of the privileges of owning your own pool."

"I've never been skinny dipping before." She'd never wanted to. She'd never had the confidence to want to put her body on display like that, but the idea of doing so with Simon was titillating rather than scary. Still... "What if Jacob came down to tell you that you had a phone message or something?"

"I'll tell him not to disturb us."

"Then he'll know what we're doing." As soon as the words left her mouth, she realized how ridiculous they sounded. It wasn't as if Jacob could actually miss the fact she'd moved into his boss's bed.

Simon didn't answer, but with an apologetic look, he lifted his watch and spoke into it. "Yes, Jacob?"

"Master Joey is on the phone."

"I'll be right up."

He looked down at Amanda. "It's my nephew. I promised to come and see him this week, but I forgot." He brushed her cheek. "Things got a little crazy."

She smiled, loving the way he made her feel when he touched her like that. "You'd better go see him today if you're going to keep your promise this week."

Simon nodded. "We'll have to put off our swim to another time. Come on, I'd better get up there before he talks Jacob into telling him another secret service story. Last time, Elaine was mad at me for a week."

"Why?" she gasped out, having to jog to keep up with Simon's long strides.

"Jacob's stories can get pretty gruesome."

She could imagine, the man loved to emote.

They reached the house a few seconds later and she left Simon to answer the phone while she went upstairs to check her email. There was a message from Jill and she answered it. There was also an email from her mother. She'd listed a condo in Amanda's building with her real estate agency and wanted to know if Amanda was interested in selling too.

Amanda deleted the message without replying. It was, after all, nothing but email solicitation and she never replied to junk mail. She ignored the twinge of pain she experienced at the knowledge that bit of salesmanship had been the first time her mother had bothered to contact her in over six months.

"Can you be ready to go in ten minutes?" Simon asked from just inside the bedroom doorway.

She turned off her computer and stood up. "Go where?"

"To see Joey, remember?"

"I didn't think you'd want to take me with you."

"Why the hell not?"

"It's a family thing. I'm not family." She wasn't treated like family by her own parents and brother, why on earth would Simon's relatives want her around?

"You're my girlfriend. That's close enough."

"Girlfriend?"

"Yes, girlfriend. Do you have a problem with that?" He looked wary.

She shook her head. "I just didn't realize you wanted anyone to know about us."

He ran his fingers back through the loose strands of his shoulder length black hair, his expression frustrated. "When have I ever said that? I love sex with you, but you're not just a business associate I happen to be screwing. I thought you realized that."

"I do." Their relationship might not be permanent, but he'd never relegated to merely sex either. She didn't know what to say to get that irritated expression off of his gorgeous features. "I'll change my clothes."

She didn't have a lot of selection to choose from, but she assumed a visit with his nephew would be pretty casual. So, she pulled out her one pair of jeans and a white button up blouse she usually wore with a suit. She cuffed the sleeves and left the top three buttons undone before slipping on a pair of white sandals.

She turned to face Simon. "I'm ready."

He had changed into a pair of black jeans and matching T-shirt. His hair was pulled back in a ponytail and he looked positively yummy.

He also looked very serious. "Amanda, are you embarrassed for my cousin to know we're together?"

"No!" She crossed the room and put her hands on his forearms. "I didn't want to intrude. That's all."

"It could be pretty awkward with your boss if he realized you were sleeping with the enemy, I suppose."

Awkward wasn't the word she would use to describe the way Daniel would respond to such news. Glee might be a better candidate. "You're not the enemy," was all she said.

"No, I'm not." He stared down at her, an enigmatic expression in his gray eyes. "I wonder if you will remember that if the merger doesn't go through."

He didn't give her a chance to reply, but pulled her out of the room. They jogged down the stairs and out through the great room onto the deck.

"Where are we going?"

He tugged her toward the stairway that connected the deck with the yard. "To my cousins."

"But the car..."

"We're taking the boat. Eric will pick us up from the pier."

"Oh." She followed Simon to the end of the deck where he lifted her onto the small yacht.

"Jacob's at the wheel, but I've got to cast off." He untied ropes that held the boat to the dock and then vaulted aboard when the last one had been loosened. He took a few minutes securing the rigging before coming back to her.

"It takes a little over an hour which isn't quite as fast as the ferry, but we don't have to worry about missing it coming home either."

"Jacob told me most of the island residents have their own boats."

"It's a matter of safety as well as necessity. You never know when ferry service is going to be interrupted."

She'd certainly found that out, not that she was complaining. "You don't have to worry about gossiping ferry officials either."

Simon's mouth quirked. "That's true."

Just as Simon had said he would be, Eric was waiting for them at the pier.

He smiled when he saw Amanda. "Hi. How are the merger negotiations going?"

Her returning smile was rueful. "Your cousin is stubborn. He listened to the proposal and all the benefits I outlined to you, but I don't think it made any difference."

Simon's arm dropped casually around her shoulder. "But she's welcome to keep trying to change my mind."

Eric looked at Simon's hold on her and then at Amanda's face with a speculative gleam, but he said nothing. He opened the back passenger door on a silver Mercedes sedan. "Elaine and Joey are waiting at home."

"What about Jacob?" Amanda asked as Simon handed her into the backseat of the luxury car.

"He'll keep himself occupied."

"Won't he feel left out?"

Eric laughed from the front seat as he started the car. "Jacob is Simon's employee, not his best friend. You don't need to worry about him, Amanda."

She didn't agree entirely with that assessment and her look to Simon told him so.

"Jacob has an old friend he likes to visit when we come to the mainland. He doesn't feel neglected at all."

"Oh. Okay then." The irascible old man irritated her no end, but she liked him.

"I imagine being on the mainland feels good after so many days on the island," Eric said to her.

"I don't know. I think I could easily live there year round. Simon does it."

Eric's laugh filled this roomy interior of the car. "Yes, but Simon doesn't look at life the same way other people do. He prefers his solitude."

She did too, when that solitude included Simon, but she didn't say it. Her first comment could be construed as a broad hint to Simon that she wanted to stay already. She didn't want to make him uncomfortable or to sound like a clinging vine.

"How's Elaine?" Simon asked.

Eric's smile slipped. "Morning sick and emotional. I feel so helpless and it only gets worse. It's a darn good thing she only wants two children. I don't think I could go through this again."

Amanda's hand slipped to her stomach. She could be pregnant with Simon's baby. Would he feel the same way about pregnancy? Would he only want one child like her parents had or two like Eric and Elaine? Maybe he didn't want any.

The sobering thought pierced the sweet bubble surrounding her. If she was pregnant, she had every intention of staying that way. She didn't see abortion as an option for birth control, not matter what the rest of the country thought. She could never get rid of Simon's baby.

For a few sweet seconds she considered what it would be like to be married to Simon and pregnant with his child. As long as she was daydreaming she might as well put a toddler on her lap and serious dark haired little boy on the seat beside her. It was positively medieval, but she would love four children...with Simon as the father.

"Amanda?"

She snapped out of her reverie.

Simon's head was turned toward her from the front. "Eric asked how soon you would have to head back to California."

She couldn't help feeling the answer should have been of more interest to Simon than Eric, but it was her lover who had asked the question.

"I... There is no set time. Upper management really wants the merger. I'm doing my other work remotely, so it's not a problem for me to stay." Well, other than a lack of clothes. Maybe she would call Jillian and ask her to Fed-ex some things up from California.

Her business suits just didn't fit her current lifestyle with Simon.

"There must be some kind of deadline," Eric probed.

She turned her face away and looked out the car window. "I'm sure there is, but I don't know what it will be."

She didn't want to leave and talking about it depressed her, but Eric was right. Her boss was bound to have some cutoff point at which he'd call her back to California.

Exploring the woods surrounding Simon's home, she seriously began to doubt that belief. Daniel had been extremely affable when she made her less than encouraging report on Monday regarding the merger.

She'd had the opportunity to discuss the merger with Eric while Simon was busy playing with his nephew. Eric had reaffirmed his interest in the proposal. However, he'd made it clear that if Simon stayed opposed to it, he would withdraw his support rather than allow a family war to start over the issue.

Which was just as she'd suspected. Yet when she'd told Daniel, he had responded as if it were a minor consideration, not the major setback it was. He had told her to keep working on Simon, but she'd gotten the distinct impression something was going on she didn't know about.

However, she'd gleaned nothing from the remainder of their conversation and her carefully worded questions.

Tuesday, she had accompanied Simon to Brant Computers. He had wanted to meet with his design teams and had invited her along. He'd made it a point to introduce her to several Brant Computers employees. The difference in how he related to them and the way Extant's Executive Management Team related to the workforce was a revelation.

He'd left her in the company of an older woman who worked in the sustaining group during his meeting. After they left the company, Simon had asked her how she would feel if that woman were one of the ones forced out of a job by the merger.

She'd been forced to acknowledge: one, it was all too likely and two, she'd feel awful.

"She's worked for us since her husband died of pancreatic cancer, leaving her a widow with two teenage children fifteen years ago. I couldn't sleep at night if she had to start working at a fast food place because we let her go."

Simon's words still echoed in her mind and she had begun to see his adamant refusal to consider the merger in a different light. He wasn't a quirky genius who didn't understand the business world well enough to function efficiently in it. He was a deeply caring man who took the plight of his company very personally and in his mind, his employees were the company.

Yet, he continued to discuss the finer points of her proposal with her. He made it a point to ask her at least one question a day, or bring up an argument which she was forced to parry. She didn't know if he did this as a sop to his conscience because of his promise to Elaine or if he just wanted to remind Amanda why she was there.

Even if that wasn't his intention, it worked. She never forgot that she was a temporary aberration in Simon's life, not a permanent fixture. The issue of her possible pregnancy had not come up again and Simon had been scrupulous about protection since that time in the shower.

Part of her was terrified she would end up pregnant. What did she know about being a decent and loving parent? A single one at that. But there was this teeny-tiny person inside her that craved having someone who belonged to her, someone to whom she could belong.

She ignored those desires while trying to understand her boss's almost complete about face. He was way too understanding about her lack of success with Simon and then today, she'd gotten an out of the office response in reply to her email asking him a question about something else.

It gave her a bad feeling.

She was afraid he had gone behind her back to talk to the other shareholders. What really preyed on her mind was the idea that she should warn Simon and Eric of the possibility. She owed Extant Corporation her loyalty as an employee and telling Simon and Eric anything would be tantamount to revealing confidential information. On the other hand, she was terrified her boss would start that family war both she and Eric were so intent on avoiding.

And if he was pursuing the other shareholders, he was violating his agreement to let her handle the merger negotiations at this point. She sighed as she stepped on a small dead branch that crackled under her feet. She felt torn apart by her divided loyalties and the impermanence of her association with Simon.

The watch on her wrist started to vibrate. Simon had given it to her on Monday. Both he and Jacob could buzz her within a mile radius via the small two-way radio that was part of the watch just like Simon's.

She lifted it and pressed a small button on the side. "Yes?"

"You got a visitor, missy."

Daniel was here! It had to be. Who else would come to see her? "I'm heading back now."

Sighing with regret, she turned back toward the house. She'd found time spent walking in Simon's woods wonderfully soothing to her confused mind and emotions. She loved the tall spindly trees that swayed like hula dancers when the wind gusted and the way their sparse branches let sunlight through, casting a dappled pattern onto the forest floor.

She approached the house from the front. The yellow Mustang convertible did not look like something her boss would rent. He drove a white BMW. It wasn't flashy, but it screamed status seeker from the polished silver door handles to its shiny black wheels.

She jogged up to the house and went in through the front door. She could hear voices from the great room, but the words were indistinguishable. However as she drew closer to the room, she could tell one of the voices was a woman. Definitely not Daniel. Maybe Elaine had come to visit.

She'd been really friendly the previous Saturday, especially after Simon made it clear he and Amanda shared more than a business relationship. Amanda had thought it odd later that neither Eric, nor Elaine were concerned she was attempting to manipulate Simon with sex.

They obviously didn't see her as Mata Hari material either.

Jacob said something and the woman laughed.

Jillian.

Amanda burst into the great room just as Jacob started laughing right along with Jillian. Dour faced Jacob laughing?

"Jill! What are you doing here?"

Jillian spun around to face Amanda. "I came to surprise you." And with her characteristic grin she flew across the room to give Amanda a hug. "I checked in to the hotel and then came right over. You wouldn't believe this guy who works at the ferry. I asked for directions and he starts pumping me for information like he's the CIA or something."

Amanda laughed. "I'd believe you, trust me."

"He didn't even recognize me."

"Most people don't and that's how you like it so don't whine."

Jillian dressed conservatively with her hair kept in an elegant up-do for her role on the soap opera, whereas in real life she tended to wear clothes that would look jarring on Madonna and let her hair riot around her head in a mass of auburn curls.

Jacob was back to looking dour. "I recognized her right away."

"You charmer, I think I'll keep you."

Red burnished Jacob's cheekbones and Amanda about fainted. The man was definitely star struck.

"Can I get you two some refreshments?" Jacob asked, at his polite best.

Amanda stifled a giggle at the amazing change in him. "Sure. I'll take Jill out to the deck. Do you know if Simon plans to surface soon?" It was just going on lunch time and he'd come out to share it with her every day so far this week.

"As I have said in the past, Ms. Zachary, Mr. Brant is not a submarine."

"Be nice to me, or I won't let Jillian talk to you."

Jillian laughed and patted Jacob on the shoulder. "Don't worry. Her bark is much worse than her bite. She hasn't muzzled me in a year at least, but I do want to meet your boss. Will he be down for lunch?"

"I believe so. He has discovered an ongoing and sufficient motivator for leaving his lab in the middle of the day." He gave Amanda a significant look and it was her turn to blush.

Because while it was true that she and Simon shared lunch every day, it was also true that wasn't the only thing they shared in the middle of the afternoon.

Jillian's brow rose. "Interesting. You two will have to be more circumspect now that I'm here, though. I'm very impressionable."

"You're impossible," Amanda replied. "Come on. Let's go out on the deck."

They were seated at the table, sipping freshly brewed ice tea with a twist of lemon when Jillian turned to Amanda, her face more serious than Amanda had ever seen it. "Tell me about this guy you're sleeping with. Are you pregnant yet?"

Chapter Sixteen

Amanda's tea went down her windpipe and she started choking.

Jill jumped up and pounded her back. "I didn't mean to kill you with the question."

Amanda tried to wheeze out an answer, but she couldn't make her voice work.

Jill stood back. "Oh, hell. It's already happened hasn't it? I knew it! You're such a babe in the woods with men. What did he do, tell you not to worry, he'd pull out?"

Amanda's face felt sunburned and her throat hurt from coughing. "It wasn't like that. Sit down, please."

Jillian shook her head, her red hair waiving wildly. "I'm going to kill him."

"Jill." Amanda reached out and grabbed her friends flailing arm at the wrist. "Stop it. I'm not pregnant."

"Are you sure about that?"

At the sound of Simon's voice, Jillian spun around, ripping her arm from Amanda's grip. "You jerk! I suppose you don't think anything of—"

Amanda's hand on Jill's mouth cut her off. She'd jumped up from her seat the minute Jillian started in on Simon. "Calm that Irish temper down or I'm going to end up eating your words and being humiliated in the process."

Jillian's eyes narrowed, but she nodded. Amanda moved her hand and turned to see Simon's reaction to her friend's outburst. He wasn't looking at Jill.

His entire attention was on Amanda. "I thought your period wasn't due for another week."

If her face had felt sunburned before, it now felt hot enough to be a three-alarm fire. "It's not."

"Then how can you be sure you aren't pregnant? Did you take a test?"

The only thing needed to make this farce more embarrassing would be for Jacob to make an appearance. "No. How could I? I doubt your local store even carries them."

He smiled cynically. "Don't be so sure about that, but if you didn't take a test, you can't know. Yet, you told your friend you're not pregnant."

"All right!" She glared at both Jillian and Simon. "I should have said I don't think I'm pregnant, okay?"

Jillian opened her mouth to say something and Amanda forestalled her. "Before you go off again, it's not Simon's fault."

"Oh really?" Jillian was at her sarcastic best. "Are you saying you had sex with someone else?"

Even the thought of another man touching her like Simon had made her sick to her stomach. "No."

Simon looked at Jillian. "It is my fault. I'm the one who forgot protection."

"And I made you forget it." She was still a little awed by that fact. Not a rational reaction, she knew, but when a woman had spent her whole life being told she didn't measure up in the female stakes, it was definitely a natural one.

"You sound proud of yourself," Jill accused.

"I noticed that too," Simon agreed laconically.

Amanda felt attacked from two sides even though, logically she knew that in their own way both Simon and Jill wanted to protect her. "How do you want me to sound? Ashamed? I left my hair shirt in California along with any false front for emotions I don't feel."

"Are you saying you want to be pregnant?" Jill practically shrieked in astonishment.

"Lunch is served." The addition of Jacob's voice to the melee was more than Amanda could handle with equanimity.

She turned on the housekeeper cum security expert with blood in her eye. "Discretion is the mark of a proper butler."

"I was being discreet. I didn't mention that pregnant women need to keep up their strength, did I? Didn't comment on the fact that a woman pushing thirty and a man already there should be a little more savvy about birth control. Now that would have been indiscreet."

Simon choked on something that sounded suspiciously like a laugh and Amanda wanted to hit him.

Jillian was busy nodding her head vehemently. "You took the words right out of my mouth. They're both old enough to know better."

"Twenty-six is not pushing thirty," Amanda informed Jacob icily. As topics for conversation went, her age outdid pregnancy by a wide margin. And she wasn't pushing thirty.

She spun on her heel and went back into the house.

"Where are you going?" Simon demanded from behind her.

"Jacob said lunch was served and as he so delicately pointed out, if I am pregnant, I need to keep up my strength."

"Uh oh..." Jill's singsong voice followed her. "I know that tone. She's really miffed. Simon, you don't have a big screen television, do you?"

"No, he doesn't, but he does have a collection of katanas that would make admirable gardening implements." Amanda didn't bother turning around when she made the threat, but she knew the people still on the deck could hear her.

"What's a katana?" Jill asked.

"A Korean sword." Surprisingly it was Jacob who answered. "The boss is partial to his collection. They're all one of kind and some are over a hundred years old."

"And no way are you using them to dig in the garden, even if you are pregnant with my baby." Simon's voice whispered in her ear as he leaned around her to pull a chair out from the dining table for her to sit in.

"That is not something I want to discuss right now." She let herself be drawn into the chair and scooted up to the table.

Jacob and Jillian came into the room.

"You're eating with us, aren't you?" she asked Jacob, thinking an obviously star struck fan would thwart Jillian's inevitable attempt to grill Amanda over the possible pregnancy.

His poorly disguised fascination with Hollywood would make an ideal topic for the lunch table.

One gray brow rose in question. "You want me to eat with you? Thought you'd be embarrassed talking about the baby in front of me."

"We are not going to discuss babies or the possibility of a pregnancy," she said repressively.

"We're not?" Jillian asked.

"No," Amanda replied firmly as Simon took the chair kitty-corner to hers. "You can tell us all about the show. Are you going to end up married to your love interest?"

The look she gave Jillian told her friend to go with the flow or else.

Jillian went, but with a look that told Amanda she wasn't done discussing the subject by a long shot.

Simon wasn't surprised when Jillian came to find him in his gym. Amanda was working on an emergency email she'd received from Extant Corporation and it was the first time Jillian had had all day to corner him alone.

"So which one of these is over a hundred years old?" she asked pointing to the wall on which his katana collection hung.

He indicated one near the center. "That one is actually three hundred years old."

"Wow. If it's more than ten years old in Hollywood, it's considered an antique." Her eyes were focused on the sword in question in definite awe.

He smiled and moved into his form.

She turned to her head toward him, her expression set. "I'm worried about Amanda."

He liked her directness.

"Me too," he admitted as he pivoted on his foot for the next step of his form.

That seemed to surprise her and she idly fingered the handgrip on one of the swords. "She's not very experienced around men. I don't think she'd like me telling you that, but you should know."

"She told me I'm the only lover she's had besides that bastard she was married to."

Jillian laughed. "He's a bastard all right and you probably don't know the half of it, but I'm glad she told you she doesn't sleep around. You won't assume she's used to life in the sexual fast lane like a lot of her counterparts back home."

"She told me." And he'd liked hearing it. He went through his entire form in a series of rapid movements that left a light sheen of sweat on his skin.

When he stopped, Jillian was eyeing him speculatively. "Are you just playing with her?"

"What is this, a rendition on the what are your intentions theme?" He grabbed a small towel and swiped at his face. "Isn't that something parents are supposed to ask?"

Jillian crossed her arms and glared at him. "Maybe it is, but Amanda's parents are dead losses where she's concerned. They were rotten to her growing up and completely wrote her off when she left Vance."

"They don't believe in divorce?" he asked, curious about every nuance of Amanda's life.

"They don't love their daughter." Jillian's voice was dripping with contempt. "They're more worried about appearances and business contacts than her happiness."

"You care about her." It wasn't a question. Jillian had flown up from Los Angeles to check on her friend. That showed genuine caring.

"I'm the only person in her life that does."

"No." He took a swig from his water bottle. "You're not."

"Then your intentions are honorable?"

"That's between Amanda and myself." And not something he could answer right now. It was too complicated. "I'm glad you care about her, but this is something you have to let her work out for herself."

"That's what I thought about Lance. I knew he was a smarmy toad, but I didn't say anything because she seemed so happy. By the time they'd been married a month, I bitterly regretted my silence."

Simon was beginning to understand Jillian's motivation for flying to her friend's rescue. "You felt responsible for her marrying someone that hurt her so much."

Her green eyes glistened with moisture. "Yes. She was so innocent and he wasn't."

"But she left him when he had an affair."

Jillian's laugh was harsh. "Lance had his first affair within months of their marriage and I think Amanda knew it, but she blamed herself for not being sexy enough. He was such a bastard. He rejected her every way a man can reject a woman and made her feel like it was her fault."

"They're divorced now." She had to have figured out at some point it wasn't her problem.

"Yes, thank God, but she's still vulnerable. She hasn't even dated since the divorce and then she falls into bed with you. Can you understand why I'm worried?"

He removed one of the katanas from the wall and began an ancient fighting routine. "She's decided to spread her wings, find out what she's been missing."

"Amanda's not like that."

He wished he shared Jillian's confidence. "Are you saying you think she's in love with me?"

Jillian's eyes averted and that said it all.

"I didn't think so. Look, I don't want to hurt her. Our relationship means a lot to me."

"I'm glad to hear that."

He finished the routine and started oiling the sword.

"What are you going to do if she turns up pregnant?"

"At the risk of repeating myself, that's between Amanda and me. You'll have to trust your friend to know what's best for herself."

"Like she did with Lance?" Bitter worry laced her voice.

He understood her pain, but he couldn't alleviate it. What he wanted and what Amanda wanted were probably two different things, but whatever happened, they had to work it out between them without anyone else's involvement.

Amanda waited with the car running for Jillian to come out of the Bed & Breakfast. She'd called her on the cell to say she was here a minute ago.

Jillian had shocked her the night before when she had refused Simon's offer to stay at his house. She'd said her clothes and everything were already unpacked in her room. Then she had asked Amanda to come over to Port Mulqueen to spend the day with her today.

Amanda couldn't say no, not even knowing it was losing a whole day of the limited time she had left with Simon. A Saturday. Jillian had flown up from Los Angeles because she was worried about Amanda. Because she cared. Amanda refused to dismiss that as unimportant. Besides a day spent with just the girls held some appeal.

For some reason she didn't understand, Simon had suggested inviting Elaine to join them. When Jillian had learned that Elaine was his cousin's wife, she'd gone along with the idea wholeheartedly. Amanda had no problem understanding what motivated her friend. She wanted to pump Elaine about Simon.

The passenger door opened and then Jillian slid in. "Sorry I didn't come right down. I had to finish making some plans."

"What plans? I thought we were just going to drive into Seattle and go shopping."

Jillian shook her head. "Change of itinerary."

"What change?"

"I'm not telling. It's a surprise."

"Does Elaine know?"

"Nope."

Amanda frowned and started the car. "She's pregnant, remember. One of your forays into extreme sports would not be the way to spend the day."

"Don't worry, we're not doing anything risky to pregnant women." Jill eyed Amanda's stomach significantly.

"Stop that. It's highly unlikely I'm pregnant."

Jillian sobered. "What happened?"

"I seduced Simon in the shower. We both forgot."

"You seduced him?" The disbelief in Jillian's voice said it all.

Her friend knew how hard initiating sex was for Amanda. "He asked me to."

"Smart man," Jillian said under her breath.

Amanda didn't reply.

"So, is it likely?"

She repeated what she'd told Simon that day in the shower to Jillian.

"Are you going to buy a pregnancy test kit while we're out and about today?"

"I'm due to start in a week."

"Do you really want to stew over it for another six or seven days."

Amanda sighed. "No, but how accurate can a test be? It has only been a week."

"There are some that claim ninety-eight percent accuracy after two days."

"How do you know?"

"Television. Some of us watch more than pre-taped programs that skip all the commercials."

"I'll think about it."

Jillian didn't push it and Amanda was grateful.

They pulled up in front of Elaine's house a few minutes later. The door opened immediately and Elaine came out. Jillian jumped out of the car and moved to the back seat so Elaine could sit up front.

Elaine smiled her thanks as she slid into her seat. "I'm not too big for the backseat yet, but I get carsick when I'm pregnant if I try to ride in the back."

"Bummer," Jillian said.

"At least I'm not morning sick all day long like I was with Joey. That was a real bummer."

"It should be against the law to be morning sick past eleven a.m.," Jill said facetiously.

They all laughed.

"So, where are we going?" Amanda asked Jillian.

"Get on I-5 going south."

"Very mysterious." She turned to Elaine. "Maybe you'd better navigate. I was on I-5 coming from the airport, but I'm not sure if I remember how to get there."

It took half and hour to reach the freeway from Port Mulqueen. Once they were headed south, Amanda asked Jillian where they were going. Jillian referred to a piece of paper she pulled from her oversized hold-all and told Amanda an exit number to take.

Elaine smiled. "This is fun."

"I'm reserving judgment," Amanda said.

Jillian snorted. "You're going to love it."

"I'm surprised you got her away from Simon. She's barely left the island since their first meeting."

Amanda felt her cheeks heat. "I was supposed to be convincing Simon about the merger."

"Oh, I could tell the merger was uppermost on both your minds last Saturday."

Remembering Simon's openly affectionate manner, she understood Elaine's teasing. "By then we'd become personally involved."

"Is that what you call it?" Jillian asked, tongue in cheek.

"What would you call it, smarty pants?" Amanda demanded.

"Incredible sex if it managed to get you off the wagon of abstinence."

"Is it incredible with Simon?" Elaine asked, sounding very disbelieving.

"Don't you know?" Amanda returned.

"No. We dated for a while, but it never got that serious."

It had been serious enough for Simon to consider marriage, but they hadn't slept together. For some reason that made Amanda feel better. "I've never experienced anything like it."

"That's the way it is with the man you love."

"Watch it you two, I think I'm too young for this conversation," Jillian piped up from the back seat.

"That will be the day," Amanda chided back.

Laughter filled the car and the tension that had held her all week long as she wondered what was going on between her and Simon and what her boss was up to dissipated a little.

Amanda pulled the car into the small strip-mall's parking lot. The gray and salmon stone buildings housed a women's only fitness facility, a bank, something called Shinga'ar and a couple of restaurants. Maybe Jill wanted to go to the women's only workout place, but Amanda hadn't brought anything to work out in and she hadn't seen a gym bag when Elaine got into the car.

"Park there in front of Shinga'ar."

Amanda obeyed Jill's command and saw that the store was actually a salon.

Jillian unclipped her seatbelt and opened the back door. "Let's go ladies, our shinga'ar awaits."

Elaine turned to Amanda. "What's a shinga'ar?"

"Beats me. Knowing Jillian, it's more than just the name of the salon."

"You're so right, Amanda. Now stop dawdling. Our appointment is for ten."

Considering the fact that it was five minutes 'til, Amanda did as Jillian suggested.

They walked into the salon and were greeted by a lovely Indian woman, dressed in a green sari outfit with a matching jewel on her forehead. A melodious tinkling accompanied her every movement.

"Good morning, you are Miss St. Clair?"

"Yes," Jillian replied, "but call me Jillian."

"And these are Miss Zachary and Mrs. Brant?"

"Please, call me Elaine."

Amanda said something similar and the woman smiled. "I am Geetha. Are you ready for your shinga'ar?"

"I don't know," Amanda said, "What is it?"

"The shinga'ar is the whole person makeover. The hair. The clothes. The jewelry. The make-up."

"You do all that?" Elaine was looking around the shop as if trying to understand how that could be so.

"Not usually, no, but your friend made special arrangements." She indicated the back room with a fluid movement of her elegant arm and her multiple bracelets clinked together softly. "I have brought in a special selection of clothes and jewelry."

"Trust you to come up with something totally unique, but I don't want my hair cut off." Simon's blatant enjoyment of her hair gave her far too much pleasure.

"Do not worry." Geetha beckoned with her perfectly manicured hand. "Come. I will show you some pictures."

Amanda followed her to the other side of the reception desk. On it was a large flat panel monitor. Geetha clicked a button and an image materialized. It was a beautiful woman, her make-up exotic, her dress alluring. That picture was followed by another and then another. Each woman looked too perfect to be real. They all had jewels on their foreheads, some wore bracelets like Geetha's, others wore sexy dangling earrings, one woman had henna tattoos on her hands, but they all had one thing in common. They were gorgeous.

She didn't think for a minute that Geetha could perform such a miraculous transformation on her, but the thought of going back to Simon tonight dressed and made up so appealingly filled her with anticipation.

"I knew you'd like the idea," Jillian said, "Your eyes are shining with a positively wicked light."

Amanda laughed and Elaine said, "This is just the sort of thing a pregnant woman needs to indulge in. How did you ever find this place?"

"I've got a friend in LA who has a sister who lives up here. She came in for Shinga'ar's Grand Opening and then told her sister all about it. Kali told me about it when she found out I was coming up here for the weekend."

"Shall we get started?" Geetha asked.

Starting meant being led to a room in the back of the salon and undergoing an all over body massage and herbal wrap. Afterward, Geetha gave them all white cotton robes to don and thongs for their feet. She then fed them a light lunch from one of the restaurants nearby.

This was followed by manicures, pedicures and makeovers. The makeovers included having their eyebrows threaded. It was like getting them waxed, but didn't hurt as much and Geetha was meticulous in shaping Amanda's eyebrows into slim, feminine curves that made her brown eyes stand out.

True to her word, Geetha did not cut Amanda's hair, but she did take it out of it's customary French twist and put it up in juice can size rollers all over Amanda's head. When she took them out, Amanda's hair fell in big curls that Geetha brushed into soft waves which she pulled back from Amanda's face with a jeweled clip.

When Amanda turned to look in the mirror, an exotic stranger stared back at her.

"Do you want henna tattoos before we select your clothes?" Geetha asked.

Elaine refused, not sure if the henna would be good for the baby. Jillian asked how long they would last and had to decline with obvious regret when Geetha said at least a week. That left the other two women looking at Amanda expectantly.

"I don't want my hands tattooed, I'm sorry." She smiled at Geetha, not wanting to offend the woman.

"What about something on your shoulder blade?" Elaine asked.

"Be daring, have her put something sexy in your cleavage." Jillian smiled devilishly.

"What about something around your belly button?" Geetha asked when Amanda remained silent.

The only person who would see it would be Simon. "Like what?"

Geetha indicated a page of swirling designs.

Amanda selected one that looked almost like lacework.

Both Jillian and Elaine insisted on watching her have it done.

When Geetha was finished, she let Amanda see in the mirror.

"All it needs is a jewel and I'd look like a belly dancer."

Geetha's soft smile shone and she left the room. She came back a moment later carrying something glittery in her hand.

She handed it to Amanda. "It has adhesive on it. If you do not submerge it, it could last for a week. If you go in the Jacuzzi or pool, it may come off sooner."

Decadent thrills were curling through Amanda and she didn't even hesitate. She took the red, ruby looking gem and put it in her belly button. "It feels funny."

With the henna tattoo and jewel, her tummy didn't look like it belonged to her.

"You need to learn to belly dance. It's too bad we don't have time today." Jillian winked.

"I think that's going to drive Simon wild," Elaine said.

Amanda blushed under the subtle makeup Geetha had applied, all the while hoping Elaine was right.

"Now the clothes and jewelry."

They followed Geetha into another room. Colorful silks filled a portable wardrobe. Amanda was surprised to see that the silks were not all Saris. Some were dresses cut in simplistic, but flattering lines. Jillian chose a flamboyant lime green and gold Sari with a gold undershirt.

Elaine opted for a Sari as well, saying the style hid the small pooch announcing her pregnancy. However, hers was a more conservative pattern in a soft yellow and tan.

Amanda was torn. Part of her wanted one of the exotic Saris, but another part of her didn't want to go the whole transformation to a woman of another culture. Geetha suggested she try on a dress in blood red. Depending on how the light hit it, it shimmered black as well. It looked demure until she got it on. The high neck was offset by a butterfly cutout right over the plunge of her cleavage.

There was almost no back at all, exposing her skin from below her shoulder blades right down to her tail bone. No way could she wear a bra with this dress. Turning to look at the side profile and the way the skirt clung to her until mid thigh where it swirled out, she thought she'd have to forego her panties as well. They were leaving a line.

"You've got to take that one," Jillian cried.

Amanda stared at the now extremely sexy, exotic woman in the mirror. "I feel practically naked." And once she got rid of her bra and panties, she would be.

"It looks beautiful on you." Elaine's voice rang with sincere admiration.

Geetha clinched it by handing her a pair of shoes that were no more than a bow and delicate heels. And they matched the two tone deep red-black of the dress.

Amanda slid them on. "How did you know to have my size?"

Jillian looked guilty. "I knew the dress I wanted you to wear. I sort of had this planned."

"But Elaine..." She could understand Jillian making plans for her and Amanda from LA, but Elaine too? That made no sense.

"Saris are one size fits all." And the simple sandals they wore with them were in neutral leather tones, easily going with any Sari selected.

Amanda turned back to the mirror. She had never looked like this in her life and she liked it. "Wow."

"Now, the jewelry."

Both Elaine and Jillian affixed jewels that matched their dresses to their foreheads.

Amanda refused one. "It wouldn't really go, and besides I've already got a jewel on."

She did, however, allow Geetha to slide about a dozen black glass bracelets on her left wrist that tinkled when she moved her arm. Elaine wanted an anklet and Jillian opted for bracelets on both arms.

When they were ready to leave, Amanda was shocked to see that it was after five.

"We'd better get back or I'll miss the last ferry back to the island tonight."

"Don't worry about it," Jillian said, "I called Simon this morning and we're all having dinner on his yacht at the Port Mulqueen pier."

"That sounds perfect." Elaine smiled. "A woman shouldn't get dressed up, just to go home and have dinner in front of the television set."

Amanda sincerely doubted that Elaine and Eric made a habit of eating in front of the TV, but she smiled too, understanding the sentiment. She even shared it, along with a certain amount of trepidation at how Simon was going to react to her makeover.

Chapter Seventeen

T he closer they got to the pier, the more nervous Amanda became.

How would Simon react to her new image? She hadn't tried anything sexy on him since the night she'd worn the cami and tap pants only to discover he'd wanted her proposal and not her. Simon seemed to prefer her naked. That had been hard enough to get used to, but the prospect of appearing before him in her almost not there dress was making her shake in her spiked heeled sandals.

She could remember times she'd gone to great lengths to look nice for Lance when he hadn't commented at all. Worse had been the times he'd found something to criticize. Simon wasn't like that. She knew he wasn't, but she couldn't seem to quiet the dancing gorillas that had taken up residence in her stomach.

She pulled her rental car into the lot attached to the pier. Jillian and Elaine got out, taking time to adjust their Saris. They looked gorgeous and mysteriously foreign. Amanda climbed out of the car and locked it.

She was afraid to look toward Simon's moorage in case he was there waiting. She wasn't ready to see him yet, to acknowledge his reaction to her new look. She approached the end of the pier where Simon docked with her eyes focused on the ground in front of her as if her life depended on watching each step. In the sexy sandals, it just might. Like a small child, she was operating on the principle that if she couldn't see him, he couldn't see her.

Elaine and Jillian discussed the merits of shopping in Seattle versus LA. Thankfully, they seemed content with her silence.

Her skin tingled and she knew he was there, watching her approach. She almost stopped walking, but she managed to keep her feet moving forward. Each step she took increased the tension inside her until she couldn't help looking up.

She had to see his reaction.

Just as she had known it would be, Simon's yacht was in its moorage and he stood on the deck waiting for them. Their eyes met across the distance separating them. His were devouring her with ravaging force.

Elaine called out a greeting to him, but he didn't respond. His eyes did not so much as flicker in their intent regard.

Jillian said something and Elaine laughed. The words didn't register for Amanda, so she had no idea what the two women found so amusing. Her attention was locked on the man standing so still on the deck. His gun metal gaze moved over every inch of her body with tactile force. Goose bumps broke out on flesh that felt as if it had been caressed.

Her mouth went dry and she tried to swallow.

She reached the yacht. She was peripherally aware of Elaine and Jillian walking up a gangplank that had not been used on the previous trip she'd taken on Simon's yacht. A male voice indicated that either Eric or Jacob had come out to greet them. Amanda could not force her attention away from Simon long enough to look and ascertain which.

She stopped at the end of the gangplank. Simon started moving toward her and she waited for him, feeling paralyzed by the look in his eyes.

When he reached her his hands came out to cup her face. "You're beautiful."

Two words that meant so much.

His head lowered and he kissed her softly, almost reverently. "I wish now that I hadn't agreed to have dinner with the others."

Her hands rose of their own volition to rest against his chest. She could feel the heat of him through the thin black silk of his dress shirt. He was wearing a pair of black slacks as well and he had pulled his hair back into a ponytail. "You look pretty nice yourself. I don't think I've ever seen you in anything but jeans."

"Right now, I want to see you out of that dress."

She tilted her head to one side, flirting in a way she'd never done. "Don't you like it?"

He laughed. "It's sexy as hell, but it does too good a job of teasing me with what is underneath."

"Not a whole lot."

His eyes closed and he tilted his head back. "I'm not going to last through dinner." Then he looked at her again, his face a study in male frustration. "What constitutes not a whole lot? I have to know so I can torment myself for the next few hours with what I can't have."

"You know the stay-ups I like to wear?"

His gaze slid down her body to her black silk clad legs and he nodded. "Uh huh."

"That's it."

His head snapped back. "Just you and a pair of thigh-highs?"

"Yep." She watched in fascination as sweat broke out on his upper lip.

"Baby, I'm not going to make it." He did sound like a man who was dying.

She inched closer so his scent and heat surrounded her. "Sure you will."

He swallowed convulsively and ran a fingertip around the cutout between her breasts. "This is nice."

She trembled. "I like butterflies."

"So do I, but I've never seen a more beautiful one." His finger rested directly on her exposed cleavage. "I want to taste you here more than I want to take my next breath."

Her breath hitched, pressing the flesh of her breasts against his fingertip. "I don't think you should do that in front of the others."

His finger ran down the line where her breasts were pressed together by the cut of the dress. "They've gone inside."

"They have?" How had he noticed? It was all she could do to remember they had even been there.

"Yes."

"Someone else might see." She was trying so hard to stay sane. He wasn't making it easy.

He looked down at the rigid peaks obvious beneath the thin material of her bodice. "I want to put my mouth over them and suck on them through your dress."

She shivered, her knees weakened and she felt herself going damp between her legs. "Stop it. I'm not going to be able to sit down pretty soon."

"I can't walk already."

She looked down and felt her insides melt at the blatant evidence that her sexy new look definitely affected Simon.

"Oh, Simon."

"Don't say my name like that."

Her head snapped up and she looked at him, half-hurt by the harsh tone in his voice. "Why not?"

"Because it makes me want to strip you naked and take you on the gangplank."

"Not a good idea cousin. You can get arrested in Port Mulqueen for stuff like that. I think it's called indecent exposure."

She peeked around Simon and there stood Eric, looking incredibly amused. She felt her face flush and looked at Simon to find a matching burnished color slashing across his cheekbones.

"Jacob's waiting to serve the appetizers until you come inside. Elaine is hungry. Pregnant women get cranky when they're hungry. She and Jacob are close to coming to blows."

"We'd better go save Elaine," Amanda said with a small smile at Simon.

Eric chuckled. "I think Jacob is in greater danger, besides our guest is waiting to say hello to Amanda."

Tension filled Simon's body at Eric's words and the look he gave his cousin could have stripped paint. Something was definitely wrong. Had he and Eric argued about the merger while the women had been gone? She could easily see Simon taking advantage of Elaine's absence to launch a full scale battle with Eric regarding Extant's proposal. Simon was protective of Elaine's feelings. He'd made that clear during their first meeting in Eric's office and again when Elaine and Eric had come to the island for dinner.

She longed to know if that was because Simon's natural protective instincts extended to her as a woman in his family or if he still cared for the woman he had once considered marrying.

Her musings stopped as Simon placed a heavily proprietary arm around her waist and began walking her up the gangplank.

Eric noted it and grinned at Simon and then winked at her.

What in the world was going on?

Simon barely controlled the urge to take off his shirt and put it around Amanda's body before letting her walk into the lounge. He'd spent the last hour in the company of her ex-husband. The guy was too smooth to be real, but his

California golden image was undeniable. A lot of women would find his looks irresistible.

Amanda had married the man.

She must have been taken in by the looks and rehearsed charm at one time. According to Jillian, she'd even stayed married to the guy after the first affair. Had she loved him that much?

He'd hurt her, but women didn't always stop loving men that hurt them, even if they worked up the emotional stamina for a divorce. And here she was looking sexier than she probably ever had. Lance Rogers was bound to be hit right in the libido with what he'd given up.

Simon was watching for it as they walked into the lounge.

Lance noticed Amanda before she noticed him and his eyes widened at the sight, an arrogant smile playing around his lips. "Hello, Amanda."

Her entire body went stiff beside Simon and she stopped dead two feet into the room. "Lance?"

Simon couldn't read anything from her voice except shock. Not welcome, not revulsion, just surprise.

Lance's smile grew. "Yes, it's me. Surprised, sweetheart?"

Simon felt his own body tense at the endearment. Damn it, no man had the right to call her sweetheart but him.

"What are you doing here?" she asked in a flat tone.

"I've been in town for the last couple of days talking over the merger with Eric." He was all golden boy charm. "You look fantastic, Amanda. Very exotic. It's a new image for you."

"You don't even work for Extant Corporation." To Simon's pleasure, she didn't respond to the compliments on her appearance.

Lance's smile was more predatory than disarming. "Not strictly, no. But they have my law firm on retainer. Your boss approached me to help negotiate the deal. Friendly mergers are one of my specialties. Eric and I have had some good discussions over the past week."

"Why wasn't I told?" Amanda asked in that same flat tone that was beginning to bother Simon.

He didn't know what it concealed.

"Is that really something you want to discuss in front of our hosts? If you insist on hearing the details right now, perhaps Simon will lend us a stateroom to talk."

The pretty boy was taking Amanda to a stateroom over Simon's dead body. His hold on her tightened.

Her head came up and her eyes met his for a brief moment, not long enough for any meaningful communication but sufficient time for him to see that she was operating in a state of contained shock.

"The details can wait." She turned toward his cousin. "You didn't mention that Lance had come to discuss the merger with you."

Eric looked discomfited by Amanda's monotone as well, or maybe it was the accusation implied by her question. "He told me you knew he was here."

"I didn't."

Lance didn't look bothered by the denial. "Let's not play games, Amanda. You knew Daniel would be sending someone." He looked significantly at Simon's hold on Amanda. "It's obvious you've lost the objectivity necessary to act as negotiator."

Amanda tensed further and pulled away, going further into the room and putting distance between her and Simon. He wanted to snatch her back, but the way she held herself so stiffly made him wary of pushing her.

"My relationship with Simon has absolutely nothing to do with the merger." At least she was admitting they had a relationship.

For a minute there, he thought she might be gearing up to deny it.

"You're right about one thing, this isn't the time or the place to discuss Extant business." She took a deep breath and let it out. "We will talk later, but I can't help wondering why I wasn't called back to California if, as you've implied, Daniel believes my professional integrity has been compromised."

"You know why, but if you really want me to spell it out to you, I'll gladly do so later." Lance's condescending tone grated on Simon's nerves.

He wondered how the pretty boy would look wet from a dunking in the Sound.

"Fine, you do that." She looked toward the doorway. "I assume that now Simon and I have arrived, Jacob is going to start serving the food?"

Whether it was because he'd been standing outside the room, listening or because of his amazing timing, Jacob came in at that moment with a tray of hors d'oeuvres. Showing intelligence, if a bit belated, he offered the tray to Elaine first.

When the tray came to Amanda, she declined anything.

"I don't know how you can wait until dinner. It's been hours since lunch, aren't you hungry?" Elaine popped a miniature puff pastry in her mouth, chewed and swallowed. "I'm starving."

Lance smiled winningly at Elaine. "With a figure like yours, you can indulge, but Amanda can't afford to partake of every course of dinner."

Fury rolled through Simon like a tidal wave and his vision of Lance was surrounded by a red haze. "That's a matter of opinion, but most men don't find a woman with Amanda's beauty a turnoff."

"Keep your opinions of Amanda's figure to yourself," Jillian added with a voice that could have shred steel.

Lance put his hands up in a gesture of surrender. "Hey, I didn't mean to offend. I was just trying to explain why Amanda hadn't taken any of the appetizers."

"I'm capable of explaining my own actions when necessary." The words were said firmly, but the look in her beautiful brown eyes was too damn vulnerable for Simon's liking.

Lance shrugged. "Sure."

Simon picked up a canapé and walked over to Amanda. He stopped in front of her and she looked up, her eyes asking a question.

"I think your body is perfect, sweetheart. Now try this, it's one of Jacob's personal concoctions."

Her mouth opened slightly, but not enough for him to slide the small goody between her luscious lips. She stared at him and suddenly he felt like he was waging a battle between the present and the past that still tormented her. Simon would win because losing was not an option. Lance had had his time with Amanda and he'd screwed it up. Simon wasn't making the same mistakes. He wasn't even tempted to.

"Open up, baby. Trust me."

Her lips parted further and he slid the morsel into her mouth. He brushed her lips with his fingertip before he withdrew his hand and signaled for Jacob to bring the tray of appetizers to him. This time he chose a mini-quiche. He put it to her lips and felt like a conquering king when she accepted it without protest.

Jacob turned away and put the tray of hors d'oeuvres on one of the small tables. "Dinner will be on the table in fifteen minutes." He left with all the dignity of a Victorian butler.

Simon winked at Amanda and her eyes warmed, though she didn't smile. "He's playing a role again," she whispered.

Simon nodded. "He's a frustrated Thespian. He never got to go undercover on his Secret Service detail and he has latent frustrated desires."

"You'd better watch out or he's going to follow Jillian back to Hollywood. Then where would you be?"

"No chance. He hates smog."

"There is that."

Good. Amanda was sounding more normal.

"So tell me about this shinga'ar thing," Eric said from his position beside Elaine on one of the small sofas.

Elaine and Jill launched into an animated description of how they had spent the day. Simon half-listened while getting a glass of wine for Amanda.

He handed it to her. "Do you want anything else?"

She shook her head. "I'll wait for dinner."

"You're not fat."

"Sometimes I see myself through other people's eyes. I don't mean to."

Looking at her incredibly sexy and downright feminine persona, he smiled. "Then see yourself through my eyes. You're perfect."

She got drawn into the conversation by Jill before she could answer.

Jacob called them into dinner a few minutes later. Lance had not said anything else offensive to Amanda, but he'd let his gaze zone in way too often on the curves he'd disparaged earlier. Amanda seemed oblivious as with each passing minute she slipped more firmly back into the to the cool, buttoned down façade she had put on when she first came to Washington.

She looked sexier than any woman Simon had ever known, but was acting as asexual as an amoeba.

He was tempted to kiss her senseless just to break through the defensive wall growing around her, but the fragility under her surface kept him from doing it. He wished he knew what was causing that fragility. Was she still susceptible to her ex-husband or was it because her company had sent him to Port Mulqueen without telling her?

She wasn't giving anything away.

Why the hell had Eric invited Lance to join them for dinner in the first place? Making up numbers. Like Jillian would have cared if she were the odd one out. That woman had enough confidence to accompany a friend on her honeymoon and still have a good time. To give his cousin credit, the first Eric had heard of Lance being Amanda's ex was when Simon had brought it up just before the women got back.

Lance sure as hell hadn't said anything. The man was obviously economical with the truth and if he was an example of Extant Corporation's management style, Simon was doubly determined to prevent any merger from taking place.

Amanda stood with Simon to see his other guests off the boat. Barely leashed tension communicated itself to her and her nerves wound another notch tighter. Was he thinking she had been aware of Daniel's plan to send Lance to meet with Eric? Was he angry with her?

He hadn't acted angry when he had been cajoling her to eat the canapé. Stress had a bad effect on her appetite, especially stress related to Lance, but Simon had been determined not to give her that coping mechanism. She was glad, but she couldn't tell what he was thinking now.

There had been times over dinner that the look in Simon's eyes had been positively violent.

He didn't like Lance. Simon was too self-contained to be obvious about something like that, but certain gestures and the measured tone he used to talk to Lance had made it clear to her.

"I didn't know he was in Washington."

Simon didn't look at her. "He said you did."

"He lied. He's good at that."

Simon's shrug said it didn't matter and cold seeped into her, making her shiver.

"It was nice of Jacob to drive Jill back to her Bed & Breakfast." No one had suggested Jillian ride with the Brants and Lance. Probably because they all wanted to avoid bloodshed.

"He's star struck."

"I thought so too." She smiled fully for the first time since seeing Lance that night. "I told you. You're going to have to watch him with Jill. She may not get him to Southern California, but she's got connections up here as well."

"He plays more roles as my employee than he could ever land in a real production."

"No doubt." She sighed and turned away from the disappearing taillights.

Simon wasn't looking at them, his eyes were on her.

"Lance is smooth."

She grimaced. "He works at it."

"He could be a model."

Too true. "He was on a Calvin Klein billboard when he was an undergraduate."

"Do you still love him?"

The question blindsided her. Hadn't Simon heard her when she told him how Lance had treated her? "No!"

"You sound adamant."

"I am." She couldn't believe he was thinking along those lines. "Simon, Lance is not a lovable person. I was more enamored with the idea of getting my family's approval than I was with him before we got married and by the time we got divorced, I despised him."

"You said he didn't want you."

"He didn't." Why was he bringing this up now? Didn't he realize that even though she was over her ex-husband, the memories of her marriage still had the power to wound. Failure hurt. Failing at the most basic definition of who you were...like being a woman, was devastatingly painful.

"His eyes were glued to your chest all night. Like hell he doesn't want you."

"What?" She felt disoriented. Simon sounded jealous, yet she couldn't believe he thought there was a need.

"He wanted to get you alone in a stateroom."

"To talk business," she said with some exasperation.

"With the way he was looking at you, I don't think business would have been the first thing on the agenda."

She'd been worried Simon thought she had been working behind his back on the merger, but instead he was suffering a bout of male possessiveness. Lance had not been possessive. It felt... She had to think about it. Different, and sort of nice.

"You think Lance would make a pass at me?" It was so laughable that she smiled. "No way." Less amusing was her next thought. "You think I would succumb?"

"I didn't say that."

"But you're jealous." Her mind boggled. Simon, the most gorgeous and masculine man she'd ever known, not to mention a lover most women would die for, was jealous.

"Yes," he bit out.

She laid her hand on his arm. "There's no need. The only man I want is you." How could he not see that? She vibrated like a tuning fork when he came into the room and wilted like a dead flower when they had to be separated.

Was he blind?

"You were married to him." It was almost an accusation.

"It was a lousy marriage."

"Jillian said you didn't divorce him after the first affair."

Jillian had a big mouth and she had a tendency to draw her own conclusions. They weren't always right.

"I didn't know about the affairs, not for sure anyway." She willed him to believe her. She'd stayed married for too long to a complete jerk, but she had not been a total doormat. "Until I walked in on him."

"That's when you realized he was having an affair?"

"Yes. I suppose I should have suspected before, the way he found it so easy to reject me physically. Maybe I was willfully blind, but I didn't know."

"What happened?"

"I went to his office on a Saturday to see if he was there. It was an off chance. He usually golfed on Saturdays, but he wasn't answering his cell. I needed something.

I can't even remember now what it was, but I remember what I saw." It still made her sick. It had been so sordid.

"He was with another woman."

She remembered Jill had said almost the same thing. "Yes, but they weren't alone."

"He had two women with him?" Simon asked with disgust.

Would that have hurt less? Maybe. If she hadn't known either of the women. "Worse."

"How?"

"I discovered my husband was bi-sexual."

"He was with a woman and a man?"

"Yes. He hadn't touched me sexually in a year and there he was with two of them. They were panting, grunting, sweaty...there was this smell, like they'd been going at it a long time. They didn't even notice me, they were so lost to reality in their lust. I left. When I told Lance I wanted a divorce, I didn't tell him what I'd seen, just that I knew he was having an affair."

She shuddered with remembered distress. "He didn't even bother to deny it. He told me it was my fault that he had to seek sexual release elsewhere. That I wasn't enough woman for him. He was furious with me for insisting on the divorce. Do you know he had the gall to suggest I get counseling?"

Simon's expression went from savage to so tender, her heart cried. "Aw, baby." He pulled her into his chest. "I'm sorry. What a bastard. If I'd known all of this before, I wouldn't have let him on my yacht."

She knew he was telling the truth. Simon wasn't Eric. He didn't allow himself to be bound by socially correct behavior.

He squeezed her tighter and incredibly, her body reacted to the pressure of his. "You're lucky you didn't end up with some disease."

"I know." She rubbed her cheek against his black silk shirt. "The Monday after I found him in his office, I went to the doctor and demanded they run every test imaginable. It was humiliating, but I couldn't live with the uncertainty." The memory wasn't as wounding in Simon's arms as it had always been before. "Who knows what level of protection he exercised in his perverse sexual games?"

"Considering his selfish arrogance, that's a damn good question." Simon's body heat surrounded her like a security blanket. "I want to hurt him." The level of fury in Simon's voice shook her.

"Don't. Please don't let it matter. It's over and now I'm really thankful he found me such a sexual turnoff."

Simon stood there rubbing her back for several minutes in silence. Thoughts of her marriage with Lance were relegated to her brain's garbage incinerator as the heat Simon's gentle touching evoked burned them up.

The cold breeze coming off the water could not diminish the lava like desire flowing through her.

She moved subtly against him and he sucked in air.

"You turn me on without trying," he said in a voice guaranteed to melt her insides to liquid honey.

Chapter Eighteen

S he didn't doubt him.

The evidence was pressing against her stomach.

"I'm glad." So very glad.

"I can't believe your family was mad at you for divorcing the bastard," Simon burst out.

She didn't want to think about it anymore, but an image of the man Lance had been with rose before her like a specter. "My parents love my brother. They don't even tolerate me."

"So?"

"The man that made up the final third of that lewd ménage et trois with Lance that day was my brother." She'd never told anyone, not even Jillian.

When she had stopped going to family events, her parents hadn't cared. She'd never been forced to explain why she couldn't stand to be in the same room as her brother. They were all too busy vilifying her for divorcing such an upwardly mobile man with all those great connections for their real estate business. She now realized her brother had pushed her at Lance to cover his own bi-sexuality. A trait that didn't go over well in the business community, even in Southern California.

Simon said something that made her ears burn.

She tilted her head back to smile at him, the pain of her brother's betrayal submerged in the pleasure she found in Simon's company.

"My thoughts exactly."

He swept her up into his arms without any warning, looking pretty fierce.

"Are we playing another fantasy? Are you the marauding privateer now?"

"Privateers were not considered marauders. Pirates marauded."

She clung to his neck. "Are you playing pirate, or just caveman...again?"

He stopped and looked down at her, his gaze silver with emotion. "Do pirates get to capture princesses?"

A lump formed in her throat. He said the most amazing things. She smiled brilliantly at him, despite the wetness she couldn't quite conceal in her eyes. "It depends."

"On what?" He'd started moving again and was carrying her along the short corridor that opened onto the staterooms.

"On what pirates do with princesses."

"Ravish them."

"In that case, I would say it's a certainty. Pirates are the very best at capturing princesses."

"Then I'm a pirate, because you, Amanda Zachary, are definitely my princess."

She wouldn't let herself believe he meant what she wanted him to mean, that she ruled his heart. But even so, the words touched her deeply. "You're a very sexy pirate. I like the fact you have both eyes and no hook."

He laughed as he leaned down to open a door. "You'll be really grateful for both hands by the time the night is over."

"Will I?" she teased, knowing his was right, but it wouldn't take all night. She was thankful right now as anticipation of what he would do with those hands rolled over her in a hot wave.

He carried her into the stateroom. It was bigger than she expected, with a custom built bed occupying most of the space. He dropped her onto the bed in a flurry of red silk. She landed with her skirt exposing the top of one of her stay-up stockings.

"I think you'd better take the dress off, captive." The words were diffident. The tone was not.

She gave him a saucy look. "Why's that?"

"Because if you don't, it's going to end up ripped."

She had never been wanted to the point of having her clothes ripped off. The concept that Simon could want her that much excited her.

She stretched back against the bed, raising her arms above her head in a way that made every curve move under the sensuous silk of the dress. "Really?"

Simon's expression turned feral. "I'm not kidding, baby."

It was a beautiful dress, but not as beautiful as the look of desire in Simon's eyes. "Show me."

His eyes widened, then narrowed and he came over her in a predatory rush that made her gasp. One of his hands slid into the butterfly cutout of her dress, straining the fabric to its limit. He cupped her ripeness. She couldn't help scooting back a couple of inches that gained her exactly nothing.

"Nervous, baby?" he asked mockingly, his hand squeezing her in erotic repetitions.

"Excited," she corrected. Conquering warrior, pirate, it didn't matter...Simon would never hurt her.

Something came over him at her response and his other hand went to join the first. When he found the opening too small for both hands, he yanked at it and the sound of rending silk filled the silence of the stateroom.

Her breasts were exposed, framed by the frayed edges of the torn red fabric.

Simon leaned back to look at her. "They're fantastic sweetheart. So beautiful they're a Heavenly work of art."

She shuddered and heat pooled between her legs as her heart swelled with emotion. "Are you going to touch me?"

Had he ripped open her bodice just to look?

His smile was all masculine sex-appeal. "Oh, yeah."

Then he started doing just that, using his mouth and his hands to tease her flesh into a state of aching need.

"Oh, Simon... Please. Yes. Don't stop."

His sensual laughter acted like a further stimulant to her senses. "I couldn't stop, baby. Not even if I wanted to and I don't. I'm going to touch you all night long."

But he did stop, long enough to tear his own shirt off, sending jet black buttons flying and then he was kicking off his pants, exposing an erection of rather daunting magnitude. It was a good thing she hadn't gotten a good look at him before they made love the first time. She would have run screaming, sure they wouldn't fit, but they did and he touched her so deeply sometimes it felt spiritual.

He came down on top of her, pressing the hot skin of his muscular chest against her soft flesh and she cried out at the indescribable feel of it. He teased her with his body, rubbing himself between her legs, the silk abrading both of them. If it felt as sensual to him as it did to her, he was going to climax before he got inside her. She felt on the verge of orgasm herself.

"You are so sexy, Amanda. So beautiful." He whispered more compliments, interspersing them with things he wanted to do to her as he kissed her face and neck and breasts.

She writhed under him, desperate for a connection he seemed intent on denying.

She wanted her dress off. Now.

Loving the freedom to touch him, she ran her nails down his back, the pirate fantasy forgotten. She didn't feel like a captive. She felt like a woman being tormented by her man.

"Simon, I want to be naked," she wailed.

The hiss of rending silk was followed by the feel of his hardness against her wet and swollen labia. He stroked his flesh against hers without penetration for several seconds.

"I want you, Simon! Now. Please..."

He reared up and backward, when he returned to her, he was holding a condom. "Put it on me."

She sat up, breathing hard, and pulled off the remnants of her dress. She discarded it, a violent ache to pleasure him holding her in its grip. She lifted the weight of each breast in her hands, then leaning forward, she rubbed her hardened nipples against his even harder erection.

He groaned.

Arrows of sensations shot straight from her stiff peaks to the very core of her.

A wantonness she'd never known pulsed with the rapid beat of her heart; she pressed her breasts around him and he shouted out.

"What are you trying to do to me?"

"Make you feel as good as you make me feel."

He choked on whatever he tried to say next as she slid the soft tunnel of her breasts up and down his length. She'd never done anything like this, but Simon made her feel wild. As her generous curves pressed against the base of his manhood, she bent her head forward and delicately licked the top.

Bucking toward her mouth, he made an inarticulate sound of need. "More, baby. I need more of you."

She understood and with one final kiss to the tip of his erection, she released his rigid flesh from its resilient prison. Excited by performing this task for the first time, she tore open the condom package. She took as much time as she dared sliding the latex down his length, wanting to prolong the touch of her fingers on him.

"I love touching you," she whispered from a throat raw with passion.

"I love your touch, but it's got to be now."

With that, he exploded into movement, lifting her up and back and pressing himself between her legs all in one desperate motion. A single rocking of his hips saw him sheathed in her heated wetness and she moaned at the pleasure of being one with him. She felt connected to him on every level at that moment.

"I love you, Simon. I love you!"

He responded in a frenzied series of thrusts that sent her into an abyss of pleasure so deep, she didn't think she'd ever come out of it. She convulsed around him, the rippling sensations going on and on and on as he continued to pound into her with driving force. Then his body bowed and he yelled her name as he came.

Afterward, she fell asleep with him still inside her.

Amanda didn't stir, even when he gently pulled himself from her body. She sprawled on top the comforter with her arms thrown wide and her legs parted in the position of their loving. One dark brown curl lay nestled around her still turgid nipple. His breathing hitched as his gaze slid lower.

An intricate pattern in red surrounded a jewel that gleamed from the center of her belly button. He reached out and gently traced the scrolling lines. It couldn't be permanent. There was no redness around it, no bandage. But even so, it moved him in wholly nonsexual way. She had done this just for him and no one else's enjoyment because no one else would see it.

He moved his hand to trace the length of dark silk strands resting against the beauty of her breast. The rest of her hair was a wild tangle around her head and she looked like an exotic queen well satisfied by her lover.

She'd been satisfied all right.

How many times had she convulsed in orgasm? He'd been too busy slamming into her with uncontrolled need to keep count, but it had seemed to last forever. And she had screamed her throat raw. He bet she didn't even realize it, but toward the end she'd done no more than croak his name.

She probably didn't realize she'd said she loved him either. Sex talk...only Amanda didn't indulge in that. Not yet anyway. That was something they could play with another time, later. If they had a later.

From the sound of things, her boss wasn't happy with her handling of the merger. What a jerk to have sent someone up to help with the negotiation and not even tell her. Especially her ex-husband. Her boss had to have the sensitivity of a rhinoceros. Or he was so displeased with Amanda's inability to get Simon to agree to the merger, these actions were like a corporate slap on her wrist. Would she be called back to California?

Could he convince her to stay?

She'd said she loved him.

In the throws of a mind-blowing climax, he reminded himself.

But she had said the words.

What did words mean?

If they were true...everything.

He made quick work of taking care of the condom and then went back in the stateroom. Not surprisingly, Amanda hadn't moved. He lifted her limp body so he could pull the covers over her, then slid into bed beside her, curling his big body around her smaller one.

Content, he slept.

Amanda laid her fork down. "When are you sailing back to the island?"

"Don't you mean we?" Simon leaned back in his chair, his empty breakfast plate pushed out of the way and measured her with a look.

She wished she did. "I have to bring my car." Too bad. She'd never made the crossing on the yacht in daylight. The view would be spectacular.

"Why don't you leave it here? You don't need it on the island. If you want to come into Port Mulqueen and I can't take you, Jacob can drive you to the ferry."

For a woman who had been fiercely independent for the past few years, the idea was much too tantalizing. "I don't know."

"You afraid of my driving, missy?" Jacob asked from his position by the galley sink.

"Of course not."

"Then leave your car here," Simon instructed.

"All right." She could always pick it up later, but the opportunity to go with Simon today was irresistible. "So, what time are we leaving?"

"Did you want to invite Jill to sail with us?" he asked instead of answering.

"I would, but she told me that she's meeting some friends from acting school in Seattle today."

"Then I guess we can leave any time."

"I need to meet with Lance before we go."

"No."

She stared at Simon, shocked at his vehement denial. Despite his tendency to want his own way, she hadn't expected him to try to interfere with her like this. Not about business.

"I need to find out what's going on with Extant."

"Call him." Simon picked up his coffee cup and took a long sip, his steady regard a little unnerving.

"I'd rather talk face-to-face." Lance lied too easily and too well. She needed all the extra help she could get and seeing his face when he answered her questions would be a step above tonal qualities over the phone lines.

"I don't want you alone with him."

"Don't be ridiculous. I've had to meet with Lance on several occasions since the divorce. Besides, that really isn't a decision for you to make."

His expression said otherwise. "I'm not trying to make the decision for you."

Right. "Like you weren't trying to make the decision for me when you kidnapped me on the island and blackmailed me into staying?"

"I lured you into staying. I didn't blackmail you."

"Semantics."

"I know he treated you like the untouchable woman while you were married and I can't pretend I'm not glad for that after what you told me last night, but he wants you now. Men recognize lust for their women in other men."

"Am I your woman?"

"Haven't we had this discussion already?"

Was he referring to their talk regarding her status as his girlfriend? She guessed he was. Only one didn't seem quite as serious as the other and she desperately wanted to know how serious about her he was.

She hadn't been so lost to passion the night before that his silence in the face of her avowal of love had gone unnoticed. No answering vow. No mention of it whatsoever in fact. Not so her temporary tattoo.

He'd made his appreciation of the body-art very clear when he woke her that morning, mapping the lines of the design with his tongue. He'd also told her he liked that it was temporary. She'd been glad. She wasn't into pain and had no desire to go through a real tattoo session.

She smiled at him. "Even if Lance is lusting, and to be honest I think your perception is biased, I don't want him. So there's no problem."

"Problem is the boss doesn't want you alone with the guy," Jacob inserted.

She turned to frown at him. "I've got enough to deal with here. I don't need your interference."

"Getting' sassy, ain't ya? See what a makeover will do for a woman?"

She let out an exaggerated sigh. "I'm not made over anymore."

"You're wearing your hair down and your face looks different. You're made over all right."

"Let me clue you into something, Jacob. I could have my hair in a bun and a bag over my head and I would still object to both your and Simon's interference in my plans."

"I want to spend the day with you and I don't want your ex-husband or your job to take any part of that away from me. Is that so much to ask? It's Sunday, Amanda. Most people take Sundays off. You don't see me headed home to my lab do you?"

No, she didn't. "Would you be if I wasn't here?"

He shrugged. "Probably. I'm working on something pretty important right now."

But spending the day with her was more important. "All right. I'll deal with it tomorrow."

Simon's smile was full of male satisfaction, but she couldn't work up any resentment because his eyes reflected a relief that touched her. He cared. He might not love her, but he cared in a way no one but Jillian ever had.

Sailing back to the island during the day turned out to be everything that Amanda imagined it would be. She loved standing at the rail, Simon behind her, surrounding her with his arms and the warmth of his body as the cold breeze off the ocean made her skin sting with awareness. The views were spectacular. They even saw whales in the distance and Jacob slowed the yacht to a crawl so Amanda could watch them play in the water.

She forced herself to forget her worries and to concentrate on being with Simon.

And true to his word, when they got home, Simon didn't disappear into his lab. He didn't disappear at all. His focus was entirely on her and she couldn't help wondering what it would be like to spend the rest of her life with this man. Late in the afternoon, he talked her into a sparring session, insisting she needed more work on her form. He touched her a lot more than was strictly necessary, but now that she did not have to hide her reaction to the brush of his body against hers, the Tae Kwon Do sessions were sheer pleasure.

He made love to her gently and slowly that night, keeping her on the brink of completion until she shouted his name and her love. He didn't return the words, but he was so gentle with her as he prepared them both for sleep that warm tears leaked out of her eyes.

He kissed them away and pulled her into his body to hold her through the night like he'd done every time they slept together since the first bout of passion they had shared.

"You said Jacob would take me to the ferry if I wanted to go into Port Mulqueen." Simon wasn't being gentle now. He was being stubborn and she wasn't having any of it. "I'll walk to the ferry terminal if I have to."

Stormy gray eyes narrowed. "It's six miles."

"Do you doubt I could do it?" In her current mood, she could jog the distance in her sensible pumps.

He leaned back against the kitchen counter and crossed his arms. "We agreed you wouldn't be alone with him."

"We agreed I would deal with it today and that's what I'm doing."

"What's the problem with calling him?"

"It's a meeting that needs to happen face-to-face." She had questions she wanted answers to, answers that would come more than just from the words Lance might say.

Simon didn't say anything, his expression set in grim lines.

She sighed. "Look, if it helps, we're meeting in a restaurant. We're not going to be alone."

"But you insist on meeting him?"

She couldn't read anything from Simon's voice. "Yes."

He straightened. "Then I guess I'll get Jacob to drive you."

He turned to go, but she reached out and touched his arm. "Simon, this has nothing to do with us."

He spun to face her with the grace and speed he showed in the gym. "That's what I'm afraid of." He grabbed her and kissed her hard, then set her away from him before leaving to get Jacob.

She stood their in bewildered surprise for several minutes until Jacob's impatient summons started her moving toward the front door.

She had a forty-five minute ferry ride to think about Simon's reaction. He was really worried about Lance and she couldn't imagine why. She wouldn't let Lance touch her with a bargepole. He was a poisonous spider under those California golden looks and she had no desire to ever again spend time in his sticky web.

Her mind was still engaged with thoughts of Simon and what his overprotectiveness could mean in terms of emotional commitment when she walked into the restaurant to meet Lance. He was sitting in a booth by the window overlooking the pier.

Sliding into the seat opposite him, she offered a polite nod, but no smile. "Hello, Lance."

"Amanda. Back to the business persona I see." He looked her over like a buyer for a used car, his expression saying there were plenty of flaws even if he hadn't found them yet. "The night before last was certainly a departure from your normal style." His gaze fixed directly on her chest in a way that it had rarely done when they were married. "That red dress had sex written all over it."

The implication was nauseating. "I'm not here to discuss my taste in clothes and I have absolutely no interest in your opinion of how I dress."

"Are you sure about that?"

She pushed her napkin and cutlery aside, and signaled to the waitress for a cup of coffee. "Very sure. The only thing about you that interests me is an explanation of what you're doing on my project and why I wasn't told you were in Port Mulqueen."

He grimaced, the perfect looks of his face marred by lines of distaste. "You're such an abrasive person, Amanda. Talking business does not preclude observing the social niceties."

"There is nothing nice about you Lance. It may have taken me a few years to figure it out, but all my blinders are off in regard to your character." She would not let him sidetrack her with his critical attitude. "Now answer my question."

She didn't care if he thought she was a female version of Attila the Hun; she wanted details.

He took a long draw on his ice tea, purposefully drawing out his answer.

When she merely sat there, silent and staring, he gave in. "You weren't getting the job done." He stopped and did that measuring thing with his eyes again. "It's easy to see why now, even if a bit difficult to believe. I never would have thought you were the type to put her personal life ahead of the job."

"Are you trying to imply that I'm somehow responsible for Simon's adamant desire to keep Brant Computers privately held?"

"Please." Lance's tone patronized her. "Your career is hinging on this deal. You want it to go through all right, but the problem lies in the fact you're obviously more concerned about getting bonked than getting the job done."

The crude accusation annoyed her, but she didn't buy it. Nothing short of a miracle was going to convince Simon Brant that Brant Computers was better off merged with its competitor, Extant Corporation. She'd tried and her failure had not been due to lack of business acumen or effort.

She relaxed against the booth. "We aren't all controlled by our libido and it's no use you trying to judge me by your standards. They don't mesh with mine."

His eyes narrowed and she knew he'd gotten the implied insult.

"If I wasn't getting the job done to Extant's satisfaction, why wasn't I told?" It really bothered her that her boss would go around her like this and undermined her trust in Daniel.

"You were left to deal with Simon, which seemed to be your preferred method of pursuing the merger." Lance's voice dripped innuendo. "Daniel thought someone else would be more effective at shoring up support from Eric Brant for the merger."

"That doesn't explain why I wasn't told."

"You didn't need to know."

"How can you say that? It's my project."

"But it's Extant's merger. You're a cog in the wheel, Amanda, not the drive-line."

The waitress laid a platter of appetizers in front of them.

Amanda ignored the food, but Lance took a sautéed mushroom and popped it in his mouth. "I don't know why you're complaining. You weren't taken off the project and you weren't required to pursue a line of inquiry other than the one you chose to do."

"I was the initial negotiator with Eric Brant and his opinion was not the one holding up forward momentum on the merger."

"The management team felt that he needed a more aggressive approach made to him."

"So they sent you?"

"I often work in a similar vein for my clients. You know that."

Lance did have experience in negotiations, but he still wasn't an employee of Extant. He was usually brought in when his clients were looking for more than a smooth negotiator. Why had upper management decided to bring in legal muscle at this juncture?

"How does Daniel think you'll succeed where I've failed?" There was a plan and she wanted to know what it was.

Lance waited to answer, taking time to eat another appetizer before talking again. "I'm working on showing Eric Brant what a visionary move the merger will be and convincing him to go ahead without Simon's endorsement."

She'd been afraid of that, knowing in her gut that a man who thought she should use sex as a manipulative tool wouldn't balk at starting a family war. She had hoped Daniel would be held back by Simon's threat to go elsewhere with his designs if the merger went through.

Apparently her hope had been in vain. "So, what are you using to convince Eric of the vision? Smoke and mirrors?"

"Not at all. Your initial proposal and subsequent number crunching were sufficient basis to begin my talks with Eric. Your analysis wasn't bad, by the way, but the presentation was too generic. I improved on it of course."

"Daniel gave you my reports without talking to me about doing so?"

Her proposal had not been in the company public domain. Those numbers and supposedly boring analysis belonged to her. Corporate common courtesy dictated Daniel ask before using them in his own work, much less giving them to someone outside the company.

Lance gave her a pitying look. "You didn't expect him to ignore their potential just because you were too busy shacking up with the competition to use them, did you?"

She ignored the comment about shacking up. For all intents and purposes, that was what she'd been doing and she could hardly take offense at the truth. However, she did not accept that her relationship with Simon had prevented her from doing her job. "I already presented that material to both Eric and Simon Brant. The potential wasn't being wasted."

"I presented it again with a few conclusions of my own." He smiled smugly. "I think we've got Eric Brant solidly in favor of the merger."

"He's always been in favor of the merger," she replied with exasperation. Didn't anyone at the head office understand that the problem was Simon, not Eric? "It's Simon who won't be budged."

"That's not a problem."

Clearly her boss was convinced of that or Lance wouldn't be in Port Mulqueen. "Did Daniel mention to you that if Brant Computers goes public, Simon will sell his new designs to the highest bidder?"

Lance shrugged. "He's bluffing and if you weren't so blinded by his personal attributes, you would realize that."

"If you make one more crude, snide or suggestive comment in regard to my relationship with Simon Brant, I'm going to make taking apart a big screen television and letting it crash to the floor seem like an act of mercy." She bared her teeth in an imitation of a smile. "As for Simon, you don't know him. He doesn't play corporate head games. It's not a bluff. He feels really strongly about keeping the company family held."

Lance shrugged again, his expression chilling in its calculation. "If Simon Brant attempts to sell his designs to the highest bidder, he'll be in for one hell of a legal battle."

"He didn't sign an intellectual property rights agreement for Brant Computers. He gives them his designs because it's his company, not because he's legally required to do so."

"There are such things as implied contracts, Amanda. Didn't you learn anything in your business law course?"

Implied contracts? She ignored the dig, feeling sick to her stomach. "What you are proposing isn't ethical."

Lance laughed and it was not a nice sound. "Grow up, Amanda."

"I am an adult. A moral adult, which is something I realize you have no familiarity with."

"Sticks and stones, sweetheart."

"Simon is not an asset on Brant Computer's spreadsheet." The nausea in her stomach increased. "You can't force him to design for the merged companies."

"We'll see."

Amanda stood up, not bothering to hide her disgust. "Yes, we will. Eric won't support a bogus lawsuit and Simon is no patsy. In fact, he's a hundred times the man you could even think of being."

Lance rolled his eyes. "Anything else, Amanda?"

"Yes." She smiled, a real smile born of joy from the experiences that led to the thought she was about to express. "You're a lousy sex partner as well as morally corrupt. I now know what it means to be satisfied by my lover and I have to wonder how much you paid the women you had affairs with because it sure as hell wasn't your prowess in the bedroom that convinced them to have sex with you."

His expression of angry shock was well worth it and the words would have been a perfect exit line if they hadn't been followed by an unexpected dash to the women's restroom where she lost her breakfast.

Chapter Nineteen

S he used her cell phone to call Daniel from the ferry.

He wasn't answering on his mobile and according to his voice mail that morning when she'd tried to reach him before going to see Lance, he was still out of town.

She closed the flip phone wishing desperately that Jillian hadn't flown back to LA the night before.

Amanda needed someone to talk to.

Her work was blowing up around her ears and she very much feared that wasn't the only thing that would be exploding in the next nine months. If that bout of nausea in the restroom meant what she thought it did, her waistline was going to do a fair amount of exploding as well.

Panic curled through her, fighting with anger for supremacy. She was furious with her boss for going behind her back and sending Lance to negotiate with Eric. It showed such a complete lack of respect for her professionally that she had to wonder why he'd sent her on the mission alone in the first place. And betrayal twisted her insides as she thought of the ammunition he'd armed Lance with...her work.

Beyond that, she was sickened by their proposed plans to use legal means to force Simon to design for the merged company. She didn't know if it would work, but it would drive a huge wedge between him and his cousin. If the merger went through, their relationship would be strained enough.

It wasn't right.

She wanted to warn Simon and tell him her suspicion that Daniel was working on the other shareholders in an attempt to override Simon at a shareholder meeting with their votes added to Eric's. Amidst all that was her worry that Extant Corporation knew details about Simon's current projects that they shouldn't. She had no idea how they'd gotten the information, but Daniel had certainly implied they had it.

But she still worked for Extant and she could not convince herself that she had the right to say anything as long as she was an employee of the company.

The fact that she wanted to say anything at all was a huge deviation from the way she would have responded before meeting Simon Brant and falling in love with him. A few weeks ago, her entire future had been bound up in her job. That wasn't true anymore. Even if Simon didn't want her as a permanent fixture in his life, she was afraid in one way or another she was going to be.

She laid her hand over her stomach, the queasy feeling not gone completely. Whether that was due to the rocking motion of the ferry or something inside her own body would be determined when she reached Simon's house and used the early pregnancy test kit she'd bought after leaving the restaurant.

"Amanda..."

At the sound of Simon calling her name, she came out of the bathroom, feeling curiously lightheaded.

All she saw was Simon's back. He'd turned around and headed back out of the room already.

"I'm right here."

He pivoted back to face here, his expression strangely blank. "So you are. Where's your watch?"

She'd forgotten to put combination watch-communication unit on that morning. "I don't know, beside the bed probably."

He turned to look and her gaze followed his. Sure enough, there it was on the nightstand.

"Simon I—"

"Eric just called," he interrupted, swinging back to face her. "Our second-cousins are demanding a special meeting of the shareholders to discuss the proposed merger with Extant Corporation."

It was her worst fears realized. Dizziness came over her and she swayed. "I see."

"Do you?"

She nodded, still too loopy from what she had learned in the bathroom to measure her responses. "I expected something like this."

"Are you saying you knew your boss was talking to the other shareholders for Brant Computers?"

Her brow wrinkled at the flat tone in Simon's voice.

"Yes." She'd known. She hadn't wanted it to be true, but she'd suspected and it turned out her suspicions were right.

"So, what was this all about?" He swept his hand toward the bed. "Your way of keeping me occupied while your boss got my cousins hot for the merger?"

"What?" His words didn't make any sense.

"You promised me you weren't using sex to manipulate me into agreeing to the merger, but I should have asked a different question, shouldn't I?"

Suddenly his meaning became clear and so did the reason why Daniel hadn't told her he was sending Lance to Washington. She had unwittingly done exactly what Simon had accused her of. Daniel had used her like a paid prostitute. Knowing she wasn't guilty in her own heart was little consolation with Simon looking at her with such a wealth of disgust in his gun metal eyes. Daniel had used her, but the possibility that Simon believed she'd done it on purpose gutted her.

She went hot, then cold with the most excruciating pain. "You think I made love to you to—" She clapped her hand over her mouth and ran back into the bathroom.

She barely made it to the sink before being sick. She hadn't eaten anything since coming back to the island, so she dry-heaved and it hurt. But then everything hurt right now. She couldn't get a deep breath and hot tears burned a path down her cheeks as she bent over the sink.

Two strong arms came around her. One held a washcloth which he wet under the tap and then used to wipe her face.

"Shh, baby. It's okay. Relax."

She closed her eyes and let him comfort her because she felt physically too week to fight him and her emotions were decimated.

Her stomach finally settled and he swept her into his arms, carrying her back into the bedroom.

He laid her gently on the bed. His hand brushed her cheek, but she kept her eyes shut. She didn't want to look at him right now, didn't want to see eyes she was used to burning with passion, humor or what she'd convinced herself was caring, now burn with resentment. It hurt.

"Amanda..."

She turned away from him and curled up on her side. "Lance thinks that if they get the merger through, the combined companies can force you to give them first option on your designs with some kind of legal injunction based on implied contracts."

She spoke quietly, but she knew he could hear her.

His hand settled on her shoulder. "Baby—"

"And I think Daniel knows whatever it is you're working on right now."

Now Simon knew it all. If Eric had waited to call just one hour, she would have told Simon everything and he would never have accused her of something so despicable. She would never have had to know what a low opinion he had of her morals, or that whatever he felt for her, it wasn't love.

You didn't think things like that about people you loved. She didn't have a lot of experience with the emotion, but she knew deep in her heart that she would not have even considered a similar scenario with Simon in the deceiving role. She'd never entertained doubts about him using sex to manipulate her either, not like he'd wondered about her in the beginning.

But then, she loved him.

"That doesn't matter." Simon's voice was gravelly above her.

She shook his hand off her shoulder. "It's all that matters."

Damn it. Why was she so weak right now? She just wanted to get up and leave, but she didn't think her legs would hold her. And where would she go? Not back to Port Mulqueen. Her job there was over. Her job was over period.

She could go home.

She was unemployed, but she still had her condo. After faxing in her resignation without giving notice, she doubted she'd get any kind of reference. It might be a while before she found another job. If things got really tight, she could list it with her mother's real estate agency and make at least one person happy.

He rolled her onto her back by exerting steady pressure on her shoulder. His gray gaze was mesmerizing. "Are you pregnant with my baby, Amanda?"

"Yes."

"I'm glad."

Was he? She guessed he could be. You didn't have to love the mother of your child to want it, did you? Simon would be a wonderful father, but that wasn't something she could deal with thinking about right now. She'd never considered being a single parent, giving birth to a child by a man who didn't love her.

"What are you going to do about the merger?"

"Eric's on his way over now. We're going to talk."

"I hope you can work it out between you."

Simon looked down at the woman he had made love to so exquisitely the night before. She had burned like living flame in his arms and told him she loved him. Her dark chocolate eyes were lifeless now, as if that incredible fire had gone out and all that remained was dead ashes.

She was talking about the merger as if it was the only thing that mattered.

As if being pregnant with his child didn't matter.

As if he didn't matter.

She wanted him and Eric to work things out, but there was no room for compromise. He couldn't agree to the merger, especially after what she'd just told him about her boss's plans. He didn't want corrupt management working with his company.

He wished he could give her what she wanted. Make it all right and make her happy, but he couldn't.

He touched her again, relieved when she didn't reject him. "I'm sorry."

"Me too."

He wanted to ask where they went from there, but she looked so fragile and he wasn't sure he could take the answer when it came. Maybe she didn't think they went anywhere. Maybe they were a done deal as far as she was concerned.

She'd admitted to knowing her boss was working behind the scenes to make the merger go ahead, but accusing her of using sex to keep him occupied in the meantime had been stupid. He was the one who had kidnapped her and convinced her to stay. She had too many hang-ups about her own ability to attract a man to have planned to use it in some nefarious manner.

He was an idiot.

And his idiocy had been born of jealousy along with a feeling of betrayal that he should not have experienced. He knew her job came first. Right from the beginning, he'd known that. But he'd wanted more and made her pay for it when he didn't get it.

Remembering the sound of her heaving over the sink, the pasty white complexion of her face and the tears, he felt like the world's biggest heel.

"You have nothing to apologize for, baby, but I do. I shouldn't have accused you of using what we have. I know it wasn't like that."

Her eyes begged him to mean it, for once her emotions as clear to him as a perfectly polished optical lens.

He pulled her into his arms, holding her so tight she squeaked.

He loosened his hold just a little. "Please, Amanda. Forgive me. I didn't mean it."

She cuddled into him and he felt like he'd cracked the secret to fiber-optic computer processing.

"Are you sure?" Her voice was muffled by his chest.

"Positive. I was the one who kidnapped you, remember?"

"I remember, but I thought you had forgotten." That was all she said, but he sensed there was more going on in her mind.

He also sensed that right now she had no intention of opening up to him.

They stayed that way for a long time, her allowing him to hold her. Finally she squirmed in his arms and he let her move back a little so he could see her face.

"Do you think you can convince Eric to vote against the merger?"

"I don't know." Remembering her word earlier, he asked, "Why did you tell me about Daniel and Lance's plans?"

"Because what they want to do is wrong. I tried to talk Daniel out of starting a family war, but he wouldn't listen."

"He doesn't care about anything but the bottom line."

Far from being offended by that indictment against her boss, she nodded her head sadly. "You're right. He even wanted me to try to convince you to change your mind using sex as my weapon."

"Is that where you got the idea I might be worried about it?"

"Yes." Her voice was small, almost like a child's.

"He's a bastard, honey."

"But a smart one. He and Lance are going to do their best to overrule you at the shareholder meeting."

"They won't be there. The only people allowed in the room are shareholders and their legal representative."

"Then be prepared for Lance suddenly taking on one of your cousins as a client."

She was right. He smiled grimly. "I'll be ready for him." He laid his hand across her belly. "Are you happy about the baby?"

"I don't know. It's all such a shock." She put her hand on top of his. "I'd rather not talk about any of that until this thing with the merger has been decided."

He almost asked her if she was going to withhold the baby from him if he succeeded in scuttling the merger, but stopped himself in time. He did not need another dumb man moment for her to file away in her memory banks and use as reference material when they did get around to talking about the baby and the future.

"Okay. Eric's going to be here soon. I'd better get downstairs."

She nodded, her expression hiding her emotions and her thoughts. "I think I'll go for a walk."

In other words, she was giving him time alone with his cousin.

Simon leaned down and kissed her, putting feelings he could not yet put into words into the pressure of his lips. Her response was everything it had always been and he shuddered inwardly with relief.

"I really am sorry for being such an idiot, baby," he said when he pulled away.

"Thank you, Simon. That means a lot to me."

He left her with a soft smile curving her lips.

Eric lounged back on the sofa, looking a hell of a lot more relaxed than Simon felt. "So you're saying Amanda told you that her boss plans to sue you for your designs if the merger goes through and you make good on your threat to put them up for the highest bidder?"

"It's not a threat, Eric."

"Yeah. I know that. You know that, but according to Amanda Extant management thinks you're bluffing."

"Right. The legal recourse is a contingency plan."

Eric nodded. "It's not a very good plan."

"They're counting on you being as numb to ethics as they are."

"Bastards."

That was pretty much what Simon thought too.

"That Lance Rogers is a smooth operator, but under the surface he's slime."

"Glad to hear you figured that out."

"I didn't like the way he treated Amanda at dinner the other night and you know how I feel about being lied to. He was so sure I wouldn't care that he'd told me she knew he was in Washington when she didn't that he didn't even bother to apologize for it."

Simon told Eric the bare bones about Amanda's marriage to Lance. He didn't expose her private pain and humiliation, but he wanted his cousin to know what kind of man Lance was. "And he's the guy Extant Corporation chose to replace Amanda as negotiator for the deal."

Arctic lights glinted in Eric's blue gaze. "A big part of my approval of this deal was wrapped up in Amanda. She's a straight player. That spoke well for Extant."

"You said was. You're no longer one-hundred percent behind the deal?"

"Are you kidding? They went behind our backs and approached the other shareholders, they sent a second negotiator who is pure slime, but their plans to try to force you to sell your designs to the merged company is the clincher for me. If this is the way Extant Corporation management operates, there's no way I'm merging my company with theirs."

Simon smiled. Extant's attempt to force his hand had backfired magnificently. "Amanda also thinks they've got some inside knowledge into what I'm working on."

Eric looked shocked. "How could they have that?"

"I'm not sure, but my guess is they've had someone monitoring my supply purchases. Some of the equipment and components I'm using right now have very limited application."

"But you don't make your purchases through the company. Even if they had an inside man and I'm not convinced they do, your activities couldn't be tracked through Brant Computers."

"But if they learned the names of my suppliers, hacked into my credit card records or even monitored deliveries via the ferry, they could get some idea."

"What are you working on right now that has Extant Corp so interested in acquiring you and Brant Computers?"

"I'm close on proof of concept on a fiber-optic processor."

Eric whistled. "The first company out with that baby is going to take over lead position in the industry."

"Yes."

"No wonder you've been so against the merger."

"I'm against it because I think it's wrong."

Eric sighed. "You've made me do a lot of thinking the past month and last week when Rogers was making such an effort to sell me on the merger, I realized how many of his arguments completely dismissed employee welfare."

"Amanda didn't. She believed that merging the companies would be best for the employees in the long run."

"Does she still believe it?"

Simon looked out the window where he could see Amanda's small figure in the distance. "I don't know, but whatever she believes, she told me what they were planning to do."

"She's in love with you."

Warmth coursed through Simon. "Yeah, I think she is."

"How do you feel about her?"

"I want her to stay. She belongs to me."

"Does she realize that?"

"I don't know. She may decide to dump me when I cost her job success."

Eric shook his head. "Are you blind? She told you what you needed to know to convince me to side with you on the merger."

"She couldn't know it would have that affect on you."

"Sure she did. Simon, Amanda and I have been talking the proposed merger for weeks. She knew me pretty well by the time she flew up from California. She knew that I would go ballistic at the idea of them trying to trump up that implied contract crap."

"You think she knew she was scuttling the last chance at the merger going through?"

Eric looked at him like he was brain-dead, which was not an expression Simon was used to receiving. "Yes."

For the first time in days, real hope took root in Simon that he and Amanda had a future. "So what do you think my chances of convincing her to stay in Washington permanently are?"

"If the question is accompanied by a marriage proposal, I'd say pretty darn good. Amanda is a traditional little thing despite the fact that she looked like sex personified the other night."

Remembering her in the dress he'd ripped from her luscious body had a predictable effect on Simon. "I think you're right."

She was not a woman who would look at single motherhood with equanimity, but his stupid accusation had made her back off from discussing the baby until after the merger issue was settled. He'd thought maybe that was because she wasn't sure how she felt about a man who would damage her career, but now he realized she didn't want him thinking their relationship had anything to do with the merger.

She really loved him and he'd screwed up. Badly.

He had to do something to make it right, something to show her how important she was to him and how much he trusted her.

"Eric, there's something I need to do."

When he was finished outlining his plan to Eric and explaining the reason it was necessary his cousin's expression was grim. "I think you're right. Women in love are vulnerable. Thinking you don't trust her is going to be tearing her apart."

Simon hated believing that, but he knew Eric was right. "You're not worried I might be making a mistake?" Simon was sure of her, but Eric wasn't in love.

"No. I trust you and you trust her. That's all I need to know."

"Okay. Let's work out the details."

Eric sat up and pulled out his PDA. "I'll take notes and then get the legal documents drawn up this afternoon."

Amanda curled into the warmth from Simon's body. The last couple of days had been strange. She hadn't told him she had resigned from her job, but instead of treating her like the enemy, he'd been gentle with her. He made no mention of the merger or the baby, but he treated her like spun glass, making love to her so tenderly she felt loved even though he never said the words.

Jill was convinced he did love her, or so she had said repeatedly during their daily phone chats. Amanda wasn't so sure. Simon would never dismiss the mother of his child. He had too much integrity. If nothing else, he would make sure they remained friends.

He hadn't felt like a mere friend last night though. He'd felt like a man who could never get enough of her. He'd woken her several times to make love throughout the night, doing little for her sleep but a great deal for her sense of value to him as a woman.

"What are you thinking about, sweetheart?" Simon's hand brushed over her stomach and came to rest just over her womb.

"You," she said honestly.

"Good thoughts?"

She wiggled her bottom against him. "Yes."

His hand moved to her hips to still her movement. "Stop that. We've got to get up. The shareholder meeting is at eleven and the crossing takes an hour."

"I remember." She rubbed her cheek against the arm under her head. "I think I'll just stay here this time. There's no reason for me to go."

"I want you with me."

Did he mean he wanted her support before and after the meeting? If so, he was showing her a certain level of trust, believing she would be there for him. Her heart desperately needed that small boost after his accusations the other day. He'd apologized, but later she'd wondered if he'd only done so because he felt guilty about upsetting her when she was pregnant with his baby.

"All right, I'll come. I can stay on the yacht while you're in the meeting."

"I've made arrangements for you to be there."

"I thought only family could be there."

"Family or shareholders."

"Well since all the shareholders are family, that's pretty much the same thing, isn't it?"

"In a way."

"So, how did you arrange for me to be there?"

"I worked it out with Eric. Don't worry about it, baby. It's all set and I'm not claiming you as my legal representative if that's what's worrying you."

"No. You don't lie. You wouldn't do that."

"But Lance Rogers would."

"I'm sure he has."

"You're right. He's the named legal counsel for Alana St. John, one of my second-cousins."

Darn Lance anyway. He was such a slimy toad. "I'm sorry, Simon."

"Don't be, baby." He hugged her. "It's going to be fine."

"You mean Eric is going to stand with you?"

He kissed the sensitive hollow behind her ear. "Did you expect anything else after telling me Extant's plans for the merged companies?"

She hadn't, but since Simon had been so silent on the merger, she had wondered if Eric had decided to back the merger regardless of the deviousness of its management. "Not really."

"That's what Eric said. He said you'd gotten to know him pretty well."

"I did. In the things that are important, you two are a lot alike."

"That's what I was counting on when I first started arguing with him about the merger. I figured given enough time, he'd come around to my point of view. It turns out your boss's belief that my cousin is as unethical as he is made my further argument unnecessary."

It was probably time to tell Simon the truth about that. "He's not my boss any more."

She found herself flipped on her back with Simon looming above her, his eyes stormy with anger. "Are you telling me they fired you over this business?"

She shook her head against the pillow and smiled up at him. He cared. He might not know it yet, or trust her as much as she trusted him, but this was not relief that she was out of the enemy camp she was seeing here. "I resigned."

"Oh, baby."

The kiss was voracious and led to other things, forcing them to take the fastest shower on record and for her to board the yacht for crossing to the mainland with wet hair.

Chapter Twenty

Amanda walked into the boardroom behind Simon and Eric. As she had expected, Lance sat at one end of the table with some people she didn't recognize. Simon's second-cousins, she surmised, the only other shareholders for which Eric did not hold proxy. No doubt Daniel was waiting somewhere close by for Lance to call with the outcome of the meeting.

Lance met her gaze with his own, his eyes reflecting both derision and certain level of smugness.

She did not acknowledge him in any way and took her seat to Simon's right. He squeezed her shoulder before sitting down himself and turning to confer briefly with Eric.

As both President of Brant Computers and Chairman of the Board, Eric called the meeting to order. "In the interests of saving time, would someone like to put forth a motion in regard to the current business on the agenda?"

The only piece of business on the agenda that Amanda was aware of was the proposed merger.

Lance raised his pen in indication he wished to be recognized by the chair.

"Yes, Mr. Rogers?"

"It is my client's understanding that Brant Computers by-laws stipulate no one outside the family and their legal representatives are allowed to attend shareholder meetings."

Eric inclined his head. "In point of fact the by-laws stipulate that no one outside the shareholders or their legal representatives may attend such meetings."

"If Ms. Zachary is attempting to pass herself off as legal representation for Simon Brant, I must point out she is neither a lawyer nor an attorney. She has no legal right to practice law in the state of Washington."

"The same could be said of you, Mr. Rogers. You've passed the California Bar not that for our state, I believe." Eric didn't fidget or indicate nervousness in any way.. "However, neither point is relevant as our by-laws do not indicate whether or not the legal representation for shareholders needs to be practicing in the law profession."

"I would like to go on record expressing my client's dissatisfaction with this proceeding."

"So noted. However, unless your client wishes to take legal issue with the ambiguity of our by-laws, I propose we move forward."

Lance turned and conferred with a dark-haired woman, presumable Alana St. John.

He turned back to face Eric. "My client is willing to allow the proceedings to go forward."

"How fortunate." The sarcasm in Eric's tone was barely perceptible.

Ms. St. John made a motion to merge Brant Computers with Extant Corporation.

In that moment, Amanda experienced an overwhelming sense of relief that Simon had convinced Eric to stand with him. He'd been right all along. Brant Computers was a family run company and the employees mattered, ethics mattered, and doing what was right mattered to the management.

Extant was interested in the bottom line only and Daniel's most recent behavior had put the difference between the two companies in stark relief.

Another second-cousin seconded the motion and Eric called for discussion.

"I move that discussion be waived and that we proceed directly to a vote." Simon's voice was even and firm with no emotional inflection whatsoever.

Lance's eyes narrowed in surprise and his gaze swung to Eric then back to Simon. "You don't want to argue against the merger?" he asked.

Simon's gray eyes were steady and unreadable. "No."

Lance's gaze swung to Amanda. She stared back. He was going to lose and in her mind it couldn't have happened to a more deserving candidate. She couldn't feel much one way or the other for the second-cousins he had duped into playing his patsies. None of them had contacted either Simon or Eric before going ahead and calling for the special shareholder meeting.

Brant Computers was an income producer for them, but they weren't close to the company or the men who ran it.

Lance said, "I would like a moment to reiterate both the short and long term benefits to Brant Computers that a merger with Extant Corporation would bring."

Eric indicated Lance should proceed.

Which he did. When he had been talking a few minutes, the secretary recording the meeting said five minutes had been reached.

"Your time is up, Mr. Rogers."

Lance stopped talking, but looked annoyed.

"Is there any rebuttal?"

No one indicated they wished to speak.

"In that case, we will move directly to the vote."

Once again, Lance's pen was in the air.

"Yes, Mr. Rogers?"

"According to parliamentary procedure, if there is no one else wishing to take the floor, I should be allowed to continue."

"If you had read the company by-laws more thoroughly, Mr. Rogers, you would have noted that our meetings are run with an adaptation of Robert's Rules. This is one of Brant Computer's adaptations."

Eric referenced a section of the by-laws which Lance immediately looked up.

He read it then lifted his head. "The adaptation is as you say."

Eric didn't bother to reply.

He called for a vote. Each of the second-cousins voted in favor.

Eric turned to Amanda. "Which way do you vote?"

"What?" For some reason she flushed with heat. "I'm not a shareholder."

"As of the day before yesterday you are. Simon Brant signed over thirty-seven percent of his stock in Brant Computers to you which constitutes eleven percent of the total company shares."

Even in the deep state of shock that Eric's words had thrown her into she could do the math. Simon had given her the deciding vote. She turned to him. He was looking at her, a warmth and trust in his eyes she could not mistake.

Tears clogged the back of her throat.

He trusted her with the future of Brant Computers in her hands, with his future as well and he had signed over those shares before she had told him about resigning from Extant.

"I vote nay." Her voice shook with emotion, but she couldn't help it.

"I also vote nay." Simon didn't look away from her as he said it and she could not look away from him.

"I vote nay as well." Eric's words were accompanied by a gasp from the other end of the table.

It was quickly followed by an eruption of gabbled voices. Evidently Lance had told the second-cousins that Eric would be voting in favor of the merger. They weren't happy.

Eric called the room to order again. "There is one more piece of business."

Looking highly irritated, Ms. St. John asked, "What is it?"

"Simon and I are prepared to buy your stock and the stock of the other shareholders at fifteen percent above market value, but only if you all agree to sell."

"What if only one of us wants to sell?" a man who looked enough like the dark-haired woman to indicate he was her brother asked.

"We will pay market value and no more."

"But you still want to buy the shares?"

"Yes. However the additional fifteen percent is only on offer until we leave this room. Once the meeting is adjourned, the offer will be withdrawn."

Amanda was still shaken from Eric's revelation that she was a shareholder. This move of his and Simon's went right over her head, just as did the second eruption of voices from the other end of the table.

"If you sell, you'll regret it. Simon Brant is working on the next generation of computer technology. If Brant Computers is the first to market with the concept your shares will increase in value astronomically."

"The operative word here is if. I won't confirm or deny the content of Simon's current experiments. His work is and has always been confidential." Eric's blue eyes were colder than Amanda had ever seen them. "Which leads to the obvious question of how you came by the belief that Simon is working on next generation technology."

Lance actually sneered. "Don't be dense. Extant Corporation would be foolish not to keep an eye on its competitors."

"Even more foolish to be slapped with an injunction and lawsuit for hacking into confidential information files." Simon spoke, having turned away from her to face Lance. "You can bet I'll know exactly who gained illegal entry into my supply records and how it was done within the next week."

Lance's expression left no one in the room in any doubt that information had been obtained in just that way. "Go for it," he said however, in a false show of bravado.

Or maybe not so false. It wasn't his neck on the line.

In the end, some of the second cousins refused to sell their stock. The others were angry they wouldn't get the extra fifteen percent, but they did negotiate for an eight percent increase over market value with the stipulation that if Brant Computers was first to market with a fiber optic processor, they would receive an additional seven percent.

"Are you sure you two won't come for dinner? Elaine and Joey would love to see you."

Simon shook his head, his hand on Amanda's shoulder. There was this irrational fear that if he didn't hold onto her, she would disappear. Until he got things settled between them, that fear was not going to go away.

"Another time. Right now, I just want to head back to the island." He turned to Amanda. "Is that all right, sweetheart?"

Her expression was sending him messages that made his knees go weak. "Yes."

Eric laughed. "You two are better entertainment than a live performance at Cheney Stadium." He squeezed Amanda's arm. "Be kind to him, honey. I never thought I'd see the day when Simon was more interested in a woman than his experiments."

She smiled, moving into Simon's side and sliding her arm around his waist. "I'll be as nice as he'll let me be."

Eric winked at Simon. "It looks like you've got it sewn up, buddy. I'll let you get to it."

He turned and walked back to his car in the pier parking lot.

Simon looked down at Amanda. She'd dressed in her buttoned-up business attire, but something was different. Maybe it was the twinkle of mischief in her eyes, or the fact that he knew the bra and panties she was wearing under the conservative gray suit was scandalous in design.

"Do I?"

She tilted her head in that adorable way she had. "Do you what?"

"Have you all sewn up?"

"Hmmm..." She thought about it and even though he knew she was teasing him, tension started to seep into his body.

"I guess it depends on what you mean by sewn up," she finally said.

"Come on." He took her hand. "I'll explain it on board." He wasn't asking the most important question of his life on the gangplank to his yacht.

She let him lead her aboard.

He stopped once they were on deck. "Do you want to stay outside for a while?" The sun was shining and she had a marked preference for the outdoors.

She nodded, but pulled her hand from his. "Let me go in and change my clothes. Then we can relax together on the forward deck, okay?"

"Sounds good." He let her go, knowing that if he went with her, the minute her clothes were off he would forget his noble intention to talk and do something far more physically active. While making love with Amanda was the most pleasure he'd ever known, settling their future was more important at the moment.

He headed to the forward deck, removing his jacket and tie along the way. He undid the first few buttons on his white silk dress shirt and cuffed the sleeves, before sitting on one of the deck loungers.

Amanda was only gone a few minutes, enough time for Jacob to have been and gone, leaving a tray of chilled water and finger size sandwiches to tempt the little mother's appetite. It wasn't exactly wine and roses, but Simon didn't want the superficial trappings of romance. He wanted the real deal and Amanda in any setting was it.

She'd taken off her shoes and thigh-highs and changed into a pair of mouth watering hip-hugging denim shorts. Her form fitting white singlet showed a tantalizing strip of skin and the top of her temporary tattoo above the waistband of her shorts as well as the shadows of two dark points that indicated she'd left her bra off.

She was beautiful.

She was pulling pins from her hair as she walked toward him, the magnificent mass of chestnut silk floating down in a cloud around her face just as she stopped in front of him. "Hi."

He had to make an effort to breathe. "Hi, baby. Nice outfit."

"Jill brought it up with the other clothes she picked up at my apartment. I wasn't going to wear it, but around you..." She shrugged, but her expression told him the rest. She trusted him not to criticize her like her ex-husband had done.

"It looks great." Better than great. "But it's going to pay hell with my desire to talk."

"I like knowing that," she admitted as she sat on the edge of the lounger beside his.

"Like you were proud of yourself you seduced me past the point of remembering protection?" He'd caught on to her.

She laughed. "Yes." The smile faded. "It was so new. I can't tell you how incredible it feels to be wholly a woman and not think there's a major part of my femaleness missing."

"And you don't mind being pregnant?"

She bit her lip. "I wish it had happened in marriage. I guess I'm old-fashioned, but I think a baby should have the benefit of two loving parents."

"Ours will. Do you doubt it?" Did she think he would dismiss his responsibility to her and the baby, leaving her to fend for herself?

She shook her head. "Oh no. I don't doubt you. You're going to be a fantastic father." She laid her hand over the tummy he loved touching. "I love the baby already. I'm going to be the best mother I can and make him or her feel so wanted."

Not like her parents had done with her. She didn't have to say it and he knew she would do it. Amanda had so much love in her small body, she radiated with it.

She smiled softly at him. "I'm really glad I'm carrying your baby."

"But you wish it had happened after we were married?"

She went completely still. "Are we getting married?"

A four letter word went zinging through his brain. He was screwing this up. He was supposed to ask her, not assume.

Operating under a compulsion stronger than any that had ever sent him disappearing into his lab, he stood up, taking her with him. He had to get this right. His whole future was at stake here.

There was one thing he had always gotten right with her and he took shameless advantage of it. Molding his mouth over her slightly parted lips, he gave her the emotion he found so difficult to vocalize.

And he found something in return. Warmth. Generosity. Love. He could taste her love. It had always been there for him, he realized now, waiting to flood his parched heart like the warmest, wettest rain.

He pulled back just far enough so he could look into the liquid depths of her Hershey brown eyes. "I love you, Amanda." It had been so easy to say. Why had he waited so long?

Those eyes drenched. "I didn't think you did." She took a shuddering breath as two rivulets of tears trickled down her face. "I told you I loved you. Over and over again, but you didn't say anything. Nobody but Jillian has ever loved me. I didn't think you could."

He wanted to dispel her fear and remembered pain. All he had was words. "Baby, how could I not love you? When I'm with you, I am whole. The shadows disappear; the frozen places in my soul melt. I've never known anything like it. Relationships before were always wrong. I didn't understand why, but now I do. Love isn't physical, though I think that's a part of it. It's spiritual and it doesn't happen just because you want it to. It's the most precious gift life has to offer."

She swiped at her eyes. "I know, believe me."

But she didn't believe he really did. Because he was the man she loved, she didn't see how inadequately he fit with the rest of the world.

"I was in college when I was fifteen."

She looked quizzical. "I remember."

"I discovered sex and older women. One woman in particular. I'd had a few girlfriends, but this woman was special. She made my head come off, or so I thought until I met you. Now I know what she gave me were minor explosions. With you, it's nuclear."

Amanda liked his description of how she affected him because it was mutual. "What happened with the woman?"

Simon's gray gaze went unfocused as he looked back into the past. His jaw tightened. "One night I went to pick her up in the dorm. I wasn't old enough to drive even, but I was having sex with this twenty year old woman. I'd go to her dorm room and she'd drive if we went out. Usually we stayed there."

"Anyway, the door was open and one of her friends was in there with her. They were joking around, talking about me and what a stud I was. At first I felt great, but then she said I was just a kid, but I knew how to use my cock and that it was big enough to really pleasure a woman. She speculated on how big I would be when I was a full grown man and then offered me to her friend when she was done with me."

The pain in Simon's voice added to the fury growing in Amanda. "That perverted, pedophile bitch!"

"She was hardly a pedophile. I was full grown physically and I lived in the adult world, Amanda."

"She hurt you and she knew what she was doing. She knew you were vulnerable and too young for her." Rage filled her on behalf of that other Simon, the one who had believed sex was love and he'd find acceptance with a woman who was using him for her own physical gratification. "What did you do?"

"I ran. I met Jacob that night. He was still in the Secret Service then, but he was on vacation where I went to college. He stopped me from doing something really stupid and helped me to refocus my energy on doing something with the amazing intellect God had given me."

"Is that when you stopped living like the rest of the world?"

"I never lived like other people, Amanda. I don't think like other men. I forget things, get lost in my experiments, work out in my gym in the middle of the night and collect ancient fighting swords because they fascinate me. I'm not normal, baby. I'll never fit."

She wrapped her arms around him and hugged him tight. "You may not be normal, but you're perfect for me. I love you so much, Simon. So, so much."

"I wasn't sure you did. I don't have a lot of experience with romance and less with love. It took me a while to figure out what I felt for you, even longer to determine you loved me."

That didn't make any sense. She'd told him. "I said it. Repeatedly."

"During lovemaking." His chin rested on top of her head. "Never any other time. I thought it was just sex talk."

She felt the heat in her cheeks from a blush as she remembered what she was usually doing when she shouted out her love for Simon. "It wasn't. I really love you."

"I figured that out." She could hear the satisfaction in his voice.

"But you accused me of using sex to keep you occupied while Daniel drummed up shareholder support for the merger," she reminded him.

"Elaine calls them dumb man moments. She says Eric has them occasionally, but she loves him anyway."

The last sounded like a question and she smiled against his shirt front. "I didn't stop loving you, but it hurt."

"I'll never do it again."

She believed him. "I know." There would be other dumb man moments, just as she would mess up, but Simon trusted her and he would never make an accusation based on a lack in that again.

He leaned back and cupped her face, his gaze intent on seeing into her soul, or so it felt. "Are you sure?"

She lifted her hands to cover his. "I'm sure. You gave me the deciding vote, Simon." Choking up with emotion again, she had to take several deep breaths before going on. "You trusted me with your future before you knew I'd quit my job. I'll never forget that."

"And will you always remember I love you?"

She tilted her pelvis forward, rubbing against the bulge that had been there since she walked outside. "How long are we talking here?"

He kissed her. Hard. When he lifted his head, they were both short of breath.

"A lifetime. Living without you is not an option I can accept." He sounded like he meant it.

She wondered what he would do if she said she had different plans. She didn't. There was nothing more she wanted out of life than to live the rest of it with Simon, but still...he was a smart, creative guy. His method of convincing her would almost be worth holding off her answer. Almost.

"When I divorced Lance, I never wanted to get married again." She'd never wanted to be that vulnerable to hurt again.

His body tensed. "I'm nothing like him."

"I know that." She brushed his chest, her hand tucking into the opening and laying against his heart. "You're so much more than any man I've ever known. You're such a gorgeous guy, I thought you had security to keep the groupies at bay." He smiled, like he thought she was joking. She wasn't.

"You have integrity I could trust my life to. You care so much for others that it humbles me." Even being a total recluse, his concern for the employees of Brant Computers had eclipsed Eric's. "You're strong physically, emotionally and mentally. You're the perfect father for my children."

Leaning forward, she kissed the exposed patch of skin in his shirt's opening. "I never want to leave you. If you need the words: I'll marry you, Simon, and spend the rest of my life glad that I did."

He shuddered, almost with relief. "I never want you to leave. I want to tie you to me with marriage, with love, with our baby. You belong to me. I belong to you. It's perfect."

She felt like crying again, she was so happy.

"Don't cry, baby." Then he kissed her, a beautiful seal to their commitment.

After several minutes of pure pleasure, he withdrew his mouth from hers. "Big or small?"

Deliberately misunderstanding him, she reached down and caressed him intimately. "It feels pretty big to me."

He growled and grabbed her wrist. "I meant the wedding."

"I don't care as long as it's soon and Jillian can be there." She'd had the big wedding and it had all been for show. They could get married in the pastor's office with Jillian and Eric as witnesses and she would feel more married, more secure than she ever had with Lance.

They got married on the yacht two weeks later. Jillian was indeed there, as were Eric, Elaine and Joey. Jacob catered the reception for the small group before scuttling everyone off the yacht. He then piloted Amanda and Simon to a deserted stretch of ocean. Amanda was finishing some final touches on the stateroom when she heard a powerboat come alongside and then leave again a few minutes later.

She looked around the room, a sense of anticipation curling through her insides. She'd set this scene once before, but this time she knew Simon wanted her. Not a business proposal. Nothing but her.

Simon tapped on the stateroom door and pushed it slowly open. Amanda had disappeared the minute they left the dock, telling him not to come down until they were at anchor. Well, they'd dropped anchor and Jacob was gone. Had she heard the boat that came to pick him up?

He wondered if she would realize it's significance, but then his brain short circuited like a wet power supply without a ground strap. The stateroom was filled with soft light, sheer scarves covering the small lamps and diffusing their glow into a golden haze. Some kind of Eastern music was playing in the background and Amanda stood in the middle of the bed looking like a pasha's favorite concubine from the harem.

Her outfit seemed to be made up of several sheer veils and scarves and not much else. When he walked in, she started swaying, clicking small gold castanets in beat with the music. The lines of her body swayed sinuously against the silk giving him a glimpse of a rosy peaked curve here and creamy white thigh there.

Blood and heat surged into his sex and he started tearing off his tuxedo. She kept dancing, her body's gyrations making sweat break out all over his body.

"Is this another fantasy?"

She shook her head, her dark hair sliding across her unfettered breasts sensually. "No. This is for real. I love you and I want to give myself to you completely. I want to be every fantasy for you. I want you to be every fantasy for me, but not live in fantasy. I want to dress up for you and dance for you and seduce you the way you seduce me."

Naked, he crossed to the bed. "Your love is the most seductive force in the world, baby, but you keep right on dancing. I'm so turned on I ache with it."

Her arms moved gracefully around her, drawing attention to different parts of her beautiful body, while she silently enticed him. Suddenly he understood the gift she was giving him. It was the same one he'd given her in the boardroom of Brant Computers. Complete trust. She trusted him to want her, to love her, to affirm her when she'd learned so well not to trust.

He couldn't help it. He swung her off the bed and into his arms. "I love you, Amanda. Everything about you."

She looped her arms around his neck. "I love you, Simon. Don't ever let go of me."

"Never. Don't ever let go of me."

Her arms tightened convulsively. "Never."

And then she kissed him, long and slow and sweet. "You're my husband."

"You're my wife." The words were sweeter to him than any decadent dessert. "We may not fit in the rest of the world, but we belong together."

Wetness burned in his eyes, but he blinked it away. "We fit."

"Perfectly."
And they proved it, once again joining body, soul and spirit.

THE END

If you enjoyed THE REAL DEAL please consider leaving a review, or rating. Thank you!
Want to read bonus content and to be kept up to date on her books? Sign up for Lucy Monroe's newsletter:
https://www.lucymonroe.com/newsletter

With more than 10 million copies of my books in print worldwide (Isn't that wild?), I'm an award winning and USA Today best-selling author with over 90 published books. My stories have been translated for sale all over the world and after a long career in traditional publishing, I've gone indie. I am loving the freedom to write the stories both me and my readers enjoy the most. My new steamy mafia romance series, Syndicate Rules features the morally gray alpha heroes and spice I love to write. I write contempo-rary, historical and paranormal romance. Some of my books have action adven-ture and intrigue. All of them are spicy and deeply emotional. I'm a voracious reader and love to talk about both my books and those I've read (or should read...good recs are always welcome) on social media. Welcome to my world where love conquers all, but not easily!

For info on my books and series extras, visit my website:
www.lucymonroe.com

Follow me on Social Media:
Facebook: LucyMonroe.Romance
Instagram: lucymonroeromance
Pinterest: lucymonroebooks
goodreads: Lucy Monroe
YouTube: @LucyMonroeBooks
TikTok: lucymonroeauthor

ALSO BY LUCY MONROE

Syndicate Rules

CONVENIENT MAFIA WIFE
URGENT VOWS
DEMANDING MOB BOSS
RUTHLESS ENFORCER
BRUTAL CAPO
FORCED VOWS

Mercenaries & Spies

READY, WILLING & AND ABLE
SATISFACTION GUARANTEED
DEAL WITH THIS
THE SPY WHO WANTS ME
WATCH OVER ME
CLOSE QUARTERS
HEAT SEEKER

CHANGE THE GAME
WIN THE GAME

Passionate Billionaires & Royalty

THE MAHARAJAH'S BILLIONAIRE HEIR
BLACKMAILED BY THE BILLIONAIRE
HER OFF LIMITS PRINCE
CINDERELLA'S JILTED BILLIONAIRE
HER GREEK BILLIONAIRE
SCORSOLINI BABY SCANDAL
THE REAL DEAL
WILD HEAT (Connected to Hot Alaska Nights - Not a Billionaire)
HOT ALASKA NIGHTS
3 Brides for 3 Bad Boys Trilogy
RAND, COLTON & CARTER

Harlequin Presents

THE GREEK TYCOON'S ULTIMATUM
THE ITALIAN'S SUITABLE WIFE
THE BILLIONAIRE'S PREGNANT MISTRESS

THE SHEIKH'S BARTERED BRIDE
THE GREEK'S INNOCENT VIRGIN
BLACKMAILED INTO MARRIAGE
THE GREEK'S CHRISTMAS BABY
WEDDING VOW OF REVENGE
THE PRINCE'S VIRGIN WIFE
HIS ROYAL LOVE-CHILD
THE SCORSOLINI MARRIAGE BARGAIN
THE PLAYBOY'S SEDUCTION
PREGNANCY OF PASSION
THE SICILIAN'S MARRIAGE ARRANGEMENT
BOUGHT: THE GREEK'S BRIDE
TAKEN: THE SPANIARD'S VIRGIN
HOT DESERT NIGHTS
THE RANCHER'S RULES
FORBIDDEN: THE BILLIONAIRE'S
VIRGIN PRINCESS
HOUSEKEEPER TO THE MILLIONAIRE
HIRED: THE SHEIKH'S SECRETARY MISTRESS
VALENTINO'S LOVE-CHILD
THE LATIN LOVER 2-IN-1 with
THE GREEK TYCOON'S INHERITED BRIDE
THE SHY BRIDE
THE GREEK'S PREGNANT LOVER
FOR DUTY'S SAKE
HEART OF A DESERT WARRIOR
NOT JUST THE GREEK'S WIFE
ONE NIGHT HEIR
PRINCE OF SECRETS
MILLION DOLLAR CHRISTMAS PROPOSAL
SHEIKH'S SCANDAL
AN HEIRESS FOR HIS EMPIRE
A VIRGIN FOR HIS PRIZE
2017 CHRISTMAS CODA: The Greek Tycoons
KOSTA'S CONVENIENT BRIDE
THE SPANIARD'S PLEASURABLE VENGEANCE
AFTER THE BILLIONAIRE'S WEDDING VOWS
QUEEN BY ROYAL APPOINTMENT
HIS MAJESTY'S HIDDEN HEIR
THE COST OF THEIR ROYAL FLING

Anthologies & Novellas

SILVER BELLA
DELICIOUS: Moon Magnetism
by Lori Foster, et. al.

HE'S THE ONE: Seducing Tabby
by Linda Lael Miller, et. al.
THE POWER OF LOVE: No Angel
by Lori Foster, et. al.
BODYGUARDS IN BED:
Who's Been Sleeping in my Brother's Bed?
by Lucy Monroe et. al.

Historical Romance

ANNABELLE'S COURTSHIP
The Langley Family Trilogy
TOUCH ME, TEMPT ME & TAKE ME
MASQUERADE IN EGYPT

Paranormal Romance

Children of the Moon Novels
MOON AWAKENING
MOON CRAVING
MOON BURNING
DRAGON'S MOON
ENTHRALLED anthology: Ecstasy Under the Moon
WARRIOR'S MOON
VIKING'S MOON
DESERT MOON
HIGHLANDER'S MOON

Montana Wolves
COME MOONRISE
MONTANA MOON